VOLUME III

The Temple Buck Quartet:
A Rocky Mountain Odyssey 1822-1837

EDWARD LOUIS HENRY

Shinin' Times!

**One trapper's personal chronicle
of the American Rocky Mountain
fur trade, 1828 – 1833**

Christopher
Matthews
Publishing

www.christophermatthewspub.com

Bozeman, Montana

ALSO BY EDWARD LOUIS HENRY

The Temple Buck Quartet
A Rocky Mountain Odyssey

Volume I: Backbone of the World
Volume II: Free Men
Volume III: Shinin' Times!
Volume IV: Glory Days Gone Under

* * *

Poredevil's Beaver Tales

Shinin' Times!

Cover design by Armen Kojoyian

ISBN: 978-0-9833164-7-3

Published by
CHRISTOPHER MATTHEWS PUBLISHING
www.christophermatthewspub.com
Bozeman, Montana
Printed in the United States of America

Dedication

For Gloria, without whom nothing would have happened, who never faltered in her faith and loving support; for Kelly, who always believed; and for all the saddle tramps and buckskinners with whom I've been privileged to share a cookfire, swapping lies and sharing friendship, throughout my life.

SHININ' TIMES!

One Trapper's Personal Chronicle
Of the American Rocky Mountain Fur Trade
1828 — 1833

by
Temple Buck, Trapper

Euphemius Hobbes, Esq.
Editor

Table of Contents

Editor's Preface

It was with no inconsiderable degree of reluctance that I returned to this task, begun nearly a decade past, of lending my services as editor of the chronicles of the exploits and misadventures of Mr. Temple Buck, who styles himself a simple trapper and sometime fur trader in the American Rocky Mountains. I must state here, as I have done in an earlier work of his, that I bear no responsibility for either the content or the language employed by Mr. Buck in his essays into literature, which flattering term I assure the reader that I use advisedly in this particular instance.

Mr. Buck insists on employing coarse, common language in presenting the speech of his companions and colleagues in the fur trade and he remains adamant in his insistence on describing in sometimes graphic detail scenes and events which would better be left to the reader's imagination or preferably not mentioned at all. He has exhibited, in this and in his earlier writing, a patent disregard for the refined and tender sensibilities of genteel readers, especially those of young ladies of proper upbringing, who, it is fervently hoped, will never cast their innocent eyes upon these pages.

In Mr. Buck's defense it should be noted, however, that he provides in his narrative a plainly-drawn picture of life as it actually exists amongst his fur-trapping brethren in the Rocky Mountain wilderness at this time, for the few readers who might entertain an interest in such matters. His earthy, often brutal, unvarnished descriptions of mountain life and the events that commonly occur in those parts will likely shock and disgust the civilized reader, but those of sturdier stomach may discover herein considerable useful instruction and perhaps even a certain degree of amusement in the recollections of Mr. Buck.

I have endeavored in vain, in this narrative as in his previous efforts, to convince Mr. Buck to allow me to assist him in beautifying his writing by incorporating those literary enhancements and ornaments so much esteemed by classical and contemporary European authors and the very best American practitioners of the Literary Art, by eliminating the quotation of ribald language and deplorable grammar employed by his comrades, as well as deleting descriptions of gross scenes and events that are thankfully foreign to civilized experience, and, finally, to improve the author's own vulgar narrative style of composition, but all to no avail. Mr. Buck merely replies that he who holds the purse strings must also guide the pen. In that crass sentiment I must perforce acquiesce and therefore confine my participation to matters of grammar, orthography, and punctuation.

So it is that you are here presented with a faithful portrait of the trials, hardships and perils, daily exigencies, frolics, and often-disappointed ambitions of those hardy trappers who provide the materials essential to the manufacture of gentlemen's beaver hats, which are worn so proudly in the glittering courts and sophisticated salons of Europe, in every fashionable thoroughfare of our own blessèd nation, and even, it is said, at the opulent levées of Oriental potentates.

I regret that you, gentle reader, must be served with the bare bones of Mr. Buck's experiences, seasoned with a sauce likely too piquant for the refined palate of the literati, instead of the sumptuous feast which I would have prepared from the author's simple woodland fare, had I been granted greater latitude in my endeavors and were it not for his obdurate refusal to elevate his homespun prose to a more dignified plane.

Euphemius Hobbes, Esq.
Editor
St. Louis, Missouri, 1833

Author's Foreword

Before I say anything else in this preamble, I reckon I need to address the use of the word **lending** by Mister Euphemius Hobbes in his foregoing editor's preface. I wish to state clearly that Mister Hobbes did not **lend** me his services in correcting my spelling and grammar and suchlike where necessary in putting this manuscript in proper form for the printer. He has been paid handsomely for every ounce and dram of effort he spent on my behalf, as he was previously paid for preparing my scribbles for the printer for the earlier two volumes of my personal history in the Rocky Mountain fur trade, *Backbone of the World* and *Free Men.* Besides which, with the aid of Mister Pierre Chouteau, Cadet, of Saint Louis, I obtained for him a respectable editorship on the staff of the *Missouri Republican,* where he prospers in much better circumstances than ever he enjoyed in Chillicothe, Ohio.

I notice that Mister Hobbes has added Esq. to his name in this book. I reckon he figures he is sufficiently distant from Ohio to allow himself to be putting on such airs, but it makes no nevermind to me.

If by some remote chance you happened to read the first two volumes of this history you may recall that Mister Hobbes and I engaged in many a skirmish concerning what I would tell of and how I might say it. You may marvel, therefore, that I would go to the trouble and expense of bringing Mister Hobbes all the way from Chillicothe, Ohio to Saint Louis, at my own expense, to assist me in preparing this manuscript, just so we might declare war on each other once again. I have often tried to unsnarl that conundrum myself, but without much success. The best reason I can offer is to quote Mister William Shakespeare, who says the most of us would "rather bear those ills we have than fly to others that we know not of." So, opinionated, stiff-necked, pernickety, and stubborn and cantankerous as he can be and mostly always is, leastaways I know Hobbes and, in some small measure, how to deal with him.

This book concerns my return to the Rocky Mountains in 1828, after a two-year absence, to resume my chosen trade, that of free trapper of beaver and other fine furs. It addresses, too, matters of my ancestry, the fortunes and misfortunes of my long-time trapping companions, myself, and others, and how the fur business has altered since I first ascended the Missouri River in 1822 under the command of Major Andrew Henry.

In the opening chapter I have done my best to carry you up to the time when this particular history commences, regarding what transpired in the earlier account of my life in Ohio, in the mountains, and upon my return to my birthplace when my mother was dying. If you are already acquainted with those events, please bear with me. I warrant I have been as brief in my telling of it as I know how to be.

Regarding that first chapter, I earnestly beg the forgiveness of the ghost of Mister Laurence Sterne for borrowing his title, *A Sentimental Journey,* for my own use herein, for that is what my return journey from Whynot, Ohio to Saint Louis Town certainly was.

Temple Buck, Trapper

Saint Louis, Missouri, 1833

Chapter I
A Sentimental Journey

My heart was big indeed within my breast, nigh full to bursting with joyful anticipation, that late-winter morning in 1828 as I completed the final preparations for my journey, snugging saddle girths and cinches on my three horses, adjusting packs, and generally readying my equipment and my animals for the long hike from Whynot, Ohio, not far north of the Ohio River, to Saint Louis Town in Missouri. My final destination was to be the Rocky Mountains and the trappers' rendezvous that would be held there sometime in July, as I reckoned, but there were many tasks that I needed to accomplish betwixt here and there before I could realize my ambition to resume my former occupation, that of free trapper in the beaver trade, and rejoin the faithful comrades with whom I had served a hard apprenticeship in that demanding trade.

My horses were in excellent fettle, for they had fed well and worked not much at all in the preceding twelve months, whilst I was healing from gunshot wounds — which I will explain later — and passing time by writing a history of my first four years in the Rocky Mountains.

I was well-mounted for my journey. All three were excellent saddle horses, but in the mountains every trapper's horse early on gets used to carrying a pack whenever required. Kumskaka, my Shawnee-bred bay gelding, a gift from the man I was now proud to call my father, bore my high-pommeled Spaniard saddle and spoke his impatience to be off upon the trail with snorts and rolling eyes and stamping hooves. The other two, Ready, awarded to me by Rotten-belly of the Crow Indian Nation, and Ashley, whom I purchased from the Missouri Militia general who also bears that name, were lightly loaded, for there was little in the way of plunder that I wished to take with me from the place of my birth and the home of my youth.

All else that I possessed — two farms, buildings, furniture, livestock, implements, and the like — I had bestowed on Toussaint and Charlotte Poitier, an honest, hard-working Métis couple, and their young children. The locally-despised French-Chippewa Poitiers had cared for my mother during the last days before her death, easing her pain and cheering her final hours. They also tended to me during my long convalescence. They deserved whatever I could give them. I was confident that, for all their dusky complexion and mixed blood, the newly-acquired wealth of the Poitiers would rapidly establish their worth and increase their social standing and acceptance amongst the purse-proud citizens of Whynot, Ohio.

Lest you think that I seek praise for my generosity, I assure the reader that I valued not a jot whatever I passed on to the Poitiers. They did me a favor by relieving me of any reason or excuse I might have entertained to return to Ohio.

What I carried away from that place burdened me and my animals but little — a handful of books from my mother's library, some extra firearms, one of them my late uncle's fine large-caliber flintlock rifle, fresh oats for my horses, and a few keepsakes, nothing more. The rest of my plunder consisted of buffalo sleep robes, camp outfit, extra clothing, and trail gear, much of which I had brought with me upon my return from the mountains. I had no use for more.

Neither was I burdened with fond memories of that place, except those of my mother and my Uncle Ben, both resting now in their graves. Those two had been the pillars upon which I had built whatever good character I possess. Now that they were gone, nothing rooted me to my native soil. A third person stirred bittersweet recollections, she who had been my youthful love. But her cold rejection of me when she learned of my true birth and descent had dissolved the only tie that might have bound me to that neighborhood.

Satisfied that my animals were ready for the trail, I returned to the cabin where I had been born and took a final turn around my mother's chamber, pausing before her well-stocked bookshelves and reflecting on how very much she had loved learning, recalling, too, the love and understanding she had lavished on me, which amounted to nearly everything good and agreeable that I could recollect of that neighborhood.

Passing by my mother's pier glass, I glimpsed my reflection and tarried a spell to appraise the man I had become in the six years since I first traveled to the Shining Mountains at the age of nineteen. The fellow who stared back at me from its blue depths had grown and changed considerably since then. The lanky youth who had run off, pursued by his own guilty imagination rather than by any real peril, had become a man ripened in freedom and seasoned by hardship. I beheld a mountaineer, a free trapper of the Rocky Mountain wilderness, clad in buckskins, girt with weapons stuck into a colorful sash, long-haired and clean-shaven, neither tall nor short, lean, clear-eyed, and, in spite of my long convalescence, weathered by sun and wind. What I saw there was by no means the portrait of an aristocrat, but I was not disappointed with the cards that nature and circumstance had dealt me.

When I emerged from Ma's chamber, Toussaint, Charlotte, and their two children greeted me in the common room with looks of sweet sorrow mixed with fond regard. I reckon some of their other feelings were included in the mix, as well. They were genuinely fond of me, but it could not be inconsiderable in their eyes that my departure and my pledge never to return thither meant that the two farms, mine and Uncle Ben's, and all that stood upon that land would from that day onward be unquestionably theirs, undreamed-of wealth for Métis farmers who had been cropping on shares, whose fondest hope theretofore had been to be employed by a benevolent landlord who wouldn't cheat them out of the measly fruits of their labor.

The Poitier family entrained at my heels and followed me into the dooryard, where we made our farewells. Charlotte, tears brimming in her dark eyes, shoved still another straw hamper of foodstuffs and kitchen dainties into my arms, declaring that I must take it with me. Whatever feeble grasp of English she owned drowned in her emotion, causing her to tumble into a torrent of French, of which I understood but little, other than, *"Tu as besoin, M'sieu, d'avoir des aliments spécials pour ton voyage, pour la santé, aussi pour rappeler aux Toussaint et Charlotte et les enfants qui t'aiment!"* I had already provided myself with the simple provisions I required for my journey, but I thanked her for her thoughtful gifts, bestowed, as she said, for the sake of my health and as a reminder of her husband and herself and the children, who loved me. Then she brought out from under her apron a pair of ankle-high moccasins, beautifully beaded in the Chippewa fashion, an intricate design of flowers and leaves, and pressed them into my hands, saying the while, *"J'espère bien que ces moccasins dirigeront tes pas ici quelquejour!"* Grateful as I was for her elegant gift, I couldn't help thinking that a herd of wild horses, let alone those moccasins, would be insufficient ever to drag my steps back to Whynot and all its painful memories.

Whilst I was stuffing Charlotte's presents into my panniers, a grinning Toussaint nudged my elbow and held up a big earthen jug that I recognized as one of those in which Pap had always stored the very best whiskey that he produced in his still. Holy water is what that old psalm-singing, Bible-thumping, skirt-chasing, bootlegging scoundrel always called it. Those particular squeezin's likely constituted the only good deed he ever did for his fellow man, but you may be sure he was careful to keep most of it for himself. "'Ere, *M'sieu*," Toussaint said with a broad wink. "Take zis, as well, in case you are bite par un serpent à *sonnettes*, 'ow you say, a rattling snake!" I joined in Toussaint's huge guffaw and added the jug to my baggage. Much as I despised its maker, the evil man who had called himself my Pap, the whiskey was too good to pass up.

As I prepared to mount Kumskaka I was nigh bowled over by the sudden onrush of the Poitier children. Jean, a boy of thirteen, and his younger sister Celeste hugged me about the waist, blubbering French pleas for me to remain with them, then stammering farewells and fond wishes in faltering English when I told them that I surely must go. I had taught them English and the Three R's as a pastime while my wounds were healing. Now I reminded them that they must continue their studies, which they solemnly promised to do. Toussaint and Charlotte would teach them all else they needed to learn.

Further goodbyes were thankfully brief. I swung up onto Kumskaka, clucked to my packhorses, and, rifle resting on my thighs, rode out of the dooryard and into the west meadow, touched by the sentiment the Poitiers had lavished on me but jubilant at commencing at last my long-delayed westward journey.

* * *

The farms that bordered the trace soon petered out and thick forest hedged the track not far after that. When I came upon a well-worn deer trail I left the main road and plunged into the woods, intent upon discharging a final obligation to the memory of her to whom I owed not only my life but nearly everything I had held dear and precious in the years of my growing up.

My mother's unmarked grave lay in the abandoned, burned-out Shawnee village where I had learned the meaning of manhood and the abiding virtues and values that a proper father teaches his son. I glimpsed through leafless branches the hard-packed village street flanked by heaps of charcoaled rubble where fourscore and more wegiwas had once sheltered Powatawa's Shawnee band. All was silent now, but, even so, I fancied that I could hear men's angry shouts and women's mourning wails echoing from a time when those original inheritors of that patch of Mother Earth were driven from their homes a decade past by white men's fear and greed.

Although no monument or sepulcher graced my mother's final resting-place, I went directly to the spot circled by four stout fire-blackened trees, where Uncle Ben, Toussaint, and I, a year before, had laid her pitifully wasted remains — she who once was so comely and vibrant, blessedly released from pain and care — precisely where she most desired to commence her journey to whatever eternity there might prove to be, but which is surely waiting for us all, be it a place of cold and sterile paradise and angels strumming on golden harps, as whitemen are often told it is, or a blank and limitless nothing.

Kneeling in that place, I conjured up the days and weeks before Ma's death, when revelations of my mother's early life and my own origins flowed from her long-locked-up thoughts like springtime freshets tumbling down a mountainside. Knowing Death was nigh, she wrenched each shred of information from deep within her heart, fearful that I might condemn her but determined at the last to tell me all her history and who and what I truly was. Her tale emerged in bits and pieces, each fragment hauled most painfully from inner vaults long sealed, not so much from shame but rather from propriety instilled by her well-bred bringing-up in a well-to-do Virginia family and genteel neighborhood.

I have no wish to retail here every jot and tittle of my mother's history, but I reckon I had best explain the gist of it, so that a reader might understand the whys and therefores of much of what occurs later in this account of my own life.

Unfounded, malicious rumor circulated by a lunatic slave woman drove my mother from her father's comfortable home in Richmond, where she had been a respected society belle, a schoolteacher, and the fiancée of a handsome young aristocrat. Even the suggestion of a Negro taint in her blood, based only in cruel gossip, was too much for either her father or fiancé to resist and overcome in that society. So, friendless, alone, desperate, and anxious to flee Richmond's venomous wagging tongues, she reluctantly accepted a proposal of marriage from Lorenzo Buck, a shiftless, conniving, unprincipled ne'er-do-well, and resigned herself to a loveless marriage on the Ohio frontier.

Amanda Temple, besides being beautiful, was possessed of remarkable intelligence and a strong character, easily a match for Lorenzo Buck's cunning and sly maneuverings. For the first few years their wedlock existed more as a convenient arrangement than what most folks consider a marriage. Then my mother met and in time fell in love with Powatawa, a handsome Shawnee warrior destined to become chief of his band, who often came to our farm to trade tobacco and suchlike with her. When my mother discovered she was with child, knowing that the white community of Whynot would never tolerate her living amongst Shawnees, she duped Lorenzo into believing that the child was his, which he never doubted right up to his dying breath. I was that child and I grew up calling him Pap and accepting, but always regretting, that Lorenzo Buck was my father.

When Ma choked out her confession that I was a bastard, that Pap was not my father, that Powatawa had sired me, I greeted her pronouncement with shock and disbelief at first, but not unhappily. Such news was too good to be true. When the surprise wore off, I gloried in that knowledge. I have regarded my bar sinister ever since as proudly as any noble knight ever flaunted his plumed crest or a redskin warrior his eagle feathers won for valor.

Powatawa and his fellow Shawnees often came to trade with Ma when I was little, but neither he nor she ever let on that there was anything betwixt the two of them. If I had guessed, I daresay I would have rejoiced, for Pap was a mean, spiteful, hateful man, a harsh taskmaster who nigh killed me with farm chores and fetching and carrying for his whiskey still from the time I was scarcely old enough to walk. That shifty hypocrite fancied himself a preacher of religion, too, which he used mainly as a dodge for his sweet-talking seductions of neighbor women. I reckon I needn't mention that he and I never got along.

Ma commenced teaching me to read and write and cipher before I was big enough to sit properly at table and when she started teaching school, about the time I was five or six, she put her foot down with Pap and insisted that I attend her classes. Which I did, in spite of Pap's grumbling.

The only bright spot in my life back then, besides Ma and schooling, was Uncle Ben, Pap's younger half-brother, who owned the farm next to ours and was married to Aunt Penny, a pretty, red-headed, scatter-brained, good-natured, kindly, all-too-generous woman. They were childless and I reckon the kindest thing I can say is that Penny had more love to give than Ben could possibly use up. Ben wasn't much of a farmer, nor much of a talker either, but he was a keen woodsman. When I was twelve, Ben told Pap that he intended to teach me woodcraft and there would be no ifs, ands, or buts about it. Which he did. I learned from Ben how to shoot and track and stalk and trap, read sign, dress hides, gather truck from the woods and meadows, and most of what a boy needs to know, living in the Ohio wilderness as we did.

I reckon I didn't learn it all, howsomever, for if it hadn't been for Powatawa happening by to save me from a sow-bear in the woods, I would have been a goner before my first peach-fuzz whiskers commenced to sprout. Even so, I was pretty badly banged up, so Powatawa fetched me to his village and kept me there until I healed.

I came to know his son Chiksika and his daughter Methotasa, both about my age, and in time we got to be right friendly — but never too friendly with Methotasa, mind you. Chiksika and Powatawa taught me a lot of things, especially about horses, but the best thing I learned from them and the other Shawnees is that the color of his hide has nothing to do with the quality of either a horse or a man.

For the next couple years, whenever I could scrape time enough away from chores, I hung around that Shawnee village. After a spell, most of those Shawnees commenced treating me as if I weren't a stranger, inviting me to play in their games and to hunt and ride with them, which I took to be a signal compliment. Which it was.

Then Pap and a money-grubbing land speculator roused the rabble of Whynot and the country thereabouts — and even the Government — into believing the Shawnees posed a murderous threat to them all and Shawnee land should rightfully belong to white men. When the bluecoats came, Powatawa wisely retreated without a fight. He knew that in the long run he couldn't win, so he led his people westward.

Where they went and where they were now, I still didn't know, but I was determined to find out.

Whilst I tarried there beside my mother's grave, I mused on the events of that day, just a year before, when Ben, Toussaint, and I buried Ma in the burned-out Shawnee village, on the site of Powatawa's wegiwa, a place forbidden to her in her lifetime but where she wished to lie in final repose. She wore no shroud, but by her own dying request Penny and Charlotte dressed her body in quilled and beaded Shawnee buckskin garments given me in my youth by Powatawa and his family. It was fitting apparel for her journey to her heart's desire.

Afterwards we rode to Ben and Penny's farm to break our fast and reminisce and jest and drink a toast or two to Ma's safe journey, in the customary manner of the living who mourn the dead but nonetheless celebrate the life and breath they themselves still possess. When it came time for me to depart, Ben walked with me into his yard, carrying a musket he meant to return to me, only to be confronted by Pap, who demanded to know where Ma was buried, which we refused to reveal. Furious, Pap rushed into Ben's cabin and emerged a moment later armed with Ben's double-barreled fowling-piece, so enraged by then that he lost all reason and balance. When Ben tried to calm his brother down, Pap shot him in the belly, then aimed the gun at me. With his dying breath and the final twitch of his trigger-finger, Ben sent the sanctimonious old wretch off to hell, but not in time to prevent him from discharging a hefty load of goose shot into my legs as he fell, a wound more grievous than any I ever suffered at the hands of either Blackfoot or Crow — native people who most white folks who never met them will tell you are nothing but savage heathens.

So ended the life of that impious Man of the Cloth, that psalm-singing, adulterous, bootlegging Bearer of the Word, who killed his own innocent brother and did his level best to kill the man he firmly believed to be his son. For once I prefer to agree with Pap. I hope that he was right in one respect — that there is in fact a hell complete with fire and brimstone and all the other diabolic furnishings he so vividly described in his ranting sermons, and that he may suffer its torments for all eternity. Nobody ever deserved more to have his bad dreams come true.

It took nigh six months time for my wounds to heal, too late for me to return to the mountains that year, so I occupied those long days and weeks in writing a history of my first four years in the Rocky Mountain fur trade, honoring a deathbed promise I made to Ma. Now it was time for me to fulfill a couple pledges I had made to myself, mainly to find my own true father and return to the only family I still had left, my fellow-trappers in the Shining Mountains.

I bade a last farewell to Ma's remains and promised that she would be forever nigh my daily thoughts, a pledge that I have kept. Then I mounted Kumskaka, clucked to the other two to follow on behind, and rode out of that dismal grove without a single backward glance.

* * *

My pace that day was rapid, for a variety of reasons — my animals' excellent condition and their lack of recent exercise, the brisk, late-winter chill, which always stimulates the spirit of a healthy horse, but most importantly because of my fervent wish to shake the dust of Whynot off my moccasins.

I rode until nearly dusk, glorying in my newly-recovered freedom, intoxicated by the clean, fresh air I gulped into my lungs, day-dreaming of Saint Louis and the Shining Mountains that lay a thousand miles or more beyond there. When it came time to halt, I rode some distance off the trace and chose a secluded little clearing in the woods, unsaddled and hobbled my horses, rubbed them down and curried their sweaty backs, treated each of them to a quart or so of grain, and turned them out to forage for whatever grass they could find beneath the skimpy blanket of snow. Then I gathered firewood and lopped off springy fir branches for my bed, then spread my buffalo robes and woolen blankets on top. The kettle was soon boiling and coffee fragrance filled the air. I had no need for cooking. Charlotte's delicious vittles, moistened with a dram or two or more of Pap's prime whiskey, filled my belly to a noble satisfaction. No wealthy English lord or eastern nabob ever supped and swilled with greater pleasure than I did that night.

When I crawled into my robes and propped my head upon my saddle, cradling my rifle at my side, I regretted not a whit the soft bed I had left behind. Stretching out on Mother Earth's firm bosom provided all the comfort a mountaineer could rightly ask. In spite of my euphoria, howsomever, the moment I closed my eyes I saw the troubled face of Sarah, beloved since my childhood, her dark eyes clouded with concern and disappointment. I could hear her single, strangled, "Oh!" that tolled the death of all her lifelong love for me, the night I proudly told her that Pap was not my father but, instead, Powatawa, a noble Shawnee chief, was the man who sired me. That choked-out "Oh!" was the final syllable that ever she addressed to me. And not many moons had waxed and waned before she wed a scion of a family that had been the mortal enemy of my true father's people.

Self-preserving practicality is a useful trait fostered by the mountain life. Rue distills into a bitter draught and I possess no taste for such. I had shed tears enough and more, bemoaning Sarah's instant disavowal of her love for me. Now I preferred to console myself with recollections of more complaisant lovers, who took me as I was and for what I have become, without regard for blood or birth, admiring those qualities in me that I value most myself. Half a dozen faces floated through my mind, resolving into only one, the golden-skinned Lucette, she of the sparkling ebon eyes and impish laughter — no better than she should be, as some might say — mercurial in temper but always mindful of reality, demanding, it is true, but generous with treasure, unfaltering affection, ready understanding, and her own delicious self.

Fond memories of Lucette provided a comforting replacement for painful recollections of Sarah and her cold dismissal of my person and devotion. Callous or capricious as you may judge me to be, that night I put aside forever all pining for the love I'd lost, contemplating in its place the renewal, leastaways for a spell, of a romantic friendship more genuine and honest and — equally important, to my practical way of thinking — possible. Borne upon a warm tide of remembered images and sensations, I drifted into peaceful slumber, free of care and almost all regret, sure within my heart that my chosen course was true.

* * *

Coals still winked and glowed amongst the ashes of my fire from the night before when I awakened in the lead-grey light of early dawn. I heaped on double handfuls of oak and maple twigs and shoved my half-filled coffee kettle nigh the blaze before I hustled off to perform my morning chore, reflecting the while on how eastern hardwoods make better cookfires than does western fir — but, for the very life of me, I couldn't conjure up a single other argument for remaining in the flatlands.

My horses nickered softly at my approach, greedy for their breakfast grain, when I retrieved them from the meadow. Whilst they munched and snorted I packed my sleep robes and camp gear, then squatted nigh the fire, warming my shanks by its friendly blaze and my belly with strong coffee, thinking of the trail ahead, wondering if I could make it to Cincinnati by nightfall. I had no clear idea of the distance that lay between Whynot and that thriving metropolis on the banks of the Ohio River. The only time I had glimpsed even the fringe of that city had occurred six years before, in the course of a nightmare journey down the Ohio, when I had been held prisoner, forced to serve as an unwilling, unpaid deckhand and all-purpose drudge aboard Mike Fink's keelboat.

I reckon it is best that I suspend my current chronicle right here and explain how it was I landed in that sorry plight, which changed the course and character of all my life thereafter.

Losing my virginity was what lit the fuse on the whole powder train of events that altered my history from what it likely would have turned out to be. It was not so much the loss itself — an experience of little consequence, eagerly anticipated and joyfully welcomed by most boys and young men when it finally occurs — but rather the peculiar circumstances which surrounded the forfeiture of my innocence. As I hinted on a previous page, my Aunt Penny was a pretty woman of certain age who was forever itching to bestow her abundant love upon her fellow man. My Uncle Ben evidently lacked sufficient appetite in that regard to satisfy her generous impulses. So it was that at the age of nineteen I chanced to come a-calling at a time when my uncle was off hunting. Before I fully grasped what was happening, Aunt Penny had transformed the boy I had been into the man I would be thereafter. Which would have been bad enough, seeing as how she was kin, even if just by marriage. But what made it worse was when Pap surprised us in bed, just as I was getting the proper hang of it all. Excitable and jealous as he was, for Aunt Penny had been generous with him as well, Pap fired off Ben's fowling-piece through the roof and commenced shouting bloody murder. I dived out the window and hotfooted it for the Ohio River, sure that Pap and Ben and all Ben's dogs were on my heels. Which they weren't, but I didn't know that at the time.

I ran all night, barefoot, clad only in a shirt and britches, until at dawn I spied a keelboat anchored in the shallows. Seeking refuge from my imaginary pursuers, I swam out, sneaked aboard the boat, and, exhausted as I was, fell sound asleep, only to be roused not long afterwards by a vicious kick, accompanied by any number of cuffs and blows, administered by the supreme bully-boy of all the rough and tough, hard-fisted Ohio riverboatmen, Mike Fink, who made up in sheer ferocity and greed whatever he lacked in charity and conscience. His two constant companions, Carpenter and Talbot, were hardly less brutal than their chief. Fink refused to put me ashore, insisting that I owed him the price of my passage and demanding that I work it out on the journey down the Ohio and up the Mississippi to Saint Louis. At first I was chained each night alongside Micah, a Negro slave whom Fink had fished out of the river after Micah's boat capsized, drowning his master and all others aboard, but after a spell Fink quit chaining me, once he extracted my promise that I would not attempt to run off. Which in any case would have been folly, for all three of those river bullies were prime marksmen. They would have considered hunting me down and killing me simply to be capital sport.

The following days and weeks melded into a single continuous horrible dream — fetching and carrying, lading and off-lading cargo at river ports, helping Micah with cooking chores for Fink and the roughneck crew he recruited in Kentucky, running the dangerous Falls of the Ohio, then rowing, poling, and hauling the keelboat up the Mississippi.

My only solace, save one other, was teaching Micah to read and write, the one opportunity available to me for revenge against Mike Fink, for bestowing literacy on a slave is contrary to law and subject to severe penalty in slave-holding states. My only other additional comfort was the bond of friendship I forged with Tuttle Thompson, a happy-go-lucky Kentucky backwoodsman, who lived for whiskey, women, and horses, whichever came first to hand. Tuttle and I tugged on the same oar, stood shoulder to shoulder poling that infernal keelboat through the Mississippi shallows, and hauled together on a towrope, often knee-deep in river muck, inching Mike Fink's miserable scow upriver to Saint Louis, where Fink was at last obliged to turn me loose. Hardship shared in such circumstances bound Tuttle and me together in lifelong brotherhood.

* * *

Such recollections occupied my thoughts all morning, whilst I maintained my horses in a steady, mile-eating trot, slowing now and then to a walk, so as to ease the muscles used in trotting, tarrying only briefly to water them at streams we crossed. Reluctantly I halted at noon in a likely meadow to allow my animals to restore themselves on winter-sered timothy grass and broke my own fast with a bait of Charlotte's delicious comestibles, although I felt little hunger for common food. That day I was content to feast on fresh air and freedom from my close confinement whilst I healed during the past year, slaking my thirst with thoughts of imminent reunion with friends and comrades whom I held supremely dear.

My contentment was, howsomever, destined to be short-lived.

That afternoon I overtook a straggling column of bluecoat infantry led by a lad I took to be an officer, judging by his tarnished epaulettes and the shiny saber that rattled at his side. Only he was mounted and except for the muskets they shouldered, slanting every whichaway, his charges might have been a convict gang, unshaven, sullen, clad in mismatched uniforms pieced out with odd bits of castoff farmer clothing, and marching out of step. I gave the rambling procession wide berth and would have ridden past, except for the leader's hailing me and bidding me to ride beside him for a spell. Unwilling though I was to slow my pace, I complied with his request and reined my Ready horse to a walk, then sidled nigh his slowly plodding nag. Close up, I saw he was hardly more than a boy who likely hadn't yet counted a full score of years, slim and gawky, well-nigh chinless, pimply-faced, awkward in voice and manner. His tone, howsomever, did not match his appearance.

"What is your destination, sir, and what is the nature of your business there?" he rapped out in a reedy voice. Stung by his forwardness, I nevertheless replied civilly that I was headed for Cincinnati but that I had no business there and would merely be passing through.

"Then what is your destination, sir, if it be not Cincinnati? Speak up and bear in mind that you are addressing an officer of the United States Army!"

I felt my temper slipping off but I held my peace for a spell, then replied as levelly as I could manage, "Where I mean to go and what I'm aimin' to do when I get there is none o' your damn business, sonny," -- I called him that although I likely had no more than half a dozen years on him — "an' I mean to keep it so! You've no call to bid me anything beyond the time o' day. I'll tell ye nothin', 'ceptin' this — if it's bullyin' ye wish to do, ye'd best go pick on one o' your sorry tramps back there!" I hooked my thumb towards his marching men. "Don't seek to puff your scrawny chest by messin' with a mountaineer!"

Even I was astonished at the vehemence of my response. The young officer was purely abashed. His watery blue eyes fairly popped. His pimples nigh disappeared on his blushing cheeks. He clamped his mouth tight shut, forestalling a reply that might have set me off again. We rode side by side in silence, I seeking to bridle my anger, he taking careful note of my person, garb, arms, and gear, obviously wishing to enquire in particular about the queer design of my Spaniard saddle and especially my percussion rifle and pistol, none of which he had likely seen before. He was careful not to do so, howsomever, lest he provoke another outburst on my part. When I reckoned I had calmed down enough, I turned and said, "I'll tell ye nothin' 'bout myself, but I'll hand ye some advice. I see you're headin' west an' the farther west ye go, the more ye'll learn your popinjay bad manners just don't shine thereabouts. An' they're apt to get ye killed. Just try, hard as ye can, to be the man ye wish ye were! All the rest comes easy. All of us'll always have a lot more to learn an' it's best ye start your own learnin' right about now."

I didn't wait for his reply. I gathered up my reins, clucked to my other horses, touched spur to Ready's flank, and galloped on ahead. I never looked back, but just as Ready surged forward, I caught a sidewise glimpse of the young officer flicking me a respectful salute.

When I reckoned I had put a decent distance betwixt myself and the marching soldiers I slowed my horses to a trot and took time to chew over my brief confrontation with the military. What surprised me most was my own hair-trigger response to the young man's impertinent inquiry, not only what I said but especially the style of speech I put to use. My angry words still echoed in my ears and they sounded more like something Tuttle or grumpy old Anse Tolliver might say than the common speech I use. Mountaineers prize their freedom far above any other wealth and the chinless wonder's officious meddling in my personal affairs had clearly trespassed on the holy precincts of my privacy. Even so, I had to admit that my response had been more than somewhat harsh, which merely firmed my resolve to get back to the mountains as soon as possible, in order to avoid such bothersome encounters.

I overtook and passed several other travelers on the trace that day, wagons loaded with potatoes or dried corn or piled high with sacks of grain, men trundling wheelbarrows covered with osnaburg sheeting to protect their merchandise against the weather, a traveling tinker, and a few who bore a pedlar's pack strapped onto their back. 'Most all of them, I reckoned, were headed for Cincinnati. I didn't slow my pace to chat, but if a salutation was offered, I returned the greeting with a friendly wave.

Cincinnati still lay beyond my reach when dusk commenced to settle on the trace ahead. I rode some distance off the track and came upon a hollow almost free of snow, with grass enough to graze my critters overnight and deadwood for my fire. It took hardly any time at all to tend to my critters and turn them out, roll out my sleep robes, and get a fire blazing. Whilst coffee bubbled in the kettle, blending its fragrance with tobacco smoke, I sipped a dram or so of Pap's prime squeezin's and let my mind run out unbridled, mulling over all that had befallen me that day, especially meeting up with that sorry troop of bluecoat foot-sloggers, then comparing such surly curs with my companions in the mountains, whom I intended to rejoin before half a dozen moons had waxed and waned.

Naturally Tuttle Thompson came first to mind. Long and stringy, rawboned, usually bewhiskered Tuttle, unwashed and profligate, who worshiped at two altars — his unquenchable thirst and never-satiated lust. Prodigal with his pelf, and often mine, he always made his debits good. Even if he hadn't done so, his simple honesty and comical good humor, his unfailing, almost casual, courage come whatever peril, fortitude in hardship, boisterous good-fellowship, and wholehearted dedication to his friends would have easily redeemed his debts.

Loved and honored though he was by me, Tuttle was but one amongst a baker's dozen of companions enshrined in my affections. Running a close second was a Len-nee Leh-nah-peh, the Delaware Indian Brass Turtle, he who had been stolen from his murdered kin and raised up to the age of twelve in abuse and servitude by whites, at which time he ran off from Pennsylvania to rejoin his people, who by then had fled their home country and sought refuge in Missouri. A natural leader of men, Brass Turtle's English was easily as good as my own, with Lén-nee Léh-nah-peh, Iroquois, and French-Canuck thrown in for boot. All those tongues were employed in his wry jests, cogent observations, and cynical remarks.

Lest you suppose that Brass Turtle was mostly mouth, I assure you that the Shining Mountains never saw a man more brave and cunning or more able in pursuit of war, resolute and steadfast, generous and helpful to his fellows, and infinitely wise beyond his thirty or so years. Remembering Turtle naturally conjured up the persons of diminutive old Foot the Healer and his hulking, good-natured apprentice Little Mountain, also Delawares, who were as handy at inflicting sudden death and wounds on enemies as they were clever in stitching up our own rips and tears and bullet holes.

Running through the pack of my remembered friends, I dwelt a spell upon Ned Godey, a gentle, good-natured man, somewhat older than the rest of us but not old, once a trader on the High Missouri, who had been our mentor in the early days when we first ascended the Big Muddy. He taught us how to trap the streams that feed the Yellowstone and Musselshell. Later, he readily blended in and learned the mountain lore alongside the rest of us, but we continued to rely on Ned's sage counsel whenever we met up with situations that called for cool and thoughtful judgment. Which circumstances occur more often than a flatlander might think.

Pictures sprang to mind of cantankerous Anse Tolliver, a scarecrow-skinny Tennessee hillbilly whose customary sour temper brings to mind a pocketful of broken glass. Anse's two great loves are mules and scraping on his fiddle. A third is without a doubt his penchant for carping and complaining, criticizing one and all. But Anse, for all his grumbling, never misses a muster when there is work or fighting to be done. His unlikely sidekick is a red-haired little Irishman, good-humored Padraic McBride, who shrugs off Anse's gibes and often turns them into compliments. Mountain life has proved our Paddy to be the rough and ready equal of any man amongst us, no matter that his Irish people's pride has been despised and trampled for untold generations.

Our trapping bunch is rounded out by Pretty Horse, a shrewd and able Iroquois, braggadocio Jim Beckwith, a Negro-Whiteman-Cherokee, who measures up to any trapper in the trade for grit and skill and bravery and who boasts of his deeds better and considerably louder than any other one of them, and Beckwith's boon companion, Cesár Pérez, a dark-hued Spaniard up from Santa Fe, whose horsemanship and roping skills provoke the admiration of all who watch him at such work.

Not every man in our bunch is a trapper. Jean-Luc L'Archévêque and Yves Dureau, a pair of half-bred French-Canucks, are content to work for wages, tending camp and doing chores a trapper considers wasteful of his time when there is beaver-trapping to be done.

There were others, long since fallen to the musket balls and arrows of Crow and Blackfoot warriors, but I swiftly turned my thoughts away from them, preferring to rejoice amongst the living rather than squander time and feeling by mourning for the dead.

How I longed with all my heart that night to be reunited with that unwashed, rowdy, polyglot, rainbow-colored crew, gorging on fresh buffalo hump and trading quips and swapping lies and treading out the lively rhythm of some hillbilly tune that Anse scraped off those magical catgut strings of his! I hadn't felt so lonely since I first parted with their company nigh two years before. Knowing that my present trail led back to them increased my need for their fellowship almost more than I could tolerate. I reckoned I surely had become some sort of herd critter — like a buffalo or wapiti who demands the society of his brethren — but all the while insisting that it must be my own particular kind of herd — Rocky Mountain trappers, hivernants, mountaineers. If such were not available, I preferred the solitary comfort of fond recollections of better times and better men than any I would likely see thereabouts.

Such memories afforded me good company whilst I munched the last scraps and shreds of Charlotte's largesse and sipped strong coffee laced with mellow whiskey, until my drooping eyelids and nodding head signaled it was well past time I roll into my robes.

One more beloved image emerged from the glowing coals of my cookfire as I settled into sleep, the lovely face and form of the adorable Lucette. Remembrance of her dusky Creole beauty, her scent and antic humor, and her ever-ready passion warmed my drowsing thoughts — and, I must confess, elsewhere as well. Lucette awaited in Saint Louis, but, I hastened to remind myself, she waited not for me. During my absence in the mountains, she at last achieved her long-desired goal of respectability by marrying a wealthy old French widower. She had closed down her famed establishment, to the disappointment of her household of filles de joie, an act which must have most certainly occasioned considerable distress, as well, amongst the cream of Saint Louis male society. Still, I might console myself with remembered pleasures of her bed. Which was nonetheless cold comfort for a healthy young fellow who possessed only his rifle to share his sleep robes.

When at last I slipped away in slumber I dreamt not of Lucette and her warm and sometimes well-nigh scalding charms, but rather of the mountains and scenes of rendezvous, where tipsy trappers frolicked and I pursued but never caught a tall Lahcotah woman who kept vanishing into the rising sun.

* * *

Mid-morning sunshine warmed my back as my critters ambled through Cincinnati's swarming, rutted thoroughfares. I gawked like the veriest backwoods yokel at the vast jumble of buildings and businesses that crowded every passageway and lane that led up from the river docks into the town, which sprawled northward out of sight — mercantiles and boat chandlers, forges and ironmongers, butchers' stalls and bakeries, saddlers' and harness-makers' shops, wheelwrights, livery barns and hay and grain merchants, cooperages, ropewalks, bootmakers, potteries, hawkers' sheds, shacks and shanties where flush-faced, red-armed laundresses plied their trade, victualers and taverns and lodging houses, and some I took to be bawdy houses from the look and manner of the scantily-clad belles who occupied the stoops, their greetings somewhat too inviting to be mistaken for mere civic hospitality.

My gawking was repaid in kind by Cincinnati's citizens I met along the way. Although mountaineers and fur traders are a common sight in Saint Louis town, my long hair and buckskin garb, weapons, and horse furniture excited curiosity that I deemed unwelcome. I hastened westwards through crowded streets, halting only long enough at a mercantile to replenish my stock of oats for my critters and foodstuffs for myself. Leastaways that was my intention, but as I was leaving the storeroom I spied a stack of well-made little iron lead-pots complete with ladles, just big enough to melt a single galena pig, so I bought half a dozen for presents for my friends in the mountains. The wily storekeeper divined my weakness and pounced. Before I made it out the door I had purchased three excellent eight-point Witney blankets, a three-legged spider, and a dozen fine English butcher knives, as well.

Munching on a stick of peppermint sweet the merchant had thrown in for boot, I urged my horses through the teeming streets as rapidly as the swirling traffic permitted, dodging 'round lumbering cargo drays and fancy carriages, threading an uncertain path through throngs of noisy, jostling, colorful humanity afoot and unconcerned with aught but their own errands and intentions. I was forced to curb my critters every stride or so, lest we trample one or more of those unmindful city folk and thereby cause additional delay.

At last we reached the western outskirts of the town, where I touched spur to flank and urged my critters onwards and away from Cincinnati's bustling bedlam, happy as Christmas to be free of city din, the overwhelming press of humanity, and cloying, crowding commerce. If I had entertained any thought of lingering nearby, a southward breeze that blew up from the river, carrying the noisome stench of a tannery to my nostrils, would have dispelled such notions. I snorted just as loudly as my horses did and galloped off along the trace until we were able once again to breathe clean, refreshing air.

* * *

My westward journey across the southern stretches of Ohio and Indiana continued without memorable incident. I avoided as best I could the larger towns, replenishing what little provisions I required at hard-scrabble farms and measly villages, remaining aloof from their residents, who were likely content that I did so. Suspicion and distrust of strangers appeared to be the watchword of such settlements and I felt no inclination to challenge their cold reserve. I marveled that there should be such poverty and ignorance and obvious ill-health amongst a people living in a country blessed with so much of nature's bounty — rich black soil and grass enough to graze at least a brace of cattle to the acre, timber trees, and water flowing in abundance. Instead of thriving farms and prosperous inhabitants I saw rude huts scattered through the woods, overrun with dirty, squalling, sickly, mostly-naked kids, indifferently mothered by vacant-eyed women grown old and haggard long before their time, lord-and-mastered by cold-eyed men, snaggle-toothed and shiftless, who apparently possessed no proper sense of self or purpose, whose only pride resided in some vague alliance with other folk who shared the color of their skin.

I could not help comparing those squalid dwellings, ill-kept fields, and unsavory residents with Powatawa's well-ordered

Shawnee village and its careful husbandry of cornfields, squash patches, meat critters, and the like, so much despised by Whynot's whites, and with the free nomadic life of wild Indians I had known in the mountains and the prairies of the West. Such idle speculation, howsomever, served no useful purpose. My best and proper course was to travel through that self-benighted country as rapidly as healthy horseflesh would allow. Which I did.

I ate well enough throughout my journey west. Approaching spring brought clouds of passenger pigeons blackening the skies and blotting out the sun, easy targets for my fowling piece, and marshes bordering the Ohio provided plump canvasback ducks in any quantity I might wish. If I hungered for solid flesh meat, I had no need to travel much distance off the trace before I bagged a tender doe. My needs were modest, my tastes were plain, and nature generously supplied me with all that I desired.

* * *

Spring came early thereabouts in 'twenty-eight. Freshets swelled the cricks and streams and every watercourse that called itself a river was running high and wild. The ferryman I met upon the Indiana bank of the Wabash was nigh beside himself with joy, contemplating windfall profits from his passengers, who were forced to gather at his wharf, and only his, from upstream and down to employ his services. He had equipped his ferryboat with stout ropes fastened onto either bank, cranked by massive windlasses, one in the bow drawing up the well-oiled rope to propel the craft across to the farther shore, while the windlass in the stern grudgingly paid out its length of rope to hold the ferry steady in the stream. From what I gathered, none of his nearby competitors had bothered to furnish their own ferryboats with such contraptions, relying instead on the customary oars and poles and sail, which were of slight utility when the Wabash rose in flood and threatened to overspill its banks.

The ferryman was a little German, by the sound of him, who glowed with satisfaction when I fished a banknote from my poke and bade him keep the change. His businesslike, brusque manner altered instantly and he immediately became my friend, leastaways for the length of our journey across the river. As we led my horses aboard and cross-tied them in the bow, he confided the secret of his success. "Alvays aheadt your t'inkin' you must do!" he solemnly proclaimed. "Take me. A purty *fraulein* I couldt haf ved, but sons der size uff me I vouldt haf got! So no! Die biggest, strongest girl I found, I picked fer marryin', undt look!" he pointed proudly towards four hulking, broad-shouldered, red-faced lads trooping aboard the ferryboat, "Dose be my boys! Not too qvick fer die t'inkin', but big enuf undt more fer die verkin' hardt! Die t'inkin' I vill do fer dem." I nodded as sagely as I could manage, saying naught and fighting to keep a straight face, which I barely succeeded in doing.

When cargo was stowed and the other passengers came aboard, the ferryman, who said his name was Dieter, cast off the mooring lines and his two biggest sons commenced to crank us across the river. The other two maintained the sternward windlass, snugging the clumsy craft to the Indiana shore against the rushing current, releasing just enough rope to make up for the length retrieved by the brothers in the prow, thus preventing the ferry from swinging downstream like a pendulum unto its sure destruction against the farther shore.

The sky was overcast, heavy as galena, and a fine drizzle commenced to fall. Then rain swept down in sheets, drenching all of us and spooking my three horses, who rolled their eyes and skittered and stamped to keep their footing on the slippery deck. We had traversed somewhat less than half the river's breadth when I felt the ferry shudder to a halt and heard the bow-line twanging like a fiddlestring, straining against the muddy surge of Wabash waters. The brothers in the bow were tugging at the windlass spindles with all their might, but the two of them, strong as they were, were powerless to gain so much as a single fathom against the flood that threatened to swamp Dieter's fragile ark.

"Gunther! Hans! *Mach schnell!* Go help yer brudders!" Dieter barked. Then he plucked at my sleeve, signaling me to help him man the windlass in the stern. I hesitated not a blink and joined him at the giant wheel, white-knuckled hands gripping a slippery spindle like grim Death itself, eyes fixed on the brothers in the bow. The younger two flew to aid their brethren, leaping high to grab an upper spindle, then pitting all their weight and strength against the river's surge to drag it downwards. Slowly, painfully we commenced to inch towards the Illinois shore, then moving somewhat faster as the four stout lads sorted themselves into a smoothly working crew, until at last we crossed the swiftly-running channel and gained calmer waters where the shallows should have been.

The clacking of the ratchets fore and aft was music in my ears, telling off each foot and yard and fathom that we gained against the river's might. The rain had quit and we relaxed somewhat, confident that we would soon set foot on solid earth in Illinois. Dieter, evidently feeling comradely after our mutual exertions, made bold enough to ask my destination. I, perhaps because of the danger we had shared, surprised myself by telling him that first I meant to travel to Saint Louis, then afterwards, on to the Shining Mountains of the West.

Through the windlass spokes and past the taut and dripping oily rope I could see old Dieter purse his lips, chewing over my reply. Then, blue eyes snapping, he demanded, "Vy you vant to do like dat? Ef'ry day I see dese traf'lers comin' here undt goin' dere undt comin' back undt neffer settlin' down! Undt vy? Nuttin' but der horse's ears dey see! Nuttin' do dey learn!" He drew a deep breath to calm himself, I reckon, and pronounced, "Vun blace iss ef'ryvere! Ef'ryblace iss no blace. Traffel der whole welt, nuttin' vot you see can you unnerstan'! Chust be sittin' by your door in your own haus undt, soon or late, der whole welt up to you comes trompin'!"

Dieter finished his sermon with a petulant glint in his eye, daring me to contradict him, which I was not about to do. Instead I replied simply, "Well, I reckon that's what makes for hoss races — diff'rent opinions." I might have added another old saw, the one about one man's meat is another man's poison, but I didn't, for fear of setting him off again.

The ferry grated against the rocky bottom and nudged into the muddy bank, prompting the other rain-bedraggled passengers to break out of their huddle in the stern — soon to become the prow for the return trip to Indiana — and scamper onto dry land. Just before I mounted Kumskaka on the slippery deck, I shook hands with Dieter, who observed, "Too badt you go to dem damn mountains. Uff you, I t'ink, ve could make a damn goot ferryman, py Gott!" I restricted my reply to a smile and a friendly clap on the shoulder. I forebore telling him that I despise any water deeper than a beaver pond. Six years before, crewing on keelboats, I had learned to loathe the Ohio, Mississippi, and Missouri. After that wild morning on the waves, I account the Wabash not a jot or tittle better.

Kumskaka plunged into hock-deep water and scrambled up the bank, Ashley and my Ready horse in tow, not one of them more grateful than I myself at feeling solid ground beneath our feet. I waved farewell and reined Kumskaka onto the trace, glad to be once again master of my circumstances, no longer flotsam at the indifferent mercy of a capricious river.

Later, hunched over my cookfire, drying out my clothes, I chewed on Dieter's proposition that one place is everywhere, everywhere is nowhere. Maybe so, but such thinking takes no account of an itchy foot or the deep-down urgent need in a certain breed of men to see the other side of the mountain. I had already seen and felt and done and learned a heap of things that never would have come to me sitting on a stoop beside the Wabash or on a farm in Whynot. Maybe Dieter had got himself a bellyful of traveling, coming from the Old Country like he did, but for my part, I still had appetite enough to chew up all the Shining Mountains and wash them down with every river in the West.

* * *

The lights of Saint Louis across the Mississippi glowed and winked a welcome to the prodigal encamped upon the Illinois shore, awaiting daybreak and the turning of another page in my history. The days and weeks of journeying had not exhausted me. Rather, every forward stride provided me with extra strength, tapping ever deeper wellsprings of hope and confidence, assuring me that my chosen course was true and that what I termed success was well within my grasp, if only I possessed grit and smarts enough to make it so.

Wavelets lapping at the foot of the low bluff on which I had pitched my simple camp lulled me into pleasant, idle thoughts, anticipating long-dreamed-of reunion with Pierre Chouteau, Cadet, my friend and benefactor, and with black Micah, my comrade in base servitude aboard the keelboat of Mike Fink, now as much a gentleman as white Saint Louis would allow him to be. If his intention had not wavered since I saw him last, I meant to help him to a state of pride and independence of which he likely hadn't dared to dream. Reunion with one other man, I hoped, awaited not far distant in the future, the Shawnee chief Powatawa, my savior, friend, and mentor, who was still unaware that now I knew him to be my father, too.

Eager as I was to see tomorrow's sun and get on with my chores, the long day's ride caught up with me and weighed my eyelids down. I burrowed deep within my robes, anticipating tomorrow's crossing over the muddy Mississippi, which at sundown had looked to be a frothy sea of café-au-lait. That shade of color brought to mind the much-desired but now out-of-reach Lucette, once my teacher in the arts of love but now respectably ensconced in holy matrimony. Still, it did no harm nor compromised her connubial virtue if I privately recalled warmer times with her and the fleshly pleasures we had shared. Which I did, until sweet slumber stole such thoughts away.

Chapter II
Old Ties Renewed

The narrow, crooked lanes and alleys of Vide Poche branched out from the dock where the ferryman had at last brought his clumsy craft ashore, a considerable distance downstream from Chouteau's wharf, which had been our intended destination. The Mississippi was running high in spring flood, cluttered with all manner of debris and great chunks of ice flung into it upstream by the Illinois and Missouri and all the rivers, cricks, and measly watercourses that drain into what some say the Indians call the Father of Waters. The ferry crew had been hard put to make it to the farther shore at all.

The captain's curses, complaining of the added cost of drayage to haul his cargo back to town, rang out above the clatter of my horses' hooves and their grateful whinnying as they scrambled onto the dock. His losses made no nevermind to me. I was simply glad to feel solid earth beneath my feet once more and eager to accomplish my errands in Saint Louis town as quickly as possible.

I snugged up girths and cinches, swung onto Kumskaka's back, and clattered off the dock, packhorses in tow. The ferry captain ignored my casual farewell. He was busy fuming at his Negro crew, as if they had connived to increase the Mississippi's flow and thereby deprive him of his profit.

We plunged into a labyrinth of winding streets and cramped alleyways called the Vide Poche, the Empty Poke, which pretty much describes the finances of most of those who frequent its saloons and bawdy houses, cookshops, and lodging-houses — river sailors, stevedores, common laborers, footpads, and faded trollops. Once I spied a solemn, buckskin-clad trapper, long rifle cradled on his arm, belt crammed full of weapons, who acknowledged my silent greeting with hardly more than a flicker of an eyelid and a brief nod, as he made his way from one low dive to another.

I urged my horses to a trot, loosened my pistol in its pommel holster, and patted the belly gun in my waistband, for even in the daylight Vide Poche is no place to linger. All too many of its residents wouldn't scruple or hesitate half a breath to plunder me of all that I possessed if they thought they might succeed. I reckoned I could deal with whatever came my way, but such an encounter would prove bothersome and likely bloody and cause delay. I was impatient to get on with the business I had come there to do. At last we came upon a byway I recalled that led up to the proper part of town. Soon my little caravan emerged onto a busy thoroughfare I recognized as one that led to Chouteau's mercantile, where I meant to pay respects and commence my chores.

I slowed my pace lest my horses trample foot-travelers, most of whom appeared to be unmindful of my critters or of one another or even of their own whereabouts, as they single-mindedly pursued their private ends, seemingly lost in a fog of their own thoughts and personal intentions, oblivious of harm or aught else around them. As we ambled at a snail's pace through the throng I consoled myself with the prospect of soon being shut of city-dwellers, of journeying to the western wilderness, where unwary folk are soon erased from all consideration.

We hadn't traveled far before I spied a house, indeed a mansion, which had often occupied my thoughts and dreams, Lucette's establishment. I expected that it would be closed and boarded up, as it had been since her marriage. But much to my surprise, a platoon of workmen swarmed about its walls and roof and spilled into its spacious gardens — masons, carpenters, and painters, gardeners planting trees and bushes, and glaziers replacing broken panes behind shutters now thrown wide, which when I last saw that place were sealed tight shut as a coffin. I reckoned Lucette had wisely decided to sell her former place of business, for such a property must be exceedingly valuable in a town growing as fast as Saint Louis appeared to be. Where I recalled vacant lots and grassy fields there now stood brand-new buildings, some still raw with lumber fresh-hauled from the mill, many of them gleaming bright with recent paint. Shrewd as she was with money, Lucette wouldn't likely let her property remain idle forever and thereby miss an opportunity to multiply her wealth.

As I made my careful way through crowded streets, heading for Chouteau's, I reflected on the first time, six years before, that I had trod those cobblestones in Tuttle's too-big cast-off moccasins, dragged along by bully-boy Mike Fink and prodded by his henchmen, ragged, scared, penniless, and — except for Tuttle Thompson and a Negro slave — friendless, without a scrap of hope for better times. Then I recalled how Lucette and le Cadet had set me on a path where I could test my mettle and prove my worth in the Shining Mountains.

Such recollections contrasted sharply with my fortunes at the moment. I was well-mounted, armed with the best of weapons, furnished with all the fixin's I could desire, healthy, and secure in the mastery of my trade. Some might consider me to be a wealthy man, thanks to my chance inheritance of all Mike Fink's ill-gotten gains and Pierre Chouteau's shrewd and careful husbandry of that windfall and the cash I earned by beaver-trapping, but such wealth was of little consequence to me.

The riches that I valued most resided in my friendships and the freedom I would soon enjoy once more in the Shining Mountains — freedom that even the richest nabob of the Orient can never know, the freedom of a Rocky Mountain trapper, who pits his brains and skill and daring against harsh Nature's law, and, if he succeeds, walks in total liberty upon the earth, unfettered by man-made laws or social custom, parochial considerations, taboos of other men's religion, or any interest but his own, relying only on his strength and skill and native cunning. Money cannot buy a penny's worth of such sweet satisfaction.

It was approaching noon when a final turn in the winding street brought me out upon the river bank. I scarcely recognized Berthold et Chouteau's imposing red-brick mercantile, crowded as it was now by new-built stores and workshops which blossomed in the open fields I recalled from just eighteen months before. I tethered my horses at the rail, entrusting them to a smiling young black man who waited there. Avoiding the double-doored entrance to the busy mercantile, I entered the building by a side door whose discreet brass plaque quietly announced Berthold et Chouteau, Commerçants.

The interior was cool and dim and the vast array of clerks' writing tables and high stools was mostly deserted, green-shaded whale-oil lamps snuffed out, except for one in front, where the sallow-faced chief clerk presided. He came forth to challenge me, a forbidding look upon his bony features, then recognized me as a client and a friend of le Cadet. His stony expression vanished instantly and he exclaimed, "Ah, M'sieu Bock, *bienvenue*! You are mos' welcome 'ere! I weel tell M'sieu Chouteau of your *arrivée*, eef you weel wait 'ere, *s'il vous plaît*." He scurried off without waiting for a reply, yanking the bombazine covers from the sleeves of his rusty black frock as he went.

Whilst I watched him hurry off, I chuckled to myself, recalling his frigid and austere reception of my early visits to those offices, until Chouteau informed him that in spite of my weather-browned features, belt-length hair, and travel-worn, sweat-stiff, bloodstained buckskin garb, I was not a renegade Métis, but in fact a man of substance, a valued client, and a friend. As I have said elsewhere, money is of slight importance to me, but at such times the reputation it conveys and the civility it commands can be most helpful and amusing.

I had not long to wait. Pierre Chouteau emerged from his workroom a moment later, slim and elegant, impeccably tailored, a smile of pleasure lighting up his hawkish features as he advanced, his hand outstretched. "*Ah, mon ami, bienvenue*! Welcome, Temple Bock!" We shook hands warmly, then he said, "Come. We mus' talk. Zere ees moch to tell." As he led me to his chamber he called back over his shoulder to his clerk, "*Café complet, Gaston, s'il vous plaît*."

Seated at his desk, sipping rich French coffee and munching flaky pastries slathered with sweet butter, I recounted as briefly as I knew how the events of the previous year and a half — my mother's illness and her death, my injuries, and the long time they took to heal, without dwelling overmuch on family matters best left unmentioned, finally declaring my firm intention to return to the mountains with the first trader's caravan headed out to rendezvous. Chouteau listened attentively, saying little until I finished. Then he said, "I believe eet ees your weesh to take our Micah wiz you to ze mountains, n'est-ce pas?" I was more than somewhat taken aback by his remark, for although that was certainly what I meant to do, I had intended to wait for a more convenient time to broach that delicate subject to Chouteau, who greatly valued the services of his former slave, now his paid employee. He would likely be loath to see him go. Le Cadet saw my look of surprise and laughed aloud. "Do not be alarm, mon ami. Eef you do not take Micah wiz you, 'e weel die of ze chagrin, 'ow you say, ze deesappointment. We 'ave talk of ziz many time, 'e and I, for Micah ees supremely *honnête, un homme de bonne foi,* and 'e would not weesh to betray me in any way. Non, eet ees bes' 'e go wiz you an' learn ze *métier du trappeur, le coureur des bois.* I 'ave a design for you an' 'eem, but we weel talk of zees at a later time." He stood up then and said, "But you mus' be *fatigué.* 'Ave you lodgings?"

I told him I had not, that I had come straightway from the ferry to see him and Micah.

"*Bien*! Ze lodgings of before, when you were last 'ere, zey were *agréable*?" I assured him that they had been more than I could wish for. He reached out to tug the bell cord that dangled beside his table, exclaiming the while, "*Bien*! You shall rest zere zis occasion as well." The funereal face of Gaston appeared in the doorway as if by magic and Chouteau rattled off instructions in rapid French. Gaston nodded and vanished and le Cadet returned his attention to me.

"Before I go," I said, "I'd like to see Micah. It's been a long time. He anywheres around?"

Chouteau smiled and replied, "*Mais non.* Now ees *l'après-midi de jeudi*, Sursday, ze 'alf-'oliday. I believe you weel find 'im wiz M'sieu 'Awken. Micah passes moch of 'ees time zere and M'sieu 'Awken esteems 'eem ver' moch. Eet appears Micah learns a new *métier* zere."

After a warm leave-taking and my promises to return at an early date, I hustled over to Jacob Hawken's shop, now tucked in amongst a passel of new-built stores, boat-chandlers' warehouses, inns, and taverns, where before, the last time I had visited there, it had stood alone in a broad, grassy field. Nothing much had changed inside the shop, howsomever, except for perhaps even more rifles, pistols, and fowling-pieces — most of them equipped with Hawken's new-fangled percussion locks — displayed floor-to-ceiling on the walls, many more than I recalled from the last time I was there.

Jake Hawken looked up from a gunstock clamped in a vise on his workbench as I came through the doorway, a huge smile spreading across his rosy features. "How d'ye do, Temple Buck!" he cried. "Ye be a sight fer sore eyes!" He jerked his thumb over his shoulder and declared, "An' there be one pair of eyes sorer'n my own fer the sight o' ye!" I looked past Hawken to half a dozen workmen busy at their benches, Micah amongst them. He was already making his way towards me, a dazzling white grin lighting up his shining black features, arms outstretched in welcome. He hugged me hard enough to make my backbone crack and I returned the favor. Then we stood back, arms still clasped, surveying each other. He appeared taller and more muscular than I recalled and now there was an air of assurance about him that he had lacked when I had seen him last, when he was newly-emancipated and uncertain of his future. We stood there beaming at each other, fumbling for words, not quite oblivious of the questioning looks of the other workmen, who were unused to such displays of affection betwixt white man and black.

Thankfully Jake broke in to introduce another man, who looked enough like Jake to be his brother, which in fact he proved to be. "Temple, I be right proud to have ye meet my brother Sam'l. Sam'l's come out to he'p me in the business." Whilst Brother Samuel and I shook hands, Jake explained, "Yep! Trade's boomin'. Too much fer just me alone anymore!" He grinned broadly, winked, and added, "'Spesh'ly now ye're fixin' to take our Micah off, traipsin' to them

Stony Mountains." This last he likely meant to be humorous flattery of Micah, which was how we took it to be.

I palavered a spell with the Hawken brothers, then, begging pardon for intruding on their labors, I led Micah outdoors, where we could talk privately. First thing he said was, "Ye have your wish. I found your friend Powatawa an' what's left o' his Shawnees, but I reckon ye won't be too happy 'bout what ye'll be seein' there. They've been suff'rin' some mortal hard times."

My initial delight was somewhat dampened by that, but my spirits rose at the thought that I would soon be reunited with Powatawa and the rest of my new-discovered kin. Micah went on to tell me that it was old Long-hair Louis Lorimier's Shawnee wife at Cape Girardeau who had directed him westwards to the heart of Missouri, where she had heard that a band of Shawnees from Ohio had settled. Chouteau had granted Micah leave from his employment — naturally docking his pay, for le Cadet was first and foremost a businessman — and my friend set out a-horseback to comb through the villages of the Kaws and the Wazhazhe that Americans call Osages until he discovered Powatawa's Shawnee band. They were suspicious of him at first, until he told them he had been sent by Temple Buck, Seewaseekau, which means A-door-opened in the Shawnee tongue. Micah said he reckons it also means Open Sesame, for as soon as he pronounced that name all their reserve melted away and from then on they treated him as an honored guest, leastaways as much as their poverty allowed. Powatawa hungered after every scrap of knowledge about me that Micah could provide and he appeared thrilled when he learned that I intended to come to him when I returned to Missouri.

Micah said he had sent me a letter more than a month before announcing his success, but slow as the post is, it was not surprising that I never received it.

"One other thing," Micah continued, "the chief's son weren't nearly so tickled as his Paw was, hearin' ye were comin' to see 'em. Don't know why, but I'm sure of it." I reckoned I could guess. Chiksika likely knew by now that I was his brother — his elder brother at that — and perhaps he was jealous that I might crowd him out of our father's affections. That wasn't likely and I had no wish to do so, but there's no accounting for another man's way of thinking.

I retailed my recent history to Micah, pretty much what I had told Chouteau, keeping it snug and avoiding the painful patches as much as I was able, not mentioning my parentage, then enquired after his activities since I had last seen him. "As ye know," he replied, "I'm still clerkin' for Berthold et Chouteau, but not so much in the mercantile nowadays. Ever since I told him I mean to go the mountains with you, if ye'll have me, le Cadet's put me to workin' more an' more on the fur side o' the trade, gradin' plews an' buyin' from traders who come in an' journeyin' out to buy fur from whosoever's got any, up an' down the River." He smiled with satisfaction and added, "Le Cadet says such learnin'll stand me in good stead once I'm in the mountains, but I reckon he's got some scheme in mind for usin' me, an' maybe you, for some adventure he's plannin' for the future. He mostly does."

I allowed that Micah's surmise was likely so, for good friend and benefactor though Pierre Chouteau had been to me, he was forever the far-thinking businessman as well. When I asked about his work with Jake Hawken, Micah's grin threatened to swallow his ears and he replied, "Well, first off, he taught me how to shoot, like you paid him to, but then I took to comin' 'round when my day's work was done over at Berthold et Chouteau's an' offerin' to help out if he'd let me. Right off he put me to smoothin' gunstocks an', when he saw I was careful an' quick, he showed me the knack o' fittin' in the locks, an' 'fore long I was makin' some o' the li'l pieces an' puttin' locks an' triggahs togethah an' helpin' out in the foundry." He smiled broadly, his teeth a dazzling snowbank in his black face. "Jake's been payin' me wages for quite a spell," he informed me proudly, then added with a grin, "Don't reckon I can make a whole rifle all by m'self, but I reckon I sure know how to go about it."

I laughed as heartily as he did, once again amazed at the distance he had come since I had first befriended him. Just six years before, he had been a scared, half-starved, abused, ignorant, illiterate, kidnapped slave aboard Mike Fink's keelboat.   If his former owner had miraculously escaped drowning and came looking for Micah in Saint Louis, he might meet up with him face to face and still never recognize him. I myself could hardly believe he was the same man.

We made our farewells then, agreeing to meet for supper at my lodgings. Micah returned to his gunsmithing chores and I retrieved my critters, then proceeded to pick my way through bustling streets and busy thoroughfares until I arrived at my lodging-house. A smiling, bowing concierge trotted into the street to greet me, announced that a comfortable chamber had been prepared for me, then ordered his lackeys to carry my packs and saddlebags upstairs to my quarters. My business at a nearby livery took but a few minutes, seeing to it that my horses were lodged in spacious stalls with dry straw and plenty of fresh hay and instructing the stableman to groom and grain them every day and to hire the services of a horse-leech to make sure they were free of worms. A long journey lay ahead and I desired their utmost good fettle. In the mountains Old Foot regularly dosed our critters, but Foot was still a long way off.

It was still only mid-afternoon by time I returned to my lodgings. I was restless and I caught myself pacing the length of my chamber, from the spacious canopied bed beside the broad bay window that overlooked a tiny garden, to the door and back again, dodging around big stuffed chairs and fussy little tables that littered the highly-polished floor. After weeks of urgent horseback riding, leisure didn't set well with me. It was still a matter of hours before Micah would arrive, so for lack of anything better to do, I reckoned I might as well indulge in a hot bath and the attentions of a barber.

A new shirt, a suit of clean buckskins, and a fresh pair of moccasins under my arm, I entered a shop whose painted sign and red-striped pole proclaimed the premises of a *Chirurgien barbier* and roused that worthy practitioner from his afternoon nap. A short spell later I was luxuriating in a great copper tub, up to my chin in near-scalding soapy water, whilst the barber expertly shaved me and lathered my hair, rattling on the while about the miracles that new commerce was bringing to the city — heretofore undreamed-of wealth in beaver furs pouring from the mountains, huge trade caravans traveling to and from the Spaniard settlement of Santa Fe, land speculation, builders and tradesmen, and a multitude of new shops come to supply the needs of fur trappers, Santa Fe traders, and the flourishing population of the town itself.

After he poured a final pail of warm water over me to rinse away the soap, he stood back to admire his handiwork and declared, "You weel do well, *m'sieu*, to theenk of going to ze *montagnes* for to make ze fortune!" I muttered something about how I might consider doing just that, toweled myself dry, and donned my clean garments, my hide still glowing from the scrubbing and doubtless considerably lighter in weight, for it was plain to see that I had left a peck or more of grime in the bath water.

Supper in my chamber with Micah was a delight, the both of us well-oiled with spirits and wine, sharp-set with appetite for the vast array of delicious eatables which the landlord sent up, and chattering a mile-a-minute, like a brace of magpies, of the past we had shared, present goings-on in Saint Louis, and our future in the mountains, this latter topic being Micah's favorite theme by more than somewhat. Most interesting to me of all our palaver, howsomever, was Micah's mentioning a scrap of information concerning the arrival in Saint Louis of Black Harris — which likely meant Bill Sublette as well — probably come to obtain trade goods from General Ashley for transport to the summer rendezvous somewhere in the mountains. Although nobody had seen Sublette, Harris, who was Bill's usual guide and guardian spirit, had dropped by the mercantile that morning on a personal errand and dropped a hint of his mission to a counter-jumper, who quickly transmitted that intelligence to his chief, who lost no time in delivering the information to the ear of Pierre Chouteau. Bill Sublette was a partner in the firm of Smith, Jackson & Sublette, which two years before had purchased the fur business from General William Ashley, although Ashley had shrewdly retained rights as sole supplier of trade goods to the new firm. Bill Sublette's arrival in Saint

Louis could mean only that a caravan to the Shining Mountains would soon be assembling, an event of prime importance to me. It would also be of considerable interest to le Cadet, who more than likely entertained thoughts of competing for trade at rendezvous through the Missouri Fur Company, in which he was known to possess a substantial financial interest.

It is well-nigh unthinkable for a small party of men, much less just a couple, to travel through the thousand miles and more of hostile wilderness that lies between Saint Louis and rendezvous, even if they know the trail, which I wasn't sure I did for certain. I aimed to join up with Sublette and his crew, reckoning that Bill might welcome, or at least tolerate, a couple more reliable riflemen, even if past history hadn't precisely forged a bond of friendship between the two of us. I determined to seek out Black Harris as soon as I could.

It was long past dark when Micah took his leave, promising to return as soon as his duties allowed, then making his tipsy way down the stairway. Whilst a lackey cleared the table and tidied up, I watched Micah out of sight and heard the door to the street close behind him. Then I retreated inside my chamber for a final sip of brandy before retiring to my robes. My actual buffalo sleep robes remained trussed in a bundle in a corner with my other plunder, for that night I intended to treat myself to the comfort of the large bed, which beckoned invitingly. That would likely be one of the few nights of luxury I would enjoy before heading west. From then on it would be God's green footstool for my pillow and a starlit sky for a counterpane, a prospect that I heartily welcomed.

I stripped and left my clothes in a heap beside the bed and crawled naked between fresh-smelling sheets as soft as eiderdown, regretting only that I had no one to share them with. Then I quickly reminded myself that I had important errands to tend to thereabouts and pleasures aplenty likely awaited at rendezvous. Remembrance of mountain pleasurings pictured my fading thoughts as I slid into deep dream-filled slumber.

* * *

Coming awake was a sight quicker. The soft click of the latch and the heavy door, carelessly left unbolted, swinging partly open on well-oiled hinges brought me to my senses as surely as a thunderbolt might have done. Four years in the mountains makes a light sleeper of any man who survives them. I fumbled amongst my clothes until I grasped the little double-barreled belly gun that was rarely out of hand's reach, then lay unmoving, alert and ready, whilst I listened to soft footsteps carefully advancing towards the bed. An unmistakable familiar fragrance preceded the intruder, howsomever, prompting me to place my pistol gently on the floor, then silently await my visitor. When the shadowy hooded figure at last reached my bedside, I shot out my arms and clasped her firmly about the waist and heaved her up beside me. It was Lucette, stark naked beneath her cloak, shrieking in surprise at first, then dissolving into fits of bubbling laughter. When at last she was able to speak, her words tumbled out in a boiling river of macaroni. "*Ah, Tompool! Tu es méchant! Un vilain absolu*! What a naughty boy you are! *Quelle vilenie* of you to fright me so! *Je veux faire une surprise à toi! Tu as gâté ma surprise*! You 'ave spoil my surprise for you!" Her sputtering halted abruptly for I quenched her protests with fervent kisses which she returned with equal ardor, nipping at my lips and ears in her excitement. In hardly any time at all I was long past mere kissing, drowning in the dizzying scent of her hair and the delicious flavor of her breasts and belly, until at last she pulled me upwards and guided me home to that treasured haven I had abandoned six years before.

Long abstinence and an excess of passion made all too short work of our first encounter, but as I slumped gasping at her side, Lucette drew me close, giggling and murmuring, "Fear not, Tompool. Be not deesappoint. Now zere ees much time for us. As much time as we can weesh." The moon had risen and a broad shaft of pearly light shone through the garden window. I could see her face, as pert and fresh as ever. Her dark eyes, huge and luminous in the half-light, sparkled with impish good humor. I marveled that her body, unseen and untouched by me in nigh six years, had not changed a whit — her saucy breasts, taut belly, firm buttocks, and strong, smooth thighs, all just as I recalled.

"You're a witch, Lucette, *une sorcière!*" I said, laughing. Then, observing a look of alarm on her face, for such charges are often made in earnest in her native New Orleans, I hastened to explain. "Ye never grow old. Ye don't change. You're the same as when I first met ye, half a dozen years since!"

Reassured, she laughed, deep and throaty, and replied, "Eet ees you, Tompool, who make me young, who breeng me back to our firs' days an' nights togezzer." I believed not a word of it, but it was pleasing to hear her say it. Then she sprang from the bed, crying, "I mus' go *m'en laver! Je reviendrai tout de suite!*" She scampered to the curtained alcove and a moment later I heard water splashing. During her brief absence I wondered idly how Lucette came to be there at all, about her husband, and what had become of her steadfast insistence on honoring her marriage vows.

She returned with a warm moist clout and bathed my nether parts, which made such questions unimportant just then, but I persisted anyhow. "What about your husband, Lucy? Won't ye be missed?"

A flicker of regret veiled her moonlit features before she replied, "*Il est mort, le pauvre.* I am *veuve,* 'ow you say, a weedow, for nearly one year." She went on to tell me that her very old and very rich husband, the eminent Marcel Marcotte, scion and paterfamilias of a powerful Saint Louis family, whom she had dearly loved and respected, had died in her arms the year before. She assured me that he had died happy, howsomever, for his demise occurred at the very moment of passionate fulfillment, which she, forever sanguine and practical, considered to be an appropriate quietus, a tribute to her affection and devotion. I could not but agree, for there are many worse ways to bid one's final farewell.

I did my best to cheer her after that and I reckon I succeeded, for we slept hardly a wink until the sun was high in the sky, bathing the rumpled bed in golden splendor. Her ardor and marvelous inventiveness kept me returning to the fray with an enthusiasm to match her own, until at last I lay with my head on her breast, drained of the ability if not the will to continue, leastaways right then. Even so, we were loath to turn loose of each other. She wriggled about to nestle in the crook of my arm, tenderly caressing my several scars and marveling that I had survived such wounds. "Ah, Tom-pool," she murmured, *"tu ne feras pas de vieux os* eef you continue so. Your body ees un journal of your catastrophes."

I chuckled and replied, "Well now, Blackfoots can't read nor write, as ye might suppose, darlin', so leavin' scars is the only way they have o' makin' their mark." As for my not "making old bones," as she put it, I said I reckoned I would take my chances on dying young rather than miss out on all the fun. She clucked her displeasure at such a notion but allowed that I would likely do as I saw fit.

The night's considerable exertions had left me with a raging hunger and Lucette announced that she, too, was famished. She swung lightly from the bed and scurried naked to the alcove. My eyes greedily drank in her supple charms until she retreated behind the curtain. A few minutes later, after a passel of splashing, she emerged clad in a simple shift, her face glowing and tousled hair combed smooth. She tugged on the bell cord as she called out for me to dress myself.

I had no sooner tended to my chore, washed up, and clothed myself than a discreet tapping at the door announced the arrival of a lackey bearing coffee and pastries, followed not long afterwards by vast quantities of eggs, flannel cakes, ham, chops, spicy sausages, rolls and butter, and a variety of conserves. The two of us wolfed down the breakfast in near silence, pausing only to express our pleasure with the welcome vittles and to favor each other with loving looks.

At last, stuffed to the gills, I fell back in my chair and regarded my companion as she leaned to refill my coffee cup. "What'll ye do now, Lucy, now that you're a wealthy widow-woman?" I asked goodnaturedly. "Spend your days in sinful leisure?" Even as I uttered the words it occurred to me that perhaps she had not inherited her late husband's wealth, for I knew the old man had had two grown sons with families of their own. The sons might have challenged the will, if in fact their father had bequeathed a substantial portion of his fortune to Lucette.

"Mais non!" she replied quickly. "I could nevair do zat! When my 'usband die, *ses fils*, 'is two boys, come to me wiz *l'avocat*. "E tell me zat I 'ave become a woman *très riche* but zat I mus' make one promesse to ze two boys, ozzerwise zey will make trouble ovair ze monnaie. Zen I ask what is zis promesse I mus' make and zose two boys zey say zat I mus' make ze promesse to open *la maison* once again! Zey bot' 'ave been excellent clients before *mon mariage* an' zey regret La Maison Lucette no longair conducts herself. *Naturellement* I agree wiz zeir demands wizzout *hésitation ou réservation!*" Lucette burst out laughing and collapsed in her chair, whilst I marveled at the complaisance of Saint Louis Frenchies, whose thirst for pleasure exceeds even their avarice.

"So," I said, "all those people buzzing about your old establishment, they work for you."

Lucette smiled and replied, "Yes, zey do so an' eet weel be soon feenish an' I weel open soon ze door for *mes* clients. Eet weel be jus' like before — *non!* bettair! — an' you, *cheri*, weel be always mos' welcome zere!" She paused and a brief frown clouded her smiling features. "But only for me! Nevair for *mes filles!*"

I laughed and assured her that she never left me with enough strength to pursue another woman, even if I wished to do so, which all-too-true remark restored her good humor.

Such prattle caused her to regard me archly and I caught her glance straying wistfully towards the bed, but she soon collected herself and briskly informed me that she must be about her affairs — returning home to dress properly, seeing a banker, prodding her workmen to ever greater zeal in accomplishing their many tasks.

She hugged me in a tight embrace, stood tip-toe to place a lingering kiss on my lips, promising to return soon, then swept her cloak about her shoulders, retrieved her reticule, and stepped into the passage, where Israel, a towering, broad-shouldered, grizzled old

Negro, her long-time majordomo and bodyguard, stood waiting. He was impeccably dressed in a startling bright green frock coat, snug doeskin britches, knee-high riding boots, and a dazzling white ruffled shirt, much the same livery he had worn when I first espied him guarding the entry to Lucette's establishment six years earlier.

Israel allowed himself a fleeting smile and a slight nod to acknowledge our acquaintance, then snapped to attention as he ushered Lucette down the staircase. As I watched them depart, I wondered how Israel could have known just when to present himself outside my door, but then, I have never understood the mysterious manner in which Lucette communicates with her efficient household or how she learns all she wishes to know of Saint Louis and its goings-on.

* * *

The sun had just begun its descent from high noon when I made my way through the dismal byways of Vide Poche and presented myself at the outer door of Madame Mathilde's establishment. A surly Negro porter bade me wait there whilst he called out my name inside. After a lengthy spell, Mathilde herself shuffled through the inner doorway, shod in carpet slippers, her considerable bulk clad in a soiled wrapper, her hard, obsidian-eyed, deeply-creased face bereft of the pound or more of cosmetics with which she painted herself during business hours. Mathilde hadn't changed a whit from when I had first met her six years before. She remained as sturdy and timeless and uncaring as a lightning-struck but surviving old hickory that the furies of neither heaven nor hell can alter. She regarded me through heavy half-closed lids, then commenced to cackle in a voice like broken glass, "Eet ees you, Tompool Bock, *l'ami de* Tootle! Tootle, 'e ees wiz you? Where ees Tootle, *hein*?" She peered suspiciously past my shoulder, as if she expected to discover Tuttle Thompson lurking there.

"No, ma'am," I replied. "I don't expect you'll find him hereabouts. Far as I know, you'll need to go to the mountains lookin' for him.

That's where we parted company nigh two years ago." Her face fell in disappointment at missing a prime customer, for Tuttle was a high, wide and handsome spender so long as his money held out. "I'm lookin' for Black Harris," I added hastily. "He around?"

"Ah, Moïse," she said, pronouncing his given name in French, calling to mind that Black's proper name is Moses. "'E was 'ere las' night but no longair. Zis morning 'e go to *ze domaine du Général Le Clerc, le patron des Indiens*, for do 'is work." I recalled that William Ashley often used some of General Clark's barns for his fur trade activities. It was likely I would find Harris there.

I thanked Mathilde for her help and politely declined to come indoors for a glass of wine and whatever else she might have had in mind when she winked broadly and rolled her black beady eyes oh-so-coquettishly. I could hear the chatter of female voices, but it was a temptation easily resisted.

William Clark's estate lay on the edge of town, too far for walking, so I hastened back to the livery barn, where I found my critters properly cared-for, bedded on clean straw, mangers over-flowing with fresh timothy, their well-curried coats gleaming in the half-light. I tossed a coin to the hostler, asked for my saddle and bridle, and led Ready out of his stall. Riding through the streets and lanes of Saint Louis, I marveled again at how much the city had grown.

General Clark's domain, howsomever, was undisturbed, its well-tended fields and gardens, groves, pastures, and paddocks remote and serene behind whitewashed fences, a tranquil island amid the city's bustle and din. A brace of buffalo stared vacantly across a lush meadow as I rode by, then dropped their massive heads and resumed their grazing.

I discovered Black Harris engaged in a heated argument with a horse trader, a wizened little Englishman, by the sound of him. Both their faces were beet-red and impassioned as they haggled over half a dozen mules tethered alongside a big barn. Neither man paid me any mind at first. I sat unnoticed for a considerable spell before Black chanced to spy me and called out, "Howdy, Temple! Hold on thar whilst I give thish'yar hossthief his comeuppance!"

The wrangling continued unabated for nigh a quarter hour, both of them roaring, arms flailing, fingers jabbing, stomping off, only to spin about and return to drive home another point about the quality and condition of the mules, until at last they fell silent and solemnly shook hands. Instantly smiles replaced scowls and Black offered a jug to the trader after first gulping a swig and wiping his lips on his sleeve, then yelling, "C'mon, Temple! Gitcherse'f off'n thet'ere hoss an' jine us! He'p us button up thish'yar deal." Which I did most gratefully. Black favored me with a rib-crunching hug, rubbing his gunpowder-pocked cheek and a week's worth of whisker against mine, exclaiming, "Hell, hoss, I been froze to see ye! It's a blessin', damn if it ain't! We thought ye'd gone under! What's took ye so long comin' back?"

His words warmed my innards as much as the whiskey did. First off, I enquired after my own particular bunch of trapping companions in the mountains. Harris assured me that, as of last summer's rendezvous, they were all present and accounted for. Then, in response to his question, I furnished a brief account of my recent life, leaving out most of it, and finished with, "Now that I'm back, Black, I'm lookin' for company headin' to rendezvous, for me and another feller. Ye know how it mostly stands 'twixt Billy Sublette an' me, but d'ye reckon he'd object to us taggin' along?"

Harris spat through his grin and replied, "Hell no! Glad to have ye 'long. We kin allus use a good hand, come trouble. "Sides, Billy ain't hyar. Reckon he be trappin' somewhars up 'round the Forks 'baout naow."

Black paused to collect his thoughts, shifted his cud and spat. "Gotta tell ye, though, thar ain't no reg'lar supply train thish'yar spring. Went up last fall. Had a helluva time, too, what with early snow an' Injun hossthieves an' sich, but we got the most of it cached fer ronnyvoo." I reckon Black noticed the puzzled look on my face, for I had supposed that Bill Sublette was in town buying supplies for the rendezvous in July. He laughed merrily and said reassuringly, "Don't ye fret none, Temple. I be headin' back soon's I buy up enough critters fer a fair price an' hire hands enough to drive 'em, 'sides pickin' up a mite o' plunder.

"Bill an' Davey Jackson an' Bobby Campbell been havin' theirse'fs a helluva good year, a galore o' beaver plew. Natcherly Crows an' Snakes been busy thievin' critters, like they allus do, so Billy be needin' more hosses an' mules fer bringin' the ketch on down to Saint Looie. I'm s'posed to meet 'em in Cache Valley."

"Cache Valley? Where's that?"

"Aw, thet's what some o' the boys commenced callin' Willer Valley arter Marshall got hisse'f kilt when the cache caved in on top o' him, couple years back. Now ever'body's callin' it thet."

I nodded, then enquired, "Ye mention Bill an' Davey. What about Jed Smith?"

"Aw, he went off to Californy agin arter rondyvoo last year. Left the most o' his men what warn't awready kilt an' all his plews thar with Harry Rogers an' come on back with jist a couple-three fellers, the lot of 'em lookin' more'n a mite peakèd an' none of 'em too flush fer cash ner plunder, neither. Then Jed got hisse'f another bunch together fer goin' back with 'im — said he figgered on collectin' his plews an' trappin' his way on back to ronnyvoo this summer." Black favored me with a quizzical grin. "Why d'ye ask? Bury the hatchet with ol' Diah, did ye? Had a change o' heart about 'im?"

I shrugged and replied, "Nope. 'Bout the same as ever. Don't hate 'im. Don't love 'im, neither."

Harris nodded. "Yep, Jed's a mite hard to git next to. Bible keeps gittin' in the way." He brightened then and added, "Fact is, ol' Diah ain't been missed overmuch. Bobby Campbell's been headin' up one o' the brigades an' doin' right handsome at it, too. Billy's come to lean on him cornsid'able of late. Now I think on it, last time I seen Tuttle an' Godey an' the rest o' yer cronies, they war trappin' purty much 'longside o' Bobby Campbell's bunch, whilst makin' a galore o' plew theirownse'fs."

I recalled Robert Campbell, a pale, sickly Irish youngster from the East, younger than I, when he came to the mountains. The trapper's life agreed with him, howsomever. His health improved and he learned to work hard and smart, staying on in the trade despite all the gossip noised about that his people were some kind of Irish lords and how his Philadelphia folks were wealthy beyond telling. Such matters make no nevermind in the mountains, howsomever. What counts is, handsome is as handsome does and, hoss, what can ye do? Evidently he was doing well enough. Tuttle and Ned and Turtle and the rest of our bunch would never trap close by a bungling brigade leader.

Black's ruined features clouded whilst he chewed something over in his mind. Then he said soberly, "Course, Sublette's payin' the bills an' as ye know, Billy's purty near with a dollar. He ain't what ye might call charitable. Ye off'rin' to work yer way?"

"Nope. I'll pay whatever it takes, cash dollars, and as ye know, I'm more'n willin' to hunt when we get to buffler country. 'Sides, ye know I ain't behindhand if it comes to an Injun fight."

Black whistled softly, looking thoughtful, and replied, "Yep. Thar'll likely be some o' thet. Them Loup Pawnee been rilin' theirse'fs somethin' fierce lately. Gittin' downright uppity! An' ye cain't never tell about the Sioux, blowin hot an' cold like they allus do. An' natcherly thar be Rees, ferever on the prod."

He didn't bother to include Blackfeet. We take Blackfoots for granted. Mention of the Pah-nee stirred a passel of painful memories in me, howsomever, concerning how they ran me ragged during my long retreat alone and afoot down the Platte, two years before. Contrary to my ordinarily peaceful nature, I found myself itching for a fair fight with that arrogant bunch. What I said was, "I ain't shy. Whatever comes, I'll be up for muster — and my pardner, too."

Harris retrieved his jug from the trader, who was paying rather too much attention to it, then turned back to me and said with a laugh, "Like I was sayin', don'tcha fret none, Temple. Glad to have ye 'long. Jes' be on hand when we pull out o' Independence in a for'night. He paused to consider, then corrected himself. "Nope. Make thet three weeks. It'll take thet long to round up all the hands an' critters an' plunder an' we dassn't git to the far prairie too early, afore thar be good graze enough. He paused, then added, "'Sides, spring rain quags it sumpin' fierce early on." He passed the jug to me and I drank to seal the bargain.

* * *

Preparing for our departure from Saint Louis was accomplished with surprisingly little trouble. After leaving Black Harris, I rode as rapidly as the city's crowded streets allowed to Berthold et Chouteau, where I found Micah sorting and grading beaver plews in a warehouse. He agreed without hesitation to show me the way to Powatawa's village, but first we had to obtain permission from le Cadet for Micah to resign his employment, which, gratefully, was granted more speedily and with greater good grace than I expected. I explained to Chouteau, lamely, that I urgently needed to visit a dear old friend from my youth, a Shawnee Indian, long unseen, before I departed Saint Louis and only Micah could guide me to him. Naturally I made no mention that my old friend was in fact my father. Chouteau smiled benignly and replied, "I am not surprise. *Naturellement*, eet ees *nécessaire* for you to make ze haste to attend your duties 'ere before you *join l'expédition aux montagnes*. Go, ze two of you, wiz my blessing."

Le Cadet supplied me then with cash money from my account — in hard coin, not banknotes, for paper is not much esteemed beyond the city — and we made our farewells. As Micah and I left the building, howsomever, reflecting on it, I was convinced that shrewd, all-knowing Pierre Chouteau had guessed precisely what my old friend was to me and that he reckoned my mission was that of a son journeying to render respect to his father. It was a sentiment that a leading member of an old, close-knit French Creole family must certainly approve. How le Cadet divined my secret I never learned, but I am sure he did so. I am a poor liar, often to my regret, which accounts for my reticence in exposing much about myself — except in these pages, which likely nobody but Euphemius Hobbes will ever read. In this case, howsomever, I didn't mind getting caught in a fib. Le Cadet keeps his own counsel. Besides, I had come to think of him as a stern but benevolent uncle.

Much still remained to be done that day. Micah and I hustled off to Jake Hawken's shop to announce our departure and to collect Micah's wages. Whilst I loitered there, waiting for Micah to make his goodbyes to the workmen, I was struck by a happy thought. When Jake returned to his workbench, I purchased from him another of his new-fangled percussion rifles of the same caliber as my own, a bullet mold, and a couple hornfuls of percussion caps, a gift for Powatawa from his homecoming son. Micah already possessed one of his own, paid for at a dollar a week by his labor in Hawken's shop. "How d'ye like your own rifle, so far?" Jake asked as he slid the new weapon into a soft buckskin sleeve.

"No complaints, at all," I replied. "She's got a long-enough reach an' shoots plumb center when it gets there an' that's as much as a sane man can properly ask of a rifle gun. Now that I got the hang o' fittin' on those little thimbles, I can prime a whole lot faster an' the wind an' damp make no nevermind to it. Yep, I reckon I'm more'n satisfied." Hawken beamed with pleasure, which prompted me to add, "Proof o' what I'm sayin', it's the gun I'll be carryin' to the mountains an', as ye know, so will Micah."

Farewells attended to, we hurried back to the mercantile, where I loaded up on all manner of presents for the Shawnees, mostly of English or French manufacture, for Indians, even wild Indians in the mountains, are shrewd judges of quality and, I'm sorry to say, most American workshops don't make goods as well as they do in Europe. Soon I accumulated a heap of good English butcher knives and tomahawks, some of the tobacco pipe variety, fishhooks and silk line, flints, gunpowder and galena, big-headed brass tacks, six-point English blankets, tobacco, coffee and sugar, vermilion, steel awls, firesteels, needles and thread, yard goods, copper kettles, sail canvas, and a passel of Venice beads, tiny looking-glasses, and other such foofurraw for the women, amongst whatever else chanced to take my fancy, including a good broad-brimmed beaver felt hat for myself — of an earthen color, for a black hat stands out like a beacon, even at a great distance. When a clerk totted it all up I was astonished at the inconsiderable cost of all that plunder, compared with mountain prices, which would have run ten or a hundred times as much or more. I made up my mind that I would buy my supplies in Saint Louis before I joined Harris and pack them to rendezvous myself.

We told the counter-jumper to parcel up our purchases and hold them against our return for them next day, then headed outdoors to pursue our errands, only to discover that the early-April daylight was nearly gone, too late to hunt up a horse-dealer in order to buy some decent horseflesh for Micah.

I realized then how hungry I was, for in pursuit of my errands I had neglected my dinner that day. I invited Micah to join me for supper at my lodgings, but he politely declined, mumbling vaguely about needing to tend to personal matters before our departure — which matters were, I supposed, likely of a feminine persuasion. I didn't meddle and we agreed to meet at my livery next morning.

I ate my solitary supper in my chamber and, thoughtfully leaving my door unbolted, retired to bed soon afterwards, the sheets still faintly recalling Lucette and our love-making. I delighted in the rare luxury of sleeping naked. Such indulgence is unwise in the mountains, where uninvited guests in the dark of night might put a full stop to your paragraph. The exertions of a mostly sleepless night before, followed by a busy day and a full belly, conspired to carry me into peaceful slumber. If I dreamed at all, I am sure my imaginings were pleasant ones.

* * *

My return to consciousness was accomplished in a sudden, pleasantly shocking manner with Lucette's icy wet arms clasping me in a tight embrace from behind, her cold and shivering naked body spooned against mine, nipples hard as unripe berries nuzzling my back, damp hair tickling my neck as she strained to reach my lips with hers. Rain volleyed against the windowpanes. Lightning flashed in the darkness and thunder crashed and rolled over the city. I squirmed around to take her in my arms, warming her chilled, quivering body with my own, kissing her soundly, then shivering myself for a rather different reason as she buried her face against my throat and reached for me. My efforts on her behalf were successful and richly compensated. Soon her trembling from the cold was replaced by a throbbing of quite a different sort, her whimpering translating to needful moans, her straying hand eagerly guiding me to a most welcome reward.

It was not until we lay clinging together and gasping for breath that either of us uttered a single word. I spoke first. "What in the world were ye doing out on a night like this, darlin'? An' how did ye get yourself so wet? Ye could catch your death!"

Lucette wriggled closer and murmured, "I could not sleep. No mattair ze wezzer, I 'ad need of you, so I come 'ere wiz Israel, but in my 'urry to see you, *mon chou,* I fall into *une flaque,* 'ow you say, a poodle, an' I am soak *des pieds à la tête!*" She nestled against my chest and added in a contented purr, "Mais, *tout est bien qui finit bien, hein?*" I could not but agree. All's well that ends well and her misadventure had ended happily for me.

Lucette was uncommonly generous with her rewards. I was amply repaid for my ministrations before a feeble dawn lightened a still lowering sky and the tempest dwindled to a gentle drizzle. Reluctantly I told her of my appointment with Micah and begged that we might rise and break our fast in time for me to meet him at the stable. She complied without demur and after giving me a final peck on the lips, she flew from the bed and fled to the alcove, pausing only to snatch up my shirt and tug on the bell cord on her way.

She had scarcely emerged from the alcove when there came a soft knock at the door and a hand slipped a parcel inside, which I correctly surmised to be dry clothes for her, brought from home by the faithful Israel. She was still fussing with her dress when the lackey wheeled in our breakfast, a feast even more sumptuous than that of the day before. There was precious little time to enjoy it, howsomever, for the brightening windowpanes and the certain knowledge that Micah would be waiting robbed me of a proper regard for what was truly an excellent repast. I hardly tasted it before I rose from my chair, gulped my coffee, stuffed a fistful of plump sausages into my belt poke, bestowed a hasty kiss on Lucette's pouting lips, begged pardon for my rudeness, grabbed up my new hat and rain-shroud, and rushed out the door.

Micah was already at the livery, his sorry old mare tethered indoors, protected from the fine drizzle that continued to dampen the city. A single glance at Micah's critter told me that the dear old nag would scarcely make the journey to Powatawa's, let alone be a fit mount for the journey to rendezvous. I held my peace on that score, howsomever, saddled my Ashley horse, bestowed a coin on the hostler for his good care of my animals, and rode out into the grey morning, Micah in tow, headed for General Clark's estate.

We made good time, for the rain-slick streets were nigh deserted at that hour, arriving at the barn just as Black's horse trader finished tethering a bunch of horses and mules to the paddock fence. Harris stepped out and waved us all inside, where a kettle of coffee boiled over a little fire. "Y'all must'a hit the groun' runnin', this early mawnin," Black remarked sourly as he passed around brimming tin cups steaming in the chill, damp air. "This'n be a day fer keepin' to yer robes." We all nodded or grunted assent as we gratefully sipped the stout black brew.

I broke the silence. "Black, this be Micah, Micah Buck. He'll be comin' along with me to rendezvous. Micah hankers to go trappin' an' I aim to give 'im his chance." Micah stood mute and expressionless, waiting for Black's reply.

Harris said nothing at first, merely appraised Micah head to foot, then addressed him directly. "Wal, ye look to be fit enough to commence tryin', anyways, an' if'n Temple hyar reckons ye got the grit fer it, he oughta know, an' thet be good enough fer me." He shoved out his hand and added, "Glad to have ye 'long!"

Micah pumped Black's arm and showed every tooth he owned in a dazzling grin, mumbling the while, "Pleased to meet ye. Much obliged."

Meanwhile, the trader, a wrinkled little man with a shrewd look about him, stepped in front of me and announced in a strong English accent, "Charlie Bowden's the name. I'm a 'orse-coper, nat'rally dealin' in mules, as well, an' if ye're lookin' to buy sound animals at a right price, I'm yer man." To which offer I carefully allowed that I might be in the market. Bowden, glancing outside and seeing that the rain had quit, said, "If ye'll just be steppin' this way, guv'nor, I b'lieve I can show ye some 'orseflesh to suit ye."

I looked to Harris, for he had first call on the trader's offerings, but Black merely shrugged and grinned and waved me out the door, saying, "I got time, Temple. I reckon you don't. He'p yerse'f."

As I followed Bowden out to the paddock I overheard Harris revealing to Micah a valuable horse-trading secret. "When ye're dealin' with a hoss-trader, ye must allus look at his left hand an' if'n thar be a patch o' hair growin' in the palm of it, he's likely honest. But if'n thar ain't, look out!"

This time the trader hadn't lied, for the stock tethered in the paddock was prime, doubtless because Harris had already refused enough of his earlier shoddy offerings to convince Bowden to bring only sound animals for sale. One horse in particular caught my eye, a line-back dark dun gelding, with all four dark-brown points and stripedy yellow hooves, sloping pasterns for an easy ride, five years old by his mouth, nearly sixteen hands and stout-built, a first-rate critter to carry Micah westwards.

Handsome is as handsome does, howsomever, so I bridled the dun and swung onto his bare back for a turn or two around the paddock at walk, trot, and lope. He lacked considerable education, but he was more than willing and his natural gaits were good. The long journey to rendezvous would provide plenty of time for schooling. Soggy saddle pads make for a good education.

When I dropped to the ground and joined my companions, I spied Micah eyeing a pair of strapping saddle mules, easily sixteen hands if they had had withers, but not coarse, full-rumped, and bright bay-colored. They showed a lot more horse than jackass in their size and looks and, if not for long ears and mutton backs, a careless glance might have mistook them for horses. Micah's discreet nod told me that he would be happy to own them if I agreed.

When I walked between the pair to mouth them, proving them both an honest six years, Charlie Bowden leaped into action. "I been a 'orse-coper, man an' boy, fer forty years an' more, like me dad an' gran'dad afore me, an' I never seen a finer matched pair o' mules in me life — 'arf-brothers they be, the both of 'em bred out o' racin' mares an' sired by an 'andsome Missourah jack. Fit fer a fine lady's coach they be! Which the very Pope o' Rome'd swap 'is bloody 'at fer these 'ere two, guv'nor!" He continued in that vein, but I paid him no further nevermind, busying myself examining feet and tendons, looking out for spavins, wervils, and such, and finding no flaw, nor a smidgeon of white sock or pink hoof betwixt them, nor in the dun gelding, either. Their manner of going when I rode them in the paddock proved them to be much more horse than mule, together with their uncommon good nature, persuaded me that the pair must be ours.

Naturally the dickering took quite a spell. It might be going on yet if Black hadn't interrupted. "Better take what he's off'rin', Charlie. I ain't about to give ye half the price Temple's awready offered to pay ye — an' ye know damn well nobody else hereabouts'll give it to ye neither." His words gave pause to the little Brit and I took that opportunity to excuse myself and step away to confer with Micah. I needed his consent to include his old mare with my offer and thereby clinch the bargain. Micah agreed without hesitation, but his eyes told me that he hated to trust his faithful critter to the tender mercies of the trader.

I returned to Bowden and said flatly, "Tell ye what, Charlie, daylight's wastin' and I got chores a-waitin'. Take what I'm offerin' ye for all three critters, the dun an' the mules, and I'll throw in the old mare for boot. That's my tender and I ain't budgin' off it. Now or never." I fingered into my belt poke and fished out a handful of coins, gold and silver, all greasy from the sausages I had plumb forgotten about, and slowly counted out the right amount into my other hand, making sure to clink the gold and silver as loudly as I could, for nothing tweaks a greedy man's interest like the sound of ready money. Bowden let on as if he didn't notice, but I daresay he was fairly twitching with lust for my cash.

"Ye'd best grab it whilst ye kin, Charlie!" Harris chimed in. "I know Temple an' he means what he sez. 'Sides, he's a sudden sort an' he ain't inclined to tarry." The dealer gave up, overcome by his avarice, and held out a grimy paw for the money, muttering the while how the old mare was fit only for the knacker, a remark I was glad that Micah couldn't overhear, for it was likely so.

Bowden wandered off to the paddock to look after his remaining stock and Black brought out his jug, waving Micah over to join us. The three of us sampled his squeezin's and Black, seeing that Charlie was returning, drawn like a magnet by sight of the jug, hastened to say, "Natcherly ye paid too much, but ye got yerse'f some prime critters." I thanked him for his help and for letting me take my pick of the animals, but Harris shrugged and said, "Naw, they be too fine jest fer packin' an' too dear fer Billy's purse, anyways. I'm glad ye got 'em."

Micah saddled the dun and we made our farewells, promising to meet at Independence in three weeks' time less a day. We hadn't reached Clark's outer gate before I reined up and said, "Micah, these critters are your own, as ye know, but I'm damned if I don't wish to trade you out o' one o' those mules! I never owned a mule o' my own. What d'ye say?"

It was unfair of me to make such a proposal, since I had gifted him with all three, but Micah just grinned and replied, "Take your pick."

Which I did, although choosing between the brothers was hard. Each one was just as desirable as the other. We named them on the spot, Remus and Romulus — names suggested by Micah, not me. In return for Remus, I offered him the horse I was riding, Kentucky-bred Ashley, which Micah happily accepted. Then he named the dun horse Buck, a suitable moniker. For two reasons, he said. The big gelding was the color of well-tanned buckskin and, handsome as he was, he deserved to be called by our surname.

Micah's saddle was a battered old dragoon, likely discarded as useless by the Army, so we rode up to the saddlery owned by an old Spaniard. We wasted no time outfitting my friend with a high-pommeled Spaniard saddle and bridle like my own, complete with alforjas saddlebags, a reata lass'rope, a brace of packsaddles and harness, and britching for the mules. Like the first time I dealt with him two years before, I wounded the old man's feelings once again — I paid his asking price, refusing to dicker — and we were on our way.

It was still early in the forenoon, so I suggested to Micah, "What say we head out now, this mornin'?" He allowed that nothing held him now. His service with Chouteau and Hawken was ended. We agreed to meet at the livery with our trail fixin's, ready to go, as soon we could.

Lucette had already gone and it was the work of only a few minutes to gather my trail gear, entrust my extra belongings to the concierge, and scribble a note to Lucette, promising to see her upon my return. When I tried to settle my account, the concierge laughed gaily, fluttering his pudgy white hands, and assured me that M'sieu Chouteau had arranged for everything.

Within the hour Micah and I had collected a stock of vittles and our gifts for the Shawnees, bundled and snugged them securely onto the packsaddles, and led our strings out of Saint Louis, heading for Powatawa's village. My heart was big at the prospect of seeing my father. Then it dwindled to pea-size when I considered what I might discover there.

* * *

Micah was no horseman but he did his manful best to match my pace as we beat along the northwestward trail to the Shawnee settlement. I dared not outdistance him, for only Micah knew the way. I begrudged every minute lost, not only because I was mortally eager to meet with Powatawa but also because Black Harris's departure from Independence, now less than three weeks off, would not be delayed. After our meeting with Powatawa, we needed to return to Saint Louis to supply ourselves for our journey to the mountains, then retrace our steps yet again and travel considerably farther to Independence on the far western side of Missouri.

Micah's early life as a slave and his years of counter-jumping and clerking for Chouteau had not prepared him for hard riding, but soon after he gained his freedom he had bought his old mare and rode whenever time allowed, thinking ahead, he told me, of a time when we would ride together in the mountains. What he lacked in horsemanship Micah made up in strength and natural grace, grit, and will. We made good time, halting only infrequently to wolf down a bait of vittles, refresh our critters, and snatch a few hours' sleep.

Switching mounts frequently helped to increase the distance we traveled each day and it served to smooth the rough edges off the new animals, as well. Micah, sore as I daresay he must have been at first, but uncomplaining, by the end of our journey was riding almost as if he had been born to the saddle. His easy grace flowed into the horse or mule he happened to be astride and he handled his bridle reins with a light but firm touch.

In the late forenoon of the third day we halted at a small stream to water the animals. Micah pointed to smoke rising from beyond a ridge and announced, "There it is, Powatawa's village." I could say nothing. My throat was choked with feeling but my heart grew big, pushing aside doubt and concern for what I might encounter there. We tarried long enough to shave our faces and sluice off a passel of trail dust. Then

I dug out my best Shoshone and Lahcotah finery, a quilled and beaded war shirt, long-fringed antelope leggin's, and quilled moccasins. Properly attired, I switched my saddle to Kumskaka and pronounced myself ready to go.

Micah was already mounted, his city clothes brushed as best he could manage. He regarded me head to toe and opined, "Ye look a proper Injun, Temple. I reckon ye'll do for payin' your respects." A quarter hour later we rode into the village.

* * *

A mob of little children heralded our arrival, scampering through the lane between a double row of wegiwas, howling words I recollected only dimly. Behind us the trail filled with grim-faced men, weapons in hand and suspicion in their eyes, flowing into view from cover behind trees and bushes. Women and old men poked their heads out from doorways and window slits. Satisfied that we meant no harm, they stepped out and followed our progress to the village center, where a goodly crowd soon gathered.

I had scarcely uttered the name Powatawa before I saw the man himself, still slim, straight-backed, and tall, a powdering of grey at his temples now, but looking as stout and resolute as ever. At the sound of my voice, his eyes lit up and a smile split asunder the gravity of his features, which he hastily tried to compose. He had little time to do so, howsomever, for I slipped from Kumskaka's back and ran to him, dropped to one knee, and taking his hand in both of mine, whispered, "Father."

Powatawa's first words were a choked, "You know?" He raised me to my feet, clasped me in a warm embrace, then held me at arm's length, surveyed me up and down, then hugged me to his breast again, murmuring contentedly the while in the Shawnee tongue. Then he stepped back and raised his arm and rattled off a string of phrases from which I was able to pick out only the name Sauwaseekau, which he had bestowed on me years before.

The mood of the Shawnees altered in a flash. At first they gasped, hands flying to their mouths, then came crowding around us, smiling and laughing now, men clapping me roughly on the shoulders, women straining to peer closely at my Shoshone garments, all of them chattering like a treeful of magpies. Here and there I recognized familiar faces from a decade before. My heart threatened to burst from my breast as memories of my early days amongst the Shawnees flooded into my mind. A young woman squirmed through the crowd and broke into the inner circle, then threw her arms around my neck, laughing and crying and sputtering a cataract of words. When I managed to wriggle halfway free I saw she was Methotasa, tomboy friend of my youth and now, I realized, my beautiful grown-up sister. I looked up from her glowing, tear-streaked face and beheld another that I knew well, but this face betrayed little feeling, one way or another. It was Chiksika, my closest friend when we hunted and fished and rode horses and frolicked together in the Ohio woods, when neither of us knew that we were brothers. Now he appeared to cloak himself in a dignity that far exceeded anything ever assumed by our father. A phrase of Uncle Ben's floated through my mind. Chiksika was "puttin' on airs." He thrust out his hand in a whiteman's handshake as if he were stabbing with a lance and confined himself to a single word, "Welcome," but there was no warmth in it.

There was no time to fret about it, for just then Powatawa took my arm and led me off to his wegiwa, waving off the well-wishers and even his children, whilst old Willoway the medicine-man, fondly remembered from my boyhood, tottered along behind, wafting fragrant smoke over me by way of welcome. As I stooped to enter the long-house I caught sight of the Shawnees pulling a startled Micah from his saddle, their smiles and good-natured laughter guaranteeing that he would be well-treated.

Inside, I saw that Powatawa's dwelling was shoddily built, much smaller than his wegiwa in Ohio, and poorly-furnished. He might have read my mind, for he said, "Here is not Ohio. All is different here. Trees are little. They grow not bark enough for walls and roof. We weave reeds now and learn new ways to make shelter and fill our bellies." His voice when he spoke in English sounded rusty, slow, as he groped for rarely-used words and sought to string them together properly, which he did admirably well, a tribute both to my mother's tutoring and his remarkable memory. He sounded weary, more despairing even than he had the day he was forced to lead his people westwards, when Ohio whites and bluebelly soldiers threatened to destroy the Shawnees.

He brightened then, howsomever, and bade me sit with him on a heap of deer hides and blankets, asking that I tell him of my history since

I had seen him last. The tale I told was chopped and pieced together like a patchwork quilt. I knew he wanted to be told about my mother, her last days and death, and how I came to learn that I was truly his son. I commenced my story there, then related as briefly as I could how Pap and Ben had killed each other, which further saddened him, for Powatawa and Ben had regarded each other with profound respect.

Just then a scratching on the deer hide dooflap announced the arrival of Methotasa. She placed gourd bowls of water and steaming succotash by our sides, bestowing loving glances on me the while and apologizing for being tardy with her hospitality. Powatawa, eager to hear the rest of my tale, shooed her off with a good-natured growl and explained, "I have no woman now. My woman died three winters since. I have no wish to take another. Methotasa brings my food and tends my wegiwa. She is a worthy daughter. She has a good man and two sons, strong boys and fair to look upon, who will never know Ohio." He lapsed into melancholy, then roused himself and asked that I resume my account. Which I did as best I could, glossing over my flight from Whynot, naturally not mentioning Aunt Penny's part in it, telling briefly of my keelboat journey down the Ohio and up the Mississippi to Saint Louis and how I joined Andrew Henry to ascend the Missouri for the purpose of trapping beaver in the Shining Mountains.

It was when I came to tell of that mountain land, the people and the animals there, buffalo and wapiti and bighorn sheep and multitudes of beaver, of running buffalo a-horseback and pony raids and battles and my beloved comrades — our bunch, Len-neh Leh-nah-pehs and Iroquois and whites and a Negro and a Spaniard all mixed up together — that his dark eyes fairly glowed. His handsome face lit up and he urged me to describe each man and critter and event in minute detail. Homesick as I was for the mountain life, that was no burdensome chore. We smoked and talked and basked in the sublime pleasure of each other's company until the failing light told us we had talked the day away. A growing din outside informed us that some kind of celebration was surely underway. Soon we heard the crackling of a bonfire in the lane and loud voices crying commands.

Powatawa called out and a moment later Chiksika, Methotasa, and Micah dodged past the doorflap and dropped to their knees beside us. My brother and sister immediately launched into a torrent of palaver, which allowed Micah to whisper, "'Pears they be fixin' some kind o' shindig for your comin' back. Hunters been out since we got here an' the women busy as broody hens. Reckon we oughta drag your presents in here for the giftin'?" I allowed that it would be a good idea to do so. After begging leave from Powatawa, I followed Micah to a nearby wegiwa to retrieve our packs. Several eager Shawnees volunteered to help and soon our plunder was stowed in Powatawa's dwelling.

The feast that night was meager compared with celebrations I recalled from the Shawnees' old Ohio hunting grounds, but the mood was merry and the flesh of a couple fat colts augmented the few scrawny deer that the hunters had been able to bring in. Micah, gnawing a meaty horse rib, favored me with a greasy grin and pronounced, "Folks're always sayin' circumstances alter cases. If ye don't have a fatted calf to kill for the prodigal son's return, I reckon hoss'll do the chore just fine."

I realized then that Methotasa or some other Shawnee had told Micah that Powatawa was in fact my father, which relieved me of a passel of explanations.

After the last shred of meat had been chewed off the bones and bowls scraped clean of porridge and succotash and dogs were fighting over scraps in the darkness, Powatawa rose to his feet and commenced a long harangue in which I heard the names Sauwaseekau and Temple Buck mentioned more than just a few times. I reckon he could have told them in just a couple phrases that I was truly his son, that I had been absent for a long spell, which they already knew, and that I had returned to him, which they also knew, but Indians of whatever stripe dearly love a flowery speech, the longer the better, and my father was not inclined to disappoint them. At last he ran out of wind. After calling me to his side and continuing his oratory a mite longer, whilst I blushed and burned with embarrassment, he embraced me and we both sat down.

It appeared this was a proper time for the gifting and when I said so to my father, he agreed. Micah and I brought out our packs and opened them in the light of the blazing fire. Naturally the first gift to be presented was Jacob Hawken's rifle, which I solemnly placed in Powatawa's hands. At first he beamed with pleasure, then looked puzzled when he saw the unfamiliar new-fangled lock, but I hastily whispered that I would explain later. His smile returned and he brandished the weapon above his head, its brand-new brass furniture gleaming in the firelight.

Naturally I expected that Powatawa would distribute the remaining gifts, but he surprised me by calling Chiksika to his side and delegating that honor to him. My younger brother was not slow to accept. As the presents were ceremoniously doled out amongst the band, each one accompanied by a flood of palaver greeted by a chorus of cheering voices, I noticed that the pile of gifts reserved for the chief was more than equaled by the heap that Chiksika held back for himself. It made no nevermind to me, so I held my tongue. Just the same, I wondered if perhaps my brother might be over-reaching himself by more than somewhat.

At last the gifting was finished. Micah and I bedded down in Powatawa's wegiwa, after promising my father that, come morning, we would show him how his new rifle worked. After two blissfully strenuous and mostly sleepless nights with Lucette and little time to rest on the trail after that, going to my robes was especially welcome. Our journey had been successful and I was overjoyed to be united with Powatawa. Whatever concern I entertained regarding Chiksika's coldness was slight, certainly not enough to keep me from plunging into a deep and dreamless slumber.

* * *

I awoke thoroughly refreshed but with an urgent need to discover the whereabouts of the midden. Neither the aroma of fresh-brewed coffee nor the sight of a smiling Methotasa swathed head to toe in her new bright-red blanket, keeping breakfast warm by a little fire, served to delay me in pursuit of my errand. I mumbled a hasty good morning, lunged out the door, and headed eastwards, for the wind is generally westerly thereabouts. I soon fell in with knots of men bent on the same purpose. Powatawa and Micah were just returning from that place as I rushed past them and they called out that they would wait for me, which they did.

When I rejoined them we strolled back through a village much different and considerably less prosperous than the one I recalled from Ohio. Shabby clothing and ramshackle wegiwas were only part of it. The people were friendly enough, but there was a woebegone air about them, as if they had been kicked in the belly one time too many. We continued along the lane past Powatawa's dwelling, then took a path that led to the men's bathing place, where we stripped and plunged into icy water just a shade removed from snow-melt. Men and boys frolicked and yelled around us, tawny hides rosy from the chill water, their laughter ringing off the rocky banks. It pleased me to see Micah joining in as if a freezing early-morning bathe amongst a passel of howling redskins was nothing new in his life.

Back in my father's wegiwa, coffee, thick and black and syrupy with sugar, drove out the chill, brightened our spirits, and loosened our tongues.   Yesterday's palaver about mountain life resumed without a hitch, encouraged even more by Micah's bottomless curiosity about the trapper's trade. Thankfully Powatawa's impatience to try his new rifle outweighed his thirst for mountain lore just then, so all three of us gathered up our weapons and fixin's and hiked off to a little glade where we set up twigs and wood chips for targets and Micah and I set ourselves to instruct my father in the mysteries of Jacob Hawken's percussion rifle.   Once he got the hang of the unfamiliar sights and fixing the tiny cap onto the nipple, Powatawa proceeded to reduce to splinters every wood chip in sight. He quickly grasped the advantage of being plagued no longer by damp priming and powder blowing out of the flintlock pan in a strong wind. His satisfied grunts and broad smile pronounced my gift to be a signal success.

Fortunately, that day all the percussion caps exploded just as they should. I saw no need to mention right then that sometimes they don't. I was mightily impressed by Micah's marksmanship, for I had never before seen him shoot. He proudly informed me that after Jake Hawken taught him how to shoot, he spent much of his spare cash on powder, caps, and lead. He improved sufficiently so that, in time, Jake entrusted him with testing the new rifles, pistols, and fowling-pieces.

Our gunshots drew a crowd of onlookers, Chiksika amongst them. Naturally he wished to try Powatawa's new rifle, which he shot very well, but which he faulted for all the usual reasons, mostly questioning what a body would do if he ran out of percussion caps. He was unconvinced by my asking what he might do if he ran out of powder and lead, as well. He returned the rifle to Powatawa with a disdainful shrug. Which in him was not surprising. For a young man, Chiksika was powerfully set in his ways.

I had thought to tell Chiksika that in the mountains I had named my favorite horse after him — in his honor, as you might say — but I changed my mind. From what I could tell, Chiksika would likely fail

to appreciate the compliment or to see the humor of it. My brother
had grown tolerably full of himself.

Micah returned to the village with Chiksika. Powatawa and I
lingered in the glade for a spell. Without prompting, my father further
expressed his discontent with his present life. "This Missourah land is
no good for Shawnee people," he declared. "Dirt here is dead for us.
The Shawnee spirit cannot grow here. In this country, we dry up and
die inside. We cannot renew in springtime and bloom as we did in the
old country. Our crops are weak and meager. They give us no
strength — not like before." I listened respectfully but said nothing.
He fell silent for a spell. Then he said, "Come. I will show you the
horses."

As we walked through winter-withered cornfields and truck
patches, Powatawa resumed his mournful discourse. "Hunting is no
good here. Deer are few and not so fat. Bears are seldom seen. Our
corn and squash and melons make no red blood in the children. This
dirt may be good for the Wazhazhe and the Kiowa. They are common.
Half-men. They know no other. But the Shawnee in this land is a fish
thrown upon the shore. He cannot breathe."

We passed through a thicket of tall bushes and came out into a
broad pasture flanked with several paddocks. A mob of horses and
mules, many more than I recalled seeing in the Shawnees' Ohio
village, milled in the paddocks and grazed on the sparse spring
meadow grass.

My father regarded them without much pleasure. "Shawnees have
become horse-sellers here," he declared. "Hunting is no good. Our
corn is without power, but our horses thrive. Mules, also. We sell
them to buy food from white men, sometimes from Wazhazhe. It is
not good to buy what once we grew in plenty." He looked thoughtful,
his eyes fixed on some faraway place, before he spoke again. "I think
horses can live well anywheres. They are not of this land. They come
from far over the water. They have forgotten their roots, so they grow
fat in this place or any place. They are never homesick. No crying for

lost land." He laughed quietly, a thin smile on his lips. "Sometimes I wish I was a horse."

My father's little jest appeared to restore some of his good humor. As we walked back to the village he commenced to pump me about the mountains once again. I told him every jot and tittle I could think of, even relating some of Tuttle Thompson's outrageous antics and pranks and the running battle of good-natured insults between Anse Tolliver and Paddy McBride. He was especially interested, howsomever, in whatever I could think of to tell him of Brass Turtle and old Foot and how in our bunch whites, Iroquois, and Delawares, even a black man and a Spaniard, lived and worked and fought together as brothers. I told him, too, of battles with Blackfoots, Big-bellies, and Rees. He chuckled and said, "That is good. A man needs fighting. He is but half a man without war."

We tarried a spell without speaking in front of his wegiwa.

My father broke the silence. "I named you well, my son," he said thoughtfully, "Sauwaseekau. A-door-opened. Too bad you must go so far, to your Shining Mountains, to do that thing."

Inside the wegiwa Methotasa had already prepared food and we ate until our bellies were nigh bursting. It was plain fare but well-seasoned with jesting and laughter, much of it provoked by my sister's shaky grasp of English, and warmed with good-fellowship. Afterwards Methotasa insisted that we come to her wegiwa to meet her husband and children. My father declined to attend us, saying that he must be alone for a spell. Naturally no one presumed to coax him to do otherwise.

Methotasa's husband was handsome, well-knit and warrior-like, quiet but friendly, and their two strapping boys, bright-eyed, intelligent, inquisitive, energetic, doing their level best to control their exuberance, more or less successfully, and conduct themselves politely, did honor to their parents. Naturally Shawnee etiquette required that we eat again and smoke with our host, whilst Methotasa interpreted the commonplaces that passed for conversation.

Afterwards, we all descended on Chiksika's wegiwa. My sister had been distressed by the coldness between her two brothers, but Chiksika was forced by custom to appear hospitable in his own dwelling. He presented his comely young wife and I complimented him on his children, a very quiet boy and a pretty girl. Then we ate and smoked and talked together in a halfway friendly manner. He loosened up considerably when I told him that Micah and I must depart next morning. I reckon that item of news relieved him of anxiety concerning any rivalry I might represent. Chiksika showed little interest in my history since the time we had sported together as boys — which was a welcome relief, for I was fairly sick of that topic. He waxed eloquent, howsomever, when he spoke of his plans and ambitions for the welfare of the band, if only he might possess power enough to make it all happen. Fact is, Chiksika grew so long-winded about his ambitions that dusk was gathering when we parted, almost amicably.

When Micah and I returned to my father's wegiwa, Powatawa was seated cross-legged by a measly little fire whose flickering blaze barely pushed back the darkness. When I squatted beside him and looked closely at his face, I was struck by the serenity of his features. He appeared ten years younger than he had that morning. Micah pleaded fatigue and retired to his robes. I seated myself at the fire and stuffed tobacco into my father's pipe and my own, prepared to talk the night away, if that were required to satisfy his curiosity about the mountain life. What he said, howsomever, startled me.

His voice was unusually gentle, contented, when he declared, "I have chosen my path. I will leave this place — with you, my first son. I must walk amongst your Shining Mountains. I must live free and hunt and fight as I did in my youth, as my fathers — your fathers — have always done. I go with you, Sauwaseekau."

I was too flabbergasted to offer a sensible reply, but I strangled out something like, "But what about your people? Who's to look after them? Who's to take over if you're not here?"

"Chiksika. Your brother has long hungered to lead this band. I never thirsted for it. The people forced the lance into my fist. I told you this when you were but a boy. Truly I am no chief, nor ever wished to be. When the Shawnee lost our war and Tecumseh died, I, also, died. I have been a hollow man from that time."

"But must you leave the village, the band?" I reckon my voice lacked conviction. I had never truly believed that he might accompany me to the mountains. Now the prospect of his doing so made my heart big indeed.

"Yes. There can be no other way. If Chiksika is to be chief, he must stand alone, with no other leader near him." When he thought that I might differ with him, Powatawa raised his hand to halt my protest. "If a bear should choose to call himself a rabbit," he explained patiently, "no other four-legged will believe he is a rabbit — especially the rabbits. So long as I stay here, Chiksika will never own the power he craves. I must go."

There was no doubt in my mind that my father, old as he was — fact is, not yet fifty years — was fit for the mountains. His skills, except perhaps for beaver-trapping, were far superior to my own. Without further hesitation and no misgivings I replied, "So be it. Come with me and welcome."

In my robes that night I thanked my stars that the men in my trapping bunch would likely make no nevermind about my showing up with a Negro and my Shawnee father. Few if any other trappers I was acquainted with would be so generous.

Next morning, Powatawa's robes were empty when Micah and I hurried by on our way to the midden. On our return we met with him and Chiksika. From my brother's cheerful face I gathered that my father had told him of his decision. This was argued further by Chiksika's hearty insistence that we break our fast in his wegiwa. Which we did, amid a passel of family and friends and a cloudburst of clashing emotions, some congratulating Chiksika on his likely elevation, others expressing deepfelt sorrow at my father's intended departure. Feelings were running high as spring flood and I had no wish to swim amid the crosscurrents of such strong sentiment mixed up with Shawnee custom and tribal politics. Micah and I privately agreed it was time we made tracks out of the village, promising to return for Powatawa in a week's time. Which we did.

Chapter III
Farewell

"Mais non, M'sieu!" the pasty-faced little concierge exclaimed, waving his little white hands excitedly, when I returned to my lodgings in Saint Louis. "Your seengs are no longair 'ere! Madame Lucette 'as order me to breeng zem to 'er *établissement* an' also to say to you zat you mus' go zere when you arrive 'ere." He frowned, evidently straining to recall Lucette's instructions precisely, then brightened as he added, "She say also zat you mus' breeng wiz you your *animaux aussi.*" I thanked the fussy little fellow for his trouble, sliding a coin across the counter as I did so, and returned to my critters tethered in the street.

Lucette's *maison* was not far distant. I supposed that in my absence construction work must have progressed sufficiently for her to occupy the premises, an event sure to gladden her heart. I thought, too, that it was just as well that I stay there with her, if only to keep her from dying of a fatal catarrh by getting soaked again in a rainstorm.

Naturally that was not my only consideration. Difficult as she could be at times, Lucette's company was always pleasurable, eagerly welcomed by me, and this occasion was no exception. I fairly bristled in anticipation of being with her again.

Micah and I had parted as soon as we arrived in the city, agreeing to meet next day at noon at Chouteau's mercantile to purchase supplies for our journey to the mountains. We had made good time returning from the Shawnees. Our critters were well-rested and lightly loaded, so we were able to shave nearly a full day off the time it had taken us to travel out there. Tired, hungry, and travel-stained as we were, the both of us were eager to have those needs, amongst whatever others, tended to as quickly as possible.

My reception at Lucette's was warm. A smiling young black stableman took charge of my animals and Israel, Lucette's faithful doorkeeper and majordomo, compromised his customary lofty dignity long enough to greet me with a friendly bow and words of welcome as he ushered me indoors. A festive air pervaded the place and all the people in it. Bright-liveried waiters bustled about their chores, some of them humming lively tunes, nearly all of them smiling. Chattering white-aproned maids, pretty black faces shining, skittered hither and thither in pursuit of their duties. Men and women both were obviously elated to be employed once again in Lucette's palatial den of iniquity.

Whilst I stood gaping at the lush new carpeting and rich velvet draperies framing tall windows in the newly-furnished ballroom, an insistent tug at my sleeve announced the arrival of Lucette. As I swung about to greet her, she strained up on tip-toe and kissed me lightly on the lips, murmuring, "At las' you are return, Tom-pool! I 'ave miss you *mos' terriblement!*" Then she sniffed and stepped back, surveying me head to foot, and exclaimed, "*Mais tu es sale!* You are ver' dirty! *Tu as besoin d'un bain!*" Although it was certainly true that I stood sorely in need of a bath and a change of clothes, especially in such luxurious surroundings, I thought that she might have been more discreet about announcing that fact to the whole world in two languages. I commenced to tell her so, but she heard not a word, occupied as she was in calling out commands to her people as she guided me to her private apartments.

By time she pushed open the heavy door to her chambers, her maids were already busy filling a big copper bathtub with pails of steaming water. I saw, too, that Lucette had refurnished her quarters in a style lavish enough to make a monarch swoon with envy. What caught my eye and held it, howsomever, was the huge canopied bed that dominated the bedchamber, a veritable altar of Venus. I confess that I felt a certain thrill at the prospect of my becoming a sacrifice upon it. Fact is, so eager was I that dismissing the maids, shaving, bathing, and the like are but a blur in my recollection, memory returning only when Lucette and I lay entwined and gasping for breath after our first encounter. After that there was time and patience enough for more leisurely and elaborate lovemaking, which we happily explored until dusk darkened the windows and Lucette reluctantly announced that her duties demanded her presence elsewhere for a spell.

Her toilette completed, Lucette positively glowed. Her smile was tender, her dark eyes soft and liquid, and roses bloomed beneath her café-au-lait complexion as she bade me a lingering farewell, as if she were to be absent a fortnight instead of merely an hour or two. Lucette is most likely a mite crazy — but then, so am I whenever she and I get together.

After her departure, I grew restless, so I dressed in clean buckskins — I owned no other clothing — and sauntered out to admire the improvements Lucette had wrought in her *maison*. Although the establishment was not yet properly open for business, several well-dressed gentlemen, most likely long-time patrons, were playing at whist or conversing quietly over their drinks, whilst attentive servingmen hovered nearby.

I was not surprised to spy Pierre Chouteau seated alone at a small table on the mezzanine, sipping cognac. He and Lucette have been fast friends for many years and are engaged in business dealings together, as well. When he caught sight of me le Cadet smiled and nodded an invitation to join him, which naturally I did. We exchanged pleasantries, chatted about my recent visit to the Shawnee village and my forthcoming journey to the mountains. Somewhere in the neighborhood of my third whiskey on an empty stomach, sentiment prevailed and I felt obliged to express my gratitude to Chouteau for his friendship and the help he had provided since I first met him six years before. I had been a scared, penniless youth on that first occasion. Now, thanks to le Cadet's kindness and his business skills, I had become a man of some substance. Leastaways I possessed enough money to finance my modest ambitions. I felt grateful to him and I told him so.

I daresay Chouteau was feeling somewhat rosy himself, for he chuckled quietly and said, "Temple Buck, do you weesh to know why eet ees zat I value you so? Why I 'ave befriend you and look after your interest zese several years? I weel tell you now." I nodded but said nothing. Le Cadet sipped his cognac and continued. "That first day when you came to our establishment with Mike Fink and his bullies, I saw that you were not of his kind, that he was using you against your will. It was none of my affair, naturally, but I gained a certain admiration for you when I saw that you had signed Fink's documents as if you were an equal partner of his, which I knew you were not. Such a bold stroke took courage and enterprise worthy of a Saint Louis Frenchman! For that reason I quickly countersigned and sealed the papers and packed them up in oilskin, so that Fink did not discover your little sin and kill you on the spot!"

Just then I realized that Chouteau had ceased speaking his customary quaint English and had switched into French, which I reckon he had known all along that I understood well enough. He smiled at my discomfort but made no comment about his change of tongue. He merely resumed his discourse. "Then when you acquired the protection of Lucette but declined to live as her parasite, preferring instead the difficult and dangerous life of a trapper, I saw in you another quality I could admire."

Le Cadet smiled to himself, as if he were recalling a pleasant incident. "When you returned from the mountains many years later, possessing all three copies of Fink's valuable documents and a boatload of furs and robes besides, my admiration of your abilities increased considerably! Moreover, your treatment of Micah speaks well of your honor and your good heart. When the time is appropriate you and I will do much good business together, Temple Buck. Now you know why I have extended to you my protection and why it is that I wish you well."

There was little I could think of to say in reply to such compliments, so I merely mumbled my thanks for his confidence and friendship, but that time I did my mumbling in French.

Before taking his leave, Chouteau invited me to visit him at his office before Micah and I departed Saint Louis, which I promised to do. Afterwards I lingered over my whiskey, lazily observing the handful of well-dressed patrons at neighboring tables and listening with half an ear to the Negro musicians rehearsing in the ballroom below. The tunes they played that evening were unlike the stately measures I recalled from my earlier stay in Lucette's establishment. This music was more common, earthier, warmer and more exciting, yet plaintive and even mournful at times. When the Negro server came to refill my glass, I told him I liked what I was hearing. "Oh, dat," he replied. "Dem's niggah tunes, lak dey play on de docks. Dey call 'em de blues. Miz Lucette she don' approve, but she ain't heah rat now."

When the music abruptly changed to what I supposed to be a European composition I reckoned that Lucette had returned from her errand. A few minutes later she and I were seated at table in her chamber, devouring a late supper. A short while after that we retired to her bed, where we did our best to devour each other as well, as only two lusty young animals untroubled by conscience can do. We might have succeeded, too, had we not fallen into exhausted slumber, thoroughly drained and contented and lovingly entwined in each other's arms.

* * *

Next morning, whilst I was saddling Kumskaka at the livery and admiring the fine workmanship of my Spaniard saddle, a random thought struck me. Instead of turning toward the river and Berthold et Chouteau, I rode in the opposite direction, leading my Remus mule, threading through ever-narrowing streets until I arrived at the alley where the leathery old Spaniard sold his wares. It took no time at all, mainly because I refused to haggle — much to the old man's displeasure — until I departed his shop with Remus loaded with a total equipage of the old gentleman's finest products, a gift for my father that would prove more valuable the longer he owned it. My heart was warm in my breast, likely less so because of filial piety than owing to the deal-sealing guzzle of *aguardiente* that I had not the heart to refuse, lest I offend the old saddler yet again.

I left Remus, the saddle and its fixin's, and the half dozen grass lasso ropes that the old man had insisted that I accept for boot in the care of the liveryman and, still grinning with satisfaction, rode on to the mercantile.

* * *

Micah was nowhere to be seen outside Berthold et Chouteau's mercantile. I was untroubled by his absence, howsomever, for farewelling to a sweetheart can be time-consuming. I decided to take this opportunity to pay my respects to le Cadet, as I had promised to do. Before I entered the building, I paused a few moments to marvel at the sight of two steamboats forging up the Mississippi. I wondered if such newfangled contraptions would ever be able to ascend the wild, snag-cluttered Missouri and dismissed the idea as impossible.

Every stool was empty in the large hall that housed the company's clerks, even that of the chief clerk Gaston, the lot of them likely enjoying their noon meal. Grateful to be relieved of Gaston's officious bustling, I presented myself at le Cadet's chamber door and rapped smartly on the well-oiled panel. "*Entrez!*" I recognized Chouteau's voice, but I was unprepared for the several other men who returned my gaze when I swung open the door, amongst whom I was startled to see General William Ashley. I daresay le Cadet was equally surprised to see me instead of Gaston, but if so, he concealed it smoothly, smiled, and waved me in, announcing the while in that French and English macaroni so common in Saint Louis, "*Messieurs*, allow me to present *mon ami* Temple Bock, *un trappeur de castor extraordinaire.* 'E weel return to 'ces *métier* in ze *montagnes* wiz-in zis week!"

He led me around the group and I shook hands in turn with Bernard Pratte, Chouteau's partner Monsieur Berthold, a smiling, buckskin-clad Frenchman named Lucien Fontenelle, a dapper, hard-eyed gentleman called Kenneth McKenzie, and then to a man who looked familiar to me. He turned out to be Etienne Provost, the French trader we had met in the camp of the Hudson's Bay partisan Peter Ogden and who later guided us to Ashley's first rendezvous in 'twenty-five. He had increased somewhat in girth since I had seen him last on the far side of the mountains, but he still appeared to be sturdy and powerful enough for whatever might come his way. Provost grasped both my hands and, beaming, announced, "I remembair you, one of zem who save *la femme* of M'sieu Ogden from *les bravaches de* Gardner when 'er 'orse 'ave run off wiz 'er *petit enfant!*" I hastily assured him that, yes, I had been one of that different party of Americans, not one of Gardner's bullies.

When I came at last to a red-faced General Ashley, he smiled wryly and declared loudly, "Oh, Mister Buck and I have been long acquainted!" Then to me: "You were one of the first bunch, I believe, Buck. In 'twenty-two, if I am not mistaken." I allowed that this was so and Ashley did what he could to stifle his embarrassment at being discovered in that particular company, pledged as he was to supply and support the firm of Smith, Jackson & Sublette. It made no nevermind to me if William Ashley undermined his successors in the fur trade, but I confess that I enjoyed observing his discomfort at being caught at it.

As I retreated towards the door, Chouteau took my arm and declared to the group, "M'sieu Bock returns to ze *montagnes* to pursue 'ees *métier* now, but I 'ave 'ope zat one day 'e weel join us in our *entreprise!*" I made my escape amid approving murmurs and the friendly smiles of all but Ashley, who seemed puzzled by my obvious warm friendship with Chouteau. At the door, in a low voice I promised le Cadet that I would visit him on a more convenient occasion, sometime before my departure. Then I hustled off to meet Micah, thinking the while how confounded Jed Smith and Bill Sublette would be if they learned that their double-dealing mentor was consorting with the enemy — but I was certain that it would never be me who would enlighten them.

Micah was waiting for me in the mercantile and we immediately set about outfitting ourselves. The mountain trade was firmly established by that time and well-understood by Saint Louis merchants, so the shelves and bins of Berthold et Chouteau's mercantile were well-stocked with everything a trader or a mountaineer might need or wish for. Prices were dirt-cheap compared with what a trader would demand — and was sure to get — in the mountains at rendezvous, so it shouldn't be surprising that I went hog-wild with my purchases. First off I furnished myself, Micah, and Powatawa each with half a dozen good English-made Manchester beaver traps and extra chain. Then I stocked up on French gunpowder and American galena pigs as well as a supply of ready-made rifle balls and birdshot, a few steel ramrods and a couple dozen hickory wiping-sticks, English flints for rifles, muskets, pistols, and firestrikers, with a gross of round firesteels to match. Before long the counter groaned under heaps of tobacco twists, woolen shirts, blanket capotes, several pairs of English Mackinaw blankets, a couple dozen calico shirts for gifts, colorful sashes and garters, coils of rope, tomahawks for smoking and some solely for persuading, fine English butcher knives and common scalpers for gifts and trade, a couple axes and short-handled spades, a pick-mattock head, small tools such as files, a hammer, pincers, several gross of awls — sixty cents the gross in Saint Louis, a dollar apiece in the mountains — harness needles and thread, whetstones and whale oil, canvas sheeting, tallow candles, fishhooks and English-made silk angling line, besides tins and bags of tea, coffee beans, sugar, black pepper and sea salt, honey, molasses, and suchlike luxuries.

Buying molasses made me grin. Four years in the trapper's trade had taught me that a mountaineer might lose his way in the mountains or lose his temper or his traps, or maybe even lose his plews and his ponies, but I never saw a single one of them in all that time lose his sweet tooth, even if mischance should leave him bereft of all his other ivories.

With that thought in mind, I added a couple large pokes of peppermint sticks to our growing heap of plunder. I purchased, too, a case of razors and a couple dozen tablets of sweet-smelling English lavender shaving soap for Tuttle Thompson, whose success in his amorous forays amongst Indian women largely depends upon his scraping off his wiry stubble beforehand.

Almost as an afterthought I purchased fistfuls of pencils and a couple thick ledger books in which I intended to keep a journal. My year-long inactivity in Whynot and writing my recollections of my years in the mountains during that time had bred a certain rude scholarship in me. Once you succumb to its wiles, writing is a difficult habit to break.

Prominent in my mind was what Black Harris had told me about Billy Sublette supplying his own company brigades the previous fall, which possibly meant that rendezvous at Willow Valley would be a measly affair for free trappers, if indeed any trade plunder at all would remain for them. Most of what I bought was not intended for my own use but would be passed out as gifts to my former companions or donated for the common use of our trapping bunch.

Naturally we also stocked up on Indian trade goods, such as Venice beads in various sizes and colors, tiny looking-glasses, vermilion and other paint powders, cock and foxtail feathers, hawk bells, a couple quarts of shiny brass tacks, nested tin-lined copper kettles, ribbon, yards of French calicos and English woolens and strouding, several pairs of scissors, coarse and fine needles and spools of silk and linen thread, besides a passel of gewgaws and trinkets — what trappers call foofurraw, calculated to tickle the fancy of dusky matrons and maidens in the Shining Mountains. I also added a couple dozen tweezers, prized by Indian men for removing the occasional whisker and, more important, by everybody for cracking greyback lice.

Micah had been a counter-jumper for Chouteau for several years, waiting on the mountain trade, so whatever I might neglect, he added to our heap of supplies. On a whim I bought a pair of curved tin canisters of five gallons each, shaped to fit the sides of a pack animal, and had them filled, one with good French brandy, the other with the best Kentucky whiskey the mercantile provided. By time we added provisions we would need for the trail until we reached buffalo country, it was plain to see that although a properly-loaded mule can pack two and a half hundredweight and a stout horse somewhat more, we would need yet a couple more mules to pack our plunder to rendezvous.

Next we paid a farewell visit to Jake Hawken's shop, where I bought a couple gallons of tiny thimble-shaped percussion caps sealed in powder horns to keep them dry and, when Micah was occupied elsewhere, two pistols like my own, gifts for Powatawa and Micah, who would be especially grateful for such weapons when we reached buffalo country, if not before, in Pah-nee territory. I thought to purchase a rifle or pistol for my brother Chiksika, as well, as a farewell gift, but, reflecting on his disdain for Powatawa's new percussion rifle, I decided that he must be content with a big brass-hafted knife the Hawkens offered. Meanwhile, Micah retrieved his kit of tools and a passel of spare parts, which, together with his gunsmithing skills, would assure him a warm reception amongst our trapping crew.

With the Hawken brothers' well-wishing still ringing in our ears, we wasted no time riding to Charlie Bowden's sale-yard. The old scoundrel was happy to oblige us, trotting out a number of acceptable animals, from which I selected two tall jack-mules I reckoned were the best of the lot. Whilst we haggled over price I learned that Black Harris had left for Independence nearly a week before, which naturally spurred my desire to be on the trail without delay.

A final visit to the old Spaniard's shop for packsaddles, hobbles, harness, and britching for the two new mules completed our needs. This time, howsomever, the wily old saddler refused to be cheated of his satisfaction. The price he named for his merchandise was so outrageously dear that, no matter how impatient I might be, I was forced to haggle, wrangling until the two of us arrived at a figure modest enough to leave me with at least a shred of self-respect. The old man cackled and grinned throughout the transaction, obviously relishing the give-and-take of the bargaining far more than he valued the money involved. When at last our deal was concluded and I was counting out the coins, he threw in a pair of sturdy pommel holsters for boot and passed around a well-worn wineskin filled with fiery Taos aguardiente brandy to seal the bargain, muttering the while in broken English how doing business was thirsty work indeed.

Micah and I parted soon afterwards, he to return to his lodgings, I to lead our new livestock to Lucette's. We agreed to meet next morning at the mercantile, there to sort and pack and load our plunder, then to bid farewell to Saint Louis and all its worldly pleasures for only God might know how many years.

* * *

Riding westwards out of town along the now-familiar trail to the Shawnee village provided ample time to muse upon the happenings of my final hours in Saint Louis town. As I had expected and dreaded, Lucette did not accept the news of my immediate departure with ladylike grace and good humor. Fact is, she threw a conniption, giving free rein to her mercurial temper, berating me one moment as a faithless scoundrel, then drowning me the next in tearful kisses, imploring me to stay, then loudly denouncing my impending desertion.

Such quarreling with Lucette has its compensations, howsomever, for the reconciliation that inevitably follows is even more intense than the squabbling. Our ardent peacemaking that night and next morning left me limp in every respect, with barely enough strength to wolf down a breakfast fit for two men and drag myself to the stables, then to ride to my meeting with Micah at Berthold et Chouteau's mercantile.

Micah wore the frowzy but contented look of a man who hadn't wasted his final hours with his ladylove in mere sleeping. The welts that laced his cheek and neck further testified to a passel of spirited farewelling.

An hour's time was occupied in dividing our plunder into six more or less equal pack-loads, taking care to distribute similar goods throughout several packs, so that the misadventure of any one pack animal might not deprive us of our entire stock of a particular item. Balancing each load and lashing them onto the packsaddles used up another hour. It was fairly late in the forenoon before our little caravan stood ready to make tracks for Independence. As if on a signal, as I prepared to mount Kumskaka, Pierre Chouteau appeared from inside the mercantile, followed by a grinning Gaston clutching a bottle in each hand. Le Cadet, dignified and well-tailored as always, beamed a warm, almost paternal, smile. "Hold, Temple!" he called out in his more-or-less English. "Zere mus' be time pour un coup de *l'étrier*, 'ow you say, a stirrup-cup!" He took the two bottles from Gaston and handed one to me, a French cognac, and the other, fine Kentucky whiskey, to Micah. "Bot because your voyage ees so longue *et difficile*, only a fool *bouteille* ees enough!" He waved away our thanks and his expression grew halfway serious when he said to me, nodding towards Micah, "Teach 'eem well, Temple. Ze two of you weel be a part of *un grand dessein au futur*."

Micah, resplendent in a spanking-new buckskin suit, beamed with pleasure and pride and I assured Chouteau that, some future grand design or not, I would look after Micah as if he were my brother, which, after all we had been through together, he practically was.

* * *

Two days' hard riding brought us to Powatawa's village, where my father greeted us with such enthusiasm that I halfway feared he might explode. Chiksika, too, was in remarkably good spirits, grinning and chuckling and rubbing his hands together, as if he could already feel the lance of leadership in his itchy palms. Only my sister Methotasa wore a long face, her red-rimmed eyes betraying her grief at the impending departure of our father and her concern for our safety.

That night Chiksika got his wish. The entire band choked the street between the rows of wegiwas, men and women scattered around a string of cookfires, where quarters of deer meat and fat colt sizzled and roasted on spits. Kettles of stout porridge and succotash bubbled on lively coals, filling the air with a delicious fragrance thick enough to chew. Then came Willoway the ancient medicine man threading his way amongst the throng, calling out in his cracked old voice that it was time for the speechifying.

Only a few women remained behind to tend the vittles and keep the dogs at bay, while the rest of the band assembled around a roaring council fire at the edge of the village. Micah and I drifted with the crowd until my father, a quilled and beaded bearskin robe draped around his shoulders, spied us and beckoned us forward to stand beside him. He gripped in his right hand a long lance elaborately decorated with all manner of feathers and claws, bands of fur, brass tacks, faded red and blue wool cloth and snakeskin wraps, and swatches of long hair that likely were scalps of long-dead enemies. He raised his left hand and the babble of voices around us ebbed and died, until the crackling fire and a nervous cough here and there were the only sounds to be heard. Powatawa commenced speaking in the high nasal ceremonial voice his people reserve for oratory, punctuating his remarks from time to time by thumping the butt of the lance on the hard-packed earth. I understood hardly anything he said, save the occasional use of my name, Sauwaseekau — A-door-opened.

At last Powatawa summoned Chiksika forward and after a passel of high-pitched formal palaver passed betwixt the two of them, Powatawa shrugged out of the bearskin, draped it over Chiksika's shoulders, and presented the lance of leadership to him. Chiksika grabbed onto it with undisguised pleasure, his grinning features reflecting not a shred of awareness of the solemn responsibility that had been bestowed upon him. Chiksika launched into a long-winded oration that had his audience shifting restlessly on their feet until old Willoway took advantage of a momentary pause for breath to cry out a command, followed by the crash of half a dozen big drums. Men and women quickly sorted themselves into a circle, bodies swaying, moccasined feet stamping, voices humming and trilling in cadence with the drumbeat, shuffling from right to left with a variety of dance steps, each person expressing himself in movement according to his own impulse. Now and again a man or woman would dart into the center, perform a passel of brief, spirited, intricate dance-steps, then duck back into the slowly spinning human wheel rotating around the council fire.

A tug on my sleeve roused me from something like a trance that watching the dancers had induced in me. Methotasa caught my hand and pulled me towards the moving circle. Her other hand pulled Micah along at the same time. "Come for dance," she called out. "Dance wiz fahzer!" She jerked her chin in the direction of the council fire. Sure enough, Powatawa was dancing alone with easy grace, smiling, lost in his rhythms, loose and playful, a man without a care in the world — he who had always appeared so stern and deliberate, clenched in the iron fist of discipline and duty, grave and dignified, bound by tradition and the demands of leadership. Methotasa grew more insistent. "Dance wiz fahzer! Now he be free! He own himself!"

I caught her meaning. Powatawa was at last released from the cares of office, free to be his own man. It was only right and proper that his eldest son rejoice with him and celebrate his father's newfound liberty. Where Micah might fit in with that line of reasoning I couldn't fathom, but we dragged him along anyway. Soon all four of us were dancing together, hands gripping one another's shoulders, moccasins tracing in the dirt the patterns of our souls, responding to the drumbeat and the beating of our hearts.

I glanced past Powatawa's smiling face, peaceful and serene in the firelight, to the place where Chiksika stood stiffly erect and alone, still gripping his precious lance, sweating under his bearskin robe, his features locked into the stern lines he deemed appropriate to his new authority. Comparing the two of them, I got an inkling of how liberated my father must feel at that moment. Better still was what I knew was coming — the mountains and all the freedom any man could wish for, if that man possessed pluck enough to reach out and grab it and hold onto it. I reckoned both Powatawa and Micah were equal to the task.

* * *

I had been dreading a passel of tearful goodbyes, but our departure next morning proved to be more festive than funereal. Even Methotasa, resplendent in a new bright green-and black-striped blanket capote with which I had gifted her that morning, joined in the general merriment.

It was understood by all the Shawnees that Powatawa wished with all his heart to travel with Micah and me to the faraway Shining Mountains. It would have shown disrespect to their long-time leader if they had begrudged him his heart's desire by too loudly lamenting his leaving them. Moreover, the night before, the band had accepted a new leader in Chiksika. It would not have been politic for anyone to show excessive grief over the former chief's departure.

The night before, once the dancing and feasting had petered out, Powatawa had drawn me aside and asked that we leave the village as quickly as possible, preferably the following morning. I needed no urging to comply with his request. Black Harris's departure from Independence was never far from my thoughts. So it was that my father's four horses, already saddled and lightly loaded with his possibles and food for the trail, were tethered at the door of his wegiwa when I scrambled from my robes next morning.

Powatawa's family members and a few close friends gathered in Chiksika's wegiwa to break our fast and bid our farewells. After we stuffed ourselves nigh to bursting, the customary gifting took place, but this time it wasn't strictly one-sided. When our presents had all been distributed amid cries of delight and grunts of satisfaction, my sister Methotasa, Chiksika's comely wife, and a couple of their women friends, amid a flurry of giggles, brought out a pair of parcels wrapped in deerhide. When they spread them open they revealed two of the prettiest doeskin shirts I had ever seen. Knee-length and soft as fresh cream, adorned with colorful, tightly-woven quills and fringed to a fare-thee-well, the garments surpassed even the best of Crow and Shoshone work I had ever seen. Methotasa, in her halting English, spoke up for her friends: "You mus' remember of zem who love you all times you put zis clozings on your arms." Then naught else would do but that Micah and I must strip off our upper garments and don our new shirts. We were still sporting those colorful duds when the three of us rode out of the Shawnee village half an hour later.

* * *

That first day on the westward trail was a short one. We made camp early so that we might repack our plunder and distribute lighter loads amongst the pack animals, now that we had the use of Powatawa's three stout horses and a mule. It was then that I gifted my father with the Spaniard saddle, until then hidden beneath one of the packs. At first he looked dubious, but Micah and I urged him to give it a fair trial.

We ate a hasty supper of vittles Methotasa had thoughtfully sent along with us and afterwards, whilst we smoked and sipped strong coffee syrupy with sugar, I presented Micah and my father each with one of the new percussion pistols I had purchased from Jake Hawken, together with the pommel holsters the old Spaniard saddler had thrown in for boot.

Admiring the pistols naturally led to talk of running buffalo a-horseback, which meandered into a discussion of desirable qualities in horses, a topic never far from the minds of men everywhere, which provides a never-ending supply of grist for disputes that are never decisively won or ever completely lost, which is likely what makes such palaver the most entertaining occupation that idle men gathered around cookfires have ever conceived, leastaways since mankind learned to stay astride a horse. Micah wasn't able to contribute much to that particular palaver, but he was an attentive listener.

When at last the talk petered out, I wished my companions pleasant dreams and went to my robes. Sleep overtook me before I was able to count the blessings bestowed on me lately, let alone those that I was sure awaited in the Shining Mountains.

Chapter IV
Westering

Three days of hard riding and little sleep brought us into Independence, man and beast alike caked with trail grit, horses and mules leg-weary and gaunt, the three of us mud-spattered hardly-humans parched as pebbles and hungry as wolves in winter. Needful as we were of rest and vittles, howsomever, we lost no time in discovering the whereabouts of Black Harris. The townsfolk whom we queried looked a mite leery at the sight of our multi-hued trio — red and black and white men riding together as equals — but we were by that time accustomed to such suspicious and reproachful looks and we paid them no nevermind. Disapproving though those people were, they pointed the way to Harris's camp on the riverbank, a rag-tag sprawl of tents and rude canvas shelters surrounding a couple of large makeshift paddocks, where more scores of horses and mules milled and neighed and brayed and snorted whilst men forked hay over peeled-pole fences.

Catching scent of the hay, our critters commenced their own whinnying and braying, which caused one of the men to swing about to confront intruders, pitchfork at the ready. Before he had turned more than halfway around, I recognized Black Harris, for hardly any man in Missouri or the mountains is as homely as Moses Harris. Many years ago a gun exploded in his hands, peppering his cheeks with gunpowder grains which he will carry to his grave, hence his nickname Black. Most of the homely disappeared, howsomever, when he saw who we were.

A huge grin spread over his features and his blue eyes twinkled as he roared, "Hell! 'Bout time ye showed up, Temple Buck! I war fixin' to leave ye 'hind!" The good-natured laugh that followed gave the lie to his threat and the grizzly hug that dragged me from my saddle erased all suspicion of it. The two of us collapsed on the ground, laughing fit to bust.

Powatawa and Micah dismounted in the ordinary fashion and Black and I scrambled to our feet, still chuckling and joshing each other. Harris already knew Micah and he greeted him warmly. "Glad to see ye come along, Micah. Lookin' for'ard to the mountains, are ye? I warrant ye won't be sorry ye went, oncet ye git the hang of it."

Micah grinned and shook Harris's outstretched hand. "Much obliged, Mistah Black. I got a heap o' learnin' to do, that's a fact, but I'll do the best I can."

"I'm sure ye will," Harris rejoined, then glanced at me. "Like I tol' ye before, if Temple hyar reckons ye got grit an' smarts enough fer the chore, I reckon I kin wager my poke on ye, too."

Powatawa remained standing nigh the horses, his face impassive, betraying no emotion whatsoever. It occurred to me that Black hadn't met my father, so I stepped forward to introduce them to each other. "Black," I said, "I'm proud for you to meet my father, Powatawa. He's a Shawnee chief — or leastaways he was until we come over here together."

Harris, always alert for a jest or a prank, cocked his head, squinted, and regarded me quizzically. "Ye don't say! Thish'yar's yer father? Yer paw? You're tellin' me yer paw's an Injun, are ye? An' I'm s'posed to b'lieve ye? That's what ye mean to tell me, is it naow?" He stepped backwards, folded his arms, and glared at me, half annoyed, half amused.

"Believe what ye wish, Black," I declared warmly. "I ain't never lied to you yet an' I don't mean to be commencin' now. Powatawa is my natural father and I'm damned proud of it!"

Something in my look or my tone must have convinced him, for Harris said not another word, but stepped forward to Powatawa and shoved out his hand. "Welcome. Glad to have ye 'long. Jist one thing. Y'oughta be teachin' thct boy o' your'n some manners!"

Powatawa took Black's hand in both of his and a broad smile lit up his face. "Thank you. I shall try to be worthy of my place in your company. I will not shame my son," he said in perfect English.

Harris's jaw dropped and he stumbled half a step backward, eyes bugging. I took pity on him and intervened. "No need to be so surprised, Black. I told ye he was a chief and a damned good one, too. My mother taught him English and how to read and write, as well. He's a first-rate hunter and as for fightin', there was a passel o' Yankee soldiers wishin' he was on their side durin' the War o' the British Return."

Black grunted and looked thoughtful before he said, "One of ol' Tecumseh's folks, was he? Thet war some doin's, I bin told." He brightened then and said, "Wal, the past be gone ferever. Water over the dam. Naow be naow."

I nodded and allowed that he was right, before I asked, "Where d'ye want us to set?" I looked past him at the Missouri flowing by behind the paddocks and added, "I'm froze to wash this muck off me, soon's I can. I swear I'm totin' half o' Missourah on my hide."

Black jerked his thumb in the direction of a dirty white tent and said, "Right over thar, next to my own lodge — pervidin' none o' ye snores louder'n me!"

I assured him that he was still likely champion in that respect, then joined my companions to lead our critters to a flat open space near Black's tent. As each animal was relieved of his burden, I watched, amused, as they sank to their knees and commenced to roll on their backs, legs thrashing, rubbing off sweat and scratching the itch from sodden saddle pads, then lurched upright onto their legs, nickering softly, letting us know that water and feed were required now.

After we watered our stock and let them roll once again in the river, we gave each critter a healthy bait of oats in a nosebag before turning them loose in one of the paddocks to forage in the timothy hay piled along the fence. Extra paddock poles and sail canvas from our packs sufficed to provide a rude shelter for ourselves and our plunder.

In no time at all, Micah and I were racing for the river. We dived in fully clothed, impatient to lave off our coat of sticky sweat and layers of trail dust and mud.

When I surfaced and shrugged my hair from my eyes, I beheld Powatawa on the bank, stripping off his clothing, then diving into the river and swimming far out, before he swam back and joined us in our frolic. Seeing him laughing and frisking like a carefree schoolboy made it difficult to recall his tight-reined former self, so grave and self-controlled and dignified. I fairly glowed with satisfaction at his transformation.

* * *

The next few days passed swiftly. Then it was time to be on our way to the West. We were giddy with excitement, infected by the uproar and near bedlam of shouting, cursing hostlers and drovers and braying, neighing, well-fed critters who humped their backs and blew up their bellies against girths and cinches, reluctant to resume their servitude. My thoughts ranged far ahead to the mountains and my old companions and whatever adventures awaited there. For a moment I chided myself for such greenhorn sentiments, but then I shrugged and surrendered to my enthusiasm.

At last Harris managed to whip his mob of more than seventy heavily-laden pack animals and a score of mounted hostlers and drovers into passable order to commence our journey. A sizeable crowd of townsfolk had come out to witness our departure, which in that sleepy little settlement amounted to a festive occasion. Bursts of laughter mixed with the curses of exasperated hostlers striving to push their equine charges into something like an orderly procession.

Strut and swagger were the watchwords of the day. Going to the mountains is considered an admirable and courageous act thereabouts. Every man in the party sported his Sunday duds and sat his horse or mule with a prideful bearing befitting a holiday parade.

We were no exception. Powatawa, Micah and I wore our colorful Shawnee war shirts and rode our best horses. Micah, in particular, looked as proud as Lucifer, astride his handsome Ashley horse, gleaming Hawken rifle across his thighs, a grin as wide as the Missouri on his shining face.

The pack train had hardly lurched into motion before it halted to retrieve some beef cattle and sheep that had strayed into the crowd of onlookers. We three took that opportunity to step down and snug up our saddle cinches. We were preparing to remount when one of the hostlers, a broad-shouldered, barrel-chested, bullet-headed ruffian called Tug Novak, swung down from his mule, shouldered his way through the milling livestock, and confronted Micah. "Hark, nigger!" he snarled. "Yer lookin' purty high an' mighty, all gussied up in them Injun duds an' settin' like a white man on thet'ere fancy Kaintuck nag o' yourn! What's a draggle-arse darky doin' 'mongst decent whitefolk, anyways? Actin' like yer betters! Reckon I oughta larn ye yer rightful place, so's ye don't never fergit it!"

For a moment I stood dumbstruck, frozen by the man's insolence. I saw Micah commence to bristle, but before either of us could make a move, a tall, lean, dark-haired drover pushed his horse through the crowd of townsfolk, stepped to the ground, and tapped Novak on the shoulder. When the bully swung about, the newcomer smashed him full in the face with a powerful punch, sending him sprawling.

Novak, sitting on the ground, his nose streaming blood, demanded, "Whad'ja do that fer, McCool? Ain't nuthin' but a goddamn nigger! Ye takin' up fer the likes o' him?"

The tall man allowed himself a paper-thin smile and asked, "Was this after bein' a private fight, me bucko, or kin anybody get in?" Novak lunged to his feet, but before he could regain his balance, McCool kicked him in the belly, knocking him down once more.

"Whatcher doin', ye stupid Mick?" Novak howled when he was able to catch his breath. "Ye ain't fightin' fair!"

"Fair, is it now? Och! I was after thinkin' t'was a fight ye was after, not dancin' a bloody minuet!" McCool reached behind his saddle and brought down what looked to be a short, heavy walking stick, actually a stout, gnarled wooden cudgel. When Novak attempted to scramble to his feet, the Irishman rained blows upon the bully's back and legs.

At last, thoroughly whipped, Novak crouched cowering in the muddy street, arms upraised, protecting his head, whimpering, "Enough! Ye win. I quit."

McCool stepped back and watched Novak scuttle amongst the silent bystanders, heading for his mule. When we lost sight of the bully in the throng, the tall Irishman turned and addressed Micah. "Finnæus McCool, at yer service. I hope ye won't be after objectin' to my interferin' in your little affair jist now — jist this one toime, mind ye. As I daresay ye know better'n me, it ain't fittin' hereabouts fer a man o' your color to be strikin' a whitey, no matter he richly desarves it. Ye kin deal wid 'im yerownsel' next toime, whin we're a ways upon the road." He gazed in the direction in which Novak had disappeared and added, "An' ye kin pledge your faith, wi' the loikes o' that blatherskite, there's sure to be a next toime."

By time Micah and I recovered our wits enough to mumble our thanks, the procession had begun to move again. McCool nodded gravely and swung smoothly into his saddle, touched a finger to his cap, and trotted off in pursuit of the cattle.

The three of us mounted, gathered our pack animals, and joined the ragged line of packhorses and mules, bawling cattle and bleating sheep, and riders threading along the bank of the Missouri.

* * *

The caravan hugged the Missouri until we came upon the Kansa River. Spring floods were still high enough to require that we ferry our stock across. Fortunately the village of Kawsmouth, a tiny mostly-French community, provided that service. The muddy lanes boiled with leather-clad *coureur dc bois* and *voyageurs*, their Indian women, and laughing, shouting children, all of them excited at our arrival.

Harris explained the importance of the village, small as it is. "Thish'yar be Kawsmouth, anuther o' the Chouteaus' tradin' forts. Ol' Auguste an' François Gesseau, the both of 'em Chouteaus, bin tradin' fer fur an' hides an' robes with the Kaw an' Ohsahdj an' Kansa an' gawd- knows-who-else fer quite a spell naow. Measly as it looks, thish'yar Kawsmouth be a proper gold mine fer 'em."

The French tongue rang off the ramshackle walls of a cluster of shacks huddled along the riverbank, mingled with the bawling of cows and steers, sheep bleating, and the shouts and curses of our hostlers and drovers who sought to keep them from straying amongst the dwellings, sure to end up in Métis cookpots if they were not quickly retrieved. Above all the din came the voice of Black Harris bellowing, "If'n ye don't hanker fer starvin', ye better git ever' one o' them'ere critters! It be a fur piece 'til we come on ter bufflers on the prairie!"

Meanwhile the rickety ferry was shuttling men, horses and mules, and cattle and sheep across the Kansa, the ferrymaster rubbing his palms together in gleeful anticipation of this early-season largesse. After hours of confusion and pandemonium amongst men and skittish animals, we were all gathered on the far bank. The bedlam continued, howsomever, whilst Harris strove to assemble his caravan into sufficient order to proceed. I had no experience of that chore, so I sat with Powatawa and Micah and watched with amusement whilst Black rode amongst his charges, roaring mostly-unheeded commands generously laced with threats and curses. At last he succeeded in getting his ark into something like marching order and the unruly column proceeded to straggle westwards.

After we achieved a respectable distance from the settlement, Black called an early halt to that day's travel. It wasn't long until our sleep robes were spread and Micah had a kettle of Powatawa's dried deer meat, corn, and beans bubbling on the coals. Whilst we waited, we smoked and palavered and watched Harris's green crew staking out saddle horses and pack animals to graze, some others herding cattle and sheep into manageable bunches for the night.

When I spied Finnæus McCool strolling nearby, on an impulse I called out to him and invited him to join us. At first he hesitated, then he shrugged and smiled and trotted over, folding his lanky frame into a comfortable squat near the fire. I reckoned we owed him a proper thankee for his earlier welcome interference, so I said, "If ye don't have a regular mess yet, Mister McCool, you're welcome here tonight. There's plenty in the kettle, likely better'n you're apt to get elsewhere, this early on the trail."

"Much obliged," he replied. "I've not yet joined a mess. I've been keepin' to mesel', fer the most part."

"It's likely just as well," I said. "Bein' alone is better'n company not to your likin'."

McCool nodded his agreement, then excused himself, explaining that he had chores to finish. Whilst he was absent, I pondered what it was about this quiet, aloof, but impulsive Irishman that inspired my trust and kindled the beginnings of friendship, if he wished to return it. Then I reminded myself that it's not necessary to eat the whole egg to know if it's rotten, or not.

McCool returned a short spell later, his club in one hand and his cup and spoon in the other. We all fell to, devouring the rich stew with keen appetite. Afterwards, we leaned against the packs to smoke our pipes and palaver of commonplaces, mostly recalling the little French-Métis village, the ferry trip across the Kansa, and the difficulty of keeping our scrambling livestock contained within the caravan.

"Sheep are the worst," Micah opined. "I'd as lief be herdin' turkeys."

"I'm supposin' we'll be after eatin' them first," McCool observed. "As much trouble as they be, I daresay Harris won't be after puttin' up with them woollies slowin' his progress more'n he needs to. Kine'll be after keepin' up better."

Knowing the impatient Harris as I did, I allowed that it was likely so, although I had no experience of pack trains coming from the settlements, bringing meat on the hoof for the early stages. Then I changed the subject by asking, "What is your aim, Mister McCool, traveling to the mountains? Wages?"

A spell of silence occurred before the Irishman replied. "No, piddlin' as the pay is, I've no wish to be makin' this jaunt more'n once. God willin', I'm after remainin' in the mountains, p'raps fer good." He fixed a twinkling eye upon me and said, "An' I'd be much obliged if ye'd be after callin' me Finn. Finn McCool. Misther McCool's me ol' da's name."

I laughed and assured him that henceforth he would be Finn McCool amongst us. Titles are best left behind in the settlements. We all fell silent and I reflected how some men know beforehand that the mountains will be right for them. I had been onesuch. Appraising Finn McCool, little as I knew of him, I reckoned he would likely do.

Dusk had turned to dark when McCool rose to his feet and prepared to depart. I said, "Why'n't ye bring your robes an' plunder over here, Finn? You'll sleep better amongst us. Better'n ye might with that bully-boy prowlin' about, maybe hopin' to even the score."

McCool hesitated a moment at the edge of the firelight. Then he smiled and shrugged and replied, "Much obliged." He disappeared into the darkness and returned a quarter-hour later, lugging his belongings, and rolled out his meager pallet alongside ours. No doubt Finn McCool had courage enough and likely some to spare, but I was pleased to see that he wasn't a damn fool.

* * *

A crimson sun barely glowed through the eastern trees before we were on the trail, bells jingling on complaining pack-animals, reluctant foodstock bleating and lowing, hostlers and drovers shouting through the uproar. I threaded my way through the unruly column, seeking Black Harris, dragging my packstring past bucking mules, loads all askew, hostlers desperately trying to hold them down whilst others fought to right their toppling burdens, snugging girths and packropes. I tried to keep a straight face, lest my amusement provoke their ire.

I discovered Black at the head of the column. I rode in beside him and observed, "I reckon your trail hands are just about as green as your critters, judgin' by the commotion back there."

Harris snorted. "Hell! It's allus like thet, early days out! Once't the critters git theirse'fs mostly trail-broke an' the hands larn packin' an' drivin', it gits a mite easier." He cocked an eyebrow and concluded, "But hell! It ain't never whatcher mought be callin' easy!" He paused long enough to spit out his tobacco cud and stuff in a fresh chaw. "Time we git to Leavenworth's fort, a couple-three days from hyar, dependin', we oughter see cornsid'able improvin'."

I could think of nothing to add to Black's remarks, so I didn't try. Instead, I asked, "How much do ye know about Finn McCool, that tall Irish hostler?"

"Nuthin' much," Harris replied. "'Ceptin' he showed up back in Independence lookin' hungry as hell an' sayin' he war willin' to work. I seed right off he war more'n a fair hand with hosses, so I hired 'im on."

I wondered if Harris knew about McCool's set-to with Novak, but he didn't mention it, so I didn't bring it up. We rode together in silence for a spell, until I bade him farewell and pulled my animals out of line and waited for Powatawa and Micah to catch up.

* * *

At day's end, after supper, whilst daylight still remained, the four of us sat around the cookfire cleaning and oiling our firearms. McCool possessed an ancient musket, which, besides being old, was in none too good a shape. The barrel and stock were badly scarred and the lock rattled when he daubed oil upon it. "Where'd ye come by your musket, Finn?" I asked, immediately regretting my words.

McCool looked surprised, then replied, "Och! I know 'tisn't much, but 't were the best I could afford. Spent me last copper on it, I did. Harris was after requirin' iv'ry man to be armed, so this'n'll hafta do, least fer now."

My thoughts ranged to the country ahead, rife with Pah-nees, then Teton Sioux, possibly Arikaras, Big-belly Grovants, and certainly Blackfoots of several different stripes when we got to the neighborhood of Willow Valley. I got to my feet, opened one of my packs, and pulled out Uncle Ben's fine large-caliber Pennsylvania rifle, together with its bullet mold and fixin's.

Presenting the rifle to McCool, I said, "Here, use this'n. That'n'll blow up in your face, like as not." When he started to protest, I said, "You'll be needin' it an' we'll sure as hell be needin' a good man with a decent gun for huntin' an' fightin'." The Irishman grinned but still sputtered protests. I cut him off. "When ye can afford it, get yourself a Hawken, like our guns — then ye can give it back. For now, it's yours." Before he could reply, I added, "'Sides, it's doin' no good ridin' on a packsaddle. Best I lighten the load."

Brushing aside McCool's protests and thankees, I finished with, "Best thing ye can do with that old fire-pipe is tradin' it to some Blackfoot Injun, if he's dumb enough to want it."

Micah and Powatawa were grinning, nodding approval, which reassured me that I had done the right thing. That night as I settled into my robes I thought of Uncle Ben and I reckoned that he would have done likewise.

* * *

Except for a now-and-then drizzle punctuated by brief heavy showers, the next day and a half on the trail was pretty much like the first day, total chaos relieved now and then by mere confusion. We were still a day or so short of Fort Leavenworth. After the nooning stop, Powatawa, Micah and I were ambling in the midst of the column when the procession halted. Pack-strings tangled and the air grew thick with hostlers' shouting and cursing. Curious about the delay, I passed the halter-shank of my string to Micah and spurred my Ready horse into a slow lope to the head of the column.

What I saw when I got there made me wish that I had remained where I was. Black Harris was kneeling in the midst of a score or more of white corpses, every one of them scalped and stripped naked, most with private parts hacked off. Broken-off arrows studded the corpses. The stench clogged my nostrils. Ready commenced to fidget something fierce, so I rode him off a distance upwind to let him graze, then trotted back to Harris.

"Sojers, I reckon," he pronounced as I knelt beside him. I nodded, although it was hard to tell, for practically nothing remained of clothing or equipment. Then I was sure of it. My gaze fixed on one body in particular. It was all that remained of the skinny young officer I had chaffed on my way to Saint Louis. He had been stripped and scalped and mutilated, but enough remained of his rusty red hair, pasty, pimply face, and pale blue eyes frozen in horror to tell me that it was the same brash young man I had met on the trace outside Cincinnati, marching his detachment westwards.

I felt a blush heating my face and a creeping sense of shame, a vague feeling of regret for treating that young officer so roughly during our brief encounter in Ohio. Still, I had warned him to pay attention and learn from others' experience, which was the best advice I knew to give him.

"Headin' fer Leavenworth, I warrant," Black opined. "Ain't no place else fer 'em to be goin' out hyar." He grunted and spat, then examined one of the ruined arrows. "Gawddamn Pawnee, fer damn sure! Gittin' all-fired uppity, they be! Settin' onto sojers so close to the fort, like they done!"

I could add naught to his verdict, so I didn't try. Harris called out to some of his hostlers who were hanging back, looking halfway scared and muttering amongst themselves. "Awright! Shake a leg! Time we git these hyar pore souls unnerground an' be gittin' on the way!" When the hostlers were slow to respond, he roared, "Less'n yer hankerin' to jinc 'em!" He didn't make it clear whether they had most to fear from the Pah-nee or from Black himself. They quickly retrieved spades from their packs and made short work of the disagreeable chore.

That spelled the end of the pleasant journey Micah, Powatawa and I had enjoyed until then. Black doubled the guard that night and we three naturally became part of it. Besides which, he appointed me to be some sort of lieutenant to himself, mostly making sure sentries weren't sleeping on post and seeing that weapons were ready for use. The penalty for a dirty rifle or musket was marching afoot next day, leading their animals. In no time at all every weapon in the outfit was clean as a tin whistle. That duty earned me not much affection, but we were all safer for it.

* * *

We passed Fort Leavenworth without stopping by. Harris accounted such a visit to be worse than a waste of time. "Cain't see them sojers doin' us a mite o' good," he averred, "afoot like the most of 'em be, an' all the Injuns a-hossback. 'Sides, we don't need 'em gittin' nosey 'bout what we be packin', pryin' out the drinkin' likker an' sich."

I shared Black's low opinion of bluecoats, recalling in particular what mountaineers call Leavenworth's Folly, the totally unsuccessful Arikara Campaign five years earlier, when Colonel Leavenworth couldn't make up his mind to attack the Rees and burn them out of their villages. The Rees went mostly unpunished for attacking General Ashley's second expedition in 'twenty-three, killing nigh a score of Americans and all the horses Ashley had traded for and making off with his trade goods. I held my peace, but Black pretty much read my mind. "As ye know, twarn't fer ol' Leavenworth shilly-shallyin' back in twenny-t'ree, we could'a taught them Rees a lesson they wouldn'a soon fergot! Haow it turned out, Rees an' Sioux an' even Pawnees hereabaouts reckon 'Mericans ain't much account." He spat and concluded, "Thar's a sight o' 'Merican ha'r hangin' in Injun lodges nowadays that wouldn't be thar, 'ceptin' fer ol' Leavenworth's circus with the Rees up thar on the Missourah!" I allowed that it was certainly so.

Just the same, Black sent an express to the fort, telling what had occurred and where, in case they wished to provide a proper burial.

* * *

Spring rains, spliced now and again with snow flurries and hailstorms, continued as we pushed westward. The prairie was fast greening up. Watery grass was belly-high, but the earth was spongy with bog and footing was often treacherous. Micah and I took to riding our saddle mules nearly every day. It wasn't long until he commenced calling Remus by the name of Lightfoot and I rechristened my own saddle mule Sugarfoot, complimenting their easy-going gaits and especially their careful way of traveling through boggy stretches and avoiding patches of quicksand.

* * *

A few days past Fort Leavenworth we were blessed with a sunny day and clear skies that lasted into the evening. Whilst we busied ourselves at our cookfire, Harris strolled by and advised us to be especially on our guard that night. "Pawnee be more'n somewhat overdue, I'm thinkin'," he said. "Weather's likely been too wet fer ther bowstrings, but a day like this'n'll sure-as-hell dry 'em out."

Powatawa nodded his assent and I suggested to my companions that we double our horse guard that night. Which we did.

Finn McCool had taken to hobbling and picketing his pack-string amongst our critters. As darkness fell, we herded the animals nigh our camp, which lay on the fringe of Harris's main bunch, and close-hobbled them to prevent their straying. Finn and Powatawa took the first watch after dark. Micah and I scattered the cookfire and moved our bedrolls away from the heap of packs and saddles, sheltering under a clump of low-hanging bushes, lest we provide tempting targets for Pah-nee arrows.

Our nerves were strung too tight for sleeping, so we lay on our robes, weapons at hand, chatting in low tones, straining eyes and ears for an unfamiliar sight or sound that might announce unwelcome visitors. In spite of my better judgment, still stung by memories of their bravos harrying my retreat down the Platte two years before, I was almost anxious to engage in a fair fight with the Pah-nee.

I was unsure how Micah might conduct himself in a fight with hostile Indians. Shooting at targets is one thing. A gunfight is considerably different. There was little anyone could tell Micah to prepare him for what might be coming, but I did what I could. In a low voice I warned him to reload as quickly as possible after each shot and never to remain in place after he fired. "One thing in our favor," I said in a low voice, "is that nearly full moon up there. I reckon Pah-nee's'd prefer doin' their raidin' in the dark o' the moon, but wet weather lately gives 'em no choice. It's now or never for them, before we move too far off from their stompin' grounds."

Micah grunted his understanding, then, "What's on their side is, the most of us are greenhorns." He sighed. I allowed that he was right, but we had to make the best of it. We fell silent and soon I heard his soft snoring. Leastaways he wasn't working up a sweat.

I was halfway drowsing myself when I heard dirt crunch beneath a boot, then felt Finn's hand on my shoulder. "Toime t'be rousin', Temple darlin'. Yer da's after thinkin' we got company."

I was rising to my knees when I heard the loud braying of a mule, then a muffled, strangled yip of pain. Before I rightly knew it, I was running towards our critters, Micah at my side, the both of us peering right and left, seeking an enemy who could be anywhere, even behind us. I slid to a halt and dropped to my knees, rifle ready, searching amongst the milling, whinnying, honking, braying herd for anything that didn't belong there.

Then I saw him, moonlight gleaming off his mostly hairless pate and his naked, bear-greased torso, lying on his side, sawing at

Kumskaka's hobbles whilst my favorite horse reared and tried to strike with his bound-together forefeet. I surprised myself by how calmly I took aim on his scalplock, then, when Kumskaka threw himself sidewise away from the intruder, I squeezed off my shot.

I skittered sidewise, hastily reloading. Rifles cracking, muskets booming, shouts and curses ripped the nighttime. I jumped to my feet and streaked towards the place where I had last seen my father. I scarcely noticed Micah sprinting at my side, until the two of us were brought up short by a pair of mostly naked Pah-nee horsethieves running out from amongst our critters, straight at us. I am not altogether sure which one of us fired first, the two explosions going off almost at once, but luckily we each picked a different target. My shot caught a stocky-built, muscular Pah-nee square in the belly, tipping him forwards, bent nearly double, his frantic rush carrying him on until he skidded and collapsed, writhing and groaning, almost at my feet. Micah shot a trifle high. His ball ripped out the other Pah-nee's throat and flung him backwards to the ground, where he lay unmoving, a butcher knife and a tomahawk still clutched in either hand.

Although it isn't my style, I was tempted to lift the scalplock of Micah's Pah-nee as a trophy of his first kill. That is, I was, until I caught sight of Micah's face, frozen in horror, his rifle dangling from clenched fingers, then falling to earth. I caught him by his shoulders, lest he fall, too, and eased him to the ground. He drooped like a broken doll, powerless, defenseless, head hanging, silent save for a strangled groan now and again.

Whilst I poured powder down my rifle bore and seated the ball, after which I loaded his, I spoke to him in the most soothing tones I could muster right then, telling him that either one of those horsethieves would have gladly sent him off to an unhappy hereafter. I pointed to the weapons gripped in the Pah-nee's stiffening fingers and explained as best I could that the life he desired in the mountains is fraught with such perils. Surviving demands prompt, almost unthinking self-defense.

"Guilt ain't in it, Micah," I told him. "That Injun would'a been proud as Lucifer, comin' home sportin' your topknot on his belt — an' mine, too! You've learned a power o' new things in your life, Micah, and ye learned 'em fast an' well, but if ye wish to keep on learnin' — an' livin' — ye'd best get used to this kind o' thing. Danger's always nigh and there ain't never time to choose 'twixt good and evil, neither one o' which count for much out thisaway, anyways. Just do what ye hafta, so's ye can see the sun come up tomorrow."

Gunfire had dwindled to naught and jubilant shouts and good-natured curses rang throughout the camp. I was relieved to see my father and Finn emerge whole and unscathed from amongst our critters, the most of which had settled down and returned to grazing. The animals were careful, howsomever, to maintain a wide berth betwixt themselves and the bodies lying nigh.

Both men saw immediately what was troubling Micah. They went to him and squatted on either side of him. Powatawa laid a gentle hand on his shoulder and Finn spoke to him in a low, comforting voice. "'Tis no crime, nor yet a sin, lad, to kill a man who means to kill you. 'Tis the first Law o' Nature and even yer God in Heaven, if ye have onesuch, will not fault ye for presarvin' the life He gave ye."

As he spoke, my mind returned to a day on the Musselshell, five years before, when I myself killed my first enemy, an Assinaboine horsethief who nearly took my life. The reassuring words of my Delaware friend Brass Turtle came back to me, not much different from Finn's soothing advice and my own clumsy counsel.

Micah roused from his stupor and I daresay there was a blush on his tear-stained cheeks, if we could have made it out beneath his dusky complexion. He mumbled apologies for his lapse from bravado — which he never displayed much of, anyway. When he spoke I noticed that his carefully-acquired diction deserted him. "Ah don' know what come ovah me. Ah nevah hurt nobody, 'ceptin' mebbe in a fistfight an' even den not much. Killin's wrong, dey say, but dat's whut I done, 'thout even thinkin'."

Finn and I stumbled over each other assuring him that it was the best way, saving his own life without weighing the right and wrong of it.   Listening to the Irishman I gathered that he himself was no stranger to killing in what he reckoned was self-defense. I wondered how many redcoat wives owed their widowhood to Finnæus McCool. Which likely explained why Finn was jaunting in the American wilderness instead of roaming about the Emerald Isle.

Harris arrived just then, making his rounds of the camp, taking stock of damage and losses. "Howdy, Temple, he called out. "I see all o' ye got through it 'thout gittin' kilt. Ye lose any critters?" We assured him that our stock and our hides were still intact. Black let his gaze linger on the two corpses, then asked me, "Ye git 'em both did ye?"

"Nope. One's mine, t'other'n's Micah's. First time for him."

Harris grinned and swung about to Micah. "Fust blood fer ye, war it, young feller? Wal, thar'll be plenty more whar that'n come from! 'Bout time ye earnt yer spurs, like they say." He regarded Micah's hang-dog look. "Don'tcha be frettin yerse'f, Micah, 'count o' killin' that'ere sumbitch. He would'a done the same fer yew, like he done them'ere sojer-boys back thar nigh the fort — him er his gawddamn kin! — skelpin' an' rippin' off yer privates, jist fer the gawddamn fun of it. That be haow it be out thisaway. Kill 'em fust, afore they git yew. Cryin' over it ain't goin' to make it no diff'ernt!" His tone softened somewhat. "Reckon ever'body gits to feelin' squarmish, fust time they put a body under, but ye'll git over it. Ever'body does, pervidin' they live long enough." Micah responded with a sickly grin and nodded, but he said naught in reply.

Harris beamed an avuncular smile on him, then turned and jerked his head sidewise, inviting me to step away from the others for a private palaver.

We strolled along the edge of the meadow to where I had seen my first Pah-nee. When Black caught sight of the body, he asked, "That'n your'n, too?" I nodded yes and he whistled softly. "Reckon ye be earnin' yer keep, Temple. Glad to have ye 'long." He walked closer for a better look, peered at the smashed skull, and observed dryly, "Hell! Ye shore-as-hell din't leave much fer takin' a skelp, did ye?" then added, "Not like thar be much skelp on these gawddamn skinhead Pawnee, anyways."

I asked him how his green crew had behaved when the Pah-nees showed up. "Better'n I could'a hoped fer. Some of 'em war a mite skittish, as ye mought expect, but not a one of 'em bolted. They stood pat an' kep' on shootin', which is all a body could ask of 'em, 'speshly this early on the trail. Din't hurt no critters, neither. I seen McCool an' yer Paw got a couple from whar they war hidin' out. One skinhead I seen war wearin' a couple arrers an' t'other'n war shot through the head. I reckon that'n war McCool's." He looked thoughtful before he said, "That Irisher'll pull his weight, gittin' on to ronnyvoo. I reckon he'll make a mountaineer yet, if'n he don't git hisse'f kilt fust."

I allowed that Finn McCool would certainly do to take along. Then I asked if he had lost any men or livestock. "Nary a one. Couple lads got banged up some — arrers — but they'll git over it. We be headin' out come sun-up." As he turned to leave, Black paused and said, "That'ere darky o' your'n, I reckon he'll do, if'n he gits time enough. Ye take good care of 'im, hyar?"

I promised that I would do so and we parted. I busied myself stripping the Pah-nee of everything worthwhile — his bow and quiver, butcher knife and tomahawk, moccasins that would likely fit McCool, and a string of bearclaws around his neck. Meanwhile I reflected on Moses Harris. Tough-talking though he mostly is, there is a tender streak in Black, an honest concern for his people that speaks well for him as a leader.

When I got back to camp and tossed the Pah-nee moccasins to Finn, I saw that my companions had not been idle. They had built up the cookfire and were pawing through a heap of plunder they had retrieved from the other corpses. A scalp lay beside Powatawa. Micah was much restored, busying himself at the cookfire. A kettle of boiling coffee wafted a welcome fragrance over the camp.

Coffee is always welcome, but I reckoned this occasion called for something stronger by way of celebration. I rummaged through my packs and half-filled a kettle with Chouteau's good Kentucky whiskey, which went a long way towards soothing frazzled nerves.

Finn provided an Irish toast, raising his cup and announcing with mock gravity, "May the Good Lord bless ye, iv'ry one, an' keep in good health the enemies of our enemies!"

Everybody laughed, the sentiment appreciated nearly as much as the excellent liquor. Even Powatawa joined in, sipping sparingly and chatting in low tones with Micah, whose spirits appeared pretty much restored by time we went to our robes.

* * *

A sullen red sun had barely risen above the eastern prairie before our caravan was on the westward trail, bells jingling on pack animals, men cursing, jesting, and bragging above the din. The last two sheep had been butchered the night before, so our progress was somewhat more rapid than it had been. A warm springtime rain commenced to drizzle. I pulled my broad-brimmed hat lower, huddled inside my rain-shroud, and let my mind stray where it might. Harris and I rode together in the lead, not talking much, each lost in his own thoughts.

There is plenty of time for wool-gathering on such a journey. I recalled Micah's behavior the night before and reflected on the transformation that I myself had undergone in the six years since I ascended the Missouri with Andrew Henry's first expedition. A set-to like last night's encounter with the Pah-nee had become almost commonplace during those years, doing what needs to be done, without hesitation, without remorse — without considering one's enemy to be anything other than a mortal threat to be dealt with swiftly and finally. It is dangerous to imagine an attacker as a loving husband, a proud father, a dutiful son, or a neighbor in his village — or even one's fellow man. Such tender thoughts will likely make you pause when there is no time for dawdling, which will get you killed. I hoped I could get such thinking across to Micah whilst he was still healthy.

It was still raining when Harris called a halt for nooning on the open prairie. There was no firewood and buffalo chips were too wet to burn. We made do with cold mutton left over from last night's supper. Afterwards I switched my saddle to Sugarfoot, for that morning's steady rain had made the prairie soggy. Kumskaka grumbled about the packsaddle and its deadweight burden, but he was getting used to it.

When I returned to our mess I saw that we had an unwelcome visitor, the hostler Tug Novak, bristling with bluster, taunting Micah with insults and challenging him to do his own fighting, if he dared to do so. Micah sat quietly between Powatawa and Finn McCool, an easy smile on his face, his long, slender body completely relaxed. Powatawa's face was a storm cloud and McCool was seething.

Micah laid a quieting hand on Finn's arm. Then, laying aside his hat, stripping off his rain shroud, and unbuckling his belt, he rose to his feet in one smooth motion, still smiling. His voice was level and soft, sunny, when he drawled, "Ah've been waitin', Mistah Tug, foh you to be sayin' somethin' new 'bout my bein' an uppity niggah and a coward an' puttin' on airs an' such that I ain't awready heard ten thousand times befoah. Ye reckon ye got any more o' that'ere trash ye been talkin' befoah we get to it?"

Novak gawped. It was likely no Negro had ever dared talk back to him before. Certainly not in that easy, confident, quietly taunting manner. "I'm through talkin', nigger! Now I got a hankerin' to turn ye inter forcemeat!" He threw a hard look at Finn and snarled, "An' you kin stay out of it, McCool! This'n's betwixt me an' the nigger!"

The Irishman shrugged. "I don't suppose Micah will be needin' any help o' me own this toime, ner any other, fer settlin' accounts wid a mis'rable bargee loike yerownsel', Novak. Have at it!"

Novak was shorter than Micah but he outweighed him by half a hundredweight. A lifetime of working on keelboats and brawling in saloons equipped him with muscle and savvy enough to make him deadly. It was likely that last night's triumph over the Pah-nee and celebratory strong spirits afterwards — and today, as well, — spurred him now into punishing Micah for his earlier disgrace.

Novak spat and ducked his head between powerful shoulders, bunching his bulk into a compact mass, preparing to spring, when I called out, "No hardware! Ye hear, Novak! No knives or nothin' else. If ye do, I'll just natcherly shoot ye dead. Ye can count on it!"

The bully glared at me, held up his meaty fists, and growled, "Don't need nuthin' but these fer killin' yer pet nigger, Mister Fancy Dan!" Without warning, he launched himself at Micah, head down, fists outstretched, legs pumping, intending to butt Micah in the belly.

Micah's languid pose evaporated. He sprang to one side, hands in the air, but Novak was an old hand at such fighting. He swerved and caught Micah on the hip, spinning him in a sidewise stumble, but not before Micah's fist smashed down upon the side of Novak's head like a sledgehammer on an anvil, sending the bully to his knees, roaring curses, blood spurting from his ruined ear.

It was plain to see that Novak's headlong rush had somewhat damaged my friend, but he whirled to face his foe with an easy grace and calm confidence. Novak scrambled to his feet and charged like a bull buffalo, arms flailing, hands reaching for a grip that would fling the two of them to the ground, where his greater weight and rough-and-tumble skill could prevail.

A paper-thin smile settled on Micah's lips. He balanced lightly on his toes, waited until the last instant, then sidestepped the rush and spun about, arms upraised, and slammed both fists into either side of the bully's lower back. A tremendous whoosh escaped Novak's mouth. He tottered, knees crumbling, then sank to his hands and knees, head bobbing as he fought to regain his breath.

His smile gone now, Micah stepped behind the hostler and delivered a powerful kick to his buttocks, then another between his legs. Novak howled and fell on his face, clutching his groin. Micah wasn't idle. He darted forward, spun about, and slammed the heel of his moccasin into Novak's face. Then he leaped behind his tormentor and punched him again in the kidneys, powerful blows, first one side, then the other.

There are times when a man's rage is his worst enemy. This was onesuch occasion. Novak struggled to his feet, one eye pasted shut, blood streaming from his smashed nose, screaming curses through mashed lips. He spat out a tooth and flung himself at Micah, fists flailing wildly, blindly, seeking a nimble target that danced out of his reach, then stabbed stinging, crushing blows to his face and belly, until Novak staggered and lurched like a drunk, still on his feet, arms hanging loose at his sides, unable to defend himself.

I knew I was witnessing the long-overdue release of Micah's pent-up anger at his boyhood in slavery, Mike Fink's derision and cruel treatment, the refusal of white society to acknowledge his manhood.

"Hold on thar, Micah! Don'tcha be killin' 'im jist yet! I'm gonna need what's left of 'im fer gittin' to ronnyvoo! Ye kin have the rest of 'im once we git thar! With my blessin's!" I realized only then that Moses Harris was standing at my side. I had been so deeply absorbed in the fight that I hadn't noticed either him or the crowd of hostlers and drovers ringed around us. Several men looked stern, grim, disapproving. Others were smiling, laughing, calling out encouraging words to the young Negro.

Micah skipped back from his bloody work, grinned and nodded, then lunged forward to smash a final powerful punch against Novak's jaw that sent the bully reeling into a crumpled heap. He lay there twitching, groaning, barely moving. Nobody offered to help him until Harris ordered a couple drovers to get him aboard his mule.

I stooped to pick up Novak's big front tooth. It would make a proper trophy for Micah's medicine poke when he acquired one. I still carry in my own little neck-bag the shriveled, leathery earlobe of a Crow Indian who stole my favorite horse and abused my woman.

* * *

When we resumed our northwestward hike I exchanged places with my father. He rode in the lead with Black Harris. I traveled alongside Micah. I reckoned Powatawa might be able to add some previously-neglected words to his American vocabulary, for Harris was cussing a blue streak at the delay in arriving at his intended overnight halt.

Our animals were pretty well trail-broke by then, following after us without lead-ropes, so they didn't interfere with our palaver. Micah appeared to be none the worse after his bout with Novak, except for skinned knuckles and a slight grimace when he mounted Lightfoot, a souvenir of the hostler's first head-butting attack. His features betrayed quiet satisfaction, but he wasn't crowing.

We rode in silence for a spell before I asked, "Where in hell did ye ever learn to fight like that, Micah? You toyed with that bully-boy like a kid with a plaything. Ye hardly ever looked even a mite flustered." Fact is, I almost envied his skill. I myself avoid fisticuffs. I rely on more serious weapons if need arises.

A dreamy look replaced his smile before he replied. "I reckon that be one more thing I need to thank M'sieu Chouteau for." My quizzical expression prompted further explanation. "When I first got to Chouteau's the others there tried me somethin' fierce. I got whupped pretty regular, for a spell. First off, I was the new boy, and besides, I couldn't speak French like they did. An' then, when they saw that I could read, they really needed to pick on me.

"I was pretty puny back then, not much more'n skin and bones, but Chouteau feeds his people proper. 'Fore long, good food an' hard work packed a deal of meat and muscle onto me and I commenced to fight back. I wasn't much good at it, but I was quick and handy an' gettin' strong. Afterwhile, the most of 'em quit pesterin' me, but not all of 'em. I reckon there's somethin' about bein' a slave, another man's property, that gives some of 'em a powerful need to be hurtin' anybody weaker'n they are. Sorta lets 'em think they amount to somethin', even if somebody does own 'em."

Micah fell silent, I daresay recollecting those early days of servitude at Berthold et Chouteau. When he resumed, his customary cheerfulness returned. "There was one man there that nobody ever bothered and he never, even once, ever picked on me. They called him Jocko and he mostly kept to himself. He wasn't a big man, but he wasn't little, either — about my own size. Jocko didn't need to be the big he-dog, but I reckon he could've been if he had a mind to.

"One time, after I got whupped to a fare-thee-well by one o' the big *bravaches*, Jocko came over and sat on my bed, where I was gettin' over my aches and pains. He told me if I was willin' to pay attention and do what he said, he reckoned he could save me a world o' hurt — and, hurtin' like I was, I just naturally told him I would do what he said."

Micah laughed out loud and went on. "And that's how I learned fisticuffs. Before Chouteau bought Jocko, his old master used to wager money on him fightin' with other slaves, so he learned all the tricks an' dodges a body needs in that kind o' work. Then his old master died and Jocko came to Chouteau's. An' then it wasn't long at all before the bullies there learned to steer wide around him.

"Jocko saw I was pretty quick on my feet an' halfway handy at getting out o' the way when need be." He grinned at me then and said, "I learned a passel o' that on ol' Fink's boat, just like you did, dodgin' ol' Mike's kicks an' slaps an' punches — an' the other'n's, too."

I remembered those days all too well, those painful recollections somewhat assuaged, howsomever, by recalling how that evil trio met their fate, killing each other off and the final one a suicide.

"So," Micah continued, "when I wasn't workin' or readin' or learnin' French, I was enjoyin' our little pastime with Jocko, learnin' how to get in and out 'thout gettin' hurt an' how and where to be hittin' an' what to be doin' with my feet, dancin' free and kickin' where it counts, an' suchlike." A dreamy look flickered over his features before he concluded, "'Fore long, hardly anybody pestered me, an' if they did, they didn't try it twice." He lapsed into silence. Then he said, "I reckon I owe a passel o' thankees to ol' Jocko. You'd'a liked him, too."

I reckon I would, indeed.

* * *

After a fortnight or more that seemed like months, trailing along the southern bank of the South Platte, we arrived at Laramie Fork. We had been beset the whole distance by rainstorms, snow flurries, and sometimes hailstones the size of musket balls that left us and our animals bruised and sometimes bleeding. Overnight halts provided little comfort. Everybody's bedding was sopping wet and rainy daytimes provided no opportunity to dry out our sleep robes. Tempers grew short and Black's hostlers grew surlier than ever. Some took out their ill-humor on the critters in their charge, but never more than once. Harris was quick to espy such behavior. Punishment was swift and harsh. A full day of slogging afoot through prairie muck, dragging their packstring, struggling to keep up with the mounted caravan, chastened even the toughest bruisers.

That night, huddled over a sputtering cookfire, I asked Harris how Laramie Forks got its name. "They tell it's 'cuz a Frenchy name o' Joe Laramie got hisse'f kilt hereabouts, back in 'twenny-one. Injuns, natcherly." He fell silent, then added sourly, "'Pears gittin' kilt be the onliest way o' gittin' yer name recomembered."

"Not necessarily, Black," I reassured him. "Sain' Looie whores'll remember ye forever. You'll be a legend in every whorehouse in Missourah. Likely ye already are."

He brightened somewhat. "Ye think so, do ye?" Then, "Speakin' of Injuns, bad as the weather be, leastaways it's been keepin' the gawddamn Pawnee in their sleep robes, on top o' their wimmenfolk an' off'n our arse."

It was true. We hadn't been pestered with Pah-nees since their first unsuccessful pony raid. Whether it was weather or the drubbing we gave them was uncertain, but it was a blessing either way.

After we crossed over to the North Platte, we traded one passel of woes for another. The rain slacked off and finally quit, which was welcome, but the lush grass disappeared, too, replaced by sparse, scrubby graze, which naturally took its toll on our animals. They had to forage harder overnight and at nooning halts for graze enough to keep them going, picking around greasewood bushes, prickly pear, and other kinds of low-growing cactus. Water was a problem. Nearly every crick was flavored with alkali. Discovering a fresh-flowing, sweetwater crick was accounted a signal triumph. Quicksand bogs were everwhere. Most of us took to riding mules every day. Even Powatawa rode a packmule instead of his own fine horses through that unfriendly country.

Alkali water took its toll. Critters' manure was loose and watery and every man amongst us had the bellyache. It sapped the strength of man and beast and shortened tempers already rubbed raw by weeks of bad weather and short rations. Fights broke out amongst the hostlers, but they didn't last long betwixt men weakened by the diarrhea.

One day we saw, off in the northern distance, a low range of scattered, chopped-up mountains. "Them'ere be the Black Hills," Harris told me.

"They name 'em after you, Black," I asked, half jesting but not altogether sure if it weren't so, considering how much Harris got around this part of the world.

"Aw, hell no," he replied with a grin. "But mebbe they should'a. Naw, it's on account of all o' them'ere cedar trees a-growin' on the sides, lookin' black like they do from fur off."

Harris did his best to jolly his people along, promising buffalo just ahead, sure to show up any day now. Game was scarce and what there was of it was skittish. Every day, Powatawa, Micah, and I ranged out in front of the column, seeking deer and pronghorn prairie goats, without much success. Whatever meat we garnered from that unforgiving landscape was greatly appreciated, but it was precious little. Our meat supply on the hoof was dwindling rapidly. Our few remaining bullocks were gant and ribby, their pace slowing more each day.

Summer was fast approaching. Soon the prairie exploded in a riot of color, flowers blooming overnight, pleasing to the eye but little valued by hungry men plagued with griping guts and pinched bellies.

The trail mostly hugged the Platte, which daily grew wider and shallower and muddier. "A mile wide and an inch deep an' it runs uphill," was how Harris described it. "Too thin fer plowin' and a mite thick fer drinkin'. But if ye hafta, best way fer drinkin' it is, ye fill yer cup, an' then ye throw it out, an' then ye fill yer cup with whiskey." The country was becoming more broken. Scattered hills, shallow ravines, gullies, and deep canyons slowed our progress.

At first we headed generally westward and northwestward. After we crossed the Platte, the trail swung generally southwest, then south. Cricks were measly and alkali more plentiful. Just about every watercourse that Harris called out aloud had something to do with poison — Pizen Crick, Pizen Spider Crick, Stinkin' Crick, Bad Water, Bitter Crick.

* * *

Powatawa spied them first. A bunch of buffalo, no more than a score, black against the desert sand, nigh a quarter-mile distant. My father's grin was wider than the Platte when he swung his arm up and pointed to those long-awaited beasts. Micah's eyes lit up. He almost jumped out of his saddle. My mouth was fairly watering. I could already taste fresh raw liver, fleece fat, and smoking hump ribs, a blessèd change from stringy beef and stinking mutton.

Buffalo or any game meat was especially welcome right then. The last of our bullocks had been slaughtered three days earlier. Sowbelly and beans are a poor substitute for red meat for hard-working men.

We rode slowly forward but a short distance before we dismounted and tethered our horses and pack animals to a clump of greasewood bushes. Crouching low, careful not to move too fast or abruptly, we made our way to a gully and slipped over the edge. Thankfully, we were downwind of the buffalo. The desert breeze thereabouts almost always blows from the southwest. I was slowly inching up the far bank, wary of dislodging loose rocks and pebbles, when I heard an ominous buzzing that nigh froze my blood. I swung about and beheld a big rattlesnake, coiled, spade head up and r'ared back, poised to strike, not six feet from Micah's moccasins. My friend stood stock-still, petrified, eyes rolling in silent alarm, which was the best thing he could have done right then.

Before I could move, I caught sight of Powatawa stepping sidewise from behind Micah, his arm a blur, his broad-bladed tomahawk flashing into the stout coils, slicing the serpent into three big chunks. It was over almost before it began.

Micah sagged at the knees, then slowly collapsed to a sitting position, a bemused look on his face, his eyes riveted on the twitching carcass. Powatawa crushed the head with a rock, scattered the remains, and retrieved his tomahawk. I peeked over the rim of the gully, made sure that our quarry, mostly young bulls, were still grazing peacefully, then slid down the bank to join my companions.

Micah needed a spell to regain his composure, so I used the time to show how to kill a buffalo. I picked up a stick and scratched in the sand a sidewise outline of a buffalo, talking in low tones, explaining where to aim in order to drop the beast in his tracks. First off, never shoot for the head. A dozen rifle balls there won't do the critter any substantial damage. Then I pointed at a spot behind the foreleg, only a hand's-breadth above the brisket. I assured them that if they hit him there they would be feasting that night on the best meat either of them had ever tasted. I advised them, as well, to shoot only young bulls. Spring is calving time. Cows are much reduced in flesh and meager of fat meat when they are nursing young'uns.

Micah's close attention to my little lesson served to wipe away his earlier fright. Both he and my father, one after the other, jabbed a forefinger at the spot I had indicated to show they understood where to aim. They were smiling broadly as they scrambled up the bank.

I tarried in the gully long enough to slice off the rattles from the snake and drop it into my pouch. It would make another fitting talisman for Micah's medicine poke, alongside Novak's tooth.

When I joined my companions we crawled on our bellies towards the grazing bunch, wriggling forward on elbows, knees, and toes, rifles cradled in the crook of our arms, head down except to snatch a brief glimpse of our prey. Fortunately for us, buffalo possess poor eyesight, but they spy movement well enough and their hearing and sense of smell are keen. We halted about a hundred yards off and carefully cocked our rifles, one after another. Even at that distance, the metallic clack caused a couple of the older bulls to raise their great shaggy heads and sniff the air, but we lay still and soon they went back to grazing. We each chose our target and took careful aim. I nodded and we all fired together.

The triple explosion naturally sent the bunch scampering, tails straight up, hoofs churning, fleeing into a nearby draw. All but three. One young bull was thrown clear off his feet and fell on his side, coughing up great gouts of blood, shaggy body jerking in the death spasm, then lay still, legs stiff as sticks. Another stumbled, sank to his knees, shoved himself up again, massive head weaving, unseeing red eyes glaring, blood gushing from his mouth. He took half a dozen faltering steps, halted and stood stiff-legged, refusing to fall, then crumpled and rolled onto his side.

The third young bull shuddered and staggered sideways when the ball smashed into his vitals, but he kept to his feet, shaking his great head, blood spraying from his open mouth, bellowing his fury, then swung about and chased after his retreating fellows.

We leaped to our feet, reloading as we ran, seeking to get a second shot. By time we reached the two downed bulls, the rest were out of range, disappearing into a narrow canyon. Powatawa wore a disgusted look on his usually tranquil face. "What's wrong, Father?" I asked, although I guessed the reason for his disappointment.

He waved towards the canyon. "My ball was off the mark. My buffalo will feed nobody this night or any other!"

I started to laugh but immediately thought better of it. Powatawa is not accustomed to coming in second best on anything he puts his hand to. "No it wasn't and yes he will!" I almost shouted. "Some bufflers take a sight more killin' than some others. I wager you threw that'n fair an' square. Just wait 'til we bring up the horses. He'll be layin' deader'n hell a ways up that draw."

And so he was. When we butchered him out, his heart was busted in half, with a hole in it as big as your thumb.

We tethered our animals upwind of the carcass. Most of them were still unused to the smell of fresh blood. We butchered Powatawa's bull first, rolling him onto his belly, legs stretched out to keep him solid, then slicing the hide down the backbone and stripping it off the flesh on one side. We took the tongue first. Then we went after the boss hump, the big hump, the hump ribs, and the fleece, by far the best of the meat, all of which was intended for our own mess. By my reckoning, to the victor belongs the spoils. Besides, Harris's greenhorns wouldn't appreciate those finer cuts of meat. Naturally Black does, but he was a frequent guest in our mess, anyways.

When we dug through to the liver, I couldn't resist slicing off big slivers still smoking hot, splashing them with gall, and offering them to my companions. Micah was a mite hesitant at first, but my father fell to with gusto. Soon the three of us were chomping away like a trio of wolves.

When we finished butchering the first bull, leaving little but bones and hide, Micah volunteered to ride back to the column and deliver the good news to Black, whilst Powatawa and I returned to the other two carcasses.

We had to drive off half a dozen wolves, surrounded at a safe distance by a score or more coyotes, whining and slavering, impatiently waiting their turn to feast on our kills. The critters had done little damage, so we proceeded with our task, parceling out a variety of cuts on each of half a dozen big squares of sail canvas for the several messes of Harris's people.

We were but halfway finished with the first bull when Black galloped up, accompanied by Micah, McCool, and a couple hostlers whom Harris immediately put to work at the butchering chore. "Don'tcha leave nuthin' but the beller an' squeal, mind ye!" he warned. "Buffler been a long time comin' an' I got me a pow'ful hankerin' fer fleece fat an' ribs! Damn if I don't!" That is all he could say right then, howsomever, for he wasted no time before he sliced off a sizeable chunk of liver and stuffed it into his mouth.

Finn was distributing meat amongst the still-steaming heaps on the canvases. I carved off a slab of liver, sprinkled it with gall, and offered it to him. The big Irishman looked doubtful when he took it from me, but I reassured him, "If ye mean to be a mountaineer, Finn, ye'd best be learnin' how to eat like one. Take it. You'll soon come to crave liver fresh off the buffler." He shrugged, bit into it, and was soon chewing happily, just as I reckoned he would.

* * *

Harris called an early halt that evening and soon the camp was redolent with the fragrance of meat roasting over half a dozen cookfires. Black joined our mess and brought with him a jug of Kentucky whiskey, "by way o' selly-brayshun fer the buffler," as he put it. There was little palaver amongst us. Everybody was too busy stowing away gobs of hump and fleece fat, chewing yards of tasty boudins sizzling hot from the spider, nibbling flavorful chunks of tongue boiling in a kettle, and gnawing meaty hump ribs.

At last, stuffed to the gills, we sprawled around the cookfire, sipping Black's whiskey, chatting idly about not much, and listening to the sounds of merriment, whoops and good-naturedcurses, coming from the hostlers' camps. "Queersome, ain't it?" Harris observed, "how buffler kin turn a bunch like our'n from actin' like a gawdfersaken fun'ral inter a gawddamn weddin'." He helped himself to another dram and continued, "Them critters be plumb magical, I'm thinkin'." He took still another sip and said, "Onliest thang lackin' naow fer a bang-up shindig is yer hillbilly fiddler Tolliver." He paused before he added wistfully, "'Ceptin', mebbe, whores."

Knowing Moses Harris as I do, I reckon the proper word was "certainly," not "maybe."

Black rose to his feet and excused himself, promising to return, explaining that he needed to make sure the horse guards were in place and wide-awake. There never comes a time on the trail or in the mountains when you can afford to forget about your critters. Indians of every stripe are drawn like a lodestone to your horses and mules, the universal coin of wealth and prestige in those parts. By then, we had likely passed beyond Pah-nee country, which meant only that we were now in Sioux and Arikara land.

Black's whiskey, full bellies, and the easy camaraderie that had grown amongst us loosened our tongues. We palavered like schoolgirls of the day's events, regaling McCool with talk about the scrape with the rattlesnake and the thrill, even for me, of the buffalo kill, promising the Irishman that he would soon have his chance to prove his mettle in making meat for the camp. Powatawa's dignified reserve had been steadily thawing and Micah's shyness amongst the nearly all-white company had all but disappeared. It made my heart big to see them taking their rightful place amongst equals.

Dusk had faded into darkness when Harris ambled into the firelight, retrieved the jug from Micah, and folded himself into a comfortable sprawl against a heap of saddles and packs. He drained a healthy swig or two, squinted owlishly at Finn McCool, and announced, "Watchin' ye today, Irish, gittin' interduced to the dee-lights o' fresh-killed buffler liver, I war 'minded of a Frenchy trapper name o' Levi LeDoux we use'ta know an' the gawdawful trouble he allus had with a differ'nt kind o' liver — his own."

I knew what was coming. Besides being a first-rate trapper, formidable Indian-fighter, redoubtable lover of Indian women and Saint Louis whores, and a guide who possesses an almost unbelievable sense of dead-reckoning, Black Harris is also the most inventive, colorful spinner of yarns and tall tales in the Rocky Mountains or, I daresay, anyplace else. I relieved him of the jug, swallowed a substantial mouthful, and passed it on to my father, then settled down to be entertained mountain-style.

"Wal now," Black continued, "ol' Levi LeDoux war allus gripin' 'bout his liver an' haow it pained 'im so, 'til one springtime it got so hellacious bad it 'peared he wouldn't even be able to keep on trappin'. Wal, that din't set too well a-tall with his Injun squaw, 'cause she war fixin' to git herse'f a heap o' foofurraw come summer ronnyvoo. They war wint'rin' with her people, a band o' Snakes down on the Popo-azhieh, so she kep' on naggin' 'im sumthin' fierce to git hisse'f on down to their healer, an ol' Shoshone medicine man name o' Mornin' Thunder, who mebbe could do ol' Levi some good, so's he could keep on trappin'.

"Naow I reckon I oughta mention that ol' Levi, 'sides the turrible trouble he allus had with his liver, he had the worst kind o' luck of any trapper anybody ever knowed. We use'ta say if it warn't fer Levi's fearsome load o' bad luck, he would'na had no luck a-tall!" Black cleared his throat, spat, and beckoned for the jug. After a swallow or two, he opined, "Thish'yar tellin' 'bout ol' Levi an' all o' his mis'ries be thirsty work indeed.

"Whar was I? Oh yeah, wal, Levi reckoned mebbe Mornin' Thunder jist mought do 'im some good an' leastaways it mought shut up his squaw fer a spell an' make her quit her naggin', so one mornin' he picks out one o' his sorriest hosses an' hikes on down to Mornin' Thunder's lodge an' they commence to hagglin' 'bout haow much it's gonna cost 'im. Naow Injun medicine don't never come too cheap, so arter Levi hikes on home an' comes on back with a couple more ponies an' a heap o' plunder, Mornin' Thunder says he'll do the chore.

"Naow I ain't precisely sartin sure jist haow Mornin' Thunder makes his medicine, but arter a spell o' drummin' an' walkin' out an' talkin' to the trees an' wavin' them'ere feather fans an' cookin' up a mess o' berries, bugs, an' roots an' such, snake spit an' gawd-knows-what-all an' smokin' over Levi in the lodge, ol' Levi LeDoux commenced to feelin' some'at better. An' then 't'warn't long afore he gits to actin' plumb spry.

"I should likely mention ri'chere that afore that'ere ol' Snake healer went to work on him, Levi war allus knowed to be the laziest, most shif'less man in camp, allus shirkin' his fair share o' work an' hidin' out whenever thar war chores what needed doin'. But naow he's doin' two men's work, shoutin' out them ol' French songs o' his'n, an' purty soon his squaw war sproutin', buffler big with child. He's trappin' better'n he ever done before. Thangs war shorely lookin' up fer ol' Levi LeDoux."

Harris paused, his face gone solemn, and allowed his gaze to rest upon each of us in turn. He sighed and then went on. "Problem war, 'spite of all his new-found bloomin' health, Levi's luck war jist as bad as ever it war. One mornin' when he war out a-runnin' his traps, he come upon a big ol' grizzle-sow a-trailin' both her cubs an' she jist natcherly riz up an' swatted ol' LeDoux into a heap o' forcemeat!

"Thar warn't hardly enough left of ol' Levi fer us to gather up fer the buryin'." Black fell silent and stared at his moccasins for a spell. Then he looked up with a sly grin and declared, "'Ceptin' fer his liver! I swear we had to kill that gawddamn liver with a stick afore we could go ahead an' bury him!"

* * *

There was no need to roust any of us from our robes next morning. Well before dawn, everybody was squatted around the cookfire gnawing on ribs, spooning cups of steaming, flavorful bone marrow, and finishing up the remains of tongue, boudins, and fleece.

Almost as good was the cheerful mood that pervaded the entire camp. Naturally there was just as much cursing as ever amongst the hostlers, but now their blasphemies were high-spirited and good-humored, lacking the poisonous sting of previous days and weeks. Their manner towards us — Micah, my father, and me — changed much for the better, as well, for it was understood that we three would be the hunters for the caravan until we arrived at rendezvous.

One exception to that general good feeling was Tug Novak, never what you might call pretty, but now considerably marred. His sneering grin was gap-toothed now and his nose more than somewhat askew. He had lost his swagger, as well as the clique of toadies who always cluster around such bullies. Novak did his glaring from afar, but Micah, my father, McCool, and I kept a watchful eye on him, for none of us doubted that he would, given half a chance, do his best to even the score. Harris, too, was mindful of the threat that Novak posed, but, short of turning him loose in the wilderness, there was little that Black could do about him right then.

* * *

We turned off from the Platte and crossed over the Sweetwater, then followed its banks generally westward. When Harris pronounced the name Sweetwater I said something about what a relief it was to be rid of alkali in the water, leastaways for a spell. Black scowled and grunted, "Sorry to disappoint ye, Temple. We ain't shet of the gawddamn alkali yet. Nope. Not by a long chalk. Reason they be callin' thish'yar crick the Sweetwater is cuz one time when a pack-train like this'n war comin' through hyar they had all o' their sugar loaded onter jist one mule an' the mule stumbled whilst he war gittin' acrost the crick an' they lost ever' gawddamn bit o' sweet'nin' they war packin'!" He chuckled and added, "Yep! We been callin' it the Sweetwater ever since."

Buffalo became increasingly plentiful. Indians, too. Even at a distance, I was able to make out what I was pretty sure were Absóraqas and what I took to be a hunting party of Snakes, both of them considerably easterly of their regular hunting grounds. A bunch of Sioux hunters brought to mind warm memories of Ahn-pah-gli-win, a Lahcotah woman who had made one particular rendezvous even more pleasant than usual. Harris identified a couple other hunting parties as Cheyennes and Arapahoes, tribes with which I was so far unfamiliar.

Their purpose in being thereabouts was hunting buffalo, but naturally our livestock and the plunder they packed made their eyes big with greed. The considerable size of our caravan discouraged a daylight attack by any one of those fairly small hunting parties, but nighttime horse-thieving is a high art amongst Indians, a matter of pride and glory, the honor to be gained thereby equaling in importance the riches represented by valuable horseflesh.   We picketed and close-hobbled our livestock and doubled, sometimes tripled, our nighttime horse guards. After half-a-dozen unsuccessful pony raids, each one repelled by a hailstorm of galena fired into the darkness, word must have got around that we were not to be trifled with.

Now that drovers were no longer needed to herd the sheep and cattle we had begun with, extra hands were available to relieve Finn McCool of his hostling duties now and then, so that he might join us on some of our daily hunts. Harris approved of Finn's intention to remain in the mountains, so he turned a deaf ear to whatever grumbling the Irishman's occasional absence from his regular chores might have provoked. "It's best the Irisher larns makin' meat soon's he kin. 'Sides, I ain't runnin' no gawddamn der-mock-racy hyar. I'm givin' the orders in thish'yar outfit an' they kin jist do like I say, like it or no."

I took Black at his word, maybe even stretched it a mite. From then on, Finn was pretty much a regular member of our hunting party. He proved to be a natural at that chore. Once he caught on to the ways of buffalo, which didn't take long, he became a reliable hunter, cool and unruffled and stealthy in stalking grazing bunches. Daily practice with Uncle Ben's rifle soon honed his aim to deadly accuracy. After a spell, he took to calling that weapon by the name of Benjamin, just as I had come to call my own rifle Jacob, after its maker, Jake Hawken. I knew, right about then, that I would never be able to reclaim that rifle from him. Which I didn't wish to do, anyway. It had found a worthy heir.

The plenteous heaps of fresh buffalo meat that we supplied to the caravan soon caused the other hostlers to abandon their resentment of McCool's frequent absences from their ranks. Full bellies make for good humor and generous judgments.

The trail continued to climb and trees grew somewhat more plentiful. I recognized certain landmarks from my eastward journey four years before. We came upon a huge grey turtleback rock thrusting out of the prairie, a hundred feet high and as big around as an Indian village, its lower sides all covered with moss. From there, we were able to make out a range of low mountains to the northwest. Harris called them the Rattlesnakes. Then he swung halfway about in his saddle and pointed out another puny range and said, "An' them'ere be the Laramies." We continued upstream along the Sweetwater until we came upon Devil's Gate, a waterfall so high it seemed to disappear into the sky, four hundred feet, maybe more. When we picked up the Sweetwater once again, about five miles above the Falls, we spied them, hazy blue and purple in the distance, snow-capped peaks barely visible, the Wind River Mountains — the Rockies at last!

I rode back to announce the good news to my father, who was already gazing in open-mouthed admiration at the measly blue ridge that barely broke the expanse of golden prairie. He, who had never seen a real mountain in all his life, understood that we were in sight of our goal, the Shining Mountains that would grant him a new life, a rebirth, as you might say.

I was scarcely less excited than he, for those still-distant mountains signaled my return to the only life I desired and reunion with companions no less dear to me than were the two beloved men whom I was bringing with me to share its pleasures and satisfactions — as well as, I reminded myself, its hardships and perils. I never doubted that either one, Powatawa or Micah, would be equal to either circumstance. Both had known danger and adversity and I was sure that the unsophisticated pleasures available in the wilderness were of a kind that both of them would come to love.

The only thing still unknown to either one was the supreme joy of absolute freedom offered by a free trapper's life to any man who possesses guts and grit enough to grab onto it and hang on, no matter what. I was confident that, different as they were from each other, they were both such men. They both needed it — Micah, who had never known freedom, and Powatawa, whose burden of being chief of his band had long ago deprived him of that precious commodity. Now it would be theirs to claim and to keep.

Powatawa, usually sparing of his words, surprised me with his almost boyish enthusiasm. "Temple, See-wau-see-kau, you truly open a door for me, your father! I have lived too long in a cave — no sunshine, no clean air! Now I see before me land like I knew when a boy, the land you told about! We are not there yet, but I feel it now! I see it! I know it! It is beautiful, even more beautiful than the pictures you painted for me that day in my wegiwa!"

I had always known that my father possesses a deep spiritual side. This far-off glimpse of the Rockies brought it gushing forth. "I reckon ye won't be disappointed when we get there, father. I wager it'll be even better'n you're thinkin' right now."

He smiled, his eyes still fixed on the misty blue-grey blur on the horizon. "Perhaps," he said, his voice distant and dreamy. "For me, what I see now is enough."

The column halted and soon Micah and Finn McCool pushed their way through the throng, pack animals trailing behind. "There's the mountains!" I called out to them, pointing to the northwest. "That's where we're headin', the Wind River Mountains! Once we get through the Pass, I reckon we'll be joinin' up with my old bunch pretty soon afterwards." Naturally I hadn't the foggiest notion where Tuttle, Godey, Brass Turtle, and the rest might be amidst thousands of miles of wilderness or when we would be able to track them down, but I was not inclined to trouble with such measly trifles right then.

Micah's eyes were shining. He fixed his gaze on that tiny sliver of blue haze. His lips were moving but he spoke no words that I could hear. At last I said, "Well, Micah, ye got your wish. Yonder's the Shinin' Mountains and beyond lies the life you've been hankerin' for. I'm hopin' it suits ye."

His reply was addressed more to himself than to me. "This'll be the first one, Temple. I never really had a life before this'n, nothin' like the life that lies up there."

"It won't be easy, ye know," I cautioned. "Life can be rough out thisaway."

"Ye told me that, back in Saint Louis, first time we ever talked about it. There's nothin'in those mountains worse'n what I'm leavin'. Wager on it, Temple. For the first time in all my life, I can be a natural man, my own man."

I thought I understood what he meant, but I'll never be sure. Tough as my own life had been at times, no one had ever owned me or despised me in the way that he had always been in his. If coming to the mountains was a rebirth for Powatawa, it was infinitely moreso for Micah.

"Well," I replied, seeking to lighten the mood, "there's no turnin' back now. No time for second thoughts. I reckon you'll be doin' just fine, else I wouldn'a brought ye along in the first place."

Micah simply nodded for reply, a half-smile on his face, but the steely glint in his usually kind eyes bespoke volumes of resolve.

* * *

Another week, maybe less, of mostly following the Sweetwater brought us to a jumble of rounded hills at the southern end of the Wind River Mountains. There lies South Pass, the gateway through the mountains, nearly twenty miles wide. It is impossible to miss, once you know where it leads.

Those final miles on the eastern side were as bad as any we had encountered. The trail is broken with deep gullies. Whatever few trickles of water we found were laden with alkali. Alkali dust blew in our faces on the southwest wind, burning our eyes and lodging in our noses and throats, all but stifling the hostlers' swearing as they struggled to shove and prod and drag their whinnying, braying charges up and through the Pass.

As our caravan snaked its painful way up the sagebrush-covered slopes sprinkled with low-growing cactus, I marveled aloud to Harris how strange it was that such a broad pathway through the mountains had gone so long undiscovered.

"Far as I know," I said, "nobody knew it was here 'til spring o' 'twenty-four. Some say Jed Smith found it. Some others, howsomever, tell me Jed was still laid up from gettin' his ear chewed off by a bear an' how it was Tom Fitzpatrick who came across it. You were with that bunch, Black. Who was it?"

Harris grinned and spat tobacco juice through cracked lips. "Wal, I reckon I kin tell yew that it war mostly Fitz what found it. But, mind ye, naowadays I be workin' fer Billy Sublette, Jed, an' Davey, so I'll natcherly be obliged if ye don't let on I said so."

He fell silent for a spell, then he said, "I reckon Tom warn't the fust, neither. Fact is, it be more'n likely some of ol' Jake Astor's men found it on their way back from Astor's fort on the West'ren Sea, arter them Nor'westers kicked 'em out 'baout twenny years ago. They din't leave no maps ner nuthin' that anybody knows of, so somebody had to find it all over agin." He swung about in his saddle, making sure that the column of pack animals was reasonably snugged up. "'Sides," he continued, "'most ever'body war keelboatin' up the Missourah back then, 'ceptin' Injuns an' some French-Canucks, so nobody went out lookin'.

We rode in silence for a spell before I asked, "Black, everybody says you're the best guide in the mountains. How do ye do it?"

As soon as the words were out, I bit my tongue, wishing to take it back. Too late. Harris favored me with a sly grin. "Aw, hell, Temple, I jist p'int my nose in the right di-rection an' then I jist natcherly follers it. Anybody kin do it."

No matter how he does it, Moses Harris delivered us to our desired destination, more or less all safe and sound. It was late in the day, two days after we came through South Pass and after crossing what he called the Little Sandy River and the Big Sandy, when we arrived at a river I knew and loved.

"Thar she be, Temple!" Black crowed. "The Siskadee! Damn if it ain't a purty sight!"

If I answered him, I don't recollect doing so. I handed my weapons to Finn McCool, riding beside us, shucked my belt and powder horn, then spurred Kumskaka straight into belly-deep water. I threw myself from the saddle and floundered about, whooping and diving and ducking my head and spewing out mouthfuls of water that bore no trace of alkali. Naturally Kumskaka took advantage of my lunacy and rolled in the water, thoroughly soaking my saddle and fixin's, but I was too elated to mind.

When I came sloshing back to the bank, sopping buckskins weighing me down, I was greeted by an array of astonished expressions. "Shee-it, Temple!" Black called out. "That ain't a damn bit like yew! Ye gone an' lost yer gawddamn senses?"

"Hell no!" I replied. "It's been two long years I ain't had a decent drink o' Rocky Mountain water an' I aim to get my fill!"

Harris snorted and grunted and grinned. He cast his gaze around the riverbank and announced, "Reckon this be as good a place as any fer beddin' down tonight. Thar's good water, lots o' deadfall, an' decent graze fer critters." Fixing his gaze on me, he said with a smile, "Reckon ye kin contain yerse'f long enough to gather up yer pards an' git us some meat?"

I allowed that I would happily do just that. I retrieved my weapons and fixin's and beckoned to Micah, McCool, and Powatawa to join me, and set off downstream. Fortune smiled on us. We hadn't traveled more than a mile before we came upon a small bunch of perhaps a score of mostly young bulls grazing in a meadow not far off the river bottom. Which allowed us to sneak afoot below the bank, downwind and concealed from their view, until we were with an easy rifle shot. Whereupon we threw four fat bulls with a single volley.

Butchering took hardly any time at all. We took the choice cuts — tongues, fleece, humpribs, backstrap, and such, and, naturally, the livers and boudins. We loaded the pack mules until they staggered, then hurried back to camp. Harris's already good humor improved remarkably when he spied our heavily-loaded pack animals coming in and his smile grew even wider at the sight of even more meat draped over our saddles. He was even more satisfied when he learned that we had killed four young bulls and suggested that he send some of his hostlers to finish butchering what we had left behind.

There had been a drouth of buffalo before we came through the Pass and on the trail past the two Sandy cricks. Sowbelly and beans no longer set well with hungry, hard-working men grown accustomed to buffalo meat. The hostlers Harris assigned to the butchering chore went whooping out of camp.

As you might imagine, merriment reigned thereabouts that night, not only because of fresh meat, but mainly for knowing that we had at last arrived properly in the Shining Mountains. A considerable journey to rendezvous still lay ahead, but everybody felt a sense of triumph at having left the barren desert behind us.

Powatawa looked serenely fulfilled and Micah couldn't keep his face straight. He was forever smiling and grinning and softly humming some personal tune that spoke a contentment that I had never before observed in him. Even the customarily stoic Finn McCool appeared relaxed and pleasantly satisfied. For my own part, the warmth I felt in my heart and soul as I burrowed inside my sleep robes that night defied the frigid breeze that swept down from the still snow-covered Wind River Mountains.

* * *

Next early morning as we prepared to set out, Harris gathered everybody together and announced, "We be in Crow country naow and I'm tellin' ye to be lookin' sharp, keepin' yer eyeballs peeled, 'speshly come dark time! Gawddamn Absorkee Injuns be ferever froze fer stealin' hosses an' they be better at it than jist abaout any Injuns yer likely to be comin' acrost. Them'ere Pawnee an' Sioux we been dealin' with up to naow ain't a patch on the arse of a gawddamn Absorkee hossthief! Crows ain't much fer killin' white-eyes, mind ye, 'though thar be some of 'em don't mind doin' that, neither. The most of 'em, howsomever, figger if'n they kill ye naow, ye won't be comin' back next year with more hosses an' plunder they kin steal! So keep on yer toes an' do yer sleepin' with one eye open. It's a gawddamn long hike to ronnyvoo from hyar an' I ain't hankerin' to be doin' it on shank's mare — an" I don't reckon none o' yew do, neither!"

That said, Harris reined his horse about and headed his unruly column west to rendezvous.

Chapter V
A Rocky Mountain Welcome

As Moses Harris had warned his crew, we still had a long trail ahead, but the days passed swiftly and pleasantly for me, in spite of my impatience to be rejoined with my old trapping bunch. Powatawa and I whiled away long days in the saddle with palaver about my boyhood in and around Whynot, reminiscences of times I spent with the Shawnees in his Ohio village, his friendships with Uncle Ben and the Whynot storekeeper Jacob Staples, and even glimpses of battles he fought against Americans before his hero Tecumseh was killed up on the Thames River in Canada.

There was little I needed to explain to my father about the country we were passing through, except to describe as best I could the different Indian tribes who generally lived and roamed through various parts of it. His bred-in-the bone knowledge of critters and woodcraft equipped him to adapt smoothly from the Ohio forest and Missouri prairie to the Shining Mountains. It was rather a different matter with Micah and especially Finn McCool, who assured me that his native Ireland harbored no snakes at all and certainly nothing like poisonous rattlesnakes.

There was any number of odd bits to impart to our two newcomers to the wilderness, such as advising them to glance back over their shoulder from time to time, not only to make sure that no enemy was stalking them, but also to see the country and landmarks from that side, in case they needed to travel back that way sometime. A trail looks a sight different when you're going the other way. Whatever I neglected to mention, Powatawa filled in for me.

I have heard it said that we learn to swim in wintertime. Tuttle Thompson, a consummate horseman, once told me that a wise horse trainer teaches a young horse everything he wishes to impart, then turns the critter out to pasture for a year or so. When the horse returns to work he knows his lessons better than he did before his holiday.

It seemed to be so in my own case. My nearly two-year absence from the mountains appeared to sharpen rather than dull my senses and honed to a keen edge the skills I had learned thereabouts. Perhaps, too, it was the example of my schoolmarm mother which enabled me to put into words and actions the patient teaching both Micah and Finn needed in order to keep them alive and healthy in places and situations neither of them had ever even imagined.

Trapping season was long over with and summer was upon us. Still, I reckoned this was as good a time as any to explain to the newcomers the habits of beavers, how it does no good to bait them with food, since they live on tender bark and shoots, of which there is a plenitude wherever they build their dams. The only thing that lures them to a trap is a tiny stick drenched in castoreum from some other beaver that we plant on the bankside of their pond, on the far side of the trap, which is placed in shallow water on a four-foot chain attached to a five-foot-or-so stake driven into the bottom of the pond. When the beaver smells that foreign odor on the bait-stick, he gets riled up about some beaver who is no part of his own family invading his bailiwick. He comes a-charging up to do battle, defending his property rights, as you might say.

If all goes well for the trapper, the beaver forgets to be cautious and plants a foot onto the trigger of the trap. When the trap snaps shut, the beaver, hurting now and scared, heads for the only place he knows where he has always been safe — deep water. When he dives, the weight of the trap holds him under and he drowns. The wooden stake floating on the pond tells us where the dead beaver is when we come around to harvest our catch.

If beavers weren't so hostile to their neighbors, a trapper's work would be a whole lot harder.

Later that day, when Powatawa and I were together, I noticed that he looked thoughtful, almost somber. When I asked him what might be troubling him, he replied, with a wistful smile, "Your talk today about beavers and how they think recalled to me our Shawnee people and our neighbors in the East."

He fell silent for a spell. I held my peace. When he resumed, he looked pained. "When Tecumseh tried to call together the Indian tribes of the East to fight the whitemen, they turned their back to him and faced their old enemies, the red teckhawk in their hand. They chose to fight their own kind over reasons long forgot, even by the oldest men." He heaved a deep sigh and continued, "The beavers you tell of are more angry with their own kind than of the men who will kill them. So it is with our red brothers. They fight old wars and never look to see their real enemy, the whiteman, who kills them off like turkeys. He has picked them off one by one, band by band, tribe by tribe, nation by nation, until now their power is broken and lost forever. Soon there will be only you and me." He paused and reflected. "And your Lénni-lénapee and Iroquois friends in these mountains." I could think of no reply. He was likely right.

Later that day, riding alone, I chewed over my father's words about how, at bottom, people and critters are much alike. Which, in the way that such random thinking is prone to stray, led me to ponder why Christian folk are so set against admitting our kinship with other critters and how humans are, leastaways used to be, after all, really a four-legged critter. Our arms aren't much different from a pair of forelegs of a horse or deer or wapiti, even frogs and toads and lizards. Our hands are pretty much the same as a critter's paws, except for our very useful thumbs.

We call them dumb animals, but anybody who pays attention knows that critters talk. Anybody who ever heard a wolf howl, bark, or growl or a horse neigh, whinney, or nicker knows they are talking to their own kind. And a cricket singing to his ladylove isn't a whole lot different from a Shoshone lad tootling a flute outside a maiden's lodge or a minstrel strumming beneath a lady's balcony, all of them with much the same lustful thoughts in mind.

One thought leads naturally to another and I commenced to add up how very much alike we two-leggeds and the four-leggeds really are. All of us have two eyes and ears and nostrils, ten fingers and toes, if you count dewclaws, and our way of begetting offspring isn't much different betwixt man and beast. It's no great wonder that Indians, who live much closer to the earth than whitemen do nowadays, thank and apologize to the critters they kill for food and clothing and such.

Then I just naturally wandered into thinking about how religious whitefolks refuse to allow four-leggeds into their Heaven, even horses. Religion surely gets in the way of common horse-sense. How could any worthwhile God create a horse, a critter that contains all those virtues that all the parsons claim to value so much, like bravery and patience and honesty and loyalty, to name just a few, then turn Himself around and shut that critter out of his Paradise? I reckon if there is a God, He loves every one of his creations, not just us two-leggeds, who likely give their Creator more trouble and heartache than all the rest lumped together.

Most whitefolks that I ever met would rather admit brotherhood with the likes of Tug Novak than with a noble critter like a horse.

Small wonder that my meandering thoughts came around to Novak. That worthy was never far from our minds. Harris, too, had marked him for a troublemaker from the get-go. Novak was stoked even hotter now, after the humiliating beating he suffered at Micah's hard and well-schooled hands and feet.

It wasn't a hard chore to keep an eye on Novak. He was always skulking around one or another of us, as if we were lodestones that drew him to us. There wasn't much that we could do about it, except to be alert, lest he try some sort of revengeful deviltry. He did his skulking at a distance, howsomever, so we had to put up with it.

* * *

Harris and I were riding together, leading the column, when he mentioned that later that day or the next we would be leaving our westward trail and cut southwestwards, in order to arrive at the rendezvous site in Cache Valley. It wasn't more than half an hour later that we were startled by a lone horseman come busting out of a thicket of scrubby willows, whooping and hollering, heading straight for us, firing his rifle in the air to show his good intentions.

Naturally we checked our mounts and signaled to our followers to halt. When the rider drew near enough for us to tell who it was, Harris and I spurred our horses forward to greet Daniel Potts, one of Billy Sublette's regulars.

"Dan'l!" Harris shouted. "What in hell ye doin' hyarabouts? Lost, are ye?"

Potts feigned to be offended. "Lost? Not me! Never on yer gawddamn life! Mebbe I been a mite confused a time or two, fer a week or so, but I ain't never been lost!" His cramped way of speaking betrayed his Pennsylvania origins.

"Wal, if'n ye ain't lost, why in hell are ye hangin' 'roun' hyar? Huntin' grizzle b'ar, are ye? Ain't a sufficiency o' them'ere critters whar ye been trappin', that it?"

Potts shrugged off Harris's joshing with a smile. "Nope. None o' those. Billy sent to tell ye we ain't meetin' at Willer Valley, or Cache Valley, or whatever-in-hell they be callin' it nowadays. The gatherin'll be on the south end o' Snake Lake, same as last year." He checked himself, then added, "That is to say, Sweet Lake, what feeds the Bear River." He allowed himself a goodnatured scowl. "Cain't hardly keep track o' the way you fellers keep changin' names on me, nowadays!"

"Don't make no nevermind," Harris replied. "One o' them'ere places be as good as t'other. Glad ye caught us afore we turned off south'ards."

"Reckon ye know the way?" Potts said, fighting back a sly grin.

"Reckon I do!" Harris snapped testily, offended that his knowledge of the country could possibly be questioned. "Jist the same, ye're welcome to ride along with us. Seen any Injun sign?"

"Reckon I have. Cain't be sartin sure jest what they be. Crow, most likely. I'd advise ye keep a close eye on yer critters hereabouts."

Once again Dan stifled a wicked grin. He fluffed up his beard to conceal his lips.

Again Black Harris rose to the bait. He roared, "Don't need no Johnny-come-lately greenhorn pork-eater like yerownse'f givin' me no advice 'bout no Injun hossthiefs. I war dodgin' Absorkees when ye war still chawin' on yer mammy's tit!"

Dan Potts fairly exploded with laughter. Those two friends were playing a long-running game, seeing which one could first rile the other. Potts had clearly won that bout.

Dan was still wiping tears from his eyes when he turned to me, looked me over top to toe, and said, "Temple Buck! Begawd, it's good to see ye back hereabouts whar ye b'long!" He stood in his stirrups, leaned out, and wrapped me in a bear hug, which I happily returned.

"It's better'n ye know, Dan'l," I replied. "I don't reckon I'll ever be leavin' again. Not if I can help it"

His gaze strayed to my Kumskaka horse and rested there a spell. "Don't s'pose ye'd be int'rested in tradin' off that hoss o' your'n, would ye?"

"Don't reckon I would, Dan'l. But thankee for offerin'," I replied, pleased with the compliment.

I noticed that Powatawa, Micah, and McCool, along with a couple of Harris's hostlers, had drifted forward and sat ringed around us, lounging in their saddles. I hastened to introduce my companions to Potts, halfway curious to see how he would greet them, especially my father, but also the other two. Neither Negroes nor Irishmen were considered to be equals with Protestant whitemen in Potts's old Pennsylvania neighborhood, any more than they were in Ohio and elsewhere in the settlements. I wondered how much of his hometown hide pride Daniel had hung onto.

Naturally Potts looked more than somewhat startled when I introduced Powatawa as my father, but he said only, "Pleased to meetcha." His response to Micah was considerably different. "Omygawd presarve us!" he roared, his eyes crinkled nearly shut with glee. "Please don't be tellin' me we got ourse'fs anuther Beckwith, come to drive us daft with his 'tarnal puffin' up hisse'f, braggin''til hell won't have it!"

I looked quickly to Micah, expecting him to look hurt or offended. Instead he was near giggling with pleasure, complimented, I reckon, to be compared with Jim Beckwith so early on in his mountain experience.

Finn McCool didn't wait to be introduced. He ambled his horse forward to Potts's mount and said, "Finnæus McCool, lately come from Ireland, at yer service." Finn's steely blue gaze dared Potts to make jest of him or in any way to treat him as an inferior.

Dan didn't take up the dare. He shoved out a meaty fist and said simply, "Welcome! If'n ye be ridin' 'longside o' Temple here, I reckon ye'll do fer the mountains. What ye don't know yet, he'll larn ye."

Harris took Potts at his word regarding Crow horsethieves. That night he doubled the night guard and ordered the livestock close-hobbled and put out to graze staked on picket pins. It was just as well, for a musket shot and a hostler's curse in the early morning darkness roused those of us not on duty from our robes and sent every man scurrying to the edge of camp, ready to fend off a raid on our critters and our plunder. Naturally we stayed put, more or less, until grey dawn assured us that the danger had passed. Powatawa discovered a spatter of blood on the grass close by the herd, which proved the hostler's judgment, as well as his aim, to be true.

* * *

Next morning on the trail Dan Potts nodded in the direction of Tug Novak and asked quietly, "What d'ye know 'bout that'ere gap-tooth feller thar, Temple, that'n what I never seen smilin', even when t'other fellers war joshin' an' jestin' 'round the cookfa'r an' him right thar amongst 'em?"

I was not surprised that Potts had taken notice of Novak's different behavior. In the mountains a man learns to notice anything unusual or out of place. "He calls himself Tug Novak," I replied, "a Miss'ippi keelboater. This is his first trip to the mountains." I went on to describe briefly Novak's history with Micah and how my black friend had given him his comeuppance.

Daniel nodded and whistled softly between his teeth. "That 'splains it, then. Las' night when the ruckus commenced an' we run out to the hosses an' hunkered down, watchin'fer Crows, I war sneakin' about, makin' sure ever'body war on the ready, when I come acrost this jaybird slippin' 'round a'hind o' yer darky. He's got his musket up, drawin' down plumb onto yer friend. He don't see me 'til I sorta coughed real quiet-like. When he seed me watchin', he ducks his haid an' skitters off inter the dark. Ye'd best be keepin' a close eye on that'n. He's like to be doin' ye harm."

I thanked Daniel, then dropped back in the column to pass on to my companions what Potts had told me. They said little in reply, but their faces spoke volumes.

* * *

We continued to push westward towards Sweet Lake. Like Dan Potts, I am more than somewhat irked by newcomers to the mountains changing perfectly good names like Willow Valley and Snake Lake to different ones. After all, we got there first and those Johnny-come-latelies have no call to be swapping our old place names for words of their own choosing.

We continued to hunt along the way, keeping bellies full of buffalo and wapiti, even deer when the other two were scarce. The column on the march made it necessary for us to ride out in advance a mile or more, lest that jangling menagerie spook whatever game might be in the neighborhood.

One day at dawn Harris and Potts mentioned over morning coffee that we were drawing near the end of our journey. Later that day or the next we would arrive at rendezvous at the south end of the lake, Snake or Sweet or maybe some other damnfool name by now.

It was still early morning when Powatawa, Potts, Micah, and I were perhaps a mile out ahead of the column, seeking game with no success, when we first heard the gunfire, much too much shooting to be coming from hunters. We were passing through a mostly forested area, so we were sure that nobody, neither Indians nor whites, could be running buffalo a-horseback thereabouts.

Powatawa, Potts, and I left our mounts and pack animals with Micah and sneaked forward afoot to discover what all the shooting was about. When I say afoot, that isn't entirely accurate. At first we trotted, then we moved ahead crouching, and as we drew nigh the fracas we were slithering on our bellies, seeking to catch a glimpse of precisely who was using up all that gunpowder and galena. It might have been a bunch of Absóraqas and Shoshones battling each other or perhaps one or the other defending themselves against a passel of Blackfoots, but it wasn't.

What we saw at last was more Blackfoots than I had ever seen in one place before, except for one time up on the Gallatin. They were ringed around a big jumble of rocks, behind which I could make out a bunch of trappers forted up, fighting for their lives against impossible odds. From where we lay there was no telling who they were, but that didn't matter. They were trappers, our own kind, and from the look of things, they were on the losing end of the battle.

"Hell!" Potts exclaimed, "Them bastards agin! Gittin' to be a reg'lar thang hereabouts!" That is all he said. There was no time for more. We hastily backed out of there and went hotfooting to where Micah was holding our critters, then rode hell-for-leather back to Harris and the caravan.

By time we reached them, Harris had already heard the shooting and had halted the column, which was milling about on the narrow trail, horses and mules by now infected by the men's alarm, r'aring and plunging and filling the air with braying and neighing, mingled with the curses of hostlers trying to control the excited beasts.

Potts was first to break the news. "Black!" he yelled. "Thar be Injuns — big bunch o' Blackfoots! — bigger'n last year! — got a passel of our boys pinned down up ahaid! We gotta go he'p 'em or they be sure'nuff goners! Hain't no time to lose!"

Harris hesitated not a jot. He swung about in his saddle and roared out to his men, "Git off yer hosses naow an' snug up them saddle girths like to cut yer critters in two! Cain't 'low them packs slippin' off! Then we're gonna ride like hell inter that'ere fightin'!"

A grumble of protest rose up from the hostlers, but Black outshouted them. "Don't nobody even thank o' turnin' tail an' runnin' off! Them Blackfoots'll hunt ye down an'pick ye off, one by one, an' skelp ye clean — an' yer balls in the bargain! Ain't nuthin' else we kin do but gittin' in on that'ere brawl up thar an' win it! Naow, git!"

Nobody had a better idea and the hostlers knew it. Quick as scat, they leaped to the ground and busied themselves yanking girths tight and making sure every pack animal was snug on its halter shank. Harris kept on bellowing. "Make sure yer shootin' irons are loaded an' primed. You're sure-as-hell gonna need 'em!

"Gawddamn heathen bastards cain't never larn nuthin'!" he roared to nobody in particular. When he noticed me at his elbow, he more or less explained. "Same as last year! Gawddamn Blackfoots jumped the whole damn ronnyvoo, same place, thar on Snake Lake. Snuck right in, they done, an' kilt a Snake an' his squaw! Then the sumbitches put up one helluva fight afore we gave 'em comeuppance! Made 'em turn tail, we done! No tellin' how many we put under! Natcherly the sumbitches hauled off them we kilt! We lost a dozen friendlies an' half a dozen trappers got banged up purty bad, but I reckon they mended — 'ceptin' fer Sam Tulloch. He ain't never gonna be usin' that hand o' his'n proper-like never no more!" He broke off, seeing his hostlers were ready to ride. "Awright, fellers!" he bawled, "Let's ride like hell an' teach them bastards a gawddamn lesson!" In no time at all we were galloping towards the fray, Harris and Potts leading the way, white-faced hostlers dragging their charges ever faster into a fight nobody wanted. Powatawa, Micah, McCool, and I rode drag, pushing up laggards, shouting and cursing and whipping up any man who might have had second thoughts about riding headlong to his suicide.

When we broke through the fringe of trees surrounding the clearing a jubilant shout went up from the men sheltered behind a barricade of huge rocks that littered the foot of a hill and scattered halfway up its slopes. We caught the attacking Blackfoots pretty much by surprise. They fell back under the hail of galena we sent their way, just long enough to allow our rag-tag rabble to race into the makeshift fortress.

Once inside the outer ring of boulders, Kumskaka skidded downhill into a large bowl at the base of the hill, where a couple hundred frantic pack animals and saddle horses and mules milled and kicked and crowded against one another, honking and whinnying, eyes rolling white in fear and excitement. I swung to the ground and turned Kumskaka and my other critters into the squealing maelstrom, then scurried back to the outer rocks, reloading as I ran.

I took cover behind a large boulder, beside two men I didn't know. They appeared to be savvy enough, taking turns, each man poking his head above the rock only occasionally, dropping to his knees or onto his belly, firing around the side of the boulder, then ducking back to reload.

The Indians had resumed their attack in earnest. Clouds of arrows clattered along the rocky hillside. Their muskets were busy, as well, showering us with rock chips and ricochets. Given a choice, it's better to fort up behind logs instead of boulders. Lead balls bury themselves in wood. Galena that hits a rock chips out hurtful splinters.

There were only two sides to the boulder, so I wasn't doing any good where I was. A nearby cluster of rocks was so far unoccupied, so I scooted across an open stretch and dived into its shelter, fetching up in a heap, bruised but still healthy. It was a good position. I could sneak a peek, aim and fire, then roll away, whilst my previous location was pelted with arrows and musket balls.

The arrival of half a hundred reinforcements appeared to dampen the ardor of the attackers not a whit. Their blood was up and they still outnumbered us several to one and no Indian could have ignored the numerous critters and rich booty we had added to the prize.

Next time I rolled to a space between a pair of rocks I beheld half a dozen Blackfoots running full tilt at my hidey-hole, firing muskets and loosing arrows as they came. They had got fed up with my potshots and aimed to eliminate the nuisance. I dropped one with a rifle shot before I jumped to my feet and scampered more or less blindly along the hillside, arrows whirring and racketing around me. I gained refuge amid a tangle of boulders and brushwood, where I tripped and went sprawling, banging my head against a rock. Half-dazed, I became aware of smelly, buckskin-clad men whose familiar accents assured me that I had literally fallen amongst friends.

"Wal, damn me if'n them'ere gawddamn Injuns ain't done gone ahaid an' kilt me daid!" The voice sounded familiar. "An' I din't even see them pearly gates whilst I war a-passin' through 'em! Lookee hyar, fellers! It's an angel, sure as hell! An' damn if'n it don't look a whole lot like ol' Temple Buck, riz up from the daid an' gone to thi'shere heaven!"

There was no mistaking the voice and the smell, even if the face was still unclear in my befuddled gaze. "Tuttle! That you?" I yelled.

"Sure as hell, that's what Mama allus called me. Never come acrost no other Tuttle, neither." I would have recognized the horse laugh that followed anywhere.

As my vision cleared I beheld the grinning whiskery face of Tuttle Thompson, big yellow horseteeth and all. His expression changed to concern. "Damn if ye ain't bleedin'!"

I looked at my leg and saw an arrow sliced through my leggin', still hanging there, blood oozing through the leather. It didn't hurt. Yet, I reminded myself.

Tuttle dropped to his knees, loosened the tie of the dagger sheath I always wear on my right leg, and yanked up my leggin', exposing a shallow slice on my calf. "Wal now, looks like thet'ere li'l toad-sticker ye carry purely saved yore laig." It was true. My poniard, a long-ago gift from Lucette, had pretty much deflected the arrow.

Tuttle continued to gaze at the ugly welts on my leg, a soft whistle escaping through his lips. "Shee-it, Temple! What in holy hell gave ye them'ere scars? T'other'n, too? Thet laig o' your'n be lookin' like forcemeat!"

"Aw hell, it's a long story an' it's only half-true," I replied. "I'll tell ye 'bout it later on." I let my gaze stray over the trappers crouched behind the boulders and saw nobody I knew well. "Where are the others, Tuttle? They all right? Anybody gone under?"

"Nope. All of 'em still kickin'. Natcherly some of 'em got theirse'fs banged up a mite, hyar an' thar. Me, too." He grinned and pulled back his sleeve. I saw a long jagged white scar on his forearm. Tuttle laughed and said, "Hell! Thet'n be a long way from muh heart an' the Injun whut done it ain't never gonna do nuthin' to nobody never no more."

"How come you're on your own over here?"

"Aw, sometimes I jest strays off. Yew know thet. Allus have. Allus will. Makes me 'preciate y'all the more when I come on back."

It is true. Faithful friend that Tuttle had always been to me and the others, there is a solitary streak in him, mostly concerning some woman he's romancing, but at other times, too.

"The rest of 'em be hyarabouts somewhars — Godey, Turtle, Paddy an' Anse, all of 'em. Bigmouth Beckwith an' his leetle Spanyard, too. Nope. Ain't nobody gone under so far. Yew'll see 'em."

"What about Chiksika? Still got 'im?"

"Ye damn betcha! An' he's better'n ever. Yew'll see. Right naow, howsomever, he's more'n a trifle gant, purty used up. All our critters be measly. Campbell's been pushin' hard, gittin' ter ronnyvoo. A week or two o' good graze an' layin' off work'll bring 'em back up to snuff."

I was glad to learn that Chiksika, the first and best horse I ever owned in the mountains, was still sound and thriving. He belonged to Tuttle now, but that diminished my affection for him not a jot.

Tuttle looked solemn. "Ye be wantin' 'im back, Temple? Natcherly he's your'n if'n ye wish.

"Hell no!" I replied. "I gave 'im to ye when I left an' I ain't the kind to be takin' 'im back! 'Sides, wait'll ye see my Kumskaka horse,

Shawnee-bred and in his prime. You an' me, we'll be ridin' together in grand style!" Tuttle looked relieved.

The blood had commenced to clot. I pulled down my leggin' and secured the poniard in place. I reloaded my rifle and pistol before I staggered to my feet. "Time I commence bein' useful, wouldn't ye say?" I announced, affecting more bravado than I really possessed just then.

"Yep, me, too. Glad to have ye back." Tuttle led me to the breastworks, where half a dozen trappers fired in relays, half of them getting off a shot whilst the other half reloaded, careful not to be shooting all at once, lest the Blackfoots catch us all with empty guns and rush us.

The field before us was alive with Indians, some a-horseback, gussied up in colorful warshirts, eagle-feather bonnets streaming, likely war-chiefs, charging back and forth just out of rifle range, shaking muskets or bows or feathered lances, howling threats and insults and shouting encouragement to comrades creeping through tall grass and shallow gullies to attack with arrows.

Now and again a horseman, likely caught up in his own bragging, came streaking almost to our barricade, brandishing his weapons, roaring challenges or singing his death-song, only to be shot out of the saddle, tumbling backwards over the crupper to lie twitching or lifeless in the tall grass.

After a time the Indians mostly shifted their attack to another quarter and things cooled down considerably. It came to me that I hadn't seen my father, Micah, or McCool since we first rode in. I bade farewell to Tuttle, who called after me, "Don't ye be fergittin', all it takes is jest one o' them leetle galena pills fer spoilin' all o' yer plans!"

I laughed and moved off in a direction where I heard heavy gunfire, dodging from one heap of boulders to another, limping across open spaces as best I could, hardly mindful of my game leg. Hot blood and fright will do that for you.

From high up amongst the rocks on the hillside I heard the wails of women and the shrieks and chatter of children, the Indian families of Company trappers hidden away out of gunshot range for safekeeping while their men did battle below.

I first saw Finn McCool, then Micah, and finally Powatawa behind a screen of brushwood heaped on a waist-high pile of rocks, taking turns shooting and reloading and firing again at an enemy whose ranks appeared never to diminish. I was struck by their calm demeanor, all three of them, intent on their chore, taking deliberate aim and squeezing off a shot at a gaily-bedecked horseman at a distance or a half-naked warrior crawling through tall grass, then coolly dropping down to recharge their weapon. I was especially impressed by Micah. This was nothing new for the other two.

They greeted me with broad grins, their teeth startling white in faces smeared black with greasy smoke and burnt gunpowder. Powatawa and Finn, that is. On Micah it was hard to tell.

I hustled in behind them, keeping low, and knelt whilst I made sure that my rifle and pistol were loaded and capped. At such times it's all too easy to forget. When my father crouched down to reload, he smiled broadly and reached out to squeeze my arm. "Good you are here, my son. My heart grows big again." He jerked his head towards the barricade and the fighting beyond it. "My blood sings now. Too many winters I have not seen fighting. My spirit was hungry, starving. Now it lives once more."

I understood what he meant, but right then I could have done with less of that particular nourishment.

Powatawa returned to his post and I greeted Micah and Finn in turn as they dropped down to reload. Both appeared exhilarated, not a trace of fright showing. Like Powatawa, their blood was up, excitement crowding out fear.

In a lull in the firing I heard men shouting nearby. I wished my companions a hasty farewell, then hurried to where I might be more helpful.

When I gained the shelter of a jumble of huge boulders I discovered a dozen or more men gathered there, Black Harris and Potts and a grim-faced Bobby Campbell amongst them. I saw, too, my old friends Brass Turtle and Ned Godey and Jim Beckwith's little Spaniard sidekick, Cesár Pérez. Several men flashed a welcoming grin and a nod but little more. They were intent on what Campbell was saying.

"We're in a tight, for damn sure," he announced, "and it's not getting any better. We need help, lots of help. We must get word to the rendezvous, else this whole shebang'll be goners for damn sure!"

Nobody disagreed.

"Somebody needs to ride through these Blackfoots an' carry the word. Rendezvous's less'n twenty miles from here. I'm willing to go, but I'll need the fastest horse we have. Any offers?" Campbell looked inquiringly around the men circled there.

I recalled Tuttle's remark that all of their horses were pretty much used up. Mostly, I prefer staying in the background, but this was no time for modesty. I stepped up to Campbell and said, loud enough for all to hear, "I've got a horse that can pert'near fly, Bobby. 'Sides, our critters are fresher'n yours. We hardly used 'em today."

A murmur of approval rippled amongst the men there. Campbell squinted at me and a smile flickered across his face. "He's fast, ye say, Temple?" Then, quietly, "By the way, good to see ye back."

"He's fast — an' handy, too," I replied. "No brag. Faster'n ye might believe." Campbell's smile broadened considerably. I reckoned he knew that I am not given to boasting. Then a new idea occurred. I had thought to lend Kumskaka to Campbell, but, instead, I said, "'Pears we've got a one-time shot. We'll not likely fool the Blackfoots twice. Best we send two men, hopin' at least one o' ye makes it through."

I raised my voice over the general babble and announced, "Some o' ye may recall Gen'ral Ashley's big Kentucky-bred chestnut! He's big an' he's fast — racin' stock! We've got 'im here." I turned to Campbell and said, "He'll carry ye to hell an' back, Bobby."

Campbell nodded and grinned. "Just to the rendezvous, thankee. I can wait to go to hell — if we're not already there."

Black Harris called out, "He's quick, that'n! That's the gawddamn truth! He'll gitcha thar!"

It came to me then that Kumskaka was a one-man horse, not likely to take to just any rider. Looking about, my eye lighted on Cesár Pérez. I stepped over to him and asked, "Ye game, Cesár? Ye willin' to go?"

The little Spaniard's face split in a grin that threatened to swallow his ears. "*Si-si, Señor* Tempo! *Gracias*! I weel ride *el Diablo* heemself *al'infierno* eef you tell me."

I asked Campbell, "Ye willin' to take Cesár along with ye, Bobby? He weighs hardly nothin' an' he's half horse himself. If anybody can get past those bastards, he can!"

Campbell nodded and called out, "It's settled! Let's get a move on! Time's wasting!" He paused, then called out again, "Pass the word about what we're doin'! Don't need gettin' shot by our own people!"

I was wondering how I would be able to lead the horses across the route I had just traveled without getting them and myself killed when Brass Turtle caught my arm and guided me through a more direct passage to the bowl where a multitude of horses and mules stamped and snorted and bumped into one another, screeching their displeasure at the crowded quarters. It was a proper equine pandemonium. Cesár tagged after us, intending to retrieve his own saddle.

On the way, Brass Turtle chuckled and said, "I tol' ye when ye left, Temple, ye got the mountains in yer blood. I knew ye couldn't stay put in Ohio."

"You're righter than ye know, Turtle. Even bein' here in this hellhole is a helluva lot better'n where I've been these past two years."

As we shouldered through the livestock in search of Kumskaka and Ashley I saw arrows sticking in the packs of several critters. Our Delaware healer, Old Foot, attended by his faithful helper Little Mountain, was tending to animals that had been skewered. I breathed a silent prayer to the Great Whoever that my canisters of booze stowed beneath a high-riding pack of other plunder had escaped unscathed.

We would need a healthy swig or several if we ever got out of there alive.

We caught up the horses, then hustled back to Campbell and the others, where we switched saddles and stripped off unnecessary gear. I passed Kumskaka's reins to Cesár and busied myself soothing the hot-blooded Ashley. Cesár commenced cooing to Kumskaka, gently stroking his cheeks and ears and blowing softly into his nostrils — introducing himself, as ye might say. Kumskaka soon settled down and nuzzled into the little Spaniard's armpit. My horse had found another friend.

Cesár had stripped off his shirt, his tawny hide no different from our Blackfoot besiegers. Campbell wore a plain buckskin shirt, for his pale Irish skin would be a certain giveaway. Each man tied a long Eagle feather in his hair. Dan Potts yelled out, "Hold on thar, afore ye go!" He pulled off his bright red shirt, tore two long strips off the bottom, and handed them to the riders. "Wrap these around yer noggins, so's we kin tell who ye be an' won't be shootin' ye! We'll tell the others!" Which several trappers trotted off to do.

As the riders leaned low in their saddles, ready to give quirt and spur to their mounts, Harris yelled, "Tell 'em Black Harris brung a passel o' booze, Bobby! That'll sure-as-hell git their arses up hyar in a hurry!'

Campbell and Pérez sped off amid a roar of laughter, which was the only sensible thing anybody could think of doing right then.

We ran to whatever vantage points our rocky fortress afforded, watching our comrades streak across the open meadow towards a fringe of forest, the while peppering the terrain with heavy gunfire in an effort to distract the Blackfoots' attention from the fleeing riders.

At last they disappeared amongst the trees. All we could do now was hold off our attackers and wait. There was no water in our rockpile. What Blackfoot arms failed to achieve, thirst might accomplish.

A nudge at my elbow announced the presence of Ned Godey. "Good to have ye back, Temple. Allus knew ye couldn't quit the mountains. But it took ye long enough."

"Too long, for damn sure," I agreed. "If we ever get out o' here, I'll tell ye the whole of it." Then, my gaze sweeping the field before us, seeking a target, I asked him, "That's one helluva bunch out there. Ye make out what kind?"

Godey chuckled, but with little good humor. "Ever' kind o' Blackfoot thar be, I reckon — Sík-si-kah, Páy-gan, Káh-i-nah — a passel o' Big-belly Grovants fer boot. Even more'n last year. They must'a learnt whar the ronnyvoo's at an' come runnin' fer takin' our plews an' plunder afore we git thar." He cursed softly and said, whilst taking aim, "Bastards don't dare hit the whole ronnyvoo. We likely 'peared like easy pickin's." He paused to trigger off his shot before he added, "Natcherly Harris showin' up with his packstring war mighty welcome."

I snorted but said nothing. From what I had seen of Black's hostlers as I scurried about the rockpile, they were of little value. Most had taken what cover they could find and hunkered down, careful not to expose themselves by shooting. It's one thing to shoot into the dark, discouraging horsethieves. It's quite another to engage in bloody warfare.

Ned and I chatted for a spell, firing only when we thought we were sure of a target, without much success that I could tell. Still, the ragged volleys from our side kept the Indians from rushing us. That was the best we could hope for until trappers from the rendezvous showed up to save our skins — if indeed they would ever arrive.

After a spell I excused myself and crawled off to see how Powatawa, Micah, and Finn might be doing. On the way, I saw Black Harris and another man bustling about, handing out powder and galena pigs. Slender columns of grey smoke were sprouting up here and there amongst the rocks as several trappers busied themselves replenishing their stock of rifle and musket balls.

As I neared their barricade, I saw my companions still defending their slice of hillside, apparently uninjured. I spied then, halfway up the slope, directly behind them, half concealed by a boulder, Tug Novak. He rose to his feet, musket snugged to his shoulder, aiming not at the meadow but at my friends crouched behind their barrier. I yelped a warning and commenced running towards them, swinging up my rifle as I floundered through slippery scree.

I never made that shot. I tripped and went sprawling. By time I twisted about and rose to my knees, Novak was tumbling headfirst down the slope. He slammed against a big rock and lay unmoving.

I shifted my gaze to the breastworks and beheld Powatawa and Finn McCool, the two of them blowing smoke from their rifle muzzles, and Micah, his back turned, intent on what might be lurking in the meadow before him.

I hastened to the barricade, where McCool — a mite piously, I thought — gravely opined, "'Twas a brave and a foolish thing for that blatherskite to be doin', defendin' us all, exposin' himself like he did, fer all o' thim redskins out yonder to see. Wasn't it now?" He sighed and shrugged, rather too dramatically. "Faith, jist the same, ye'd have to be sayin' he was after dyin' like a hero, wouldn't ye now?"

Powatawa nodded in solemn agreement, his face as impassive as the rocks around us. I allowed that it was likely so. Some matters are best left like that.

* * *

The following several hours contained more of the same, a tedious siege punctuated by half-hearted charges quickly discouraged by our gunfire. Our best hope lay in that we had seen no jubilant chief come riding out waving a pair of bloody scalps. Still, we remained trapped, our throats dry as dust.

I stayed with my father and the others, taking my turn at the breastworks, anxiously peering past the meadow to the treeline, where the trappers from rendezvous would likely appear.

After a time Tuttle scuttled into our little refuge, accompanied by a rattle of arrows skittering off the rocks. He appeared uninjured, howsomever, and his hearty horselaugh confirmed it. "Missed me, sure as hell! They must be gittin' tuckered. Cain't blame 'em. Me, too!" He glanced from one to another of my companions and, not recognizing any of them, even Micah, looked to me."

"This is Tuttle Thompson," I announced, "my oldest friend in the mountains. We've been pards from the get-go." Then, "Tuttle, you oughta recall Micah here. From Fink's hell-boat in 'twenty-two?'"

Tuttle gawped, passed his hand across his eyes and squinted closely at Micah. "Wal, damn if it ain't!" He shoved out his hand, a smile breaking across his stubbly features. "Gawddamn, Micah! Ye 'pear t'growed up ter twicet what ye war back then! Whatcher been eatin'? Giant beans?"

Micah laughed out loud, his teeth flashing in a broad grin, and pumped Tuttle's hand. "Whatever I've been eatin', it's a deal better than what I ever got from Mike Fink's stingy hand." They laughed together and Tuttle pounded Micah's back, muttering welcoming sentiments the while.

Powatawa was on watch at the wall, so I introduced the Irishman next. "This's Finn McCool, come all the way from Ireland." As they shook hands I was struck by how much alike they were, both tall, rangy and muscular, both secure in themselves. To his credit, McCool differs considerably in matters of hygiene. "Finn's come up with Black, hostlin' a packstring," I went on, "but he reckons he'll be stayin' on hereabouts. Reckon he'll fit with the rest o' the bunch?"

Tuttle stepped back and appraised McCool head to foot in a comical fashion. Then he guffawed and said, "Reckon so, pervidin' he don't snore no louder'n me! Glad to meetcha!"

Finn's customary reserve melted. A smile overspread his features and he replied, "The playshure's me own, Tuttle Thompson, and I'll be tryin' me best not to be outdoin' ye in the snorin'." He winked at Micah and me and added, "But no promises, mind ye."

I took a moment to apologize to Micah for volunteering his Ashley horse without asking him first. His smile and friendly clap on the shoulder assured me that he took no umbrage, that he understood that there hadn't been time for such niceties.

Micah relieved Powatawa then and I presented my father to my friend. "Tuttle, I want ye to meet my father, Powatawa. You've heard a lot about him from me over the years. Here he is."

Tuttle stumbled backwards a step, dumbfounded, eyes bulging, mouth agape, this time sincerely. He swallowed hard and strangled out, "Yer father, ye say? Yer daddy? Y'ain't funnin' me, Temple?"

Powatawa allowed a thin smile to play on his lips. "No, he is not, he speaks true, Tuttle Thompson. I have heard much of you from my son. My heart is big to see you at last."

My father's quiet dignity and his carefully measured speech disturbed Tuttle nearly as much as my announcement, but at length he regained his composure. He extended both hands in welcome, mumbling the while, "Wal, I be damned an' double-damned if'n thi'shere don't beat all! Jest the same, I be happy as hell to be meetin' ye, sir." I was myself surprised right then. I had never witnessed Tuttle Thompson sirring anybody, no matter who it was — leastaways not since Major Henry returned to the settlements four years before.

Tuttle and Powatawa continued to chat until a barely audible cough from Micah called McCool and my father to his side. When Tuttle was satisfied that Micah's signal meant no immediate danger, he nodded sidewise and led me as far away from the others as that hidey-hole allowed.

Tuttle wasted no time getting to the point. "Don'tcha be frettin' none 'bout yer daddy bein' Shawnee, Temple." He looked about, making sure we were out of earshot. "Fact is, thar war some folks back home in Kaintuck said Mama had Cherokee in her blood. Natcherly if Daddy heared 'em, he jest natcherly whupped hell out'n 'em an' ther most of 'em quit sech gossipin', but Mama never let on, nohaow, one way or t'other. She'd jest smile, quiet-like, an' say it takes all kinds, don't it? I don't know nuthin' fer sartin sure, mind ye, but I wouldn't be a tall bit surrounded if it war so. Don't care, neither. Like Mama use'ter say, don't make no nevermind what ye mought be puttin' in the dressin, so long as it tastes good — an' ther turkey don't give a gawddamn, nohaow."

I could barely contain my mirth at his concern for my heritage. Fighting to keep a straight face, I said, "No way, Tuttle. I've never been prouder in my life. Ye know damn well how I felt about Pap an' how I always looked up to Powatawa. Ye don't know the half of it concernin' Pap. I'll be tellin' ye when there's time. For right now, just rest yourself that I reckon I've been gifted with the best father a man could ever wish for."

Tuttle nodded and said, "Amen." He might have said more but just then the whole hillside exploded in hoarse shouts and nigh-hysterical laughter. We rushed to the barricade and heard a pandemonium of shooting coming from the tree-fringe on the far side of the meadow. Nobody needed to say it. Trappers and a passel of friendly Indians had arrived from rendezvous.

Word passed quickly along our hillside and amongst the Blackfoots. Suddenly half the meadow erupted in half-naked redskins jumping to their feet and racing for the treeline where their horses were tethered. Naturally we did our best to speed them on their way. Every rifle, musket, and pistol on our side belched fire and galena — without, howsomever, doing much damage that I could see.

Here and there I caught a glimpse of mounted trappers amongst the trees, rifles and pistols spouting smoke. The tables had turned. Our attackers found themselves trapped in a crossfire betwixt our rescuers and us. Suddenly I beheld a most curious and fearsome sight. A double score or more of horseback Indians, mostly chiefs from the look of their fancy get-ups, were gathering on the far side of the field, yelling and pointing towards our hillside. Then they all busted loose at once and came galloping straight for us, firing muskets and loosing a cloud of arrows, shaking lances aloft, screaming insults and challenges and singing death-songs, a wave of horseflesh and eagle feathers and wild-eyed painted savages that threatened to engulf our rocky garrison.

What they might have had in mind, if anything in particular, nobody will ever know. Blackfoots on the prod are mostly daft, anyway. Perhaps they sought to occupy our fortress and defend it against our rescuers. More likely their intention was to overwhelm us and grab whatever plunder and ponies they could snatch up and make off with in their retreat. Whatever their aim, we were surely goners if they succeeded.

What happened next took no time at all. A withering fire from our side emptied half their saddles in mid-field, but it didn't faze the rest of them. They kept on charging, unmindful of comrades toppling from their mounts, bloodlust, excitement, and crazy pride goading them onwards.

An eerie lull in our own shooting told us that gut-wrenching excitement and fright on our side made us violate our own iron rule. Every man was firing as fast he could trigger and reload. Most of us were caught with empty weapons. It didn't last long, but it was long enough. The Blackfoots gobbled up the remaining ground whilst we dumped in powder and ball and primed, in a fever to re-arm ourselves. Most of us abandoned our rocky defenses and stood up to receive the charge. In a flash of recollection that sometimes returns after a moment of fright, I recall Micah standing unflinching beside me.

A sheet of flame blasted from rifles and muskets all along our front, sweeping most of our attackers and many horses to the ground, but not all. Through a pall of gunsmoke I beheld one warrior, painted face twisted in hatred, down-pointing lance clamped under his arm, lifting his wide-eyed piebald horse in a high-arcing leap over our barricade.

A hoof punched my shoulder, spinning me sidewise to the ground, my rifle bouncing amongst the scree. Half-dazed, I tugged at the pistol in my sash, but too late. Micah, too, had been thrown onto his back by the charging horse. He twisted halfway about, pistol in hand, then fire flashed from the muzzle. The heavy ball, fired from only a yard away, ploughed into the Blackfoot's belly and swept him from his saddle, flinging him backwards onto the stony earth. His horse, mostly unhurt, clattered halfway up the hillside before excitement deserted him.

Finn McCool brushed past me, vaulted the low barricade, and hotfooted out to the meadow, where he snatched up the rein of a good-size bay pony grazing there, then ran back with him to where we stood.

"I'll be after needin' a horse o' me own when I bid farewell to Misther Harris," he explained matter-of-factly as he stooped to examine a shallow gash in the critter's shoulder.

Tuttle returned from the hillside just then, leading the fallen warrior's horse. He passed the reins to Micah. "Reckon ye sure-as-hell earnt this'n, Micah. He be your'n, natcherly."

Micah hesitated not a jot. He took a step towards McCool and handed the reins to the Irishman. "Here, Finn. I've got critters enough. You'll be needin' more'n one." His generous act was powerful testimony to the solid bond that had grown amongst those three newcomers to the Shining Mountains. Besides his rifle, a horse is the most valuable single item a man can own in the mountains and Micah knew it — except for friendship, and I am sure that Micah knew that, too.

Tuttle was gazing into the meadow, watching our trappers, white and Indian alike, stripping bodies that the Blackfeet had been unable to haul off. Suddenly he tugged at McCool's sleeve. "C'mon, Irisher! Ye need new duds! Ye look like a gawddamn raggedy doll! Git a move on, 'fore they be all gone!" He grabbed the reins away from Finn, handed them to me, and hustled McCool out to the battlefield.

Which reminded me of the Indian who lay at our feet. He had likely been some sort of war chief, judging by his fancy get-up, all quilled and beaded and fringed to a fare-thee-well, as well as by his recent reckless behavior. He looked to be about the same size as Micah, so I entrusted the horses to my father, stooped down, and proceeded to strip the body clean — a butter-soft doeskin shirt, antelope leggin's, britchclout, his belt with all its bags and hardware, quill-encrusted moccasins, and even his finely-quilled medicine poke — which, when you think about it, hadn't done him much good.

When I held out the armload of clothing to Micah, he recoiled somewhat, but I reassured him, "Hell, Micah, he'd be doin' the same for you, if he could, an' he'd be takin' your balls along for boot. 'Sides, from the look o' these duds, they're most likely Absóraqa, anyways. That's how he got 'em." Micah accepted the clothes with a sickly grin, but he took them.

I wandered off a stride or two and discreetly emptied the little medicine poke of its contents, which I buried. Then I stuffed into it Tug Novak's tooth and the snake rattle. When I returned and draped the thong around Micah's neck, I told him, "That's just for a start. You'll know what to add, if and when."

I noticed Tuttle standing somewhat apart, gazing over the recent battlefield, now and then licking his lips, a faraway look in his eyes. Concerned, I asked if anything was amiss. "Aw, hell no, Temple," he replied wistfully, "but I shorely would like to come a-callin' on some o' them 'ere Blackfoot lodges arter this'n. Thar's gonna be a passel o' grievin' widders sorely in need o' comfortin' an' I jest natcherly be the right feller fer thet kind o' chore."

We drifted along the hillside to where Robert Campbell was trying to assemble the company. Ned Godey fell in with us and said to me, "Warn't but two fellers got theirse'fs kilt, which is surprisin', consid'rin' all the arrers an' lead flyin' about — yer hostler an' Bobby's Frenchy cook — never did catch his moniker. He war packin' a deal o' suet, Bobby's cook war, an' he war a mite too slow gittin' to the rocks."

One of Campbell's trappers put in, "That'n war Looie Boldue. Yep, he war more'n some'at heavy, which ain't surprisin' in a feller what allus had fust grab on the vittles."

Black's hostlers buried the bodies under a cover of scree and rocks to keep the coyotes off. If anybody said the Words over them, I never heard about it.

Cesár Pérez, grinning fit to bust, trotted up on Kumskaka and slid to the ground. Whilst he was loosing the cinchas, he turned to me and positively crowed, "Yer 'orse, *su caballo*, 'e fly like a, *un pajáro*, a bird, *Señor* Tempo! *El jefe*, Don Roberto, 'e cannot stay wees me! I mus' slow por heem. Even so, *los Indios*, we leave zem far be'ind!" He patted Kumskaka's cheek, then he flung his arms around my horse's neck and kissed his nostril. "'E ees *magnífico*!" Even if it was mostly about Kumskaka, I have received few compliments better than that one and none more heartfelt.

* * *

Bobby Campbell wasted no time in gathering us all — free trappers, his own Company men and their families, those who rode to our aid, Harris's packers, and our tagalong quartet — and setting out for the rendezvous, lest the Blackfoots entertain second thoughts and return.

All the way, I greeted old friends and comrades. Our little redheaded Irishman Paddy McBride fairly bubbled. "Sure'n ye've made this troublous day a happy one altogether, Temple darlin', comin' amongst us once again. There's been a fearsome hole in our pleasure this long while ye've been gone from us."

Even sour Anse Tolliver put aside his acidulous humor. "'Baout time ye showed up, Buck. Ye been missed." This constituted a warm welcome from crabby Anse Tolliver. I wondered what he would say when I introduced my Shawnee father, a Negro, and another Irishman, one who would likely never put up with the dour Tennesseean's sharp tongue, as long-suffering Paddy had tolerated for years. "We reckoned ye might'a gone an' turned yerse'f inter one o' them'ere greyback farmers back thar."

"Not a chance," I replied, thinking the while that I might have done precisely that, if Sarah Rutledge hadn't cast me aside in horror when she learned that my true father was a Shawnee Indian.

I observed with pleasure Major Henry's fiddle case, much scarred now, bobbing behind Anse's saddle, promising merriment at rendezvous tonight. And I felt a certain sneaky satisfaction that his saddle now was of the Spaniard kind. When Tuttle and I first swapped our old dragoons for Spaniard saddles, Anse had sneered at such foreign contraptions. I kept that thought to myself.

Anse kept sneaking envious looks at my mule Sugarfoot, careful, howsomever, not to display too much interest. At length, he could contain himself no longer. With an air of exaggerated disinterest, he ventured, "Fine-lookin' mule ye got thar, Buck." I allowed that I thought so, too. Then, "Likely could use some proper trainin' up by somebody knows mules," he harrumphed, greed kindling in his flinty eyes. "Ye care to swap?"

I laughed aloud. "Nope. Not a chance. He's mine an' he'll remain so. I reckon ol' Sugarfoot here must'a saved me from drownin' in bogs a dozen times, gettin' up here." Anse made no reply. He merely sighed, set his jaw, and lapsed into his customary gloom.

I spied big Jim Beckwith at a distance, riding amongst trappers I didn't know. He was smiling broadly and gesturing wildly, doubtless spinning one of his self-congratulating yarns. I didn't intrude. There would be time enough to renew acquaintance at rendezvous.

My companions were riding with Harris's packstring. I bade so-long to Anse and fell out of the column to wait for them to come up. Whilst I tarried, I saw that my old bunch had harvested a galore of beaver plews. Their pack animals fairly staggered under swaying, high-piled bundles of fur that threatened to topple. Even humorless Bill Sublette might be inclined to crack a smile or two when he calculated the profit he would make on such a haul, once he got it to Saint Louis.

As they passed by, I exchanged greetings with our French-Canuck campkeepers Yves Dureau and Jean-Luc L'Archévêque, their pack animals also burdened with packs of plews riding atop their camp utensils. It had truly been a good couple seasons. They filled the air with enthusiastic bienvenues, waving and promising good vittles when we arrived in camp. I feasted my eyes on my old trapping bunch as they filed by, our Delawares Old Foot, Little Mountain, and Pretty

Horse, then the Iroquois Acorn and Stone Bird, every one of them loyal friends and often our mentors in the early days. Indian-like, most of them were reserved in their greetings, but their nods and brief smiles assured me that my return ws welcome. Only Little Mountain broke ranks to greet me, leaning far out of his saddle to wrap me in a huge embrace, smothering me in sweaty buckskin, babbling, "Too many moons you don't come, Tom-pool! Your sittin'-place long-time empty," and such-like welcoming nonsense.

When Black Harris came into view, I clucked to my pack animals, nudged Kumskaka, and rode to meet him. He hailed me with a smile and called out, "I put yer pards to work ridin' drag, in case them Seek-see-kahs ain't had theirse'fs a bellyful o' fightin' fer one day. Yer ol' dad's got a keen eye, fer damn sure."

I allowed that he did. Then, "Ye lose anything, Black? Still got all your plunder?"

"Nope an' yep. Come through clean as a hound's tooth. Got it all. Arrers punched some holes, but nuthin' serious."

"Same here, best I can tell." I refrained from mentioning my concern about my booze canisters, but it did no good.

"Good. Lookin' for'ard to helpin' myse'f to some o' them Kaintuck squeezin's ye be packin'." He licked his lips, longing in his eyes. "An' mebbe a tetch o' that'ere Frenchy brandy arterwards."

I groaned inwardly. Moses Harris possesses thirst enough to drain entire oceans. But I said, "Ye know you're always welcome, Black," hoping I sounded sincere. We didn't mention Tug Novak.

I reined about and joined my companions at the rear of the column. Micah and Powatawa rode together, Micah in high spirits, chattering a mile-a-minute, eyes dancing, still excited from the battle, pride in having done well swelling his chest. My father, calm as always, smiled and nodded, letting my friend get it out of his system.

McCool was riding his new Piebald, who was restive with the unfamiliar whiteman odor, wrestling with his packstring and his other Blackfoot horse, a tall bay, surging and yanking on his haltershank, rolling his eyes and now and then letting out a nervous whinney.

"Got your hands full, I see," I called out to him.

McCool threw me an exasperated look. "Ye might be sayin' that. It'll be takin' a bit o' toime 'til they accept me."

"No offense, but it's the smell o' ye that's got 'em riled. Ye lack a sufficiency of bear grease an' Blackfoot sweat. They never met a Mick before now."

He grinned. "Which is altogether indade their own pathetic loss. Ere long, I warrant, the sweet smell of Ireland'll be perfume in their haythen noses. Nothin' plaises an equine better'n a whiff o' the Ould Sod!"

We continued such frivolous banter until we caught sight of Snake Lake glimmering golden in sunshine and a cluster of tall tipis and white tents gleaming amidst a sea of green grass. Rendezvous at last!

Battered and used up though most of the party was, a general whoop echoed throughout the column. As if on a signal, trappers spurred their horses into a gallop, long hair and eagle feathers flying out behind them, yelling like lunatics and firing rifles and pistols skywards, thundering towards the camp, yanking pack animals in their wake. There was naught else for it. I abandoned my comrades and urged Kumskaka into the thick of it, his strength flowing into me and coursing through my blood, hollering and shooting with the others, thrilling to the color and excitement and the promise of the long-dreamed-of rendezvous.

Charging through the Indian encampments, we scattered laughing young women and kids and barking dogs, jumping over logs, dodging excited prized buffalo horses broken loose from their tethers and running free. We roared into trappers' camps, shouting hoarse halloos and laughing our heads off, giddy with joy for just being alive.

Chapter VI
Sweet LakeRendezvous

Snake Lake or Sweet Lake, whichever or whatever you choose to call it, is an excellent site for a rendezvous. Lush graze extends for miles. The pine and aspen treeline is thick with deadfall for fires. Still more driftwood clutters the shoreline. Buffalo and wapiti not yet spooked by the smoke and stir wandered and grazed within view of camp when we arrived.

In 'twenty-five, our bunch had wintered farther north on its eastern shore, nearby a good-size Shoshone band, not greatly distant from Captain Weber's headquarters camp on the Bear. We called it Snake Lake then. It was even more beautiful now in early summer.

Several different Indian bands had already arrived for the trading, their lodges set up in areas distinctly separate from one another. Some tribes were traditional enemies of others there, but they tolerated no hostilities at rendezvous. The business of trading for whitemen's plunder was far more important than counting coup on an enemy. That could be done at another time.

I recognized the encampments of Shoshones, the Gaí-bi-shuh we mostly call Bannocks, Absóraqas, and Nez Percés. Tuttle jerked his chin towards a sizeable collection of lodges neatly arranged in a circle. "Them's the Eutaws," he said admiringly. "Them'ere Injuns saved our lily-white arses last year! Fought like them'ere 'vengin' angels in ther Good Book, they did! Kilt more Blackfoots'n the rest of us all put together!"

Another camp, located beside the Nez Percé encampment, was unfamiliar to me. Tuttle said they were Flatheads, generally a goodnatured bunch, down from the North. He went on to extol the beauty, desirability, and complaisance of their women, which is what you might expect to rank at the top of Tuttle's personal values.

It required little time for our bunch to establish ourselves nearby the free trappers' camp on the lakeshore, clusters of brush and sailcloth bowers, small Indian lodges scattered amongst them. Many trappers had taken Indian wives. Little brown children scampered and hooted amongst the dwellings. None of our own people had married yet, but I reckoned it wouldn't be long until some of us would acquire families.

A pang of regret stabbed me. It had been my intention to bring Night-eyes with me two years before. Her death, suffered defending my life, was a sorrow I would carry forever.

Introductions were in order. Reactions amongst my old trapping bunch ran the gamut from warm approval to consternation, depending upon the bred-in-the-bone bias of my various comrades. Universal amazement greeted my announcing that Powatawa was my Shawnee father. Brass Turtle fairly howled. "I allus knew ye had some good in ye, Temple! Injun blood! That's what it war all along! I should'a knowed!" He stepped forward, extending both hands to Powatawa, who took them in his own, smiling but saying naught. "Glad to have ye. Yer boy hyar allus did need some lookin' after!"

The whites, once they got over their surprise, extended a warm welcome to Powatawa. Our Indians — except for Brass Turtle, who always does his own thinking — Delawares and Iroquois alike, were at first passive, cool, uncertain how to greet this newcomer. I reckon the spectre of Tecumseh loomed in their memory, even those who themselves had been too young to witness the Shawnee leader's mostly-ignored call to arms against the Americans. Their people had come to rue their reluctance to join Tecumseh's resistance. Now they were exiles in their own land. Perhaps they were wary of reproach from this Shawnee arriving in their midst. Their standoffishness didn't last long. Brass Turtle, who stood with a foot in both worlds, red and white, soon jollied them out of their uncertainty. Before long they were hobnobbing with my father like old friends.

Micah was a different matter. A Negro was nothing new amongst our bunch. First there was Eddard Rose, who saved our bacon time and again in the early days with savvy gained from years of trading with the tribes on the Missouri, then living amongst the Crows as a respected war chief. When most of us were still green as grass, Rose's wise counsel and unassuming leadership taught us life-saving lessons about surviving in the wilderness. Surly and distant though he often was, every man amongst us owed a substantial debt to Eddard Rose.

Then there was big Jim Beckwith, a loudmouth braggart, to be sure, but Jim had proved his mettle in every fight and hard circumstance we encountered since he and Cesár Pérez joined our bunch three years before. I often wondered if Jim's colorful boasting of his exploits, his constant embroidering upon what he did, wasn't just his way of whistling past a cemetery, a need in him to assert his right to be considered an equal amongst the whites in our bunch. Bragging is common amongst trappers. Beckwith is a master at it.

Most of our people knew a little something of Micah from odd bits that Tuttle and I had mentioned in previous years, chiefly concerning our journey on Mike Fink's keelboat down the Ohio and up the Mississippi. Tuttle swept away any doubts about Micah when he announced, "Thi'shere darky — this man ri'chere! — war standin' hard as hick'ry back thar agin them'ere Blackfoots this mawnin'! I seen 'im! Fightin' jest as good, mebbe better, as ary man amongst us! I be proud to call 'im one of our own!" He paused for breath, then finished with, "'Sides, if Temple hyar sez he be fittin', thet's good 'nough fer me!"

Micah hung his head through it all, shifting uncomfortably at Tuttle's rough-hewn praise. I daresay he was blushing, if we had been able to tell. Approval rippled amongst the group. Ned Godey called out, "Glad to have ye!" and several other voices echoed that sentiment.

Only Jim Beckwith stood aloof and silent, staring straight ahead, face hard as granite. He made no objection, but he offered no welcoming smile or handshake, either. Once again I wondered at what might be going on in his mind. Until now Beckwith had been the only black man in the fur trade — now that Eddard Rose had returned to the Crows — although Jim always referred to himself as a whiteman. Like Rose, Beckwith was a mixture of races — white father, Negro-Cherokee mother — and his complexion was hardly darker than the rest of us, weathered as we were by sun and wind. Micah, fine-featured though he is, is black as ebony. I reckon Jim feared that now he might be lumped together with Micah as just another blackman. I reckoned, howsomever, it had to be Beckwith's personal conundrum. Only he could untangle it.

Finn McCool was still beholden to Black Harris and Bill Sublette for chores in the trader camp, so he wasn't present. Tuttle Thompson, howsomever, was not inclined to put off what might prove to be a difficult task. He stepped forward once again and said in a loud voice, "Shee-it! Let's be gittin' thi'shere interducin' bizness over an' done with! I been with thi'shere bunch since the fust giddy-up, so I reckon I got some kind o' say-so, once't'awhile, 'long with the rest o' ye. Thar be one more o' Temple's piebald menagerie what he brung along. He be workin' right naow fer Black an' Billy, so he cain't be talkin' fer hisownse'f right naow, but I reckon I kin be talkin' fer him, leastaways 'til he gits hyar. He be an Irisher name o' Finn McSumthin' an' I know as much about 'im as ever I need to. Hell! Ye don't hafta eat the whole buffler to larn if'n it be spiled! Thet'ere Irisher be one helluva Injun-fighter an' he hates Britishers an' he sure-as-hell knows hosses an' thet's enough fer me! What he don't know 'bout trappin' plews, we kin teach 'im, like I reckon we'll hafta fer Temple's paw and Micah hyar. I say we open the door fer all three of 'em an' git on with what we come hyar fer! Gittin' drunk an' laid! What'say?"

I reckon the gang was as flabbergasted as I was at Tuttle's oration, reluctant as he mostly is to be making long speeches. A roar of laughter and general assent greeted his words. It was time to put a lid on that confabulation. I called out, "Anybody thirsty?"

Micah and I hotfooted to our heap of packsaddles and rummaged amongst them, unearthing the tin canisters of booze, both of which had thankfully escaped Blackfoot arrows.

Two things are rarely distant from a trapper's grasp, his gun and his cup, especially the latter at rendezvous. I sloshed generous splashes of whiskey into each cup and Micah passed them on to their owners, which helped to assure their early acceptance of him.

As I have observed before, Black Harris is a first-rate trail boss, an unerring guide in the mountains or on the trackless prairie, and a consummate story-teller. He also possesses a nose as keen as any wapiti or buffalo if the faintest fragrance of booze happens to be floating on the breeze. In no time at all, Harris came trotting up, cup at the ready, grinning and fidgeting and urging me to greater haste as he impatiently waited his turn. Finn McCool stood behind him. Beyond them, loitering at the edge of camp, was Bill Sublette.

This was no time to be cultivating ancient grudges. Besides, I harbored no personal hard feelings towards Bill Sublette. Tough skinflint toady though he usually was, Bill had never done me harm. I hailed him with a smile and a friendly wave. "C'mon, Bill! Join us for a drink!"

"Don't mind if I do," he replied with a grin, padding forward, cup extended. I poured him a brimming cupful, served Harris and Finn, then filled my own before settling back on my heels and raising my cup in a toast.

"Here's to a long, hard ride thankfully completed an' better days ahead!" I swallowed a deep draught of Chouteau's best Kentucky whiskey, glorying in its golden fire as it burned through my gullet.

"Amen," Sublette concurred. Then, his face betraying difficulty in saying thankee, likely lest a show of gratitude might cost him something, he said, "Much obliged for helpin' out on the trail. Black's been tellin' me 'bout you an' yer pards an' what ye did gittin' up here."

I shrugged. "Same to you for lettin' us tag along. It's a fair swap. 'Pears we both got the best hoss."

Harris and McCool had wandered off, one greeting old friends, the other meeting new ones. Sublette let his gaze stray over our plenitude of bulging packs, doubtless imagining what they might contain, which was likely what had drawn him to our camp in the first place. At length he said cautiously, "Figgerin' on doin' some tradin' on yer own hook, are ye, Buck?"

I let him stew for a spell before I replied, purely enjoying his uneasiness. "Nope. Not at all. I'll be leavin' such doin's to you an' your pards, Bill. You're good at it. I ain't, nor wish to be."

Sublette's relief was obvious. I continued. "Naw, all o' that is presents for my ol' pards — plunder an' foofurraw ye likely don't carry in your trade goods, anyways." That wasn't precisely true, but it appeared to reassure Sublette considerably. "Nope," I went on, "I'm set on gettin' back to trappin', nothin' else — that an' teachin' Powatawa, Micah, an' McCool the beaver trade." Sublette was visibly brightening, which prompted me to add, "Which'll likely put some extra dollars in your poke, Bill, once they get the hang of it."

I refilled Sublette's cup and my own before I mentioned, "Naturally I'm hopin' ye won't be causin' Finn McCool any trouble 'bout not goin' back with your packstring. 'Pears there's always a few who don't find the mountains to their likin'. They can take his place. Ain't it so?"

Sublette swallowed hard and allowed that it was so. We touched cups to signify agreement, drained a final mouthful of Kentucky's superior squeezin's, and parted on better terms than I had ever enjoyed before with any of General Ashley's favorites.

Straight Kentucky corn whiskey is a couple-three times stronger than the trader's booze commonly served up at rendezvous, which is customarily well-watered straight grain alcohol flavored with plug tobacco, hot red peppers, and, some say, a couple rattlesnake heads thrown in for extra bite. By time I poured a couple more rounds for our bunch and a few other good friends, the whiskey canister was getting shallow and everybody was unsteady on his feet. Tough and young and healthy though trappers mostly are, a year-long alcohol drouth reduces any man's capacity for booze. It was time for the gifting.

Father Christmas could have felt no more pride and satisfaction than I did when Micah and I threw open our bales and distributed a cornucopia of clothing, carrots of tobacco, gunpowder and galena, knives and tools and other hardware, sailcloth, stout manila rope, and a galore of Indian trade goods for every man. Foodstuffs went to our campkeepers, Yves Dureau and Jean-Luc, who knew best how to put it to proper use for everybody's benefit. There was more than enough to go around. Nobody minded holes punched into shirts and capotes by Blackfoot arrows. Rendezvous is a time for strut and swagger. A rip here and there in colorful new clothing makes no nevermind.

Naturally I held back a tidy store for Powatawa, Micah, Finn, and myself, as well as an extra stock of Indian goods for Tuttle. His amorous forays require a plenitude of foofurraw to supplement his dubious charms. Even so, much of my plunder remained unspent.

When I presented Tuttle with the case of English razors, together with a poke filled with English lavender shaving soap tablets, he sniffed at the soap, then exploded in a horse laugh. "Shee-it, Temple! I purely don't know if'n I oughter be usin' thi'shere cornfection fer shavin' or jest go ahead an' eat it!"

The gifting at an end, I admitted my discomfort with the greasy gunsmoke from that morning's battle that still smeared my hands and arms. My face and neck itched with it. I kicked off my moccasins, stripped off my clothes, and sprinted for the lakeshore. I dropped my britchclout and plunged into the chill waters, amongst Brass Turtle and our other Indians, who never miss their daily bathe if opportunity affords.

I plumbed the depths, kicking my way to the bottom, scooped up handfuls of fine sand, and scraped my hide head to foot. At last, lungs fairly bursting, I broke the surface, skin tingling, gasping and sputtering, laughing out loud at simply being alive and amongst my friends.

Reluctant to quit the water, I struck out for a tree-shaded headland jutting out from the shore, glorying in the clean cold water, surprising strength flowing into my sweeping arms and scissoring legs, my body as buoyant as my soaring spirits, now and then diving and gliding beneath the surface, seeking glimpses of fish and plants, marveling at that underwater world.

When at last I surfaced I saw that I had passed around the point. I floated just outside a sheltered cove, where I spied a dozen or more naked golden-skinned women frolicking and splashing in the shallows, bosoms and bottoms jiggling delightfully, some of them slender and lithe a few somewhat plump, some downright chubby, others rather more so, all of them enchanting. I felt myself blushing. I chided myself for being a Peeping Tom. Still, I tarried, in spite of my conscience. It had been many months since I bade farewell to Lucette.

An alarmed shriek announced that I had been discovered. Then, oh what a divine spectacle there was of bouncing and jouncing and gelatinous elasticity as the ladies scurried for cover!

I watched the last coppery bottom out of sight, heaved a deep sigh, and prepared to swim back to camp, when the water just in front of me burst open and a golden-skinned naiad shot straight up out of it, for an instant exposed to her thighs, jaunty breasts streaming droplets, flaring hips framing a delicious dark triangle, long hair clinging to shapely shoulders, then all too quickly she was gone.

Stunned, I treaded water until she surfaced thirty feet away, eyes wide with fright, her expression terrified. Seeking to reassure her, I waved feebly and swam a stroke or two away from her. Her features softened and she almost smiled before flipping over like a diving otter and disappearing once again. The final image I retained of her was a pair of delicious golden moons vanishing into the depths.

When I rounded the point I discovered Brass Turtle floating on his back, waiting for me. "I war gittin' halfway concerned fer ye, bein' gone so long, so I follered along, jist in case."

"Ye saw all that, did ye?" I replied, somewhat disappointed but not surprised that he had shared my vision. Turtle rarely misses anything worthwhile.

"Reckon I did." He grinned. "Speakin' o' which, that'ere Flathead village'll bear lookin' into, wouldn't ye say?"

I allowed that it certainly would. Then we raced each other back to our own patch of shoreline. He won, but not by much.

* * *

Camp was busy as a kicked-over anthill. Pretty Horse and Little Mountain had gone out and killed a brace of buffalo cows. They spilled a heap of choice cuts and innards — tongue and liver, boudins, hump ribs and backstrap — onto a square of sailcloth next to a driftwood fire already crumbling to glowing coals. Yves and Jean-Luc, sporting colorful new shirts, sashes, and garters, bustled about skewering great gobbets of meat onto steel ramrods and putting chunks of tongue to boil in new tin-lined copper kettles. Ned Godey, clean-shaven now, clad in a new shirt and clean leathers, still somewhat tipsy from his libations, hailed me with a lopsided smile. "Ye done yerse'f proud, Temple, haulin' all o' that'ere plunder up hyar like ye done! Ever'body's lookin' like Chris'mas and Easter an' birthday all t'run together in them fancy new duds ye been spreadin' 'round. Much obliged!"

My face was burning. "Hell, Ned," I stammered, "it's nothin' much. Glad to do it," and other such nonsense.

Micah and my father were nowheres about. I spied their plunder and saddles stowed neatly together in a bower, sailcloth snugged expertly over a clutch of arching willows. Far off I could hear what was likely Anse Tolliver's fiddle scraping out a lively jig. I reckoned my companions were out and about, discovering the pleasures of rendezvous.

Searching for my own plunder, I spied Tuttle Thompson hunkered down, peering into a tiny looking-glass, his lean jaws slathered with soapy suds, earnestly scraping off his stubble. All of my property was heaped on one side of his bower. At my approach he sat back on his heels and brayed, "'Baout time ye war comin' home! Whar ye been? Thought ye might'a gone an' got yerse'fs drowneded, yew an' Turtle both!"

"No such luck, Tuttle," I replied. "I'm here to stay. You're stuck with me, like it or not!"

"Reckon I be, an' I'll jest haft'a try an' make the best of it," he grumbled in mock sorrow. He waved his razor towards my stack of goods and gear. "Ye can thank me fer totin' all o' yer plunder over hyar whilst ye war sportin' about with Turtle. I figgered ye'd be wishin' to be takin' up housekeepin' whar we left off when ye went back to the settlements, so I brung ever'thin' over hyar."

Fact is, I hadn't given it any thought at all, but since Powatawa and Micah had decided to pair up, returning to my old arrangement with Tuttle suited me. "Yep," I told him, "I reckon I can put up with ye, leastaways for a spell."

He burst into a horselaugh. "Yep, I reckon ye kin." Then, returning to his shaving chore, he said, "Much obliged, Temple, fer thi'shere razor an' all what goes with it. Makes shavin' plumb tol'able." His eyes went dreamy for an instant, then he added, "'Spesh'ly when I think on why I'm doin' it."

He continued scraping, wholly engrossed in removing every wiry whisker, marveling aloud the while at the keenness of the blade. At last he beamed into the mirror and exclaimed, "By gawd if'n I ain't the purtiest thang in thi'shere whole damn con-gree-gayshun! Whatcher mought be callin' plumb pluperfec' handsome! That's what I be, fer a fac'!"

I struck whilst the iron was hot. "Well now, if you're seekin' perfection, y'oughta trot on down to the lake there an' bathe yourself all over with some o' that sweet-smellin' soap. There's nary an Injun woman anywheres in all o' these mountains that could say no to ye if ye do that!"

Tuttle looked dubious. "Ye truly think so, Temple? This ain't one o' yer sly schemes to git me in the water?"

"Course not! Why, just smellin' that soap from your shavin' has got even me just about giddy already. Ain't a woman ever been born who could say ye nay after a whole bath of it!"

Now, Tuttle Thompson is not a stupid man. Far from it. You will likely never find a shrewder gambler or a more savvy horse trader in all your travels. But just thinking about women, especially after a long dry spell, gets him purely addled. I could almost see the wheels turning in his head.

"By gawd, it mought be so! I'll do 'er!" he exclaimed, snatching up a tablet of lavender soap and darting out of the bower without another word. I watched him, arms pumping, long legs scissoring, shedding his grimy leathers as he ran, until he leaped off the bank and splashed into the lake. "Well," I told myself, "it couldn't hurt." Even if he met with resistance from his intended conquests, sharing sleeping quarters with him would be much more pleasant.

In his absence, I lathered my face with his brush and shaved my scanty beard with his English razor, which surprisingly still possessed a fairly keen edge after harvesting Tuttle's formidable stubble. Shaving never takes me long. I have never grown much hair on my face or elsewhere on my body. Now I knew why, considering my paternity.

As I rummaged through my packs in search of my Sunday best, I came across the booze canisters buried beneath my other plunder. Tuttle had resisted his ever-present thirst for strong spirits, a remarkable sign of respect for which I felt immensely flattered. Tuttle never hesitates to rifle my plunder in search of foofurraw to further his courting of Indian women, but he always replaces whatever he takes, come next rendezvous. This was different. He knew that replacing honest-to-goodness Kentucky whiskey or French brandy can't be done in the mountains, so he left it untouched.

I filled two cups brimful of Kentucky's best as a reward for my comrade's admirable forbearance. Besides which, my earlier indulgence had commenced to wear off and I intended to make the most of this rendezvous, for which I had longed so desperately during the past two years.

By time Tuttle returned dripping from the lake, I had dressed in Snowflower's quilled antelope leggin's, Night-eyes' beautifully beaded moccasins, and a clean britchclout, topped with a bright-blue calico shirt cinched with a crisp new sash. Tuttle paused only long enough to don a britchclout before he snatched up his cup, clinked it against my own, gulped half its contents, and strangled out, "Hyar's to ye, pard. Good to have ye back!"

"Same to ye!" I replied simply, for I knew no words to tell him just how happy I was to be reunited with my own rowdy bunch of mountaineers.

Tuttle held out his cup for a second toast. "Wish me luck tonight, Temple. I be headin' fer ther Snake camp, callin' on a little widder woman from last year. I spied her agin today an' she gave me ther glad-eye, so I reckon I won't be troublin' ye with muh snorin'."

Mention of the Snake camp put me in mind of Snowflower, my winter-long lover of four years before. After we clinked cups again, I said, trying to make it sound like an idle question, "Ye seen Wáh-shah-kee here with his band?"

Tuttle sniggered. "Naw. He ain't. An' neither is thet li'l Flower Gal o' your'n. Ain't seen none of 'em since we wintered with 'em on the Popo Azhieh in 'twenny-four."

I stifled a sigh and admitted to myself that the Rocky Mountains cover a lot of country. It was unlikely that I would ever meet up with Snowflower again. I consoled myself with Tuttle's philosophy: There's always tomorrow, but more important and better — and sooner — there's tonight.

* * *

Throughout the late afternoon and early evening, small parties of free trappers, a brigade of Company men led by Tom Fitzpatrick and Jim Bridger, and some late-coming Indians straggled into rendezvous.

One of the last to arrive that day was a party of traders from Missouri Fur captained by our old friend Joshua Pilcher. He had altered considerably since we had last seen him in spring of 'twenty-four. He was no longer the sleek, ebullient, confident leader of men we recalled. Now he appeared fatigued by more than the journey, whipped and discouraged by high hopes frequently dashed by misfortunes that are all too common in the Rockies.

We learned that this year his cache of trade goods at South Pass had been nearly destroyed by springtime floods. What they were able to salvage would produce little profit for his outfit. Our bunch recalled Pilcher's good-natured generosity at a time when we sorely needed it and it was generally agreed that we would trade with him for whatever he had left that we could use. Naturally Powatawa, Micah, Finn, and I had no plews to trade this year, but I possessed hard cash aplenty, which would be a sight easier for him to carry back to the settlements.

Most of our people had returned to camp and gathered around the cookfire. Great chunks of hump and loin sputtered and dripped rich fat onto the coals. Coils of tasty boudins sizzled in three-legged spiders, and buffalo tongue bobbed in bubbling kettles. It had been a long, hungry day, so there was little palaver just then. Every man was busy stuffing himself, suspending his gobbling only long enough to step forward to slice off another slab of meat from the spit or spear yet one more tender morsel of tongue from a kettle.

At last I could hold no more. An antic thought occurred to me then. Sublette's trade tents had not opened that day. Bill was waiting for all the trappers to show up. No trader's booze was available. I lacked sufficient whiskey to satisfy that many thirsty gullets, but I recalled a drink I had enjoyed at Lucette's.

I obtained a large kettle, a pound of sugar, and a cupful of molasses from Jean-Luc and trotted back to my bower, where I mixed the remainder of my whiskey and the sugar and molasses in the kettle, then filled it to the brim with lake water. Likely it wasn't the best julep in the world, but there was enough to go around. Anyways, my people wouldn't know the difference.

"I reckon ye be gittin' back amongst us jest in time, Temple!" Tuttle exclaimed, waving his cup. "We feared ye war turnin' inter one o' them'ere Sain' Looie dandies, what with sech fancy drammin'! 'Pears ye war gittin entirely too civvy-lized fer mountain livin'!" He peered into his empty cup and added, "Ye got any more?"

Finn McCool, released for a spell from his duties with Sublette and Davey Jackson, raised his cup and announced, "I'm wishin' to be makin' a toast!" Weaving slightly, he bellowed out, "And on the last day, God made man — the Eye-talians fer their beauty — the French fer their dee-licious foine vittles — the Swedes fer intelligence — the Jews fer religion — and on and on, until He took a look at all thim He'd been after creatin' — an' He said, 'These craychures may be all very well, but nobody's havin' any fun! I'm thinkin' I need to be makin' Meself some Irishmen!' Drink up, lads!"

The chorus of laughter — Paddy McBride's the loudest of all — that greeted Finn's mock-serious toast provided assurance that I hadn't erred in bringing McCool into the bunch.

Paddy, the shortest man amongst us but apparently unaware of it, swaggered up to McCool, who towered a foot or more over him, and demanded, "Finn McCool, is it now? I've been hearin' about ye since I was a pup, I have, an' from all they was tellin', I'm thinkin' ye've been shrinkin' more'n somewhat of late, ain't ye?"

Paddy's sally was apparently a stale jest for Finnæus McCool, who had been named after the mythical Irish giant Finn McCool, but he responded in good grace. "Aye," he replied with a wry smile. "'Tis eatin' naught but taties in the Auld Sod that's done it. P'raps a sufficiency o' buffler meat'll be after restorin me former self."

Paddy barked an appreciative laugh and extended a welcoming handshake to his countryman.

Their bellies full, most of our bunch wandered off, Anse Tolliver amongst them, his rifle slung, fiddle case dangling from one hand, a still-smoking buffalo rib in the other. Brass Turtle caught my sleeve and asked, "What'say we take ourse'fs over yonder to that'ere Flathead camp an' see what we kin see?" I agreed, delaying only long enough to stop by my bower to pick up a few firesteels, some English flints, and half a dozen steel awls. I added a string of pretty sky-blue beads, then stuffed it all into my belt poke. I harbored a vague notion somewheres in the back of my head that I had unfinished business over there, although I knew not what it might be.

On the way to the Flathead camp I asked Turtle, "Have ye seen Jim Clyman yet?"

"Nope. An' it ain't likely we'll be seein' no more of 'im, neither. Ol' Jim went back to the settlements with Sublette arter ronnyvoo last year. Sez he's quittin' the mountains fer good."

"How come?" I asked, surprised. "That doesn't sound like Jim, of all people."

"Hard to say," Turtle replied. "Best I kin figger, it might'a been what happened to him an' ol' Pierre Tivanitagon, that'ere Oneida Iroquois trapper what jumped off o' Pete Ogden's Canucks an' come trappin' on our side. He be the one we been callin' Pierre's Hole arter. The way Clyman war tellin' it, him an' Pierre got to feelin' sassy an' went trappin' on their own hook purty far north inter Blackfoot country, whar the most of us don't hanker to be strayin' on our own, no matter how good the trappin' be."

I was not surprised to hear that. Generally quiet, good-humored Jim Clyman possesses a bold, resolute streak that he mostly hides under a witty, easy-going manner. Jim had been a good frind and valued companion ever since we first met him during the Arikara Campaign in 'twenty-three.

"Wal, Jim an' ol' Pierre —" Turtle pronounced the name Peer, as most of us do, "the two of 'em war gittin' rich up thar, hidin' out durin' the day an' runnin' their traps only fust thing at daylight an' jist afore dark, stayin' shy o' Blackfoots, movin' camp reg'lar, an' keepin' to the willers 'longside o' the cricks they war workin'."

Turtle allowed himself a wry chuckle. "Like I say, they war storin' up a gawdawful passel o' plews an' cachin' 'em hyar an' thar, all the time congratulatin' theirsef's on outsmartin' the Blackfoots, until one time they war ridin' in some heavy timber whar they cain't see much, when they realize they've gone an' rode straight into a whole gawddamn camp o' Píkunis!"

Turtle barked out a short, dry laugh. "Wal, like Jim told it, thar warn't nothin' else they could do jist then but ride straight up to the big lodge they reckoned b'longed to the chief, claimin' in hand-talk that they done it a-purpose, aimin' to pass the night with 'im, countin' on him respectin' their gall an' bein' obliged to show 'em some proper horsepitality.

"Accordin' to Jim, that'ere Piegan chief din't look none too happy, but he war sorta caught in a crack, 'twixt showin' respect fer their nerve an' takin' their ha'r. Howsomever, he tol' his women to sarve up some vittles, which Clyman an' Pierre, even hungry like they war, din't have a deal of appetite fer, jist then. Arterwards, a bunch o' them'ere Píkunis come inter the lodge an' commenced palaverin', which neither Clyman ner Pierre savvied, but they caught on from the chief's hand-talk that he reckoned they oughta be kilt.

"Natcherly thar warn't nothin' they could do right then, but jist afore dark, the two of 'em hotfooted fer the trees, arrers an' galena flying all about 'em, an' ran fer the river. Clyman lost track o' Pierre about then. He jumped inter the crick an' swum acrost an' hid hisse'f under the bank 'til the Blackfoots gave up lookin' fer 'im. Jim sez he never seen Pierre arter that — reckons he went under whilst they war runnin' off."

We were by then nearing the outskirts of the Salish camp. Turtle hastened to finish his tale. "That warn't the end of it fer Clyman, howsomever. Lackin' nigh all o' his plunder an' his critters, too, he hiked on down thisaway 'til he run inter some trappers an' got an outfit together. Then he rode back up thar an' got all o' them'ere plews an' brung 'em on down hyar to ronnyvoo. He din't trade 'em off, though. He carried the lot of 'em off to Sain' Looie on his own hook, so's he could sell 'em off by hisownse'f, which natcherly din't happify Billy Sublette nohaow, as ye might be supposin'. Jim said he din't reckon he'd ever be comin' back to the mountains, much as he loves 'em."

Although I regretted losing Jim Clyman's witty companionship, his keen mind, and unwavering loyalty to his fellows, I wished him well in whatever new pursuit he fancied.

* * *

There is a feeling you get when you enter an Indian camp, a certain sensation that tells you if you're welcome or not. Bannocks and Lahcotahs make you wary, suspicion and hostility seeming to hang in the air. Snakes generally make you feel warm, as if you had been invited, even if you weren't. The Flatheads appeared to be the latter sort, even though I knew that every eye in their encampment was taking note of everything Turtle and I did as we ambled idly amongst the neatly-aligned lodges, nodding and smiling at the older folk, careful not to stare at the younger women, dodging unruly hordes of shouting, laughing, healthy-looking kids and their dogs, pausing now and again to inhale flavorful aromas floating from a double score of cookfires, stirring appetite I had supposed had been more than sated by our own feast, then resuming our unhurried stroll towards the center of camp.

"Why do ye reckon they call these people Flatheads, Turtle?" I asked. "I haven't spied a single one of 'em lookin' like that. Fact is, they look to be a handsome lot."

He snorted. "Whiteman foolishness, I reckon. Mebbe the fust one o' these hyar partic'lar Injuns some white-eyes ever seen had a funny-lookin' head, so natcherly, bein' the way whites mostly be, they jist kept on callin' 'em so ever since. Hell! Like they don't call us Len-ah-pee! 'Stead, they call us Delawares, arter some white'arse guv'nor we never even heard of! These hyar Injuns call theirse'fs the Sah-lish. An' you're right. They be a good-lookin' bunch, ain't they? 'Speshly the womenfolk."

We halted at a sizeable open space, where a driftwood fire was burning. In no time at all three middle-aged, well-dressed men, likely headmen from their appearance and manner, emerged from a lodge and approached us. One of them spoke to us in a pleasant-sounding language I had never heard before, at the same signing a welcome, which I did understand. Even if I hadn't, his smiling features bespoke friendliness.

Turtle responded, speaking English slowly and smoothly signing what he was saying, how we had come to pay our respects and to show our friendship for the Sah-lish people, how we hoped that these men would come to our lodges one day and share meat with us, and a passel of other sociable flim-flam.

It is doubtful that any of the three headmen understood a single syllable of Brass Turtle's English, but their smiles grew broader as he spoke and gestured. Whatever whitemen they had previously encountered had likely been rough and ready trappers, untutored in the etiquette of the redman. Turtle, on the other hand, was smooth and mannerly, properly respectful, but dignified in the fashion of a man who knows his own worth.

Naturally it didn't hurt that Turtle was himself an Indian, albeit of a far-off nation unknown to the Sah-lish. And I wasn't too far off the mark, either, thanks to Powatawa.

When the palaver slowed to a halt, Turtle reached into his pouch and presented a sizeable twist of tobacco to each of the headmen and I lost no time in stepping forward to gift them each with a firesteel and a large English flint. They all spoke at once, babbling away in their ear-pleasing tongue, meanwhile signing that we must come to their lodge to eat and smoke. Which naturally we did.

The appetite of a Rocky Mountain trapper is a prodigy that will likely never be understood by folks in the settlements. No matter that he has just eaten to a surfeit, if there is meat to be had, a mountaineer will just naturally surround it. Stuffed to the gills though we had been only an hour earlier, I daresay we did ourselves proud, gnawing our way through a respectable stack of buffalo ribs, after which we smoked with our hosts, all of us signing mutual friendship and respect for one another.

When at last we emerged from the lodge the sun was dipping behind the western mountains. It was still daylight, howsomever, so Turtle and I were in no hurry as we made our way through the lanes. We could tell that word of the headmen's hospitality had spread throughout the band, for the mood of the Sah-lish had altered. Where before there had been quiet, aloof reserve, now we were greeted with friendly nods and smiles, even by some of the women.

But not all of them. I spied one woman who instantly absorbed all my attention. Even through her loose deerhide work dress I descried the shapely form of my naiad of the lake. She was kneeling, head bowed, intent upon her chore, fleshing a fresh buffalo hide, but when she sneaked a furtive glance at us, I was sure of it. No other woman that I had seen in all that camp possessed her fine dark eyes, sleek facial planes, full rosy lips, and graceful neck. Abandoning all caution and whatever better judgment I possess, I went to her, dropped to one knee, and commenced signing an apology for intruding upon her and the other women earlier that day, doing my best to declare my innocence, hoping the while that the longing that must be flowing from my eyes would not belie my sincerity.

At first she recoiled, startled, falling back upon her heels, twisting slightly as if to flee, but she didn't. As I babbled nonsense in my own tongue, my hands and fingers continued to flutter and fly with skill I never knew I possessed. Sign language, howsomever, useful as it is, severely limits the depth and color of what you wish to say, so I found myself simply repeating what I had already told her. By time I found myself rendering the same apologies for the third or fourth time, I saw that she was paying less attention to my hands and was gazing more upon my face. At last she raised her hand to check my protestations. Her face softened almost to a smile and she signed that she bore me no ill will.

Relieved, I fell silent, my hands at rest, bereft of any idea of what to do or say next. Which, the more I pondered it, was nothing. I had taken my best shot. Unsure if my gesture would be well-received, I dug into my pouch and placed the string of blue beads on the buffalo hide, together with a scatter of awls, then rolled back onto my feet and with a final awkward bow retreated to where Brass Turtle stood, laughing and chatting in signs with a number of other women.

"Ye reckon ye got 'er done, pard?" he asked with a chuckle.

I nodded and replied, "Best I know how, anyways. P'raps we best be makin' tracks outa here. Sorta let it simmer, as ye might say."

Turtle grunted his assent and we resumed our stroll. Before we passed out of sight amongst the lodges, howsomever, I stole a final peek at my naiad. She was smiling now with a kind of wonder in her eyes. The blue beads lay untouched before her, but, I consoled myself, leastaways she hadn't thrown them in my face.

We walked on in silence for a spell. I admitted to myself that I was truly smitten, that all my apologizing was in fact a manner of courting. I wondered if she thought so, too. At length I blurted, "Hell, I don't even know if she's got a man of her own!"

"Nope. She don't. She's a widder. I ain't been idle, Temple. Them other women tol' me so. Blackfoots kilt her man more'n a year ago. That's her daddy's buffler hide she war a-chorin' on."

Hope surged in me for a moment, then doubt set in. I realized that even if my naiad were unencumbered with a husband, I didn't really know how to go about wooing her. The bred-in-the-bone casual courtship skills of, say, Tuttle and Brass Turtle, for two excellent examples, were mostly a mystery to me.

We marched on without saying anything more, until I said, "Ye know, I don't even know her name."

"They call 'er somethin' like Rainbow Minner, best I can make out from the signin'," Turtle replied promptly. "Couldn't catch how ye say it in Sah-lish, but that's what it means. Comes from how she loves swimmin' an' how she's good at it."

Rainbow Minnow had a pleasant sound to it, but, I reflected with an inward chuckle, my naiad had long since become a delightfully grown-up mermaid indeed.

As we neared the outer ring of lodges I became aware that we were being followed. I called it to Turtle's attention.

"Yep, I seen 'em," he said. "Kids. Likely they're doggin' us hopin' fer a handout. Ye got somethin' fer 'em?"

"Reckon I do, but they'll need to follow us back to camp."

"Reckon they will. If fer nothin' else, jist to see how we live. Don't reckon these hyar Sah-lish've had much truck a-tall with trappers."

A few rods outside the Sah-lish encampment I turned and beckoned to the children, letting them know that they had been discovered and that they were at liberty to follow us home. Which they did.

Tuttle was absent from the bower, but that surprised me not all. Inside, aided by the last glimmer of sunset, I pawed through my plunder, at last unearthing a poke of peppermint sticks. At first the little boys looked puzzled, uncertain what to do with the candy, until I retrieved a stick from one lad, bit off a morsel, and grinned at them. They quickly got the idea and ran off into the gathering darkness shrieking gleefully.

Satisfied that at least I had made my peace with my naiad, I reckoned the occasion called for a toast to that minor success. Brass Turtle enthusiastically concurred. I filled our cups with fine French cognac, which restored glorious sunshine to my belly if not to the sky, then, adhering to the principle that it is unwise to try to fly on one wing, we indulged in a second cupful.

As we chatted about the evening's events I noticed that Turtle was becoming distracted. At length he confessed that he might have some unfinished business back in the Sah-lish camp. Again I was not surprised. As he had said earlier, he hadn't been idle whilst I was occupied with my apologies. I bade him Godspeed and my Delaware friend lost no time in disappearing into the night.

It had been a long, hard day, overflowing with enough adventures to fill an ordinary week. I was bone-weary. Sleep beckoned and I saluted its authority. I laid my pistol, horn, and pouches aside, then, taking advantage of the relative safety of rendezvous, where such affectations may be tolerated, I shucked my moccasins, slipped out of my clothes, and crawled onto my sleeprobes.

A maelstrom of images whirled through my mind — the charge through Blackfoot ranks, the battle, Novak tumbling headfirst downhill, reunion with my bunch, pride in my comrades and my father, the gifting, and myriad others — and, at the vortex, a glorious naiad emerging from the deep, golden and shimmering, smiling now, taking my hand and leading me off into a fathomless, dreamless sleep.

* * *

Leastaways it was dreamless at first, as far as I can tell, but at some point I became aware that Lucette had entered my slumber, snuggling her body against my back, her breath warming my neck, recalling fleshly pleasures now a thousand miles away. It was only when a gently searching hand stole across my midriff and grasped my private part that I fled that pleasant dreamland and struggled to rise up, terrified that my bower had been invaded, that an enemy meant me mortal harm of the worst possible sort. A restraining arm of surprising strength held me down and I heard a soft voice murmuring reassuring syllables in a tongue unknown to me. I fell back, reason replacing fright, realizing that if this were indeed a foe, establishing a truce might be a most agreeable chore.

I swiveled to face the invader, immediately reassured that this was no Blackfoot warrior when she pressed her full, firm breasts against my chest, clasping me close, her face against my throat, the fragrance of her hair making me giddy with desire. A waxing three-quarter moon had risen in a cloudless sky, bathing the bower in a pearly glow. Reluctantly I thrust my all-too-welcome captor from me, just far enough to let me know that my visitor was indeed my naiad, all the goddess that I could possibly wish for. No ancient Greek was ever more generously blessed than I just then.

Impulsively I leaned to kiss her, but as our lips touched she twisted away with a startled yelp. I grinned, reassured that she had never before been with a whiteman. Kissing was unknown to her, so also were the venereal maladies too often bestowed on Indian women by trappers and traders. So far I had avoided such blights and I intended to continue thus.

I began again, this time nuzzling her neck, then nibbling her ear, pressing my lips to her cheek and letting my tongue stray, until at last

I kissed her gently, softly resting my lips against hers. Her resistance melted and soon she joined in this whiteman's foolishness with enthusiasm, exploring its many pleasing possibilities with the zeal of a convert.

I found myself in conflict. Saint Louis was a long way away, both in distance and in time. It seemed a lifetime since I had been with a woman. I needed desperately to plunge, to quench without delay the fire this woman ignited in me, yet I was unwilling to forego the delight of exploring her magnificent body, bringing to bloom every possible shred of pleasure and passion.

Reluctantly I abandoned her lips and kissed her neck, the hollow place at her throat, her firm but yielding breasts, first one, then the other, teasing her pert nipples, hard as unripe berries, then descending to savor the fragrance, the clean, exciting woman smell and taste of her muscular belly, her navel, at last to lose myself in the enchanting bouquet of her most secret place. I could barely hear her groans of fulfillment until she caught hold of my shoulders and hauled me onto her breast, guiding me home, gripping me ever closer, kissing and nipping my lips and ears and neck, the two of us squirming and plunging and lunging and thrusting, until at last we thrashed our way to a groaning, shrieking, shuddering mutual arrival in paradise.

We lay entwined, panting, both of us slick with sweat and shivering in the chill night air, locked in a tight embrace neither of us wished to loosen, she cooing soft words into my ear that for once I was sure I understood.

All too soon she wriggled from my arms and slipped out of the bower. A pang of disappointment was swiftly quelled when I caught sight of her dress and moccasins carelessly discarded beside my pallet. I lay marveling at my good fortune, hardly daring to ponder how it had come about, lest I break the spell and frighten it away, revisiting each delicious moment and sensation, yearning for her return.

Which wasn't long in coming. She ducked into the bower, bearing my kettle, then dropped to her knees and proceeded to lave my sweaty body, head to toe and every nook and cranny, with a swatch of soft-tanned deerskin, pausing now and again to lean over me to kiss my lips. She glistened in the moonlight, her lithe body still dripping from her visit to the lake, the sight of her limned against the starry sky arousing me, mind and body, recently so completely limp from our exertions, now anything but.

Her ministrations completed, she put aside her utensils and returned to my side, threw herself onto me and straddled my mid-section, pinning me down, kissing and caressing my face and throat, my chest and beyond, her lips and artful hands and busy fingers returning the favor I had recently bestowed on her. She returned that favor so expertly, with such inspired fervor, that in a fleeting moment of lucidity I caught myself hoping that I had done nearly half so well by her.

Sensing that I was near bursting, she tried to fling herself onto her knees beside me, head down, inviting me to enter in the fashion of her people. I refused, hauling her back instead and restoring her to her former perch, achieving our joining, grasping her hips, encouraging her to ride her mount to a standstill. Which she did, admirably, crowing and laughing aloud at yet another example of whitemen's peculiar ways, smothering my face with kisses, shuddering with delight as I attended to her delicious nipples, until with a throaty cry she collapsed upon my chest just as I was able to restrain myself no longer.

That wasn't the end of it, not by a long chalk, but from then on we were more leisurely in our attentions, exploring and learning by heart the geography of her body and she of mine, discovering what pleased the other best, and how we might achieve our mutual pleasure.

After each love-making she led me to the lake. We frolicked like otter pups, recalling my first glimpse of her half a day before. Then, giggling, she raced me back to our robes, where we eagerly resumed our lessons.

At last I fell into exhausted slumber, holding her close, my face buried in her hair, lost in the natural perfume of this healthy young woman of the mountains, wishing for no better mate or companion, now and again praying to I-know-not-Whom that she felt likewise.

* * *

I awakened sweating, hot sunshine streaming into the bower, Tuttle Thompson's twanging voice ringing in my ears. "Like I tol' ye an' I tol' ye, time an' agin, Temple! 'Tain't fittin' fer ye to be layin' about whar ever'body kin see ye in jest yer bare-nekkid hide! Makes 'em feel bad, jealous, don'tcha know!" I squinted up at him leaning into the open front of our shelter, a huge horse-toothed grin nigh splitting his face. "Like it says right thar in ther Good Book, it's pride what makes ye fall off'n yer hoss — er somethin' like thet!" He let out a huge guffaw. "Preacher-raised like ye war, y'oughta know thet!"

I clutched at my nether parts, snatched up my britchclout, and exploded past him, racing to the lakeshore, loudly cussing him and his comicality all the way. The cold water instantly restored my respectability, allowing me to swim back to shore, retrieve my britchclout, and return to the bower. I found Tuttle inside, sniffing about in an exaggerated fashion, grinning like a crazy ape. "So ye ain't been lonesome whilst I was out an' about, upholdin' whatcha mought be callin' the fambly honor, warn't ye?" He sniffed again, elaborately. "I kin tell! I got a nose fer sech thangs! C'mon! Ye kin tell yer ol' pard!"

I allowed that I hadn't been lonely in the least, especially not by being deprived of the dubious pleasure of his company. He roared loud enough to make the bower tremble. Then, "Hell! I reckon ye desarve some corn-gratchulations! Din't take ye no time a-tall, gittin' back inter mountain-style! I be proud o' ye!" He sniffed again, this time in the direction of the cookfire. "Reckon we both be needin' a bellyful o' vittles. Let's be gittin' over thar, 'fore it's all gone! Swivin' be hungry work an' it 'pears we both be needin' to be keepin' up our stren'th!"

I heartily agreed. I was famished. When I grabbed up my shirt, a string of blue beads and half-a-dozen awls fell to the ground. I was puzzled. Then I took it to mean that she was telling me that it was honest desire for me, neither gratitude nor greed, that brought her to my bed and kept her there last night.

Now it was I who was grinning like a crazy ape when I joined Tuttle and trotted off to break our fast.

On the way I spied a score of pack animals loaded with bulging packs of beaver plews, Tuttle's amongst them, picketed outside our camp, ready for the trading that morning.

Knowing grins greeted us when we squatted at the cookfire and helped ourselves to the plentiful remains of last night's feast and a cupful of Jean-Luc's newly-made pease-porridge, liberally laced with crispy bits of buffalo meat.

"'Bout time yew two showed yerse'fs hyarabouts," Anse Tolliver declared sternly. "Y'oughter be'shamed o' yerse'fs, sleepin' away Gawd's own daylight like ye done." Then, riveting his gaze upon me, evil humor dancing in his flinty blue eyes, "An' yew, Temple Buck, y'ain't even 'pologizin' fer deprivin' honest trappers o' their rightful sleepin', cavortin' like a gawddamn horny mink-critter like ye war doin' all night long, makin' sech a racket an' excitin' sinful thinkin' 'mongst yer innercent pardners thet'll sartinly lead to more o' thet'ere mortal sinnin', givin' ary oppi'tunity!" Tolliver's bony jaws snapped shut, his thin lips compressed to stifle a snicker. He failed. He broke into a raucous cackle, totally destroying his comical attempt to express preacher-like righteous indignation.

Even so, I blushed in spite of myself. Concern about disturbing my neighbors had been the farthest thought from my mind the night before. Now I felt somewhat embarrassed by our noisy coupling, but not much. It had been worth it. What I might have replied was lost in laughter at Anse's mock-pious sermon and my own discomfiture. "Don't let 'im josh ye, Temple," Ned Godey called out. "He's jist feelin' green 'cause ye beat 'im to it!"

"Thar's all kinds o' fiddlin', Anse!" Brass Turtle put in. "You do your'n an' we'll do our'n!" Except for a scratch or two on his neck, he appeared to be none the worse for completing his unfinished business.

"Let us all be after learnin' a lesson from Temple's teachin'!" Paddy McBride announced with burlesque solemnity. "He's after breakin' trail fer the rest of us laggards an' I, fer one, promise to be profitin' by his good example!"

Micah, Finn, and my father sat amongst the others, not contributing to the jesting but apparently enjoying it. Powatawa was smiling broadly, perhaps recalling his own youth and thinking, like father, like son. I dismissed the thought with still another blush. Cesár Pérez squatted with them, eyes crinkled and lips twitching in quiet amusement. Jim Beckwith was nowheres about.

Our Iroquois and Delawares, except for Little Mountain, were for the most part silent, permitting themselves only fleeting grins, sly looks in my direction, and rapid exchanges in their own tongues. They, and Cesár, too, had acquired a passel of American palaver during my absence.

Whoops and shouts from the direction of Sublette's trade tents signaled the opening of trading. As if a giant hand swept them away, our camp emptied of all but us newcomers and the campkeepers, everyone else grabbing up their loaded pack animals and racing to join the crowd gathering at the traders.

I refilled my cup with pease-porridge and joined my companions. "Well, what d'ye think of rendezvous so far?" I asked.

Finn was first to reply. "'Tis a pleasant gatherin', to be sure, Temple, but it's not the Donnybrook Fair ye were tellin' us about, comin' up here."

I laughed. "Just wait 'til this bunch gets a skinful o' Sublette's rotgut. That'll light the fuse on the powder keg. I daresay ye'll consider your Irish brawls to be a Sunday School picnic, next to the goin's-on hereabouts."

McCool grinned. "I'm devoutly hopin' so. Och, it's been intirely too long that it's been all dry work an' no play a'tall fer this partic'lar Mick."

Neither Powatawa nor Micah had anything to say on the matter. They were content to wait and see. I had no idea if either of them would join in the coming merriment. It was up to them.

I excused myself and returned to my bower. I had naught better to do just then and, recalling Finn's eager anticipation of tying on a proper Irish drunk and guessing where the bulk of his meager wages would go, now was as good a time as any to provide him with the basic tools of his intended trade. After that, he must be on his own. I buckled on my knife and pouches, shoved my pistol into my belt, and set off for Missouri Fur's little trade camp.

It was nearly deserted. Most trappers were by then clustered around Smith, Jackson, & Sublette's much larger establishment. A dour Joshua Pilcher stood behind a counter of rough-hewn planks. I greeted him with "Good mornin', Major Pilcher," employing the title he had borne during the disastrous Arikara Campaign in 'twenty-three. The salt-and-pepper beard I remembered was now mostly white. The snapping black eyes had lost much of their lustre.

A flickering smile graced his lips, howsomever, when he replied, "Mornin', Mister Buck. Yes, you were there. Seems like long ago, doesn't it?" I allowed that it did, mouthing some nonsense about water over the dam or under the bridge or wherever. Then, ever the businessman, he asked, "An' what may I do for ye this mornin'?"

"Well, first of all, would ye be willin' to trade for hard money? I have no plews this year. I've just come up from the settlements myself." His interest kindled at the mention of cash. "'Pears to me gold coin'll tote a sight easier'n plews anyhow, "I added.

He allowed that one was as good as the other, providing there was enough of either one. Looking over his pitiful stock of trade goods, much reduced by the ravages of the spring flood, I was hard put to discover enough useful items to make a decent purchase. Bolts of trade cloth and spools of ribbon and thread were faded and frayed with rot. Foodstuffs were absent. Metal items — knives, tomahawks, guns, copper kettles, and the like — were mostly flecked with rust or green with corrosion. Even so, I found a sufficiency of useful goods to make the transaction worthwhile for our former benefactor, chiefly, half-a-dozen used but serviceable English-made beaver traps of Manchester manufacture, galena pigs, several horns of gunpowder sealed against the damp, a couple kettles, and a passel of glass beads, brass tacks, and other foofurraw.

Whilst a clerk bundled my plunder into croker sacks, two men entered the trade tent. Pilcher introduced a stocky sandy-haired man as Andy Drips, the other he called Major Vanderburgh. Addressing the major, he said, "And this is Mister Temple Buck, one of Andy Henry's trappers who fought so well agin the Rees in Leavenworth's fiasco in 'twenty-three. Reckon you didn't get to know 'em, busy as you were with your cannons and such." Vanderburgh smiled and nodded politely but said nothing. After a brief word with Pilcher, they departed.

Pilcher and I dickered not at all. The figure he named for the lot was surprisingly modest for a Rocky Mountain trader. I paid without protest. When the clerk took my plunder outdoors, Pilcher quietly informed me that this would be Missouri Fur's final foray into the mountains. The Rockies had whipped him. There was naught I knew to say that might comfort him. Besides, it would have been presumptuous of me to try. Defeated though he was, Joshua Pilcher is a man of great pride and noble bearing. I would not demean him with expressions of sympathy.

Outside, as I prepared to return to camp, I chanced to spy a handsome long-barreled flintlock pistol stuck into the sash of the man Pilcher had called Andy Drips. Fortunately it was a .54-caliber, the same bore as our Hawken percussion weapons. Naturally Drips was reluctant to part with his pistol, bullet mold, and fixin's, but the gold coins I offered, worth three or four such pistols in Saint Louis, swiftly changed his mind. Gold outweighs gunmetal every time.

Thoroughly satisfied with my visit, I bade Major Pilcher and his people farewell and, my belt bristling with hardware, lugged my sacks back to my bower.

* * *

"Been over to Pilcher's, have ye?" Tuttle demanded affably. His slurred speech and the half-empty kettle of booze at his side testified to his successful visit to Sublette's trade tents. "He got much plunder, do'ee?"

I dropped my sacks with a clattering thud and allowed that he had some, but likely not nearly as much as Sublette.

"'Tain't hardly so. Ol' Billy's stock be purty measly this year. Mostly jest what's left o' what he cached last fall. T'warn't fer what you an' Black fetched up hyar, we'd'a been hard put fer gittin' through two whole seasons comin' up, 'speshly us free trappers. Natcherly Billy be lookin' after his own Comp'ny men fust. Free men be suckin' hind tit."

"Ye get any plunder from Billy last fall, when he came up from Missourah?"

"Naw. We din't jine up with Bobby Campbell 'til winter camp an' then it war too late, 'ceptin' fer some powder an' lead we got from Bobby. We had ourse'fs a coupl'a good harvests, but ye'd hardly know it, ragged-arse poor like we be!"

"Ye'd best git on over to Pilcher, then. He's still got powder an' galena an' some foofurraw for Injun trade. It'll be enough to get us through 'til next year. 'Twon't be fat cow, but we likely won't be starvin', neither." Then, knowing Tuttle as I do, I asked, "Got any plews left ye ain't traded yet?"

"Yep. Plenty. An' not only thet, I got a heap more credit on Billy's cipher book right naow'n I ever done afore! Ain't had time to drink it up!" He commenced laughing, then choked off, a pained look on his face. "Ye don't 'spose mebbe Billy's runnin' short o' likker, too, do ye?" Gloom shrouded his spirit. "If thet be so, thi'shere ronnyvoo's gonna go daown in hist'ry as the stingiest, measliest, wust ronnyvoo thar ever war!"

Tuttle tipped up his kettle and gulped a substantial swig, then offered it to me. Naturally I accepted, the fiery brew searing a furrow through my gullet and into my belly, arguing convincingly that Sublette's clerks had indeed flavored it with rattlesnake heads.

My friend rose unsteadily to his feet and announced, "I best be gittin' over yonder to Pilcher's, afore what he's got left be all gone." He lurched outdoors, grabbed up the tether of his packhorse, and headed for Missouri Fur.

Our camp was mostly deserted, Powatawa and Micah nowheres in sight. I had nothing to do, so I stripped down to my britchclout and trotted down to the shore. I swam straight for the wooded jut of land nigh the Flathead camp, but a quick look-about there produced no sign of my naiad. Disappointed, I swam slowly back, wondering the while if she would ever visit me again.

As midday approached, our people commenced straggling back to camp, most of them staggering somewhat, toting kettles, laughing and jesting and hallooing hoarse greetings to long-unseen friends they spied along the way. Yves and Jean-Luc puttered about the cookfire, serving up the remains of yesterday's buffalo. Appetizing aromas drifted on the light breeze, reminding me that I was hungry again

Whilst I gnawed at a hump rib, Micah and Powatawa returned, helped themselves from the fast-dwindling meat supply, and joined me. I was restless, not yet ready to plunge into rendezvous frolics. "Meat's gettin' scant," I said. "What'say we ride out and get ourselves a couple buffler 'fore they're all spooked clean out o' the valley?" They nodded enthusiastic assent.

"I've been wantin' to go out huntin', all mornin' long, Temple," Micah replied when he finished chewing, "but I reckoned you might have other business in mind." He sniggered and poked Powatawa in the ribs. They laughed.

"Fact is, I did and I still do," I said, trying to face them down. "But it'll hafta wait, leastaways 'til dark." Then, "And it wouldn't do you any harm to get yourself over to one o' the Injun camps. It'll be a long dry spell for everybody, once rendezvous's over." I directed my remark mainly to Micah, but I secretly hoped that my father might take still another step away from the austere discipline he had imposed upon himself amongst his Shawnee band.

Powatawa's expression grew serious, but his dark eyes were twinkling. "All things in their time," he said, the smile returning to his face. "New country, new life, new ways. Who can know?"

A quarter-hour later we were riding across the valley, pack animals in tow. The buffalo had drifted off the prairie, into brushy draws that bordered the broad valley, shunning the bustle and din of the rendezvous. A mile or so distant from camp we discovered a good-size bull and his harem of mostly fat young cows grazing in a grassy glade surrounded by a stand of lodgepole and quakies. We dismounted downwind, tethered our critters, and crept to the edge of the clearing, screened by trees and high grass. We each chose a young cow, hardly much bigger than heifers but promising a plenitude of tender fat meat.

At my nod, we fired together. The hillside rang with the blast of three heavy rifles going off at once. Two cows, Powatawa'a and mine, immediately crumpled to their knees, shaggy heads swaying, coughing blood through nose and mouth. The rest thundered off, tails sticking straight up, churning through the tall grass, Micah's cow with them, lagging somewhat behind.

"Damn!" he cried, sheer anguish in his voice. "Missed her! How'd I do that?"

"Don't be so sure," I cautioned. "Some buffler take more killin' than some others."

Before I got all the words out, Micah's cow skidded to a halt, bearded chin plowing a bloody furrow in the grass, collapsed in a heap, and lay unmoving, hardly three rods distant from where she had been shot.

"Like I said," I crowed, "ye got 'er plumb center! I'll wager on it! She just had a sight more sand than t'other'ns!"

Micah was skeptical, but when we butchered her out we saw that his ball had ripped through her lungs and busted her heart. Nobody could ask for a better shot.

We butchered the first two cows first, naturally taking time out to slice off mouthfuls of fresh liver, still smoking hot, sprinkled with gall, the hunter's just reward. We were working on Micah's cow when a horrendous snarling roar froze us at our chore. A huge grizzly boar, shaggy hide shimmering silver in the sunshine, came lumbering through the grass not thirty yards away, pausing every few yards to r'are up on his hocks and bellow homicidal threats.

Our first impulse, quickly abandoned, was to run for the trees, but the bear would surely have run one of us down before we could shinny to safety.

Every grizzly bear looks huge when first you see him, but this one required no exaggerating. We dived for our guns, then jumped behind the buffalo carcass, trying to put some kind of barrier between Old Ephraim and ourselves, no matter how futile that might be. "Try to hit 'im in the mouth when he hollers!" I called out without thinking, in my excitement harking back to Uncle Ben's advice concerning black bears when I was a lad back in Ohio.

I fired first. My ball thudded into his chest. He hardly faltered, just kept plodding on, bawling his displeasure. I was dumping powder down the bore, my still-bloody fingers fumbling for a second ball, when Powatawa fired. His ball ripped into the brute's throat, throwing him sidewise for a moment but halting his charge hardly at at all.

"In the mouth, ye say?" Micah yelled. Ephraim was barely half a dozen strides away from us when he r'ared up to his full height. He looked to be tree-top high, snarling and bellowing, piggy little red eyes glaring, wicked, long-clawed paws batting the air, letting out an ear-splitting roar that nearly drowned out the blast from Micah's rifle.

Gunsmoke blotted out our vision for an instant. When it drifted off the grizzly still loomed erect before us, tottering, blood spewing through shattered teeth, hairy arms and knife-sharp claws sweeping in menacing arcs, his roaring reduced to a gurgle. He slowly folded into himself and fell forward, the fearsome jaws no more than a foot away from the half-butchered buffalo cow.

We stood like rocks, petrified with slowly draining fright, trembling like aspens, gazing in awe at the grizzly twitching in his final tremors. Suddenly I yelped with relief and pounded Micah on his back, praising him for his cool courage and his unerring aim. Even my father abandoned his reserve and hugged our companion.

When I recovered my wits, I asked him, "Why in hell did ye wait so long before ye shot, Micah?"

"Well, ye said to shoot 'im in the mouth and I surely didn't want to miss, him movin' about so crazy-like."

Trappers often describe a man of exceptional courage as having "the hair of the bear" in him. Micah certainly possesses that particular commodity in abundance — and, for boot, Old Ephraim's balls, as well!

We made short work of the third cow, taking all the choice cuts, but anxious to get out of that glade, lest our hairy visitor had a friend nearby.

Still, we were reluctant to leave all that rich bear meat for the wolves. We butchered Old Ephraim, also, removing the best parts and enough thick fat to render out a couple gallons of oil. As a final gesture I sliced into a forepaw and whittled out a claw full six inches long. "Here, Micah, stuff this into your medicine-poke, if it'll fit," I told him. "It'll be good medicine an' you surely deserve it." Micah accepted the token with a big grin, allowing that he would certainly make room for it.

Our saddlehorses and pack animals gave us a heap of trouble when we tried to load the bear meat, r'aring back, neighing in terror, eyes rolling white. Only one of them had ever smelled a grizzly bear, but instinct told the others that such a critter meant trouble. Only Micah's high-strung Kentucky-bred Ashley horse minded his manners. He had been in the mountains before with the General, but even he trembled and stamped his hooves.

We had garnered more meat than the pack animals could carry, so we loaded up our saddle horses, too, then hoofed it back to camp, happy to get out of that meadow.

We left our loaded critters with the campkeepers. Then, their mercis and formidables ringing in our ears, we trotted to the lakeshore and threw ourselves into the water, washing sweat and sticky blood and whatever else off our hides and clothes — especially our britchclouts.

* * *

It was late afternoon by time we got ourselves dressed, stuffed ourselves at the cookfire, and set out for a look-see at the rendezvous. It was in full swing. Tipsy trappers mingled with Indians of every stripe, men and women alike, at the trade tents, stocking up on essentials for the coming season and filling their kettles with Sublette's well-watered but still deadly trader's booze. I caught sight of two of the Sah-lish headmen from the evening before, but my naiad was nowheres around.

Naturally I bought a kettleful of spirits. Davey Jackson generously accepted my coins for the purchase, which his clerk was reluctant to do. Precious alcohol is meant to buy plews.

I espied Finn McCool, still engaged to Smith, Jackson & Sublette, tugging at a big log press, baling plews — fifty stiff-cured hides, ninety pounds to the pack, two of which make a pack-horse load, besides whatever else he can carry. I asked my companions to tarry and beckoned to McCool.

When he joined us, I asked, "That saddle you've been riding, is it your own?"

The Irishman frowned. "No,'tis not. When I hired on I lacked all but the clothes I was standin' up in. Harris provided the saddle and all else I needed for hostlin', but I don't own it. The musket, as ye know, I bought with me last few coppers. I'll be after buyin' the saddle when Sublette settles up me wages."

"Don't bother," I told him. "You'll get no bargains from Bill Sublette. Besides, that worn-out old dragoon is worthless." I fingered a couple-three gold coins out of my poke and pressed them into his hand. "Here, take these an' buy yourself a Spaniard saddle like ours. You'll need it, come trappin' time." McCool started to protest, but I insisted. "When Davey turns ye loose today, find yourself one o' Billy's Spaniard hostlers an' get him drunk, if he ain't already, then dazzle 'im with those gold-pieces until he sells ye his saddle. He'll do it if ye get 'im drunk enough." I waved away his objections and turned to join my companions, adding only, "Make sure it's a good'un." Which was unnecessary. Finnæus McCool possesses an expert's eye for horseflesh and all that goes with it.

Beehives and kicked-over anthills came to mind when we melted into the throng. The camp was feverish with activity, a colorful blur of every kind of merriment. Red-faced trappers competed in catch-as-catch-can wrestling bouts, foot races, and horse races, shooting rifles and pistols at a mark, chucking knives and tomahawks at a stump, and, inevitable amongst exhuberant young men suddenly released from the harsh discipline of the wilderness, outright brawls, drunken, wild-eyed men trading kicks and punches until their comrades stepped in and broke them up.

The trapper ranks had swollen during my two-year absence, especially amongst Company men. There was a time when I knew just about everybody at rendezvous. Now there were scores of new faces. Manners had altered, as well. We had always been a rough and ready breed, but decently respectful of our fellows. Now there was a harsh, brutal quality in many of the newcomers, loud-mouthed bullies, men who, it was easy to imagine, had fled to the mountains only a step ahead of the law, packing with them the same criminal impulses that had driven them from their hometowns. The friendly camaraderie that existed amongst us in the early days, when we were only a few, relying on one another for survival, was diluted by this new element. Only the fact that every trapper was well-armed and accustomed to defending his life and property would keep them in check.

One bully was all too familiar. Peeking through a circle of excited men, I spied the rugged features of Hugh Glass, a veteran of our first expedition up the Missouri in 1822. Glass was bare to the waist, crouched over a fallen log, red-faced, eyes squinched shut, sweat rolling into his grizzled beard, teeth clenched tight on a willow twig, silent except for an agonized grunt now and again as a trapper sliced and probed and wiggled a broken-off arrow shaft lodged in his horribly-scarred back. The mountaineer surgeon, equipped only with a razor and a pen-knife, persisted with his grisly chore, pausing now and then only to wipe his bloody hands on his leggin's. At last he whooped in triumph, tugged the arrow-point free, and brandished it above his head. When the bloody iron came loose, Glass shuddered and sagged over the log, but he didn't collapse. He caught his breath, looked up through pain-glazed eyes, and grinned.

"Feller sez ol' Glass rode seven hunnerd miles all the way up hyar with that'ere arrer stickin' out'n his back," the man standing next to me volunteered. "Some doin's, huh?"

I allowed that it was indeed some doin's. As I retreated from the circle of cheering men, I saw a man slosh a cupful of trader's booze into the bleeding wound. Another trapper offered a second cup to Glass, which he grabbed and drained dry.

I never liked Hugh Glass. Hardly anybody did. He was a brutal bully, one of Mike Fink's toadies, but I had to admire his fortitude. As we moved off, I briefly related to Powatawa and Micah the story of Glass getting himself mauled into forcemeat by a bear after the Arikara battle in 'twenty-three and how Jim Bridger and a trapper named Fitzgerald stayed a couple days with his mangled body until it was plain that he must certainly die. Where they were was swarming with Rees, so when they saw his condition was hopeless, they left Glass where he lay and hotfooted back to their brigade. Problem was, by some miracle, Glass didn't die. Lacking even a knife, he crawled five hundred miles, living off bugs and grubs and carrion when he could get it, until he hauled himself into an Army post, where they patched him up.

Next spring, sure as hell, Glass showed up with blood in his eye, seeking revenge. By then, Fitzgerald had run off and joined the Army. Glass grudgingly admitted that Jim Bridger had been a green-as-grass youngster at the time and forgave him. Jim felt mortally bad about the affair, but, as Tuttle and I told him, Hugh Glass never would have waited even five minutes with a wounded comrade if it meant risking his own hide. After a spell, Jim appeared to get over it. But perhaps he never did.Fiddles scraping out lively tunes mingled with hoarse shouting and hallooing of greetings, gunshots, winners' shrieks of triumph, the clatter of kettles and tinware being being hauled back to various camps, distant Indian drums, and a hundred other ingredients of that merry pandemonium. We turned our steps towards the music, passing along the way clusters of grave-faced trappers and Indian men sitting cross-legged, gambling at Old Sledge or the Indian hand-game, Black Harris holding forth on a log, surrounded by a rapt audience, spinning one of his fanciful yarns, coveys of chattering young Indian girls, pretty faces flushed with unaccustomed spirits, shyly flirting with eager young Americans, and squads of mostly-naked little brown-skinned boys darting like minnows through the crowd, begging or snatching up whatever wasn't nailed down.

Anse Tolliver was in the midst of the fiddlers, gleefully sawing out lively tunes, an unaccustomed smile pasted across his usually sour phiz. Anse's musical sidekick, our campkeeper Yves Dureau with his little French squeeze-box, was absent, busy with supper chores, but he was sure to join in as soon as he was free to do so. A grinning Cesár Pérez tootled on a little clay sweet potato and a number of other men donated to the din, blowing on Indian flutes or banging away on Indian hand-drums and copper kettles. Paddy McBride and half a dozen other flush-faced trappers flung themselves about in high-kicking dances, laughing and dropping out only long enough to gulp a couple mouthfuls of trader's booze, then plunging back into the musical melee.

One of the fiddlers standing next to Anse caught my eye, as much for his unusual appearance as the total abandon with which he chastised his battered old instrument, dancing in place, occasionally cavorting wildly in a circle, whilst he swept a tattered horsehair bow across the strings, red-faced, head flung back and bellowing out the words in an unmistakeable German accent to whatever song they were playing. Rusty red ringlets straggled out from under what I took to be a sea captain's cap, one eye concealed by a black eye-patch. His buckskins were mostly covered by a seaman's short blue coat, replete with a double row of tarnished brass buttons, but I saw he wore a britchclout and moccasins, so I reckoned he had been up thisaway for a spell. I shook my head in wonder, marveling at how much our fraternity had altered in my absence.

Strangest of all, howsomever, was Henry Fraeb, a German trapper everybody calls Frapp, jigging amongst the dancers and banging on the most curious musical device ever imagined at rendezvous or anywheres else, a five-foot length of skinny lodgepole surmounted by a pair of cymbals and festooned with an Indian hand-drum, a cowbell, and a hollow wooden block, all of which he thumped upon with a foot-long stick, more or less in time with the music.

I had seen the thing before but I was no less fascinated than Powatawa and Micah were. When Fraeb quit long enough to catch his breath, I caught his attention and offered my kettle, which he happily accepted. After he gargled down a pint or so, I asked, "Frapp, I saw ye punishin' that contraption o' yours a couple years back. What d'ye call it? Ye told me then, but I forgot."

"Ja, in Chermany ve call it a *teufelgeigenspieler*, vat you say, der Debbil's play-toy! I got Black to fetch der moosicals up from Sain' Looie und I carry 'em 'long in my sattlebags ven ve aind't rondayvoosin'."

The fiddlers swung into another tune just then. Frapp pricked up his ears. "Goot t'see ya, Buck. Gotta go. Dey're playin' a goot vun, ja?" He leaped back into the maelstrom, banging wildly on his infernal machine, and disappeared amongst the dancers.

Once again Tuttle Thompson proved that somewhere in his ancestry there must have been a bird-dog. Even in that crowd his keen nose picked up the scent of my booze. A freshly-shaved Tuttle, resplendent in a clean red calico shirt and redolent of lavender, pushed through the press of frolicking humanity and, without a word of greeting, relieved me of my kettle. Only after his third deep draught did he croak out a thankee. Then, "Whar ye been? Lookin' all over fer ye. Folks been askin' after ye."

"An' who would that be?"

"Aw, Bridger, Fitz, an' thet leetle Missourah Frenchie, whaddayacall'im, LeBref — 'mongst some others. They heared ye come back."

As we sauntered through the noisy, colorful mob, I mentioned the red-headed fiddler. "Oh, thet'n! Thet be Cap'n Billy Sump'in'er-other. Come up last year with the pack train — mappin' the country, some say. Found he likes these'hyar mountains better'n sea-goin' an' stayed on fer trappin', mostly with Frapp. Fitz sez he's a purty fair hand — fer a one-eyed lefty, thet is t'say."

The sound of gunfire drew us to the edge of camp. Several men were shooting at marks tacked to trees, showing off their marksmanship, whilst others wagered on their favorites. Micah and Powatawa had fallen somewhat behind Tuttle and me. I took that opportunity to brag on Micah's shooting skill and steady nerves, earlier that day with the grizzly. Tuttle was mightily impressed. "Whar'd he larn shootin' like thet? Back home, darkies warn't never 'lowed no shootin' irons. Hell, din't even dare be seen pickin' up a musket."

I explained how Micah had worked for Jake Hawken back in Saint Louis after I bought his freedom from Chouteau. "I reckon he got a lot o' practice, testin' out Jake's hardware. Not only that, he learnt how to make 'em and fix 'em. In case ye bust a lock or somethin', he's your man."

Tuttle whistled softly and looked thoughtful, but he said no more. I should have guessed what was going on in his mind. Tuttle Thompson is a consummate gambler. If he isn't skinning men at Old

Sledge or outfoxing Indians at the hand game, Tuttle will bet on which bird will be first to fly off a tree branch.

We watched the contests for a spell, men shooting at sixty paces at a wood chip not much bigger than a dollar. The longer we watched, the more agitated Tuttle became. When he was about to burst, he strode into the midst of the marksmen and yelled out, "Hell! Thet ain't nuthin'! I got a feller hyar kin put all o' yew boys in the shade!"

A murmur of consternation rippled through the crowd. Tuttle paid it no heed. "Y'all put up yer irons fer a minute an' I'll be showin' ye some real shootin'!" With that he hiked out to the target tree, picked up a splintered chip half the size of the regular mark, then trotted out another twenty paces and fixed it to a tree trunk.

Micah had already divined what Tuttle had in mind and had begun to move off, but Tuttle loped on back, caught up with Micah, and commenced talking a mile a minute. At length he led Micah back to where the shooters were gathered. My black friend stood with his head bowed, scraping the toe of his moccasin in the dust, no doubt wishing he could be anywheres else but where he was.

"Awright!" Tuttle announced, "I'm takin' all o' yer wagers agin thi'shere feller winnin' thi'shere shootin' match! Any takers?" I was absolutely sure just whose stock of coin would be reduced if Micah failed to win.

Some of the shooters, sensing a ringer, moved off, but some others, convinced that no Negro could possibly be as skillful with firearms as they themselves were, stepped up to take their place. Half a dozen trappers assembled to prove their prowess against the uppity darky.

Micah, standing somewhat apart, reluctantly unslung his rifle and fitted a percussion cap onto the nipple, then stood quietly, waiting for the other shooters to take their turn, whilst Tuttle hustled amongst the marksmen and through the crowd, making bets.

The tiny distant target, overconfidence born of hide-pride, disdain for Micah's new-fangled percussion gun, and, no doubt, considerable imbibing of trader's booze, all took their toll. Everybody missed the nearly-invisible wood chip. Except Micah. He wasted no time taking aim.   He casually swung his rifle to his shoulder, sighted, and squeezed off his shot. When the smoke cleared, the chip was gone.

A roar of protest erupted, but quickly died, replaced by a buzz of wonderment. A gleeful, crowing Tuttle bustled amongst the crowd collecting wagers. Micah slung his rifle and commenced to retreat, when one of the bettors, one of Sublette's Company men, leaped forward and grabbed his arm, growling, "No gawddamn nigger's goin' ter fleece thi'shere ol' boy! I aim ter whup some manners inter yer uppity gawddamn black arse! Damn ef I ain't!"

Before I even knew it, I had flung myself betwixt the two of them, calling for calm and fair play, but the disappointment amongst the spectators at seeing their favorites bested, especially by a Negro, was too great to be denied. Cries of "Let 'em fight!" and "We'll see who's best!" and suchlike sentiments prevailed. The red-faced challenger stood half-a-head taller than either Micah or me and outweighed my friend by half a hundredweight or more. His breath reeked of booze, which reassured me somewhat, for a fight looked to be unavoidable. Micah was cold sober.

The crowd had grown considerably. I spied Bridger, LeBref, and Fitzpatrick shouldering their way to the inner circle. Finn McCool appeared behind us, a thundercloud on his features, the gnarled, wicked-looking club he called a shillelagh dangling from his wrist. Godey, Brass Turtle, and Little Mountain followed close behind him. Now I felt better about it all. None of those hearties would stand by to allow a mobbing.

Like it or not, I was a reluctant referee, but there was no getting out of it. "All right," I shouted above the din. "Shuck your hardware! Nothin' but what God gave ye!" Micah was already passing his rifle, pistol, horn, and belt to McCool. I stepped close to the big trapper and said in a low voice, "I warn ye. This black feller can hurt ye bad." Just as I had reckoned it would, this bit of honesty merely inflamed the bully further, likely making him even more reckless.

I retreated to Micah's side and counseled, "Make it quick, Micah. Don't toy with him. Hurt him quick and put 'im down." Micah nodded, his face unsmiling, grave, eyes steady, sizing up his opponent.

The bully ripped off his belt and flung it into the crowd, then, head-down, loosing a string of curses, he charged like a maddened buffalo bull. It was Tug Novak all over again. Micah balanced on his toes like a dancer, side-stepped the charge, and slammed the sole of his foot against the big fellow's ear, bowling him sidewise into the dirt. Before he could rise, Micah leaped high in the air and landed on the bully's back, smashing both feet into the man's kidneys. The whoosh expelled from the big trapper's mouth could have pushed a keelboat a mile up the Missouri. Micah appeared to float over the fallen man's head, spun about, and kicked him solidly under the chin, snapping his head back. It was over. The brawler lay facedown in the dirt, panting and groaning, blood oozing from his broken lips, spread-eagled arms and legs twitching, all the fight gone out of him.

Micah stepped back amongst us, buckled on his belt, and retrieved his weapons. We wasted no time making our exit, our bunch flanking the two of us. As we passed Fitz and Bridger, Jim called out, "Reckon yer feller'll do, Buck! Best keep 'im around!" Considering Bridger's feelings about people of color, except for Delawares and Indian women, it was a high compliment indeed.

Micah's only comment as we walked off was, "No sense wreckin' my hands. Didn't need 'em this time." Later, as we neared our camp, he brightened and said to nobody in particular, "Reckon this is why I come to the mountains. All my life I never been 'lowed to fight back, 'ceptin' with niggers. Now I can."

Tuttle caught up with us at the cookfire, grinning happily, his pouch jingling. He explained his tardiness. "Had to hang around a spell 'til thet'ere big feller got hisse'f together 'fore I could collect on his wager. He didn't much care fer payin' up, but he warn't in no corn-dishun fer argyfyin'."

* * *

Boudins simmering in buttery bear grease, fat hump ribs and tender backstrap, and tongue flavored with wild onions bubbling in kettles made a proper victory banquet.

"Don'tcha be worryin' none 'bout what happened over yonder, Micah," Ned Godey opined. "Thar's many'll give ye good marks fer givin' that'ere sumbitch a righteous comeuppance. Them as don't'll be walkin' wide around ye, jist the same, lest ye be givin' them the same medicine. Ye made yer mark this day!"

Approving grunts and nods greeted Ned's assessment. The trapping fraternity lives by harsh laws, but it respects courage, skill, and fortitude. Weaklings don't last long. What counts is what works. Settlement rules don't signify in the mountains. In the end, it's handsome is as handsome does and, hoss, what can ye do? Micah went a long way to proving himself that day. Micah appeared to grow in stature. His early shyness mostly drained away, replaced by a quiet confidence that he was worthy to join our rag-tag ranks.

Tuttle tossed a gnawed-over rib into the fire, wiped his greasy fingers on his leggin's, and announced, "'Pears to me, Micah, y'oughter git some kind o' ree-ward fer whatcha done. What'say we take a stroll over thar 'mongst the Snakes arter we git done fillin' our bellies? I be knowin' a coupl'a Snake ladies what'll jest abaout fit yore pistol!" Approving laughter resounded around the cookfire. Micah grinned and nodded.

Half an hour later a half-dozen of us, clean-shaven and gussied up in our Sunday-best rendezvous duds, were on our way to the Shoshone camp. It was still early evening, with plenty of time to return to my bower by nightfall, so I tagged along to witness what Tuttle was calling Micah's Rocky Mountain christening, leastaways the early stages.

I had made sure that Micah's belt pouch was stuffed with beads and awls, firesteels, shiny brass thimbles and hawkbells, tiny looking-glasses, a couple bright bandannas, and whatever other foofurraw it would hold. Romance has its price in the Rockies, as it does everyplace else. Only the specie differs.

Such material inducements proved to be mostly unnecessary. Micah's unusual appearance instantly captivated the Shoshone women, several of whom were soon tipsy from sips of trader's booze provided by Godey, Paddy, and Tuttle. They clustered around him, stroking his smooth ebon cheeks to see if the color would come off, running their fingers through his kinky hair, and babbling their wonder at this very different black-whiteman. His shy smile flashing in his dark face and the sturdy, strong-limbed rest of him didn't hurt matters either.

Tuttle wriggled free of the chattering women and trotted back to where Powatawa and I stood, apart from the merry throng. "Ain't gonna be no trouble a-tall gittin' ol' Micah laid. They been callin' him Young Buffler Bull an' sech — on account o' thet woolly hair o' his'n. Onliest problem's gonna be whittlin' them wimmen down to mebbe jest a couple-three. 'Pears all of 'em want a shot at 'im."

I had seen enough. It was time to leave Micah in Tuttle's capable hands and tend to my own affairs. I wished them all success and turned away, looking for Powatawa. He was nowheres in sight. I chuckled and shrugged. My years with Tuttle had taught me not to be my brother's keeper. I was not about to take on that chore with my father.

As I moved off, Tuttle called after me, "Don'tcha be waitin' up fer me an' frettin, mind ye, Temple! Reckon I'll be hangin' on somewhars hyarabouts!"

Brass Turtle joined me on the hike back to camp, leastaways part of the way. "Ye done good, Temple, fetchin' that'ere Micah 'long with ye. Once he larns the trade, I reckon he'll be fittin' right in, likely takin' Beckwith's place 'thout ary trouble." I threw him a sharp look, but said naught. Turtle caught my unspoken question. "Yep, I got me a hunch ol' Jim's thinkin' 'bout splittin' off, likely headin' back to the Crows. Yer bringin' another darky up hyar likely only clinched what he's been ponderin' anyways."

My own instincts had told me as much. Turtle's words backed it up. I said only, "We'll see."

Just outside the trapper's camp we encountered Tom Fitzpatrick and Jim Bridger, kettles in hand, apparently headed for the Crow camp. "Thar ye be, Buck!" Jim called out. "'Bout time we see ye close up. Good to see ye back." I have always been fond of that strapping Missouri blacksmith and I warmed to his welcome.

"Indeed it is," Fitz put in. "Us originals need to be maintainin' the quality o' the brotherhood. Too many furriners comin' up are dilutin' the standards." I smiled but said naught, reflecting that Fitz himself had emigrated from Ireland not long before he joined Ashley's second expedition in 'twenty-three.

Jim Bridger had done a heap of growing-up in the two years since I had seen him last, not only in height and muscle, but also in manner. He was still the bluff, goodnatured, fun-loving, irreverent trapper he had always been, but now he fairly radiated leadership and natural authority, that indefinable quality that makes most men content to rely on his judgment and follow his orders.

I am neither kind. I wish to boss no man, but, equally, obeying another man's commands without question or choice is something I can never do again. Our free-trapping, leaderless bunch is the only place for me.

Tom Fitzpatrick had changed little. From the start we knew him for an educated man of courage, knowledge and understanding and cool judgment, adept in mountain skills and gifted with wry good humor. Besides, he is a first-rate horseman.

We were chatting about trapping, fur prices, the rendezvous, and such when I chanced to mention that I hadn't seen Jedediah Smith around camp. "Ye miss 'im, do ye, Temple?" Bridger asked wih a wink, doubtless recalling that Smith and I have never been friendly, especially since, five years before, he had tried unsuccessfully to commandeer for his own use my personal, bought-and-paid-for Chiksika horse.

"Not so's ye'd notice it," I replied, "but seein' as how he's partners with Bill an' Davey, I reckoned he'd be somewheres hereabouts."

"Nope. Not since last year," Jim said. "Headed out with a brigade o' men fer Californy, right arter ronnyvoo." He looked solemn. "From whut we heared, he run into a world o' hurt 'gin a passel o' bare-arse Injuns out in the desert afore he hardly got started. Lost ten men kilt an' a bunch o' hosses an' the rest of 'em starvin', livin' on bugs an' suchlike."

"Grover Weed carried the word back," Fitz put in. "He and Hiram Scott and another fellow — all of 'em free men, trappin' on their own hook — got their fill o' such doin's an' quit. No question o' desertin', mind ye, free trappers as they be. Weed sez they got to where they were after suckin' blood from their critters and eatin' ants an' snakes an' lizards — an' glad to get 'em, too." He chuckled wickedly. "The lads've lately gone to callin' ould Grover by the name o' Buzzard."

We shared a laugh about that. I didn't say it, but I wondered why Jedediah Smith thought he needed to go all the way to California to trap beaver. So much of the Rockies is still unexplored and cricks and streams hereabouts provide a plenitude of plews. Perhaps the answer to that conundrum is somewheres in that Book of his. Perhaps not.

Brass Turtle made no comment concerning Smith's whereabouts. He was becoming impatient. We wished Jim and Fitz happy hunting amongst the Absóraqas and took our leave. Before we parted, Turtle to the Flathead camp, me to my bower, he observed drily, "Ol' Diah 'pears to be marchin' to a drum ain't nobody but him kin hear. Ever wonder who might be doin' the beatin' on it?"

* * *

Shrinking daylight hurried my preparations for the return of my Lady of the Lake. I had amongst my plunder a book from my mother's library that possessed that very same title, written by a popular English author, Sir Walter Scott. I had never even opened it, but I promised myself that I would do so. This was not the time, howsomever. It would soon be dark and I had much to do.

I rummaged through my packs, pulling out tallow candles, trade items, yard goods, and foofurraw, stowing it all next to my pallet. Then, so I would be able to light a candle, I heaped up char and tinder and laid a flint and fire-striker beside it. I felt a powerful need to talk with my visitor and hand-signs don't work in the dark.

Naturally I couldn't be sure that she would come to me that night or any other, but it seemed to me there had been a quality in our love-making much different from the usual casual coupling betwixt trappers and Indian women. She had sent the little boys to learn the whereabouts of my bower and she had come to me without my invitation to do so. For my part, I had been powerfully drawn to her from the moment she first exploded from the deep.

There was naught to do now but wait. Which wasn't easy. I puttered about, filling two cups with cognac, draining one of them, then refilling it, stoking my pipe, sitting in the doorway, smoking, half-hearing the faraway din of the rendezvous and drums and barking dogs in the Indian camps, staring out over the lake, silver in starlight, recalling the long, lean, smooth length of her rising before me in a shower of glistening droplets, then sliding downward, her long unbound hair flowering on the surface before she disappeared.

I heard her light footstep only a second before she touched my shoulder and slid under my arm, her lips reaching up to caress my cheek, moving on to nibble my ear, then drawing my face down with two strong hands to drown me in a lingering kiss. It was worth the wait.

Waiting, howsomever, was a thing neither she nor I wished to do. Unwilling to turn each other loose, we scrabbled into the bower to my robes, lips locked, tongues probing, hands frantically searching, seizing, wriggling free of garments, clasped together, locked into a single striving, panting, heaving, gnawing, clawing, honest, natural animal worthy of the wild mountains we called our home, until moaning, groaning, whimpering release returned us to earth and halfway to our senses.

It seemed no time at all until we resumed, more leisurely now but nonetheless spurred on by a primal need to possess each other thoroughly, completely, exploring every part and pleasurable sensation, until, exhausted, we fell apart, but only a hand's breadth, drenched in sweat in spite of the cool breeze from the lake, breath mingling, fingers entwined, eyes straining in pearlescent moon glow to know the other.

At last she rose in one fluid motion and tugged me to my feet. She led me to the shore and into the chill water, pressing me down and laving away both sweat and the cobwebs cluttering my mind, restoring at least a part of my commonsense. Now more than ever I needed to learn as much about this woman as I possibly could.

I took her hand and returned to shore, up the bank, and into the bower. We sat facing, cross-legged, naked, silent, grateful for the dim light of the rising moon, until I saw her shiver. I fetched a blanket from my bed, draped it about her shoulders, and retrieved the cups of cognac. She shivered again and grimaced at her first taste, then sipped again and smiled as liquid sunshine warmed her belly. She giggled and drank a little more, eyes glowing, lips pursed then spreading into a broad smile as she savored the golden magic from a faraway land.

Naturally I joined her. We touched our cups together in a toast to our mutual affection, although I am sure such a gesture was certainly unknown to her until that moment. Reluctantly, I broke the spell, rising to strike a tiny blaze in the little heap of char and tinder, lighting a pair of stout tallow candles, and returned to place them between us. The bower was bright enough now to assure me that my lips and hands had not deceived me. She was even more beautiful than I had recalled.

We commenced by exchanging our names in hand-signs, the universal language of the mountains and the prairies. We spoke in our own tongue as we gestured. Her name, as Brass Turtle had told me, was something like Rainbow Fish, because of, she explained, her love of swimming. The unfamiliar sounds of Sah-lish speech eluded my tongue. I decided, then, simply to call her Rainbow until I might learn to wrap my tongue around those alien syllables. My own name, Temple Buck, translates in finger-talk to a buck deer or a bull wapiti. After several tries, she pronounced my name Tompo, which was close enough.

I learned that she lived with and cared for her father — her mother had died two years before — and that she herself was a widow, her husband of only two years killed by Blackfeet nearly a year ago.

It wasn't easy to concentrate on her finger-signs. As she spoke and fluttered her hands, the blanket kept falling away, exposing her smooth shoulders and her delicious breasts, which jiggled my attention away from our talk and drew my thoughts to my robes. Hard as it was, I put the impulse aside. I needed to know how it was that she had been drawn to me, why she had chosen me, come to me without my asking, how she was sure of what kind of man I am.

Sign-talk, useful as it is, lacks the facility of speech. After several unsuccessful attempts, I was mostly able to get my questions across to her. Answering them was, for her, almost as hard. Time and again I had to ask her to repeat the signs. What I finally made sense of was that it all started with our first glimpse of each other, when she shot up like a geyser before me. Naturally she was scared and ducked back down and swam off, but when she came up again, she saw that I wasn't chasing her.

She laughed at that point in her story and made backstroking motions, showing how I had retreated. I especially liked that part, for the blanket completely fell away, exposing most of her slim, well-muscled body. She clucked mild disapproval at my staring, retrieved the blanket, and continued her tale, enchanting me the while with the warm, liquid tones of the Sah-lish tongue as her fingers darted and curled, forming her thought.

She described my visit to her village, when Brass Turtle and I first paid our respects to the headmen and when I made my fumbling, schoolboyish apologies to her, blushing and repeating myself endlessly in my rusty hand-talk. She made signs that said there was no evil in my thinking. When I left my gifts with her but asked naught in return, she was sure of it. She told me, too, that she had been to rendezvous before and my behavior was not like that of whiteman trappers she had seen there.

Now it was her turn to blush, but only slightly, for Indian women are pretty straightforward about expressing their desires. She went on to tell me that she saw that I was strong and she considered me handsome, that the scars she could see testified that I was a brave warrior, that I was different from any men she knew of, red or white, and, finally, that it had been a long time since she had enjoyed robe games. She had sent the little boys after me to learn where I lived, so that she might see if she were correct in her appraisal.

She laughed, showing perfect white teeth, blushed again, and shrugged, signing one last time that she was content with her choice.

I yelped with glee, scooped her up, and carried her to my robes, where we passed the remaining dark hours in discovering and refining our mutual pleasures.

When at last moonlight retreated before grey dawn, she let me know that she must depart. I insisted that she must accept my gifts, sweeping the lot into a sizeable length of red woolen stroud. She resisted at first, but I settled the matter by placing atop the bundle a shiny brass pipe-tomahawk, signing that it was a gift for her father. She relented, flung her arms about me, and drew me to her for a last lingering kiss. Then she was gone.

* * *

The sun was high in a cloudless sky by time I dragged myself away from my dreams and threw my blanket aside. I had made sure to cover myself, lest I be once again the butt of Tuttle's witticisms. Outside, our camp bustled with activity and, far off, at least one fiddle scratched and squeaked above the caterwauling shouts of roistering trappers.

After my morning chore and a quick splash in the lake, I trotted to the cookfire, my belly griping with hunger. Even before I got there,

Jean-Luc was already filling a large cup with his pease-porridge. He held it out to me, winked broadly, and said slyly, "Bon jour, M'sieu Temple, tu as besoin des aliments, je crois. Tu as fait tous tes efforts hier soir, hein?" I grabbed the cup away from him and replied huffily that I certainly did have an appetite and that I was sure he had better things to do than to be concerning himself with my exertions, day or night. Unabashed, he guffawed, turned away, and busied himself with his chores, still cackling.

Two cups of steaming porridge and a meaty hump rib restored my good humor. Most of our people were scattered about camp in small groups, smoking and talking, choring at repairs to their gear, or sleeping off last night's revelry. Micah and Brass Turtle sat under a tree, totally engrossed, exchanging hand-signs. As I approached, they greeted me with some nonsense about it being about time I was rising. Micah volunteered, "Reckon I'd best be learnin' the sign-talk. It would'a come in right handy las' night."

Turtle sniggered and opined, "Mebbe so. Mebbe not. Thar be a time fer talkin' an' a time fer doin'. What I been hearin', you di'n't have no time fer talkin', anyways."

Micah laughed aloud. "That's a fact! Just the same, I reckon I'll be needin' it next time I get a hankerin' for such company." It warmed me to see how smoothly Micah was fitting into our bunch. It was time to quit worrying about him.

The same with Powatawa. I spied my father seated amongst a circle of our Indians, smiling and talking and fluttering his hands like a fieldful of butterflies. I couldn't tell what he was saying, but the approving nods and grins of the others assured me that he had found acceptance amongst them. Both he and Micah were able, resourceful men. Their apprenticeship in the trade wouldn't take long.

Brass Turtle jerked his chin in the direction of the Snake camp. "Hyar comes Tuttle — big as life an' lookin' none too sprightly, fer a fact." It was true. My good friend was approaching from the direction of the Shoshone camp, his customary coltish gait replaced by dragging footsteps, a woebegone frown pasted on his normally cheerful features. He tarried at the cookfire just long enough to fill his cup with porridge, then ambled over to where we sat. As he drew near I saw that his stubbly jaws looked unusually puffy, but I chalked it up to last night's excesses.

Ned Godey joined us at the same time. He threw himself down in our midst, squinted up at Tuttle, and enquired, "Drank yerse'f a leetle too much o' Billy's popskull las' night, did ye, Tuttle?"

Tuttle snorted. "Nope, never done no sech a thang! I drank not a drop! Reckon some sumbitch must'a gone an' unscrewed ther top o' my haid an' poured it in!" He smiled ruefully, then, "Ain't complainin' though. I woke up in ther lovin' arms o' one o' them'ere Snake women this mawnin'."

"Purty woman, war she?" Turtle asked.

"Wal, tellin' truth, I'd hafta say she warn't precisely ther belle o' ther ball. Ye mought better be callin' 'er ther ho' o' the hoedown!" When our chuckles subsided, he added, "But she'll do. 'T'war a long chalk better'n lonely robes." He fell silent, turning his attention to his porridge, spooning it in until his spoon rattled in the cup, then shambling off to the cookfire for more. I watched him with pleasure, reflecting on our long friendship, forged in our earliest meeting on Fink's keelboat, and how it had enriched my life since then.

Ned broke into my reverie. "Hey, Temple, what'say we git out amongst 'em? Thar'll be more'n time enough to be hangin' with our own kind purty soon, once't we git to trappin'."

I agreed that it was so, bade him wait whilst I got some clothes on, and soon joined him for a stroll through the rendezvous. It was even more frenetic, if that were possible, than the day before — throngs of trappers and colorful Indians, men and women of half a dozen tribes, clustered at the trade tents or wandering amongst the crude mountaineer shelters, others eagerly crowding in amongst gamblers at Old Sledge or the hand game, some sprawled wherever they had fallen, sleeping off last night's drunk. Fervent young whitemen pursued giggling young Indian girls who were not seriously trying to escape. The din was fearsome, exhilarating, a Babel of half a dozen

Indian tongues, a proper fricassee of English, French, Spaniard, and European accents and dialects, fiddles scraping and trappers howling ballads off-key, gunshots from the target range, gleeful shouts and encouraging yells from the horse-race course, and somewheres out of sight, a caterwauling Scottish bagpipe. Over it all wafted the aroma of roasting meat from half a hundred cookfires. Naturally we tarried, now and then, to carve off a bait of buffalo hump or tender cow wapiti.

We tarried a spell nigh a bunch of free trappers gathered around a remarkably-recovered Hugh Glass seated on a log He looked now as tough and mean and dangerous as ever he did. The boys were saying how they were fed up with high prices and Smith, Jackson & Sublette's high-handed take-it-or-leave it policy. They were urging Glass to return to the Missouri and invite Kenneth McKenzie and American Fur to come trade in the mountains. It appeared that old Hugh Glass was more than willing to do just that.

As we meandered on, Ned observed, "Hell! I don't give a damn who's buyin' my plews. Top dollar gits mine, an' that's a fact." I couldn't disagree.   Ess-Jay-&-Ess had never tried to endear themselves with us trappers. They were in it solely for themselves, squeezing out every possible dollar. I smiled, thinking that Pierre Chouteau would be glad to hear that sentiment.

Wandering into the Crow camp, we almost collided with big Jim Beckwith thrusting his broad shoulders through the door flap of a lodge. "Wal, howdy, Jim!" Godey said with a grin. "Fancy meetin' ye hyarabouts! Ain't hardly seen ye 'round our cookfa'r since we got hyar."

Ned's remark was innocent enough, gentle joshing at worst, but Jim responded with a sheepish, hangdog look. "Aw, 'tain't nuthin' pers'nal, jist brushin' up my Absóraqa, don'tcha know." He lapsed into uncomfortable silence.

Godey, sensing a deeper reason, backed off. "Sure 'nough, Jimbo. Practicin' don't nevcr hurt nuthin'." He paused, then tacked on, "Good as ye be awready with Crow-talkin', anyways." He trailed off awkwardly.

Seeking to lessen the tension, I chimed in with, "Rotten Belly anywheres around this year, Jim?"

Beckwith's eyes sort of hooded over and he looked down at his moccasins, which I noticed were bright with new beadwork. "Nope. He ain't. Likely doin' his tradin' over on the Missourah."

I was surprised by Jim's short answers. His customary garrulous nature appeared damped down to disappearing and he seemed anxious to be rid of us. At last, mumbling some nonsense about having some business elsewhere, he trotted off amongst the Absóraqa lodges.

Ned and I stood dumbstruck, staring after him. Ned broke the silence. "Sumpin' queersome's goin' on with ol' Jimbo, I'm thinkin', him not spoutin' off like usual." He frowned, then snorted, "Hell! ol' Jim ain't never content usin' only jist one word when a couple dozen'll fit! Mark me, he's up to sumpin'!"

I was tempted to mention my suspicions that resentment of Micah might be at the bottom of Jim's odd behavior, but I held my tongue. I wasn't sure, so I kept my own counsel.

Ned shrugged. "Wal, whate'er it be, I reckon he'll git over it." I nodded my assent. He brightened. "Time we be gittin' on. Thar's a whole bang-up rendezvous waitin' out thar an' we be wastin' a passel o' pleasurin'." That made sense, so that is what we did.

* * *

It was mid-afternoon by time Ned and I reeled back to camp, more than somewhat tipsy from sipping from a score of comradely kettles as well our own. I looked about for Tuttle. He was nowhere to be seen amongst our people. Our bower was unoccupied. Recalling his quiet behavior that morning, I became concerned. Naturally he could be anywhere, likely frolicking in the robes of one of his paramours. Just the same, I sobered up somewhat and set off to search him out.

I discovered him in a clump of willows on the lakeshore, his face half-submerged in a mud puddle. Drawing near, I was shocked. His swollen cheeks looked like a greedy chipmunk gorging on seeds, his red, bleary eyes nigh disappeared in the swelling. "Tuttle," I choked out, "what's wrong?"

He roused and tried to sit up, then sank down. "Aw, I got the gawddamn toothache," he slurred, "an' thar ain't booze enough in thi'shere whole gawddamn ronnyvoo fer killin' it. I know! I been tryin', sure as hell."

I cursed the unkind fate that had laid my friend low. In all the battles and scrapes we had been through together and all the wounds he had suffered, I had never seen Tuttle so miserable, so whipped and defenseless, so pitiful. Anger gave way to despair. Where in the entire rendezvous was someone to relieve Tuttle's agony? The answer was plain. Nobody.

Even so, something had to be done, even, like they say, even if it's wrong. I dragged Tuttle out of the puddle, lest he drown, then hotfooted back to camp for help.

The first man I encountered was Finn McCool, released just that day from his clerking chores with Bill Sublette. "Hullo, Temple," he called out affably. He saw the look on my face. "What ever is the trouble, man? Ye're looking uncommonly distressed."

"It's Tuttle," I blurted. "He's hurtin' bad — got the toothache! A bad 'un an' it's like to kill 'im! We gotta get him back to camp." I must have spoken louder than I thought. Half a dozen of our bunch — Powatawa, Micah, and Turtle amongst them — came trotting to where we stood. I hastily described Tuttle's state. A few minutes later we half-carried a protesting Tuttle out of the willows and up to the cookfire, where he lay curled in a ball.

"Ain't no use," he mumbled. "Ain't nuthin' ye kin do. Jest as soon shoot m'se'f."

"Perhaps we'll come to that," McCool replied, "but let's be after takin' a look at the problem before we go to providin' ye with a pistol."

Tuttle regarded his new-found Irish friend with glazed eyes, a twisted grin on his bulging cheeks. "An' whadda'ye know abaout sech matters, ye dumb Mick?" he strangled out.

A flush crept over Finn's hawkish features. He hesitated a mite, then said quietly, "I was two years studyin' medicine at Trinity College before the bloody Brits tumbled to my politics and set me on the run. I'm no certified doctor, mind ye, but I know more about the matter than you do, hillbilly." So quit yer blatherin', ye ninny, an' open yer mouth, lest ye die o' yer foolishness."

Something in McCool's eyes and in his tone convinced Tuttle that the Irisher might be his only hope. He closed his eyes, beckoned feebly, and muttered, "Go fer it."

Finn knelt and pried Tuttle's jaws open, peered into his mouth, then released him, sat back on his heels, and looked up. "'Tis as I supposed. It's his wisdom teeth. They must come out or they'll poison 'im."

Gallows humor is a plentiful commodity amongst mountaineers. "Wisdom teeth?" Brass Turtle piped up. "Hell, McCool, that cain't be it! Ever'body knows Tuttle owns not a speck o' wisdom!"

A ripple of laughter flowed amongst us. Even Tuttle appeared to smirk. The smile disappeared from McCool's face. Looking glum, he announced, "The difficulty is that I have no instruments, no tools, and furthermore, I am no surgeon, nor even a barber."

Micah was kneeling beside Tuttle. He looked up, his expression almost as pained as Tuttle's, and said, "I have some tools — not the right kind — but I yanked a few teeth at Chouteau's. You show me which ones and I'll do what I can."

A sigh of relief that rippled the grass went up from us. This was truly a case of "in the kingdom of the blind, the one-eyed man is king." In that particular case, two kings. Tuttle looked up at Micah and muttered through cracked, swollen lips, "Do whatcher hafta."

Micah scuttled back, rose to his feet, and raced for his bower, returning a couple minutes later with his box of gunsmithing tools. Ned Godey's booze kettle dangled from his hand. "Ye'd best be givin' Tuttle some spirits," Micah advised. "All he can hold. This'll be hurtin' more'n somewhat."

Micah sloshed pliers, pincers, and an awl in Ned's kettle and wiped them clean on his shirt. He looked grim, doubtless wishing he were somewheres else. Ned poured booze down Tuttle's gullet until he mostly settled down. Then Finn knelt, pried open Tuttle's jaw, then reached into his mouth and lightly tapped a tooth with the awl.

Tuttle fairly exploded. He jackknifed nearly double, flailing his arms and kicking out like a crazy mule, screaming with pain, scattering Micah, Finn, and the rest of us like startled quail. When at last he settled down, Micah and Finn looked at each other and shrugged, as if to say there was naught they could do. As Tuttle himself had said, there wasn't enough booze in all the rendezvous to do him any good.

Just then our Delaware healer Old Foot wriggled past the watching men, whose numbers had increased greatly. He knelt at Tuttle's head, a wooden bowl in hand, and commenced to spoon one of his evil mixtures into Tuttle's mouth, all the while crooning some Lénni-Lénapee nonsense. At first Tuttle grimaced and tried to spit, but soon he relaxed. In no time at all his stentorian snoring set the aspen leaves a-quaking. Foot grinned, twinkling eyes nigh disappearing, and beckoned to Finn and Micah. "Dream-vittle, he make sleep. You work now," he told them. "Horseface no fight no more."

Extracting the wisdom teeth — all four of them, just for luck — took less time than it had required to prepare Tuttle for the operation. Micah's steady hand on the pincers grasped each tooth that Finn pointed out and wiggled it loose. Each time, Tuttle groaned and surged upwards, but quickly settled down, allowing Finn to stanch the bleeding. As I watched, I wondered if Tuttle knew that our Delawares called him Horseface. If not, I wasn't about to tell him.

We lugged Tuttle's unconscious body into the bower and onto his robes, after which I rewarded our trio of surgeons with brimming cups of fine cognac, a couple of which I drained myself. I was purely shaken.

Finn excused himself and trotted off to his bower, returning a few minutes later, lugging a worn but serviceable Spaniard saddle, a fancy apishamore saddle pad, a headstall the Spaniards call a bosal, and a pair of big-roweled spurs. "There now!" he crowed, dumping the lot in front of me, "I'm equipped to ride to hell an' back wi' the best o'ye!" He laughed aloud, fished around in his poke, and handed me two gold pieces. "Thankee, Temple. I needed but one o' yer coins! Spaniards have no head a-tall for holdin' their poteen!"

* * *

Rainbow and I made love that night on a buffalo robe spread in a willow grove at the lake's edge. Tough as I knew Tuttle to be, I was not about to risk his rousing from his stupor and witnessing our intimacy.

Our coupling was less energetic than it had been, but infinitely more intense, deeper, warm and comforting, infused with emotion I was sure I had never known before. I sensed that she, too, felt something new and more valuable between us. I longed to know her thoughts. More than ever, I wished for a common language. But even if my wish had been granted, I couldn't have expressed what I was feeling right then, even to myself.

In that shadowy glade, our sign talk was limited. Even so, our entwined bodies and the heat of our embraces welded us into a single being that needed no words.

Bathing from time to time in the chill water of the lake did not lessen our ardor, but rather increased it. We clung together, shivering, until youthful nature signaled a hasty return to the robe.

When at last she slipped into the fading darkness to return to her village, there was a hollow place inside me that I reckoned only she could fill.

* * *

Tuttle's ordeal with the toothache bore valuable fruit. If there had been any lingering reluctance to accept another Negro and an

Irishman into our bunch, such reservations evaporated like morning mist. Every trapper fears the toothache with anxiety unmatched by his concern for wounds he might suffer in combat. Wounds, if not mortal, will heal. A man is defenseless against the dreaded toothache. The presence of Finn and Micah, together with Foot's mysterious brews, insured us against the terrors of the toothache.

It was late in the forenoon before Tuttle poked his tousled head out of the bower. He still resembled a chipmunk, but one not so greedy as the day before. The swelling had lessened and his lopsided grin assured us that yesterday's pain had abated as well. "Mawnin'!" he called out in a voice like a pokeful of broken glass and rusty razors. He squinted into the sunshine. "Thet yew, Temple?" I allowed that it was. "I got me a pow'ful heap o' thirsty," he implored. "Only a dram o' thet'ere Frenchy brandy o' your'n kin cure it. What'say?"

Seeing him up and about, I was too pleased to argue. "I reckon ye got it comin'", I replied, shouldering past him. "How're ye feelin'?"

"Better'n I got ary right to, thet be sartin." He held out his cup, which I filled brimful, then splashed a healthy snort into my own. We clinked and drank. I half expected Tuttle to jump with pain when the cognac washed over his recent wounds, but he showed no sign of discomfort. When I commented on it, he shrugged. "Yep, it's a-painin' some'at, but, hell! thi'shere ain't nuthin' a-tall, nex'ter ther gawddamn toothache. Naow thet be whatcher mought call hurtin'!"

Then he did a most un-Tuttle-like thing. He reached out and wrapped me in a grizzly hug, rasping my cheek with his, and muttered, "Thankee, pard, fer doin' whatcher did yestiddy. I won't ever fergit it."

Stunned by such unaccustomed tenderness, I was lost for a reply. He turned me loose and announced, "Time we be gittin' out o' hyar an' git to surroundin' a peck o' vittles!" Which we did.

* * *

The Sweet Lake rendezvous ran its customary course, winding down steadily as Sublette's booze became increasingly diluted. Traders' wares dwindled, trappers turned their thoughts to the fall hunt, and Indians packed up and set off for their home country.

It was about time. The stench produced by that large assemblage was getting to be overpowering, especially when a breeze came up. I visited Josh Pilcher's forlorn establishment a time or two more, pawing through his meager stock for whatever our bunch might find useful. Although I had never come to know him well, I felt respect and affection for Pilcher, mostly due to his honorable code of fair play in matters of trade and for his courage and leadership in the Arikara affair in 'twenty-three. It was proper that I help him out however I could.

Observing that my rifle and pistol were percussion weapons, he offered, "I brought up a fair supply of caps, but there's not much call for 'em hereabouts. The boys are pretty much stickin' to their flintlocks. If you can use 'em, I'll make you a fair price." I hesitated, for I had carried a goodly quantity of percussion caps from Saint Louis. Before I could reply, he added, "Tell ye what, I've got a passel o' percussion locks for rifles — and pistols, too — a mite rusty from the cache, but they'll clean up just fine. I'll throw 'em in for boot."

I thought of Micah's gunsmithing skills, recalling that he had brought a few spare percussion locks along with his tools. I reckoned he knew how to replace flintlocks with the new kind. Besides, after rendezvous, gold coin had little value in the mountains. "Done," I replied. "Name your price, Major." Which he did — and a very fair price it was, too, hardly more than I had paid Jake Hawken in Saint Louis, not even counting the boot.

By time I finished I had purchased half a hundredweight of galena and thirty pounds of gunpowder, besides a gallon of percussion caps, some not-too-rusty butcher knives, and other odds and ends of trade goods. It was too much for me to tote, so Pilcher ordered one of his people to load it all onto a mule and deliver it to camp.

As I prepared to depart, I said in farewell, "See ye next year, Major."

"No, ye won't, Mister Buck. Missouri Fur's goin' belly-up. All we got out of this whole rendezvous is a measly seventeen packs of plews, not nearly enough to make expenses." He sighed deeply and added, "It's past time we admit we're whupped." I could find no words to reply. Pilcher stared off into the distance and added, "I've got only one small card left to play — with Aitch-bee-cee, but I'm not hopeful."

I mumbled some parting nonsense and retreated as fast as I was able, deeply saddened by that noble man's defeat.

* * *

The Flatheads and the Nez Percés, still selling horses to trappers, were among the last tribes to quit the rendezvous, for which I was grateful. Brass Turtle and I paid a final visit to the Sah-lish camp, gifting the headmen, of whom, I learned, Rainbow's father was one, with blankets, knives, tobacco, gunpowder and lead, and what-all, in gratitude for their hospitality — naturally not mentioning what that hospitality might have consisted of.

Rainbow's father accepted my gifts with quiet grace, but his knowing gaze let me know that he was well-aware of my relations with his daughter. For once I was content that I couldn't speak their language. As it was, my cheeks were burning as I fumbled with the farewell signs.

Rainbow and I made love in those final nights with alternating frenzy and tender devotion. Often I lay quietly with her in a close embrace, tracing with my fingers her dips and hollows, the sleek planes of her arms and thighs and muscular back and buttocks, her swelling breasts and taut belly, nuzzling her neck and kissing her eyes and burying my face in her sweet-smelling hair, seeking to memorize every precious inch of her before she disappeared from my life. Her caresses told me that she was doing much the same.

I agonized over asking her to come with me. It meant abandoning her father and her people, all that she had ever known, to embark on an unknown, unforeseeable adventure with me. I had no experience of traveling in a perilous wilderness with a woman — and perhaps a child someday — nor did my companions. I wrestled over that decision and at last I held my peace.

Overriding her protests, I heaped a galore of trade goods upon her — woolen strouding and calicos, blankets, knives and kettles and all manner of hardware, a tomahawk, belt axe and whetstone, beads and all manner of other foofurraw — but the one gift that she desired, myself, I withheld, unable, even for her, to forfeit the wild, utterly free, unencumbered life that I had so recently regained.

Then one morning she and all of her people were gone, as we had known must come to pass. There were no final goodbyes. When I roused from my robes one forenoon I discovered, heaped in a corner of the bower, raiment worthy of a chieftain — butter-soft doeskin shirts richly quilled and beaded, antelope leggin's adorned with horsehair, quills, and hawk bells, britchclouts, and half-a-dozen pairs of moccasins, some sturdy, others light as sunshine, all encrusted with tiny quills and colorful beadwork.

There was no need to run to her village. The Flatheads had departed.

* * *

Rendezvous was dwindling rapidly. Every day Company brigades were forming, accompanied by free trappers, some already heading out, others still wrangling over where the best country lay for a rich fall harvest. Our own bunch was undecided, a few choosing to go it alone to the Seeds-kee-dee, others arguing for hitching onto a Company brigade for sake of safety in numbers against Blackfoot and Grovant attacks and horse-raiding Crows.

Powatawa, Micah, McCool, and I stayed pretty much out of the arguefying, until Brass Turtle heatedly made a case for attaching ourselves to the brigade Davey Jackson and Tom Fitzpatrick were taking north to Flathead country. I jumped into the fray with both feet, seconding Turtle, and my three newcomers voted with me, along with a sufficient number of the others to carry the day for Turtle. It was settled. We were going north with Fitz and Davey. There were no really strong opposing opinions, so there was no serious grumbling, except from Anse Tolliver, who hates to lose a contest even if he doesn't care that much about winning it.

I still possessed entirely too much plunder, in spite of my free-handed gifting at the start of rendezvous. Once trapping commenced, our critters would be needed mostly to pack beaver plews. We needed to cache our extra supplies against a time when our bunch would need them, as is almost always the case, come winter.

First off, I lessened my load a mite by equipping McCool with the pistol and the extra traps I had bought from Pilcher and I handed over the percussion locks to Micah, for only he knew what to do with them. He pronounced them serviceable and stowed them away with his tools, along with those he had brought up from Hawken's shop.

That made hardly a dent in the heap of extra goods. Turtle and I enlisted half a dozen of our people to load the lot onto pack animals and head out to build a cache. Half a day's travel took us to a high grassy bank, well-screened with trees, overlooking one of the many streams that feed Sweet Lake, a spot safe from springtime flooding.

Locating a cache so that it can be found again requires four landmarks — in that case, a lightning-struck tree, a couple odd-shaped big rocks, a far-off peak, none of them likely to move or wash away — located roughly in four different directions. Then by drawing an imaginary line from each opposing landmark, say, north to south and east to west, the cache is located where the lines cross. That's the easy part.

First, you must carefully remove a two-foot-square of sod, complcte with roots, preferably in one piece, put it aside, and keep it well-watered. Then you dig a straight-sided chimney about two feet deep before you commence widening the hole outward underground, forming a jug large enough to store your plunder, say, four to six feet in diameter and deep enough to let a man work standing or crouching on the bottom.

The dirt you dig out of the hole must be carefully placed on a hide, then toted to the riverbank and dumped into the stream, lest its presence betray your hidey-hole. Lacking nearby running water, you need to scatter the dirt in the air a goodly distance from the cache, but that requires a lot of extra work.

Next, it's necessary to build a sturdy lattice-work flooring of inter-laced saplings suspended a foot or so off the bottom of the cache to allow drainage from the surrounding soil and then to line the hole with more saplings to protect your goods from seepage from the walls. Harvesting saplings — willows are best — must be done far enough away from the cache to avoid arousing the curiosity of passers-by. Never take too many from one place. Cut them close to the ground and daub the stumps with dirt to deceive prying eyes.

After you deposit your plunder in the cache, stacking it up to the chimney-hole, cover it with hides or heavy canvas, build a strong lattice of sturdy saplings over the hides, lay one more hide over the lattice, then fill in the chimney-hole with well-tamped dirt and replace the sod precisely as it was before you removed it. Tramping about afoot or horseback is advisable.

Then, barring the myriad misfortunes that dog a trapper's life, you have a pretty good chance of preserving your plews and plunder from the elements, thieving Indians, and the Competition.

* * *

By time we got back to rendezvous, dog-tired and filthy, it was hard to believe that just a few days earlier the southern shore of Sweet Lake had swarmed with a noisy, colorful mob of Indians, trappers, and traders. Now it was nearly deserted. The pack train had already departed for Saint Louis and most of the brigades had scattered to the four winds. We were relieved, howsomever, to spy Jackson's people still gathered near the spot where Sublette's trade tents had stood.

As we passed by, Tom Fitzpatrick hailed us. "Welcome back, me buckos! We just about gave up on ye!" He surveyed our muddy clothing and dirty faces with a grin. "Ye'd best be puttin' yersel's to rights an' get to packin' yer plunder. We'll be leavin' crack o' daylight tomorra!"

Our own camp was stripped down to bare bones. The campkeepers, Dureau and L'Archevêque, had packed most of their gear into loads ready to be slung onto packsaddles. Horses and mules had been brought in from the broad pastures and were grazing nearby under the care of Acorn, Pretty Horse, and Little Mountain.

"'Bout time ye be showin' yer sorry-arse se'fs!" Anse Tolliver screeched. "Damn lucky ye ain't findin' us all skelped an' picked over by ther gawddamn buzzards whilst ye war out frolickin'!"

"Frolickin', hell!" Brass Turtle rejoined sharply. "Ye'll be goddamn glad, Tolliver, come skinny times, that we put some plunder by fer when we'll be needin'it!" Anse clammed up under Turtle's glare. "'Sides, I di'nt hear you off'rin' to help with the diggin', 'stead o' fiddlin' an' drammin' an' whorin' back hyar!"

Matters might have become ugly had not Ned Godey intervened. "Awright,'nuff said! Our bunch is plumb wore out. Ever'body's edgy! Let it go! We be hyar now an' so's Davey. We'll be ready to ride when he is, so no harm done."

That quelled the dispute. Our cache-building crew scattered to unsaddle, drop off the digging tools with the campkeepers, and turn out our critters to graze. Tuttle had packed most of my belongings as well as his own. I stripped off my dirty clothes and dived into the lake to wash off the grime I had accumulated inside the cache.

When I returned dripping to the bower, Tuttle greeted me with a broad grin. "Feelin' better, are ye?" I nodded my assent. "'Pears ye could be usin' a dram or two o' thct'crc Frenchy boozc o' your'n, don'tcha think? I kep' it out fer ye." I laughed and allowed that a snort might very well be in order just about then and, although I was absolutely certain of his reply, enquired if he might be willing to join me. "Wal, naow, cain't letch'er be drinkin' alone by yerownse'f. 'Tain't proper. Don't mind ef I do."

Chapter VII
The Flathead

By time we halted for nooning we had been on the move for half-a-dozen hours, much of it occupied with frequent dismounts to cinch up packsaddles, adjusting and repacking loads, and chasing errant pack animals intent on suicide on the narrow trails we were snaking through on our way north from rendezvous. A fortnight on the lush graze at Sweet Lake and little or no work during that time made them frisky, forgetful of their schooling, and resentful of servitude, especially the mules, most of whom bucked and kicked and sought to scrape off their loads on trees and boulders. In spite of the extra work, I had to admire their free spirit, much like our own refusal to knuckle under to any man's authority.

Our bunch numbered eighteen now, fifteen seasoned mountaineers and three likely newcomers. I harbored no doubt that Micah and Finn McCool would soon get the hang of their new life. Both were tough, intelligent, and quick to learn whatever it takes to survive. Powatawa had little to learn except the new country and the art of beaver-trapping, which I was sure would come easy for him. He would have many good teachers, especially amongst our Delawares and Iroquois.

Our little caravan tagged a quarter mile or so behind Jackson's brigade, which numbered no more than sixty trappers in all, some of them accompanied by their Indian women and little kids. The pace was as brisk as the country allowed, for Davey and Tom Fitzpatrick made no allowance for the distaff side. They didn't need to do so, either. From my earliest experience, 'way back on the Yellowstone in 'twenty-two, I have been continually impressed by the speed at which Indians can travel — whole villages lugging tipi poles, squalling babes swinging on cradle boards from their mothers' saddles, old folks and youngsters too young to ride and mountains of plunder heaped onto travois drags, huge horse herds tended by stripling boys, the whole shebang led and flanked by the men, chiefs and warriors, who never turn a hand to help with chores, which they consider to be women's work, unworthy labor for a hunter or a fighting man. It is the women who move the village, never the men.

Davey's brigade was measly, only sixty men, a mix of mostly engagés and a few free trappers, especially considering that we were heading north into country that bordered the Blackfoot domain. It was the hunting grounds of the Sah-lish and Kootenai, Pend d'Oreilles, and a scattering of other smaller tribes, all of whom are generally tolerant of trappers. Just the same, Blackfoots can be anywhere. No wonder Fitz and Davey welcomed our company, nigh a score of reliable extra guns.

In the manner of men on the move, I found myself visiting now with one man, then another, as we dealt with difficult trails and stubborn pack animals. The customary gloom was settling on my old companions, some doubtless regretting the loss of rendezvous pleasures, all of them regaining the suspicious vigilance that enables a trapper to survive in a hostile wilderness.

My three new companions were so far unaffected. They had enjoyed the rendezvous, but its delights had meant less to them than it had to the old-timers, who were looking forward now to yet another year of peril and likely privation — certainly and especially an absence of booze. The newcomers were so far mostly ignorant of the manifold dangers ever present in the Rockies. Our various hostile encounters on the westward trail had helped to prepare them for more of the same, but the deeply-ingrained refusal of seasoned trappers to trust anything or anyone had not yet permeated their character. That would come soon enough.

When I chanced to fall in with Tuttle and Finn McCool, they appeared cheerful enough. "I see ye war lookin' arter thi'shere Irisher proper-like, Temple," Tuttle declared, "gittin' him thet'ere Spanyard saddle, like ye done."

I shrugged. McCool was quick to add his approval. "Indeed, Temple, I owe ye a plenitude o' thankees. I niver would'a thought o' tradin' that sojer saddle for one o' these. Once I got meself accustomed to the diff'rence of it, I warrant ye me arse thanks ye kindly, especially fer climbin' hills." He reflected a moment and added, "Me 'orses'll be thankin' ye, as well. Such a saddle is eversomuch aisier on their backs."

"Nex' thang," Tuttle cut in, "we need to be teachin' 'im haow to be flangin' one a them'ere reata ropes, afore we be countin' 'im some kind o' mountaineer."

I had to smile. It was plain that Tuttle had pretty much adopted the Irish greenhorn, just as he had done for me, back on Mike Fink's keelboat. Finn McCool could have done a great deal worse.

Later, coming up behind Micah and Cesár Pérez, before they noticed my presence, I heard them chattering away in the Spaniard tongue. We had entered a broad meadow, which allowed me to ride up beside them. When they became aware of me, they switched over to English, or what passed for it with Cesár. "I didn't know you could palaver in the Spaniard lingo, Micah," I commented. "Where'd ye learn to do that?"

Micah grinned sheepishly. "Well, not very well, so far. I picked up a smatter o' Spanish working for Chouteau — leastwise the way the Mexicans speak it." He saw the question in my eyes. "A passel o' Chouteau's kinfolk are up to their ears in the Santa Fe trade, so you can wager M'sieu Pierre has a hand in it, too. About half the time, for a spell there, he had me workin' furs an' silver and all manner o' goods the Spaniards were bringin' in from Santa Fe." He laughed self-consciously. "I reckon I just sort'a picked it up without hardly even knowin' I was doin' it." He laughed again. "Maybe now, with Cesár here, I'll learn it better."

Once again I breathed a silent prayer of thanks to Pierre Chouteau. No matter his self-interested motives, le Cadet had exposed Micah to an education that I myself might have envied, had I not been content with Ma's teaching and the lessons I had learned in the Rocky Mountain School of Hard Knocks.

Looking about, I saw no sign of Jim Beckwith. Formerly, he had almost always ridden nearby Cesár when our bunch was on the move. Now, even at the nooning halt, Jim had sat off by himself, munching cold vittles, talking to no one, until it was time to mount and get on the trail once more. Beckwith was likely traveling up front with Jackson's people. Which made no nevermind to me, right then.

* * *

Our journey led pretty much due north and somewhat west, but naturally our actual passage was nowhere near a straight line. We zig-zagged one way and another, seeking mountain passes, skirting thick forests where deadfall makes progress impossible, and avoiding, when we could, desert land bereft of water and graze for our critters, as well as the buffalo on which we depend for meat.

I often rode with the Company men up front, mostly with Tom Fitzpatrick, when he wasn't busy with one chore or another, mainly keeping men and animals snugged up on the trail. Straggling is a sure invitation to horsethieves to come swooping out of ambush and making off with pack animals and plunder and killing their owner for boot, if opportunity affords. The Indian horsethief likely knows the country and the traveler mostly doesn't, so if the thief can put enough ground betwixt himself and his pursuers, he'll likely be successful, even if he hasn't already set up a second ambush.

Each day, Fitz grew a mite more edgy, constantly scanning every ridge and hollow, forever cautioning his greenhorns, and doubling horse guards at night. "It's grateful I am to be havin' your bunch bringin' up the rear o' this bloody menagerie. We've too many new men and not enough old hands amongst us. Snake country's mostly behind us. Now we're amongst the bloody Bannacks. Be after keepin' yer eyes skinned, day an' night. They're a villainous lot!" I needed no such admonition, but I nodded and assured him that I would do just that.

Our critters were trail-broke by then, capable of traveling free and sticking close. Even so, we kept them on haltershanks, snugged head to tail, lest marauders spook and scatter them. At night we kept them close-hobbled and staked on picket-pins and we stood horse-guard in pairs. Either Powatawa or I accompanied Micah, for, naturally sharp as he is, night sounds in the mountains were still new to him. A hoot or a chitter might signal an impending attack. Tuttle paired with Finn for the same reason.

At Davey Jackson's request, we camped at night nearby his brigade. He wished to have as many seasoned men as possible gathered in case of a raid. Just the same, we camped just outside the main group, our critters separate from theirs, maintaining our own cookfire.

We were still in Bannack country when, one late forenoon, Powatawa beckoned me to ride nigh him. "We are not lonesome," he said quietly, slightly lifting his chin towards a nearby ridge. After a decent interval I glanced in that direction but I saw nothing. "He is gone now," he said matter-of-factly, "but three times this day I have seen a short-hair, a Gah'ee-bee-shuh, what you call a Bannock. We will know him better this night." I accepted my father's warning as gospel. There was no doubting which Indians were shadowing our column. Bannack men I had seen at Sweet Lake wore their hair loose, chopped off shoulder-length and tied down with a band of leather or cloth. Even at rendezvous, they were a troublesome lot.

I drifted back in our column to let Brass Turtle in on Powatawa's discovery. He nodded. "I seen 'em, too, this mornin'. Din't say nothin' yet, lest we scare 'em off by lookin' 'round too much." I gigged Kumskaka into a faster walk to where Tuttle and Godey led our procession. They received my muttered words calmly, without question, careful not to scan the hilltops right then. Still trailing my pack animals, I rode forward to the brigade at an easy-going trot to inform Fitzpatrick of our discovery, advising that he refrain from letting his greenhorns in on the secret, lest they show excitement and spoil our surprise. Fitz chuckled and replied, "Och, Temple, you're right. 'Tis best we welcome thim haythens on our own terms, lettin' 'em be thinkin' they've got the drop on us and us none the wiser. I'll be tellin' only thim as know what they're about in sich circumstances. Much obliged."

After the nooning halt we came out upon a broad stretch of prairie. We spied, at a considerable distance, a small bunch of buffalo grazing, unconcerned about our cavalcade. Tuttle, Micah, and I detached from the column, each leading a pack horse, and ambled out to them, staying downwind. We dismounted within a long rifle shot, took careful aim, and, upon Tuttle's nod, we fired at once and dropped three cows in a span of no more than a couple rods. Naturally the rest took fright and thundered off, great shaggy heads swinging, tails straight up as ramrods, hooves churning, flinging sod every whichaway.

We butchered only one cow, for Fitz had dispatched several men from his column to retrieve the meat from the other two. We made short work of the chore, tarrying only to savor the smoking-hot liver, loaded our pack animals, and hastened back to our comrades, mouths watering at the prospect of fresh hump ribs, tongue, and boudins that night. Fresh-killed meat had been a seldom thing during our journey through mostly forested areas up to then.

Supper was a merry affair, not only on account of fresh meat sizzling over the coals, but mostly because every one of us was halfway giddy at the prospect of ridding ourselves of the hovering horsethieves who had likely dogged our trail ever since rendezvous. Even if we hadn't spied them, it was a fair bet they had been there.

We made ourselves an inviting target that night. We camped in a fair-size meadow fringed with close-grown forest that ran up the surrounding hillsides. The brigade camped farther out in the meadow, away from the trees. Powatawa, Brass Turtle, and most of our Indians elected to gather deadwood for the cookfire, each of them meanwhile selecting a hidey-hole with a clear view of the deer trails that meandered amongst the trees and thick underbrush.

We gorged on tender cow and afterwards Anse Tolliver unlimbered his fiddle and sawed out cheerful tunes, accompanied by Yves Dureau on his squeezebox concertina and Cesár tootling on his little earthen yam. Paddy McBride and Micah leaped and cavorted in a wild dance in the firelight. A distant watcher might have supposed that this was another drunken revelry, much like rendezvous.

When at last the merry-making ended, we retired to our robes, scattered away from the firelight, as our custom is. Horse-guards relieved their fellows, the cookfire burned to glowing coals, and silence soon settled over the camp.

Every man was sober and alert, eyes and ears straining into the darkness, firearms primed and ready to hand. A slim sickle moon cast barely enough light to see my outstretched hand. Micah and I slithered out of our robes and crawled a roundabout way to the edge of our staked and hobbled livestock. We stationed ourselves a rod or so apart, lying flat in the grass, and waited, the only sounds the snorting and stamping and chomping of our grazing critters. Minutes passed, then an hour, maybe more. I commenced to wonder if the watchers had tumbled to our scheme.

An agonized yip from the hillside first broke the stillness, then another barking grunt, followed by a flurry of shouts and gunshots. A shadowy figure erupted from inside the herd and ran towards the trees, then another. I rose to my knees and fired at the first runner. He slid headlong into the tall grass. Before the report of my rifle had quite faded, Micah's shot rang out. I spun about in time to see the second horsethief throw up his hands, totter forwards a step or two and crumple to earth.

All hell broke loose just then, gunshots and frenzied yelling from every quarter. I threw myself flat on the ground, lest a stray ball put a full stop to my paragraph. It was quickly over, Indian yips and jubilant American shouts and Christian curses replacing the gunfire. Reloading my rifle, I stayed put for a spell, in case a lingering marauder still remained amidst the neighing, braying critters who r'ared and strained against their picket ropes, but no enemy appeared. I rose and joined Micah, Tuttle, Finn, and Anse. We did our best to calm our rattled livestock, knot together slashed picket ropes, and replace severed hobbles. The critters settled down soon enough, howsomever, and resumed their grazing.

The cookfire was blazing now. Soon, our Indians straggled out from amongst the trees and into the firelight, teeth flashing in broad grins, bows still strung, several flaunting fresh scalps, mincing about in dainty dance steps. Powatawa carried two scalps, which, together with his cheerful smile, attested to his successful marksmanship.

Naturally nobody could sleep after that. We still had coffee beans from rendezvous and soon the kettle was boiling. The air was fat with marvelous accounts of the battle, each telling of it more outrageous than its predecessor. I commenced to wonder if the encounter of which they spoke was the same one that I had witnessed.

After a spell, Fitz and Davey Jackson strolled into camp, helped themselves to coffee, hunkered down, lighted their pipes, and listened to the wonderful exploits of my comrades. At last Fitz knocked the dottle from his pipe and observed drily, "'Pears ye've been after exterminatin' the intire Bannack nation, from the sound of it."

"Oh, don'tcha be worryin' none, Fitz," Tuttle assured him, "these hyar yarns're jest a-bornin' naow. They'll be gittin' a whole lot bigger an' better afore long."

"Ye kin count on it," Godey observed. Then, "How'd it go 'mongst yer men, Davey? Anybody hurt? Lose any stock?"

"Nope," Jackson replied. "'Pears you got the most of it. Caught two of 'em 'mongst the critters what won't be stealin' no more hosses."

"That's purty much how we figgered it," Brass Turtle offered. "It's why we set up ri'chere, so's they couldn't do hardly nuthin' else but comin' thisaway, gittin' off o' that'ere hill."

And so it went, rehashing the fight until dawn fingered into the eastern sky, time to saddle up and push northwards.

Just before we mounted up, Brass Turtle tossed a double handful of clotted scalps onto the smouldering coals. "Din't really want 'em," he announced. "Jist wanted to teach 'em an extry lesson 'bout messin' with mountaineers." He swung aboard his horse and called out, "Best we be movin' out, 'fore we git the gawddamn Bannack stink on us!" And so we did.

* * *

The way north widened into a broad prairie flanked on the east by the distant Tetons, when you could see them through low-hanging clouds. Our pace was more leisurely now that Bannock bandits no longer threatened, although there never comes a time anywhere in that country when you dare relax your vigilance. Horses and mules are the common cash of the mountains and plains and the unwary traveler will soon be set afoot, even by Indians who are otherwise friendly.

It was still midsummer and the prairie was often black with buffalo. Cows had mostly weaned their calves by that time and were rolling fat on the rich graze thereabouts. We got spoiled by the plenitude of buffalo and spurned even young bulls in favor of their sisters and dams.

It was time to lay in a stock of dried meat for winter. Memories of deep snow and pinched bellies prompted even Jackson and Fitzpatrick, anxious as they were to reach the Flathead, to tarry long enough to harvest meat. Until then, we had been content with picking off stragglers from the big herds, shooting from a distance, mostly afoot and from cover, but now the great shaggy multitudes drifting southwards offered not only meat but sport. It was time to introduce our newcomers to running buffalo.

We awoke one morning to the lowing and grunting of ten thousand or more buffalo moving in a grand procession past our overnight crick-bottom camp, hardly a quarter-mile distant. Opportunity had arrived! Fitz and Davey required no persuading to delay our travels. They were as greedy as the rest of us, not only for the meat, but also the excitement of running it down a-horseback.

On the long westward journey from Independence and in recent days I had often relieved the tedium of the trail by describing to the new men the best ways to shoot buffalo from the back of a galloping horse. Naturally, Tuttle, as always, was happy to chip in his two-cents-worth. Running buffalo is a common topic of mountaineer palaver, but talk is a flimsy substitute for experience. Learning by doing is the rule.

The camp fairly buzzed. We stripped off all excess from saddles, cleaned rifles, muskets, and pistols that were already clean and oiled, filled powderhorns and bullet pouches to the brim, and snugged cinchas tight — then, after a spell, even tighter.

I chose Kumskaka for the chore, even though he had never before engaged in that pursuit. Starting with the first buffaloes we harvested on the westering trail, I had taken care to load him and Micah's dun with the bloody fresh buffalo hides, getting them accustomed to the smell. Handy and courageous as I knew Kumskaka to be, I was confident that he would be equal to the task.

Tuttle was already astride Chiksika, my gift to him when I returned to Ohio. Chiksika was the very first horse I owned in the mountains, already a seasoned buffalo-runner when I bought him. Paddy waved from the back of Jake, another fine buffalo-runner, my trophy from our first fight with the Absóraqas on the Yellowstone. Brass Turtle was soothing the piebald Patch, my reward from the Snake chief Wah-shah-kee after a battle with a Crow raiding party on the Popo-azhieh. Looking at those horses was like reading pages in my own history in the mountains.

Our neophytes were itching to get into the fray, Micah aboard his big dun and Finn mounted on the tall bay horse he had claimed after the Blackfoot battle. My father lounged quietly on one of his sturdy piebalds. All of our Indians were ready, rifles or muskets slung next to their quivers.

Ready as ever we would be, we trotted out of camp, headed for the brown ocean of woolly humps and tossing horns lumbering southwards. I thrilled at the sight of them. A score of riders led by Jackson and Fitzgerald streamed out of the brigade camp. We had agreed that one of them would signal when the chase should commence.

Nobody galloped or loped to close with the herd, lest we spook them into a headlong rush before we were ready. A sedate trot brought us nigh its flanks soon enough. Company men and our bunch strung out several rods distant from the shaggy parade. The outer critters commenced bawling nervously and tried to shove into the herd, away from us. Every eye was fixed on Davey Jackson. Tuttle called out to Finn and Micah, "Best ye rest easy hyar fer a spell, so's ye kin see how it's done!" He might have been talking to the wind. When Davey stood in his stirrups and fired his pistol, they were off and running with the rest of us.

Kumskaka surged like an ocean wave and flew headlong into the hairy throng. I did naught to check him, glorying in the sheer ecstasy of the chase, in his flying mane and hammering hooves, his powerful shoulders pouring strength and excitement into my thighs and my very soul.

When buffalo move in big herds they don't travel in a close-packed solid mass, as they appear to do when you're looking from the outside. They are constantly grazing on the move, keeping a comfortable distance between one bunch and another.

Once the chase commences and you get inside the herd, they still don't bunch up. Old cows haze their younger charges together and the seed bulls come on behind, protecting their harems. Bachelor bulls run hither and thither, singly or in pairs or threes.

I chose a fat young cow and urged Kumskaka to close on her off side. As we came up with her I brought my rifle to bear just above and behind her pumping foreleg, an easy downward heart and lung shot. Which it would have been had not my uneducated horse allowed himself to crowd too close to her wildly swinging head. She banged his shoulder with her cheek and the flat of her horn, bowling him sidewise and nearly off his feet. My shot went wild and I nearly flew out of the saddle, cussing all the way. When I caught my breath, I reminded myself that this was Kumskaka's schooling time and a plenitude of buffalo and rifle balls still remained.

I recharged my rifle and fitted on a percussion cap as we closed upon the off side of another well-padded young cow. This time Kumskaka kept a respectful distance from the swinging horns, matching her speed and holding steady half a head behind hers, allowing me to bring the muzzle within a foot of her and fire. She ran no more than a stride and a half before she collapsed and skidded to a halt, bearded chin ploughing a furrow, great gouts of blood spewing from mouth and nostrils.

Still at a gallop, we set off in pursuit of another cluster of cows, careful to dodge wide around the huge seed bull trailing behind, as well as the shaggy old cow chaperoning them. I slung my rifle and pulled my pistol from its saddle holster, the while offering a prayer of thanks to Jacob Hawken for his shorter-barreled rifle and his tight-fitting percussion caps. This time we came up on the near side of a portly young cow. Kumskaka matched her pace, ever wary of her swinging head and sharp horns. I swung the long-barreled pistol out at arm's-length and sent the heavy ball cleanly through her heart and lungs, or so I reckoned from her sudden loss of interest in the race.

I slowed somewhat to an easy lope in an open space whilst I reloaded and primed rifle and pistol, meanwhile watching Micah kill a fine, fat cow, then swing wide out of reach of the big bull charging close behind, proving once again that my friend is a quick-learner. Our Indians trailed us whites, spread pretty much across the galloping herd, harvesting meat but also loosing arrows into the carcasses of our kills, thereby scotching future disputes with Company men over who killed which buffalo.

Swinging my gaze about, seeking a likely target, I saw Finn McCool, well ahead, topple a good-size cow, then spur his tall, leggy bay horse in a wide arc to evade the mothering cow and the big bull rushing close behind her. He slung his rifle, yanked his pistol from its saddle holster, and set off after another bunch. My heart warmed to see the Irishman take so handily to mountain ways.

What happened next took no more than a hundredth of the time it takes to tell it. McCool's horse, fairly flying in an all-out gallop, hooves barely touching the ground, constantly changing leads on the uneven prairie, suddenly misstepped on a loose rock or a shallow hole, stumbled to his knees, and turned topsy-turvy, his forward speed propelling his hindquarters in a soaring arc over his head and, as I supposed, surely breaking his neck. Which, howsomever, by some freak of good fortune, he didn't. Finn flew from the saddle, long arms thrashing, skinny legs scissoring skywards, looking for all the world like an octopus falling out of a tree, still clutching his pistol, and lit flat upon his back and onto his still-slung rifle, as well.

The bay horse scrambled to his feet, somehow dodged an oncoming bull, and disappeared amongst the woolly humps and tossing horns and straight-up tails fluttering like pennants.

A cluster of buffalo veered between the Irishman and me, certain to run over him before I could reach him. Somehow, they didn't. Finn staggered to his feet, dazed, shaking his head, befuddled, striving to get his bearings. My thoughts flashed to my first buffalo-running on the Yellowstone and Jake Yancy trampled to strawberry jam when his horse fell in the midst of a stampeding herd.

Finn stumbled about in a tight circle, his slung rifle sticking out above his head, pistol still clutched in his fist. I spurred Kumskaka into an even faster gallop, despairing the while of reaching him in time, try as I might. Then, over the thunder of hooves and snorting, bawling buffalo, I heard a screaming war-whoop. I swung my gaze to behold Powatawa, standing in his stirrups, crouched over his horse's neck, streaking towards McCool, swinging a saddle blanket around his head, scattering oncoming buffalo just enough to open a space between himself and Finn.

Hardly breaking stride, Powatawa swooped like an eagle skimming a fish from a lake, grabbed McCool under the arms, clasped him to his hip, and sped off just in time to dodge the horns of still another bunch of charging buffalo, Finn flopping like a raggedy doll, his slung rifle banging his head and my father's face, as well, whilst Powatawa threaded the big piebald out of the herd to the safety of the open prairie.

By time I got loose from the woolly torrent and trotted back to them, Finn and Powatawa were seated face to face on the ground. The sweat-drenched spotted horse stood splay-legged, trembling, head hanging, gasping for breath. Blood oozed from gashes on my father's cheek and forehead, but it didn't obscure his jubilant grin. McCool sat hunched over, breathing heavily, rifle across his knees, a mournful look on his lean Irish mug.

"Would'ja be lookin' at this, now," he wailed, holding up the rifle. "'Tis ruint beyond savin'! Yer sainted uncle's rifle gun! Busted to rubbish, it is!" I glanced at the rifle and saw that the lock was indeed smashed beyond repair.

"It's only a gun, McCool!" I yelled at him. "Ye could'a been tromped to jelly out there, if not for Powatawa here savin' your skinny Irish arse!" It felt good to release my feelings by shouting. I had been scared nearly to death for the both of them.

"Och, I've already been after givin' my thanks to this darlin' man! I'll niver be thankin' 'im enough. He owns me body an' soul from this day onwards!"

A smiling, nodding Powatawa confirmed the truth of Finn's declaration. "He thanks too much," he said. "One time is enough."

"But would ye be after lookin' at what's left o' yer dear uncle's foine rifle gun!" he lamented. "'Twas yer heirloom, Temple darlin', it was, an' now 'tis fit only fer the dustbin!"

I squatted to inspect the rifle. Only the lock was smashed beyond repair, naught else. Even the trigger and its guard were intact. "What would ye say if I told ye this was a happy accident?" I said, rising. "I daresay Micah'll have ye shootin' better'n ever afore ye know it."

Finn stared in disbelief. "Are ye daft, man? Where d'ye propose to be findin' a gunsmith shop in this benighted wilderness?"

"You'll see," I replied. Further talk was cut off by Paddy McBride's arrival. He was leading McCool's bay horse, who looked hardly the worse for wear. The saddle was scuffed but undamaged.

When he spied Finn, unhurt, sprawling on the turf, Paddy blew out a great breath of obvious relief before he roared, "Saints presarve us! Here ye be, ye great ninny, lollin' here like a Sassenach lord, ye be, whin half the camp is after huntin' yer sorry remains to stuff in a saddle-poke so's ye might be after gittin' a daycent buryin'!

"Thank ye kindly, Padraic," Finn replied with a wry smile, "but I'm needin' nayther priest ner parson just yet. Misther Powatawer here saved me arse this day, else ye'd surely be after performin' a spadin' job o' work."

Paddy told how he had spied Finn's riderless horse roaming amongst the buffalo and Finn related all he could recollect about Powatawa's remarkable rescue, by which time the herd had mostly disappeared into the distance, all except a few bachelor bulls who trotted forlornly in its wake. Rich as we were with fat cow, no one bothered them.

Most of our bunch drifted by and naturally the story needed to be told again and again, each time with increasingly colorful flourishes, until Ned Godey gestured towards our camp and announced, "Fun part's over! Time we be commencin' the hard work!" The campkeepers were leading pack animals onto the prairie. It was indeed time to begin the real work of butchering out our kills.

* * *

More than a hundred shaggy carcasses littered the plain, spread over a distance of five miles or more. Iroquois and Delaware arrows told us which ones were ours, so we suffered no conflicts with Company men. There was more than enough for everybody. We commenced the bloody task in mid-forenoon and the sun was dipping towards the Tetons before we led the last of our pack critters into camp and dumped their loads onto the huge heap of still-steaming meat beside the crick.

I lost no time before jumping into the crick, fully clothed, joining my father, Brass Turtle, and our other Indians. In no time at all, Micah and the rest of our whites were frolicking in the water. Even Tuttle and Anse strolled into the shallows and sedately seated themselves up to their armpits, which was in itself some sort of prodigy. Itchy prairie loam and sticky warm blood mixed with a plenitude of sweat encouraged even the most reluctant bather to indulge in cleanliness, however temporary.

Merriment reigned at supper that night. We stuffed ourselves with tender, fat-larded hump ribs, tongue, boudins, and razor-thin-sliced liver simmering in the spiders. The air was rife with recountings of the chase, each one more elaborate in the re-telling, tales of close calls and near things and impossible shots that proved successful. I sneaked a cup of my precious French cognac each to McCool and Powatawa and naturally I poured one for myself. As you might suppose, Tuttle's keen nose penetrated my stealth, so he got a cupful, as well.

When I crawled into my robes under a cloudless, starlit sky, I tried to revisit Rainbow in our bower at rendezvous, but my reverie was brief. If I dreamed at all, I had no recollection of it next morning.

* * *

Naked save for britchclouts, early in the morning we plunged into the task of drying our plentiful meat harvest, some gathering willows along the crick bottom and fashioning a long line of spindly drying-racks lashed together with bark stripped from the saplings, the rest slicing the meat into thin strips and draping it on the racks. The butchering of so much meat appeared to be an endless chore, but necessary, for a long winter and the likely scarcity of game loomed in every man's mind.

Old Foot called Micah and me away from our labors and led us to the edge of the prairie, where he pointed to several grizzly bears gorging on yesterday's leavings. "Need one bear now," he told us. "You go shoot plenty-damn-quick foh me." When I started to object that we already possessed a plenitude of meat, Finn McCool, who had joined us, explained that bear fat was required for horse medicines that he and Foot were concocting.

"We'll be renderin' the fat into oil for the makin' of a physic for the equines," he said, "but first we need the bear. And lackin' a rifle-gun as I am, as ye know, 'tis best ye go out an' perform the task."

Bears — black, brown, cinnamon, or silvertips — have been my personal anathema ever since my boyhood. No Blackfoot warrior has ever stirred in me the unreasoning fear that a bear of any sort can do. So far, my encounters with bears have been fortunately few and I much prefer to keep it that way. The purpose of their request, in aid of our livestock, was, howsomever, undeniable, so, after enlisting the assistance of Godey and Tuttle, Micah and I armed ourselves, saddled up, and, four-strong, rode out to harvest a great white bear for our medicos.

As it was, four good marksmen, shooting from a safe distance, made short work of a big grizzly, who, occupied as he was with his breakfast, paid us little attention until a volley sent him off to his ursine Happy Hunting Ground. Naturally we lingered long enough for a pipeful before approaching the carcass and butchering out gobs of rich summertime fat meat. Then we loaded our packmules and returned to camp and the seemingly never-ending job of jerking meat.

* * *

Next day I spelled myself from my butchering chores long enough to visit Foot and McCool, busy at mixing handfuls of grass seed and various other dried herbs into clear bear oil, as well as saturating quantities of shredded tobacco with molasses. When they spied me standing by, they lost no time in commandeering my help in dosing every one of our critters with both concoctions. As I fed sweetened tobacco into one horse or mule after another, all of them eager to gobble the treat, I called over to McCool, "I know about tobacco riddin' 'em of worms, Finn, but what's the other'n for?"

"Och, 'tis a recipe Misther Foot an' meself have been after puttin' together fer relievin' 'em o' sand they're always takin' up with the grass they're eatin' on the prairie. 'Tis a cathartic fer cleanin' 'em out — clean as a tin whistle, it does." He chuckled. "Mind ye be careful o' walkin' behind 'em after the dosin', though, lest ye wish to be runnin' to the crick fer a bathe!"

When all of our more than five dozen horses and mules had been treated, I saw Finn and Old Foot, kettles in hand, hiking downstream to the brigade camp to share what remained of their medicines with the Company men.

Later, when we moved the animals to fresh grazing, the ground was slick with liquid manure and wriggling with long ugly white worms. Looking closely, you could see little red ones, as well.

After supper Finn and I were smoking a pipeful when he said, "'Tis remarkable how much medical knowledge that savage ould Injun has accumulated, Temple. Why, I warrant ye, our darlin' Ould Misther Foot could be teachin' lessons to many a certified medical doctor at Trinity itself!"

I snickered and replied, "Not surprising, Finn. I daresay his people have been attendin' their school long before yours ever did."

McCool laughed aloud. "I warrant you're right! An' I count meself lucky to be sittin' here in his classroom!"

* * *

The crisp, dry air of the high prairie quickly dried the jerk meat to leather. Three days after the buffalo running we were in the saddle, leading our heavily-laden pack animals northwards. Our bunch had trapped the Flathead country the year before with Fitz and Davey, but the trail was a new one for me.

"Enjoy yer ridin' 'long as ye kin, Temple," Tuttle advised. "Arter a couple days, it gits a mite hairy, as ye mought say." He offered to say no more and I didn't coax him. I merely nodded, slowed my Ready horse, and fell back to join Micah and McCool.

Finn was still gloating over his newly-restored rifle, fitted now with a percussion lock. Once the butchering and drying chore was completed, Micah had removed the smashed flintlock from my uncle's rifle and replaced it with one of the percussion locks he had brought with him from the Hawkens' shop. It had taken Micah the best part of a day to complete the job, drilling screw-holes and tapping the new lock into a proper fit on the little anvil he carried with him. When it was finished it was hard to tell that the rifle had ever been a flintlock. McCool was ecstatic, not only by regaining the rifle he had thought was destroyed, but also by the ease and speed of priming it. He became an instant convert to the art of Jacob Hawken and was loud in his praise of Micah to anybody who would listen. "You'll be extra glad when you're huntin' in wet weather," I advised him, "but even so, ye'd best keep a cow-hock over the lock, same as a flintlock."

Two nights later we camped by a mere trickle of a stream that meandered through the increasingly dry plain. "Drink deep whilst ye can," Tom Fitzpatrick advised when he visited our camp, "an' do yer best to fill up your craytchers like a parcel o' camels. Startin' tomorra, it'll be dry doin's fer the next coupl'a days."

By then I had learned that a stretch of godforsaken country lay ahead that would tax both man and beast. "Best ye commence ridin' that purty mule o' your'n," Anse Tolliver counseled, "leastaways 'til we git past that'ere patch. Ain't nuthin' like a good mule fer gittin' through bad footin'." Anse is never free with advice. I took his words to heart.

Next morning I swung onto Sugarfoot when the column headed out. Micah rode my mule's half-brother Lightfoot. We halted early for the nooning, at the edge of a vast ocean of jagged black rock barren of vegetation save random tufts of coarse prairie grass and prickly pear clinging desperately to patches of scanty windblown sandy soil. A more desolate region this side of hell was hard to imagine. Dinner was a hasty affair and we set off as soon as our animals had rested and grazed on the skimpy forage that bordered that seemingly unending sea of porous black and dull grey rock and scattered drifts of sand.

We traveled mostly single file through narrow passages betwixt heaped-up mounds of ashy rock and along the rims of deep craters.

Inside that no-man's-land the air was deadly still. Heat shimmered off the walls of our stony prison. Once, when the sandy trail widened enough to allow riding two abreast, Finn McCool opined, "Would'ja be lookin' at that now? This intire country was surely once a huge volcano, it was. 'Tis lava rock we're ridin' through, dead and lifeless lava rock. 'Tis surely like trav'lin' on the moon, it is."

"It's a helluva lot wuss'n thet," grumbled Tuttle, who had crowded up behind us. "Leastaways the moon be made o' green cheese. Ye could be eatin' thet, if'n ye could git to it. Thi'shere hell-hole ain't no good fer nuthin'!" Finn and I laughed, but I wasn't sure if Tuttle really meant it about the green cheese. With Tuttle Thompson, you can never tell.

When the trail narrowed and we were again riding single file, I thought about Finn's calling the lava rock "dead and lifeless." He was likely right. I had lived amongst Indians long enough to accept their belief that even rocks have a soul. This rubble, howsomever, could surely harbor no living spirit, except, perhaps, an evil one.

We plodded through the old volcano's serpentine passages until nearly dark, at which time word passed along the line for each man to halt and bed down wherever he could find room enough to stretch out, for there was no place in that enormous labyrinth to pitch a camp. Naturally there was neither water nor graze for the critters. The only bright spot was Tuttle's reassurance that we would likely reach the far side of hell sometime the next day.

Which we did. Jackson's brigade and our bunch straggled out of that rocky stewpot in late afternoon, every man and beast footsore and drenched in sweat, moccasins in tatters and every critter limping on hooves cracked and shredded by sharp-edged lava rock.

If I were a religious man who believed the fire-and-brimstone claptrap that Pap used to shout about on the Sabbath, I would be absolutely sure that I will go to heaven, for I have surely been to hell and back and once is enough for any sinner.

* * *

We halted a couple days at the Snake whilst our scouts roamed its banks seeking a shallow crossing where we might safely ford that broad river. Late in summer as it was by then, before autumn rains, the Snake's normal strong flow was greatly reduced. The delay afforded a welcome respite for all concerned. Graze was abundant for the critters and the river coaxed stray bunches of buffalo to linger along its shore, so it was with full bellies and replenished spirits that we made our crossing without incident and resumed our northward march.

We skirted forested areas scattered over the plain when we could. Dense deadfall slows progress or makes it impossible, but once we arrived at the foothills of a high mountain chain there was naught else to do but follow deer trails that wind through the thickly-wooded slopes and finger randomly towards the summit. We took turns at swinging axes to clear a path through downed trees. Agile deer are able to sneak through but our livestock were denied passage until we hewed out a trail.

We ate well enough, for, although buffalo avoid such country, the high mountain meadows teem with gangs of wapiti — and tender cow elk makes for a toothsome supper. We also harvested a couple cow moose, which provide delicious meat when taken high in the mountains. It is much less appetizing if they have been feeding in lowland swamps.

For all its difficulties, journeying through thick woods makes it unlikely that you will encounter raiding parties. There is little to attract them to such places. They thirst after horses and plunder and sometimes captive women, none of which are common commodities in the forest. So, besides the benefit of traveling a more or less direct route to our destination, avoiding a fight was a welcome dividend.

After we cleared the summit we came upon an increasingly broad, fast-running river flowing northwards. We followed it as best we could until it spilled out onto a fairly level plain. There was beaver sign aplenty on the cricks and streams that fed that clear-running river, but my companions assured me that even better trapping lay ahead. Just the same, I scribbled a note in my mind to find my way back to that country when the rich bonanza of plews of which they spoke petered out, as it inevitably must.

When at last we made our descent through the northern foothills, we spied, here and there, lone Indians marking our progress. They kept their distance and we offered them no challenge.

Once we arrived upon the plain we discovered scattered bands of buffalo. The lure of fresh meat was too great to be denied. Half a dozen of us delivered our pack strings to our fellows and set off in pursuit of a long-overdue feast. Which we harvested in practically no time at all. We donated four of the six fat cows to the brigade, which still left our bunch a plenitude of choice cuts on which to feast.

Davey and Fitz called an early halt beside a crick and soon the cookfires were blazing, the heady aroma of roasting meat intoxicating us all. That heavenly fragrance must have wafted over the entire prairie, for it wasn't long before we were visited by half a dozen neatly-dressed Indians. They halted their ponies a hundred yards from camp and fired their guns in the air, then advanced slowly, arms upraised, palms outward, in a sign of peace. "Kootenai," Ned Godey pronounced. "They be friendlies." They proved to be exceedingly so.

Some Indians on the plains, such as the warlike Sioux and the Pani, insolently demand tribute from any whitemen who intrude on land they like to call their own. Others, like these unthreatening Kootenai warriors, wish only to be gifted with presents. Which really amounts to the same thing.

Naturally we offered tobacco, a few awls, flints and firesteels, some beads, and suchlike, which they happily accepted. And naturally we invited them to supper, for we had meat aplenty. They were a jolly lot, laughing and hand-signing amicable sentiments and pledging eternal friendship to all whitemen who entered their precincts. And when they had stuffed themselves to bursting and had wrapped several of our number in a final greasy hug before they departed, we naturally tripled our horse guard and naturally we caught every one of our affable guests trying to steal our horses.

Nobody was surprised or even particularly angry, for horse-thieving is as natural as breathing amongst nomadic Indians. It is neither a sin nor a crime, but rather a mark of pride in one's prowess. They didn't even particularly mind the cudgeling they received when they were apprehended by Little Mountain, Turtle, and several others of our bunch, nor were they noticeably shamefaced when we relieved them of the knives, powder horns, shot pouches, bullet molds, and other items they had pilfered from our persons in the course of their final heartfelt embraces.

Still laughing, they retreated into the darkness and soon we heard their ponies drumming across the prairie.

* * *

At length we came upon a large lake called the Flathead by those who had been there the year before. It stretched northwards for several miles. Whilst we rode beside its western shore my mind was powerfully drawn to memories of another lake and the naiad I had encountered there. We must certainly be in the country of her people. I wondered if I would ever see her again.

Once past the lake and several days travel along a good-size south-flowing river, Davey Jackson called a halt at what he determined was a good place to build his headquarters. It wasn't precisely what you would call a fort. It was rather a breastwork of close-set logs with a couple lean-tos and room enough inside its walls to gather livestock in case of a serious Indian attack. The structure ran all the way to the river's edge, a worthy consideration in the event of a siege. The river valley afforded good graze and a plenitude of sweet cottonwoods for winter horse feed. Although we were somewhat south and east of the Blackfoots' home country, their warriors can show up anywhere. Naturally our trapping parties would range far away from that spot, harvesting the cricks and streams that feed the river and the lake, but it was somewhat reassuring to have a place to retreat to if an enemy attacked in large numbers.

As our custom is, we pitched camp half a mile upstream of Jackson's brigade in a grove of sweet cottonwoods that straggled alongside the river, interspersed with grassy clearings, assuring critter feed for the fall and for later on when the snow fell. It was still a mite early for trapping — early-autumn plews run too sparse to be worthwhile — so we set about digging dugouts with willow-frame bowers overhead, caching most of our winter meat, gathering firewood, and generally getting ready for the harvest, when there would be little time for camp chores.

Whilst the rest of the bunch were busy chipping last season's rust off their traps, I showed our three newcomers how to cut and sew wool blankets into winter leggin's for trapping. Soaking-wet buckskin quickly freezes into icy armor. Wool isn't perfect, but it's a sight better than icicles.

We kept a watchful eye on the cricks and ponds as the weather chilled. When overnight ice commenced to form on the edges, it was time to commence practicing our trade.

* * *

Our neophytes were apt pupils. Surrounded as they were by a dozen seasoned teachers, they quickly picked up the basic skills of the trade — how and where to set their traps, securely planting the float-stick, properly placing the bait peg doused in castoreum, skinning and fleshing their catch, stretching plews on a willow hoop for curing, and burning their personal mark on the plew with a smoldering stick. The most difficult part for Micah and McCool, as it had been for me, was getting accustomed to wading hip-deep in icy ponds or sloshing about in cricks and streams when they were setting traps near bankside burrows and beaver slides. If Powatawa minded the cold, he never showed it.

I enlisted Brass Turtle to counsel Finn and Micah on "rising above it," that is, simply putting aside your thinking about the cold, as he had instructed me in our first winter on the Yellowstone. There is nothing magical about it and it takes a spell before it works, but after a time a greenhorn trapper overcomes his reluctance to wade into icy water to do his chores, although, to tell the truth, I never got to like it.

Fitz and Davey had chosen well. That country fairly crawled with beaver. In the beginning, nearly every well-set trap was full when we ran our traplines. Our greed allowed no time for hunting, so we lived mostly on beaver flesh, which isn't too bad, except for the tail, tough gristle as it is. Some trappers claim beaver tail roasted in coals tastes like bacon, but I have never thought so.

As you might suppose, sixteen trappers will soon trap out any neighborhood, no matter how rich in beaver it was at first. We ranged ever farther afield, probing upwards along the watercourses that feed the river. In time it became impractical to return to camp each day after running our traplines, so we cached our winter meat, the plews we had taken so far, and extra plunder, abandoned the camp, and split into smaller bunches of four or five men each.

Cesár Pérez and Micah had become thick as thieves ever since rendezvous, so I invited big Jim Beckwith to join Tuttle and me and those two. "Don't reckon so," he replied coldly. "Ol' Caesar kin do what he likes, but I figger I'll jist be trappin' on my own hook from here on." I was flabbergasted. So far on the Flathead, we had been lucky, without a single hostile attempt on our livestock or our lives, but such good fortune was not likely to last.

"You mean to say you mean to go trappin' without somebody watchin' your back, Jim?"

"That's perzackly what I mean to do. Won't be the fust to go it alone, neither. Plenty other'ns do it. I kin, too."

"Yep, some do. An' most of 'em lose their hair, too." I wanted to say more, but let it go with a shrug. This wasn't the Jim Beckwith I had known before I left the mountains two years before, the braggadocio Merry Andrew who had shown up uninvited with Cesár on the prairie and bulled his way into our bunch, then proved his mettle by trapping and hunting and fighting with the best of the rest of us, all the while displaying unfailing loyalty and courage and wild good humor. I should have bit my tongue, but instead I asked, "Is it Micah that's got ye riled, Jim?"

He looked past me for a spell before he replied. "Nah. Don't make no nevermind to me 'bout yer pet nigger. Jist don't go lumpin' me an' him together, nohow."

I dropped it then and there. Jim Beckwith could do as he liked. I wished him good luck, but I didn't say it out loud.

* * *

Powatawa elected to join Brass Turtle's Indian bunch and Finn McCool came along with us. Naturally Yves Dureau stuck with his musical mentor Anse Tolliver, together with Paddy, Godey, Little Mountain, and Old Foot, so Jean-Luc L'Archévêque became our campkeeper.

The morning the bunch split up, Jim Beckwith was nowheres about. "He go in nighttime," Little Mountain informed us. "Take hoss, plundah, eb'ryt'ing. Go by lonesome."

"Good riddance!" Anse growled. "Been actin' queer as all hell ever since ronnyvoo. Don't trust that sumbitch nohaow no more!"

* * *

We took the west side of the river and scoured every pond and likely stream that flowed to it, reaping rich rewards for our industry, working from dawn to dusk, running traplines, then skinning, scraping, and stretching hides, every man amongst us aware that each plew represented more than a month's wages for a greyback farmhand back in the Settlements — that is, until it comes time to buy next year's supplies from the skinflint trader at rendezvous. Then those newfound fortunes rapidly melt away until there is little more left than enough to buy a grand and glorious drunk before heading out in the fall.

We worked in pairs, one man standing guard against hostile Indians, bears, or painters, whilst the other tended to his traps. Cesár joined one or the other pair each day and Finn and Micah switched between Tuttle and me, picking up whatever odd bits of knowledge we were able to impart, mostly by example. One pair remained in camp with Jean-Luc each morning whilst the others ran their traplines. Guarding our livestock was always the paramount consideration. Losing our critters would be the greatest misfortune, reducing the rewards of our labors to naught. Moreover, a mountaineer afoot is easy prey.

When the first pair returned to camp with their catch, the others set out to run their own traps and the early-morning trappers went to work preparing their plews for curing. That chore is ordinarily the job of the campkeepers, but our harvest that season was too much for Jean-Luc alone. He did what he could, working from morning to night — from can to can't, as the saying goes — but the plenitude of plews overwhelmed him, so we all pitched in on camp chores.

We moved camp every couple-three days as we trapped out each drainage and also because remaining in one place too long is an invitation to unwelcome visitors. For the same reason we leave no gut-piles on the banks of streams and ponds, lest they attract bears or alert a hostile passer-by to our presence. Beaver-trapping is honest work, but our furtive behavior might be considered more appropriate to thieves and footpads.

Depending on distance and terrain, some days we rode horseback to our traplines, on others we tramped through the deepening snow. Winter was fast approaching. Each day proved more difficult to break the ice on the ponds and small cricks commenced to freeze over, which made beavers less adventurous. They preferred to remain in their lodges and bankside burrows, chewing on the tender bark they had stored up in warm weather.

Moving camp as often as we did, we took to erecting only a single shelter — most often a lean-to propped against a bank. Four of us huddled together for sleeping, much like a litter of puppies, while one man tended the fire and another stood horse guard for a two-hour stint. As the early-December temperature plunged, sleeping together for warmth became increasingly desirable. The cold made the proximity of all those unwashed bodies somewhat less noisome.

* * *

One night Tuttle and I sat together at the fire, huddled inside our capotes, heads bowed against a fierce north wind that rattled the elk hides and canvas on the lean-to and threatened to blow the whole shebang into the crick. It was almost time for Tuttle to relieve Finn McCool on horse guard and I had squirmed out from under the sleep-robes to take over the fire chore.

"By gawd, it's cold!" he grumbled. "Cold as a step-mother's tit, it shorely be! An' thi'shere gawddamn wind! Never seen the like! Hell! I reckon I kin surely spit a gawddamn mile." To prove it, he spat a stream of tobacco juice that whisked off into the darkness.

I myself had given up trying to smoke my pipe. As fast as I tamped tobacco into the bowl, the wind plucked it out and blew it away. It was too cold and windy for palaver, so we sat silent, cold and miserable, wishing for daylight and for the wind to quit.

At length Tuttle struggled to his feet, slung his rifle, and announced, "Time I spell ol' Finn afore he freezes inter a lump. I'll be waitin' fer ye, pard, when muh time is up." I watched him fade into the grey-to-black darkness. The windswept sky was cloudless, lit by a cold half-moon.

It wasn't half a minute before I heard Tuttle's strangled curse. "Dirty gawddamn bastards gone an' kilt McCool! The Irisher's daid!

An' they stole all ther gawddamn hosses!" There followed a string of curses that I am not sure I know how to spell. I grabbed up my rifle and hotfooted to the meadow where we had hobbled and staked out our horses and mules. Every one of them gone. Tuttle crouched over Finn McCool's body, a dark blur half covered with drifted snow, holding up the Irishman's head, shouting into his face, as if his imprecations would bring our comrade back to life. It must have worked. Next thing, I heard Tuttle roaring, "He's movin'! He ain't kilt! He's movin'!"

By time we lugged McCool back to the fire the rest of our crew were up and about, their curses and questions barely audible, swept away by the wind. Lying close to the warming fire as he was, a wicked gash on the back of Finn's head commenced bleeding through his hair. He stirred and groaned, tried to rise, but fell back. Tuttle, always noisy but usually exasperatingly calm, was half out of his head, calling for aid for McCool, then yelling that we must go after the critters, both excellent suggestions but he was doing naught to accomplish either one. I realized then how strong was the bond of friendship that had been forged between those two men in the past half-year.

Jean-Luc knelt by McCool and lifted his head, then whipped off the sash from around his middle and bound it tightly around the Irishman's head, chattering the while, *"J'aurai soin de lui! Allez, donc! Il faut retrouver les animaux! Allez, mes amis! Je promesse, j'aurai le bon soin de lui! Vraiment!"*

Jean-Luc was right. Lacking the medical skills of Old Foot, Little Mountain, or Finn McCool himself, L'Archévêque was likely the best physician we had amongst us. He was doubly right. The only useful thing we could do just then was to pursue the horsethieves before they put too much distance behind them.

If we succeeded in overtaking the horsethieves, there would likely be more of them than the four of us. There was sure to be a gun battle. We armed ourselves with every gun we possessed and filled powder horns and bullet pouches. As we prepared to depart, a random thought struck me. I yelled, "Hold up!" and ran off to where McCool's hody had lain. Kicking about in the snow, I discovered Uncle Ben's rifle, grabbed it up, and rushed back to the fire. In the flickering firelight I saw that Finn had thoughtfully tied a leather patch over the muzzle to keep snow out of the barrel, for which I blessed him.

I thrust the rifle into Tuttle's hands, saying, "Here, take this'n! Leave your own rifle back! You'll never be able to keep powder in the pan long enough to get the frizzen down!" Tuttle stared, uncertain about what I meant, but he unslung his flintlock and shoved it into the lean-to. I stooped and removed Finn's bullet pouch from his belt, hefted it to make sure it contained a sufficiency of balls, then snatched up his little horn of percussion caps and tossed the both of them to Tuttle. "All right!" I screamed into the wind. "Time we go!"

Cesár led the way. He was by far the best tracker in our bunch, even better than the Delawares. As I trotted beside Tuttle I leaned close to his ear and yelled, "Shee-it, Tuttle! I couldn't keep tobacco in my pipe long enough to smoke it! Ye'd never be able to prime your flintlock, once ye shoot it!"

I was barely able to see his grin in the pale moonlight when he grunted, "Thet be why I keep ye 'roun', Temple. Ye be allus thinkin' a step ahead!"

The extreme cold had frozen the snow into a solid sheet and mostly kept it from drifting, in spite of the gale that threatened to sweep us off our feet. As it turned out, Cesár's skill was mostly wasted. Even without him we could have followed the trail. A score of horses and mules had created a veritable king's highway across the prairie. The broad, well-trodden swath also made it easier for us to maintain a jogging pace instead of floundering through crusty, knee-deep snow.

I am not sure how much ground we covered that night, but I was supremely happy when Cesár signaled a halt. Far ahead I was able to make out a faint glimmer amongst a sizeable stand of trees. Cesár motioned for us to wait where we were, then trotted off into the darkness. When he returned, he announced, "Ees *no mas que* one, two, four — *ocho*, eight *indios* — Píkuni, I seenk so." Just for luck, he held up eight fingers. "*Vamonos*! Ees time we keel zem!" Nobody disagreed with that sentiment. We trotted off behind him.

When we neared the grove of cottonwoods straggling alongside a puny crick, at first we saw no horses. "Los caballos y los mulos are zere," he said, pointing to the trees. Without another word, as if we had planned it beforehand, which we hadn't, Tuttle and Cesár, crouching low, trotted off to the right. Micah and I headed left, dropping to our bellies just inside the fringe of trees, somewhat behind the fire, lest our own crossfire kill one of us. Not thirty yards away I counted all eight Blackfoots gathered together, feasting on a deer haunch skewered on a ramrod over a blazing fire. They were a merry crew, as well they should have been, considering the magnificent haul of horseflesh they had just stolen. The wind swept away their shouts and laughter, but their broad smiles and antic gestures bespoke triumphant hilarity.

I leaned close to Micah's ear. "Aim a mite upwind of 'em, best ye can." He nodded and held up two fingers, indicating which man he intended to shoot. I chose the next one on our side of the circle.

We waited what felt like an hour or two, letting Tuttle and Pérez commence shooting. When the crack of their rifles going off almost as one sliced through the howling wind, we triggered off our own. One man r'ared up and fell face-first into the fire. A second slumped forwards and joined his companion. A third fell sidewise, scrabbling for his musket. I cupped my hand over the muzzle and dumped powder down the barrel, then the ball, and slammed the butt into the hard-packed snow to seat the charge. My chilblained fingers fumbled away a couple caps before I got my rifle primed, instinctively ducking whilst the remaining five, maybe six, horsethieves fired wildly at our muzzle flashes, then scrambled for cover out of the firelight. Two of them never made it, pitching headlong into the snow when we returned their fire.

I reloaded and primed as fast as I was able, the while peering into the pale moonlit brush surrounding the fire, seeking a target, anxious to learn if they were able to charge their muskets in the whipping wind. There was no returning fire and still we waited, straining to discover a form or unusual movement in the low-growing brush. First one, then two figures rose to their knees and loosed arrows in our direction that likely went flying downwind onto the prairie long before they came nigh to where we lay. I daresay their bowstrings were still twanging when our gunfire, Micah's and my own and one muzzle flash from the far side, toppled them both into the snow.

We charged our rifles and I made sure that my pistol was capped and ready, meanwhile turning my head from side to side, trying to pick up movement from the tail of my eyes. Then I saw him, a tall figure, capote flapping in the wind, sprinting for the trees where the critters were tethered. I swung my rifle, trying to get a bead on him, when I jerked it skywards and strangled out a warning to Micah not to shoot. From the treeline on the far side of the fire, a squat figure was racing in pursuit of the fleeing Blackfoot. It was Cesár, swinging the short, heavy, broad-bladed sword he called a machete, dashing after his prey. He caught up just as the Indian reached the horses. The blade flashed once, twice in the firelight and the Indian crumpled onto the snow.

Before I knew it I was on my feet, Micah beside me, struggling knee-deep through crusty snow, trying to get to the fire, lest a surviving Blackfoot attack Cesár from behind. There was no need for concern. Only one horsethief showed any sign of life. Cesár sent him off to the Sand Hills with a single savage chop.

A grinning Tuttle Thompson emerged from amongst the trees, rifle ready but strolling contentedly in Cesár's wake as if he were on a maywalk. When we came nigh each other he leaned towards me and shouted into the wind, "Reckon we larned 'em a thang or two, din't we, ol' hoss!" I nodded but I wondered how much good those bloody lessons would do those horsethieves as they traveled to their Grey Land.

Right then, howsomever, the main concern was our critters. I floundered through deep snow to the cottonwood grove where they neighed and honked and whinneyed and stamped and strained against their tethers. As best I could tell in the dim light, all of our critters were there, as well as a dozen or so horses that belonged to our recently departed, unlamented foes.

Assured that our livestock was safe and accounted for, I was heading back to the fire when I nearly stumbled over a body in the snow. Alarmed that it might be one of the Blackfoots who had crawled towards the horses trying to escape, I yanked my pistol from my sash and brought it to bear on the still form lying there. My fears were ungrounded. Even in the shadowy light I could see that the man in the snow was trussed like a Christmas goose. When I dropped to my knees and turned him onto his back, he uttered a faint groan.

Crunching footsteps at my back told me that Micah had followed me out to the critters. Together we slashed the rawhide cords that bound the man, then half-carried, half-dragged him to the fire. He was naked save for a britchclout, his hide blue in the firelight. We stripped a capote off a dead Blackfoot and wrapped him in it, then laid him beside the fire on a couple of their blankets. "Cain't feature them Blackfoots treatin' one o' their own like thet, no matter how much they mought be dislikin' 'im," Tuttle opined. "Nekkid like he be, cain't tell from his git-up whar he be comin' from, but thar ain't no doubtin' he b'longs to some other people what ain't frien'ly to Blackfoots." That appeared to be the case to the rest of us, as well, so, abiding by the principle that the enemy of my enemy is my friend, we felt obliged to render aid and comfort to the prisoner.

Comfort was a pretty scanty commodity right then and there, but we did the best we could. When the fire's warmth thawed him out somewhat and he commenced to stir, we got him dressed in a leather shirt and leggin's and moccasins from one of the Blackfoots who wouldn't be needing his fancies anymore, then bundled him back into the capote and laid him down again beside the fire.

Whilst we were at it, we stripped the clothes and other belongings off the rest of the dead men. Nothing goes to waste in the mountains. What we couldn't use ourselves would come in handy as trade goods when we next encountered a friendly Indian band. We were struck by the excellent quality and nearly-new condition of their muskets. Even the brass tacks that studded the stocks were still shiny.

"Whar do ye reckon them Injuns got a-holt o' them'ere purty guns, Temple?" Tuttle asked, his grin betraying his opinion of what that source most likely was.

"Nobody else but the Aitch-bee-cee," I replied, mostly for Micah's benefit. "Damn Britishers'd rather let Blackfoots kill us off than meetin' us head-on."

"Reckon so," he agreed. Then, "Let's be gittin' ourse'fs a bait o' thet'ere meat what's a-hangin' thar." He jerked his chin towards the deer quarter suspended over the fire. Which we did.

Grey daylight reduced the wind to a chill breeze, which aided our labors in loading our new-found plunder onto the Indian ponies. The prisoner had revived considerably but he was still too weak to ride, so we slung him over Ready's back and roped him down for the short trip back to camp. Nobody was disposed to bury the Blackfoot bodies. We left them where they had fallen. I would have left their hair intact, which was more kindness than they deserved. Tuttle and Cesár were not so generous.

On the way, I mentioned to Tuttle, "Did ye notice how young those Píkunis were? Not much more'n boys, by the look of 'em."

"Reckon I did. Don't s'pose we would'a had sech luck whuppin' 'em so easy ef'n they war growed-up Injuns an' knew a li'l sumpin'. Hell! Fust off, they din't kill ol' Finn. Jest left 'im a-layin' thar! Din't skelp 'im ner think to look fer his rifle gun, neither." He warmed to his subject. "An' then, arter they went an' stole our critters, they got to feelin' plumb neighborly an' set their camp no fu'ther'n a long spit from our'n." He spat disgustedly. "An' they got to corngratchulatin' theirse'fs 'baout what big ol' he-dogs they war an' din't even keep an eye peeled fer us comin' arter 'em!" He fell silent for a spell. "Shee-it! Even ther gawddamn Blackfoots're better off 'thout sech a passel o' snot-noses!"

In camp, Jean-Luc fussed over the prisoner like a mother hen, first preparing a rich broth of fat beaver meat and the last of our dried peas. He dug into his possibles and produced a box of healing ointment, then boiled up an embrocation with which he laved off the dried blood and blackened scabs that covered the poor wretch from head to foot. By time L'Archévêque finished tending to him, the young man, bruised and battered though he was, looked halfway presentable, although he was still too weak and groggy to tell us who he was and what had happened to him.

Finn McCool's well-being, howsomever, was of much more importance to us, but we soon learned that Jean-Luc's ministrations had worked wonders for our wounded Irishman, as well. When we drove the critters into camp, he tottered out to greet us, pale and still shaky, his head wrapped in a colorful turban made of our campkeeper's sash, but smiling through his months-old growth of whiskers. "How're ye feelin', Finn?" Micah asked him, concern in his eyes.

"Och, it'll be more'n a knock on the head to put Finnæus McCool down fer long! They're not after callin' us hard-headed Micks fer nothin', mind ye!"

After we filled our bellies with the last of the beaver meat, it was time for serious palaver. I started off with, "We've been sayin' how it was their foolish greed that let us whup those Píkuni young'uns the way we did. We can learn something from that. We've trapped more plews this fall than we ever did before. Let's not be greedy. I say we pack up an' get the hell out o' here before some proper Blackfoots come lookin' for their young'uns and find us instead."

Tuttle jumped in before I hardly got the words out of my mouth. "Good fer ye, Temple! I been thinkin' ther se'f-same thang. Ain't no use pilin' up a heap o' plews jest to be losin' 'em to Injuns — 'long with our critters an' our gawddamn hair inter the bargain!" He turned to our little Spaniard. "Whatcher say, Caesar? Ain't it so?"

"*Si*! We 'ave already *muchas piels de castor*. I weesh to spend zem wiz *el cabello en la cabeza*." General laughter greeted his words. Truly, it is better to enjoy your profits with your hair still where it belongs.

Neither Micah nor Finn had much to say. They both had done well for their first season and they appeared relieved that now they were not likely to lose those hard-won plews.

Within' two hours' time we had struck camp, loaded up, and were on the downstream trail with a rich autumn harvest, a dozen captured ponies, a heap of trade plunder, and a passel of new muskets, with our scalps intact. Which was especially appreciated in Finn's case.

* * *

It was a pleasure to be a-horseback again instead of up to our arse in freezing beaver ponds. Moreover, wapiti pushed down from high mountain meadows by winter snows provided a welcome improvement on beaver meat. The first day or so we had taken turns propping up in his saddle the young Indian we had rescued from the Blackfoots. Thanks to Jean-Luc's mothering attentions, howsomever, he soon regained strength enough to ride on his own and to let us know his name and how he had come to be in the sorry state in which we had found him.

We possessed no common spoken language but hand-talk sufficed to inform us that he was a Flathead called Fast Horse and that he and his three hunting companions had been attacked and captured by the Blackfoots. The other three had been killed out of hand, but that jolly pack of Píkunis had chosen to spare his life for a spell and carry him home to their village, where the squaws could carve him up for their amusement.

Even through his scabs and bruises it was plain to see that he was a well-put-together young man of about my own age, his manner forthright and resolute. By signs he let us know that one particular piebald horse in the captured bunch was his own, asserting, as well, that he was sufficiently restored to ride that horse. Naturally we granted both requests.

At a supper cookfire we divvied up the horses and plunder we had taken from the Blackfoots. We returned to Fast Horse his own belongings before sharing out the rest. The Flathead got an equal portion. We reckoned that his suffering at the hands of our common enemy had earned him a fair share. Each of us claimed one of the fine English muskets and we drew straws for the eighth one, which went to Tuttle. Most pleased of all was Jean-Luc. He sat marveling at the excellent workmanship of the weapon resting on his knees, infinitely superior to any firearm he ever expected to own.

I drew the short straw for first pick amongst the captured horses, which surprised me. I have never been lucky at gambling, which is why I rarely wager. I chose a sturdy, deep-chested, six-year-old bay, whom I christened Punch, for no special reason. "Gawddamnit, Temple!" Tuttle groaned good-naturedly. "I larn't ye too damn good fer my own good! I been a-hankerin' fer thet'ere partic'lar critter myownse'f ever since we taken 'em up. Damn ef he ain't a jim-dandy, sure as hell!"

After the first seven horses were chosen, we drew straws for the remaing four. I lucked out again, this time picking a short-coupled sunburnt black. Tuttle, McCool, and Fast Horse got the remaining three. I suspect the Flathead was careful not to choose ponies that had belonged to his deceased companions, lest their relatives claim them.

The remaing plunder was sorted out to everybody's satisfaction. Redistributing the loads amongst the new critters, which made the packs lighter, let us make rapid progress to Jackson's camp. Our hearts were big as we galloped into the clearing, whooping and hollering, firing guns in the air, and yelling greetings. All of us were rich in plews, horses, weapons, and trade goods, the only wealth that counts for aught in the Shining Mountains.

* * *

Brass Turtle was first to greet us. When he beheld Fast Horse, his broad smile disappeared, fading into a quizzical grin. "Whar in hell did ye come by that'n, Temple?" he asked, the while taking stock of the young Flathead warrior, still much the worse for wear. I laid out the bare bones of our skirmish with the Píkuni and told how we had freed their Salish prisoner, who had been destined for a slow, painful death in the Blackfoot village. "An' ye still don't know who the hell he is, do ye?" Turtle's grin slid into a smirk.

"No, and I don't suppose it matters much," I replied. "Does it?"

Turtle chuckled. "Nope. Not to nobody else 'sides yerownself, Temple Buck. Leastaways not as much."

I dismounted and faced him, my curiosity aroused. "C'mon, Turtle. It's been a long ride and I'm too whupped for conundrums. What're ye gettin' at?"

He burst out laughing. When he recovered he informed me, "Why, that'ere young feller, sorry-lookin' as he be right now, is the brother of your own swimmin' lady from rendezvous!"

I gawped like a ninny, which sent Turtle off into another spate of laughter. When he quieted, I demanded, "How d'ye know that?" But before he could answer I recalled that Brass Turtle had spent much more time in the Salish camp at rendezvous than I had. Rainbow had always come to me. It was Turtle who had gone a-calling on his Flathead light-o'-love.

Just then Fast Horse called out something in his tongue. He was staring straight at Brass Turtle and smiling, chin wagging, hands flying like a covey of startled quail. Turtle's hands were equally busy, but he addressed his words me. "He's tellin' that he recollects me from rendezvous an' if I be your friend, then he be my friend, too." He beamed at me. "'Pears ye made a good impression on 'im. Seein' who he be, ye might be luckier'n ye think." He paused, thinking over what he had said. Then, "P'raps fer the whole bunch, afore it's over."

My father, Godey, Anse and Paddy, and the others came crowding about, stalling further palaver. The drift of Turtle's remarks, howsomever, commenced to take shape. Passing the winter in a Salish village, not even considering renewing my tie with Rainbow, was vastly preferable to scrabbling for a living with Fitz and Davey's brigade. Just the same, it was best to let Fast Horse make the first move.

Naturally there was a heap of bragging on the magnificent haul of beaver. Everybody was calling the fall harvest shinin' times! Company men as well as our own bunch. And nobody had gone under. Jackson's brigade had fought off Blackfoot raiders during the harvest and lost two packhorses and a mule, but not a single hair from their heads. The horsethieves hadn't been so fortunate. Several fresh scalps fluttered in the crisp December breeze and my father sported a long-haired trophy on his belt.

Small bunches of south'ard-bound buffalo had been drifting down the west side of the river valley, so there was plenty of meat roasting over the cookfires. Whilst I filled my belly I observed that the customary good-fellowship betwixt our campkeepers Yves Dureau and Jean-Luc was sorely lacking. L'Archévêque was cheerful enough, but Dureau was snappish and short with his partner. Tuttle, squatting beside me, noticed it, too. After a spell, Tuttle rose to his feet, strolled off to his packs, and returned toting one of the Aitch-bee-cee muskets we had taken from the Blackfoots. He walked directly to Yves, thrust the musket into his hands, and growled, "Hyar ye be, Dureau. This'n be your'n. See thet ye larn to use it better'n thet'ere blanket gun ye been totin'!" When Yves tried to sputter his gratitude, Tuttle snapped, "Ye kin save yer gawddamn mercies, but see ye mind yer manners with Larchyveck hyar!" Without waiting for a reply, he spun about and returned to my side. Dureau's face lit up like a bonfire as he gazed admiringly at the shiny new trade gun in his hands. Tuttle carved off a rib from the hump hanging over the cookfire and commenced chewing, saying not a word, keeping an eye on the campkeepers, whose manner towards each other visibly softened and warmed. "Thar now!" Tuttle snorted. "Cain't be 'lowin' ol' Dureau to be poutin' like a gawddamn schoolgirl an' them two a-pickin' at each other. Gotta keep peace in the fambly!" He gnawed off a chunk of meat, gulped it down, and observed, "'Sides, a couple extry guns mought be comin' in handy." He paused, then added gloomily, "Ef'n them'ere Frenchies ever larn to use 'em proper an' don't go ter hidin' out when trouble starts."

I made no reply. He had said it all. I marveled that rough-hewn, happy-go-lucky Tuttle Thompson could be so delicately attuned to the moods and relationships of our fellows.

Perhaps because our whole bunch had turned up safe, Anse Tolliver unlimbered his fiddle as dusk gathered. Soon his merry tunes lured half a hundred trappers from Jackson's brigade to our cookfire, along with some of their women and young'uns. His chores finished and his good humor restored, Yves Dureau dug out his little musical squeezebox. Before long a rude orchestra of tootling Indian flutes, hand drums, wooden spoons banging on kettles, and hoarse voices raised in half-remembered song rang out over the snow-covered valley. They were still at it when I returned from my stint at horse-guard and rolled into my sleep-robes to close my eyes and recall Rainbow's warm embrace, which appeared to be not so distant now.

* * *

I awakened to the startling sight of Anse Tolliver's blood-shot eyes and the warmth of his boozy breath close to my face. "C'mon, Temple," he whined. "Cain't be sleepin' yer life away. We need'ja out thar. Sumpin' y'oughta be hearin'. Sumpin' ye likely won't be mindin', neither."

Wondering the while where Anse had managed to get hold of ardent spirits after months of dry since rendezvous, I slithered out of my robes and into a cold grey dawn. The fire was blazing high and our entire bunch was gathered around Brass Turtle and Fast Horse seated cross-legged on one side of it. Turtle beckoned me to join them. "Mornin', Temple!" he called out. "Ol' Fast Horse here's been tellin' us somethin' I reckon ye won't be objectin' to." He grinned slyly, an expression he is good at. "He's been sayin' there ain't no doubtin' we'd be more'n welcome fer passin' the winter 'mongst his people, no more'n a couple days' ridin' from hyar. Just us, not Jackson's people, mind ye.   So whadda'ye think?"   A murmur of approval rippled amongst my comrades.

I nearly choked on my reply. "Ye damn betcha!" I strangled out, my heart growing big enough in my chest to burst me wide open.

"Thought so!" Turtle crowed. "Ain't no cause fer talkin' fu'ther! Best we git to packin' up!"

We informed Davey Jackson and Tom Fitzpatrick of our intention to spend the winter with the Flatheads and assured them that we would join them for the spring hunt. There was little else to do than retrieve our winter meat and extra plunder from our cache upstream. We debated for a spell about using that cache to store our plews, but decided against it. Clannish as our bunch had become, we didn't altogether trust even our fellow Americans not to help themselves to such valuable booty. Digging another cache in frozen ground elsewhere meant a lot more work, but the peace of mind it provided made it worthwhile.

Riding back to camp I sidled up to Anse Tolliver, a question rankling in my mind. "I gotta ask ye somethin', Anse. Where in hell did ye get hold o' that booze ye were blowin' in my face this mornin'?"

He grinned and spat a brown stream into the snow. "Aw, hell, thar ain't no myst'ry to it a-tall. Been doin' it all along. Oncet I git to sawin' music an' the boys git to likin' it enough, I jist natcherly offer to quit unless somebody kin wet muh dry. Ye'd be surprised how quick one feller er some other'n kin dig a leetle squeezin's from out his possibles!" He let out a sharp guffaw that startled even his placid old mule. "Like they say, ther workman's worthy of his hire an' I don't never fancy workin' fer nuthin'!"

* * *

Davey and Fitz and a few old hands came to bid us farewell next morning. "Now don't ye be after thinkin' o' turnin' Injun on us whilst ye be livin' the sweet life of O'Riley amongst thim haythen Flatheads all winter," Tom Fitzpatrick warned, his blue eyes twinkling. "We'll jist natcherly be obliged to come after ye for convertin' ye back to proper Christian ways."

"Hell, Tom!" Brass Turtle piped up, jerking his thumb towards the white-eyes in our bunch. "Jist look at 'em! There ain't hardly one of 'em that ain't awready more Injun than us what were born to it!" We departed amid chuckles and here and there a spirited huzzah from one or another old friend. We made good time all that day through hock-deep snow, Fast Horse pointing the way, until we made camp in early afternoon beside a measly frozen stream bordered by a grove of sweet cottonwoods. After we broke the ice and watered the stock we busied ourselves digging a cache and hauling dirt to the water, lest it betray our hidey-hole. We required a sizeable cache, for the harvest had been generous to every one of us. As they say, many hands make short work. The chore was finished by nightfall. The aroma of jerked meat boiling in half a dozen kettles hastened our final efforts before we lost the final shreds of daylight.

Bellies full, we sprawled around the cookfire, peeling cottonwood bark for the animals and speculating on what the coming months might hold for us amongst the Flatheads. "Well now," Ned Godey opined, "much as they might be thankin' us fer bringin' home their prodigal son, ol' Fast Hoss hyar, I reckon nigh a score of extry guns fer fightin' off Blackfoots'd count cornsidable fer lettin' 'em make us feel at home amongst 'em."

"Yep, an' from what I been hearin'," Tuttle put in, "ain't nobody ever heared o' Flatheads ever killin' a white man." He snickered and shot a sly glance at Brass Turtle. "Course, ye cain't never be sure jest how they mought be treatin' a passel o' yew civvy-lized Injuns."

Turtle refused to take the bait. "Hell, I reckon they'll be takin' to us jist fine, figgerin' how we'll be improvin' the breed."

"Speakin' o' which," Paddy McBride declared, "there's a disgraceful lack o' red hair amongst the natives hereabouts, which I'm pledgin' to correct to the best o' me consid'rable abilities!"

Such observations made it plain to see where the minds of my companions were headed. It had been a long spell since rendezvous.

But I heard no more of it just then. Finn McCool and I rose to take our turn at horse guard. We made our way to the cottonwood grove and scattered armloads of sweet bark amongst the critters before we relieved Anse and Micah at their posts.

Squatting beside a tree, huddled inside my capote, alert to any unusual movement or alien sound, my thoughts inevitably strayed to the days ahead, wondering if the balmy summer nights at rendezvous might be recaptured amidst the wintering village of Rainbow's own people. Perhaps she had taken up with a Salish warrior. Maybe she considered now that our shared passion had been merely a pleasant fling. It was possible that her duty to her people precluded further commerce with the likes of me. Such torturing self-doubt owned my mind until I heard moccasins crunching in the snow and Brass Turtle saying, "'Pears the Great Spirit's smilin' on us, Temple. Snow's fallin' hard enough so's even we won't be able to find the cache, come morning'."

* * *

We pushed hard next day through deepening snow until we halted at dusk in a cottonwood grove and made camp. Fast Horse wasn't the only one who was disappointed that we hadn't reached his village, but he signed that, deep snow or not, we would get there the following day.

By time I awakened next morning Tuttle was already crouched over a steaming kettle, squinting into a tiny trade mirror and sawing at his bristling beard with a pair of my scissors. "What in the name o' hell are ye doin', Tuttle?" I demanded.

He gave me a withering look. "Mama allus tol' me it be the fust impression whut counts," he informed me with a superior air, "an' I don't aim to be behindhand nohaow when we git ourse'fs amongst ol' Fast Hoss's people, 'speshly ther widder-wimmen." With an appraising glance at my face, he added, "An' ye wouldn't be hurtin' yerownse'f none, neither, ef'n ye got rid o' thet'ere peach fuzz on yer phiz."

My hand darted to my chin and I daresay I blushed. Even though I have never produced much in the way of whiskers, it had been several months since I had used a razor. "All right, Mister Smart-aleck, I reckon this time you're right," I declared lamely, "but I'll be slick as a tin whistle whilst you're still scrapin' your face."

"Reckon so," he replied with mock hauteur, "but yew ain't never gonna be as purty as ol' Tuttle Thompson!"

"Beauty is in the eye of the beholder, Tuttle. Ye dast not be lettin' go o' that lookin'-glass!"

I dodged a snowball that whizzed past my ear and ran to get my own kettle, fill it with snow, and hustle off to the fire.

As I had said, I was freshly-shaved and togged out in the quilled doeskin shirt and leggin's and fancy moccasins I had received from Rainbow at rendezvous whilst Tuttle was still battling his blue-black stubble. He was suffering enough, so I refrained from further gibes.

Chapter VIII
Flatheads

A festive air prevailed in camp that early morning. Snowfall had dwindled away overnight and my companions had donned what you might call their Sunday best. My father was resplendent in soft white quilled and beaded buckskins, moccasins to match, and Micah and McCool strutted in the Blackfoot finery they had taken in battle. Fast Horse was not to be outdone. He had sorted through his Píkuni plunder that morning and found enough frippery to satisfy even a young warrior's need for showy garb. Ours would be a colorful entry into the Salish village.

And it was. Scouts and sentries had long since alerted the people to our impending arrival. They had announced, as well, that Fast Horse was leading our procession. A couple hundred yards outside the camp we broke into a gallop, whooping and hollering our heads off and firing guns in the air, until we pulled up at the outer ring of lodges and proceeded at a stately walk. Fast Horse urged his spotted horse a few paces in front and advanced with tiny, mincing steps, whirling and curvetting his mount, grinning wide enough to burst his handsome face, the lower part of which was painted black in mourning for his murdered comrades. He still bore the marks of ill-treatment, but Jean-Luc's attentions had mostly restored his features. Every man, woman, child, and barking dog in the village flanked our path. Their cries and ululations — those throaty, trilling howls that signify either profound grief or unrestrained joy — rose to a deafening pitch that made my temples throb. At last we arrived at the center of nigh a hundred lodges, the mob trailing in our wake. A huge council fire blazed high in the crisp mountain air. Five dignified, mature men waited there, afoot, erect as ramrods, solemn as the Sabbath. In their center I recognized the man I knew to be Rainbow's father.

A hush fell over the crowd. Fast Horse halted his mount and slipped to the ground. He advanced, head bowed, and sank to his knees before his father. The old warrior bent down to clasp his son by the shoulders and raise him to his feet, then drew him to his breast in a hearty embrace. I never saw his lips move, but the gesture spoke volumes of thanksgiving.

The people went nearly crazy then, filling the air with shouts and those long trilling wails. They whirled about and stamped their feet in the snow, throwing their hands skyward in wild abandon. Our bunch sat quietly in our saddles, empty rifles on our thighs, trying to look solemn, as dignified as a passel of scruffy trappers can look.

When I wasn't trying to seek out Rainbow's face amongst the milling women, at which I was so far unsuccessful, my gaze strayed over my comrades. Circumstances considered, we were a presentable lot, dressed in our Sunday-go-to-meetin' quilled and beaded and painted leathers, the whites smooth-cheeked and rosy under leathery tans, long hair adorned with trailing eagle feathers, strings of trade beads at our throats, many with cheeks and brows streaked with bright red vermilion. Even our saddle horses were bedaubed with painted designs. We were a far cry from the green hands who landed at the mouth of the Yellowstone in 'twenty-two. I reckoned we would pass muster amongst the Flatheads.

A murmur swelled to a dull roar when Fast Horse stepped away from his father and proceeded to limp around the council fire, the while calling out his story and repeating it with rapid hand gestures as he spoke. The Flatheads fell silent as he related his tale. Even prattling children hushed their chatter. Only the jingling of bridle bits and the snuffling of our critters vied with his speech. A universal groan and a passel of wailing erupted when he told of the deaths of his three hunting companions at the hands of the Píkunis. Cries of consternation greeted his words concerning his capture and the fate that had been intended for him. When he came to his rescue and release he faced us and first pointed out Micah and me, then Cesár and Tuttle, after which he swept his arm to include the rest of our bunch. He made a special fuss over L'Archévêque before thanking and praising all of us for his deliverance and our generosity in restoring his property fivefold. Which wasn't precisely accurate, but it's the thought that counts.

I sidled Kumskaka next to Tuttle and murmured, "How in hell does he know it was me that found him in the snow? He was out cold as a rock when we dragged him to the fire. I never said and neither did Micah."

Tuttle leaned close and replied, "Ye kin be thankin' ol' Larchyveck fer thet. The two of 'em got to be right frien'ly comin' back."

In the manner of Indians everywhere in the mountains, telling a story just a single time is never sufficient, but at last Fast Horse threw his arms wide as if to embrace the lot of us and entreated his listeners to treat us as their honored guests.

The crowd commenced to drift off and two of the elders came to us signing that we could dismount and stow our plunder in a couple-three big lodges he pointed out in the second circle beyond the fire. As I prepared to step down I spied her standing before the doorflap of a lodge nearby those assigned to our bunch. She wasn't precisely smiling but the eager look on her face when she caught my eye promised a welcome.

We had barely time enough to strip off saddles and packs and turn our critters over to the herd boys before we were summoned to the big council lodge facing the fire. We filed in, mindful of etiquette, choosing the right side of the circle to enter and being careful not to step between a seated man and the small fire that burned in the center. Our bunch outnumbered the Flatheads there by nearly twice, so the pipe ritual — drawing a mouthful of smoke and pointing the pipestem skywards, to the earth, and to the four directions — took up quite a spell and used up several pipefuls of strong tobacco before each of us was able to pay his respects.

When Fast Horse's father commenced the palaver I found myself charmed by the soft liquid syllables. They put me in mind of a gently-flowing brook tumbling over smooth pebbles. I was only vaguely conscious of his hand-signs thanking us for returning his son and welcoming us to all that the village could offer. I reckon he could guess what such an invitation might mean to a bunch of horny young trappers, but he laid down no rules or prohibitions. Naturally each of the other four elders had to have his say, but they were mercifully brief. Soon a procession of women filed inside, bearing bark platters heaped with steaming elk and buffalo meat, which did wonders to loosen up the formal atmosphere of the gathering.

Goodnatured laughter rang out as Flatheads and trappers exchanged ribald jests in greasy-fingered hand-talk whilst chomping away at an endless supply of hump ribs, backstrap, and tongue. Meanwhile Fast Horse circulated amongst our people, collecting the Blackfoot scalps that some of our number had on them and asking that he be provided with any such hair that remained with our plunder.

*　*　*

Darkness had hardly fallen before we were were summoned from our lodge once again, this time, we knew, for the inevitable scalp dancing. This was not the first such celebration I had attended, but it was the most welcome one, for it meant that I was almost certain to see Rainbow. I was fairly tingling at the prospect. It had been all I could do to restrain myself from trotting over to the lodge where I had seen her earlier that day.

A big drum was already booming and a huge bonfire sent sparks and burning embers spiraling into a starry winter sky when we straggled through the door-flap and made our way to the fire, where most of the village had already assembled. They greeted us with smiles, parted ranks, and pushed us into the inner circle, where we sat or squatted, huddled in our capotes, and watched the smiling, joshing drummers at their chore and boys hauling great boughs and whole tree trunks to the fire.

A staccato rattle on the drumhead announced the arrival of the crier clad in a buffalo coat and a horned headdress. He pranced about the circle, haranguing the people, doubtless telling what was coming, which I daresay they already knew. He was soon followed by Fast Horse, a striking figure in creamy leathers encrusted with quillwork, wearing a big round bonnet of magpie feathers, his face cleansed now of the black paint he had worn earlier that day. In spite of his lameness he darted from one side of the circle to the other, pretty much repeating his first oration, although, from what I could make out from his gestures, rather more elaborately this time. I reckon it's the same with Indians as it is with trappers — the more often you tell a story, the better it gets.

When his yelling commenced to drain away into a hoarse gurgle, Fast Horse suddenly quit, chopped one hand downwards, and beckoned into the darkness. The big drum burst into a thunderclap, echoing off the hillsides, speeding up into a frenzied rhythm that fairly shook the ground beneath my hams. On the far side of the circle the people parted and a serpentine procession of women threaded into the circle, shaking aloft war lances festooned with fluttering scalp hair. They weaved patterns amongst one another, bending low then leaping high in the firelight, crouching nigh to the ground and shuffling onward around the circle, their moccasined feet never losing the beat of the thundering drum.

I strained to discover Rainbow in that colorful maelstrom of women grown frantic in the joy of celebration. And then I spied her, whirling and bobbing and leaping in their center, as befitted the sister of the warrior who had been returned to them from the Grey Land of the Dead. I watched fascinated as she swooped and gyrated in time to the drumbeat, until the rhythm suddenly altered and slowed and the women scattered out of the firelight and scurried to our side of the circle. They were smiling now as they reached out to haul this or that trapper to his feet.

I had donated no scalps but I needn't have worried. Rainbow made a beeline for where I sat, her dark eyes sparkling, luscious lips parted, breathless from her wild dancing, smiling and laughing and brandishing a feathered lance that bore two scalps. I shrugged out of my capote and leaped to my feet, eager as never before to join in a dance.

She faced me and writhed in sinuous rhythm, the while shaking the the long-haired scalps above my head, smiling and tilting backwards, inviting me closer, never losing the beat of the drumming that filled my ears and my very soul and nigh made me drunk with feeling. For the first time in my life I lost all my shyness and gave myself up to the dance, shuffling and mincing and whirling about and kicking high above my head as the spirit and the drumbeat moved me, whilst my soul, the very core of my being, was drawn unresisting ever deeper into the liquid depths of her eyes.

As we bobbed and twirled I caught sight of my comrades matching their steps to those of the women who shook their trophies over each trapper's head, our Indians and our French-Cree engagés graceful in their movements, the whites considerably less so, except for red-haired Paddy McBride, who leaped and cavorted and spun about like a creature possessed, laughing and crowing and catching his partner by the waist to whirl her about in a wild Irish reel that brought many a Salish hand to mouth in astonishment. His stocky little partner fought to maintain her dignity but failed, at last giving herself up to Paddy's frenzied gyrations, matching his steps and laughing aloud in what I daresay her neighbors thought was a most unseemly fashion.

My father, graceful as ever, emulated his partner's every elegant move, his coal-black eyes dancing in the firelight, a faint smile on his clean-cut features, appearing more free of duty and care than I had ever known him to be. Micah displayed his customary athletic grace, reflecting mirror-like his woman's traditional dancing, while she — in spite of herself, I am sure — could not resist reaching out to stroke his cheek from time to time to see if his ebony color would rub off.

And then it was over. The drumming ceased with one enormous thud. Silence reigned, but only for an instant. A mighty cheer erupted from the spectators and they rushed into the firelit circle, engulfing us trappers in a press of happy humanity that threatened to crush us. The scalp-dancing women retreated hastily, Rainbow amongst them, but as she fled past the bonfire she threw me a look that promised that the night was not over for us.

* * *

Once I freed myself from the rather too grateful Flatheads I scurried back to the lodge I shared with Micah, Tuttle, Cesár, Godey, and L'Archévêque. I plunged past the doorflap, tossed some smallwood onto the smoldering fire, and commenced digging into my possibles.

"Goin' somewhars, are ye?" Ned Godey asked from somewhere in the shadows. The flimsy sticks caught fire and blazed up, revealing him sprawled against a backrest.

"Reckon I am," I replied, continuing to rummage through one of my packs. "How come you're mopin' in here, 'stead of out there with the rest?"

"It's been a long day," he said wearily and yawned. "Reckon whatever's out thar'll keep 'til tomorry. 'Sides, I din't cotton much to that'ere scalp-woman I war dancin' 'longside of."

"*Dans le nuit, tous les chats sont gris.*" Jean-Luc's cackle came out of the dark. His understanding of English had improved greatly in my absence, but he preferred to speak in French.

"Reckon so," Ned said with a chuckle. "Like the Frenchy says, all cats are grey in the dark, but I'll jist bide my time an' find m'se'f a kitty to suit me, day or night."

"Like ye say, Ned, I reckon it'll keep, but tonight'll never come again. Make hay whilst the sun shines, like they say, even if it ain't."

Ned wished me well and I thanked him for the thought. I had found the tallow candles I sought, stuffed them into my poke, and departed.

I lingered in the shadow of the lodge, unsure if she meant for me to come to her lodge or if she would come to me — or if I would be seeing her at all. I shivered in the cold night air but my ardor remained unchilled. Then I heard her moccasin scrape on the hard-packed snow behind me and felt her hand slip into mine, tugging me towards her lodge.

We ducked through the doorway into a good-sized lodge dimly lit by a small fire burning beneath the smoke-hole. She knelt and I heard the scrape of the crossed sticks she was placing in front of the doorflap, advising neighbors not to come a-calling. She rose, smiling, and came to me, pulled me close, and snuggled her face into the bosom of my capote, her warm breath making me totter almost to falling off my feet, before pulling me down onto the pallet spread beside the fire.

Later, lying naked in her robes, marveling at her passion, still breathless from the savage force of our initial encounter, I watched her face limned against the flickering firelight, admiring her high cheekbones and deepset eyes, large and dark and mysterious as enchanted wells, her broad, smooth brow coppery in the fire's glow, framed by her tumbled hair flowing free over delicate ears, the flat planes of her cheeks, her full lips and firm chin, and the gentle hollow in her throat that never failed to respond to my kisses.

My fingers traced the miracle of her long, lithe body, the lean, hard-muscled thighs and rounded calves, swelling buttocks firm as green apples, sculptured into flaring hips and strong, wide-shouldered back. I knew the power of her arms clasping me close and the strength of her work-toughened hands that could be as gentle as zephyrs when she caressed me. Here was truly a child of the high, wild mountains, the mighty rivers, and the warming west wind, all that was honest and good and eternal in the untamed land that I had chosen for my own, a woman born and bred to be the mate of a wilderness man.

Naturally my explorations aroused my interest in more immediate considerations. I trailed my lips and fingertips over her swelling bosom, rather fuller now than I recalled from our summertime trysts, and her flat, taut-muscled belly, somewhat more rounded now. I chalked it up to enforced inactivity. Winter's cold and ice-covered rivers and lakes must certainly interfere with her swimming.

My wonderments evaporated like a bursting soap bubble, howsomever, when she responded to my overtures with a passion that startled me. We embarked on a second journey made more delightful by a lessened urgency, each of us revisiting those summertime pleasures that most satisfied the other, until at last we lay panting in a close embrace, murmuring endearments understood only by tone and circumstance, unheedful of aught that might exist outside our private universe.

Our passionate trembling, howsomever, was replaced ere long by another sort of shivering as nighttime chill invaded the lodge. Our mutual exertions had flung the sleep robes every whichaway and the fire had dwindled to coals. Rainbow rolled to her knees and added more wood. Then she took up the copper kettle warming nearby the fire and laved my nether parts and her own with a soft deerskin clout, after which she draped a blanket over my shoulders and another around her own. As the fire blazed up we were able to see well enough to exchange hand-signs. Rainbow had a passel of questions for me and I needed answers for a few of my own.

Crouched facing each other on the pallet, our fingers flew like startled grasshoppers, canceling each other, getting nowhere, until I surrendered and folded my hands and let her have her say. First off, she insisted that I tell her the story of her brother's rescue, although Fast Horse himself had already described that event with more than enough detail. I complied, trimming my narrative to the bare bones, less because of my reluctance to appear a braggart than the fact that my signing was considerably less efficient than hers. She kept interrupting, prying out every tiny detail — the Blackfoots' numbers, how big they were, their age, their weapons, and suchlike — until she exhausted all I could possibly remember or invent. Then, before I could take my turn, she demanded to know how it was that not one of our trapping bunch had a woman of his own, since she had seen many trappers at rendezvous with their wives and children.

I did my best to explain that they likely hadn't got around to it yet, that sooner or later some of my comrades would probably take a wife, but so far they had been too busy trapping beaver. Rainbow appeared dissatisfied with that response and clucked her displeasure, but she went on with her queries about how we lived in winter, what we ate and who cooked it, who made and mended our clothes and moccasins, and a passel of other questions, mostly about what you might call our housekeeping. I tried to respond, but I kept getting flustered by her beauty, glowing like burnished bronze in the flickering firelight, and even more distracted when her blanket slipped away from her delicious bosom when she became excited, which was often. At last she ran out of questions and let me ask some of my own.

Right off I wanted to know how it was that she lived by herself in a lodge of her own. Few Indian women are allowed to do so. She quickly explained that she was the widow of a brave warrior who had been killed by Blackfoots only the winter before, that her father was an important man in their band, and that her brother Fast Horse was an up-and-coming war chief, which gave her protection enough to do pretty much as she wished. She told me, too, that she worked hard for her father and brother and they, in turn, provided her with meat and whatever else she required.

When the fire commenced to crumble into embers, I dug out the candles from my poke so that we might continue our palaver. Much as I wanted to grab hold of her and roll back into the sleep robes, I fought back that desire and resumed my questioning. This was a woman whose charm and value far exceeded robe games, important as those pleasures are. I needed to know everything I could learn about her. Which I mostly did that night.

I learned that she was four winters younger than I was and that so far she was childless, that her father was called Iron Bow because, long ago, he had been the first Flathead ever who owned a gun, which he took off a Blackfoot warrior he killed, and much more of her proud family history than I really needed to know.

Fact is, I learned rather more than I was prepared for right then. The last thing she told me was that she was nigh six moons along with child and that the child was mine.

I was stunned, as you might suppose. I sat there speechless, staring without seeing much of anything. Rainbow came to my rescue, explaining matter-of-factly that she expected naught of me, that her people needed all the children they could come by, and that I was not obliged to do or say anything right then or ever. She told me all that with a calm expression on her comely features, her hand-signs slow and deliberate, her voice low, without emotion, as she spoke along with her gestures. Then, bursting into laughter, she grasped my shoulders and tipped me over onto the pallet. The last thing she signed in the guttering candlelight was that we should not waste our pleasure. Which we didn't.

* * *

Daylight was fingering into a galena-grey sky when I dodged into the lodge I shared with Ned and the others. Tuttle was already there and L'Archévêque was fussing with the fire. A kettle was steaming, filling the air with welcome coffee smell. "Hyar ye be," Tuttle greeted me, grinning. "Sleep much, did ye?"

"Not much," I grunted. You?"

"Me neither. Thar's allus time fer sleepin' when thar ain't nuthin' else doin'."

I dipped out a cupful from the kettle and hunkered down beside the fire, inhaling the delicious fragrance, my mind straying over the delights of the night before and trying pretty much unsuccessfully to wrap my mind around the disturbing fact of my siring a child.

The rattle of the doorflap announced Micah's arrival. He ducked through the low opening and headed straight for the kettle before he squatted amongst us, warming his hands on the steaming cup and gratefully breathing in the aroma.

"Wal, naow, Micah," Godey demanded with a chuckle, "did that'ere woman ever git the color rubbed off'n ye?" He craned his neck comically to peer at Micah's face.

"Reckon not," Micah replied sheepishly, pretending to hang his head. Then, looking up with an impish grin, "No, she didn't get it off my face, as I'm sure ye can see. And I ain't about to show ye if she got it rubbed off my belly!"

Such light-hearted banter continued until a scratching on the lodgeskin summoned us to break our fast in the council lodge where we had feasted the day before. Food was no less plentiful that morning, smoking-hot elk and buffalo meat and boudins and a tasty pease porridge laced with crispy meat bits. Whilst we filled our bellies there was much talk amongst us trappers about forming up hunting parties, lest we wear out our welcome in a hurry. Nigh a score of hearty new appetites would likely strain the Flatheads' larder and their hospitality, in short order.

We needn't have worried, howsomever, for by time we straggled out of the council lodge, Little Mountain, Pretty Horse, and Acorn rode into the village with three loaded-down packhorses and even more meat slung across their saddles. The approving murmurs and nods of the onlookers told us that such donations in future would assure our continued welcome amongst our Salish hosts.

Little Mountain swung off his horse, his big grin framed by bloody cheeks, attesting to his early breakfast of fresh-killed buffalo liver. "What you teenk o' dat, Tompo?" he crowed. "Ain't nobody say we same-like Big-belly Grovants, eh? Like dey eat you last morceau, den say bye-bye, see you nex' time!" He roared at his own jest and clapped me on the shoulder with a huge still-bloody hand, which nearly buckled my knees.

"No, they can't be sayin' no such a thing, Mountain. Thankee," I replied, laughing. "Ye'd best be gettin' inside, howsomever, before Tuttle eats up all that's left."

Little Mountain burlesqued mock concern. "You right! Ol' Hoss-face he got big belly — like sumbitch Atsína! Bettah go!"

The women had already commenced unloading the meat and carrying it off, smiling and chattering and casting back admiring looks at our hunters, who lost no time hustling into the council lodge. A couple herd-boys led their animals towards the cottonwood grove where our critters were gathered. Having nothing better to do just then, I followed them.

I passed a couple hours with the herd-boys, propped against a tree, stripping tender bark off lengths of sweet cottonwood, which makes excellent winter horse feed when deep snow puts grass out of reach. It's a mindless chore but it provided time to sort out my jumbled thoughts. Which wasn't very successful. The only thing I puzzled out for sure was that it would be a good idea for me to be paying my respects to Rainbow's father.

I had no illusions that he could be unaware of where I had spent the previous night or even about our trysts at rendezvous. There are few secrets in an Indian village and this matter concerned his own daughter. All I could do was to try to convince him of my good intentions, even though right then I was woefully unsure of what my intentions really were.

Just the same, I trotted back to the village, determined to do something, even if it proved to be wrong. When I stepped into our lodge I discovered my father seated alone by the fire, wearing his customary serene expression, smoking a short briar pipe I had given him. He greeted me with, "I wish you a good today, my son. You went to the horses?" I allowed that I had been there and assured him that all was well with our livestock. "I know," he replied. "The Turtle and I and the healer went to them before first light, the time stealers like most." He trained a steady gaze upon me, searching in my eyes, before he declared, "You are troubled, Sauwaseekau, my son — Temple."

At first I tried to deny it, laughing unconvincingly, even to my own ears, before I gave it up and blurted out the cause of my quandary. He was silent a long while, staring into the fire, drawing on his pipe, his face unreadable. At last he turned to me, a faint smile playing on his lips, his eyes softer than I ever recalled them to be. "What is it you fear, Sauwaseekau?" he asked quietly.

"Nothing," I replied too quickly. "Well, not much." I fumbled about in my mind, grasping at thoughts that slipped away like quicksilver. Then I said, "When I came back to the mountains all I wanted was the free life I have known here, my old friends, and you and Micah to share it with." I ran out of words about that time and fell silent. Powatawa remained silent, his eyes fixed on mine. I squirmed, less because of his gaze than for what was thrashing about in my mind. The words came tumbling out, unprepared, unthought about, surprising myself more than I daresay they did my father. "But now it's just not enough. I won't ever give up this life, these mountains, my friends, and you — the only things that ever made me happy — exceptin' for Ma, nat'rally — but now there's a hole in it somewheres," I finished lamely.

Powatawa made no reply. Only his knowing eyes invited me to continue. I struggled against what was taking shape in my mind, reluctant to admit the truth of it. My father's thin smile tickled his lips ever so slightly. Under his steady gaze, it was too much for me to hold in. "Like I said," I strangled out, "it ain't nearly enough anymore! I want that woman more than I want my own life! An' now she's carryin' my child!" I almost added, "Leastaways I think she is," but I didn't.

Powatawa's smile lit up his face — fact is, the whole lodge. Still he said nothing until he refilled his pipe, picked up a hot coal in his fingers, and placed it atop the tobacco. He inhaled a deep draught and let the smoke trickle out his nostrils, then handed the pipe to me. We passed the pipe back and forth a time or two before he said, "What will you do, my son?"

I was not prepared to answer, even to myself. Do? That was a formidable thing to decide. Do? Doing anything meant altering forever the free, unfettered, irresponsible life I cherished, but not doing anything at all was unthinkable. We smoked in silence for a spell whilst I juggled my thoughts first one way, then another, all the while being dragged, kicking and hollering mercy, to the only possible choice I could make. "I reckon I'll make her my woman," I said at last, "if she'll have me."

His smile broadened. "She will have you." He shrugged and added smugly, "You are my son."

I had to laugh at that, but he was likely right. We continued to sit without speaking, conflicting thoughts still whirling in my head, Powatawa appearing to drift off into his own world. At length he roused and broke the silence. "You have grown much today, Sauwaseekau. Today you left your robes a boy. Now I smoke with a man."

Startled, I stared at him. He continued. "A man must take his woman. Until he does that thing, he is but a part of what he will be. Only in his children and their children can he live forever. Only his woman can give him that — not war, not hunting, not honor from his people — only his woman."

He lapsed into silence, absorbed in his thoughts, whilst I chewed over what he had said and realized the truth in it. Then he said, "When I gave you the name Sauwaseekau, which you know means A-door-opened in our Shawnee tongue, I wished that you might, one day, open the door between whitemen and redmen, showing the whites that Indians are worthy equals. Your mother wished this thing perhaps more than I. We were young. We were blind. We were wrong. That will not happen in your life — not if you see one hundred winters before you die.

"Now I believe it is best if you open the door of the Indian. You live in two wegiwas — lodges — a red one and a white. Teach your children well, Sauwaseekau. Teach them what is best in the two lodges, my son, for only in that way will our grandchildren catch hold of happiness." He fell silent for a spell, staring into the fire, absorbed in his thoughts. Then, in a hollow voice, he said, "Before peace can come betwixt red man and white, the Indian must put away as childish playthings his old hatreds of other Indians. Tecumseh told them that. They laughed at him. They refused to come together and fight the whiteman. Tecumseh died. They lost their land. Maybe someday they will learn, before all the land is eaten up by whitemen."

I am still chewing that one over. It would be, as Mister Shakespeare said, "a consummation devoutly to be wished." But making it happen will be a tough chore. Even aside from simple greed and bloodlust, there is deep-seated hide-pride. Hardheaded people on both sides, inwardly unsure of their own worth, need to claim that their particular skin color makes only their own kind the big he-dog, so they can feel good about themselves.

I shoved that conundrum out of my mind, lest further delay melt my resolve. I excused myself and retreated to my heap of baggage, where I dug out a carrot of tobacco and the fine Aitch-bee-cee musket and its fixin's. I reckoned old Iron Bow deserved a worthy weapon, considering how he had earned his name. On my way out of the lodge I caught sight of my father's faint smile and what I took to be a reassuring wink.

When I scratched on the lodge-skin a woman poked her head out, then threw the doorflap aside and stepped back. At the far end of the lodge, seated on his sleep-robes, was Rainbow's father. He called out something to the woman and beckoned me to enter, motioning me to sit by his side. As I did so I heard the woman leave the lodge, then the scrape of cross-sticks being placed over the doorway. It was plain to see that my visit was not unexpected.

When I was seated at his left, the musket across my thighs, Iron Bow signed that first we must smoke. Which we did, observing the ritual of the six directions, then passing the pipe between us until the tobacco burned away. It gave me time to study the man who had sired the woman I had chosen to be my mate. I knew him to be a village elder, but he was not old. He was a handsome, still-vigorous, warrior-like man, and as I judged, not much older than Powatawa.

When he put the pipe aside, I laid my gifts on the ground before him, first the tobacco, then the musket and fixin's. His eyes widened when he realized the musket was intended for him. Rarely does a mountaineer — or an Indian in a camp not his own — go about unarmed, so he likely assumed the weapon was my own. As I was memorizing the signs I needed to tell him what amounted to a jest concerning the musket and his own name, the doorflap banged open and two women entered, bearing steaming platters of meat. Iron Bow signed that we would talk later. Eating was more important now. I needed no urging and we emptied the platters down to the greasy bark.

Not to be deprived of my jest, I hastily gestured my carefully-rehearsed signs. Iron Bow rewarded me with an appreciative grin before he took over the palaver. Naturally there are no actual words that I can write here, for we shared no common language, but our hand-talk went pretty much like this:

Iron Bow: "You come to ask me to give you my daughter. Is it not so?"

Temple, flabbergasted, but relieved at not being required to present a long proposal: "Yes."

Iron Bow: "You are sure that you want this strong-headed woman?" He tapped his temple, then made the sign for rock.

Temple, smiling in spite of himself: "Yes, I know. She is not a leaf trembling on a tree limb."

Iron Bow: "You will take her with you when you go?"

Temple: "Yes."

Iron Bow: "She will be missed. She is a good worker."

Temple: "I will pay. How many horses do you ask?"

Iron Bow: "No horses. I have many horses. You have not so many. Also, I got many horses from him who was her man before."

Temple: "What do you wish? Name your price. I will give it."

Iron Bow: "You have given it already."

Temple: "You mean the gun? It is a small thing. She is worth more."

Iron Bow: "You have given me my son, returned him from the Grey Land."

Temple: "I ask nothing for that. Fast Horse is a good man."

Iron Bow: "You give me a child. Perhaps a brave warrior. Perhaps a good woman, someday." He gestured a round belly, then the birthing sign.

I could think of no reply right then. I felt my cheeks burning but I continued to stare into his eyes, black and hard as arrow-points but with good humor crinkling the corners.

Iron Bow waved his hand as if to scatter away further discussion. It had been a topsy-turvy kind of talk, our traditional positions totally reversed — my insisting that I pay for his daughter, he refusing to accept anything from me in return for her, a most un-Indian thing for him to do.

He brought out the pipe again, tamped down some of my tobacco, and placed a coal on top. We smoked it to the dottle, sealing the bargain, as you might say. As I made my exit I was careful not to appear too grateful, lest I lose whatever shreds of dignity I still possessed.

Outside, I felt light-headed, unsure of what had just happened and uncertain if I should break the news to Rainbow or let the family tell her. It was bound to prove awkward, so I took the coward's course and hustled off to find Tuttle.

On the way I encountered my father, who merely glanced at my face before he said, "You have done well, Sauwaseekau. With such a mother my grandchildren will make me proud." He invited me to walk with him to the horses, which I did. On the way I learned that he had been making inquiries about Rainbow amongst the Flatheads. I was not surprised to learn that she was highly-regarded for her industry and her character. No mention was made of her beauty, but I needed no reassurance on that score.

I left him at the edge of the cottonwood grove. When I returned to my own lodge I discovered Tuttle Thompson snoozing on his robes, his stentorian snoring rattling the lodgepoles. It quit as soon as I touched the doorflap. He cracked open one eye and greeted me with, "Whar the hell ye been?" I told him as briefly as I could what I had done. "So thet's it. Sorta thought so. Thet's why she come in hyar trailin' a passel o' li'l boys an' taken off ever' scrap o' yer plunder."

I glanced at my sleeping place. It was completely bare. "And you didn't stop her?"

"Hell no! I warn't abaout to git in her way, nohaow. Purty gal like thet — I reckon she knows what she's abaout. Fact is, I he'ped her some, p'intin' out all o' yer b'longin's."

I failed to understand why Rainbow's good looks had anything to do with her absconding with my property, but then, Tuttle Thompson's logic has always been a mystery to me. I let it go. "So what d'ye think? About my takin' up with just one woman? From here on out."

Tuttle snorted and grinned. "I say it's abaout time. Ye been moonin' over thet'ere woman ever since ronnyvoo an', 'pears to me, thet'n'll be ready fer anythin' what comes up next."

"What about the others? Think they'll mind if I bring her along, come spring? An' don't forget, there'll be a young'un, too."

"Shee-it, Temple! Thet don't make no nevermind. Injuns do it all the time." He looked reflective for a moment. Then, "Hell! I wouldn't be a tall bit surrounded ef'n some other'n's'll be teamin' up theirownse'fs afore green-up!"

That was reassuring. Then I asked, "How about you? Ye got intentions?"

Tuttle looked startled, then indignant. "Natcherly I ain't gonna do no sech a thang!" He assumed a pious expression. "'Sides, like I been tellin' ye fer years, Temple, it be my bounden Christian duty to be comfortin' all o' them'ere grievin' widder-wimmen hyar in thish'yar gawdfersaken wilderness. Ain't nobody kin do it better'n me."

I allowed that it was likely so and bade him farewell, supremely confident that Tuttle Thompson would never neglect that particular duty.

* * *

When I neared Rainbow's lodge I spied Kumskaka, up to his knees in prairie hay and cottonwood bark, tethered at the doorway, announcing to all the village that she was no longer a widow but a wife. He nickered at my approach and I stopped to scratch his ears, suddenly shy about entering her lodge, which, I reminded myself, was now my own.

When I stepped inside she greeted me with a shy look I had never seen on her face before. I went to her, tilted up her chin, and kissed her soundly, which changed everything. Her face was suddenly wreathed in a brilliant smile, like summer sunshine, and I realized that I had seen her in daylight only once before. We had always met in darkness, lit only by firelight or a flickering candle. This was a definite improvement. Today she was clad in holiday raiment, soft golden doeskins crusted with colorful quillwork, her face rosy and glowing, full lips parted over perfect white teeth.

Without a word or sign she caught both my hands in hers and led me to the sleep robes at the far end of the lodge and gently pushed me down before she retreated to the doorway and fixed the cross-sticks outside the flap. When she returned she knelt to take off my moccasins, then my leggin's and the rest of my clothing before she removed all of her own.

Thus it was that we celebrated our marriage and embarked on our honeymoon. No parson or priest ever sanctified a more perfect union.

* * *

Winter wore on, mostly mild, sometimes with welcome heavy snows, which helped to keep Blackfoot raiding parties at home in their lodges, although you can never be sure of it. This was the farthest north and west that we had ever wintered, closer to Blackfoot home country than ever been before. The village moved twice, westwards along the broad valley, when forage grass and sweet cottonwood bark for the horses and mules grew meager, when game critters got pretty much used up thereabouts, and the middens built up and became rather too much to bear whenever the wind shifted to the east or warming Chinooks blew gently from the north.

Like most winters, our bunch had little to do besides hunting for meat and dragging in a-horseback great bundles of firewood, using the grass ropes I had got from Pilcher. Even the customary chores of repairing moccasins and clothing were taken over by the women most of my companions had taken up with. The communal lodges provided for us by the elders were pretty much empty come nightfall as my comrades sought the sleeprobes and warm comfort of their various light-o'-loves.

There was plenty of time for pastimes. Naturally Tuttle kept himself busy perfecting his skill at the hand game and instructing eager Flatheads in the mysteries of Old Sledge. I had time to put a fine edge on my two new ponies, the bay horse Punch and the sunburnt black I called Rowdy. He was a proper handful at first, but a stern hand coupled with loving attention soon gentled him out.

Only Micah was deprived of his daytime leisure. He was besieged by a steady stream of trappers taking advantage of his gunsmithing skills, some asking him to repair damaged locks and triggers and sights lost or bent askew, most to replace their flintlocks with the new percussion locks he had brought up from Hawken's shop and those from Joshua Pilcher. Tuttle had been the first, vaunting the virtues of what he called "them leetle nipple-huggers" and endlessly recounting his experience the windy night we rescued Fast Horse from the Blackfoots. Before long almost every trapper was clamoring for the new-fangled locks, first for their rifles, then their pistols.

As you might suppose, Anse Tolliver, set in his ways as he is, at first sneered at such affectations, advancing all the usual arguments about the unavailability in the mountains of "them'ere teensy li'l thimbles" and suchlike, but in the end sheepishly asking Micah to modify his "shootin' arns."

I thanked my stars that I had bought a generous supply of caps from Jake Hawken and then more than doubled that amount when I traded with Pilcher. It was truly a case of well-meant charity returning manifold and fat chickens coming home to roost. Sometimes virtue is truly its own reward.

* * *

Buffalo straggling southwards from deepening snows in Grandfather's Land provided meat aplenty for the village. Nearly every day half of our bunch joined Flathead hunters in a rich harvest of meat and hides. Every mild day, women all over camp were busy slicing meat into slender strips and drying it on long racks or kneeling on bloody hides, scraping off bits of meat and tallow, turning them into robes for use at home or for trade.

Rainbow was amongst them, her increasing belly resting on her thighs as she tugged the scraper in smooth, even strokes, preparing the hide for curing and tanning. Concerned for her well-being, I tried to make her quit, but she brushed me away as if I were a pesky fly, signing that this was women's work and that I would be better occupied smoking and telling lies with my fellows.

On days when strong winds and heavy snowfall prevented hunting and outdoor chores, she and I would remain snug in our lodge, me reading English novels from my mother's library, scribbling notes in my journal, or cleaning weapons, she mending or making moccasins and colorful clothing from the woolens I had given her. She marveled at the needles and fine silk thread I provided and her cries of delight when she discovered the use of scissors almost made me think that she was right to call such a common tool magical.

From time to time we would put aside our chores and go to school. Sign-talk is eminently useful when you are learning a spoken language, for it is exceedingly helpful to know beforehand the meaning of the slippery word or phrase you are trying to wrap your tongue around. Rainbow was much more successful in learning my language than my tongue-tied attempts to learn hers. I am not sure if Salish is easier to learn than other Indian tongues or if learning from her just made it easier, but as the winter wore on I got a fair grasp of those slick, sonorous syllables.

Sometimes we would, by mutual consent, retire to our robes, where we would continue our language lessons as well as those which require no words.

Often, in the early evening, half a dozen of my mountaineer companions would crowd into our lodge to eat and palaver and jest. During such times Rainbow was an attentive listener. Afterwards I did my best to expunge from her new vocabulary such gems as "sumbitch" and "bahstohd" and other choice cusswords, with but little success. I am convinced that the tone and unconscious emphasis one applies to scurrilous speech makes it memorable, no matter how casually we use it.

Other nights, Anse Tolliver would tote his fiddle to the big council lodge and hold forth, to the great amusement and admiration of the Flatheads, who crowded inside until the lodgepoles threatened to splinter, whilst a throng gathered outdoors, grinning and stamping and performing dance steps to the unfamiliar music. Naturally Yves Dureau and his little squeezebox provided welcome accompaniment and often Turtle, Cesár, and several others of our bunch joined in with flutes and hand-drums and suchlike.

We all took our turn at horse guard nearly every night, putting in a two-hour stint, huddled in capotes or buffalo greatcoats, crouched in the snow, mostly silent, straining our ears for an unfamiliar sound. When I returned to the lodge, chilled to the bone, Rainbow would kneel before me, remove my moccasins, and bathe my feet with a warm, moist deerskin clout, before taking me to our robes to restore the rest of me. Such attentions go a long way towards convincing a mountaineer that giving up some of his freedom might be well worth it.

Wintry days slid into weeks, then months of peaceful living amongst the Flatheads, which caused us mountaineers and I daresay our Indian hosts, as well, to become uneasy, suspicious of our good fortune. All of us felt in our bones that a visit by a Blackfoot raiding party was sure to come. "T'won't be long," Brass Turtle warned solemnly, "afore them greedy bastards h'ist their arse outa their robes an' come runnin' on down thisaway fer their fun."

"Ye kin bet yer arse on it!" Ned Godey agreed. "I been expectin' it long since. We been lucky so far, but thar's no way it kin last."

"Ye reckon these hyar Flatheads'll put up a decent fight?" Tuttle wanted to know.

"Reckon so!" Godey replied emphatically. "Close as they be livin' 'longside o' Blackfoot stompin' grounds, thar wouldn't be no Flatheads hereabouts nohow if'n they war short on spunk!"

"Let'em be comin' on, then!" Paddy McBride declared warmly. "'Tis intirely too bloody long, anyways, since we had oursel's a proper donnybrook!" Anse Tolliver grunted and looked even more sour than he usually does.

I had nothing useful to contribute to what had already been said and Micah, McCool, and Powatawa held their peace as well, but all three faces told me that they were more than ready for a fight.

* * *

Ice on nearby beaver ponds commenced to grow spongy, thanks to a chinook that hung around for several days. Sober, strained looks appeared on the faces of the normally easy-going Flatheads. Every man bristled with weapons. Horse guard was doubled in daytime and tripled at night. Most of us took to sleeping fully-dressed and shod.

Rainbow was nearing her time. She assured me, howsomever, that the birthing was nearly a month off. Naturally my concern for her dampened whatever ardor I might have conjured up for a brawl with Blackfoots. Which even in the most carefree times of my life was never much.

* * *

The attack came at false dawn, not quite daylight, with a rush of four horsemen bursting through the cottonwoods, yipping and howling and swinging blankets around their heads, spooking our critters, which r'ared and plunged and fought their tethers and hobbles. A few broke loose and rushed about wildly, screaming in fright, crashing into still-tethered animals, bowling them over, ripping up picket-pins, skidding and sprawling on the slippery snow, struggling to their feet and racing about in circles, a proper maelstrom of hysterical horseflesh.

When all hell broke loose, Tuttle, Micah, and I were together, cached in a clump of spindly cottonwoods, nearly finished with our spell of guard duty. At first we were unable to shoot, lest we hit our own critters or the herd-boys, who were scurrying about like startled minnows, doing their best to catch hold of trailing tether-ropes. Only when the raiders swung about and joined together to drive loose animals from the grove could we take careful aim and sweep three of them from their saddles. Two of them lay still. A third one flopped about like a catfish thrown upon a bank.

Micah brushed past me and went high-stepping through the trampled snow, his pistol held aloft, until he was but half a rod distant from the remaining mounted horsethief, who was frantically trying to unsling his musket. He never did. Micah's pistol shot toppled him from his horse and he lay unmoving in the snow, his head half-buried in a heap of steaming manure donated by one of his frightened prey. Micah caught up the rein of the Blackfoot's pony and handed him over to one of the grinning herd-boys before he trudged back to our post.

In the distance, farther down the cottonwood grove, I heard gunfire and angry shouts, where I reckoned Flatheads and some of our bunch were fending off other invaders.

I had been so occupied with reloading and watching Micah that I lost track of Tuttle. Now I spied him, a scalp in one hand, hiking back from the fallen Blackfoot, who was no longer thrashing about. He halted before me, bent to wipe his bloody blade on his leggin', and announced happily, "Cain't see no need a-tall fer wastin' good galena on thet'n!"

By then several Flatheads and some of our own, alerted by the gunshots, came streaming into the grove, some a-horseback, most afoot. Our greetings were cut off by a rattle of gunfire in the village. A fearful thought stabbed into my brain. I fled from the grove, legs pumping, floundering through the snow, racing as best I could to my lodge and Rainbow, cursing the while that I had walked instead of riding to my post. As I topped the rise to the village street I beheld several burning lodges, a dozen mounted Blackfoots belting their horses through a mob of Flatheads shooting and lunging at the raiders with lances, arrows flying in every direction, terrified women running past me, clutching babes to their breast and dragging little ones by the hand as they sought refuge from the blood-bath. It made me think of a school of pike ripping through a pondful of frantic chubs.

I was some fity yards off from our lodge when I spied a Blackfoot slashing Kumskaka's tether, attempting to lead him off. My horse had other intentions, r'aring and striking with his forefeet at the horsethief. Without thinking, I dropped to one knee and brought Jacob Hawken's Best to bear on the interloper. The din was so great that I scarcely heard the report of my rifle, but I saw the result. The ball must have caught him low in the back. His legs shot skywards and he flopped upon his back and lay still. Kumskaka ran off and disappeared in the seething mass of angry, frightened humanity and frantic horseflesh.

There was no time to reload. I slung my rifle, jerked the pistol from my sash, and sprinted for the lodge. Twenty yards off I slipped on an icy patch and went sprawling on my belly, just as a big Blackfoot warrior exploded through the doorflap of our lodge, arms flapping, then collapsed and lay unmoving on his back, half in, half out of the doorway. I struggled to my feet and closed the remaining distance, but not before a second Blackfoot ran up and attempted to drag his fellow free. He was bent double, his back to me, grunting and jabbering as he tugged and strained to move the dead man. Without forethought I shoved my pistol through the back slit of his capote and jammed the muzzle squarely into his arse, triggering the charge as I did so.

Even excited as I was I could not fail to marvel when the ball shattered his skull, blowing it to smithereens in a bloody spew of bone and brains. The scalp was a total loss.

There was no time for either gloating or regret. I shoved the body aside and tromped over the dead man cluttering the entrance, ducking low out of habit, although his hasty exit had ripped loose the lacing-pins, leaving the lodge gaping wide open. When I straightened I beheld Rainbow, tottering but on her feet, staring vacantly, horrified, my blanket gun dangling from one hand, her other arm flung protectively across her bulging belly, mumbling words I doubt even she understood.

I caught her before she fell and half-carried her to our sleeprobes. I laid her down and gently loosed her fingers from the gun, blabbering the while a spate of foolishness about how she was safe now and that I would always defend her and I don't know what-all.

Gradually the terror faded from her eyes. She smiled faintly and reached up to stroke my cheek. She closed her eyes then and appeared to drift off to sleep, which I fervently wished she would do.

I bethought myself that it was past time that I reloaded my weapons. This was no time to be caught unarmed. Which I did before advancing carefully to the wide-open doorway. The bodies still littered the entrance but the scene past the inner ring of lodges had altered remarkably. The shooting had for the most part ceased. No longer were women scampering frantically for safety. Now they were cautiously threading their way amongst the lodges, returning home. Young girls clung to their mothers' skirts, but wide-eyed little boys darted hither and thither, inspecting corpses, crowing when they discovered a dead Blackfoot and snatching valuables from the body.

I stood there uncertainly, anxious to learn the result of the battle but reluctant to abandon Rainbow. First one, then the other of the two women from Iron Bow's lodge — Rainbow's aunts, I learned later

— bumped me aside and rushed to Rainbow's side, cackling their concern for her well-being and shooing me off. Assured that she was likely in better hands than my own, I was about to depart, but first I needed to remove the dead man from the doorway. He was a big fellow, not old, a Káinah, judging by his clothing, his painted face frozen in what I took to be horrified surprise, a single eagle feather tangled in a wealth of long black hair, his belly ripped open by a close-up charge of goose shot.

I pried his tack-studded musket loose from his rigid hands and chucked it into the lodge before I hauled him into the narrow walkway, then to the side of the lodge. An antic thought occurred. Contrary to my custom, I drew my knife, grabbed a handful of hair, traced a wide circle around his crown, and yanked off the scalp. It came free with a sickening plop. Grisly as the action was, I felt a pleasing warm glow. Rainbow had earned her trophy. I tossed it into the lodge before I trotted off to discover what damage the Blackfoot raid had caused.

It was considerable. Everywhere I looked, it seemed, women and old men, most with faces daubed black in mourning, knelt beside the bodies of slain loved ones, some weeping quietly, others howling their grief, hacking off great hanks of their own hair, some throwing themselves across the still forms in a final embrace. Neither sex nor age had been spared by the marauders. The bodies of women and children outnumbered men.

Scattered here and there in the council clearing lay the bodies of dead Blackfoots, unattended except for passers-by halting to kick them or spit upon them.

Finn McCool was kneeling beside a prostrate Iron Bow, probing his thigh for a musket ball which came free just as I arrived. The old warrior merely grunted as Finn gouged a final time and flipped the bloody ball onto the blood-stained snow. Finn flashed a fleeting grin as he bent to staunch the blood which flowed from the wound, smeared on a greenish paste, then wrapped the leg tightly with a wide strip of deerhide. "Don't ye be after worryin' none about your Da-in-law, Temple," he advised. "He's tough as a hussar's boot. The ball damaged nothin' serious." He smiled at Iron Bow, patted him on the shoulder, then scurried off to assist Old Foot, who was similarly engaged.

I tarried a moment with my father-in-law, who struggled to a sitting position, tilted his head towards his shiny new musket, and grinned at me, as if to say that his new weapon had served him well. I offered my hand to help him rise, but he merely tossed his head, spun about, and heaved himself erect. Still smiling, using his musket as a staff, he limped off to his lodge.

I passed the forenoon running errands for Foot and McCool and helping when I could, interrupted only by the triumphant arrival of Brass Turtle and Fast Horse, most of our Delawares and Iroquois, and a passel of Flatheads driving before them a score and more riderless horses burdened with clothing, blankets, muskets, bows, and quivers lashed onto their hair-pad saddles.

Turtle was giddy with excitement, beaming with satisfaction. He threw a fistful of scalps onto the snow and announced, "Reckon that'll larn 'em somethin'! Time they got their gawddamn comeuppance! B'lievin' their own braggin' got them sumbitches kilt!" He described how, when the shooting commenced, a previously-picked crew mounted up and raced to ambush the raiders when they retreated. "Thar war a sufficiency o' guns an' arrers hyar to hold 'em off an' make 'em turn tail. Stayin' hyarabouts, we'd'a jist got in the way. Soon as they backed off, we hit 'em hard!" He confessed that a few got away, but not many. "When they're lickin' their gawddamn wounds up thar, they'll be thinkin' twicet about comin' down thisaway agin!."

By mid-afternoon the wounded had been patched up and the Salish dead removed to their lodges to be prepared for their final rest. Blackfoot bodies, scalped and stripped to the hide, few if any intact by now, had been dragged onto the prairie to feed the ravens. It was time to see to Rainbow.

When I arrived at our lodge a ten-year-old boy was teetering high on a lodgepole, replacing the lace-pins. Even before I got inside I heard Rainbow's groans and stifled yelps. I wormed past half a dozen chattering women hovering around her and knelt by her side. Her hair was soaked with sweat, her face drawn and strained.

Little as I knew of such matters, it was plain even to me that fright and excitement had brought on the birthing before its time. The women crowded around, gabbling like a yardful of geese, making unfamiliar hand-signs but making it plain that something had gone terribly wrong. When I gently lifted her head she opened her eyes and tried to smile, mumbling incoherent words cut off by a sudden painful yelp. Scared half to death, I bent to kiss her feverish brow, then rolled back on my heels and raced outdoors to find Foot and McCool, who might be able to help the woman I loved.

I found them at the crick, cleansing off blood from their earlier chores. Somehow I managed to babble enough sense to describe Rainbow's plight, telling them they were needed at her side, now! Finn's face clouded with concern. He snatched up his little bag of medical tools and hotfooted off to my lodge. Foot betrayed no emotion that I could see, but he lost no time trotting after McCool.

Naturally the Flathead women raised all kinds of hell when Finn and Foot shouldered in amongst them, clucking and shrilling their disapproval. Birthing is women's work. Men should take no part in it. Foot growled and signed menacingly enough to scatter them off. I hung back at the doorway, hearing my woman's torment, powerless to do aught, wishing I knew how to pray and, if I could master that part, where I should direct my pleas.

After a spell Finn led me outside and said gravely, "'Tis a sorry state she's in, Temple. The child is breeched." When he saw my uncomprehending look he explained, "The babe is turned about all topsy-turvy, not coming on headfirst as is proper."

Somehow I strangled out, "Rainbow? Will she die? Is there naught ye can do?"

He sighed. "Ye can be sure I'll be doin' whatever my poor trainin' allows, my friend. 'Tis niver a lost cause whilst there's life remainin'.

We'll be hopin' together." With that, he wheeled and plunged back into the lodge.

I have no idea how many hours I sat in the snow outdoors, numb to my surroundings, cursing myself for being the author of her suffering, listening to her muffled cries and choking whimpers and McCool's occasional grunts and grumbling curses. I was hardly aware of the awkward sympathy my comrades sought to offer. At last I heard her throaty shriek and anguished moan, followed soon after by McCool's triumphant bellow, a mewling, squalling cry, then a cackle of nervous laughter from the attending women.

Afraid to hope, I poked my head inside and saw in the light of the blazing fire a grin on Old Foot's leathery face, then a reassuring wink when he spied me in the doorway. Finn shifted about on his knees and held up a tiny squirming still-bloody naked squawking bundle shining in the firelight. When he spied me he called out, "Ye've sired a bee-yoo-ti-ful colleen, Temple, me lad!"

"And Rainbow?" I choked out. I confess that I had given little thought to the child, only to my woman.

"Och, she'll be doin' jist fine! Don't ye be after worryin' yersel', now the birthin's past." I scrambled forward on hands and knees, eager first to see Rainbow, who lay smiling weakly, giggling softly, stretching out her arms for the child, who was receiving the attentions of the women laving off blood and mucous from her tiny body, then swaddling her in a blanket before they placed the little bundle in my woman's arms.

In my mother's books I had often seen tinted pictures of Italian Madonnas, but none so beautiful as the glowing woman who cradled our child on her breast. She and I exchanged no words or signs, but her contented smile spoke volumes of love and trust and satisfaction. She reached out and squeezed my hand, then closed her eyes and drifted into slumber.

When I emerged from the lodge I was greeted by Iron Bow and Fast Horse and all of our bunch who weren't on horse guard, even our Indians. Little Mountain was first to step forward and clap a comforting hand on my shoulder. "Too bad," he said soothingly, "dis time no man-chile. Nex' time mebbe fer damn-sure." I burst out laughing, choosing not to tell him that, boy or girl, it made no nevermind. Everybody gathered around, showering good wishes and congratulations on me, as if it had been I and not Rainbow who had survived the birthing ordeal. Shaky as I was, perhaps they were right to do so.

When the crowd commenced to break up and drift off, Iron Bow beckoned me to follow him to his lodge. Which I did.

When I entered, Brass Turtle, my father, Micah, Fast Horse, and Finn McCool were already seated. Iron Bow waved me forward to sit at his left side, then prepared the pipe, which we smoked and passed around in thoughtful silence. Little was said afterwards, either. For the most part we just grinned at one another until a scratching on the lodgeskin announced the arrival of vittles. Food was indeed welcome. I realized then that I hadn't eaten a morsel for a day and a half. Heaps of smoking hump ribs, steaming boiled tongue, and sizzling boudins loosened our tongues as much as trader's booze ever did. Soon the lodge rang with rude jests and laughter. Knives flashed in the firelight as we carved off great gobbets of meat and declared our relief and our joy with greasy finger-signs, celebrating both a costly triumph over our enemy and the arrival of one more Human Being to insure the survival of the Salish Nation.

I was not inclined to quibble that point. Rainbow had paid a far greater price for that honor than I ever could.

I should mention that in most Indian tongues the title of Human Being is restricted only to members of that particular tribe or nation. All other two-leggeds are considered to be somewhat less than human. Naturally the precise parentage of my daughter was discreetly left unspecified.

It was broad daylight and a warm breeze bathed the village by time we left Iron Bow's lodge. The others straggled off to their various dwellings, but my father tarried with me, reluctant to depart without a glimpse of his grandchild. We walked to our lodge, where I bade him wait a spell whilst I went inside to wish Rainbow good morning and get a proper look at my daughter.

Rainbow lay on our sleeprobes, propped against a willow backrest, suckling our child, her face glowing with pride and contentment. She broke into a broad smile when I succeeded in wriggling past the gaggle of attending women and knelt beside her. She waved away my concerns for her well-being and signed that she should be up and about her chores. Her aunts and the other women wouldn't allow it, for which I silently thanked them. The babe gave up her sucking for a moment and Rainbow held her out at arm's length, inviting me to hold her, which I did, albeit hesitantly, for I feared that I might break that precious bundle.

Even swaddled in a woolen blanket, she weighed next to naught. All I could see was a tiny red face, eyes squinted tight shut against the bright sunlight that streamed through the smoke-flaps stretched wide open on their poles. I shifted about to put her in the shade of my body and she opened her eyes. I almost dropped her.

Her eyes were deepest blue blending into violet and the dark purple that you see when you peer downwards from a high mountain trail into a shadowed valley far below, the enchanting hue when a still drowsy sun first pokes a shy finger into the black velvet of a starless early-morning sky, the mysterious color that I had seen in the eyes of only one other person, my mother.

If I had ever had any doubt that it was I who had sired Rainbow's child, such wonderments vanished. I reckon I did, a time or two, although I didn't much care one way or another. Every man hears all too often sly remarks about how it's a wise child that knows its father. Now I could be certain she was my own, for whatever that might be worth.

I ducked through the doorway and thrust the babe into Powatawa's waiting arms. "There's your granddaughter, father!" I almost shouted. "What do ye see?" Naturally my newborn child resented such rough handling and commenced to wail, squinching her eyes in the sunshine and howling.

Most uncharacteristically, Powatawa rocked the little one in his arms, cooing and clucking the while, and moved into the shade of the lodge, where she soon quieted and opened her eyes. His jaw dropped. Then he said, "Your mother is with us once more, Sauwaseekau. She has returned." He continued to stare into the tiny red wrinkled face, at last declaring, "I shall call her Kay-sah-kee Wah-thay-yaw. She will bring us out of darkness. You may call her Morning Light, if it pleases you."

About then Finn McCool showed up, red-faced and bleary-eyed from lack of sleep. "I've been after makin' me rounds this early mornin'," he informed us, "makin' sure me patients are still alive an' kickin'. This'll be me last stop afore I git some shut-eye." He took the baby from Powatawa, stooped low, and entered the lodge. A moment later the aunts and other women hurriedly emerged, cackling furiously, again resentful of his intrusion into their precincts.

Powatawa went on his way and I waited alone until Finn invited me to enter. The baby was nuzzling Rainbow's breast whilst McCool stowed his medico tools in his rusty little satchel. "Well now," he said, "I'm pleased to be tellin' ye that all's well with the both o' thim. Yer woman lost much blood in the birthin', but she'll likely be herownsel' again after half a week, if ye can keep her abed that long." He glanced towards the mother and child. "An' yer pretty colleen is all ye could iver be askin' for, possessin' all her proper parts an' healthy as a high-bred filly, bright as a shiny new shillin'!"

Finn's face darkened. "This last I'd rather not be tellin' ye, Temple, but ye might as well be knowin' it all." I braced myself for bad news, although I couldn't imagine what it might be after what he had just told me. "The birthin' was hard, as ye know. The child was all askew in there an' there was likely some serious damage done in gittin' her turned about." He sighed deeply before he announced, "It's doubtful yer darlin' Rainbow'll iver be conceivin' another child. Does that matter to ye, Temple?"

I hesitated not a jot before I replied. "No, it doesn't. I have the two of them. That's enough."

Relieved, Finn brightened and asked, "So what'll ye be namin' the child? Ye can't be forever callin' her the baby an' such, ye know."

I hadn't given a moment's thought to the baby's name. Rainbow had likely already named her something in her own tongue, but the child required a name that I and my friends could pronounce. "Well," I began uncertainly, "it ought to be something connected with Rainbow herself. As you know better than anybody, she had a lot more to do with it all than I did."

Finn reflected for a spell before he exclaimed, "I've got it! Why not call her Iris? 'Tis the name of the Greek goddess of the rainbow, sure enough, an' she the beloved messenger of the gods!"

It was perfect. "Done!" I cried. "Iris it is!" McCool grinned with obvious pleasure, bade me farewell, and went on his way.

A minute later I informed Rainbow that our daughter's American name would be Iris. She smiled and nodded her agreement, happy, I reckon, that I cared enough about a girl-child to involve myself in her naming.

Problem was, Rainbow could never quite pronounce our daughter's name correctly. It always came out Irish, which pleased Finn McCool and Paddy McBride to no small degree, as you might suppose.

* * *

That night, in the early darkness, the great drum thundered out its call to the people to come to the scalp dancing. All day long the women had been busy preparing fallen family members for burial, dressing them in their finest raiment, together with their favorite weapons or household tools, wrapping them in buffalo robes or blankets, lashing the bodies onto wooden frames, and placing them high amongst tree branches, safe from prowling critters until the earth thawed sufficiently to permit a proper burial.

Now it was time to put aside grief, leastaways for a spell, and celebrate victory over their enemy, for several more Blackfoot raiders than Salish warriors and women had gone to the Grey Land the day before. It was time to glory in whatever triumph they could persuade themselves to claim, parading captured horses, ignoring their own shorn tresses and gashed faces and arms, and to forget for a spell the forever-after absence of beloved members of families and clans.

When the big drum commenced its hollow beat and high-pitched chanting pierced the darkness Rainbow struggled to rise and join her family and neighbors, but I refused to allow it. Then she urged me to go alone and strut my prowess — for the sake of our family honor, as I interpreted her signing — but I declined. Without her, such boasting would be was empty. At last she gave up, reluctantly, and sulked.

The great council fire blazed high, coloring our lodgeskin bright orange, casting giant shadows as our neighbors scurried to join the celebration. The booming, throbbing, thrumming of the drum and quavering male voices extolling their courage and warlike skill filled our ears and made our skin tingle. It was impossible to ignore.

I commenced to fidget, then to pace about. Then a fanciful thought occurred to me. I reached behind the woodpile nigh the doorway and retrieved the Káinah's musket and blood-crusted scalp that I had thrown there the day before. Plucking a fringe from my leggin' I tied the scalp to the muzzle, then proceeded to cavort and caper about our own fire, imitating as best I knew how the howling braggadocio of Flathead warriors, crouching and leaping and mincing dainty dance-steps, brandishing the musket and its grisly long-haired trophy over Rainbow's head and brushing her face with the flowing hair.

At first she frowned and clucked her displeasure at my buffoonery, but I refused to quit until at last she relented and burst out laughing, holding up our daughter to witness her father's insanity. I laid the musket aside then and signed that it was she, not I, who had killed the big Blackfoot and thus deserved the honor.

Rainbow reached out and drew me to a close embrace, kissed me soundly on the lips, and murmured sweetly in my ear, "Bastohd! Sumbitch! You a dammit!"

Chapter IX
Double-harness

This time, farewelling the Flatheads required considerably more time and confusion than it usually did in getting our outfit on the trail. Naturally there was a passel of weeping and embracing and last-minute gifting, repacking loads, and settling down critters grown fractious and independent during their long winter layoff, but at last we were ready to set out to rejoin Fitz and Davey Jackson at the lake we called the Flathead.

As it turned out, Rainbow wasn't the only woman in our party. Paddy McBride's pretty little scalp-dancing woman, already bulging noticeably at the midriff, sat astride a prancing piebald pony, alternately giggling and sobbing as she made her good-byes to tearful family members and friends. Paddy had announced to me only that morning, "I dassn't be leavin' her behind, brimmin' wid me own child loike she be, as ye can plainly see, fer a red-headed young'un's sure to be a figger o' fun amongst these dark folk. Meself's put up wid more'n me share o' sich funnin' most o' me loife. I can't abide inflictin' more o' the same on me own kid. Besides, mind ye, I've grown fond o' the woman — Molly, I'm callin' her, fer I can't, fer the loife o' me, harness me tongue to be sayin' her proper name loike she calls it."

Ned Godey, too, had a woman in tow, a tall, slim, dark-eyed beauty. She sat quietly in her saddle, tight-lipped and solemn, brushing away an occasional tear and nodding to her well-wishers. "We made up our minds only last night," Ned told me, laughing nervously. "Like I told ye when we fust got hyar, Temple, I'd not be settlin' fer jist any woman an' I din't hafta, as ye kin plainly see." He cast an admiring glance at his handsome spouse — if that's the proper word. "An' she's jist as good as she looks, too. Ain't no way I'm leavin' her behind — same as you. She lost her man and a young'un to

Blackfoots sometime back," he went on hurriedly, "so I promised I'd give her another'n soon's I kin."

We chuckled over that one. For lack of anything better, I said, "Reckon you will, Ned, and happily, too."

Rainbow sat serene, unruffled, aboard my sturdy new bay horse Punch, our month-old daughter swinging gently in her cradleboard from her mother's high-pommeled saddle, snoozing peacefully, blissfully unaware of the surrounding hubbub. Rainbow had earlier made her good-byes to her father and brother. Now they stood solemnly with the other elders and young chiefs, faces impassive, betraying not a whit of feeling.

At last our braying, neighing, bell-jingling, critter-cursing caravan got underway, three of the packhorses dragging travois poles, the rest only lightly loaded. Our fall harvest and what was left of the jerked meat had been cached on our way to the Flathead village. At first the welfare of the women occupied our concern, but before the day was was half done, we knew they required no coddling. They were seasoned travelers, each the equal of any of us in that regard.

We had departed the village well before the spring harvest. Ponds and streams were still frozen. The Salish are much more enterprising in beaver-trapping than most other tribes, so we reckoned it best not to compete with them when the spring thaw occurred. They had been friendly, generous hosts. We owed them that much and more.

We raised the cache on the second day out and reached Jackson's flimsy fort early on the fourth. As usual, we announced our arrival in mountaineer fashion, firing off our guns, galloping the last few hundred yards, whooping and hollering and yelling out greetings to old friends. I was riding drag and it was a memorable sight to behold our women in the thick of it, adding high-pitched voices to the shouting, their travois bouncing and swaying and jouncing over snowy ground, then bringing their critters to an abrupt halt behind the leaders.

Davey and Tom Fitzpatrick stood before the welcoming crowd. "Glad to see ye made it through the cold," Fitz called out. "The lot o' ye lookin' all fat an' sassy to boot! 'Pears ye wintered well."

"Likely better'n y'all," Tuttle replied, his gaze straying over the assembled men, noting several with bandaged heads or arms in slings. "Had trouble, did ye?"

"Some, jist a week back," Fitz admitted. "'Twas nothing we couldn't handle. We lost not a man — ner woman or child, nayther." He spat tobacco juice. "Bloody Grovants they were, but we gave 'em proper comeuppance! Now there be some'at fewer Big-bellies bringin' grief to the loikes of us." He grinned. "Moreover, the bloody bastards donated nine good ponies after the fray, 'though surely 'twasn't their intention!"

"I see ye've added to your numbers," Davey broke in, his gaze resting upon our women.

"Indade we have!" Paddy crowed. "Temple an' Godey've taken up wives an' meownself soon to be a proud papa!"

"Och!" Fitz cried out in mock horror. "Not another one loike yerownself clutterin' the face o' the airth! May the Lord presarve us!" Fortunately the two Irishmen had long before mended their differences. The jibe elicited only laughter.

Pitching camp inside the enclosure was easier than it had been ever before, lestaways for us married men. Rainbow shooed me off, insisting that such labor was women's work, unseemly for menfolk to do. Our lodge was less spacious now than hers had been. It consisted of only four poles and a lodgeskin to fit, but it was more than adequate for the two of us and the child.

Ned, Paddy, and I amused ourselves by offering advice to our fellows building makeshift bowers, the while dodging sticks and gobs of mud they threw at us.

* * *

Ice was fast disappearing. We were preparing to split with Jackson's brigade and pursue the spring hunt on our own, when gaunt, travel-worn Jedediah Smith arrived with only three companions. The jubilation amongst men who knew him was, howsomever, short-lived, replaced with ill-concealed consternation when they learned that more than a score of trappers who had gone to California with Smith had perished at the hands of Indians. Only the four of them survived.

He brought no plews with him, but word was that he presented Davey Jackson with a draught for a couple thousand dollars or so, drawn on a London bank, payment by the Aitch-bee-cee for the furs and other property recovered by the Brits from the Indians who had robbed Smith and killed all but three of his men.

"Ol' Diah must be mostly cat," Brass Turtle observed drily, "seein'" how he keeps swappin' them nine lives o' his'n fer comin' out with a whole hide." He made a sour face. "Too bad he cain't be teachin' his people how he does it."

"Yep," Tuttle agreed mournfully. "I'd as lief be sleepin' 'longside o' grizzle b'ars as follerin' a'hind o' Jed Smith." He heaved a deep sigh. "Ye know Tom Virgin war amongst them as din't make it."

"Ye reckon it's on account o' that'ere Bible book Diah's allus totin' along?" Anse Tolliver enquired seriously. "Ain't never seed 'im without it."

"Well now, Misther Fiddler," Paddy McBride shouted gleefully, "if that's the truth of it, the Good Book'll be doin' the loikes o' you no good a-tall a-tall! Consid'rin' ye can't read a solitary word of it!" He dodged a flaming firebrand that Anse flung at him and capered out of range, cackling wildly, doubtless congratulating himself on his own hard-won ability to read and write, acquired at great pains one winter in the Rocky Mountain College.

* * *

Pierre's Hole on the Popo-azhieh had been selected for the 1829 rendezvous, so we trapped the watercourses generally southwards for our spring hunt. As we usually did, we separated from Davey Jackson's brigade, so as not to interfere with his trappers, but we stayed close enough to join up with them in case of a serious Indian attack. It was understood that Smith, Jackson & Sublette would have first call on our plews, providing they paid top dollar at rendezvous.

We split our own bunch into three trapping parties in order to cover the country most thoroughly as we moved southwards. This time there was no question about Powatawa joining our crew. He refused to be separated from his tiny granddaughter. Tuttle, Micah, and Cesár made up the rest and Jean-Luc L'Archévêque came along as campkeeper.

Godey joined Paddy and Anse, for Ned's woman wished to be near Paddy's pregnant little Molly, just in case. So did Finn McCool, for much the same reason. Brass Turtle went along because, as he put it, "Somebody's gotta keep an eye out fer these white-eyes whilst they're lookin' arter the womenfolk." Tolliver joined them and Dureau, never content being far off from Anse's fiddle, was their campkeeper.

The other Delawares — Little Mountain, Foot, and Pretty Horse — and the Iroquois Stone Bird and Acorn made up the third trapper camp.

Rainbow didn't mind being the only woman in our party. Strong and self-confident, she required no feminine companionship to keep up her spirits, although she and Godey's woman had formed a close bond since we left the Salish village. Ned called his woman Kathleen — his grandmother's name, he said — but it wasn't long until we all called her Cat, an apt nickname for that slim, sinuous, independent dark beauty. Cat was deeply devoted to Ned, but there was no doubting that she was definitely her own woman.

As for me, Rainbow filled in every corner of my life. She rejoiced in her labors, cheerfully sharing cooking chores with Jean-Luc, gathering firewood, searching out wild peas and roots for porridge, fleshing and stretching beaver plews, making and mending moccasins whilst she nursed our daughter, and moving camp every couple-three days. There is no proper telling of my pleasure when I returned each day in the gathering dusk from running my trapline, soaked to the waist, shivering with cold, ice crusting my leggin's, and beheld the yellow glow of our little lodge, glorying in her warm embrace and ardent kisses before she stripped off my moccasins and chafed feeling back into my feet and legs. Over her objections at first, we ate together and afterwards we played with little Iris, encouraging her to crawl, the two of us delighting in her birdlike chirping, then gently lacing her into her cradleboard for the night. Afterwards, in our sleeprobes, my woman provided warmth and satisfaction I had never dreamed possible.

Whitemen's ways were good for Rainbow. Warrior training and lifelong discipline squeezes out much of the tenderness in Indian men. I had no need to dominate or be the boss. In the beginning she wondered at my easiness, but in time she understood and accepted that I could be firm and resolute without bullying her or anyone else.

The fur harvest of the previous fall had been abundant, one of the best we had ever had, but that spring was even better, producing a galore of rich, deep-piled plews. "These shorely be shinin' times!" Tuttle crowed. "Hain't even so froze fer ronnyvoo, like I mostly be. Heapin' up plews 'til hell won't have it, like we been doin', is purely glorifyin'!"

It was no exaggeration. We had amassed so many fine plews that the tremendous swaying loads threatened to topple our pack animals. Late in spring, Tom Fitzpatrick came to our aid. Jackson's brigade had been equally successful. Davey and Fitz decided to send their harvest ahead to Campbell's much larger brigade and Bobby would carry it to rendezvous. "'Tis best we get this king's ransom o' plews out o' this country as soon as we can," Fitz explained, "lest we lose the lot to the bloody Blackfoots. We've been fortunate so far, but there's no p'int in temptin' fate. You're welcome to send your peltries along with us, if ye choose. Thanks to the bloody Grovants, I've animals enough to carry 'em an' men enough keep 'em safe." Noticing some of our people's reluctance to let their peltry out of their own keeping, he added briskly, "Suit yoursel's, but ye'd best make up yer minds. Toime's wastin'."

There was no reasonable objecting to Tom's generous and very welcome offer. He wrote out receipts for every man and it was short work to gather up our bales of plews, already branded with each trapper's personal mark, and load them onto Jackson's extra pack animals.

That spring we ran pretty much between the raindrops. We scotched two feeble Grovant attempts to run off our horses. Nothing more. Davey's much larger brigade drew most of the Blackfoots' attention. Our bunch was able to trap and travel largely undisturbed, reaping a second rich harvest of deep-piled springtime plews as we forged our way ever southwards.

* * *

Springtime warmth steadily winnowed out the thick beaver fur until it was hardly worth trapping such measly plews. "Best we leave the rest fer seed," Brass Turtle opined when our three parties joined up. "Thar ain't ha'r enough in a plew fer buyin' a swaller o' squeezin's, nohow, come ronnyvoo!"

"Been thinkin' likewise myownse'f fer a spell naow," Tuttle agreed. "Time we be gittin' ourse'fs some fat buffler. I'm tired o' livin' on beaver an' ther jerkmeat's mostly gone. 'Sides, we oughter be gittin' on ter ronnyvoo afore them'ere Comp'ny men git it all drunk up." Nothing puts the spur to Tuttle Thompson like the prospect of traders running out of liquor.

"Indade we should," Paddy piped up. "Me darlin' Moll kin hardly fit into her saddle as it is and us still a fearsome ways off from the Popo-adjie." It was true. The little woman's bulging belly could barely squeeze between the high pommel and cantle of her saddle. McCool and Godey nodded gravely, both of them concerned for her health and the well-being of her unborn child.

Anse hammered in the final nail. "An' 'nuther thang. We best be stickin' together from hyar on. Injuns'll be roamin' thicker'n greybacks, naow it be hottin' up, pickin' us off like turkey-birds, ef'n we ain't j'ined up."

Nobody disagreed. We stowed our traps and set out directly for the Popo-azhieh, leastaways as directly as that broken country and rivers still running high permitted.

Rainbow took to riding my Sugarfoot mule, and sometimes Micah's Lightfoot, for their gaits were smoother and their footing more sure than those of our horses. As days became weeks she put away the pretty cradleboard and carried our crowing, gurgling daughter astride on the saddlebow or cradled in her arms as she gave the child her breast. Whenever I rode beside them I found myself captivated by my daughter's mysterious, seemingly-all-knowing deep blue eyes almost lost in her coppery chubby cheeks.

It was a pleasant journey. Nursing buffalo cows were still puny, but fat young bulls placidly grazing northwards provided succulent feasting along the way. Our critters prospered, too. Coarse green prairie grass spread an unending carpet through the valleys. Whenever we halted the women busied themselves collecting bird and duck eggs and raiding the burrows of mice and voles, stealing the little critters' hoards of stored-up peas.

There was much more time, too, to play with my daughter, encouraging her to crawl from one of us to another. My father was most attentive, constantly repeating, *"Pay-ah-ah-lah, Oh-tan-ay-tha Maht-squah-thay"* — which is to say, "Come here, granddaughter — and beaming broadly when Iris responded, however accidentally. The child was an attractive novelty amongst all of our bunch, even the Indians. Tuttle and Micah both insisted upon calling themselves her godfather and Cesár Pérez was forever busy carving rattles and toys for her amusement. But only Rainbow herself exceeded Godey's Cat Woman in lavishing loving attention upon little Iris. Cat's devotion likely stemmed from memories of her own lost child and because she herself had so far failed to become pregnant.

Here and there we spied small bands of Indians we took to be hostiles, but our numbers were sufficient to discourage daylight attacks and nighttime attempts to steal our critters came to naught. Our Iroquois and Delawares and my Shawnee father derived no small degree of pleasure from thwarting such efforts and never failed to scalp and strip the interlopers if they caught them, as a warning to others.

It is no wonder that booshways prize so highly their trappers from those three nations, born and bred as they are to be canny woodsmen, hardy horsemen and tireless runners, and fierce warriors. In the Rockies, they have no distracting tribal allegiances and they glory in making war. I have known many able and courageous whitemen in the mountains, but few who equal and none who outshine those dispossessed Indians from the East. We owe a tremendous debt to Brass Turtle for bringing his fellows into our bunch.

* * *

In spite of the breathtaking beauty of the place, Pierre's Hole in late July was disappointing. Belly-high grass sprinkled with colorful flowers, shimmering crystal-clear waters of the swift-flowing Popoazhieh — Head River in the Absóraqa tongue — a plenitude of buffalo, wapiti, and deer grazing in far-off meadows and along the treeline, walled on the east by the magnificent thrust of the rugged Tetons and the unforgettable *Trois Tetons* couched in their midst all faded to unimportance. Bill Sublette's white trade tents were absent. Only a scatter of rude trappers' digs and the separate encampments of half-a-dozen Indian tribes lined the riverbank.

Our customary jubilant headlong charge into camp, shooting off guns, yipping and howling and roaring out greetings to long-unseen *compañeros* met with a half-hearted, almost sullen response. Some trappers had been there since June. There was still no sign of Billy Sublette's pack train from Saint Louis.

We had feared that we might arrive too late. Now our hearts grew small at the possibility that this year there would be no rendezvous at all. Speculation was rife, everybody recollecting the Blackfoot attacks of 'twenty-seven and 'twenty-eight, wondering if the hostiles had amassed enough warriors to wipe out Sublette's entire caravan. "Cain't feature Billy jest not comin' this year," Tuttle mourned. "Cain't find a dram ner drop o' likker in thi'shere whole gawddamn shebang!"

"They'll be comin'" Brass Turtle assured. "They been late afore this. 'Sides, his pards Smith an' Jackson're up thisaway, too, same as us. Sublette ain't likely fergittin' them two ner what they be totin'."

"Speakin' o' which," Ned Godey said gloomily, "whar the hell's Davey an' Fitz? They're packin' nigh ever' gawddamn plew we took this whole gawddamn year!"

"Fitz'll bring 'em in," I said loyally, but without much confidence. Too many perils lurk in the mountains.

"Well, hell!" Anse barked. "Jawin' ain't gonna change matters nohaow! Time we git to plantin' ourse'fs somewhars in thi'shere ronnyvoo!"

Which we did, selecting a shady spot considerably upstream of the camp and the horse herd. After we unloaded the packs and turned most of the critters out to graze, Rainbow and Cat first put up Paddy and Molly's lodge, whilst the pretty little woman scampered clumsily about, both hands holding up her sagging belly, protesting loudly that she could do that chore herself. They paid her no nevermind and made short work of the job before setting up their own lodges.

Once our dwellings were in place and plunder safely stowed inside, Cat and Rainbow boosted Molly into her saddle and, little Iris bobbing on Rainbow's saddlebow, they made a beeline for the Flathead camp. I daresay they were content to be living with our bunch, but family ties are strong amongst Indians, especially the womenfolk.

* * *

Days became weeks that slid into August. Still there was no sign of Sublette's packtrain. At first we solaced ourselves with tremendous feasts of buffalo and wapiti and amused ourselves by swimming and fishing for firm-fleshed trout in the icy Popo-azhieh, but the situation became deadly serious when tobacco ran out. The Indians grew increasingly stingy with their native tobacco, demanding ever higher prices from trappers who were painfully short of trade goods, even though most of us were wealthy in unsold beaver plews. Tempers grew short and fights broke out amongst free-roving young men forced into idleness and deprived of their vices and entertainments.

For Tuttle, Billy Sublette's nonappearance was a triple curse. Not only was he deprived of trader's booze and tobacco, but his nighttime forays after feminine companionship had lately proved fruitless. "Gawddamn wimmen're gittin' jest like a passel o' skinflint counter-jumpers! Even ther Snakes! Won't even cornsider givin' a feller no credit no more!" he complained. "'Tain't neighborly ner civerlized, thet's whut it ain't!"

We talked of sending a party to Sweet Lake to lift our cache, but that was a long way off. We sat tight, nursing dwindling hopes, forever scanning the eastern passes.

A welcome distraction occurred in the middle of the night. Paddy McBride roused our whole camp with his yelling, running from our lodge to Godey's to Finn McCool and to the bower of Foot and Little Mountain and back again, imploring our women and everyone else to come to the aid of his Molly. "She's after birthin' the child this very minute!" he lamented at the top of his voice, "an' I know nothin' a-tall a-tall o' sich doin's!"

Rainbow and Cat scurried to Molly's side and Finn hung around outside the lodge in case his help was required. Which it wasn't. After a string of Molly's strangled yelps and grunts, we heard the lusty squalling of the newborn McBride over the delighted chattering of the attending women. After a spell, Rainbow poked her head past the doorflap and beckoned for Paddy to enter. Which he did, reluctantly, almost fearfully.

Next thing, we heard Paddy's triumphant bellow. "Praise be! 'Tis a boy! I've sired a man-child, I have! An' a bee-yoo-ti-ful Mick he is, too! Would'ja be lookin' at 'im, would'ja!" He burst from the doorway, the squalling, blanketed baby in his arms, calling out to us, "Come see 'im! Me son! Scraymin' loike a bloody banshee he is! Do ye hear 'im? This'n's a true McBride, if ever I heard one! An' I've heard a good many! None o' me own, mind ye. This'n's me first — that I'm sure of — but me sisters back in the Auld Sod're after delightin' the priest no end wi' their everlastin' whelpin'!"

When daylight came, he was at it again, parading amongst us with the baby in his arms. "Take a look, would'ja," he crowed, pulling aside the blanket, revealing the tiny red crinkled face. "There's no doubtin' he's me own!" It was true. The hair on the little fellow's head, what there was of it, was unmistakeably red.

* * *

The mob of frenzied horsemen who thundered out to greet the packtrain when it finally arrived in late August must have struck terror into the hearts of Sublette's greenhorn hostlers. Every man of our bunch was amongst the welcoming horde, firing off guns and shouting greetings and good-naured Christian and heathen curses, melding amongst the newcomers in a maelstrom of snorting, r'aring horseflesh, dragging old *compañeros* from their saddles with grizzly hugs, and rolling on the ground with them in nigh-hysterical jubilation.

As I galloped past the leaders I saw with satisfaction that a grinning Tom Fitzpatrick was amongst them, together with Davey and Smith, Bobby Campbell, and an unsmiling Bill Sublette, anxious as always to maintain his fragile dignity. Kumskaka's headlong rush carried me into a bedlam of braying, bucking packmules and beleaguered hostlers scrambling to control them. As I swept past, I exchanged waves with Jim Bridger and Milton Sublette, laughing their heads off at the melee and doing naught to help out. At last I pulled up in the midst of Henry Fraeb, Louie Vasquez, and Jean Gervais, riding alongside my bookish friend Etienne LeBref. *"Voila!* There you are!" he greeted me, smiling. "I feared you had perhaps gone under, you and all *vos compagnons,* when you failed to appear at Davey's *vallée."*

"So that's where ye've been!" I replied testily. "Nobody told us! We've been growin' roots right here for more'n a month!"

"Iss goot you vaited," Frapp put in sourly. "Sublette goes ven undt vere he vishes. He knows ve mus' vait, 'cause ve need 'im, py Gott." The others nodded gloomy agreement. He brightened considerably then and added, "But now ve gonna haf *der* beeg shindy, *ja?"*

I allowed that nigh a hundred trappers and thrice that many Indians waiting in Pierre's Hole were purely itching to do just that. Etienne and I chatted for a spell, promising to swap books later, before I checked Kumskaka and fell back, greeting old friends and observing that Sublette had brought with him more than half a hundred men and three times that many pack animals, many of which were already loaded with plews.

In camp, there was no shortage of willing hands eager to help Sublette set up his trade tents and unpack his goods. As usual, Billy put off serving up liquor until the next day, but he did break out a plenitude of tobacco from his packs, even before his canvas went up.

The waiting had put a fine edge on everybody's appetite for rendezvous. When booze commenced to flow next day the merriment kicked off in fine style, wilder and noisier than ever before. Billy's greenhorns wandered amongst us wide-eyed with wonder, astonished at trappers' antics. The surrounding hills rang with gunshots from shooting matches and triumphant yells and disappointed groans at horse races. Fiddles scraped out rip-roarious tunes night and day and booming Indian drums from half-a-dozen encampments provided a heartbeat for the festivities. Clusters of gamblers absorbed in Old Sledge or the hand game cluttered nearly every walkway betwixt the trappers' rude shelters. Wrestling matches and foot races sprang up amongst young men anxious to exhibit their manly prowess in front of doe-eyed Indian maidens who were likely more impressed with Saint Louis foofurraw and gimcrackery than whitemen's muscles.

Throngs of trappers and Indians crowded the trade tents, swapping their peltries first for essential goods such as gunpowder, galena and shot, firearms, traps, knives, tomahawks, whale oil, and other crucial hardware, and then for luxuries — shirts, blankets, kettles, coffee, tea, sugar, molasses, beans and flour, and whatever other settlement plunder Sublette's clerks spilled onto the plank tables, and finally much-prized trade goods — lengths of woolen stroud and calico, silk squares, gobs of colorful beads, Chinese vermilion, ribbon, needles, thread, shiny brass thimbles, beeswax, showy horse trappings, fishhooks and silk line, hawk bells and myriad trinkets, just about anything that glittered and shined — even bales of used clothing gleaned from Saint Louis attics.

Our women were not behindhand in besieging Sublette's counter-jumpers. Trappers' wives feel entitled to flaunt their exalted position amongst their less fortunate stay-at-home sisters and Rainbow, Cat, and Molly made the most of it. Every day they tugged us married men along to Ess-Jay&Ess's cornucopia to amass ever more settlement treasures, until we three benedicts wondered if there would be enough left over from that year's magnificent harvest of beaver plews to permit a proper drunken spree.

There was — and we, too, made the most of it. Indian women don't interfere with masculine pleasures. Even so, I made it back to my hearth each night, albeit unsteadily, and so did Godey. Paddy was rather more difficult to keep track of, so we didn't try.

Despite all the palaver last year about American Fur offering competition, Ess-Jay&Ess had it all to themselves this year and the outrageous prices they charged showed that they knew it. Josh Pilcher could have made a killing if he had been there, but his attempt to make a deal with Hudson's Bay had come to naught. Missouri Fur was history.

Grumble as we might about high prices, trappers bought Sublette's trade goods down to the bare planks and we stoked our long-awaited drunken binge as long as the increasingly watered-down booze continued to flow.

Rainbow and I passed most daytimes together, playing with Iris, encouraging her first faltering steps until she was able to toddle back and forth between us. Naturally my father was tireless in that activity, praising her extravagantly and lavishing loving caresses upon her in a most unchieftain-like manner. Having severed ties with his Shawnee band and his children in Missouri, Powatawa's new family in the mountains was paramount now.

Rainbow was constantly busy sewing garments for herself and me and making moccasins crusted with quills and beads. Every morning she combed and plaited my hair in long braids wrapped with otterskin and red wool, so that I might make her proud when I promenaded through the rendezvous with her or by myself. Growing up threadbare and shabby as I had, I did naught to discourage her.

Summertime leisure gave us plenty of time to talk, as well. Rainbow picked up American lingo at an astonishing rate, so much that I practically gave up trying to acquire the Salish tongue. English grammar remained forever a mystery to her, but such niceties are of little account in the mountains.

One day our doorway was cast into shadow by a tall young greenhorn tentatively scratching on the lodgeskin and bashfully inquiring if my wife might make some clothing for him. I had seen him before. He was hard to miss — six-foot-two at least, broad-shouldered and sturdy, with a shock of black hair and a goodnatured, open countenance. He introduced himself as Joe Meek, from Virginny, one of Bill Sublette's hostlers. "I seen ye walkin' aboot, lookin' mighty fine in yer Injun duds. I could'a took ye fer a sure'nough Injun," he began uncertainly. Naturally I enjoyed the compliment. "So," he stumbled on, "I figgered I'd be askin' if yer woman might be willin' to make me some, too." He trailed off, looking uncomfortable, holding out a handful of beads, presumably in payment for her services.

He certainly needed new clothing. His settlement duds were all rags and tatters, his boots broken, soles flapping, exposing his toes. Rainbow understood his request. Waving away the proffered beads and turning her head to hide her smile, she rummaged amongst her plunder and brought out a length of smokehole buffalo hide, then swiftly outlined Joe's foot with a charred stick, cut out the sole, flipped it over for the other foot, measured his arch, and cut out the uppers. Half-an-hour later Joe Meek was properly shod for the mountains, leastaways for a start.

Whilst Rainbow punched with her awl and whipped soles to uppers with sinew, Joe told me something of himself. He came from a large, apparently well-to-do Virginia family. He had received some schooling but learned absolutely nothing and he cared not at all for farm work. "Hell! — pardon, ma'am," he said, excusing himself to Rainbow, "Pappy's slaves kin do sech toilin' a heap better'n me, so I never got a taste fer it." I learned, too, big as he was, he was just nineteen, the same age I myself had been the year I came to the mountains, seven years before. Green though he was, I believed him when he declared earnestly, "I'm set on stayin' hyar in ther mountains, larnin' ther trappin' trade, an' gittin' to be a mountaineer, jis' like y'all."

I showed him how get into his moccasins, pulling the toe snug before he slipped the back part over his heel. Whilst Rainbow took his measurements, clucking the while at the immense length and bulk of him, Joe flexed his toes and stamped, getting accustomed to the feel of the earth beneath his feet. "Once ye get used to moccasins," I told him, "you'll get to know Mother Earth. She'll tell ye a lot ye need to know." I let it go at that. Joe appeared canny enough to puzzle it out for himself. We agreed that he would return next day for his shirt, britchclout, leggin's, and a couple more pairs of moccasins. As he prepared to depart, he again held out his handful of beads to Rainbow. "Keep 'em, Joe," I advised. "We don't need 'em. Besides, you'll be needin' 'em to get yourself laid." Joe blushed and Rainbow clucked before she tittered, but it was true.

Joe returned next day with another greenhorn in tow, a quiet, alert, well-set-up young fellow whom Joe introduced as Doc Newell, his "pard." Whilst Rainbow measured the newcomer for moccasins and leggin's I asked Newell how he came to be called Doc. "Aw, I sure ain't nothin' like no doctor," he replied, blushing. "Some o' the fellers commenced callin' me that 'cause I can read. I been writin' letters home for them as can't, lettin' their kin know they got to the mountains 'thout gittin' kilt an' how they reckon they'll be stayin' on hereabouts for a spell." He shot a playful glance at Meek and added, "Joe got it all started an' the rest of 'em just natcherly piled on after that."

After they departed, promising to return on the morrow, I reflected that Joe Meek, for all his lack of book-learning, was shrewd enough to choose a worthy man to partner him as he set out on a career in the Shining Mountains.

* * *

Strolling through rendezvous, Tuttle, Godey, and I amused ourselves by assessing the qualities of Sublette's hostlers, judging their ability to survive in the mountains if they chose to remain behind when the packtrain returned to the settlements. "Naow, thet'n," Tuttle observed, jerking his chin towards a lanky, stoop-shouldered, pimply chinless wonder, "ef'n he hangs on hyarabouts, thet'n'll shore-as-hell be wolf bait afore nex' green-up." Ned and I merely grunted. It was hard to disagree.

The sound of lively music and and a strong voice singing in a shadowed glade hastened our steps thither. When we emerged into a clearing we spied the errant seaman called Cap'n Billy sawing on his fiddle alongside a tall, well-built young man seated on a log. He was plucking and strumming on a most remarkable musical instrument resting on his lap, a sort of big wooden pear laced with a dozen strings along its long neck, his big, deep voice raised in song, a rousing sea-chantey echoing off the hillside. "Whut in holy hell be thet'ere moosical corntraption?" Tuttle wanted to know. "Ain't never seen the like."

"That'd be what they be callin' a cittern — mebbe a cither — some kind o' old English, mebbe Irish, insterment," Ned volunteered. "I seen a couple-three like that'n over on the Muddy. Saltwater sailors had 'em."

By the cut of his patched and threadbare clothes and his tarred pigtail, it was plain that the young musician had done his share of saltwater sailing. Etienne LeBref joined us and we all stood silent, enjoying the young man's full-throated singing. At length I asked Etienne, "Ye know who that is?"

"*Enfin,* I do," he replied in his precise, well-studied English, sprinkled with his native French. "*Le ménetrier,* the fiddler, *le Capitaine* Billy, told me of him just this morning. His proper name is Harry Yeats, *un Irlandais,* an Irishman, but they call 'im Harry Harpoon. Billy says they sailed together on whaling ships. Billy says Harry was the best harpoon-thrower of them all."

"What's he doin' up here?" I enquired. "Whales are scarce as hell hereabouts."

Etienne chuckled. "As Cap'n Billy tells it, Harry was the best — strong as a young bull, without fear, an eye like *un faucon,* able to sink his iron deep, where he means it to go. *D'ailleurs,* he was *très populaire* with his messmates, always laughing, always singing. Whaling ships competed for him."

"If he was that good," I demanded, "why would he come to the mountains?"

Etienne roared with laughter. When he recovered, tears in his eyes, he said, "Cap'n Billy says that no matter how good at throwing the harpoon he was, Harry Harpoon was cursed with *mal de mer!* He was forever seasick! He swears he will never go to the sea again!"

Moving off, Tuttle opined, "Don't know 'im, natcherly, but seasick or no, I'm wagerin' thct'n'll bc up tcr bcaver 'fore long."

"Cain't find no fault with that," Ned agreed. "He's got the look." I agreed with them, so I simply nodded and said naught.

Resuming our promenade, tarrying now and again to share a dram with long-unseen friends and helping ourselves here and there to a bait of roasting hump or sizzling boudins, we continued to exchange opinions about the new men we saw along the way. The long and short of it was, although many of the newcomers would be welcome additions to the trapping fraternity — such as big, goodnatured Joe Meek and his friend Doc Newell and likely the Irish harpooner who had strayed so far off-course — there was another element common amongst the new crowd that was far less welcome — hard-eyed, loudmouth bullies, rude, selfish scoundrels likely no more than half-a-step ahead of the law. Tuttle summed it up. "I'd as lief be trustin' Grovants more'n some o' these hyar scamps!"

We had always had such men amongst us. Mike Fink, Carpenter, and Talbot and their hangers-on Hugh Glass and John Fitzgerald stirred unpleasant memories, but they were the few amongst a majority of good men with whom we had plied the trapper's trade from the first giddyap in 'twenty-two. "Thank yer stars," Ned Godey opined, "that we be free-trappin' mountaineers, not obliged to be rubbin' elbows with the likes o' sich trash in some booshway's brigade."

It was in the course of that particular stroll through the camp that we were harshly reminded that certain men of that selfish, unfeeling stripe who had been amongst us from the start still held sway.

Tuttle's kettle had gone dry, so we sauntered over to a trade tent to fill it, lest Tuttle die of a conniption. Whilst we waited in a queue, goodnatured Grover Weed happened by. "Hey, Buzzard!" Tuttle called out. "Whar ye bin? Ain't seen yew ner yer pard Hi Scott neither, thi'shere whole intire ronnyvoo! Whar yew fellers bin keepin' yerse'fs?"

The welcoming smile abruptly slid off Grover's unshaven face. "Ye ain't heared abaout it?" he demanded earnestly. "Ye don't know 'baout what happened to Hiram las' year arter ronnyvoo, headin' back to Sain' Looie?"

"No, we don't," Godey put in. "What happened? Whar is he?"

"He be daid," Grover said grimly. "Wolf bait, likely." A steely glint crept into his normally smiling eyes. "An' we kin be thankin' Bill Sublette fer the doin' of it."

Naturally we threw a heap of questions at Grover, until he held up his hand for silence, then proceeded to explain what had occurred the year before. "Las' year at Sweet Lake, Hiram he got hisse'f a letter up from the settlements. Don' know what it said. Cain't read, m'se'f. Likely concernin' fambly matters, best I kin tell. Hiram din't 'zackly say, but he rode off with Sublette when they headed back with the peltries. That be the last I ever seed of 'im."

Grover swallowed hard, as much from anger, I surmised, as from grief over the loss of his friend. "Black tol' me haow it come abaout. 'Pears one mawnin', arter they got through South Pass, some'eres out on the prairie, ol' Hiram woke up with a turrible gripin' o' the guts — all bent over, he war, couldn't stand up straight, couldn't git on his hoss er nuthin' else." Weed heaved a deep sigh and clenched his jaw. "The short of it war, Sublette hung abaout no more'n an hour afore he sez Hiram's likely bin drinkin' bad likker an' he'll likely git over it, so they best let 'im be an' git on to gittin' on to Sain' Louie. They jist left 'im thar layin' on the prairie an' that be the last anybody ever seed o' Hiram Scott!" He cleared his throat and spat. "'Ceptin' fer thi'shere spring, when they war comin' back an' found all what war left of 'im — jist his bones — but not whar they left 'im! Black sez he reckons Hiram crawled mebbe sixty mile afore he quit an' give up the ghost!"

Grover turned his back to us — lest we see tears in his eyes, I reckon — and bade us farewell in a broken voice as he shambled off.

The three of us remained silent for a spell as we shuffled forward in the queue, until Ned Godey asked in a mock parson-like tone, "An' what lesson do we learn from this?"

Tuttle was first to reply. "What ever'body has allus knowed from the git-go. Don'tcha never git yorese'f 'twixt Bill Sublette an' a dollar, else ye kin be damn sure ye'll git yorese'f run over!"

Naturally none of us knew what had ailed Hiram Scott or what might have been done for him, but we agreed that Sublette's actions had been mighty cold.

* * *

September was mostly used up and the rendezvous was dwindling. Trader's booze had grown increasingly watery. Free trappers stowed their coxcombry, colorful duds calculated to catch the eye of Indian women, and donned once again work-stained leathers more suitable for travel and trapping. Indian camps thinned out as various tribes returned to their home grounds, their furs and extra horses long since traded off for whitemen's goods and drunken sprees. Bobby Campbell had departed nearly a month before, leading the fur-rich pack train back to Saint Louis. Still our bunch lingered, uncertain where to head for our fall hunt.

Word was that Jed Smith had made a promise to the Aitch-bee-cee that Ess-Jay&Ess would refrain that year from trapping west of the Divide in gratitude for the generous treatment Smith had received at the hands of the boss man of the Brits. Naturally such promises made no nevermind to us free trappers, but we were still divided amongst ourselves about which country might provide the best harvest. Some wanted to return to the Flathead, where beaver were still plentiful — and naturally our women favored that choice — but Anse and some others argued that Blackfoots were increasingly on the prod up thataway and Crow country to the east had lain pretty much fallow for a decent spell, offering rich rewards for our labors. In spite of Rainbow's persuasions, it was a conundrum that I myself had no strong wish to unravel.

I reckon the sheer beauty of Pierre's Hole, lying as it does at the foot of the *Trois Tetons* and lush with Nature's bounties, had much to do with our reluctance to come to a decision and depart that earthly paradise. Undecided as we were, we were easy prey for Milton Sublette's invitation to join him that fall, couched in his glowing description of the Wind River country nowadays and the plenitude of beaver there. Naturally he didn't mention that Brother Bill had saddled him with a brigade composed mostly of greenhorns and that a score of savvy trappers who know the use of guns would be a most welcome addition to his company.

I should mention here that two brothers, William and Milton Sublette, could hardly be more unlike each other than those two are. As crabby, cold, distant, calculating and conniving, grasping, and selfish as Bill Sublette mostly is, Milton balances the scale with his warmth and generosity, madcap enthusiasms, hearty appetites for food, drink, and women, and he offers unswerving loyalty and good humor for boot. Neither brother lacks for courage in a scrape, but Bill won't waste many tears over your death. On the other hand, Milt will risk his own life to save yours.

The generally high regard in which we hold Milton tipped the scales in favor of heading east with him. As it turned out, Jed Smith's arguefying won out and Bill Sublette and Davey Jackson agreed to stick to the east side of the Divide, leastaways for that year.

So it was that when we pulled out of Pierre's Hole we were part of a sizeable cavalcade of trappers, their Indian families, *engagés*, and a scattering of Crow tribesmen who had lingered too long at the fair. Bill Sublette intended peel off his brigade at Henry's Fork of the Snake, then trap his way up to the headwaters of the Madison, whilst the rest of us continued eastwards, our numbers dwindling as each brigade dropped off to work its particular patch of country.

The whole shebang was still together, howsomever, on Andy's Fork of the Snake when all hell broke loose one early morning, just as grey dawn was chasing off darkness. Most of the camp was still asleep. I was, too, when the hollow boom of a musket and Jim Bridger's *"Levez! Levez! ye* sons-o'-bitches! Injuns!" brought me hurtling out of my robes, grabbing up rifle and pistol, horn and belt, and bursting stark naked out of our lodge, just in time to behold a scene of utter pandemonium — the bang and rattle of fusees and the heavier reports of a score of rifles and muskets, terrified neighing and braying of our critters, clouds of white smoke parting to reveal half a hundred screaming mounted Indians waving blankets in the midst of our hobbled and picketed horse herd, flashes of gunfire, and half-clad trappers rushing in amongst the critters to do battle with the invaders. Some of the critters had yanked up their picket pins and, still hobbled, lurched crazily back into the camp, crashing into tents and bowers, trampling cookfires, scattering saddles and packs, careening into yelling men and Indian women trying to catch hold of them.

I ran to the edge of the herd, buckling on my belt as I did so, peering through a cloud of swirling dust and gunsmoke, seeking a target, halting when a half-naked horseman swinging a blanket over his head loomed out of the murk not half-a-dozen paces from where I stood. My shot caught him squarely in the belly and he toppled off his wild-eyed pony to fall under the hooves of bucking, rearing horses and mules fighting to get free of their tethers.

I backed off, lest I myself suffer the horsethief's fate. Reloading as I went, I trotted to a clearing where I spied a half-naked Tom Fitzpatrick astride a bareback horse coursing the fringes of our herd, yelling his head off, cursing and calling for help to haze critters that had yanked up their picket pins and were running loose. Fitz's horse suddenly checked, stumbled, and sprawled, pitching Tom over his head. The Irishman rolled onto his bare feet, howsomever, grabbed onto a loose horse, swung onto his back, and disappeared into the surging mass of horseflesh, a picket pin trailing in his wake.

Failing to spot a target, I slung my rifle, shoved my pistol deeper into my belt, and caught up a free-running horse, sliced his hobbles, grabbed a handful of mane, and leaped aboard, painfully reminded as I did so that I wasn't wearing so much as a britchclout. Yanking his head to one side and the other with the picket rope, I guided my mount to the outside edge of that boiling equine cauldron, yelling my throat ragged, hazing horses and mules into a hairy maelstrom, punching and kicking at them when they tried to break out from the throng, squinting into the swirling dust. When I saw him, certainly a Blackfoot, likely a Blood, bringing his fusee to his shoulder, he was no more than a horse-length in front of me. There was no time to unsling my rifle nor to pull my pistol loose. Curses stuck in my throat as I slammed both heels into my horse's ribs, yanked his head straight, and drove headlong into his spotted pony's side, tumbling the two of them onto the turf. By time I was able to wheel my mount and return, the Indian was on his knees, scrabbling for his weapon. My pistol shot settled the matter.

It was broad daylight now. Men a-horseback ringed the herd, some gathering strays, others pursuing runaways heading for the prairie. I bethought myself that it was time that I get myself decent, now that others appeared to have the situation sufficiently in hand.

I had no more than swung to earth and turned the pony into the herd when I heard Tuttle Thompson's horselaugh strangled in a snort. "Like I tol' ye an' I tol' ye, Temple, Gawd only knows haow many times, 'tain't fittin' fer ye to be paradin' abaout 'thout no clothes on, excitin' unchristian envy amongst yer companyeros an' arousin' sinful desires amongst ther wimmenfolks! It's a plumb disgrace to pious folks like myownse'f!"

I muttered a fervent curse on Tuttle and all his clan, clutched my nether parts, and hotfooted to my lodge. Which resulted in hardly any improvement.

When I burst past the doorflap I was greeted not only by Rainbow but also by Cat and Molly, who had gathered there for mutual protection against the marauders. When they spied my naked state their hands flew to their mouths in shock, immediately followed by titters, then outright laughter — all of them, even Rainbow. Naturally I grabbed at my loins again before I commenced yelling, ordering them out of my sanctum, telling them they ought to be ashamed of their unladylike behavior, and a passel of other nonsense.

As the visitors filed past me, they barely contained their giggles, and little Molly actually grinned and winked at me.

* * *

Whilst I sat yanking on my leggin's and moccasins, Rainbow chided me for my prudery. "Why you crazy-mad?" she demanded. "I no shame for you! Why you shame for you? I am walk high for you! I proud for you! Be happy Spirit give you heem, beeg so you can use heem for — ." Words failed her. She finished by making the hand-sign for counting coup.

I burst out laughing, blushing at what I took to be a compliment, and reached out my arms for her. She laughed, too, as she dropped to her knees and planted a big kiss on my mouth and hugged me to her bosom. Then she rolled back on her heels, slithered about, and rummaged in the *parfleche* case we used for a food-box, coming up wih a meaty buffalo rib left over from the day before. "Now," she commanded, "you mus' eat! More work dere!" She gestured towards the door-flap. She was right. The chore with the raiding Blackfoots wasn't finished. A steady rattle of distant gunfire whilst I got myself dressed testified to that.

Decently attired now with britchclout and shirt, I buckled on my belt, retrieved my weapons, kissed Rainbow one more time, and left the lodge, still gnawing on the buffalo rib.

A smiling Little Mountain greeted me in the alleyway between the close-packed bowers and lodges. He brought good news. "You hoss all good. All critter b'long us okay-you-betcha! No sumbitch Káinah git 'em, by goddamn! Kilt one, mebbe two sumbitch." Reassured that my most important property was safe, I thanked him and trotted off to where a cluster of men were gathered at the edge of the clearing.

"'T'war a gawddamn good thang them'ere bastards jumped the gun so early this mawnin'," Jim Bridger was saying, "afore we war up an' about an' turnin' critters loose."

"Indade," Fitzpatrick agreed. "Pickets an'hobbles slowed 'em more'n some'at, grantin' toime fer foilin' their haythenish scheme."

Bridger spied me, came to my side, and said in a voice loud enough for the others to hear, "We kin be thankin Turtle an' yer darky feller fer lettin' us know, fust off, what war goin' on. 'T'war them two as spied 'em fust an' commenced the shootin' this mawnin'. Had'n'a been fer them two, we'd'a lost half o' the critters." I nodded my thanks to Jim for including Micah, who still had not gained the respect he deserved amongst most of the whites, including Bridger himself. Brass Turtle had long ago earned their esteem by his savvy, skill, and courage.

"Best we be gittin' to yon gulch an' lend a hand," Bridger declared, jerking his head in the direction of the firing. "Boys got 'em backed up, 'thout no gittin' out, fur as we kin see."

Most of our people were scattered along a slope that led to a narrow ravine where the Blackfoot raiders had holed up amongst big rocks, exchanging gunfire whenever a possible target offered itself, mostly no more than a fleeting glimpse of a man shrouded in white smoke or arrows sent aloft from behind boulders. I crawled the last few rods to the ragged firing line, where I discovered the eager young greenhorn Joe Meek and his partner Doc Newell lying on their bellies nearby Tuttle and Finn McCool. The new men had already learned not to remain in place after they fired a shot, lest the gunsmoke give away their position. Meek, in particular, was getting fed up with the lack of success in dislodging the Blackfoots. "Reckon we oughta jist git up an' run 'em outa thar?" he asked of nobody in particular.

"Not on yer gawddamn life!" Tuttle called out. "Yew jest leave thet'ere kind o' damnfoolery to sojer boys — which we ain't! Ain't nohaow wuth gittin' kilt jest fer gittin' a mite more Injun ha'r!" McCool and I quickly and loudly seconded Tuttle's warning. This was neither the time nor place for bravado. Cowed, the young Viginian bit his tongue and went back to shooting where puffs of smoke blossomed, like the rest of us were doing.

The forenoon wore on without any visible success on our part, save a diminishing response from Blackfoot musketry and fewer arrows clattering off the rocks. At last it dwindled to none. Still we waited. At length we realized that the unsuccessful horsethieves were no longer bottled up in their hidey-hole. They had discovered a way out of the canyon. When we cautiously entered their makeshift fortress all we found were a few blood-spattered rocks and some cast-off moccasins. The Káinah, if that is what all of them were, had carried off their dead, if any, and made their escape. Our own damage was slight, mostly from rock chips and ricochets, nothing fatal.

Hot, thirsty, and hungry, we retired to our lodges, satisfied that we had taught the raiders a proper lesson. Besides the half-dozen warriors we killed, they had lost more horses than they succeeded in stealing. On the way out of the canyon I heard Finn McCool advising Joe Meek, "'Tis better by far, me young spalpeen, to be leavin' the heroics to thim as don't wish to go on livin'."

As I approached my lodge I spied a spotted horse tethered there and two bloody long-haired scalps lying near the doorway. Rainbow told me that the horse and the scalps had been left there by our Delaware Pretty Horse. He told her that the spoils were rightfully mine and that the other horse, the bay ridden by the first Blackfoot I shot, had been commandeered by Bill Sublette to replace some of the stock he had lost. I hadn't expected any reward for my morning chore, so I didn't begrudge Sublette recouping his losses. I was mildly surprised that anybody had taken note of my earlier activities, but then, Indians don't miss much of what they consider important.

* * *

As we journeyed eastward, the various brigades — first Bill Sublette's, then Jackson's, Fitz's, and Bridger's — dropped off to trap the neighborhoods they had chosen. The cavalcade dwindled to just Milton's company, our own bunch trailing behind. It was mid-October. An early-morning skim of ice fringed the crick banks by time we arrived in Wind River country, which more than lived up to Milt's extravagant claims concerning the galore of beaver awaiting there.

That was the most happifying trapping season we had ever known. The women, familiar now with the chores of a beaver camp, relieved the campkeepers of a goodly portion of their labor. Nobody was overworked. Everybody remained in good humor. Vittles were tastier, too. We ate mostly beaver, but now the women spiced up the stews in ways that our French-Canucks never bothered to do.

Little Iris was growing up fast, toddling about and chattering an incomprehensible macaroni of Salish and English and a smattering of Shawnee that pleased us all. As usual, we kept our distance from the company brigade, scattering out through a generous slice of territory that Milt had consigned to our bunch. Best of all, we stayed clear of Indian forays, our three trapping crews moving every couple-three days, each one small enough to avoid attracting the attention of horse-thieving Crows and vengeful Blackfoots.

Naturally the water was just as cold and mishaps as plentiful as ever, but for me and the other married men such hardships were easily forgotten when, tired out and shivering, we returned to camp to be coddled and comforted in our robes by our helpmeets — which blessings did not go unnoticed by the bachelors in our bunch.

We trapped well into December, the while rejoicing in the plenitude of plews we amassed. At last ice became too thick on the ponds and streams. Beaver retired to their lodges and burrows in the banks to pass the winter gnawing on stored-up bark. It was time to come together and join Milton's brigade for winter camp.

On the way we tarried long enough to cache our plews. There was no profit in carrying such a load along and risking their loss to raiding Indians or even trappers anxious to increase their haul, although every cured pelt was clearly branded with each trapper's personal mark.

By time we discovered Milton's camp it was teeming with trappers from the brigades of Bill Sublette, Davey Jackson, Bridger, and Fitzpatrick. They had come east to gather on the Wind for mutual protection, increasing distance from Blackfoot stomping grounds, even though Blackfoots can be anyplace they take a notion to go.

First to greet me was Black Harris. "'Bout time you're showin' up, Buck!" he called out. "Thought ye might'a gone under! Had a good season, did ye?" Then, eyeing our lightly-loaded pack-animals, "See ye cached yer plews along the way. Did ye?"

"Better safe than sorry," I replied. "'Sides, there's no profit in loadin' the critters down. We'll raise 'em, time for rendezvous."

"Reckon so," he said. "Couldn't feature ye come up short, not this year. Ever'body's happified as hell! Best year ever! Shinin' times fer damnn sure!" He sidled up beside Kumskaka, reaching inside his capote. "Why'n'tcha step on down an' jine me fer a li'l snort fer ol' time's sake?" It was a welcome offer and I did.

Amongst the swarm of trappers gathered there I ran into the young Virginian Joe Meek, but it was no longer proper to call him a greenhorn. He told me that on the eastward track he had been sent out to hunt, got lost for several days, starved and had to kill his mule for food — though he asked me not to tell Bill Sublette, who owned the mule — and wandered in amongst the boiling springs nigh the upper Yellowstone, where a couple of his *compañeros* found him. Amazed at his survival, they were calling him Ol' Joe now, which pretty much qualified him to shuck the greenhorn tag.

It was nearly Christmas and bitter cold along the Wind, but we made the best of it, celebrating the holiday along with Finn and Paddy, Cesár, Anse and Godey and our Catholic campkeepers with whatever festive edibles and potables we still had amongst our plunder. If Micah is religious, he has never mentioned it. It was a meager feast. Game was scarce in that neighborhood to start with and the multitude of trappers gathered there soon used up the little there was.

Bill Sublette — in my personal opinion — bestowed a Christmas gift upon us all. The day after Christmas he set out for Saint Louis on snowshoes, accompanied only by Black Harris and a dog to pack supplies and likely to provide a bait of stringy vittles when they ran out of food. I was sorry to see Black go, but if anybody could get through, Moses Harris was the man to do it.

It didn't take long for that mob to exhaust the game and graze thereabouts. Even sweet cottonwood bark to feed the critters soon became scant. Snow was falling in abundance and starvation was a likelihood. Our bunch was considering pulling out and seeking a better neighborhood when Jed Smith and Davey Jackson called a meeting. "There's no sense in hangin' 'round hereabouts," Davey declared. "We'll starvin', sure as hell, lest we pack up an' git over the hill to the Powder. The sooner the better, 'fore snow gets deeper an' the critters tucker out."

I am usually reluctant to follow anybody's orders, but Jackson's words amounted to pearls of wisdom. Not a solitary dissenting voice was raised amongst the trappers. We would leave that camp on the Wind first thing in the morning.

I likely should mention here, howsomever, that the "hill" Davey was talking about is one godawful high mountain and the trail to get there and through the pass is long and treacherous. Still, it was the only way out of what would likely prove to be our graveyard.

It was no great chore to gather our plunder and ready the packs, in which we stowed every mouthfulof meat. We swiftly stripped every sweet cottonwood of its branches and everybody spent the night shaving off tender bark and carrying it in blankets to the critters. They would need every ounce of strength for the hike and there would be little or no graze on those rugged mountainsides. What our critters didn't eat we stuffed into hastily-stitched panniers for future use. Another packhorse was loaded with a pair of panniers filled with deadwood sticks for cooking and to warm our lodges at night, leastaways whilst they lasted. These were feeble preparations, but it was the best we could do. We congratulated ourselves for caching our plews. Lightly-loaded stock would stand a better chance for survival. The other brigades also cached their plews in that neighborhood, which was happifying. We wouldn't need to travel far in order to retrieve our own peltry in time for summer rendezvous on the Wind.

* * *

The journey through the Big Horns was a fortnight-long white nightmare. Rainbow and Molly rode Sugarfoot and Lightfoot and Cat used one or another of Godey's saddle mules. The women faced each day's trial from dawn-to-dusk with fortitude that would do any trapper proud.   Rainbow and Molly swaddled their squirming youngsters in the bosom of their capotes during the long day's ride. Cat spelled each of them from time to time. It was the women who hustled to throw up a lodge for nighttime shelter before they cooked whatever scraps we had into watery stews and measly thin broth for the whole bunch, before the lot of us crowded into a single lodge for mutual warmth and fell into exhausted sleep until stingy dawnlight summoned us to another day of wintry hell.

The column stretched along the craggy trail for a mile or more. Men constantly trudged forward afoot to spell the men in front at digging through mounds of drifted snow, battling to gain just one more foot or yard towards the summit, which loomed forever distant, seemingly unattainable. Bone-chilling western wind was forever at our back. Stinging snow and numbing cold, snow-burned eyes and wind-chapped lips and faces, and chilblains tingling feet and hands plagued us all, but there was naught else to do than forge forever upwards. Critters became gant, their necks sunken and scrawny, their hips knobby, every rib showing plain enough to count, tottering with every step they took. Some died, which was a blessing. Not a single pound of meat went to waste.

At last we reached the summit. The valley below lay hidden in a sea of emerald firs and pines stretching downwards to our goal. Snow was not nearly as deep and the wind lessened once we attained the leeward side. We made camp and indulged ourselves with a roaring bonfire, for the forest floor was littered with deadwood aplenty. We were still cold and hungry upon that mountaintop, but when we crowded in together and burrowed into our robes that night not a soul amongst us, including myownself, failed to give thanks to some Great Whoever for seeing us through Grandfather Winter's ordeal of snow and ice.

Chapter X
Winter Camp

There was likely more than just a few trappers who lost a mite of admiration for Jedediah Smith for pledging to the Aitch-bee-cee that Americans would refrain from trapping west of the Divide that year, but it is the nature of our kind rarely to dwell on past matters. The here and now is our concern and dealing with it generally takes up most of a trapper's time and attention.

Winter camp on the Powder made up for the hardship of getting there. Graze was plentiful for our starved-out stock. All of our own had survived the rigors of the trail. Before long their ribs and hips disappeared under healthy flesh and hard fat. Far-reaching groves of sweet cottonwood promised ample nourishment for them when the grass got eaten up. Buffalo and wapiti and deer were drawn to the grassy prairie alongside the river for shelter and graze. They wandered close to camp and sometimes even within it. It was no great chore to keep great gobbets of meat sizzling over the cookfires, wafting a delicious fragrance over the ever-growing assemblage of bowers, tents, and tipis. When we arrived, our train of nigh two hundred trappers and their families settled in alongside a band of Snakes. Shortly afterwards, a band of Crows, then another, showed up and set their villages on the other side of us. Although they didn't mix, Grandfather Winter's harsh discipline caused those Indians to put aside their traditional enmities, leastaways until spring.

For me, foremost amongst the pleasures of this winter camp was being alone once again with Rainbow in our lodge. I reckon she felt the same. Our lovemaking was as warm as in our first encounters — even better, for we had learned our mutual arithmetics. Our ciphering was less frantic now but much more pleasurable, more satisfying in arriving at the sum.

There was time, too, simply to be together, playing with Iris and encouraging her to talk, trying mostly unsuccessfully to separate her English from her mother's and Cat's and Molly's Salish. Rainbow profited hugely from those lessons, acquiring my tongue much more rapidly than she likely would have done only from our talking together. I confess that I was laggardly in learning hers, relying instead on her increasing knowledge of English and the hand-talk.

Other times, whilst Iris napped, we enjoyed bathing together and grooming each other's hair, washing and brushing and plaiting, the while plucking out the ever-present greyback lice and cracking them with tweezers, which is preferable to the Indian method of cracking them between your teeth.

In many ways, winter camp in such a desirable place is an improvement even on rendezvous. Trappers' behavior is not so hectic. There is no need to cram into a single fortnight all the rude delights and entertainments for which every trapper yearns. Winter holds the land in thrall for at least two months, most often three, so there is ample time for swapping brags and outrageous tales, for thoughtful palaver, reading for those who can, gambling at cards and the hand game, competing in games of skill and athletic prowess, and especially for strutting through the Indian camps, a talent at which trappers excel, attired in their most extravagant coxcombry, adorned with all manner of foofurraw, intent on attracting the attention and achieving the complaisance of doe-eyed Indian maidens and those who can no longer claim that status.

Micah, Finn, and even my father were becoming adept at such pursuits, although in the case of my father I preferred not to enquire too closely into whatever success he might be achieving. Micah, in particular, had transformed himself remarkably for the better during the nearly two years since he had come to the mountains. His shoulders had broadened considerably and rippling muscle padded his sleek black torso and arms. His hair was long now, usually plaited in braids wrapped in otter skin, bobcat or civet tails dangling from the ends. He exuded quiet self-confidence and friendliness, unless challenged or insulted, which occurred all too frequently, especially on the part of newcomers, who soon learned to put aside their assumptions of lily-white superiority, leastaways in regard to Micah.

He was popular in the Indian camps, where his kinky hair inevitably got him tagged him with names concerning buffalo. Women, in particular, could rarely resist running their fingers over his smooth ebony cheeks and doubtless over other portions of his hide in more intimate circumstances. His easy-going but resolute manner and especially his physical skills in wrestling, foot-racing, and various games, as well his remarkable ability to mimic their speech, gained their respect and acceptance. It was plain to see that my earliest friend had found a home in the Shining Mountains.

A scarcity of booze also contributes to good-fellowship in winter camp, unlike summer rendezvous, where almost every trapper can hardly wait to get a skinful of rotgut squeezin's, which commonly results in hair-trigger tempers and drunken brawls. Naturally there was still some alcohol amongst such a mob. Tuttle and Anse Tolliver succeeded in maintaining a rosy glow most of the time, Anse by means of his fiddling, Tuttle by his uncanny skill at Old Sledge and the hand game.

* * *

It was booze that saddled me with a pleasant chore at that winter camp. One day young Joe Meek scratched on our door-flap and earnestly requested that I teach him how to read. "Ever since I come up thisaway," he told me, "I been thinkin' I ain't never goin' to 'mount to much if'n I cain't read writin'. Never could 'bide larnin' it back home in Virginny, when I had ther chance, but up hyar I see nigh ever'body wuthwhile kin read — 'ceptin' fer Bridger an' mebbe some others — an' I cain't."

I didn't reply immediately, so Joe stumbled on. "Fust off, I asked Doc to larn me readin', like he kin do, but he tol' me it be one thang to be doin' it an' somethin' a whole stretch differ'nt to be teachin' it. Said he war much obliged fer my askin', but he'd jist as soon pass." The embarrassed blush on his cheeks faded somewhat as he warmed to his subject. "So I hunted up a feller name o' Reuben Green an' he 'lowed he'd be willin' to be larnin' me readin' an' mebbe some writin' if'n I paid 'im off in plew, come spring trappin', an' I tol' 'im I'd be willin' to be doin' that, so we commenced my book-larnin' thar an' then." I smiled at that and Joe took it as a sign of encouragement. "Wal, ol' Reuben had hisse'f a book by a feller name o' Shakespeare an' we got right to it, fust me larnin' my letters an' then puzzlin' out the words, which warn't like any talk I ever heared nobody talkin', but I reckon that's what book-larnin's all about. Ain't it?"

I chuckled at that, breaking Meek's train of thought, but I urged him to continue. "Wal, we war goin' at it 'most ever' day an' I war gittin' ther hang of it purty good — makin' sounds outa them'ere words, even if I din't rightly unnerstan' what ther most of 'em war s'posed to mean, 'speshly ther big'uns — when this other feller come along an' tol' ol' Reuben that he wants to larn readin', too, 'stid o' me, an' he's got hisse'f a coupl'a jugs o' squeezin's to pay fer it!"

Joe snorted and fell silent. I surmised what was coming next, but I waited for him to resume. "Wal, dry as thi'shere camp mostly be an' thirsty as ol' Reuben allus is, thar warn't no contest nohow 'bout who war goin' to git ther book-larnin'. Ol' Reuben Green he jist sent me down ther road an' takes up with that'ere other feller, tellin' me I kin fergit about ther plews come spring, 'cause a coupl'a jugs'll more'n make up fer ther time he passed larnin' me."

"So what brought ye to me, Joe?"

"Wal, I war natcherly feelin' more'n some'at blue 'bout losin' out, when I got to talkin' with Tuttle an' that li'l red-headed Irisher an' they tol' me you larnt ther both of 'em readin' — an' writin', too." His look was imploring. "I'd be obliged if'n ye'd take me on, Temple, Mister Buck. I'll pay ye what ye ask, soon's I kin."

There was no way I could turn him down, dedicated as he appeared to be. I told him that I would do it. "As for payin' me, howsomever," I added, "there's nothin' much I need right now, so let's let it be for now. Ye can pay me back sometime when I might be needin' help." Joe Meek must have been desperate indeed about learning to read for him to be calling anybody mister. I told him, "An', Joe, there ain't any misters in the mountains. Just call me Temple."

I told Joe to come back next morning. After he departed, I ransacked my plunder for books that I had brought from my mother's library. Then I hunted up Etienne LeBref to see if he still possessed the copy of Henry Fielding's *Tom Jones* that I had swapped to him several years earlier. He still had it. After some goodnatured haggling I returned to my lodge with the desired *Tom Jones,* having surrendered in exchange a still-unread copy of Scott's *Quentin Durward* and a couple Peacock novels that I held in little esteem. Etienne threw in for boot Fielding's *Joseph Andrews,* which I hadn't read until that time.

When Meek showed up at my lodge next morning, we immediately set to work unraveling the mysteries of the alphabet. *Tom Jones* threw open the door to the marvelous world of the written word that William Shakespeare, for all his magnificent genius, had barred. Shakespeare's sonorous phrases might as well have been written in Chinese, for all the sense that an unlettered Virginia farm-boy could make of them. Fielding, although he wrote a hundred years ago, used the common language of his time, which wasn't a great deal different from the way older educated folks talk nowadays. After I explained that words that were printed "a———, d————ed, h———, and wh——re" actually meant arse, damned, hell, and whore, Joe plunged ahead with renewed enthusiasm for the art of reading. The racy nature of Fielding's narrative appealed to Joe's earthy humor and sped him along the path to literacy. In time he gave up reading with his finger and let himself enjoy the story. Naturally there were many words that were as remote from Joe's experience as Greek and Latin, but he blithely ignored such obstacles and skipped happily through the tale.

Writing was a tougher chore. Try as he might, the complexities of English spelling and niceties of expression eluded him. To be sure, his spelling is often remarkably creative, but now he can make himself understood on paper by scribbling his own everyday way of talking, which is what most of the literate people I know do, anyway. He will likely never be a scholar, but now nobody can rightly call Joe Meek uneducated.

Weeks later, when I declared him a success, Joe showered me with a heap of gratitude, but it was I who owed him a debt. Instructing that very intelligent, infinitely-curious young man carried me back to my mother's little classroom and the happiness I had known there. My satisfaction with Joe's hard-won literacy was much like Ma's when she transformed one more crude young animal into a literate human being capable of acquiring knowledge and understanding.

* * *

Naturally Joe and I didn't work all day at his learning chores. Young and tough though he was, a couple-three hours of brain-work wore him out. Besides, he was still obliged to jump whenever Smith or Jackson called out a command. There was plenty to do otherwise — looking after critters, hunting meat, cleaning and oiling weapons and traps, honing knives and tomahawks and other tools, making and repairing harness, and half a hundred other tasks a trapper needs to do to earn his living. Being a married man, I was relieved of mending moccasins, making clothes, and the like. Any Indian woman will take it ill if her man invades her rightful domestic territory. Rainbow was no exception.

On days when snow was falling heavily, several of us men often gathered in my lodge to smoke and read and engage in yarning and endless palaver. Sometimes one of us read aloud from our scanty store of books. Often Finn McCool would recite from memory passages from Shakespeare, especially the soliloquies, his fine Irish tenor voice flavored by his educated brogue lilting through the beautiful lines, revealing by his tone and pauses and emphasizing meanings that are often undiscovered in silent reading. I myself have never been good at memorizing, but I often read aloud from my favorites.

Brass Turtle particularly enjoyed listening to Jonathan Swift's *Gulliver's Travels,* which appeals to our Delaware friend's caustic wit and cynical outlook on whitemen's pretensions. He often borrowed that volume from me to read at his leisure. Ned Godey, my father, Tuttle, and Paddy were attentive listeners and they were never behindhand in the often heated discussions that followed the readings.

Whenever Etienne LeBref stopped by he would cite in English the writings of French authors, notably Voltaire and Rousseau. Turtle loved Voltaire's acid satire, but he scoffed at Rousseau's *naïveté* when that insulated Frenchman described the Noble Red Man.

* * *

It was unwise to pasture livestock far out on the prairie, when graze nearby camp became measly, lest they be carried off by hostiles — or even by our friendly Indian neighbors, for whom horse-thieving is an admired art, even a virtue. We gathered daily to provide sweet cottonwood bark for the critters, seated in a circle, peeling tender bark from green branches, accumulating heaps of it on blankets, engaging the while in lively palaver. I'm not sure how much wisdom we acquired, but our livestock grew seal-fat as a result of those pleasant get-togethers.

There was quiet time, too, for me to scribble in my journal, recording significant events as well as my personal thoughts and wonderments and feelings.

The women were constantly busy butchering and drying meat in the cold, dry air, scraping and tanning hides, making clothes and stitching up *parfleche* boxes, foraging for roots and berries and such beneath the snow, cooking, gathering firewood, and shooing away our campkeepers when they tried to help. L'Archévêque hovered nearby at first, fearful that we might decide that his services were no longer needed and turn him adrift, but Yves Dureau happily tripped off, his battered little squeeze-box in hand, to join Anse in the music-making.

We amused ourselves teaching L'Archévêque and Dureau to shoot at a mark, although Tuttle was skeptical about their being of much value if it came to a fight. "Don't hurt nuthin' showin' 'em haow to shoot an' sech, but I ain't countin' on 'em stayin' put ef'n some real shootin' starts. Hain't in their gawddamn nature!"

When our women saw us teaching marksmanship to the campkeepers naught else would do but that we instruct them, as well. All three were apt pupils, delighted to acquire a skill denied them amongst their own people.

There was always plenty of music. Cap'n Billy was usually not far off from Anse, together with the Irish harpooner, his cittern, and his fine baritone voice, as well as half a dozen other fiddlers of varying ability and a passel of whitemen and Indians joining in on familiar tunes, tootling flutes and beating on hand-drums and kettles. Sobriety improved the cacophony and sometimes the musicians on the fringe actually kept the beat. Sometimes it seemed that the critters, too, were joining in, when neighing and braying rolled in from nearby pastures.

There was plenty of music and dancing in the Indian camps. Trappers togged out in colorful finery joined their Indian hosts, shuffling their moccasins in time with the drumbeat, nasal Indian voices raised in quavering chant, wailing flutes, and swishing rattles, the while keeping an eye out for approving glances from Indian women gathered at the edge of the crowd. Neither Crows nor Snakes are particularly mindful of their women's virtue, providing that amorous impulses are mutual and the women return home with sufficient plunder.

Most of us joined in, from time to time, in games the Indians played with bows and arrows, shooting guns, chucking knives and tomahawks at a mark, foot-racing, and horseback contests. The young Irish whaler constantly astonished us all with his almost unbelievable accuracy at throwing a lance or a staff through a fast-rolling hoop, even at impossible distances.

Strolling through the Shoshone and Absóraqa camps, it came to me that the Indians of either tribe lumped all of us trappers together, regardless of the color of our hides — whites, Delawares and Iroquois and my Shawnee father, the Spaniard Cesár Pérez of whatever mixed origins, and black-skinned Micah. We are all acceptable to them under most circumstances, but they consider all of us to be somewhat less than completely human. The name they use to designate their own tribe translates to the word in their tongue that means human beings. I smiled to think that hereabouts Micah has achieved equality with his white brethren that is denied him in the settlements.

Not all trappers' liaisons were casual and temporary. By early March several rude bowers in camp were replaced by small Indian lodges of the traveling sort and their new owners were spending more time in camp than theretofore. Two of the most surprising benedicts were Tuttle Thompson and Brass Turtle.

When I braced Tuttle on his new-found status, he blushed and replied, "Aw, hell! Temple. I been seein' haow easy yore livin' be naowadays, naow ye gotcherse'f a woman fer the chorin' an' sech — an' her bein' handy to ye all o' the time. An' 'sides, I do b'lieve I found m'se'f a woman what kin keep up with me in ther robes." He looked thoughtful before he added, "Ef'n she don't wear out." Which he punctuated with a snort and a loud horselaugh. He called her Dolly, "fer she be purty as a poppet." She is, too.

Turtle was somewhat more serious in his reply. "Reckon it be time I be thinkin' on makin' a couple more Delawares. Ain't too many of us Lenni-Lenapees out thisaway an' it be only fair I improve the breed hyarabouts." He chuckled and added, "An' when I seen Tuttle war willin' to jump the broom — an' with a Shoshone woman, too — it 'peared to me that takin' a woman o' my own won't be hurtin' nothin'. Them two kin be keepin' each other comp'ny an' not gittin' lonesome, seein's how they be from the same bunch o' Snakes."

When I enquired after her name he replied, "I been callin' her Tallymesko — that be Lenni-Lenapee fer 'I'll go'. I asked her did she wanta come along with me an' all she said war, "I'll go" in sign an' Shoshone talk. An' then she told me that wherever I go a-traipsin', that's whar she'll be goin', too." He grinned. "The fellers'll jist likely be callin' 'er Tally, which'll do." He was right. Tally it was. Although it just as well might have been Ruth. Like in the Bible.

The Iroquois Stone Bird and the Delaware Pretty Horse also took up with permanent helpmeets that winter, one of whom brought along her young son, both of them from the Absóraqa camp. Those two Crows were anything but crows. Both were strikingly good-looking.

Our Flathead wives were standoffish at first, but in no time at all they were trading chores and chattering like a yardful of hens, hands flying in the hand-talk, their speech a polyglot peppered with American words, many of which are unacceptable in polite society. Which, naturally, our society is not.

* * *

Pleasant as life was at that winter camp, too much leisure commenced to gnaw at every trapper. We itched for the spring harvest. The Powder and its tributaries teemed with beaver and nobody had trapped there in recent years. Grandfather Frost had other ideas, howsomever. He held us fast in his icy fist throughout all of March. There was no profit in heading out whilst ponds and streams were locked with ice and castors stayed snug in their dens and lodges. Fidget though we might, we were obliged to wait.

During one of my aimless daily strolls through the trappers' camp, it came home to me that something was afoot. Nearly every day I saw Tom Fitzpatrick, Jim Bridger, Milt Sublette, Frapp, and a Frenchy trapper, Jean Gervais, huddled together, deep in earnest palaver. It would have meant naught to me if not for their sudden silence at my approach, their strained smiles, false cheerfulness, and brittle chatter whilst I tarried there, and their obvious relief when I moved on. Apart from piquing my curiosity, whatever it was likely made no nevermind to me, so I gave it little thought.

As the month of March dwindled, snowfall tapered off and sunny days shallowed the prairie's white blanket. The camp came alive with new excitement. Spring trapping was at hand. Smith and Jackson roamed the camp recruiting free trappers for their respective brigades. Diah was heading north to country where Blackfoots sprout like weeds. Davey and Milton aimed first to trap the Powder, then work west to Snake territory. Rendezvous in June or July would take place on the Wind, nigh the upper Popo-azhieh.

It appeared that Jed's promise to the Aitch-Bee-Cee meant only the fall hunt — or, more than likely, Bill Sublette's and Davey Jackson's hard-headed arguments had prevailed. No matter what caused it, a free-for-all west of the Divide was about to commence.

Jedediah assumed command of Bill Sublette's brigades and naturally Joe Meek, Doc, Cap'n Billy, and the Irish harpooner Harry Yeats were amongst his people. Whilst they were readying for departure I sought out young Joe and handed him the copy of *Tom Jones*. "Don't reckon you'll be findin' much time for readin', come trappin' time, Joe," I told him, but maybe ye can squeeze out enough daylight to find out how it all comes out." He thanked me profusely and promised to take good care of the book and return it next summer. Which he did. The copy was somewhat the worse for wear, but he kept his word.

Deciding to throw in with Jackson and Milt Sublette for the spring hunt took no time at all. None of our bunch had any stomach to place ourselves under Jed Smith's authority.

Not long after Smith's departure, we abandoned winter camp and tagged along after Milt's brigade, trapping the feeders along the Powder. Davey took his people back over the mountain, a much easier journey now in springtime, to so-far-untrapped streams and cricks that feed the Wind.

As usual we kept a comfortable distance from Milt's main bunch, reaping a glorious harvest of rich fur grown deep in winter's bitter cold, our efforts increasingly successful as cricks and ponds surrendered their protective armor to warming weather. Ice on the ponds was growing spongy and commencing to break up. Beaver ventured from their cozy lodges and commenced to patrol the borders of their domain, falling prey to curiosity, their selfish lack of hospitality, and the baited twigs and traps we placed at the shoreline to deceive them.

One early evening Powatawa and I were trudging back to camp, each with a burden of bloody plews slung over our shoulders. I looked him up and down, taking note of his greasy leather shirt, sopping-wet blanket leggin's, squirting moccasins, and dirty, blood-smeared face and hands. How different he was now from the immaculate, dignified man of authority he had been when he first saved my life and carried me to his Shawnee village in Ohio. "Do ye ever regret leavin' your old life, father," I asked him, "comin' to the mountains to follow the trappin' trade? It's got to be a whole lot diff'rent for ye."

He halted and swung about to face me, eyes twinkling. "Different, yes. Regret, never!" He brushed away a straggling strand of hair from his brow and grinned. "You have stolen twenty winters from me. I am young once more. I thank you for that, my son. I do now what I hungered for, worthy work, man's work in a land the Shawnee can only dream of now. Regret? No. I left regret on the shore of the Great River." I laughed and we plodded on, both of us content with the life we had chosen.

* * *

Jean-Luc needn't have worried. There was no lack of work to be done in our trapping camp, what with a constant supply of fresh plews to be fleshed and stretched on willow hoops to dry and cure in the crisp mountain air, the never-ending chore of peeling green bark for the livestock, gathering firewood, the women foraging under the retreating snow for tender shoots and winter-dried berries and peas to supplement and flavor our monotonous diet of beaver stew in the cookpots, and every one of us always on the look-out for Indians on the prowl for critters and maybe our hair in the bargain.

Naturally, as the main work of trapping permitted, we kept an eye out for deer or wapiti for the cookfire and the stewpot, but we were reluctant to do much shooting, lest we alert unfriendly ears to our presence. Bows and silent arrows were much preferred for that chore.

Our three separate camps moved on every couple-three days, scouring the ponds and watercourses of our allotted chunk of Powder River country until we pretty much winnowed out the beaver, leaving behind enough for seed but not enough to make further trapping worthwhile. We joined together and sought out Milt Sublette, who also was ready to move on to fresh territory and rich pickings to the west.

Milton was purely happified with the harvest so far. A healthy slice of the profit from the takings of his brigade went to him. He was happy about about something else, as well, I reckoned, but whatever it might be, he kept his own counsel and I didn't pry. "Somethin's in the wind," Brass Turtle surmised. "Ye kin wager yer clout on it. Thar's goin' to be a change in the weather hyarabouts."

As we moved westwards into Snake country such concerns made no nevermind. We were harvesting a galore of plews the like of which we had never taken before. "Less'n ol' Bill ups the price o' likker to ther gawddamn sky," Tuttle crowed, "I reckon even thi'shere chile ain't gonna be able to drink up all o' this year's ketch!"

"Reckon ye won't," Turtle observed dryly. "Yer woman's goin' to grab onto the most of it fer foofurraw an' such!"

Tuttle sobered, suddenly stricken. "Omigawd! I warn't thinkin' o' thet!" He shrugged, then set his jaw and declared, "Wal, we'll jest be seein' abaout thet! Reckon I'll be showin' 'er who's ther boss!"

"Yep, you do that," Turtle taunted, "an' she'll cut ye off, sure as hell. An' she'll make yer life mis'rable if ye try any o' yer tipi-creepin'!"

Tuttle already looked miserable. "Wal," he mumbled, "reckon we kin work somethin' out."

"Reckon ye'll hafta," Turtle replied, turning his face away to hide his smile.

* * *

Following mostly in the wake of Jackson's brigade, Milton's company and our bunch trapped a wider swath than Davey's men had done, spreading out north and south of his westward passage through Snake country. Nevertheless, from time to time we met up with Jackson or Fitz and their people. We usually stopped with them overnight when we did so, for the pleasure of different company and for a respite from our constant vigilance against horsethieves.

On one such occasion, Davey invited me to share his flask, which I did most happily. It had been a long spell between drinks for me. It was plain to see that he had been tippling for a spell before I got there. His voice was mildly boozy, his mood sentimental, neither of which was customary with that steady, reliable leader of men. Davey was the mountain mainstay of EssJay&Ess. Without David Jackson that outfit would have gone broke, what with Bill Sublette passing half his time in the settlements tending to business and Jed Smith traipsing off to god-knows-where looking for god-knows-what, beaver apparently amongst the least of his concerns.

We palavered for a spell about the harvest, which we agreed was the best either of us had ever known, shining times indeed. Which naturally led us back over the years to the commencement of it all, 1822, when we were together on Henry's keelboat snailing up the Muddy.

After we drank a snort or two or maybe three, he lowered his voice. "I rightly shouldn't be sayin' none o' this, Buck, but I've knowed ye since the fust git-go an' I know ye fer a feller what chaws the gristle quiet-like, inside o' yerse'f. Ye don't mind keepin' yer thinkin' to ycrownsc'f." He heaved a sigh and went on. "I been gittin' a proper bellyful o' Billy's graspin' an' Diah's 'tarnal preachin' an' gittin' good men kilt off like they ain't wuth a damn. Don't cotton nohow to leavin' ol' Hiram out thar by his lonesome, like Billy done, neither." He paused for another sip. "Cain't fault 'em none fer makin' money, mind ye. Mostly Bill. Got more in my poke than I ever b'lieved I'd be takin' out o' the mountains. Jist the same, I been thinkin' on mebbe sellin' out an' headin' west to Californy. 'Pears to be some purty good doin's tharabouts, 'cordin' to what some what've gone thar with Diah been tellin' about."

I made no reply. I had enough trouble at the time just keeping my face straight. Davey caught himself up short. "Likely been talkin' too much. I'd be obliged if ye keep it to yerse'f, Temple. Once't'awhile, a feller's got to git it said out loud on account o' blowin' the steam off, don'tcha know?"

We drained what remained in his flask. Before we parted I assured him that what he had said was safe with me. Which it was.

* * *

The remainder of the spring hunt was successful and largely uneventful, save for a couple of attempts to steal our horses by otherwise friendly Snakes who were nonetheless obliged as a matter of custom and prestige to give it a try. The first was foiled by Micah and my father, the second by Rainbow, Cat, and Dolly, who chanced to be strolling at dawn and raised the alarm. A volley of our gunshots routed the thieves with no more damage than a few slashed hobbles and picket ropes on our part and naught but disappointment for the interlopers.

Warming weather pushed us to grab as many plews as we could before the rich underfur shedded out, but by the end of May we stowed our traps and let ourselves enjoy the easy living that the Wind River country affords in abundance. No longer did beaver occupy the stewpots. We feasted instead on solid meat of young buffalo bulls, increasing bunches of which wandered not far off, grazing their way northwards.

Rainbow and I swam together in the icy waters of the Wind or in deep holes in its many feeder streams, much to the disapproval of Tuttle, who railed, "Thar ye go agin, Temple, makin' ther rest of us lookin' bad to our wimmen, settin' a bad example an' washin' off yer natcher'l pertection agin the cold an' sech! 'T'ain't Christian!"

As usual I paid him no nevermind. Shivering in the cold mountain air, teeth chattering, was a paltry price to pay for the glorious sight of Rainbow's lithe, tawny, naked body, rosy with cold, water drops glistening on her smooth skin in the pale springtime sun. Afterwards we would scamper back to our lodge to make love. Cat or Molly looked after our daughter until we put aside the crossed sticks at the doorway.

All of the women and all of our Indians bathed every day, albeit separately from their spouses. The whites and Cesár were of Tuttle's persuasion and steadfastly retained their odoriferous accumulation.

Iris was growing like a weed, looking more like her beautiful mother every day, scurrying from one lodge and bower to another, getting into everything, prattling a jumble of even more tongues than before, now that she was hearing a passel of Shoshone and Absóraqa, especially from Pretty Horse's adopted son, who was about her own age. Finn assured me that she would sort it out in time, but right then it appeared that I had sired a Daughter of Babel.

It was still too soon to travel to rendezvous. We tarried in that mountain Eden, the valley of the Wind, moving camp when graze and firewood grew scant, hunting when we chose to do so, choring at repairing harness and suchlike, some of us reading, and in my case, catching up on my journal. Naturally we engaged in endless yarning and palavering about nothing all of us didn't already know.

For all the occasional pain, peril, hunger, and hardship, the life of a mountaineer is an easy one. Trapping occupies less than half the year. The rest we spend living off a land lavish in abundance, once you learn its ways and master the skills needed to survive and prosper there.

"Och, 'tis infernitely pref'rable to be livin' the loife we've got hereabouts," Paddy McBride observed contentedly one afternoon, tapping the dottle from his pipe. "'Tis much better'n spadin' taties mornin', noon', an' night, back in the Auld Sod, dodgin' the landlord, an' doin' yer unsuccessful best to keep yer backbone from scrapin' holes in yer belly."

"'Deed you're right," Ned Godey agreed. "An' we best keep on doin' what we do. Ain't a one of us fit to make his livin' anymore amongst settlement greybacks. Livin's plumb easy hyarabouts — once ye git the hang of it. Workin' a Missourah farm'd kill the most of us, I'm thinkin'."

"Don't rightly know ef'n it'd kill me, Ned," Tuttle put in, "but I reckon I'd be killin' myownse'f afore I go to plowin' an' pickin' ever agin!"

Tolliver looked thoughtful, almost wistful. "Reckon I cain't be faultin' ye none fer whatcha say, mostly, 'ceptin' I shorely miss 'stillin' muh own squeezin's, like I useta." Which remark produced general laughter and ardent wishes that he might resume his former trade right there in the mountains. The sooner the better.

* * *

We dawdled thereabouts until the middle of June, enjoying warm sunshine, feasting hugely, hunting and fishing, and passing the daylight hours in pleasant converse with our women and easy-going banter amongst the men. The presence of women amongst us altered our character — and much for the better. Once they saw how we treated our women, even the two stand-offish Crow women warmed up. They put aside their lifelong humble behavior in the presence of men. They joined in the horseplay and exchanged taunts and humorous, frequently bawdy, insults with us, by hand-signs at first, but soon in often-hilarious broken English.

Nights, except for my necessary stints at horse guard, were a constant delight. Rainbow was more beautiful than ever and I cannot imagine a more perfect lover. I had never known her to be so happy. Every day, my heart was big. Never before had I been so content and satisfied with my life.

There was ample time to play with my daughter, teaching her to speak my tongue, to swing her onto the saddle bow and carry her a-horseback about the valley, coaxing her to repeat in English the names of critters and other things we saw along the way. She was eager to please and quick to learn. Now that she could walk and talk, I discovered the true joy of being her father. I confess that up to then she had been for me little more than a precious responsibility.

Good fortune caused us bid farewell to our pleasant valley sooner than we might have done. Rendezvous that year was not far off from where we were, but our haul of plews just from the spring harvest already had our pack animals laboring. We needed to make two trips — first to carry our springtime plews, plunder, and people to rendezvous, then some of us would have to ride out again to raise our cache from the autumn hunt. It was a delightful nuisance. No trapper had ever amassed such a store of wealth in just a single year.

Chapter XI
A Season of Prodigies

Rainbow, Cat, and Molly were hugely happified when we first caught sight of what there was of the rendezvous so far. Iron Bow's village was already there. And what a frolicsome greeting we received as our overloaded column filed out of the surrounding woods! Fast Horse led a colorful mob of warriors, firing guns and waving feathered lances and coup-sticks, dashing in amongst us, scattering our critters and leaning off their horses to embrace us like long-lost prodigal sons. Fast Horse tumbled the both of us to the ground, hugging and laughing fit to bust.

We accepted the Flatheads invitation to pitch camp with them, even though Tally and Dolly's Snake village had also arrived. Brass Turtle and Tuttle surmised that their own critters and plunder might be safe enough with the Snakes, but the rest of us might not fare so well with young men anxious to increase their wealth in horses and mules. On the other hand, the winter we had passed with Iron Bow's people had forged many friendships and mutual respect. We were better off with the Flatheads.

A plenitude of buffalo grazed their way through the valley of the Wind. We feasted morning, noon, and night on juicy hump and ribs. Boudins sizzled on the coals and tender tongue boiled in every copper kettle. Naturally Iron Bow's women fussed delightedly over Iris and Molly's son Sean. At first, the older women were unimpressed and not a little distressed by my daughter's wealth of alien vocabulary, which she strewed throughout her shaky Salish, but they got over it. Sometimes I spied a wistful look on Cat's beautiful face. So far she hadn't a child of her own to be praised and admired and coddled by family and friends. Cat's sensible, generous nature quickly swept away such feelings, howsomever, and she pitched into the general merriment with as much enthusiasm as Rainbow and Molly.

Ned Godey went about with the same happy, contented look that he had worn ever since he took his beautiful Kathleen to wife, which I ascribed to Cat's passionate attempts to get herself with child. Naturally I kept such suppositions to myself.

Rendezvous continued to fill up with brigades and free trappers streaming in from their various hunting grounds, each party whooping and hollering and trailing strings of pack animals wobbling under swaying loads of plews. It was shinin' times for all concerned.

After a few days we got itchy to raise our cache of autumn plews, lest Sublette's packtrain show up in our absence. Tuttle, in particular, worried that booze might be in short supply and he wasn't about to be cheated of his fair share. Our women and children were safe in the Salish and Shoshone camps. When the families of the wives of Pretty Horse and Stone Bird arrived with a large band of Crows and established a separate village, guaranteeing safe haven, we were free to go. We had dubbed Pretty Horse's woman Nettie, from the Delaware word Nettaqueathy, which means Bashful, which she rarely was anymore, and we called Stone Bird's woman Sally, for no particular reason that I know.

* * *

Three days of hard riding, trailing packstrings carrying saddles and little else, brought us to our Wind River cache, which had happily gone undiscovered. A single day sufficed to raise the cache and distribute the loads. The return trip took rather longer. The packs were heavy and cumbersome on the brushy trails. The main reason for delay, howsomever, was an encounter with a small party of Grovants who pounced upon Pretty Horse and Stone Bird who were lagging behind and out of sight of our main column.

Gunshots, shouts, and war-whoops alerted us. We swung about and bunched up our critters. Then most of us charged upon our back-trail. We soon spied the two laggards pelting hell-for-leather to catch up with us, tugging wild-eyed pack critters in their wake. A dozen howling, then very surprised, Big-bellies were in close pursuit, but they jerked their ponies to a rearing halt when a volley of gunshots emptied a couple saddles. The others scooped up their wounded comrades at a high lope and fled.

After that we proceeded with rather more caution, keeping the column snugged up, with lookouts ahead and behind, doing whatever we could to discourage ambitious Blackfoots seeking easy pickings.

* * *

We needn't have worried about Sublette's arriving in our absence. Still no Billy. Nearly every trapper that I knew was already there. The camp boiled with fanciful rumors concerning all the mishaps that might have befallen the packtrain. Each day hatched new fears — Indian raids, quicksand bogs that swallowed the entire caravan, cholera and smallpox plagues, and other even more horrendous catastrophes. The absence of booze and tobacco running out served to feed the flames of such fanciful fictions.

We thanked the Flatheads and moved upstream of the trappers' camp on the bank of the Popo-azhieh. The women were reluctant to leave their kin, but they made the best of it, returning every day to visit their respective Flathead, Snake, and Crow friends and relations. Micah, Finn, my father, and I went after buffalo most days, returning sweaty and blood-spattered, anxious to cleanse ourselves in the chill waters of the river. I rarely joined them, preferring to swim with Rainbow in a secluded cove, glorying in the sight of her, recalling our first encounter, when I thought of her as my beautiful naiad. She still was, but infinitely more precious now.

Independence Day was a dismal affair that year, bereft as it was of booze, always a vital ingredient of a mountaineer's patriotic fervor.

Joe Meek showed up one forenoon whilst we were lazing around the cookfire. He was leaner now, stronger-looking, his manner self-assured, as well it should have been. He had by then trapped two seasons in the mountains and survived the winter. He had been blooded in battle more than once and not found wanting.

"Thar ye be, young Joe!" Tuttle greeted him. "Happy to see ye ain't gone under. How'd yer springtime go?"

Meek grinned. "Wal, I still be hyar, though thar war a time or two when I had no great hopes fer it."

"Injuns, ye mean?" Godey enquired.

"Wal, them, too. But Injuns warn't the wust of it."

"Ye went along with Diah, din'tcha?" Brass Turtle asked. "How'dja do?"

Joe nodded in response to the first question. "Yep, I war in Jed Smith's outfit. An' seein' as how I'm still hyar, I kin count m'se'f lucky."

There appeared to be a good yarn or two in what the young Virginian implied. We urged him to expain. He begged a pipeful of tobacco, settled by the cookfire, and launched into what would have been a proper jeremiad if he hadn't been so goodnatured about it. "Wal, as ye know, arter winter camp we headed up nawth fer spring trappin', which war better'n purty good, once ice got off'n ther water. Ever'body said so. That is to say, it war more'n purty good 'til snow come on agin, up whar we war along what they be callin' ther Big Horn — a lot o' snow! An' then, natcherly thar warn't no trappin' fer a spell — an' no eatin', neither! 'Ceptin' fer b'ilin' mockersins an' sich."

Joe pulled a deep drag from his pipe and leaned forward, warming to his tale. "Wal, arter too long a spell, it quit snowin' an' warmed up cornsid'able an' we got ourse'fs a coupl'a deer an' some porkypines, which he'ped to git our backbones off'n our bellies. Then ther booshway sez we best be gittin' on, which warn't bad thinkin', cornsid'rin' what we jist been through whar we war.

"Arter a spell we come onto what they call Bovey's Fork, which ther free men war tellin' me warn't nuthin' but a piddly-arse crick, but by time we got thar it war runnin' overtop ther banks, lookin' like ther gawddamn Missy-sip! Which made no nevermind to ol' Smith, ther booshway, howsomever, 'cause he war in some hellish kind o' hurry. Sez we kin swim ther critters acrost it, 'thout waitin' to build no bullboats, like ther free men war tellin' 'im to."

Joe paused, looking dreamy, likely calling up the picture in his mind. "Natcherly I had no call 'cept to do what he said, but, jist the same, I sorta hung back with ther free men whilst ther whole shebang o' Comp'ny men jist jumped off ther gawddamn bank on their hosses an' mules an' draggin' ther pack-critters a'hind 'em an' went a-sailin' on down that'ere branch 'til they fetched up agin some big ol' trees an' war able to climb out'n ther water!"

Joe cadged another pipeful, confident, I daresay, that no one could refuse him, anxious as we were to hear the rest of his story. "Wal, ther long an' short of it war, we lost thutty head o' hosses an' mules an' three hunnerd traps an' most o' whut else they war packin'! Lord knows why nobody got hisse'f drowneded — 'ceptin' ther critters, mind ye!"

Joe paused again, lips still moving, likely cursing under his breath. "Wal, arter they got theirse'fs mostly dried out an' quit shiv'rin', Smith put us all to buildin' bullboats, like ther free men said we should'a done in ther fust place, an' we war able to git on." When the laughter died down and everybody had his say about haste making waste and suchlike, Joe resumed his account of Jed Smith's spring hunt.   "I m'se'f din't lose muh traps ner muh plunder, but, as ye mought s'pose, ol' Smith he jist natcherly took muh traps fer hisownse'f an' when we warn't fightin' off ther gawddamn Blackfoots an' went to trappin' agin, I war in the same fix as all ther other fellers. 'Stid o' trappin' like we war s'posed to, the booshway put us to diggin' inter crick banks an' bustin' up dams an' drainin' ponds an' bustin' inter lodges an' clubbin' them pore critters to death!" Joe fell silent, looking mournful. I thought I heard a catch in his voice when he continued. "Pore li'l critters, lookin' at ye with them'ere sorryful brown eyes, not even fightin' back when ye hit 'em! Din't care fer it one gawddamn bit! Don't mind trappin' 'em, mind ye. They be dead by time ye see 'em, but killin' 'em thataway, wal, it like to made me sick!"

He quit talking for a spell before he brightened and said, "Jist the same, fer all o' that'ere clubbin' bizness, we baled up a plenitude o' plews doin' it thataway. Ol' Smith war lookin' purty sassy by time spring trappin' war over an' done with."

"Did'ja ever git yore traps back, Joe?" Tuttle wanted to know.

"Shee-it! Hell, no, I din't! Ain't about to ask 'im fer 'em, neither, ther way he be. Reckon they b'long to ther comp'ny, anyways."

Turtle chimed in with, "Don'tcha let 'em be chargin' ye fer them'ere traps, neither, mind ye, Joe! Billy Sublette don't never miss grabbin' up a gawddamn nickel!"

Naturally, palaver buzzed considerably amongst the rest of us, hashing over what Joe had told us, until Godey said, "Wal, Joe, all's well that be endin' well. Leastaways ye got out of it with a whole hide."

Meek snorted. "Not perzackly! That war only ther half of it! Come quittin' time fer harvestin' plews an' headin fer ronnyvoo, we natcherly war 'bliged to raise the cache o' fall plews afore we come down hyar." Joe spat and looked grim. "I'd been on hoss guard ther night afore we come onto ther cache an' then Smith sent me an' Doc out huntin' meat ther next mawnin', so I reckoned I had some time to ketch up on muh readin' in that'ere Tom Jones book o' your'n, Temple," he said, smiling in my direction. "Wal, whilst I war restin' up an' readin', the booshway he comes moseyin' by an' sees what I'm readin' ain't ther Good Book, he yells at me to shake a leg an' git to work diggin' out the cache. Which natcherly I do, jumpin' down in ther hole, 'longside a Frenchy name o' Ponto, an' we go to spadin' inter the cache, when ther whole shebang cuts loose an' all ther gawddamn dirt in ther whole gawddamn world comes fallin' down on the two of us! An' that war the last thing I kin recollect o' what happened thar'aboots!"

"Didja git kilt, Joe?" Tuttle asked, eyes twinkling.

"Mebbe," Joe replied in kind.

When the laughter subsided, Meek went on, serious again. "When I come to, Doc's a-shakin' me an' tellin' me not to die an' I'm a-spittin' dirt an' hurtin' all over an' thinkin' mebbe dyin' mought be better'n what I'm feelin' right aboot then.

"When I come to agin an' I'm able to take nourishment, Doc tells me ol' Ponto got kilt an' ever'body reckoned I did, too, 'ceptin' Doc, 'cause he knows I'm too orn'ry fer that. Then next mawnin' the booshway comes by an' asks me kin I ride an' I say if he kin, I kin, too. So, muh thanks to Doc fer helpin' me up on muh mule fer a couple days, that's how I come to be hyar amongst y'all." Joe let his gaze rove over each of us before he said fervently, "Cain't hardly wait fer jist one more year to be up afore I kin git to call m'se'f a free trapper!"

We said amen to that sentiment. "Ye'll make a good'un, Joe. That's fer sartin sure!" Ned Godey said.

"Proud to have ye 'mongst us," Tuttle assured him.

"Damn lucky Diah din't leave ye out thar fer the buzzards, Joe," Brass Turtle said sourly. "'Twouldn't be the first time fer that outfit."

After Joe begged another pipeful and wandered off, we chewed over what he had been telling. Anse Tolliver, who had remained silent throughout Joe's long history of his travails, averred, "That'n's shore-as-hell up ta beaver. He'll do." A chorus of nods endorsed that sentiment.

"Three hunnerd traps!" Ned Godey, ever practical, exploded. "That be a passel! Costin' ten dollars apiece, even in Sain' Looie, that'd come to three thousand dollars! Ol' Billy ain't gonna like hearin' 'bout nothin' like that! Ner Davey neither."

"An' thutty head o' critters!" Tuttle threw in. "Thet'll shore as hell be usin' up a passel o' plunder, tradin' fer thet many hosses with Injuns!"

"An' precious little plunder he still had left, mind ye, like Joe war sayin'," Brass Turtle added. "Cain't be knowin' how many plews he got, but thar's sure goin' to be a helluva hole in the profits, once they tot it all up. That's a passel o' ponies, traps, an' trade plunder to be makin' up fer."

"Haste makes waste," Finn McCool observed. "T'would appear Misther Smith was after tryin' to recover the losses he suffered in all his California jaunting. I doubt he succeeded."

I kept my own counsel, but it appeared that EssJay&Ess's boat had sprung a couple leaks.

* * *

The week after Independence Day the whole camp wallowed in the doldrums. Tempers were short, fights broke out for no good reason, and gloomy rumors flew like flocks of ill-omened ravens. Bill Sublette ran off with all the partners' money. Pawnees attacked the packtrain and grabbed all the plunder. God was trying to save the beaver by forcing us out of the mountains. The most fanciful I heard — lightning struck the cavalcade and killed every man in it and all the critters, too.

What we saw, howsomever, when Bill Sublette arrived at last, was hardly less fantastic.

Word came from a trapper out hunting east of camp. The rendezvous emptied like water pouring out of a boot. Every trapper swung onto a horse or mule, most of them bareback, and raced eastward to greet the supply train. Even some foofurraw-starved Indian women rode amongst the hysterically happy buckskin horde streaming out to catch a first glimpse of the horseborne cornucopia from which all good things flow. And naturally every man of our bunch was in the midst of the pell-mell charge to welcome our saviors.

A rattle of gunshots from the leaders of the mob signaled the first sighting of the supply train. Then they reined to an abrupt halt. A queersome hush settled upon the restive throng. Welcoming yells squelched into murmurs and muffled curses. I crowded to the front and beheld the prodigy that Bill Sublette had somehow brought across the plains and mountains to our Rocky Mountain rendezvous. Indian women clapped hands to mouth, lest their souls fly off. I felt much the same.

Bill Sublette on a piebald pony led the caravan, his lantern-jawed face split in an uncharacteristic grin. Behind him stretched a train of wagons, ten in all, each one drawn by five mules, shepherded by hostlers mounted on mules. Bringing up the rear were two light dearborn carriages lurching crazily over the uneven trail. Behind them, trudging amongst the spare mules and saddle horses, were four beef cattle and, unbelievably, a curly-horned brindle Guernsey milch cow!

If the usually humorless Bill Sublette had intended to make up for all his years of saturnine seriousness with one gigantic prank, he succeeded beyond his wildest dreams. Tuttle Thompson stared open-mouthed, Adam's apple bobbing, eyes bugging, his face pale under his leathery hide. "Shee-it! Cain't b'lieve it!" he gasped. "A gawddamn sure-'nough milkin' caow ri'chere in ther gawddamn mountains!"

I was scarcely less dumbstruck. It was an impossible feat — wagons traveling across mucky prairies and through steep and narrow mountain passes I remembered from my journey only two years before. Yet Bill Sublette had done it. Ocular proof was rumbling past us into rendezvous.

Most of us regarded the phenomenon with a mixture of wonder and amusement. Ned Godey took a different view. And not a happy one. "Ye be lookin' at the beginnin' of the end, fellers," he announced solemnly.

"How so?" Tuttle wanted to know.

"Wagons comin' to the mountains! What's next?" Nobody offered a reply. "I'll tell ye! Oncet word gits about, thar'll be pilgrims movin' west, that's what! Killin' off game an' farmin' an' civilizin' an' makin' laws an' killin' off ever'thin' we been lovin' ever since we come up thisaway. That's what! An' I, fer one, sure as hell don't cotton to it nohow!"

It was a sobering thought if you took what he said seriously, but naturally nobody did. This was rendezvous and our thirst had remained too long unslaked.

We fell in behind the caravan, still stunned by the spectacle, not saying much. Brass Turtle overtook us and rode in between us. "Ye think that be somethin', whatcher seein' jist now?" he said, smiling broadly. "Jist you wait 'til the Injuns git an eyeful o' them'ere wagons comin' in amongst 'em! An' that ol' milker, too! Craziest-lookin' buffler they ever did see!"

* * *

As you might expect, next day, the thirsty, plunder-hungry mob besieged EssJay&Ess's trade tents, our women amongst them, dragging us along to exchange our plews for all manner of useful goods and gobs of frilly, shiny foofurraw they were dying to flaunt before their stay-at-home sisters. There was a plenitude of staples and luxuries to choose from, far more than ever before, heaped upon the rough planks of the booshway's trestle tables. Prices were higher than ever before, too, but that meant little to trappers bent on showing off their new-found wealth and strutting, bedizening their woman with showy garb and ornaments or acquiring the temporary favors of dusky maidens easily tempted by foofurraw, the tawdrier the better.

"Thutty thousand dollars wuth," Black Harris informed me. "More'n ol' Billy ever put up afore. He be fixin' to make hisse'f a killin' thi'shere year, scrapin' up ever' gawddamn plew afore the compertishun kin git up thisaway."

"Competition?" I asked. "Who else is comin' up for tradin'?"

"Who ain't!" Harris laughed. "Jist abaout ever'body as kin lay hands on cash enough to buy up plunder an' git together men an' critters enough to git a packtrain on the trail. That's who!"

"All right, but precisely who's doin' it?"

"Wal," Black responded, taking a healthy swig from his kettle and passing it to me, which I gratefully accepted. "Let's see. Fust of all, thar's Amurrican Fur, ol' Jake Astor's outfit — Andy Drips an' that Frenchy Fontenelle callin' the tune — lef' Sain' Looie even afore we did, back in Feb-yoo-rary, headin' fer the Seeds-kee-dee."

"Why there? I asked. "We're all here."

Harris grinned slyly. "Don't rightly know." He chuckled. "'Course it mighta been 'cause they heared us sayin' that war whar the ronnyvoo war gonna be. Ye think?" He broke into a laugh, which he drowned in another deep swallow from the kettle.

"Who else, then?"

"Wal, as ye mought s'pose, your ol' pal Chouteau ain't never behindhand whar thar's money to be had. He be headin' up ol' Astor's inter'sts out thisaway naowadays, but jis the same, he war fixin' to send still anuther train up hyar, on his own hook, with Joe Robidoux, when we left in April. Way it looked to me, howsomever, don't reckon they got off afore sometime in May. I 'spect they won't be gittin' hyar afore y'all're gone the hell outa hyar fer fall trappin'."

"Anybody else?"

"Yep. We run onto ol' Hugh Glass on the way up hyar — come into camp one night, purty as ye please, outa nowheres — an' he told us ol' high-an'-mighty Kenny McKenzie, what be callin' hisse'f King o' the Missourah naowadays, he be sendin' up anuther bunch under Major Vanderburgh fer tradin' at thish'hyar ronnyvoo an' then' fer trappin' arterwards. Ye recollect Vanderburgh, do ye? That'ere sojer-boy runnin' the cannons when we war fussin' agin the Rees back in 'twenny-three?" I assured Black that I recalled Major Vanderburgh all too well, especially because several days of bombardment by all his Army artillery had inflicted no serious damage on the two Arikara villages.

"Wal, half a year back, Jake Astor bought out Columbia Fur an' him an' Chouteau put Kenny McKenzie in charge. They be callin' theirse'fs the Upper Missourah Outfit naow, tradin' outa Andy Henry's ol' fort on the Yellerstone. They call it Fort Union naow, spreadin' best they kin all the way up the Missourah, even tradin' with Blackfoots!" Harris snorted, looking grim. "Tradin' guns to them sumbitches, mind ye!" He loosed a string of curses. "They'll be gawddamn sorry when them red niggers turn them guns on their own trappers! Mark my words!"

Black soothed his ire with copious draughts from his kettle and naturally I could not, in good conscience, let him drink alone.

Tipsy though I was, stumbling home to my lodge, I was sharply aware that this was the passing of an era in the Rocky Mountain fur trade. Never before had the booshway, either Ashley or EssJay&Ess, suffered serious competition from anyone. The measly efforts of Josh Pilcher's Missouri Fur hardly counted. Now, from what Harris had said, we would see a cutthroat struggle for beaver plews. The mountains breed hard men and greed makes them harder. Trappers might, for a spell, gain some small advantage from competition amongst the traders, but I reckoned that wouldn't last long.

* * *

The rendezvous launched into frenzy. Fiddles scraped and squeaked day and night. The woods rang all day long with the gunfire of marksmen striving to prove themselves best — many of them, I noticed, shooting caplock rifles now in place of flintlocks. Long queues snaked out from every trade tent. A wealth of prime fur piled up behind the plank tables. Grinning trappers, their women, and Indians from the camps of Snakes, Crows, Flatheads, Nez Percés, and minor tribes staggered homewards under armloads of woolen cloth and all manner of foofurraw, sugar and coffee, and essentials such as muskets, knives, tomahawks and axes, gunpowder, and galena. That year had yielded the richest harvest of prime beaver fur ever seen. It would bestow on the partners an even richer harvest of dollars. Word was that beaver was fetching higher prices in eastern markets than ever before.

Bill Sublette rarely misses a chance to turn a profit. He auctioned off his four remaining beeves to the Indians, shrewdly making sure to part with all four critters at the same time. Indians had never seen such queersome buffalo. They were curious to learn how the meat tasted. Sublette was sure they would be disappointed, but by that time it would be too late.

The Indians were equally fascinated by the big wagons and the gaily-painted dearborn carriages, but those vehicles were not for sale. They were needed for hauling the huge harvest of plews back to Saint Louis.

Early on, we stocked up with gunpowder, lead, percussion caps and good English flints, and other gun fixin's we needed, as well as replacing lost, stolen, or damaged traps, six to a man, and other hardware we required for use or for trade. Then we gave free rein to our women to indulge themselves with coffee, sugar, and molasses, flour, dried beans and fruits unknown in the mountains, vermilion and other powdered paints and dyes, yards of woolen stroud, calico, osnaburg, silk, and satin cloth, colored beads and thread, hawk bells, gaudy horse trappings, and a wealth of glittery trinkets and baubles.

Although our own women resisted such fooleries, here and there throughout the throng bobbed colorful parasols proudly displayed by Indian belles whose dusky complexions would acquire no useful benefit from such protection from the sun.

Until the traders' stocks ran out, we happily paid extra for metheglin, a pleasant mixture of honey mead and trader's booze. After that, I preferred to lace EssJay&Ess's throat-scalding spirits with blackstrap molasses.

Anse Tolliver and Yves Dureau were rarely in camp, but nobody objected to the campkeeper's absence. They were off scraping and squawking, contributing to the general merriment, which is what rendezvous is all about. There would be time enough for chores when the autumn harvest commenced.

Strolling through the colorful swarm, togged out in my best finery, sidestepping brawls and wrestling bouts, my ears besieged with half a hundred tongues and dialects roared out from drunken throats, I enjoyed that rendezvous more than ever before. They are my people — leathery whitemen hardly distinguishable from redmen and those who are brown, black, or mixtures of all four. I am proud to be one of them. I gloried in the uncivilized hubbub, a well-earned saturnalia for hard-working men and women who suffer perils and hardships unimagined in the settlements. No one who knows us can deny us our brief excesses at rendezvous.

Drunkenness at rendezvous is well-nigh universal amongst trappers and Indian men and many women, too, but there is a markèd difference betwixt whites and the redfolk. Ardent spirits mostly stimulate trappers to hilarious high good humor and wild physical activity, now and then sparking belligerence that usually drains off when friends haul the brawlers aside and give them time to cool off.

Indians are different. Liquor was unknown to them before we came to the mountains. They can't handle it. When in their cups, too many Indian men become murderous, slaking an unquenchable thirst at the expense of everything they own, stumbling and reeling and picking fights until they collaps in a sodden heap and know no more. It is just as well that rendezvous and trader's booze are confined to a fortnight or so, once a year. If not, all of us might die.

Crows are a happy exception. Long ago the Absóraqa Nation became disgusted with the bloody excesses brought on by alcohol. The elders forbade their young men to use it. It is a rare thing to see a drunken Crow at rendezvous or anyplace else. Such virtue almost makes up for their penchant for stealing horses.

Even amidst all that jollity I realized how much of my contentment stemmed from my new-found happiness with Rainbow and our child. I still possessed the freedom I had found in the mountains and the camaraderie of my brothers in our bunch, but now I was further enriched by my woman and all she had brought into my life. Nothing lacked.

Best of all is meeting up with old friends. I have known some of them since the hard early days of 'twenty-two. My heart is big when I hear them call out, "Temple Buck! Good to see ye! Glad ye ain't gone under! Gitcherse'f a bait o' grub! He'p yerse'f to squeezin's!" Ours is a hard trade. Each year we hear of good comrades gone under, but, Indian-like, their names are rarely mentioned afterwards and most of us don't dwell overlong upon their fate.

A mild disappointment that year was the frequent absence of a handful of valued friends who are usually in the thick of the merrymaking, particularly Jim Bridger and especially Milton Sublette, who always lives up to his nickname, the Thunderbolt. Tom Fitzpatrick, too, was rarely seen that year, except in company with the other two in the precincts of EssJay&Ess. Even then Fitz usually wore a long face and a preoccupied air. And the musicians mostly had to do without Frapp and his diabolical musical contraption that year, most likely gratefully. He, too, was mostly to be found within the traders' ring of tents. When I mentioned my wonderment to Black Harris, he looked mysterious, but all he would tell me was, "Sum'pin's in the wind. Count on it."

* * *

The mystery was solved when rendezvous dwindled to near-sobriety. Booze was hardly more than water and planks showed on the trading tables. A wealth of civilized plunder had been carried off to lodges, tents, and bowers by then. For days the traders' lackeys had been stuffing tight-pressed bales of plews into the high-wheeled wagons, stacking them clear to the iron hoops overhead and bulging out the canvas sides. Even the two dearborn carriages sagged under a burden of fur. One by one, trade tents were collapsed and stowed or sold off for their canvas, until hardly anything remained of the booshways' camp.

I was in my lodge, breaking fast with Rainbow, Iris, and my father, when word came that a meeting had been called at the booshways' circle. I reckoned all it amounted to was Sublette bidding us farewell and departing, but, just the same, I dressed and hustled along with the rest of the bunch to hear what he had to say.

The five-mule wagon teams, sleek and seal-fat now from a fortnight and more on lush graze, were already harnessed and in the traces, wagon wheels still dripping from standing in the river, soaking spokes and felloes. Spare mules and horses and the one lonesome curly-horn milch cow were bunched together, held in place by hostlers riding circles around them. Bill Sublette was about to bid farewell for another year.

He was already clambering up upon the tailboard of a wagon by time we joined the throng of trappers. That morning his long horseface wore an unaccustomed lopsided smile under his battered beaver topper. He was clad in well-worn, travel-stained buckskin clothes, pouches and weapons belted at his waist, ready for the trail.

Davey Jackson and Jed Smith stood quietly beside a rear wheel of the wagon, their saddle horses tethered to the spokes. Both wore a sober expression, like men bearing witness to something important. We hadn't long to wait.

Once he was satisfied that just about every trapper sober enough to get there was present, Bill spread his arms for quiet and commenced his speechifying in that high-pitched, ringing, anvil-pounding voice he uses whenever he addresses his listeners with something he considers important. "Thankee, one an' all, for the fine job ye done this year! It's a prodigy! The stock won't be thankin' ye" — he waved his arm towards the mules fidgeting in their traces — "but we do! It's been a helluva good year!"

A chorus of cheers bellowed from a hundred throats. Bill signaled for quiet and resumed. "A helluva rendezvous, too!" More cheers, but not so much this time. "And it's been a helluva good run for Smith, Jackson and Sublette, too, for all these years!" A few weak cheers disappeared in a questioning rumble as the possible meaning of his words sank in. Trappers are rough but we aren't dumb. Stupid men die off early on. Something was afoot.

"But like they say, all good things do come to an end. It's time to be movin' on! Doin' other things. Smith, Jackson an' Sublette are quittin' the mountains, sellin' out!"

Pandemonium broke out. Yells and curses split the air. Shouted questions about the future tumbled one over another, mostly drowned in the hubbub. The jovial mood turned ugly, menacing. I glanced at Diah and Davey. Their faces betrayed nothing.

Sublette gestured for quiet, a mite disturbed but still hanging onto his counterfeit grin. His outstretched arms commanded silence. The noisy crowd, still restive, quieted enough for him to go on. "But we ain't about to leave ye high an' dry! Nosirree! We're leavin' ye in good hands — hands ye already know! Hands ye can trust, like ye always could Smith, Jackson, and Sublette!" This last remark provoked a ripple of snickers and goodnatured curses. Sublette ignored them. "I'm proud to tell ye the new owners, what'll be callin' theirselves the Rocky Mountain Fur Company, are men ye've been trappin' with from the get-go!" He swung about and beckoned to the far side of the wagon, calling out, "C'mon up here, fellers." He wheeled to address the crowd as five men we knew well stepped into view and announced, "Here they be! The new owners! Tom Fitzpatrick, Jim Bridger, an' my own little brother Milton!"

A roar of laughter greeted the last introduction. Big, broad-shouldered Milton nearly dwarfed his tall but lean elder brother. Bill signaled for quiet. "An' that ain't all — not by a long shot! Fer boot ye're getting' good ol' Frapp, Henry Fraeb, an' Jean-Baptiste Gervais! Ev'ry man-jack of 'em a man ye can count on! All five of 'em hivernants an' mountaineers through thick an' thin! That's the new company an' ye can be proud to be workin' with ever' one of 'em!"

The five new partners were grinning, but in their case the grins were genuine. Sublette stepped down from the wagon and formally shook the hand of each of the new owners. Bill Sublette can be quite the showman when he chooses to be. Naturally a deal of back-slapping and spirited well-wishing was going on when I caught up with Davey Jackson, who had moved away from Jed Smith. "I reckon ye meant what ye said last spring, Davey," I told him, "when ye said you had a hankerin' for Californy. Ye goin'?"

Davey wore an almost bashful look when he replied, "Mebbe so. Ain't quite made up muh mind, but mebbe so." His gaze strayed over the green prairie and rolling hills and the hazy blue, snow-capped mountains beyond. A gentle smile wreathed his handsome face. "It ain't easy, mind ye, sayin' g'bye to all o' this, but mebbe so." I shook his hand and thanked him in mumbled, inadequate words for his comradeship over the years, ever since he and I clerked for Andrew Henry, coming up the Missouri in 'twenty-two.

We separated amid a press of smiling men jostling to congratulate and perhaps scrape a mite of future good will with the freshly-minted partners. They had all been brigade leaders at one time or another, but now the partners assumed a much greater importance in the affairs of every trapper, freemen and engagés alike. At length I came upon a cluster of my own people, Black Harris amongst them, all of them chattering like magpies.

"Told'ja so," Brass Turtle was saying smugly. "Thar war too many leaks in that'ere boat to keep it floatin' much longer."

Tuttle asked me, "What'd'ja think o' thet'ere corn-fab-yoo-layshun ol' Billy war spoutin'? Warn't he sumpin'? Ther gawddamn birds war a-fallin' out o' ther trees, jest hearin' 'im talkin'!" I allowed that I had been mightily impressed.

Tuttle guffawed at my lack of sincerity. "Yep, ol' Billy's jaw gonna be painin' him halfway to Missourah, hangin' onter thet'ere shit-eatin' grin on his phiz like he war, all ther way whilst he war speechifyin'! 'Tain't like him, nohaow!"

"He oughta be grinnin'," Ned Godey opined, "haulin outa hyar that'ere heap o' prime plews they got fer theirse'fs this time around."

"Ye damn betcha!" Brass Turtle asserted. "A hunnerd an' seventy packs, one o' the clarks tol' me. Biggest haul ever, by a long chalk! Like ye say, he oughta be dancin' jigs an' howlin' at the moon!"

"Reckon Billy's through with the mountains, do ye?" Anse Tolliver wanted to know.

Black Harris snorted. "Don'tcha never letcherse'f be thinkin' so. Ol' Billy ain't never goin' to be shet o' these hyar mountains so long as thar's one single copper left that he kin git his paws on!" Nobody offered any objection. We knew Sublette too well. "'Sides, he awready made them new pardners promise to git their trade goods offa him an' t'others, leastaways 'til they pay up what's still owin' — 'bout fifteen thousand dollars, I'm hearin'." He allowed himself an evil chuckle.

"Same deal as ol' Gin'ral Ashley laid onter EssJay-an'-Ess in 'twenny-six. Billy's a quick larner. He don't never let nuthin' git away easy-like."

"Are ye after goin' back with 'em, Black," Paddy McBride enquired.

"Not this time," Harris replied. "Reckon they kin find the way by theirownse'fs 'thout me traipsin' along." He grinned and rubbed his thumb against his forefinger. "Nope. It be time fer makin' money. Reckon I'll hang aroun' hyarabouts 'til spring. Mebbe trappin'with ya'll, if'n ye don't mind." He looked wistful for a spell before he added, "Jist the same, I'll be missin' one partic'lar li'l gal in Sain' Looie."

Before we could assure him that he would be welcome amongst us, which I reckon he knew anyways, shouts and whipcracks and the braying of mules erupted from the wagon train. "Reckon they be pullin' out," Tuttle said. "Let's go see 'em off."

By time we got there, mules were lunging into their collars, budging the tall iron-shod wheels from muddy ruts. Smiling wagoners were cursing, purely from habit, whips cracking harmlessly in the air. Mounted hostlers crowded packmules and loose stock into an unruly queue behind the dearborns.

Sublette, Davey, and Smith were mounted now, rifles slung, Jed and Bill trotting forward to lead the train, Jackson hanging back with the herders. Sublette's feigned affability had vanished, replaced by his customary stern expression, appropriate, as I reckon he saw it, to a leader bearing great responsibilities. Diah wore his usual remote, unreadable expression. Of the three partners, only Davey Jackson was smiling, waving to friends, and leaning from his saddle for final handshakes and well-wishing.

"Ye mark thet, do ye?" Tuttle observed. "Outa ther three of 'em, Davey be the onliest reg'lar mountaineer amongst 'em. He be, fer gawddamn sure, one of our kind. T'other two ain't!"

One by one, the straining mules jerked the heavy wagons loose. Wheels commenced rolling along the rocky trail, axles creaking, harness and trace chains jingling, wagons jouncing and swaying under high-piled loads, the much-lighter single-mule dearborns bouncing in their wake, wagoners spewing a never-ending litany of harmless curses and cracking whips just for the sheer joy of doing it. Packhorses trudged at the rear under towering white-canvas loads, followed by a still-unruly mob of loose animals not yet settled into the discipline of the trail. Last in the procession was the lonesome brindle Guernsey milch cow, patiently plodding back to Missouri, still a mystery as to why they brought her up there in the first place.

She would have been last, that is, except for Black Harris. He galloped up to us, reined in, and yelled out, "Sorry, fellers! Cain't feature hangin' with ye thi'shere winter! That'ere li'l whore back in Looie'll be pinin' fer me somethin' awful if'n I ain't 'longside o' Billy when he gits thar!" Without waiting for a reply, he put spurs to his horse and, trailing his protesting packmule, rode off to catch up with the caravan.

We watched them out of sight, until the final squeaks and jingles and colorful cusswords faded from hearing, until the last bustling horseback hostler disappeared around a bend in the trail.

"Well now," Ned Godey opined softly, "that's sartinly the end o' somethin', ain't it?" He brightened. "An' the start o' somethin' bran'-new! Fer my part, I'm likin' what I see comin' on, leastaways fer right now. I'll take this new bunch fer mine — Fitz an' Jim an' the rest."

"Amen," Brass Turtle assented. "We oughta he'p 'em make a go of it. They gotta be better'n what we been puttin' up with." Nobody differed. The new partners would likely be an improvement over Sublette and Smith.

Joe Meek, wearing a long face, joined us as we meandered back to camp. "What'say, Joe?" Tuttle asked him. "Ye be lookin' kinda mournful."

The young Virginian sighed. "I be wond'rin' what all o' this's gonna be meanin' fer me an' Doc an' ther Irisher Harry, that's what."

"Mean?" Turtle told him, laughing. "What it means is ye got yer wish! An' a whole year early! Ye be a free man, Joe, if ye wanta be. A free trapper, trappin' on yer own hook an' takin' yer own chances! Else ye kin sign on with Fitz an' Milt an' the others."

"Ye mean I ain't bound no more?" Joe demanded, beaming.

"Hell, no!" Godey replied. "Ye made yer deal with Billy an' he's long gone outa hyar. All bets are off. You're on yer own — an' so's yer pards!"

Joe leaped in the air and clicked his heels — or he would have done, had he been wearing boots — and, thanking us through his laughter, rushed off to his friends to spread the good news.

All in all, from what we could tell, this rendezvous had been one of the best.

Chapter XII
Three Forks

For the next several days we scoured the surrounding prairie and draws amongst the hills for buffalo grown fat on summer graze. The camp was festooned with jerked meat draped on willow racks and over cords strung from every nearby tree branch and smokeflap pole. We needed a lot of meat for the journey we would soon be making. There would likely be precious little time to hunt when we arrived at our destination,

It was right and proper that we help the new Rocky Mountain Fur Company succeed. The partners had been our friends since our early days on the Missouri. When Jim Bridger came by and asked that we trail along with his brigade that fall, it would have been difficult to tell him no.

Rocky Mountain Fur planned to go to the headwaters of the Missouri, called the Three Forks, for their autumn hunt. The sizeable debt they owed to EssJay&Ess, payable in just one year, prompted their decision to trap those beaver-rich streams in Blackfoot country. A bountiful harvest was a sure thing, but just as sure would be the Blackfoots' determined effort to keep us from getting it. Good intentions towards RMF aside, arriving at a decision to join them produced a plenitude of conflicting palaver.

"Ye got any idée, do ye," Anse Tolliver demanded in that high, cracked voice of his, "'bout whut kind o' hornet's nest yew'll be kickin' over up thar? That'ere be the wust kind o' sitchee-ayshun! Ye mought's well go crawlin' inter them Blackfoots' lodges an' beddin' down with 'em! That'ere be their own pers'nal stompin' ground!"

Anse was right. We had all heard tell of the bloody results of attempts to trap that beaver-rich country, starting with Andrew Henry being run out of there a dozen years before our bunch first came up the Missouri, then again in 'twenty-three, when he tried it a second time and failed with heavy losses.

"Mebbe so," Tuttle countered, "but thar's sure to be plews aplenty fer easy takin' up thar. Ain't nobody ever done no trappin' thar'abaouts thet I ever heared of."

"An' fer good reason," Godey advised. "Ol' Beelzebub's Boys claim that whole country fer their own partic'lar dooryard an' they don't take kindly to trappers or nobody else comin' in — Injuns same as us. Feller I useta work fer, ol' Manuel Lisa, tried sendin' men fer trappin' thar a coupl'a times. Lost his shirt an' a passel o' good men ever' time!"

Tuttle bristled. "Bub's Boys er Bug's Boys er whatchamever ye mought be callin' 'em, I ain't afeared of 'em — not enough, anyways, to pass up all o' them prime plews jest a-waitin' thar fer the pickin'!."

"Hold on thar!" Anse countered hotly. "I got as much guts as yew ever did, Tuttle Thompson, so don't ye be callin' me yeller! Jist the same, I don't fancy seein' my guts spillin' onter muh britchclout fer the sake o' plews!"

"Fer what it's wuth," Brass Turtle declared, "an' it's wuth consid'rable — the fellers an' me been jawin' 'bout goin' up thataway. We reckon it's past time we be givin' them sumbitches comeuppance in their own home-patch, 'stid o' waitin' fer 'em comin' down thisaway, pickin' on us like they allus do!"

"Ye kin betcher sweet arse," Paddy McBride threw in, "this Mick'll not be hangin' back whin there's fightin' to be done! I'll not soon be fergittin' how thim blaggards run us ragged in 'twenny-five, purty nigh thim selfsame T'ree Farks, whin there wuz but a score of us. Let 'em try it now, fightin' agin a couple hunnerd guns! This toime we'll whup 'em fair an' square!"

McCool, my father, Micah, and I held our peace. Certainly the sheer numbers of Blackfoots was worrisome, but greed and bravado arc powerful persuaders. In the end we chose to accompany RMF to the Three Forks of the Missouri.

Warmly contested as that decision had been, convincing our women to remain behind was an even more difficult chore. It made no nevermind to them that Rainbow and Molly had young children, that Tally and Dolly were both far along with child, and that the Crow women might also be in a family way by then. They were all determined to go with us, no matter the danger. Long nights of wrangling, sulking, and renewed domestic combat each morning came to an end only when we were able to convince them that we men would be in greater peril if we were burdened with worry over our women and children's well-being. At last they surrendered. The women would stay with their respective bands during the autumn harvest. We would retrieve them on the way to winter camp.

When it came time for departure, Jim Bridger showed up in camp seeking a favor. He was obviously uncomfortable when he drew Ned, Paddy, and me aside and said, "Hate to be askin' ye this, but I ain't hankerin' fer carryin' muh Flathead woman inter that'ere country. Too dangerous. Her band ain't hyar, so I'm askin' kin she mebbe go along home with yer wimmen 'til fall trappin's over." Naturally we consented, shuddering the while at the cost in even more foofurraw, come next rendezvous, that this additional concession would exact from us. Fact is, howsomever, they already knew Bridger's woman and happily welcomed her.

* * *

Iron Bow's band traveled alongside us until we came nigh Flathead country, where they parted from our cavalcade of a couple hundred trappers — white and red and a passel of in-betweens, Company men, free trappers, *engagés,* some still with their women and kids, trundling travois heaped with their lodges and plunder. Most of us, howsomever, were burdened only with essentials on lightly-loaded pack animals. I hated to see the Flatheads go, carrying with them our women and children, but I was nonetheless relieved, reasonably sure that my loved ones would be much safer with their people in winter camp than with us in a hotbed of hostile Blackfoots that surely awaited us at the headwaters of the Missouri.

That final night before parting from Rainbow was memorable for the intensity of our passion, coupling with almost insane frenzy, then, breathless and gasping, murmuring endearments and clinging together in sweaty embrace, reluctant to pull apart lest we sacrifice even a moment of being close. Sweaty and sleepless, we were wide-eyed when Bridger's battered bugle broke the stillness, summoning us to the trail.

At rendezvous I had heard several men refer to Jim Bridger as Gabe, but I hadn't bothered to enquire why they called him so. The first morning on the northward journey dispelled the mystery. Somewhere in his travels Jim had traded for an old Army bugle, tarnished and dented but still able to make a braying mule melodious by comparison. He blew it every morning, rousing his brigade from their robes with more alacrity than they might have displayed otherwise, just to make him quit. If the Angel Gabriel summons the Faithful to Eternal Bliss on Judgment Day with such cacophony, I'd as lief pass,

Bidding farewell to my little daughter was even more painful than parting with Rainbow. Indian-like, she didn't cry, but tears gathered in the corners of her wondrous deep-blue eyes and her final hug threatened to choke me.

Bridger, burdened now with new responsibilities, had said his goodbyes to his woman earlier. Paddy and Ned, along with my father, Micah, and Finn McCool, lingered with me until the Flatheads departed, heading westwards, travois drags stirring up trail dust, outriders ranging ahead and alongside the colorful column, a few at the rear urging laggards forward. We strained to catch a final glimpse of our women and children. At last I espied Rainbow, erect in her saddle, eyes fixed straight ahead, expressionless, little Iris straddling the saddle bow, twisting about and peering past her mother's shoulder, seeking me out. When she caught sight of me, her face lit up and she waved, continuing until the shifting stream of riders obscured them from view.

"'Tis a hard thing to be sayin' farewell to your dear ones," Finn said quietly, "trustin' them to others' care. Even so, 'tis a far better choice than puttin' them in harm's way where we're after goin'."

"Ye be right on all counts," Ned agreed. "Toughest part of it war gittin' Cat to see it thataway."

Grunts and nods affirmed that we had chosen the best course. "Well now," Paddy declared, brushing his sleeve across his glistening eyes, "'tis a done thing! We'd best be after catchin' up wi' the others, lest the bloody Blackfoots catch the measly few of us out here by oursel's an' make widders an' orphans of 'em all!"

It was sound advice and so we did.

* * *

Anse Tolliver's oft-repeated dictum that "thar's safety in numbers" held true on our journey north and west. Our vast caravan, numbering nigh two hundred trappers, not counting the women and children still amongst us, discouraged Blackfoots and Grovants from attacking in force. They prefer long odds on their side. Now they contented themselves with mostly unsuccessful nighttime horse-thieving, now and then taking potshots from cover, unfailingly answered by a volley of gunfire which convinced them, after a spell, that such sniping was suicidal.

Buffalo migrating southwards kept our numerous company well-fed. Plentiful grass, crisping by then in warm, dry, early-autumn air, maintained our stock in good fettle. It was a pleasant journey, allowing plenty of time for jawing with long-time friends, mulling over my own private thoughts, and sometimes for a few of us to gallop out from the column to run small bunches of buffalo for both pleasure and provender.

Three of the RMF partners led our expedition — Fitzpatrick, Bridger, and Milton Sublette. Frapp and Jean Gervais, with a smaller force, had remained in Snake country for their fall harvest. When we neared the sources of the three rivers that join to form the headwaters of the Missouri, the partners called for a parley to determine the best route northwards. Five years earlier our bunch had made a journey on our own down the easternmost of the three rivers, through the steep-sided canyon of the Gallatin, which narrows and widens for nigh a hundred miles, affording decent graze for a fast-moving traveling party in the broad bottomlands and defendable terrain in the narrow parts, where a party might fort up in case of major attack. None of the leaders had traveled any of the three river valleys — the Gallatin, Madison, and Jefferson — so when we recommended what we knew, the Gallatin, they took us at our word.

Finn McCool, the most scholarly man amongst us, had suggested, "In case of attack, the narrow parts of the canyon will surely provide us with much the same advantage the Spartans enjoyed when defendin' agin' the Persians at Thermopylae, don't ye know." It is doubtful that either Bridger or Milton knew what in hell he was talking about and Fitz merely nodded. Finn and I refrained from mentioning that all of the Spartans had perished.

As it turned out, our caravan made it through the canyon of the Gallatin unchallenged, in three days' time, emerging into a broad valley at the northern end which stirred unpleasant memories. Our bunch had been attacked and besieged there five years before.

"Och, man, ye should'a been here that toime," Paddy McBride was telling McCool. "T'ree days we went, dyin' fer water we wuz, but stackin' up Blackfoots loike faggots fer the fire, we wuz, killin' 'em loike hawgs at Killarney Fair, we wuz, an' still the bloody blatherskites kep' comin' on, a couple t'ousand of 'em, they wuz, an' no gettin' loose of 'em, mind ye, fer they wuz iv'ryplace around us, 'til ten t'ousand buffler come runnin' 'cross the lea an' thim greedy spalpeens rode out an' kilt a couple hunnert o' thim bufflers an' went to gorgin' thimsel's loike stuffin' a Chris'mus goose, they done, mind ye, eatin' 'til they could hardly move a foot or a finger an' the lot of 'em wuz after fallin' to sleep, they wuz, which is how we got out o' this very place, mind ye,

McCool, iv'ry man of us escapin' thim bloody red niggers with a whole hide or mostly!" Paddy looked to me for confirmation. "Ain't it so, Temple?" I nodded and bit my tongue and allowed that, yes, it had been something like that.

Fortunately history didn't repeat itself. We passed through the broad valley unscathed, some of us wondering if perhaps we had been overcautious in leaving our womenfolk behind. The next couple months, howsomever, confirmed the wisdom of our original decision.

Another thirty miles brought us to the Three Forks of the Missouri, where three sizeable rivers flowing northwards — the Gallatin, Madison, and Jefferson — meet to form what becomes the mighty Missouri River, which gathers size and power from hundreds of tributaries on its way east, until it spills into the Mississippi just above Saint Louis. Three Forks itself is a broad, mostly marshy area several miles wide, abounding in beaver dams and ponds and burrows dug into crick banks. It promised more riches in plews than any of us had ever dared dream of. No wonder Andrew Henry and many other traders and trappers had risked their lives there to reap a golden harvest in fur, willing to brave the bloody onslaughts of Blackfoots dedicated to driving them out of that treasure trove. Until now, the Blackfoots had always prevailed.

"We been lucky so far," Brass Turtle opined, "trav'lin' like a gawddamn army. This is whar the fun commences, once we split up fer trappin'." He brushed away a mosquito teasing his eye. "Think the skeeters are bad? Jist wait 'til we git to work. I warrant thar'll be a heap more Blackfoots than skeeters pesterin' us, by a long chalk!"

"Thet ain't s'prisin'," Tuttle replied. "Ef'n it war gonna be easy, thar wouldn't be nuthin' left o' beaver hyarabouts. They'd'a been trapped out to nuthin' twenny year ago!"

"That's so," Godey agreed. "Ol' Lisa tried it a couple-three times, once with Andy Henry. Injuns kilt half of 'em an' run 'em out ever' time."

"Best we kin do," Anse advised, "is we bunch up fer trappin', mebbe four-five men together, an' allus keepin' enough fellers in camp, lookin' arter critters an' plunder." He swept his gaze over the mostly swampy land, dotted with islands overgrown with cottonwoods and willows. "Doin' it thataway'll likely slow us up some, but it 'pears thar's a sufficiency o' beaver out thar to make up fer what time we mought be losin'."

"Indade!" Paddy exclaimed. "Wouldja be lookin' at all o' thim willers an' barky trees, will ye! 'Tis surely a heaven fer castors!"

* * *

Milton Sublette had proved to be a good brigade leader the previous year, so we stuck with him at the Forks. Joe Meek, a free trapper now, had attached himself to Milt, which wasn't surprising. They shared a madcap streak fortunately well-seasoned with commonsense. Milton had long ago earned the nickname Thunderbolt and it appeared that Joe was determined to compete for that title.

Milt assigned us a desirable parcel of territory sufficiently removed from his own brigade to prevent squabbles. We were pretty much on our own regarding hostile attacks, but we saw nothing wrong about that. If things got too hot we could always retreat to the crude fort and breastworks the Company men were building.

Early-morning ice already frosted the shores of ponds and waterways. It was time to commence trapping, even if those early plews were still far from prime. Establishing our first camp occupied less than a day. First we chose a clear-running stream with enough level ground on the bank and built our bowers with canvas and hides, bordered with plentiful sweet cottonwood and willows. Then we built a rude paddock for our livestock and gathered dry firewood and sweet cottonwood bark for critter feed. Little else is required for a trapping camp. The surrounding woods and meadows teemed with grazing buffalo, wapiti, and deer and entirely too much bear sign for my taste.

Whilst we busied ourselves with domestic chores we could hear beaver in the surrounding ponds and streams slapping their tails on the water, alerting their brethren to our intrusion. The invitation was too much to resist. As soon as necessary tasks were completed, a half-dozen of us sallied forth to set our traps in likely spots. Next morning we were rewarded with sixteen beaver, a fortuitous beginning to what promised to be the best harvest yet.

Mindful of Anse Tolliver's advice, we doubled our usual trapping pairs, three of us standing guard on shore while the fourth man tended his traps, everyone alert for any alien sound or movement. Even so, not one of us escaped that harvest with a whole hide. Blackfoots were everywhere, more deadly bothersome than ever, resisting our intrusion into that marshy ground as a matter of tribal honor.

Fear was every man's constant companion. Bravado withered under constant forays against us, day and night, whilst we set and lifted our traps, stood horse guard, hunted, and gathered firewood, and in camp. We maintained a heavy guard, taking turns at lying concealed in hidey-holes whilst a few men gulped a hasty bait of grub and snatched a few winks of sleep before relieving the sentinels. Tempers grew short. Pointless quarrels flared up and sputtered out. Harmless witticisms often provoked a savage response amongst friends whose nerves were rubbed raw by constant vigilance and fear.

"Thi'shere's like shootin' fish in a bar'l," Tuttle opined one time, "an' I be gittin' gawddamn fed up o' bein' ther gawddamn fish!"

Gunfire echoed often in the woods and across the meadows from the skirmishing. Blackfoot scalps became a glut on the market. No matter how many bravos we killed, there appeared to be an endless supply of foolish young men itching to replace them, earning eagle feathers, proving their worthiness.

And still, every day, every man reaped a harvest of beaver fur unthought-of in any year before or any other place. Often, as I worked my traps or crouched alone in cover, straining to spy out an enemy, I weighed the value of our princely haul against the deadly risks we ran every minute of the day and night and decided that no amount of profit was worth my life. Yet there was no choice but to stick with it. Even if our entire bunch agreed to give it up and retreat, a mere score of men would be easy pickin's for the horde of Blackfoots that would likely descend upon us. Only the RMF partners could make that decision. We were stuck, so we might as well make the best of it.

We dug down a couple-three feet deep inside the bowers and heaped up the extra dirt on the outside as a barricade against musket balls and arrows that often came whistling through the canvas above.

Bad as the constant vigilance was, the worst of it was the smell. Even Brass Turtle, my father, and our other redskin brethren were forced to forego their daily bathe. Nobody dared expose himself by swimming in the chill waters around us. We slept fitfully in our clothes and moccasins, weapons no more than a hand's-breadth distant. In time, even Tuttle Thompson was no more odoriferous than I was.

Attacks when we were tending our traplines were commonplace. Foot and Finn stayed busy patching up bullet scrapes and digging out arrow points, Foot muttering the while his reassuring singsong, "Be long vay from yer heart." Scabbed up though we were, our homespun medicos kept us reasonably mended and able to do our chores.

Blackfoots weren't the only problem. As weather worsened and hivernation time grew nigh, the woods swarmed with bears, black and grizzly, gobbling up every edible morsel. Gut-piles were their favorite snack, but their appetite recognized no boundaries. They were just as likely to invade our camp, drawn by hanging meat and cooking smells, as they were to forage for berries or rip up rotten logs in search of ants and grubs. Men always remained on guard in camp, day and night, rifles ready, to defend against hungry bears as much as Indian horsethieves and scalp-collectors out to make a name for themselves.

Without dwelling on each and every narrow scrape, it's worthwhile recounting here a few that will likely survive for a spell amongst mountaineers yarning alongside cookfires.

At daybreak one snowy morning, we were huddled around the cookfire, sipping the last of our coffee, choosing who would go together to run traplines. Suddenly our whole world exploded with the terrified screams of our critters and half a dozen equally frightened Blackfoots charging into camp. Every man snatched up his rifle or musket, but before we could use them it was plain to see those Indians meant no harm to us, leastaways right then. Their only wish was to escape whatever was behind them. A couple-three stampeded through camp, jumped into the crick, floundered across, and disappeared into the woods beyond.

A pair of half-grown grizzly cubs bounded out of the brush and a bellowing, slavering grizzly sow shambled into view. She reared onto her hocks, pawing the air, then dropped to all fours and went after her errant offspring. The remaining Blackfoots worried us less than the enraged sow-bear. They stood dumbstruck, frozen in place. She swatted one of them with a paw like a fistful of daggers and he caromed into the crick, his head half torn off. Another met his fate when our campkeeper L'Archévêque, never notable for his courage, swung up his precious new musket — intending, he said later, to shoot the bear — and nigh cut the warrior in two with a charge of buckshot.

A dozen heavy rifle balls despatched the sow and a few more took care of the cubs. As the grizzly crumpled to earth, the remaining Blackfoot recovered his wits and fled across the crick. Nobody bothered to fire a parting shot.

Once we settled down, we reckoned the event was a blessing. The Blackfoots had done us no harm and maybe they carried with them a superstitious notion that we were protected by grizzlies. Either way, the plenitude of rich bear meat provided a welcome change from a monotonous diet of beaver.

Brass Turtle, my father, Little Mountain, and a couple others hotfooted into the woods and returned shortly, leading seven Blackfoot ponies and toting three new-looking muskets, bows and quivers, and various items of hardware. The guns immediately captured our attention.

Tuttle studied the marking on the barrel, tossed the musket to Turtle, and snarled, "Amurrican-made, by Gawd! "Whar'd'ja s'pose them'ere Píkunis got a-holt o' 'Murrican guns, all alike an' bran'-new?"

"Ain't likely Aitch-bee-cee's been shoppin' in New Jersey," Brass Turtle opined wryly, passing the weapon on.

"Nope," Godey assented. "Ain't nowhars else'n from ol' McKenzie down on the Missourah!"

A spate of curses sputtered amongst us. "Bad enough the gawddamn Brits been sellin' guns to 'em!" Anse growled. "Naow we got a 'Murrican doin' likewise!"

"His chickens'll soon be comin' home to roost, I'm thinkin'," McCool observed. "Now that Misther McKenzie's after sendin' his own trappers out, Beelzebub's boys'll be regardin' them no more kindly than they do the rest of us."

It was fact. Gratitude is not a common trait in the Blackfoot character. They tolerate traders, but any trapper who invades what they fancy is their domain is fair game, the Upper Missouri Outfit included.

* * *

Joe Meek and his friend Doc Newell gifted us with a couple good yarns when they happened by one day. Naturally we regaled them with the tale of the Blackfoots and the bears. The number of Blackfoots had increased from half a dozen to nigh a score in the telling, but no matter. It makes for a better story.

"Speakin' o' b'ars," Joe said, "a comical thang happened a coupl'a days back, when me an' Milt Sublette war out huntin'. Him an' me, we come upon a leetle bunch o' young buffler bulls feedin' in a clearin' an', not wishin' to spook 'em, we got down off'n our hosses an' went to sneakin' up on 'em. Ol' Milt war purty fur ahead o' me, gittin' on t'other side o' them'ere bufflers, when I spy a big ol' grizzle b'ar come jumpin' out'n some bushes, hollerin' sumpin' dreadful, an' headin' straight fer Milt. Natcherly Milton sees 'im, too, an' he ups an' shoots at ther b'ar, but, pressed like he war, he jist nicks 'im, makin' ol' Ephraim even madder'n he awready war."

Joe paused to pluck a coal from the cookfire and drop it onto the bowl of his pipe, taking his time, whilst we all leaned forward, anxious to hear the rest of his story. Young as he is, Meek has acquired the tricks of a good tale-teller. "Wal naow," he resumed, "ol' Milt jist natcherly slings his empty gun an' hotfoots fer a big ol' cottonwood that war a-standin' thar an' ther grizzle boar comes a-runnin' arter him, a-screechin' an' a-bawlin' 'til hell won't have it! I ain't payin' hardly no nevermind to Milt jist then, 'cause I reckon I best be killin' that ol' b'ar, lest he be eatin' ther both of us!"

He paused again and let his gaze drift around the circle of eager listeners. "Wal, like I said, I got eyes fer nothin' else'n that ol' b'ar right aboot then. I gits close as I dare, takin' a bead on his eyeball, and drops 'im purty as ye please!" Joe leaned back with a triumphant grin, as if he expected applause, which was not forthcoming.

"What abaout Milt?" Tuttle wanted to know.

"I'm a-comin' to that," Joe replied. "By time I git done loadin' up agin, lest ther ba'r ain't daid, I go to lookin' up inter that'ere tree fer Milt, but he warn't nowhars up thar! An' then I spy 'im sittin' flat-arse on ther ground, a-huggin' that'ere tree like it's his mama! 'Hey, Milt,' I yell, 'do ye allus climb a tree thataway? Ye went an' grabbed onter the wrong end of it, Milton!'

"Wal, Milt he gits all red-faced an' he says, 'I'll be gawddamned, Meek, if'n I din't think I war twenny feet up thi'shere tree when ye took yer shot!'"

When the laughter subsided, Joe added, "Natcherly that'n be too good a yarn to keep to m'se'f, even it's true. I reckon ol' Milt's gonna be hearin' it fer some time to come."

"How's that young Irisher that war runnin' with ye, the spear-throwin' feller?" Ned Godey asked. "He gone under yet?"

"Not hardly!" Doc Newell replied warmly. "An' he ain't likely to, neither! Harry's takin' to these mountains like a babe to mammy's pap!"

"Glad to hear it," Brass Turtle said. "He war lookin' good, playin' Injun games, las' winter camp."

"He ain't playin' no games nowadays," Doc assured us. "He's trappin' an' stayin' alive an' doin' a purty good job o' both. Lemme tell ye 'bout what he did about a month back."

It sounded like another yarn coming. Naturally we cheered him on.

"I reckon ye know Harry was what they call a harpooner, sailin' on whalin' ships along with Cap'n Billy. Billy says Harry was the best he ever seen at throwin' them big spears for catchin' whales. But Harry got sick an' tired of always gettin' seasick, so he come on up thisaway for makin' a livin'.'"

"We know," Godey told him. "Billy or somebody awready said so."

"Well now," Doc resumed, "the four of us were out trappin' over on the Gallatin and ol'Harry got somewhat separated from the rest of us. He was wadin' out to get a beaver that ripped the float-stick loose before he drowned, when an arrow plunks into the water right in front of him. Nat'rally Harry lets out a holler an' looks up to see an Injun on the bank, reachin' for another arrow. The both o' them are too far away for us to take a shot, so we come runnin', fast as we can, but all the while knowin' it's gonna be too late!

"Nat'rally Harry's got his rifle slung — so's he can use both hands for the beaver, don'tcha know — an' he can't get at it fast enough, an' we're still too far off to be helpin'! It sure-as-hell looked like we're gonna be short o' one Irisher."

"What happened?" Tuttle demanded. "He daid?"

"Nope! I awready told ye he ain't," Doc replied with a grin. "Quick as scat, faster'n ye'd think, ol' Harry yanks the float-stick out o' the trap ring and heaves it at the Injun 'fore he can get another arrow off. Plugs 'im square in the belly, he done, right through his capote an' all, spits 'im like a goddamn chicken! A float-stick, mind ye! The sharp end, right through the belly!"

"Anse was skeptical. "Yew funnin' us, Doc? Sounds purty gawddamn tall to me!"

"Swear to God!" Doc replied earnestly. "He done it, sure as hell! Me an' t'others saw 'im do it! It's a goddamn fact!"

"I warn't thar," Joe put in, "but all of 'em're sayin' it's so. I'm takin' it fer true. An' ther Irisher ain't daid!"

True or not, another cookfire yarn was born for the edification and mystification of the Rocky Mountain fur-trapping fraternity.

Afterwards, Tuttle opined, "I reckon lyin' fer fun jest comes natcher'l-like fer Joe an' Doc. Bein' up hyar 'mongst ther likes of us jest hones an edge onto what they war awready born with."

"Sure an' makin' a good story better is a God-granted talent," Finn agreed. "Joe Meek'll niver be shunnin' such gifts o' the Lord."

* * *

Deepening snow and increasing cold at the Missouri Forks did little to slow either Blackfoot attacks or the abundant harvest. The heap of cured plews got to be a burden and a peril. Moving that many hides from one camp to another was trouble enough, but such wealth was also an inviting target, not only for hostile Indians but also trappers of the Upper Missouri Outfit tempted to help themselves to our gains. We thought it best to deposit our plews at Rocky Mountain Fur's stockade for safekeeping.

UMO trappers had been crowding into territory we considered our own. Save their few free trappers, they were a clumsy lot, new to the trade, anxious to profit from our skill, respecting naught, often setting their traps within a rod of our own. It was hard to restrain Tuttle and hotheaded Paddy and most of our Indians from declaring outright war. Tempers were strained enough without such provocation.

Oddly, it was acid-tongued, usually-bellicose Anse Tolliver who preached toleration of the interlopers. "'Tain't right," he averred, "fer whitemen to be killin' each other, nohaow, consarnin' plews ner nuthin' else!"

"Ye be includin' Injuns, are ye, Anse?" Brass Turtle taunted. "How 'bout us? Ye reckon it's awright fer us Injuns to run their arse out'n our trappin' ground, killin' 'em or mebbe jist gittin' 'em bleedin' bad?"

"Ye know better'n that, Turtle," Anse replied huffily. "It be all the same, white er Injun! Our bunch dassn't be killin' no other trappers, neither whites ner tame Injuns like yerownse'f!" It was an unfortunate choice of words.

"Tame?" Little Mountain exploded, jumping to his feet. "Ye callin' me *tame!* Ye wanta see how *tame* we be, nex' time we fight Síksikah? I t'inkin' mebbe no!"

Fortunately cooler heads prevailed. Anse mumbled an apology for his ill-chosen word and admitted that our often bloodthirsty red brethren were largely responsible for the happy fact that our bunch was still alive and kicking. Which somewhat mollified the bristling Delawares and Iroquois.

We continued to put up with the UMO nuisance, which was nearly as bad as the constant harassment we suffered from Blackfoots. Only the daily accumulation of prime fur made it tolerable.

Next time we moved camp, several of us loaded up a packstring with a mountain of plews, each one marked with the owner's brand, and headed for the RMF stockade. Tending the packstring, numerous as it was, didn't require seven of us for the chore, but the fortune in plews we carried warranted serious protection.

We arrived at the headquarters camp unchallenged, availed ourselves of the Company's hide press to squeeze the plews into manageable packs of sixty each, and entrusted them to RMF's protection.

It was late in the day by time our chore was completed. Tuttle and Anse claimed they suffered a life-threatening thirst, so we stayed overnight. Naturally Tolliver carried his fiddle and Tuttle is never without his greasy pack of cards, so those two worthies were assured of booze from Company men starved for music and others eager to test their skill at Old Sledge against Tuttle, which is never a wise thing to do.

None of us went dry. When Fitzpatrick and Bridger laid eyes on the wealth of rich fur we brought in, they weren't inclined to be stingy.

They sloshed our cups to the brim with proper Kentucky whiskey, as much for bonhomie as greed.

"Ye be lookin' fit enough," Fitz remarked. "Anybody gone under?"

"Bunged up some'at, ther most of us," Tuttle replied, "but so fur, so good."

"Glad to hear it," Jim said. "We awready lost three o' the new men an' thar's a passel more hurtin' purty good, but they'll likely git over it."

"What about thi'shere Upper Missourah bunch?" Turtle wanted to know. "They be damn near as bad as gawddamn Blackfoots! Pesky as skeeters!"

Fitz sighed and shrugged. "I fear 'tis a circumstance we'll hafta put up with. Times are changin'. Competition'll be a fact o' loife from here on. Best we can do is slow 'em down."

Bridger barked out a laugh. "Ol' Fitz hyar be doin' some fust-rate slowin' 'em, too! Ever since they come 'round, Tom's been busy as a whore on payday a-stealin' off green trappers Vanderburgh brung up!"

"Vanderburgh, ye say?" Anse put in. "The Army feller? Him what run the cannons fer Leavenworth in that'ere fracas wi' the Rees down on the Muddy?"

"The same," Fitzpatrick acknowledged. "He's headin' up McKenzie's trappin' brigade nowadays, doggin' our steps, cuttin' in on the harvest." He shrugged. "Save for startin' a shootin' war, the best we can do is convincin' his people they're better off with us."

Bridger laughed again. "Damn right! Ain't nobody better at sich convincin' than ol' Tom hyar. An' fer boot, the most of 'em been bringin' with 'em what plews they awready took!" He grew halfway serious. "Blackfoots been he'pin', too. Most o' them'ere new men reckon we kin he'p 'em keep their ha'r better'n Vanderburgh kin."

Which was likely so. Afterwards, strolling about the compound, I fell into conversation with one of the trappers newly-recruited from Vanderburgh's brigade, a tall, spare Pennsylvanian by name of Simon Pence. He was new to the mountains, but he had the look of a man who was no stranger to the wilderness. His buckskin clothes were shabby and worn but well-made, his weapons scarred with hard use but clean and well-oiled.

At first he was slow to engage in palaver, but once he realized I had no wish to vaunt my longer experience in the trapping trade, as many others do, he loosened up. I asked why he had chosen to abandon Vanderburgh's brigade and sign up with Fitz, Jim, and Milton. "'Pears to me trappin' fur be only a part of it," he replied. "Survivin' Injuns an' eatin' reg'lar be the most of it, hennit? There be a heap o' larnin' a feller needs hereabouts an' the Major don't know much more about it'n we'uns what jist come up. Sojerin' hain't the same as mountaineerin', hennit?"

I laughed and told him I agreed completely. "From what I've seen," I said, "soldiers hafta live by a passel o' rules. Up here, rules don't much apply. It's more about learnin' on your own from men who've been hereabouts for a spell that lets ye keep on livin', more'n followin' rules. Bein' amongst trappers that've learned the hard way is the best schoolin' you're apt to get."

Pence grunted assent. I couldn't help comparing this Pennsylvanian with John Smiley, who also had come from that country. Smiley, for all his woodcraft and steadiness, was a hardhead, stubbornly wedded to Pennsylvania customs and prejudice, unwilling to bend and accept the lessons of mountain life. That mulish insistence on holding onto his old ways had cost John his life. Simon Pence appeared to be of a different stamp, one that spoke well for his chance of survival.

Pence opened up. "What drove in the bung an' made up muh mind was the Injun fight we'uns got into, soon as we got up thisaway. I reckon ye could say we'uns won, if ye can call it such. We lost three good men kilt doin' it an' a bunch more tore up purty bad. Then arterwards we'uns larn them Injuns been killin' us with guns they got from McKenzie down on the Missourah!" He paused and spat. "Hain't right, sellin' guns to Injuns ye know're bound to use 'em fer killin' yer own kind! Hennit?"

Again, I could only agree. The only surprise was that Vanderburgh's entire brigade hadn't deserted *en masse* and come over to Rocky Mountain Fur. Still, most men lack imagination and will enough to make hard choices. Fortunately for him, Simon Pence wasn't onesuch.

* * *

At length, our bunch had it to the gills with Upper Missouri men trapping our swatch of the Forks. We let Milton know our decision, then packed up in the dead of night and moved out, heading up the Jefferson, trapping the beaver-rich feeders as we climbed towards the Divide, each day adding ever more plews to our harvest. We were bothered less by Blackfoots there, the most of them content to bedevil trappers at the headwaters. Which is not to say that we were ever completely free of them, either.

* * *

Winter clamped down in earnest and thick ice covered the ponds. Even the fast-flowing Jefferson froze. It was time to make tracks for Iron Bow's village, reunite with Rainbow, Cat, and Molly, then catch up with Rocky Mountain Fur and go into winter camp on the Yellowstone.

This had been the most successful fall hunt yet — and the most taxing. Only after it was at an end did I dare admit how much I had missed my wife and daughter. If I could have done, I would have galloped all the way to Iron Bow's village.

Chapter XIII
The Cache

It was nearly the new year by time we rode into winter camp in Crow country, where the Powder spills into the Yellowstone, a capital place to while away winter months. It provides good graze and sweet cottonwood for horse feed when grass runs out, firewood aplenty, and a plenitude of game, mostly buffalo wintering on abundant prairie grass. Even some two hundred trappers and their families didn't spook them off that lush winter pasture.

I had eyes for little else besides Rainbow and my daughter. Until the fall hunt, we had never been apart since I took her to wife. The warmth of Rainbow's greeting in Iron Bow's winter village never cooled, amounting to one long honeymoon throughout the long, hard weeks of snowy travel from the Flathead to the Yellowstone, increased somewhat by a detour into Snake country to retrieve the wives and newborn babes of Tuttle and Turtle.

I was confounded by how much Iris had grown up in my absence and enchanted by her constant chatter, sometimes in jumbled English, sometimes mostly Salish, often in an incomprehensible macaroni of several tongues. She was nearly two, frisky as a colt, forever yammering and scurrying about our lodge or fidgeting when she rode upon her mother's, my father's, or my own saddlebow during the long days a-horseback. Powatawa never tired of her prattle and her endless pranks. I marveled at his patience. The mountains had stripped decades from him, revealing a man almost too young and vital to be my father.

Winter camp on the Yellowstone was made up of the brigades of Fitzpatrick, Bridger, and Milton Sublette, a considerable number of free trappers, and the inevitable camps of Absóraqas who drifted in for trading and handouts. The brigades of Fraeb and Gervais wintered that year in Willow Valley, the area they had trapped in the fall when the rest of us went to the Missouri Forks.

Full bellies and a scarcity of booze made for a goodnatured camp during the two months we wintered on the Powder. There was time for reading and scratching at my journal, romping in the snow with Iris and Paddy's little boy Sean, and leisurely afternoons in our lodge making love with Rainbow, while Cat generously looked after our daughter. Naturally there was work to be done — hunting, cleaning and oiling weapons, refurbishing worn gear, and standing horse guard in turn. The women and our campkeepers did everything else. Which definitely recommends the married state.

Our considerable numbers discouraged Blackfoot raiding parties. One untroubled week slid into another, spiced only by an occasional irate Absóraqa husband objecting to his complaisant woman giving in to some trapper's charms — or more likely, the shiny foofurraw he dangled before her eyes.

The camp was redolent of meat roasting on spits. Music floated on the air day and night, Indian drumbeat and quavering chant and fiddles scraping lively tunes, accompanied by makeshift musical instruments and hoarse male voices raised in song. There was plenty of time for bragging and yarning, endless palaver, and reading aloud to illiterate men. There was time, too, for deepening friendship with one's trusted comrades, whom wilderness and peril bring closer than most brothers ever get to be.

Considering where we were, the weather was mild. Occasional snowfalls mostly preserved the camp in a pristine white counterpane splashed with colorful blankets and bright-hued capotes. The pleasant memory still lingers.

* * *

In early March Tom Fitzpatrick and three of his Company men departed on a long, hard journey to Saint Louis to obtain supplies for the summer rendezvous. They traveled first by bullboat down the Big

Horn, thereby avoiding treacherous rapids on the upper Yellowstone, then to the Yellowstone and on to the Missouri. They carried no furs.

After winter camp broke up and the visiting Crows drifted off to their spring hunting grounds, RMF cached its abundant autumn harvest. Our bunch, confident of the trustworthiness of the new partners, added the remainder of our fall catch to the RMF cache.

We were already there, so Bridger and Milt chose to trap the east side of the Divide. It was mostly Crow country, less likely to be troubled by Blackfoots, although nothing is ever certain in that regard. Its streams had lain mostly fallow for several years, untrapped by any large brigades. Their decision appeared to be sound, so we tagged along.

Trapping had hardly commenced when one of the worst misfortunes that can befall a trapper was visited upon us. Our horses were stolen. Leastaways, most of them, my darling Kumskaka, my Sugarfoot mule, and my prized bay horse Punch amongst them. Micah lost all of his and Tuttle cursed the loss of his beloved Chiksika, amongst several others. No one in our bunch came off unscathed. The horse guards had been knocked unconscious but none of them killed, which suggested that Crows, not Blackfoots, had made off with our critters.

The loudest cursing erupted from Gabe Bridger and Milton Sublette. Rocky Mountain Fur lost nearly all their stock, more than three hundred head, a crippling loss that would surely destroy their fledgling outfit. They lost no time in assembling a pursuit. Every able-bodied man capable of chasing the horsethieves afoot, nigh fourscore men, was ordered into service.

Naturally we weren't about to shirk. Brass Turtle, Little Mountain, Pretty Horse, Tuttle, Cesár, Micah, Finn, and I volunteered. Everyody wanted to go, but some had to stay behind in order to safeguard our women and children. Hardest to convince was Old Foot. He insisted that he was still the fleetest Delaware ever hatched.

Several free trappers who were stringing along with RMF got off scot-free. They lost nary a critter. They just laughed when Gabe tried to enlist them.

We set off immediately, carrying not much more than our weapons, extra moccasins, an Indian-style rope or leather bridle, and a poke of pemmican. Rainbow beamed when she bestowed a final hug and a fervent kiss on me, proud that her man was amongst the war party.

The booshways named a sturdy young French-Iroquois, Antoine Godin, to head up the pursuers. Joe Meek and his constant companion Doc Newell trotted at by Antoine's side.

There was no difficulty in following the trail left by nigh four hundred critters. Trail sign confirmed that the horsethieves were Absóraqas, at least twoscore men. Driving that many animals slowed them somewhat, but they were able to make better time than we did. We dog-trotted through snow and slush and mud, splashing across cricks, halting only to gulp a few mouthfuls of water and chew a bait of pemmican, then doubling our pace to catch up. Only nighfall forced Antoine to call a halt near a fast-running stream.

Most of us dropped in our tracks, grateful at last to rest our aching legs. When he caught his breath, Tuttle grinned and said through parched lips, "Sorta takes ye back, don't it, Temple? Time we chased arter thet'ere other bunch o' Crows, back on ther Yellerstone."

"It surely does," I replied. "An' I'm hopin' this time'll work out as good as that'n did."

"Aw, I reckon it'll be awright, 'less'n we cain't ketch 'em afore they git all ther way home." His grin was barely visible in the falling dusk. "Course, thi'shyar time we got ourse'fs nigh a hunnerd men along, pert'near enough to be takin' on ther whole gawddamn Crow Nation, don'tcha think?"

I laughed and allowed that it might be so. That other time we chased Crow horsethieves afoot, in 'twenty-two, a mere dozen of us, green as we were then, were willing to confront an entire Absóraqa village in order to reclaim our horses. And we succeeded.

When we returned from slaking our thirst at the crick, we were joined by Brass Turtle and Little Mountain. "How fur do ye reckon we come today?" Tuttle asked.

"Mebbe thutty mile, give or take," Turtle replied.

Tuttle grunted assent. "We oughter do some'at better tomorry, cornsid'rin' we got a late start this mawnin'."

I groaned inwardly. The last time I pursued horsethieves afoot for such a distance had been nearly a decade earlier, before I had acquired a passel of gunshot and arrow wounds. Naturally I said nothing about that.

"I been kickin' m'se'f fer lettin' them gawddamn Crows git away wi' this," Turtle lamented. "I should'a knowed better, the way them young bucks war allus eye-ballin' our critters in winter camp."

"'Tain't nobody's fault, perzackly," Tuttle assured him. "Reckon it comes from sharin' robes with a warm woman. It be dreadful hard keepin' yer mind on hosses at sech a time."

When the chuckles subsided Little Mountain observed grimly, "Dem Absorka no be t'inkin' woman ner hoss, needer, purty quick, I be t'inkin'. Dey be t'inkin' keepin' ha'r an' nuttin' else!"

That was a sentiment shared by everyone. I soon fell into deep sleep, huddled inside my capote, uncaring of chill night breezes and damp that seeped up from the soggy ground.

* * *

We were on our feet before dawn and on the track as soon as there was light enough to see, trotting out our aches and cramps, falling into a mindless rhythm of putting one muddy, soggy, slimy moccasin out in front of its mate, eyes fixed on the colorful capotes of the leaders, striving to pass the man in front or leastaways not to fall behind, letting your mind roam into a thousand nooks and crannies.

There was little palaver whenever Antoine called a halt for water and a brief respite from our everlasting trotting. Wetting and soothing parched throats and restoring our breathing took precedence over jesting and bragging about what we might do when we caught up with the Crows. Every time we halted, a couple-three men stayed behind, too exhausted to continue. Nobody blamed them.

Both days we ran past the ashes of half a dozen cookfires and an acre or more of trampled snow, where the horsethieves had spent the night before resuming their homeward flight.

When we quit at darktime, Pretty Horse, our best tracker, held up his hands, fingers splayed, six times, informing us that our quarry numbered sixty Crow warriors, half again as many as we had thought at first. By that time, howsomever, not a man amongst us would have cared if there were six hundred fire-breathing Absóraqas waiting ahead, so eager were we to end the pursuit. Fighting was infinitely preferable to dying from exhaustion.

* * *

Near the close of the third day, a dull orange springtime sun was dipping into the western hills when our stumbling mob came to lurching halt, the men in front holding a finger to their lips, signaling silence. Whispered word quickly spread amongst us that the chase was ended. The Crows, confident that they had safely outdistanced pursuit, had killed a buffalo or two and camped for the night.

After I rested I made my way through the crowd and up a slope to where Godin a few others were sprawled on the snowy ground. Antoine saw me coming and waved me on, signing to be quiet. I crawled on my belly the last few yards to the lip of an overhanging bluff. On the other side of a measly little crick was a rude log fort enclosing seven or eight crackling cookfires and more happy Indians than you'd expect to find on that windswept prairie. They were all young men, doubtless congratulating themselves on making their fortune at the expense of the hapless white-eyes. Pretty Horse hadn't erred. Easily sixty able warriors were stuffing themselves with fresh-killed meat.

Ranged along the crick, tethered to the willows, was what appeared to be an endless string of tethered horses and mules grazing on whatever grass or leaves they could forage. My pinched belly griped at the smell of roasting meat. Right then, I would have been happy take on that whole lot of Crows single-handed, just for a mouthful of smoking-hot hump.

Naturally I did no such a thing. I crawled to Godin's side. In a low voice he said, "Eet ees good you are yet wiv us, Tompo. We 'ave need of you an' *vos camarades. S'il vous plait,* choose t'ree *ou* four of zem for takin' *les* animaux from ze *crique. D'accord?* I cannot trus' zese *blanc-becs. Hein?"*

I told Antoine that I would be happy to choose a few men from our bunch to retrieve the animals from alongside the crick and that I would join my fellows in that worthy endeavor, especially considering that he didn't trust his greenhorns. Fact is, it was a risky chore. Godin didn't wish to lose any RMF men in the attempt. So much for flattery.   Just the same, I was happy to take part in getting our critters back. We couldn't afford to fail and I didn't trust most of his greenhorns, either.

I crawled away from the bluff and hastened to my people. Brass Turtle, Little Mountain, Pretty Horse, Cesár, and I, together with Godin and whomever he picked, would steal across the crick, cut the tethers, and drive the horses and mules up the bank to our waiting comrades. Micah wanted to come along, but getting our livestock away from the Crows might turn into a bloody affair. I wasn't sure that Micah had the stomach for the kind of killing that would likely occur, so I refused. Fact is, I wasn't altogether sure that I did, either.

As always, waiting to go was almost as bad as doing the chore, but at last the cookfires burned to coals and the Crows, confident that no white-eyes pursuers could have closed the distance, rolled up in their robes.

The camp settled into silence. Authority and discipline are civilized affectations virtually unknown amongst Plains Indians. Individual bravery is what counts. It's mostly a matter of every man for himself. Sentries are usually voluntary and because these Crows appeared to be all grown men, with no half-grown boys assigned to watch the herd, there was a good chance that our initial efforts would go undetected. Leastaways, we hoped so.

After an eternity of waiting, Antoine gave the signal. Besides himself, Godin had chosen Meek and Doc, the Irish singer, and a few other Company men, one of whom, I noticed with satisafaction, was the tall, lean Pennsylvanian Simon Pence. Then, rifles slung, primed pistols snug in our belts, we cautiously made our way down the bank and waded across the crick. We quickly spread out, slashing every picket line we encountered. Once freed, the thirsty horses naturally headed for water, crowding into the crick. Later arrivals pushed the leaders onto the far bank, where eager hands grabbed up their tie-ropes and trappers led them up the slope. It was lonely work. Ears straining for a cry of alarm, I worked feverishly, slicing tethers with my knife and chopping with my tomahawk, until I bumped into Little Mountain.

His teeth flashed in a grin in the faint light of a mere sliver of moon. "I be t'inkin' mebbe we got all of 'em," he growled. "Ye kilt some Absorka?" I told him that I hadn't. He sighed. "Me needer. Mebbe purty quick we git to killin' some. Ye t'ink, mebbe?" I did not share his disappointment. We parted, each of us scurrying along the bank, making sure that no critter had been overlooked.

I was slicing the tie-rope of the last remaining horse I had discovered when the inevitable whoop of alarm stabbed through the darkness, followed by a babble of yips and angry shouts from the Crow camp, then the drum of hoofbeats and Antoine Godin's triumphant yell as he thundered past me, waving a long-haired scalp, streaking for a break in the willows along the crick. Immediately behind him were Meek, Newell, and Yeats, also a-horseback, laughing like loons. Simon Pence brought up the rear, elbows cocked, capote flapping, a veritable equestrian scarecrow.

I looped the tie-rope around the pony's jaw for a makeshift bridle and grabbed a fistful of mane, preparing to mount, when a thunderous volley of gunshots erupted from the bank above. I swung aboard, wincing as I landed upon the pony's sharp backbone, then, yanking his head one way and another, drumming my heels on his bony ribs, I raced for the opening on the streambank, whooping and hollering, crowding the last few laggardly horses and mules across the water and up the bank.

By time I reached level ground, only scattered gunshots, the sharp crack of rifles and hollow reports of muskets, came from the ridge — then silence, save the outraged shouts of Absóraqas in their fort. Half a hundred trappers streamed off the ridge and disappeared into the mob of milling horses, held more or less in place by riders doing their best to herd them together.

A grinning Brass Turtle appeared out of the gloom. "Best we git ever' last critter," he yelled, "so's them Crows cain't be comin' arter us!" He burst into laughter. "Let them gawddamn sumbitches be walkin' home!"

Which we succeeded in doing. We saw neither hide nor hair of the Crows after that.

* * *

When every trapper was mounted, we pushed the herd southwards. With so many drovers it was not difficult to keep the tired critters moving together. As soon as I could, I swapped my bony Indian nag for another, but he was hardly better. The Crows had pushed the stolen herd to the limit and beyond, rarely letting them drink and close-herding them during their brief overnight halts, so they were unable to graze. They were gant, spiritless, weak as cats, many hardly able to bear the weight of a rider.

That first night we were no kinder to the critters than the Crows had been, anxious as we were to put miles between ourselves and the Crows. So far I hadn't come across any of my own horses or my Sugarfoot mule, but when daylight poked above the eastern rim I spied Kumskaka. I could have wept. His proud head drooped and his sunken flanks and neck and ribby barrel showed the loss of a hundredweight of flesh or more. I didn't ride him, reckoning that RMF owed me the use of their nags for the return journey.

When Tuttle spied me he urged his mount through the herd to join me, a huge grin stretching his stubbly cheeks. "Happy to see ye, hoss!" he crowed. "Ye look like ye come through it 'thout nuthin' bad happ'nin' to ye!" I assured him that it was so, that I hadn't even laid eyes on a Crow. "Wal, I shore as hell did!" he cackled. "A gawddamn passel of 'em! When them Injuns heared ther critters makin' sech a racket a-splashin' inter ther crick, them sumbitches come a-b'ilin' out'n thet'ere piddly-arse fort o' their'n like piss-ants spillin' out'n a holler log. Thet's when we opened up on 'em from up on ther ridge! Ever'body shootin' all at oncet! Galena flyin' ever'whar! Like shootin' fish in a bar'l! Begawd, it war a purty sight! Dead hossthiefs fallin' daown ever'whar!"

A year or so later we learned that the Absóraqa loss amounted to seven dead and many more wounded. Our little army got off with nary a scratch.

Whilst we trotted southwards I gathered the rest of my critters, lest someone choose one of them for a mount. All the free men did the same, cutting their own critters out of the herd and riding the RMF stock, swapping mounts frequently. Bridger and Milt would have done likewise. Sugarfoot showed less wear and tear than the horses, which wasn't surprising. Mules are easier keepers than horses. Even so, I didn't ride him, either.

My poke of pemmican was long since used up, but, hungry as I was, I would have gladly swapped all of next week's vittles for a saddle. The critters' bony backbones threatened to unman me. Straddling my capote helped somewhat, but trotting without stirrups over that snowy, mucky prairie was still painful. Walking was too slow to stay ahead and loping was out of the question if we hoped to deliver our starveling charges to the Company.

When the sun was high in the sky that first day we spied a little bunch of buffalo. Several of us immediately rode out and killed half a dozen. The meat, hastily roasted over sagebrush fires, was charred and half raw, but Lucullus never dined as happily as our mob did that day.

The journey we had accomplished afoot in three days required more than a week for the horseback return, by which time we mud-spattered trappers weren't much fatter than our scrawny charges. Happily, we had lost not a single critter and we delivered sixty-three Crow ponies for boot.

No army's triumphant return from the wars ever provoked a more enthusiastic welcome from the stay-at-homes than ours did when we pushed nigh four hundred rack-ribbed horses and mules into camp on the eighth day. Men cheered and women trilled happified hosannas to our success. Smiling Powatawa held my daughter high above his head and the rest of our bunch swarmed to greet us, dragging us to the ground, smothering us with grizzly hugs. Gabe Bridger and Milt Sublette were downright delirious at the sight of their precious herd, but not nearly as happy as Rainbow was to welcome me or I to be reunited with her. Filthy and bone-tired though I was, I could not decline her ardent embraces that night, leastaways until I passed out in the midst of our love-making.

* * *

We remained pretty much in that neighborhood for nigh a fortnight, moving every day or so to fresh graze for the livestock. Day and night herd guards were tripled, lest the Absóraqa seek revenge, but it appeared they had learned a hard lesson, leastaways for a spell. Rainbow coddled me with rich broths and stuffed me with as much fat meat as I could hold. In our robes she clasped me in close embrace throughout the night, murmuring Salish lovetalk and running her fingers over my gaunt ribs, clucking her displeasure.

My daughter had somehow divined the gravity of our mission against the Crows. She refused to let me out of her sight, clutching my hand and toddling beside me as I went about my chores, her prattle now mostly in English, to please me, I reckon. She was fully two years old by then, growing like a weed and becoming more precious every day.

"I'm thinkin' we oughter go chasin' arter hossthiefs ever' once't'awhile," Tuttle opined one day whilst we lounged around a cookfire, peeling bark for horse feed. "Muh Dolly cain't be doin' enough fer me, day an' night, naow we're back. A feller gits right fond o' thet'ere kind o' 'tention, don'tcha know."

"Enjoy your en-joys whilst ye kin, Tuttle," Brass Turtle observed wryly. "Time's a-wastin' fer the spring hunt. Purty soon thar won't be time fer nothin''sides beaver, fer man ner woman, neither." His tone softened, howsomever, when he added, "Which ain't to say, mind ye, I ain't 'preciatin' all the extry lovin' I been gittin' from Tally."

No work and ample feed soon let the critters regain their fettle. Ribs disappeared under hard fat, necks and flanks filled out, and heads were once again held high. Trapping time could commence.

Our bunch chose to go along with Milton Sublette for the spring hunt. We had enjoyed good luck with Milt. He had never failed to give us a proper patch of territory that repaid hard work with a bountiful harvest. Wild as Milton often is on his own, he is always a thoughtful, caring leader of his brigade.

The day before we quit camp, Gabe Bridger and Milton and a couple other men rode in, leading eight stout horses. "Ain't nothin' but fair y'oughter git some gain fer yer good work, follerin' arter them'ere Crows like ye done," Jim announced. "These hyar be some o' them Absorkee ponies y'all brung back along with our'n."

"Damn betcha!" Milton seconded. "Ye be desarvin' more, but it'll hafta wait 'til ronnyvoo! We'll be makin' it up to ye come summer."

Those of us who had gone on the raid drew lots for the critters. I got to choose a handsome piebald mare, which I gifted to Rainbow. Fact was, howsomever, I already had more critters than I needed or wished to look after. That was also the case with Tuttle, Turtle, and Cesár. After supper I cut out of our cavvy the tall sorrel gelding I had acquired at the Forks. Then the four of us led gift horses over to the

Company. When I presented the sorrel to Simon Pence, at first he refused to accept the horse. "Take 'im," I insisted. "Ye deserve to own a critter of your own. You owe me nothin'. Thankee for comin' along, chasin' Crows an' doin' what ye did." At last he took hold of the lead rope and mumbled his thanks as we parted.

Riding back to our camp I learned that Meek and Doc and the Irish spear-chucker were now horse-owners, as well. They had earned every hoof and hide that scary night in the Crow camp.

* * *

Absóraqa country was no longer a good place to ply our trade that spring, but greed prevailed and we didn't retreat to the west immediately. The RMF brigades, with us free trappers alongside, spread out to trap the streams on the eastern side of the Divide before we topped the long belt of mountains the Indians call the Backbone of the World and descended into the country of the usually-friendly Snakes.

Whilst we were still on the eastern side of the Divide, combing the canyons for dammed-up ponds and bankside burrows, every day adding fresh beaver plews to the already sizeable clutter of hides curing on willow hoops in camp, we came upon a most remarkable prodigy. I was tending traps that day with my father and Ned Godey, nearly finished with our chore, congratulating ourselves on our successful haul, when the wind shifted to the south. Powatawa wrinkled his nose and spat. "That be one bad stink," he pronounced. Ned and I smelled it, too, immediately recalling a similar rotten-egg odor we had encountered years before near one of the streams that feed the Yellowstone. Powatawa hadn't been with us at that time, so we told him about it, the while itching to learn the source of the familiar stench. It drew us like a lodestone.

We slung our bloody plews from a high branch for safekeeping and trotted off in the direction of the dreadful smell. A quarter-mile hike dispelled our wondering. We came upon a murky blue-green crick reeking of sulphur, spilling out from between high canyon walls on which not a single tree or shrub was growing. Inching our way upstream on a narrow ledge through the gap, the stink growing ever stronger, our ears beset with increasing din, we soon discovered the source of the malodorous emanations.

The ravine abruptly opened into a large flat bowl that justified and exceeded by far the dire predictions of hellfire preachers haranguing and cowing their errant flocks with threats of Divine punishment. Powatawa's hand flew to his mouth as he beheld the precincts of every evil spirit enshrined in Shawnee religious lore and likely several other imps so far unmentioned by the medicine men.

We confronted gurgling, hissing pools of bubbling blue-green water, half-blinding and choking us with sulphurous yellow steam, gigantic spouts of boiling water and gobs of mud shooting skywards, ear-splitting explosions and ominous underground rumblings, whistling shrieks of ten thousand teakettles gone mad, and smoking tar pits spewing sizzling black pitch onto barren ground. Coughing and spitting, we hastily retreated. Our moccasins broke through crusty earth, scalding our feet in muddy hot water, as we mostly felt our way along the riverbank and gained safety on the other side of the gap.

Without a word spoken amongst us, we took to our heels and ran back to the stream where we had inhaled our first whiff of Satan's fetid breath. Up to our waists in clear-flowing water, drenching off the sulphurous stink, we laughed like coyotes, splashing one another and congratulating ourselves on having gone to hell and back.

On the bank, shaking off water like wet dogs, we recounted what each of us had seen and felt in Lucifer's stomping ground. Ned suddenly grew half-serious. "Gawddamn! I'm wond'rin' if'n we ain't jist been whar ol' John Colter said he war, back when he war workin' fer ol' Lisa, lookin' up Crow winter camps an' tellin' 'em to come in fer tradin', 'stid o' whar we war on the Yellerstone back in 'twenny-six."

Ned and I told my father at greater length how we had once found refuge from a large Blackfoot war party by retreating into such a place of boiling waterspouts, hot sulphur springs, and suchlike, which the Blackfoots refused to enter on account of evil spirits dwelling there. We assured him, howsomever, that that place had not been nearly so fearsome as what we had just witnessed and that it turned out to be downright pleasant, once you got used to all the noise and hot water.

"Yep," Godey averred, "I'm wagerin' this'n be whar he war, 'stid of our'n. Ol' Manuel built hisse'f a tradin' fort right whar the Big Horn gits to the Yellerstone, not too fur off from hyar."

From everything that Ned had learned when he worked for Manuel Lisa, a few years after Colter quit the mountains and returned to the settlements, it appeared that what we had seen had been a glimpse into John Colter's Hell. "Maybe so," I told Ned, "but ye can be pretty sure nobody'll believe we saw hell on earth today, any more'n they did old Mister Colter."

Which was so, back in camp, until our comrades took to sniffing the sulphur smell on our clothes and allowed that perhaps we were telling the truth, after all.

* * *

As it always is, the spring harvest was a frenzied rush to grab every possible close-haired plew from the chill waters of every pond and along the streambanks before summer warmth thinned the fur. Those were shining times indeed and much safer than the Three Forks. "Thim little darlin's are drawin' straws, I tell ye," Paddy McBride insisted, "seein' who's to be first into me traps!" He wasn't far off the mark.

Once over the summit, in Snake country, we all breathed a little easier by day and slept more soundly in our robes. Granted, Shoshones, too, will steal your horses. Given half a chance, all Indians will. It's a matter of challenge and daring, pride, wealth, and prestige with them. But the Snakes bore no recent grudges against the likes of us, leastaways none that we knew about.

When Rocky Mountain Fur moved off towards the Seeds-kee-dee we remained in the high country, scouring headwater cricks and streams that no American trapper had ever seen. Beaver abounded. Ere long our pack animals struggled under unwieldy loads whenever we moved from one camp to another, seeking graze for our critters and ever more plews. Indians on the move generally travel along buffalo trails, but there are few buffalo in that high, broken country, where grass is scant, so we escaped the notice of Blackfoot raiders and ambitious Shoshone horsethieves alike. We lived mostly on beaver and an occasional deer or wapiti — and one grizzly bear that unwisely wandered into camp — but nobody minded. Come rendezvous, there would be fat hump and meaty ribs aplenty.

Hard as trapper's work is, our women worked much harder, scraping and stretching pelts when they weren't cooking and mending, tidying lodges, making and washing clothes, foraging for roots and berries, and tending critters, besides looking after the little ones and us men. Before we wived, we had shifted well enough for ourselves, but now, if we tried to lend a hand, they shooed us off with sharp words, declaring that such work isn't proper for men to do. The women's attitude was a powerful argument for wedlock for the bachelors amongst us. Only the campkeepers, Dureau and L'Archévêque, were allowed to join the women in their labors.

In spite of her exertions during daylight hours, Rainbow reached into what seemed to be a bottomless well of strength to comfort me each day when I returned from my trapline, stripping off my sodden moccasins and iced-over leggin's, rubbing warmth into my half-frozen feet and legs, feeding me rich broths, meaty soups thick with flavorful roots and herbs, and fat meat, and later, when Iris drifted off into slumber, arousing me with robe games that never failed to surprise and delight.

As you might suppose, traveling in double harness wasn't always smooth going for all of our benedicts. The buffalo-hide walls of lodges grant little privacy when tempers flare. Only Ned Godey and Cat appeared to have no difficulties — except for Cat's continued childless state, which Rainbow told me was a matter of constant regret for her. The miffs and spats of the others were usually short-lived, resulting in hardly more than a brief spell of yelling and long faces. Once they take an Indian wife, few trappers are willing to forego the comforts provided by their bedmate and slavey. And most Indian women agree that no matter how coarse and uncaring her trapper man might be, she is still likely better off with him than with his redskin counterpart.

* * *

Even though winter snows clung to the mountain slopes much longer than on the plains, springtime warmth thinned out beaver plews at last. Sometime in mid-May, Brass Turtle opined, "Time we be thinkin' on leavin' some fer seed an' gittin' on down to ronnyvoo." It was a welcome suggestion. Even greed has its limits.

"Indade! 'Tis a capital thought!" Finn McCool declared. "'Tis intirely too long I've denied me appetites! 'Tis past toime I be indulgin' some of 'em!" He paused dramatically and added, "P'raps all of 'em — an' possibly a few I've not yet acquired."

"The critters'll be thankin' ye, too," Micah said with a grin. "Many more plews'll surely be breakin' their backs. Enough's enough."

Micah and Finn had both altered tremendously during their three years in the mountains, especially Micah. His shyness had disappeared, replaced by confidence in his own ability, bolstered by the acceptance he earned amongst our bunch and from trappers who know and respect him for his cool courage and his many skills. Unlike Jim Beckwith, there is no brag in Micah. Newcomers to the mountains are often advised early-on to put aside their fancied superiority over the color of his hide, lest they learn otherwise the hard way.

The Irishman has never suffered from a lack of self-assurance. Finn came to the mountains well-equipped with what he needed to survive and prosper — flexible intelligence and an open mind, strength and endurance, steadfastness and bravery when required, ever-ready good humor, and what Tuttle and I reckon to be equally important, an innate love and understanding of horses. He tolerates no settlement nonsense about his Irishness and he is quick — often eager — to discourage such foolishness amongst ignorant greenhorns. An Irishman dearly loves a brawl.

My other protégé, my father, slid almost seanmlessly into mountain life, new knowledge and custom melding smoothly with what he had known and done almost from birth, possibly what he inherited in his blood. The principal and most remarkable change in Powatawa is that he appears to grow younger every year, sloughing off the stiff dignity and restraint that burdened him during the long years of his reluctant leadership of his Shawnee band.

Naturally our women were delighted to be going to rendezvous, expecting to see their people again. The camp disappeared almost by magic, the packs sorted and assembled in no time at all, and our sizeable caravan set upon the trail to Willow Valley the following day.

The descent from the high mountain slopes was a pleasant one, especially when we spied our first small bunch of buffalo. Our first feast on young bull was a merry affair. We gorged ourselves on fat hump ribs and tender backstrap, fresh liver gobbled up raw, tongue bubbling in kettles, and boudins sizzling in spiders or on the coals. We were in no hurry, so we indulged ourselves in many such wilderness banquets as we made our way to the appointed gathering place.

Long hours in the saddle every day passed swiftly for me, entertained as I was with my daughter straddling my saddle bow and prattling excitedly about everything she spied along the way, easy-going palaver and swapping jests and yarns with my fellows, and sometimes merely feasting my eyes on the sight of Rainbow, relieved now of hard chores in trapping camp, riding serenely alone, a quiet smile on her beautiful face, wrapped in her thoughts or gossiping with Cat and the other women.

As we dropped lower on the trail and the weather warmed, we often chose to forego the privacy of our lodge, simply spreading our robes under trees or in a grassy glade, apart from the others, making love under a counterpane of diamonds flung onto endless black velvet, afterwards chatting softly of simple things in our personal language pieced together from her native tongue and my own. When at last she slept, I often lay awake, gazing at the beauty of her face and form limned in moonlight, marveling that I should be gifted with such a miracle.

Naturally we became increasingly alert as we neared the prairies, although we are never free of caution. Springtime fosters not only green grass and aspen leaves, but also Blackfoots on the prowl for plunder and glory. On nights when I finished my stint at horse guard and crept into our robes, Rainbow was always awake, welcoming me into her arms, nuzzling my throat and laving me with kisses, inviting further intimacy. The hard parts of mountain life disappear in memories of such natural delights.

* * *

Riding pell-mell and hell-for-leather into rendezvous, dressed in our best, long hair and feathers flying, shooting guns in the air and whooping like a band of Indians — which more than half of us really are — proved to be a disappointment. The white trade tents surrounded by a scattering of trappers' bowers and Indian encampments were not those of Rocky Mountain Fur. They belonged instead to Pierre Chouteau's two brigades, American Fur's under Lucien Fontenelle and Andrew Drips, the other commanded by Cadet's shirttail relative Joseph Robidoux.

These were Cadet's long-lost trading missions that failed to arrive in time for last summer's rendezvous on the Popo-azhieh. Reluctant to return to Saint Louis empty-handed, they elected to hang around the neighborhood, trapping with their crew of hostlers and other greenhorns and the few free trappers who tagged along with them. Which activity turned out mostly unsuccessful. They wintered in Willow Valley and returned there after a meager spring harvest.

Problem was, most of their trade goods had been used up by their own men during the fall, winter, and spring, leastaways the kind of supplies that trappers need to survive and continue trapping. Yard goods and foofurraw can't replace gunpowder and galena.

Their liquor was mostly used up, as well, which was also a cause of considerable disappointment. Not only for trappers. The Indians grumbled, too, but there was no remedy available. "Ain't nuthin' else fer it," Ned counseled. "We jist gotta put a poultice on it an' keep on waitin' fer Fitz." It was sound advice but nonetheless a bitter pill to swallow.

Weeks dragged into a month and more and still no sign of the packtrain. Grover Weed, who by then everybody called Buzzard, and several other free men rode in one day and told us that Gabe and Milt and their brigades were waiting on the Seeds-kee-dee, but Fitzpatrick had failed to show up there, either. Trappers, RMF and free men alike, were getting uneasy. The fall hunt was fast approaching and powder and lead were running low for everybody, let alone all the other necessary plunder trappers need to survive in the mountains.

Naturally we were just as short of needed goods and just as thirsty as everybody else, but fortunately we had an ace up our sleeve. We could get by in the skinny months ahead. We still had our cache near Sweet Lake, untouched in three years, which contained much of what I had brought to the mountains in 'twenty-eight. My companions and I had stocked up on Bill Sublette's supplies at that rendezvous and put by my gifts against future skinny times. The cache, if it was still there, not robbed or flooded out, might provide enough plunder to let us scrape through the autumn harvest.

Naturally we did a little trading with American Fur and Robidoux, rewarding our women for their hard work with yard goods and gewgaws, but we held back most of our plews for RMF. The new partners had treated us honestly and well. We believed that we owed our trade to our old friends.

Summer was drawing down by time we bade farewell to Fontenelle and Andy Drips and Joe Robidoux and set off for Sweet Lake. They were decent enough men, but our loyalty lay elsewhere. Besides, McKenzie's trading guns to Blackfoots still rankled. Iron Bow's Flathead band had failed to show at Willow Valley and so had the Crows. The Snakes, disappointed by the lack of arms, proper trade goods, and booze, had already departed. All of our women came with us, which was just as well, for we intended to go directly to join RMF on the Seeds-kee-dee after we raised our cache.

On the way, at a place sufficiently distant from Willow Valley, we cached our plews, intending to retrieve them on our return trip. They were an unnecessary burden and an inviting target for Indian raiders. From there on we made good time, but we didn't hurry. We took time each day to harvest a buffalo and give the women a chance to forage for roots and herbs, nuts and berries, and other truck they use in our daily fare. Now and then they clubbed a porcupine for its quills and the rich fat meat provided a welcome stew.

That journey stands out in memory as the best traveling I have ever done. Food never tasted so good before or since, meat never so tender and flavorful, colors never again so vivid and vibrant, the sounds of forest and prairie, the camp and the trail, so resonant with natural music — birdsong and the ring of an axe biting into firewood, the grunting of buffalo and the jingle of hawkbells on leggin's and saddlepads, an Irish voice raised in carefree song, Tolliver's sweet fiddle whenever he surrendered to tender feeling, the plaintive paeans of coyotes at dusk — and especially the sound of Rainbow's voice, her crystal-pure laughter when she and Cat shared a jest, her throaty murmurs when we coupled in darkness in a faraway land that only she and I will ever know. Even the palaver of my comrades returns in memory as more witty, profound, and penetrating than from any other time and place.

Or perhaps it merely appears that way in recollection, compared with the end of that idyllic journey. But that will come later.

A time or two our outriders spied what appeared to be an Indian raiding party on the move. At such times we halted, concealed in a forest or a deep coulee, and waited until they passed.

Our leisurely pace allowed Rainbow and me to enjoy each other's company, day and night, as well as sharing our daughter's delight in discovering the miracles she spied along the way. How I could have though myself happy before I teamed up with Rainbow was, and still is, a mystery. So much so that I blundered into saying as much to sour Anse Tolliver one day while we rode side by side. I went even further when I carelessly remarked, "It's a puzzle, Anse. How come ye haven't taken up with a woman of your own by now."

I immediately regretted my words. He harrumphed and swung a steely gaze my way. The damage was done. "Swivin' don't hafta lead to wivin', nohaow, Temple Buck! Me an' muh fiddle gits all the squars we're wantin', come ronnyvoo an' winter camp, 'thout draggin' one of 'em along when I don't want 'er 'round! Don't mind cookin' an' fetchin' fer myownse'f, like I allus done, an' I shore-as-hell don't need no sniv'lin' brats snatchin' at muh claout an' callin' me pappy!"

He paused to catch his breath, but he wasn't finished. "Wivin' ain't fer ever'body! Take yer pard Tuttle, fer one! 'Tain't all huggin' an' kissin' fer him, no more, as I daresay ye awready know! Thar's a ruckus comin' out'n that'ere lodge o his'n ever' gawddamn night, 'count o' his squar raisin' hell 'baout Tuttle allus slippin' 'round them Injun camps at ronnyvoo an' winter camp!"

I sighed and nodded agreement. Anse was right. Old habits are hard to break and Tuttle's go all the way to the bone. Whiskey, gambling, horses, and an endless variety of women are the air that Tuttle breathes. No man could ask for a better companion than Tuttle Thompson, but his appetites don't fit well with connubial felicity.

Anse was still muttering his disapproval of the married state. "Me? I'd be lodgepolin' 'er, like Injuns do, 'til she shets up, but I cain't feature Thompson doin' it! Tough as he kin be when he has to, Tuttle's got a soft spot fer squars. He'll be puttin' up with 'er 'til she quits 'im! Yew'll see." Anse paused and allowed himself an evil grin. "Yep, Thompson's got hisse'f a soft spot fer squars, awright, but whar-in-hell he keeps it shorely ain't under his britchclaout!" He broke into a wild cackle, overcome by his own witticism, spun his saddle mule about, and, still chuckling, rode back to look after his pack animals.

I mused over Anse's remarks. It's true, double harness isn't right for everybody. Godey and I were blessed with good, beautiful women. Paddy couldn't be happier than he is with his plump little Molly. Tuttle will likely never find just one woman to satisfy him. Brass Turtle, quick as he is to speak his mind, is, howsomever, private about the life he leads in Tallymesko's lodge. The domestic situations of Pretty Horse and Stone Bird will remain forever a mystery. And that is just as well.

Our bachelors appeared to be content with their single state. No new liaisons had occurred at Willow Valley, leastaways not lasting ones. Some of them just weren't ready. Some never will be. It is unwise to inquire about such matters. I reflected ruefully on my palaver with Anse. I had got what I deserved. I had stepped over the line. Uncle Ben would have chided me for "meddlin'."

Thinking about Tuttle's woman Dolly and her jealous assertion of her rights, objecting to Tuttle's philandering in a manner that would never be tolerated by an Indian husband, led me to a recollection of something I had read long before by the French *philosophe* Rousseau, who argued that revolutions are born out of hope, not despair.

Dolly, released from the iron traditions and restrictive customs of her Shoshone bringing-up, was tasting freedom for the first time. She was absolutely drunk on it. Problem was, like most drunks, she was having trouble finding her way home. Difficult as living with Tuttle's philandering might be for her, going back to the Snakes meant losing her new-found freedom, likely returning to a life of thankless hard work and abuse. It was a conundrum that only Dolly would solve, if she could.

Thinking on it, it came to me that Dolly's plight wasn't much different from that of all of us mountaineers. Our life is fraught with peril. Sudden death might show up at any moment. Hardship and privation are commonplace. Which might be avoided by returning to the safety of the settlements. Safe as that might be, it means losing the absolute freedom we know and cherish in the mountains, trading our precious liberty for a life of toil and drudgery and bowing to a boss. No mountaineer worth his salt would give it a second thought. We'll be staying in the mountains, thankee.

* * *

The cache had suffered little in three years. The canvas scraps and hides at the mouth were moldy and rotten, but the plunder below had been well-protected from seeping moisture by the carefully-woven latticework of willows on the sides and ground beneath. Most welcome was the plenitude of gunpowder, galena, shot, and percussion caps. A trapper might yearn for all manner of settlement goods, but he can do without all of it, save for a reliable, plumb-center-shooting gun, ammunition, and a good knife or two. With those items in hand he can live well enough and even prosper Indian-fashion. Without them, he is doomed.

There was tobacco and well-made English knives, sturdy Manchester traps to replace those stolen at the Forks and the few carried off into deep water by beaver not yet drowned, trade goods and tools, harness needles and packthread, all sorts of yard goods, needles and thread, and foofurraw for the women, coffee, tea, sugar, honey and molasses, black pepper and sea salt, dried beans and such, and much else. Best of all was the curved metal keg, still nearly half-full of fine French brandy, that I had carried up from Saint Louis three years before.

Our Irishmen were most vocal in their appreciation of those excellent spirits. "May the rainbow be sure to follow each rainstorm that falls upon ye," McCool solemnly pronounced. "And may that rain fall soft upon your back an' the sun shine warm upon your face."

Not to be outdone, Paddy chimed in with, "An' may the wind be fair and always at your back an' the road rise up to meet ye!" He swigged a gulp and added, "But not too quick or steep, mind ye!"

"Naow, Tuttle," Ned Godey called out, raising his brimming cup in a toast of his own, "ain'tcha glad ye din't drink up all o' thi'shere fine Frenchy booze, back thar on Sweet Lake?"

Tuttle didn't reply immediately. He looked thoughtful before he said seriously, "Mebbe so. Right naow, I be, fer damn sure. But livin' hyarabaouts makes a feller like me grab onto whatever pleasurin' comes along, right naow, 'thout no savin' up an' puttin' by. Ain't no tellin' ef'n you're still gonna be livin' later on, what with Injuns an' grizzle b'ars, catamounts an' snakes, an' gawd-knows-what-else a-waitin' jest a-hind o' ye, fixin' to put a stop to all o' yer earthly pleasures. Ever' swaller an' ev'ry new woman ye bed mought be ther last'un you're ever gonna git! Best ye git yer en-joys whilst ye kin!" He fell silent, staring at the ground, then raised his head and grinned and lifted his cup. "So what the hell! Drink up! Ain't nobody what kin be sure abaout tomorry!"

A few chuckles greeted his unexpectedly serious pronouncement, then grew to general laughter and scattered remarks such as "Damn right!" Tuttle had voiced what we all knew was so. In the mountains, we live on a razor's edge betwixt hearty, healthy living and eternal nothingness. It's best to live that life to the fullest while we still can.

The women joined us men in repeated toasts to our regained riches. Even little Iris was permitted a sip or two from her mother's cup, which soon caused her eyelids to droop. Which was not unwelcome. Rainbow and I continued our celebration in our robes soon afterwards.

Before we retired, Rainbow presented me with a beautiful padded apishamore, a saddlepad decorated with intricate, colorful quillwork, fringed with shiny, tinkling hawkbells, the product of many hours stolen from her labors when I was out of sight. Her dark eyes glowed with pleasure in the flickering firelight as I expressed my delight with that handsome and useful token of her affection. Its beauty faded to unimportance, howsomever, when she slipped her dress over her head and I beheld her slim, full-breasted, naked body before she took me in her arms and drew me down beside her in our robes.

* * *

Rainbow was already at the cookfire, preparing a tasty pease porridge, when I slipped out of the lodge and trotted to a nearby thicket to perform my morning chore. Before we ate, howsomever, she caught my hand and pulled me along to a secluded spot on the crick, where we swam and frolicked like a pair of young otters in the chill water, her nipples hardening like unripe berries, which, naturally, I did not neglect to taste.

Afterwards, we sat in the bright sunshine, wolfing down our porridge. We were soon joined by Micah and Turtle and his woman, who finished off the kettle. Whilst Rainbow and Tallymesko carried the cups and such to the crick, we men lazed about, drinking coffee thick with long-untasted sugar, smoking and talking about the best route to the Seeds-kee-dee.

The sharp chatter of a magpie stilled our palaver, alerting us to visitors espied by the horse guards. We grabbed up our rifles, never far from a trapper's hand, and listened for another signal. A second magpie squawk followed by a songbird's trill prompted Turtle to say in a low voice, "Thar be Gai-bi-shuh, Bannocks, comin' on. Best we git ready fer 'em."

All over camp our people were doing just that, men darting into bowers and lodges, emerging with belts and sashes bristling with weapons. Cat and Molly and the other women swept up the children and carried them out of sight. Men scattered along the edge of camp, watching a score of horsemen walking their mounts across the prairie, calling out and firing their muskets in the air to show peaceful intent, as they drew nigh. We saw, howsomever, that they reloaded before they dismounted and advanced, broad smiles on their faces, hands held high in friendly gesture.

They appeared to be a jolly bunch, young men in their early twenties, if even that old, but not a man amongst us failed to recall our last brush with Bannocks three years earlier. It had been a bloody encounter, not one that the Gai-bi-shuh were likely to forget. Still, we were in a quandary. Short of declaring war and opening fire, we were obliged to put up with them as long as they minded their manners.

Brass Turtle, Ned Godey, and Pretty Horse walked out to meet them, rifles slung, signing peace. Turtle presented a carrot of tobacco to their apparent leader, a big, ugly buck, who pulled out a pipe from his otterskin pipebag, then folded into a sitting position, along with a couple other Bannocks, and filled his pipe. Our greeters did likewise, sitting on the prairie, passing the pipe, palavering in signs, whilst the rest of us looked on, trigger-fingers itching, but obliged to wait it out.

At last they all got to their feet and our diplomats returned to camp, a half-dozen Bannocks on their heels, the unwelcome visitors looking as cheerful as parsons come for Sunday dinner. When our women saw them coming, they scurried about scooping up kettles, cups, bridles, axes, and anything else that our long-fingered guests might take a fancy to. Always curious, my daughter kept darting from behind Rainbow's skirts to see the visitors, only to be hauled back by her mother, suspicious as all Indians are of any people but their own.

Brass Turtle came nigh and growled, "Don'tcha take yer eyes off'n 'em fer so much as a blink — an' keep yer irons primed. I'd as lief shoot 'em now, but if'n we do, some of our own blood'll be runnin' with their'n." It was a sound assessment. We were whipsawed. Our women and children put us at a disadvantage.

At first the Bannocks were reasonably respectful, wandering amongst our people, smiling and chatting in sign, peering into bowers like curious kids at a fair. I stuck close to our lodge, alert, nerves strung tight as a bowstring. Rainbow shooed Iris inside and followed her there, pulling the flap closed as she did.

Before long a bare-chested young buck, clad only in britchclout and leggin's, bow and quiver slung over his back, sauntered nigh and asked me in sign where we had come from and where we might be going, making what you might call small-talk. Before I could reply, Iris streaked out of the lodge, anxious to get a better look at the unfamiliar Indian, closely followed by her irate mother. Mildly startled at first, the Bannock quickly recovered and grinned, showing broken, blackened teeth, when he got a proper look at my pretty wife, who had caught hold of my daughter and was pulling her back to the lodge.

The buck's hands flew in a flurry of obscene finger-signs and he burst into raucous laughter at his daring wit. Rainbow never tolerated disrespect from any man, Indian or White. Red-faced, she turned Iris loose and responded with gestures that questioned the Bannock's manhood and his ability to perform what he offered. Before I could move, he swung his arm and slashed her cheek with the riding whip dangling from his wrist. Rainbow fell back with a howl and a whimper. Before I quite knew what I did, I smashed my rifle butt against the buck's head, sending him sprawling, likely dead.

I leaped towards my woman as an arrow whirred past me and struck Rainbow in the breast, embedded nigh to the feathers. I whirled to see another grinning Bannock nocking a second arrow to his bowstring. Without conscious thought I fired a shot that took him plumb in the belly, sending him into a crazy backward dance until he fell writhing upon his back, then lay unmoving. Suddenly the whole camp boiled with yelling Bannocks running wild, brandishing muskets, knives, and bows. Gunfire erupted from every quarter and the hostiles' angry shouts were equaled by those of our own people.

As I turned to go to Rainbow's aid I caught sight of the first buck, the one who had started it all, trying to rise to his feet. I jerked my pistol from my sash and sent him off to the Grey Land, carrying a pistol ball in his head.

Again I turned to Rainbow, but I suddenly froze. Still another Bannock, a big, paint-smeared ruffian, was roaring with laughter as he caught up my little daughter by the ankles and proceeded to swing her in a wide arc, intending to smash her head against a tree trunk. Both of my guns were empty. I yanked my knife from my belt, grabbed at my tomahawk, and lunged at him, but before I could close the distance the Bannock suddenly straightened to his full height and dropped my squalling offspring to the earth. He wilted, eyes bugging, yellow teeth showing in a ghastly grin before they disappeared in a bloody gush spewing from his mouth. He crumpled inside himself, legs wobbling, deserting him as he fell headlong.

Only then did I see Cat crouched behind the marauder, eyes blazing, lips twisted in a snarl, yanking a long-bladed knife out of his back, then sinking it time and again into the corpse, screaming Flathead curses at his departed spirit.

Iris was shaken but undamaged, weeping softly and clinging to me until Cat swept her up and ran off into the willows beside the crick. I ran to Rainbow's side, but she was no longer there. Only her lifeless body remained, eyes staring in horror, lips parted in a voiceless scream. I closed her eyes, clutched her to my breast, and bent to kiss her delicious lips already growing cold.

* * *

That is all that I recall of that fateful day until I came to my senses, trussed like a goose at market, the gunmetal taste of fury still poisoning my mouth.

The grey blur slowly resolved into daylight. The throbbing of ten thousand grumbling imps gradually translated into familiar voices. Micah, my father, Brass Turtle, Tuttle, and Finn McCool huddled around me, looking grim, until Tuttle exclaimed, "Lookee! He be comin' 'round!"

An excited babble subsided into comprehensible fragments like "Thank Gawd," "He's gonna be awright naow!" and "Lord be praised!" I struggled at my bonds and tried to speak, but my tongue was thick and dry, my throat parched, my jaw aching.

Tuttle leaned in, his stubbled chin brushing my cheek. "Ye reckon ye be settled daown naow, Temple, so's we kin turn ye loose?"

I nodded as well as I was able, hoping my eyes, so close to his, could speak for me. Evidently my imploring gaze succeeded. Tuttle announced, "Yep! Reckon ther crazies done left 'im! He be rightly civer-lized naow!"

They loosened the ropes that bound me, but my companions stayed close, lest I revert to dangerous insane behavior. I managed to strangle out the word "Water!" quickly echoed by half a dozen voices. Cat's strained, anxious face leaned over me. She murmured gentle Salish words as she poured cool water into my mouth, laving away the foul taste of blood and bile, soothing my swollen tongue and ragged throat, until I was able to ask, "What happened?"

My friends fell silent. Finn McCool shouldered into view and knelt beside me. "How much do ye recollect, Temple," he asked in a soft voice. "Your woman? Your wife? An' do ye know your darlin' babe is safe and sound as sterlin'?"

I shuddered with an agonizing chill akin to the ague, but I was able to tell him yes, I remembered Rainbow's death and Cat's heroic rescue of my daughter. "And after that, Temple lad, what d'ye recall?"

I must have stared at him blankly. My mind was completely bereft of anything that happened from the moment I last embraced my Rainbow until just a few minutes earlier. I shook my head. "So ye know naught of what ye did after ye kilt thim two Injuns and discovered your dear dyin' wife, do ye?"

"No. Nothin' at all." I struggled to sit upright, just as Molly squirmed through the throng, clutching a willow backrest. A dozen hands reached out to help. "What happened? What'd I do?"

They all vied to describe my insane behavior when I took leave of my senses. Finn's voice sliced through the rest. "No Viking berserker iver done as much damage in so short a toime as ye done this mornin', Temple! Ye went totally daft, man! Runnin' this way an' that, slashin' an' stabbin' an' choppin' loike a madman! Which I daresay ye were at the toime."

"'Thout even a gun, mind ye!" Tuttle put in. "Jest yer tommyhawk an' yer knife! Done yer killin' close up, pers'nal-like, fer a fac'!"

"'Tis truly charmed, ye be, Temple darlin'!" Paddy McBride called out. "'Tis a blessèd miracle the blaggards din't kill ye, but the blood you're wearin' is all theirs an' none o' yer own!" Only then did I take stock of my person. My shirt was in tatters, leggin's ripped, one moccasin gone, legs crusted with blood. So were my hands and arms and face. My hair was stiff and sticky with the stuff. But Paddy was nearly right. Except for a few scrapes and scratches, my hide was mostly unscathed.

The crowd parted to let Ned Godey come to my side. "Hyar ye be, Temple," he said, smiling, shoving a tin-lined copper cup into my hand, "I reckon this'll be welcome 'bout naow. I war able to shake a coupl'a drams out'n yer keg that Tuttle din't git."

Tuttle's guffaw exploded. "Reckon I be losin' muh smeller! Don't hardly never pass nuthin' up!"

The delicious cognac, pure liquid sunshine, was indeed welcome, spreading warmth all the way to my guts, for a moment almost laving away the grief that clouded my spirit.

Everybody threw in his two cents worth. I learned that I ran from my lodge into the thick of the fighting, armed only with a knife and tomahawk, and plunged amongst the Bannocks, chopping and stabbing and screaming my head off.

"Gawddamn Injuns din't know what to make o' ye!" Godey observed. "Figgered ye'd been tetched by the Sperrit, I reckon, which might'a slowed 'em up somewhat, 'til it war too late fer 'em!"

"Gawddamn lucky fer yew, Buck, one of us din't shoot ye, ourownse'fs — not meanin' to, mind ye — the way ye war runnin' amongst 'em!" Anse Tolliver called out. "The two o' ye! Yew an' that crazy li'l Spanyard, choppin' like a looney with that'ere sword o' his'n!"

I learned that I had killed four more Bannocks during my unconscious escapade. The last, one of the horse-tenders, trying to run off our livestock during the confusion.

"Shee-it!" Brass Turtle told me. "I couldn't hardly b'lieve it — runnin' out thar like ye done! Sprung yerse'f clean onter his hoss an' knocked him off, ye done, jabbin' and choppin' all the way! We like to never got ye off'n that'ere hossthievin' bastard, carvin' at 'im like ye war, purely makin' forcemeat out'n 'im!" He paused, looking me over, head to toe, appraisingly, mock-seriously, taking stock. "Never knew ye had it in ye, Temple! Must be the Injun comin' out! Good fer ye!"

Even when he smiled, which he was doing then, there was a hard, brittle edge to it. "Hadn'a been we tied ye up, we warn't none of us sure ye wouldn'a turned on yer pards, all het up like ye war."

If what they said was true, such savagery was more surprising to me than it was for them. I am not behindhand in a fight, but I have never shared the high hilarity that some of the others — especially our Indians and Tuttle — derive from battle and crowing about it afterwards. With me, it's mostly saving my skin and dealing out just deserts.

The crowd had mostly drifted off when Little Mountain arrived with an unappetizing handful. With a grand gesture he scattered half a dozen bloody, bobtail scalps beside me. "Heah," he informed me with a broad smile, "dese you ha'r. You pa say dis time you gotta take 'em — fer rememb'rin' you woman. Godey Cat-woman say udder one ha'r b'long she."

I have rarely enjoyed scalp-taking. This time was different. I thanked the big Delaware and scrambled to my feet, scooping up the scalps as I did so, and trotted off to my lodge, where I tossed them aside before heading for the crick to wash away the bloody souvenirs of the carnage I had authored.

* * *

My father, Micah, Ned and Cat helped me dig Rainbow's grave. Nobody spoke the Words when we buried her deep in the woods, far from camp. Each of us was thinking his own farewell. There was no need to say anything aloud. Cat had dressed her in her very best doeskin dress, leggin's, and moccasins. Together we wrapped her body in her silken Chinese shawl from the Popo-azhieh rendezvous.

Cat chose the items from our household to bury with her, things that Rainbow would need in the spirit world. I added her pretty ornamented saddle to the heap. Then, before Micah and Ned filled the deep grave, I laid the six Bannock scalps at her feet and Cat placed her own trophy on the grisly pile.

While Ned and Micah completed their chore, I walked off to stand between Kumskaka and Rainbow's favorite horse Punch, saying naught, not even to Powatawa, who understands such things better than most. I possessed hardly any feelings right then. I was numb. The grieving had not yet begun.

* * *

I slept not at all that first night. I volunteered to stand horse guard. When Acorn and later Micah came to relieve me, I waved them away, unwilling to talk or to hear their words of sympathy. I have no memory now of what I was thinking during those dark hours. Likely nothing useful.

The first faint glimmer of daylight roused the camp into a bustle of departure, women chattering whilst they took down lodges and bundled belongings onto travois, kids squalling, men cursing without purpose, stripping bowers, catching up critters, saddling and loading, grabbing a mouthful of breakfast on the fly. By time I led my animals from the meadow, my lodge was down, the poles lashed together for a travois, and my possessions all neatly gathered in packs, ready to load.

Ned and and a hollow-eyed Cat were standing nigh. "If'n it be awright with you, Temple," Ned began uncertainly, "Cat an' me'd be proud to be lookin' arter yer little'un fer naow." He swallowed hard, looking uncomfortable. "Leastaways 'til ye figger out whatcher gonna do."

I confess that until that moment I had not considered how I would care for my two-year-old daughter. I shrugged out of my lethargy long enough to tell them yes, I was grateful for their offer, that I would do whatever I could to help out. My faltering response produced the first faint smile on Cat's face that I had seen since Rainbow's death. Ned smiled broadly, saying, "Don'tcha fret none, Temple. We'll be takin' good care o' her. Ye kin be sure of it."

Whilst I saddled and loaded my packstring, Iris kept hugging my knees, asking after her mother, whimpering softly, her eyes vacant, the truth slowly dawning that Rainbow was not coming back. I could offer no helpful words, just hugs and reassuring noises that likely did little good. At last Cat rescued me. She gathered Iris in her arms and swung her up to perch upon Cat's own saddle.

* * *

Most of the journey to the Seeds-kee-dee blurs in memory, collapsing into a grey jumble of trails, landmarks, overnight camps, and chill weather. When hoarfrost and early snow skiffed the land and morning ice crisped the crickbanks, we tarried now and then to trap along the way, grudgingly grateful for the Bannock ponies to carry the new harvest of plews.

Early on I gifted Cat with most of Rainbow's belongings. She saved some valuable items for my daughter and distributed the rest amongst the other women. From what I could see, she kept naught for herself.

During those days I thought often of the Grey Land that Indians in that country consider their destination after death. Sometimes I wondered if I hadn't already gone there. The delicious taste of life, all the delicious flavors on which I had gorged since I first came to the mountains, turned to cold ashes. Colors faded to gunmetal grey. Prairies, forests, hills, and mountains, even the sky, were all lifeless now. Golden sunshine flattened to a dull, colorless glare. Once-treasured sounds, birdsong and chittering varmints, rang harsh and tinny on my ear. I was short-tempered, impatient, even with my favorite critters. I held my comrades at arm's length, refusing to let them come nigh to render comfort, try as they might.

I couldn't even mourn properly. Rainbow's living image kept slipping from view. It faded into a picture of her lifeless body, stark and stiffening and cold, drawn in harsh charcoal on flat white canvas, not the warm, vibrant colors she had worn in life.

I kept the little traveling lodge she and I had shared. In time, my father, Finn, and Micah joined me in it. Even then I couldn't be sociable. I kept myself to myself. I moped, chewing my soul to shreds.

The world about me receded. I saw it as through the wrong end of a spyglass, visible but remote. It had naught to do with me, as if I were stranded on a sandbar amidst muddy, roiling waters, within sight of my comrades on a distant shore but unable to reach them or even to call out to them.

Nights were the worst. Dreams tormented me. They contained no pleasant memories. They were furnished instead with serpents writhing in a black morass, dark forests where slavering wolves and catamounts stalked, peopled by the likes of Pap and Mike Fink. I woke up often in the night, shivering in cold sweat, grabbed up my weapons, and raced out to the herd, preferring to stand guard until daybreak, lest I return to such nightmares.

One night when I was standing guard the herd was struck by half a dozen raiders. I dimly recall rising to my feet, taking slow, deliberate aim, and shooting a mounted horsethief off his critter's back, then, still standing, reloading my rifle until Micah yanked me to the ground. He gave me hell for offering myself as an easy target.

Iris had many foster mothers besides Cat. Molly and the other women showered her with attention. They fed her tasty tidbits and talked with her in their respective tongues. As the weeks passed, she was able to glide smoothly amongst Salish, Absóraqa, Shoshone, and English. She always called herself Irish, howsomever, which greatly amused Paddy and Finn.

Iris also had an attentive uncle in Cesár. He devoted much of his spare time to carving little toys for her — burros, birds, buffaloes, and suchlike.

The poisonous miasma lifted slowly from my mind. At first, a wraithelike Rainbow visited my dreams only rarely. After a spell she returned more often, her presence increasing each time she appeared. At length I felt her warm breath on my face and tasted her fragrance. When I awoke I was hard where a man ought to be hard. I revealed nothing of this, but I thanked her for that gift.

In time my festering grief scabbed over and appeared to heal, leaving only a dull ache. If I dreamed at all, it was of common things. I no longer dreaded nightfall. I took pleasure once more in my horses and my Sugarfoot mule. The palaver of my comrades gradually warmed in my ears. A good day's harvest gave me pleasure and bringing down meat with a difficult shot — a wapiti or fat doe or a straggling buffalo — provided satisfaction that had long been a stranger.

Powatawa didn't presume to offer counsel or comfort during my time of torment. He understood that only time and I myself could heal me. His presence and the love I knew he bore me, howsomever, bolstered my will and let me find my own way out of my slough of despair.

By time we trapped our zigzag way to the Seeds-kee-dee, scouring every likely crick and stream, I was mostly healed. Or so I thought.

Chapter XIV
Skinny Doin's

When Stone Bird and Pretty Horse rode into camp nigh the Seeds-kee-dee and reported that the RMF brigades were gathered not faroff, we tarried long enough to dig a cache for the plews we had taken during the spring and fall seasons. It needed to be a large one. Both harvests had been abundant. The chore was more difficult than usual. It was by then mid-November. The snow-covered earth was iron-hard and disposing of the dug-out soil was difficult because ice choked the nearby crick. Scattering the dirt on the prairie or in the woods was out of the question. Its presence on the snow would have been a sure giveaway of our hidey-hole. We made do with the crick. Fortunately it snowed again the night after we completed the chore, covering evidence of our labor.

Whilst most of us toiled, Ned and Brass Turtle rode ahead to the RMF camp. They returned looking glum. So far, Tom Fitzpatrick had failed to arrive with a packtrain from Saint Louis. The RMF Company men were in a mutinous mood, although what good that might have done was hard to see. The annual packtrain is our only lifeline, our only source of vital supplies — gunpowder, galena, knives, traps, blankets. Trappers can't survive without such plunder. Tobacco and booze are almost as important. Some might say moreso.

Naturally we congratulated ourselves on opening the Sweet Lake cache. Leastaways, for now, we had powder and lead and caps enough for hunting and keeping our hair, but we, too, had looked to rendezvous and its promised plenty like Hebrews seeking the Promised Land.

When we joined the Company, whatever gloom I still entertained was overmatched by that of the trappers gathered on the Seeds-kee-dee. Going dry and tobaccoless was bad enough, but lacking gunpowder and lead could prove fatal. Most free trappers had conserved enough to get by, but many Company men, some of whom were but a year in the mountains, hadn't learned the lesson of thrift. Now they were desperate for enough ammunition to feed themselves or to put up a defense if need be.

As you might expect, happy-go-lucky Joe Meek was onesuch. Forever optimistic, unconcerned about tomorrow, Joe was bereft of powder, lead, and caps, as well as his next bait of vittles. In much the same boat were his close companions, Doc Newell, Simon Pence, and the carefree harpooner Harry Yeats. Naturally we shared some of our own with the four of them, which likely further confirmed Joe in his cheerful expectation of smiling good fortune always waiting around the next bend to rescue him.

If an expedition of American Fur or one of Pierre Chouteau's other enterprises had arrived in that camp, they would have made a killing in beaver fur and established themselves firmly in the mountain trade, but no packtrain showed up.

The mood in the scattered-out trapper camp was sullen. Pessimism reigned. Even the camps of the Crows and the Snakes who had gathered there were wrapped in gloom. Hardly more sanguine were the four partners of Rocky Mountain Fur. Jim Bridger, Milton Sublette, Jean Gervais, and Henry Frae had come together to await Fitzpatrick, leaving many of their men in the field to finish up the fall trapping. As weeks wore into a month and more, they became increasingly anxious that no support would arrive that year. From time to time, each partner led out a small party to greet Fitz's column on his likely westward trail. Each time they returned empty-handed, deeply disappointed.

At length Frapp, reckoning he didn't have much to lose, gifted a couple spotted ponies to a respected Absóraqa medicine man, who told him that Fitz was neither dead nor precisely lost. He was merely on the wrong trail.

Frapp believed what the Crow healer told him. He lost no time in setting out with a party of men to meet up with Fitzpatrick. Which he did, somewheres on the Sweetwater. The old Crow's medicine and Frapp's trail-savvy paid off. A fortnight later, Frapp rode into camp at the head of a train of Mexican mules loaded with plunder, forty or so hostlers, and, most welcome of all, reasonably fresh tobacco and an ocean of *aguardiente,* fiery Spaniard brandy that, even watered-down, is considerably better than common trader's booze.

Although his packs lacked considerably in foofurraw, which disappointed the womenfolk, we obtained enough necessaries to let us hold out until summer.

Almost as welcome as the goods he brought was all the news that Frapp had learned from Fitzpatrick when they met on the trail. It wasn't all good. Much had changed since Fitz set out for Saint Louis nearly a year before. Winter snows forced him to travel afoot much of the way. By time Fitzpatrick arrived in Saint Louis in May of 1831, Smith, Jackson, and Bill Sublette had already departed for Santa Fe to launch a new business venture.

"Vell now," Frapp told us, "natcherly Fitz don't got no money — ner beafer plews, needer — fer tradin' in Sain' Looie, so he got no uddervize t'ing he kin do but goin' chasin' after dem t'ree all der vay to Sandy Fay fer gittin' der plunder ve be needin' *hier.* Undt ven Fitz he got dere dey tell 'im dey haf busted der partnership. Dere aind't no Ess-Jay-an'-Ess no more undt Schmidt aind't even wid 'em no more! He be dead!"

Fraeb barely acknowledged our astonishment at hearing that news. "Aind't no surprisin' dey busted up, needer, I be t'inkin'! Ef'ry year vas *wanderjahre mit* Diah, traipsin' off fer Californy like he vas alvays doin', ven beafers enuf fer ef'rybody ve got right hier!

"Den Davey sez to Fitz he aind't schtickin' 'round no more, needer. Sez he got a bellyful o' Veeli Sublette all o' time ge-squ'veezin' vun more dollar out'n der trappers! Sez he got enuf money fer two men awready undt he be goin' to Californy undt he's gonna schtay dere!"

I was not surprised to learn that Davey Jackson was heading west and not coming back. He had told me as much nigh two years earlier, along with expressing his disgust with Sublette's avarice and his impatience with Jed Smith's unprofitable wanderlust and disregard for the men who followed him on his wild-goose chases.

Unraveling Frapp's thick German accent, we learned that on the long, hard, dangerous journey across desert land to Santa Fe, the partners had quarreled, mainly over Sublette and Jackson's unhappiness with Jedediah's constant wanderings westwards, losing too many men, and failing to produce enough beaver fur to hold up his end of their bargain. From what we could puzzle out of Frapp's sketchy account, Smith had split off from the main party and proceeded with a small bunch of his own. They had run out of water and whilst Jed was alone, seeking a waterhole, he was attacked and killed by Indians. Which likelihood was borne out by Smith's guns and some of his possibles turning up in Santa Fe in the hands of Spaniard traders making trade with those particular Indians, who were bragging on their prowess, although, Indian-like, they admitted that Diah managed to take a couple of their warriors along with him.

Tom Fitzpatrick didn't return with Fraeb. Instead, he went back to Saint Louis to arrange for supplies for next summer's rendezvous in Pierre's Hole.

Strolling back to our camp alongside Jim Bridger I learned more unwelcome news. "Afore ye come up," Jim confided, "Frapp war tellin' 'bout what happened when Fitz caught up with Billy in Santy Fee. 'Pears ol' Bill's been honin' his choppers more'n some'at since we seen 'im last." He swallowed hard and gritted his teeth whilst I awaited what promised to be disturbing news. It was. "When Fitz got thar," he continued glumly, "natcherly he din't have no cash, ner plews fer tradin', neither, an' naow with Diah an' Davey out o' the pitcher, thar warn't nobody gittin' in the way o' Billy's appertite fer cash money!"

Bridger paused, his anger building. "Long an' short of it be, Billy give us credit, awright, but stric'ly on his own gawddamn hard-as-hell terms! Inter'st's out o' sight an' Bill Sublette'll be the onliest one carryin' goods to ronnyvoo in Pier's Hole nex' summer an', arter that, ferever! Not us!"

Jim fell silent, staring straight ahead at nothing in particular. Then, "All o' them'ere years o' workin' together out hyar don't 'mount to a pile o' shit fer him! By gawd! He be swivin' his own gawddamn flesh-an'-blood brother Milt! But nuthin' else matters 'sides hard cash dollars fer good ol' Billy Sublette!" After another long silence, he muttered, "Hyar we be, sittin' on a mountain o' prime fur an' him treatin' us like ragged-arse niggers! Ain't likely Rocky Mountain Fur'll be survivin' this'n!" He spat and stalked off.

In our camp the air buzzed with palaver concerning the prodigies that Frapp had related. Naturally Jed Smith's death topped the heap. "Ol' Diah din't pay 'nough attention to what war writ right thar in that'ere Good Book o' his'n," Ned Godey declared. "Frapp be tellin' Jed war all by his lonesome out thar, 'thout nobody backin' 'im up, when them'ere Injuns jumped 'im an' put 'im under. Hell! Even Jesus allus kep' a passel o' 'postles around Hisse'f — fer coverin' His back, don'tcha know!"

Tuttle expressed a more practical view. "Reckon thar's a passel o' men thet won't be gittin' theirse'fs kilt naow," he opined. "Follerin' along a'hind o' Jed Smith could purely put an end to all o' yer earthly pleasures!" He heaved a sigh, looking glum. "Ol' Diah war allus usin' up his people like as if a man warn't wuth no more'n a pokeful o' pemmican!" He spat out his cud and added bittrly, "Shee-it! Not even thet much!"

Anse Tolliver, who values even those mountaineers he doesn't like — which, being Anse, is likely most of them — averred sourly, "Ef ol' Diah had'a skelped all o' them'ere good men he got kilt with his gawddamn gallivantin' ter hell an' back, he wouldn'a had room on his belt fer all o' them'ere skelps!"

"Yep," Turtle agreed, "any Blackfoot would'a been proud as Lucifer fer killin' so many white-eyes on his own hook! He'd'a needed a couple-three lances fer sportin' 'em."

Turtle lapsed into silence then, holding his peace until the others had their say. When talk tailed off, he said seriously, "Ye reckon Dave an' Billy never tumbled to what Diah war really after? Thar ain't no b'lievin' Smith war goin' all the long way to Californy, time an' agin, jist fer trappin' plews! Ashley an' the gawddamn Guv'mint's a'hind it all! Mark me! The Guv'mint's got eyes fer Californy an' Smith's been givin' 'em the lay o' the land! Beaver warn't never hardly in it!"

It was food for thought, but none of us knew enough to make up our minds one way or another.

When I related what Jim Bridger had told me about Bill Sublette grinding out a deal that would make him sole supplier for future RMF rendezvous the camp rang with yells of disapproval. "Saints presarve us!" Paddy McBride lamented. "Jist whin we're thinkin' we're shut o' that connivin' blatherskite dippin' into our purse 'til nothin' remains, along he comes agin, stalkin' us like the hellacious sarpint he be, grabbin' up iv'ry copper in sight! He's worse'n a bloody Irish landlord!"

Nobody countered Paddy's sentiments. Free as we consider ourselves to be in the mountains, the likes of William Ashley and Bill Sublette will be forever conniving schemes to put us in their thrall.

* * *

Frapp and the other RMF partners carried much-needed supplies out to their trappers, extending the harvest until cricks and ponds froze solid and trapping became impossible. Then the whole shebang drifted into camp on the Seeds-kee-dee. A riotous good time ensued, celebrating Christmas and a belated rendezvous rolled in together. One item in abundance in Santa Fe and Taos is throat-scalding *aguardiente* and Fitz had acquired a generous supply. Merriment reigned unrestrained for several days and nights in the trapper camp, until Frapp ordered the bungs hammered back into the kegs and word went quietly about that we were quitting the Seeds-kee-dee.

One reason for pulling up stakes was lack of game. A couple hundred meat-eating trappers, many of them with families, will soon exhaust amost any neighborhood of buffalo, wapiti, and even deer, especially in wintertime. The main reason, howsomever, was the recent arrival of unwelcome neighbors. American Fur's Major Vanderburgh and Andy Drips had brought their brigades to the Seeds-kee-dee and settled in, cheek-by-jowl, alongside Rocky Mountain Fur.

Hospitality or the lack of it had naught to do with RMF's decision to move out. American Fur's inexperienced leaders and their greenhorn trappers couldn't find prime beaver country on their own. Come spring trapping, they meant to dog our trail and help themselves to a healthy share of our rightful harvest. Short of declaring outright war, RMF's only choice was to retreat and leave American Fur high and dry.

Our bunch chose to stick with Rocky Mountain Fur, if for no better reason than Tuttle's dubious pledge of loyalty, which ran, "Hell! So long as ol' Frapp's still got some o' thet'ere *argewenty,* I reckon thi'shere ol' coon'll be follerin' 'im anywheres he goes!"

On the first night of a decent snowfall we dropped our shelters, packed our ponies, and decamped. By time an uncertain sun poked a finger through a leaden sky we were miles away, snow still falling heavily enough to cover travois tracks a hundred yards behind us.

Our party was swelled considerably by the forty or so hostlers that Fitz had recruited in Santa Fe and Taos, most of them Spaniards. There would be no packtrain returning to the settlements until late summer, so, like it or not, they were obliged to learn the trapper's trade, leastaways for a spell.

Not all of the new men were greenhorns, howsomever. Several of them had worked beaver streams in the southern Rockies. Onesuch was a remarkably short-statured, fair-haired young fellow who more than made up for what he lacked in size by what he brought to a brawl, as a couple of Company bullies discovered early on when they chided him about his size and tried to take advantage. Short he was, but wiry and tough as a jackscrew, with grit and smarts to match.

He and I often fell in together on the westward trail. He picked my brain concerning the Salmon River country we were heading to and I learned much about Santa Fe and Taos and beaver-trapping in those parts. He said his name was Christopher Carson, but just Kit would do. Young as he was — about twenty at the time — Kit was no stranger to our trade. He had trapped the southern desert cricks and streams for three years, from Taos all the way to California, with a booshway name of Ewing Young. When Tom Fitzpatrick offered a chance to see our northern country, he jumped at the chance. An itchy foot and a hankering for the other side of the next ridge is a large part of what keeps many of us in the mountains.

Huddled inside my capote, horses plodding along snowy trails, palavering about this and that helped pass time during long days in the saddle. Down deep, I was still hurting. It was easier for me to talk with a stranger like Carson than with men in our bunch, who were sure to bring up painful memories. Before long the two of us were swapping histories. He had been apprenticed to a saddler in Missouri but had run off when he was just fourteen. We shared a laugh when he recalled that the saddler had offered a reward of only one cent for his capture and return. Odd jobs, mostly working as a cook and a teamster in and around Santa Fe and Taos for the next three years, kept body and soul together, until Ewing Young took him on and taught him trapping.

Kit had no particular ties to anyone in the party, so he took to hanging with our bunch when we camped overnight on the trail, sharing our vittles and contributing more than his fair share of game he shot as we pushed on to the Salmon. Tuttle and Anse thought he might be a welcome addition to our crew, but I doubted Carson's wanderlust would let him hang with any one bunch for long.

I rode often alongside Ned and Cat, with Iris, almost three years old now, straddling before me on the saddle. She chattered excitedly about every new thing she spied along the trail, what we saw on the snowy prairie, in the forests, or climbing through steep mountain passes. She was forever curious, her questions almost always echoing the last answer I supplied. Her curiosity was inexhaustible. I had known such women before. I came to realize that in this precious bundle, this wondrous child, I still retained the spirits of the two most important women in my life, Rainbow and my mother.

* * *

Wintering alongside the Salmon River was a considerable improvement over the Seeds-kee-dee. Weather was milder and game and good graze for the critters more plentiful. Before long bands of friendly Indians drifted in, including Iron Bow's Salish band, as well as Kootenays, Nez Percés, and Pend d'Oreilles. Naturally there was a great lamentation when the Flatheads learned of Rainbow's death. Naught else would do but that I join Iron Bow and Fast Horse in the sweat lodge, blacken my face as they did theirs, and sit through some old healer's endless rituals. All that fuss served only to deepen my melancholy, but I did it anyway. Word got around amongst them — likely spread by Brass Turtle — about my crazy killing spree after Rainbow's death, which happified my in-laws considerably.

Indians prize their children above all things and Iris's recent orphaning earned her even more attention and coddling amongst the female kin than ever before. I rarely saw my daughter until Cat collected her from her doting aunts and female cousins and returned her to Godey's lodge at bedtime. Which left me ample time to hunt with my father, Micah, and frequently with Carson. Buffalo and wapiti were plentiful and even the large congregation of hungry mouths thereabouts failed to diminish their numbers enough to matter.

There was time, too, for reading and recording events in my journal, no matter how painful that chore proved to be at first. In a way, it was helpful. It drained away some of the hurt by forcing me to take a clear-eyed view of it, inditing all that I could recall — somewhat, as I understand it, like confessing your sins to a priest relieves the burden of your wrongdoing, as Paddy and Finn described it to me.

Naturally Rocky Mountain Fur made trade with the Indians as much as their meager store of goods allowed. When their stock was exhausted, our bunch swapped what plunder we could spare for their plews and fine fur, but RMF's hopes of getting what was left at next summer's rendezvous were dashed when American Fur showed up on the Salmon.

Vanderburgh and Drips were determined to dog us to prime trapping grounds, come spring. They also needed to know where rendezvous would be held, so they might lure free trappers and Indians to their trade tents.

Getting ahold of such information was no great chore for them. Keeping secrets in that close-knit society was like toting water in a sieve. Free trappers and Company men were easily bribed with booze and foofurraw. Several RMF men even sneaked away their plews and sold them to their booshways' rivals.

Free trapper though he was, Joe Meek was likely the most loyal man amongst RMF's regulars. Even before the new partners bought out EssJay&Ess, Joe and Milton Sublette had bonded in close friendship, doubtless born of mutual respect and likely because the two of them possessed much the same madcap personality backed up by skill, strength, fairness, daredevil courage, wild good humor, and intelligence. Joe was already some sort of legend because of his foolhardy but so far successful exploits with grizzly bears. Milton was forever ready, even eager, to meet whatever challenge that chanced his way. What occurred at that winter camp on the Salmon tested their friendship beyond all imagining.

Winter camp, as I have mentioned elsewhere, is a time of abundant leisure, without much of the frantic pleasure-seeking of summertime rendezvous. Hunting meat along the Salmon and refurbishing gear for the coming season occupied but little time. There was time aplenty for lusty young trappers to go a-courting amongst the lodges of friendly Indians encamped nearby. Unfortunately, a few RMF Company men chose, instead, to visit the American Fur encampment in search of amorous dalliance.

Most of the trappers' children were too young to be of interest to our would-be Lotharios, but amongst American Fur's recruits was a band of Iroquois breeds ramrodded by a tough, surly trapper who went by the English name of John Grey, whose very pretty, nearly-grown-up daughter was eminently eligible in the eyes of a few of our slavering swains. Inevitably, one or more of the RMF lads went too far, too fast, in seeking her complaisance and all hell broke loose.

We first heard of it when Little Mountain galloped into camp shouting, "Goddamn 'Murrican breeds killin' our fellers over dar!" Naturally a couple score RMF men, free men, and several from our bunch, including myself, leaped into the saddle and made haste to intervene. Milton Sublette led the pack.

When we arrived on the scene, just at dusk, we discovered three bloody but mostly unhurt Rocky Mountain Fur greenhorns cowering under the kicks and punches administered by the irate, outraged *paterfamilias* John Grey. Milton swung off his horse and stepped into the fray, seeking to calm matters, but Grey would have none of it. Instead, he swung about and lunged at Sublette, his dirk glittering in the firelight. Sublette backed and dodged, the while trying to talk sense into the frothing Iroquois, but to no avail. Milt Sublette was no stranger to rough-and-tumble fracases, but before he could retrieve his own blade, John Grey threw himself at Milton and stabbed him in the thigh.

A grunting roar rose up from both sides. Our people surged into the firelit circle, rifles and pistols leveled, eager to even the score and then some.

Suddenly Major Vandenburgh and Andy Drips rushed into the narrowing gap between their men and ours, shouting commands, waving their people away, ordering them to return to their shelters. Which most of them did. Even John Grey was suddenly calm, if not cowed. He backed away from the fallen Sublette, a smirk frozen on his craggy features, then slunk off into the darkness.

Milton lay sprawled in the snow, blood spreading rapidly onto the whiteness, his knife in his hand now, cursing and struggling to rise and do battle. McCool and Old Foot rushed to his side, dragged him close to the fire, stripped away his leggin', and laid bare his thigh. Blood gushed from the wound in ugly gouts, more blood than any man can afford to lose, no matter how tough he is.

Finn ripped loose his own neck scarf and bound a tourniquet above the gash, then laved away the blood with snow. Foot sprinkled a handful of some sort of powder into the wound before he fixed a poultice of spiderwebs in place with strips of hide from Milton's leggin'. McCool loosed the tourniquet, lest it cause Milt's flesh to rot. Now only a tiny trickle oozed from beneath the poultice.

"'Tis best we get 'im to our camp," Finn announced, "where we can be tendin' to 'im proper-like. 'Tis no good remainin' here." A dozen eager hands reached out to lift Milton and carry him to his horse, ordinarily a high-spirited, frisky steed, but not that night. The tall lineback dun stood stock-still, head hanging down, muscles quivering but otherwise unmoving, whilst we got Sublette into the saddle. Several men held him erect from either side. Another man led the horse across the snowy expanse to our camp. Old Foot and Finn kept them close company.

Joe Meek didn't go with his friend. He was too busy, I reckon, inventing brand-new curses as he bundled the miscreants who had caused it all aboard their mules. The trio was somewhat the worse for wear but healthy enough, which apparently infuriated Joe. He cuffed each of them soundly before he threw them onto their saddles. His ire grew with each one, so much so that he pitched the final Casanova clean over his mount and sent him sprawling in the snow. The fellow wisely declined to renew acquaintance with Meek just then. He scrambled more or less upright and scampered off afoot.

* * *

Morning revealed a haggard, hollow-eyed Finn McCool emerging from my lodge, where he and Foot had been ministering to Milton throughout the night. I had surrendered my quarters to them and passed the night with Ned and Cat, sharing my daughter's robes for the few catnaps I was able to capture. Finn gratefully accepted coffee, but the steaming brew failed to brighten his mood.

"'Tis a bloody deep wound Milton has suffered," Finn declared glumly, "too deep for Foot's magical powders to reach to the bottom, try as he might to blow them in with that little reed of his." He sighed and stared into his cup. "I fear infection will come of it. Fortunately, the blade missed the femoral artery, which would've killed 'im surely, but it nicked the thigh bone. Try as we will, we can't get hold o' the chip to remove it. It'll be after causin' all manner o' mischief unless we do."

Micah, Ned, Paddy, and Anse listened with close attention, saying naught, but their worried looks spoke volumes.

Finn might have told us more, but just then a mob of horsemen galloped into camp and pulled up at our cookfire. They were a grim-looking bunch — Joe Meek, Brass Turtle, Little Mountain, Powatawa, Cesár, Tuttle, and nigh a dozen men from Milton's trapping brigade — all of them armed to the teeth, everybody except my father cursing a blue streak.

"Sons-o'-bitches got plumb away las' night!" Turtle announced, flinging himself from the saddle.

"Gawddamn Eerie-quah bastards hadn't balls enough to hang on fer fightin' fair an' square," Tuttle bellowed, "'stid o' runnin' off in ther dark, arter what thet'ere gawddamn Eerie-quah Grey done to Milton!"

Nearly every one of them had his say, until Joe Meek, his still-boyish face a thundercloud, his voice ominously quiet, declared, "He kin run all he wants, but I'll be findin' 'im yet an' settlin' 'counts, oncet fer all!" Nobody doubted that Joe would do just that, no matter how long it took.

When the threats petered out we learned that our avengers had arrived in the American Fur camp too late to confront John Grey and his Iroquois breeds. Vanderburgh and Drips had met them at the edge of camp, expressed their regret at Milton's injury, and declared that the troublemakers had been ordered to leave shortly after the brawl and, no, they didn't know where they went. Short of scouring the country in every direction, there was naught our people could do.

Afterwards, Anse expressed relief at the outcome, a view many of us privately shared. "Wal, p'raps it's best the way it come out. 'Tain't no good, trappers fightin' an' killin' one t'other, even Eerie-quahs. We awready got a sufficiency o' Blackfoots ready an' willin' fer that kind o' chore."

The only good thing that came out of it all was that Drips and Vanderburgh agreed with Tolliver regarding open conflicts amongst American trappers, possibly because our people outnumbered theirs by more than somewhat. Whatever their reasons, they decamped within the week, headed towards Sweet Lake.

* * *

Sublette's wound was slow to heal, if it ever did. Joe Meek hovered nigh my lodge until Milt was sufficiently recovered to move to their own digs. Milton, a supremely active man now unable to do much of anything useful, was bitter. "Christamighty, this's what I git fer tryin' to be some kind o' gawddamn peacemaker!" he lamented loudly. "Should'a ripped his gawddamn gizzard in the fust place!"

There wasn't much to do along the Salmon, besides keeping our bellies full and restoring our livestock, first with good graze, then with sweet cottonwood bark when grass became measly. Iris was nearly three by then, so, when I wasn't reading to her or telling her stories I had learned from my mother, I took to teaching her her letters and simple ciphering, as my mother had done when I was that age. I daresay it was a chore more pleasant for me than it was for Iris, but we made a game of it and she appeared thoroughly to enjoy my company.

The most difficult obstacle to her learning was the multiplicity of languages, dialects, and accents that abounded around us. American English as I speak it was only one tongue amongst a dozen or more in which she was fairly fluent — and not the most useful or important one, at that. We persisted, howsomever, and before long she was puzzling out and pronouncing the words and phrases I wrote out for her. Later, she was able to scribble some of her own with charcoal on swatches of tree bark. The fast-filling pages of my ledgers were too precious to be used for that purpose.

Cat was an attentive witness to Iris's schooling. When her chores permitted, she sat quietly by, mouthing and quietly pronouncing every syllable I spoke and inscribed. Sometimes she traced the letters with a charred stick on bark or on the earth. Once she asked, diffidently, "Mebbe sometime, Tompo, you teach me talkin' leaves, same like Irish, huh?" I assured her that I would do so, happily, but, fact is, she had already begun that chore.

* * *

Naturally there was a deal of loud lamentation amongst Iron Bow's family and the rest of Rainbow's kin when it came time for us to bid farewell for a spell and head for the spring harvest. We promised, howsomever, that they would have the prickly pleasure of my daughter's rascally company, come summer rendezvous in Pierre's Hole. Which mollified them somewhat.

Cat, too, shed a passel of tears at parting with her kinfolk, but there was no doubting where her loyalties lay. Like Rainbow, Cat had chosen the trail she would follow. Nothing could pry her loose from Ned Godey and our harum-scarum bunch. Molly, too, by now the mother of two rusty-haired toddlers, was completely devoted to Paddy and he to her — except, perhaps, occasionally at rendezvous.

Ice was already rotting, breaking up, and drifting down the Salmon. It was high time to head for the mountains south and east of Sweet Lake for our spring hunt. Quitting winter camp was difficult. It meant leaving Milton Sublette behind. His wound hadn't healed sufficiently for him to undertake the journey. Rocky Mountain Fur had no choice. Delaying the harvest amounted to suicide for the fledgling company. Notes held by Brother Bill were coming due, some of them already past due, and the elder Sublette isn't known for his generosity in money matters or much else.

Milton himself was loudest in urging the Company to get a move on and commence the harvest. He insisted that he could fend for himself, although it was impossible to see how he could do so.

Nobody was surprised when Joe Meek announced that he would remain with Milton until he either mended or died. As he put it, "I ain't aboot to leave Milton layin' hyar fer wolf bait. We'll see 'er through, one way or t'other!" He spat out his chaw and added, "Or mebbe we won't. But we'll be doin' it together."

Many of us gifted the pair with all the necessaries we could spare, as well as the few luxuries we still possessed. When sight of their little camp disappeared behind the first rise in the prairie, not many believed that we would ever see either of them again.

* * *

The journey south and eastwards was mostly unremarkable. A party of nigh two hundred trappers was too big for most Blackfoots to consider easy pickin's, which is what they prefer. Here and there we paused a couple days to trap likely streams and refresh our livestock before moving on. As we penetrated deeper into Shoshone country, it was Snake horsethieves, not Blackfoot raiders, who proved to be most troublesome. A few brief gunfire exchanges and doubling the nighttime horse guard discouraged all but the most ambitious thieves, howsomever, so we kept our livestock.

Jim Bridger headed the expedition. I was impressed with his almost unerring sense of direction and choice of trails, as well as his easy-going but firm command of the ill-assorted mob of strong-minded rowdies that made up our company, what Jim Clyman once described as Falstaff's Battalion. My mind often returned to those early days on the Musselshell, when Jim and I were fresh-faced kids just learning the trapper's trade. I marveled at the change in him. Illiterate though he is, Jim is a natural-born leader. I am not, but neither am I a follower, unless it suits me to do so. I thank my stars that I fell in with our bunch of like-minded loners, men who neither give nor follow orders.

Once arrived at our mountain destination, our bunch split off from the RMF and trapped a sizeable patch of country that Bridger allotted to us. He knew we would scour every nook and cranny for beaver and that the RMF would get almost every plew we took, at least that year. We are free trappers, beholden to no one, but that year we reckoned we owed our loyalty to our old companions.

That season was much like the others before it, long days filled with wading icy ponds and streams, gutting the catch and hauling it back to camp, skinning and fleshing plews, then going out at day's end to run traplines once again. It is mindless work, but a man had better keep his wits about him. Peril is ever-present. We are never free of catamounts, hungry bears newly come from hivernation, or Indians who wish to settle old grudges, lift your hair for the pure fun of it, or to acquire your gun and plunder, likely all three.

That high, rugged country, remote from well-traveled trails, let us avoid Indian depredations and our few encounters with bears provided a welcome change from our daily diet of beaver flesh. Women in camp lessened the labor, greatly improved vittles, and generally made life more pleasant. Their constant chatter and bursts of laughter lent gaiety to our society, an improvement on grumpy, bone-tired bachelors whose customary communication is mostly threadbare curses.

I missed Rainbow desperately during those months, yearning for her warmth and good humor, her loving attention, especially at night. Now, cold and shivering, alone and wanting in my robes, I longed for her fragrant breath on my throat, her firm, warm flesh pressed against the length of me, soft syllables whispering loving nonsense. I wondered if I would ever be rid of the cold emptiness in my gut and I mostly decided that it was here to stay.

Cat did what she could to comfort me, but she was Ned's woman. I am sure it was her abiding love for Rainbow that prompted her to drag me to their cookfire to break my fast and join them at supper, even as she mothered my daughter as if Iris were her own child.

Often I would sit apart in their lodge, silent and smoking my pipe, admiring in the cookfire's glow her lithe, catlike movements, her slim, supple form graceful beneath a shapeless buckskin dress, the dramatic planes of her face, high cheekbones and mysterious coal-back eyes that could suddenly catch fire with laughter or fleeting displeasure.

At such times I would catch myself up, blushing with guilt, reproving myself for such feelings, reminding myself that Cat was Ned's woman. Such sentiment, no matter that it was born of honest admiration and simple gratitude, is unworthy. If Cat was ever aware of my torment, she gave no hint of it.

* * *

In time the plenitude of plews we had garnered thus far became a nuisance. They cluttered the camp and it became a serious chore to haul them from one campsite to another. Also, such wealth was an all-too-attractive temptation, both for Indians roaming the neighborhood and for greedy American Fur trappers, most of them new to the trade and unconcerned with the rough code by which we old-timers live. Vanderburgh and Drips had sniffed out RMF's trapping grounds and were crowding in. So far they hadn't troubled our bunch, but it was only a matter of time until they did so.

As we had done before, we baled up our cured plews, clearly marked with each man's brand, and hauled them off to Bridger's headquarters camp for safekeeping and later for transport to rendezvous. The rich, still-unsold haul we had gained from previous seasons, still cached nigh the Seeds-kee-dee, would tax our packstrings to the utmost.

The air in Bridger's camp was blue with curses and outright threats concerning American Fur. Jim was hard put to prevent that sputtering discontent from exploding into outright war. Likely his personal feeling was to have at it with Drips and Vanderburgh, but he knew that a shooting war with the opposition would destroy Rocky Mountain Fur. Vanderburgh had already protested the deaths of a couple-three of his trappers found dead in the woods, but Jim had so far been able to shrug off the charges, laying the blame on marauding Indians.

The gloom in Bridger's camp was lifted for a spell by the arrival of Joe Meek and Milton Sublette, especially when Jim saw fit to celebrate their deliverance with his remaining kegs of *aguardiente*. Everybody clamored to hear the tale of their ordeal on the Salmon and the journey that brought them back to us. Naturally Joe Meek was happy to oblige.

"Wal, now, it's a long story — an' likely only half-true — but I'll do ther best I kin to tell ye haow it war, baby-nursin' ol' Milt daown on ther Salmon an' gittin' his sorry arse up hyar, so's I kin be shet o' his 'tarnal bawlin' an' bitchin', once an' fer all!" Joe paused to bestow a sly glance at Milton, who merely laughed at him and urged him to go on. "Wal, thar I war, arter y'all packed up an' rode out an' lef' me lookin' arter ol' Milt 'til he got hisse'f mended er kicked off, one — me, a free trapper what din't have no time fer trappin' ner nuthin' else besides, 'ceptin' list'nin' to Milton frettin' an' complainin' 'baout ever'thin' I done or din't do! An' no matter what I done fer 'im, it war wrong! Fer forty days an' forty nights, jist like in ther Good Book, thar I war, fetchin' an' totin' an' movin' camp' an' Milton 'long with it an' huntin' an' cookin' an' puttin' up with his bitchin' aboot how I war cookin' the meat too much er not enough an' cuttin' it all wrong, besides, an' helpin' 'im with his sore laig an' gawd-knows-what-all! I war tellin' 'im ever' jest an' tale I ever heard of an' makin' up some when I run out, jist to keep 'im quiet, but nary a thankee did I ever git from him!"

Joe quit long enough to drain his cup and hold it out for more. "I'd shore 'preciate a dram er two o' that'ere argeewenty fer wettin' muh dry, thankee." Bridger complied. Joe drew a deep breath and plunged on. "When I go under, I'm sure to be goin' straight up through them'ere Pearly Gates an' settin my arse down in Heaven fer good an' all, 'cause I awready been to Hell fer forty days an' forty nights, like I been tellin'!"

When the laughter died down, Joe guzzled another swallow and went on. "So, ye kin plainly see what I been puttin' up with all thi'shere time. Wal, arter forty days an' forty nights, like I war sayin', 'spite o' ever'thin', Milton's nasty ol' laig healed up enough so's he could ride his hoss good enough fer us to be gittin' shet o' that'ere gawdfersaken camp on the river an' we traipsed on out o' thar, puttin' as many miles a'hind us ever' day as Milt could be standin', tryin', best we kin, to ketch up with y'all."

Milton held up his hand, interrupting, "Hold on, Joe! Let me be tellin' the best part. I reckon the boys hyar'll be grantin' ye'll be gittin your ree-ward in Heaven fer all ye done back thar."

Joe grinned and waved him on. "Hell! I war jist warmin' up, but yew kin have yore say. Go on."

"Wal, now, like Joe war a-tellin', we war makin' ever' mile we could ever' day, pushin' the critters hard an' not payin' 'nough mind to what we should'a been watchin' fer, when we come out o' some woods an' run into a passel o' Snakes in a medder, all of 'em painted up fer goin' to war, war what it looked like to the both of us. An', soon's they spied us, they come on a-whoopin' an' a hollerin' an' wavin' their guns an' bows an' sich! But they ain't shootin' in the air, which tells us they ain't inclined to be friendly!

"Wal, our critters war purty well tuckered an' muh laig warn't doin' too good yet, neither — fer fast ridin' fer long, mind ye — so me an' Joe, we high-tailed it fer the village we spied on t'other side o' the medder. We come bustin' in 'mongst the lodges, raisin' hell with all the wimmen an' kids an' dogs, an' shootin' in the air fer showin' we don't have no bad intentions, when we spy a big ol' lodge in the middle what likely b'longs to the chief or somebody wuthwhile, so we jist natcherly head straight fer it, jumpin' off our hosses and divin' past the doorflap an' runnin' to the right an' settin' down, purty as ye please.

"Wal, as ye mought be s'posin', 't'warn't no time a-tall afore the ol' chief comes a-pokin' through the door an' gives us a hard look afore he goes to take his seat in back o' the f'ar, which tells us we war right. That'ere lodge b'longed to some kind o' head man. Which warn't nohow comfortin', mind ye, 'cause right then I see that'ere head man war ol' Bad Goatcha, the same ol' Shoshone pirate what kilt a passel o' ol' Provo's men an' pert'near kilt Provo hisownse'f!"

Many of us were familiar with the story of EtienneProvost, who, many years before, had parleyed with that particular renegade Shoshone chief — known as Mauvais Gauche because of a severely crippled left hand — who had insisted that the whitemen lay aside their arms during the talking, because, the old chief told them, his personal medicine forbade the presence of iron anywhere near his person. As soon as Etienne and his comrades complied, Mauvais Gauche gave the signal and his warriors fell upon the whitemen and killed most of them. Provost, a remarkably strong man, was lucky enough to fight them off and escape with his life.

"As ye kin be imaginin'," Milt continued, "our hearts war purty small, 'bout then, sittin' next to sich a rascal, don'tcha know, but thar warn't no he'pin' it. We had to see it through.

"Jist then, a passel o' bucks come a-stormin' inter the lodge, all painted up an' loaded fer b'ar, fixin' to be takin' our ha'r, fer damn sure! Joe an' me war bracin' fer a fight, though it din't 'pear we could git out o' thar alive, when ol' Goatcha holds up his good hand and commences palaverin' a mile-a-minute, puttin' the kibosh on any o' them'ere young bucks what dared to be talkin' back.

"Joe an' me, we both savvy enough Snake lingo, 'sides the hand-talk, to know he's tellin' 'em they dassn't kill us right naow, 'cause he's gotta give it a good thinkin' an' do the job right. The young fellers din't like it much, but, arter a spell o' hollerin', they backed off an' let 'im have his way an' purty soon they left.

"The ol' rogue grins arter they leave an' lights his pipe an' then — damn if he don't hand the pipe over to Joe an' me an' we go to passin' that'ere pipe back an' forth fer a spell. Arter that, he calls out somethin' in Snake an' 'fore long the purtiest li'l Injun gal ye ever did see comes in totin' vittles an' all three of us go to dippin' in to 'em, sorta like we be fambly, even if we ain't. Ol' Joe hyar tol' me he din't have much appertite, cornsid'rin' whar we war an' all, an' neither did I, but we et, anyways, jist fer bein' perlite, don'tcha know.

"Arter we et, the ol' boy gits up, never sayin' nothin', an' goes out, leavin' us thar, 'thout even takin' our guns er nothin', an' we keep on a-sittin' thar, not knowin' percisely what we oughta do, but corngratcherlatin' ourse'fs on so far, so good. Natcherly it war gittin' dark all that time an' we're gittin' purty itchy, what with all the racket them'ere young bucks war makin' outside, 'speshly when their whole gawddamn hoss herd plumb busted loose an' run off!

"The two of us war thinkin' on makin' a run fer it, even lackin' hosses an' consid'rin muh bad laig an' all, when ol' Bad Goatcha comes back an' tells us mostly in sign that it be time we be gittin' out o' thar an' whar our critters'll be waitin' an' we best be ridin' like hell all night an' not stoppin' even when it's daylight! He tells us whar his daughter'll be holdin' the hosses an' we best not be meddlin' with 'er, neither. Which we tell 'im the thought never crossed our mind, even if it did more'n somewhat.

"Then he goes to the back o' the lodge an' slits the hide big enough to crawl through an' waves us goodbye, never hardly crackin' a smile the whole gawddamn time! Natcherly we waste no time hotfootin' it to whar he tol' us the hosses war an', sure enough, thar she war, that purty li'l gal, smilin' an' tellin' us to git a move on! Which we sure-as-hell done!"

Joe Meek had been hopping about like a cricket on a griddle. At last he could contain himself no longer. "Like hell we did!" he hollered. "Thi'shere damn fool, 'stid o' gittin' out o' thar quick as we can, hangs around long enough to ask that'ere purty gal what's her name, which she tells 'im is somethin' like Mountain Lamb er somethin' like, an' Milton tells 'er he'll be comin' back fer her, one o' these days, 'cause he wants her fer his own woman!"

Milt Sublette actually blushed, but he kept mum, in spite of everybody demanding to know if it was true, what Joe said about him and the Indian girl called Mountain Lamb.

It was a good story, worthy of a Rocky Mountain yarn-spinner, and those two scamps rank amongst the best in that line of work. Naturally it could have happened more or less the way they told it, but, equally, they could easily have concocted their fantastic escapade during long days in the saddle on the trail. The tale did have a familiar ring, with echos of Jim Clyman's adventure with Pierrre Tivanitagon in the Blackfoot camp. Sometimes it's best not to know for sure.

* * *

Days were getting longer, the weather warmer, and the underfur of the plews we had taken lately was getting measly. It was time to quit trapping and think about rendezvous. "An' we shorely had best be gittin' a move on," Tuttle observed. "We got a helluva roundybout way o' gittin' thar, cornsid'rin' we got to raise thet'ere cache on ther Seeds-kee-dee afore we kin be gittin' on ter ronnyvoo."

Nobody had a differing view. All of us were restless, ready for new country. Springtime produces such feelings. The women were no less enthusiastic about abandoning the daily drudgery of fleshing and curing plews, on top of foraging, cooking chores, chasing after children, and catering to their dirty, dog-tired men at day's end.

Merriment reigned as we pulled up stakes, assembled travois for goods and kids, loaded packstrings, and prepared to pay a final visit to Rocky Mountain Fur. Even crabby Anse Tolliver betrayed a glimmer of pleasure. He allowed a grin to slip onto his craggy phiz, which prompted Tuttle to ask, "What's happened, Anse? Ye run out o' them'ere green p'simmons ye 'pear to be mostly livin' on?" Much as I wish to tell it like it is, Tolliver's reply was unfit even for these pages.

A good portion of Anse's good humor was revealed next day in the RMF camp. Most of the free trappers and Company men had abandoned the harvest and come together in preparation for the journey to rendezvous. The Irish harpooner Harry Yeats was already there with his cittern and baritone voice. Frapp had put together the infernal musical machine he calls his *teufelgeigenspieler* and all manner of Indian flutes, hand-drums, little washboards, and a passel of makeshift musical noisemakers appeared out of saddlebags and possibles sacks. Even usually somber Simon Pence lingered on the fringe of the musical crowd with a well-used pair of silver spoons clinking between his fingers. Tolliver was untying his battered fiddle case from behind his saddle even as he entered camp and our campkeeper Yves Dureau already had his little Frenchy squeezebox in hand. It had been a cold, sometimes dangerous, hardworking winter for everyone. Now it was time to celebrate.

The general mood of jollity was shared by the booshways. Their fondest expectations had been exceeded by the harvest. Jim Bridger's grin grew even wider when we thumped one pack of prime fur after another on the rude trestle table he had set up in front of his lodge. "Ye been busy, I see," he said, smiling broadly as he pawed through the towering pile of deep, rich-furred plews, sorting and grading and calling out to his clerk, who recorded the owner and value of each stiff hide. Jim, for all his keen knowledge of our trade and the mountains, is unable to read or write.

"An' that ain't hardly the half of it," Brass Turtle told him. "We be headin' fer the Seeds-kee-dee fer raisin' a cache what's got a heap more'n this in it." Bridger's grin grew even wider.

When the tedious chore was completed, Jim invited us into the lodge, where he generously filled our cups with fiery *aguardiente* from a nearly empty keg. "Yep!" he announced. "Booze be pert'near gone, but it don't matter. Thar'll be plenty more come ronnyvoo, if'n Fitz an' Billy don't lose the way an' Cap'n Clark don't go to countin' the boatmen too close."

We all had a good laugh over that. What Bridger meant about Captain Clark, who is actually a general now, was that although it is forbidden to bring ardent spirits to the mountains, lest liquor be traded to Indians and thereby corrupt them, it is permissible for traders to provide a daily ration of alcohol for the boatmen who row, pole, and drag keelboats up the Missouri. Apparently it makes no nevermind that the mountain trade has been served by overland caravans of packhorses and mules, and lately of wagons, ever since South Pass was discovered in 'twenty-three. Only trading forts established on the Missouri rely on keelboats anymore, but naturally nobody is inclined to point that out to Indian Commissioner Clark and he is apparently too polite to enquire into the matter.

"Yep, it's been a damn good year," Bridger declared. "We got what we come fer, thankees to y'all. We're set to be pullin' stakes t'morry er next day an' Amurrican Fur is welcome to our leavin's!" He refilled our cups and his own and all of us fervently toasted that sentiment. We had been thorough. There wasn't much in the way of fur left in that neighborhood.

Chapter XV
Fort Nonsense

"That'ere popskull argeewenty shorely gives ye a helluva wallop, don't it naow?" Anse Tolliver observed as he guided his packstring of lightly-loaded mules through a narrow place on the trail. "Ain't complainin', mind ye," he added cheerfully — for him, that is. "Them'ere Spanyard squeezin's shorely warmed muh soul whilst I war fiddlin' with the fellers las' night."

"Ye git yorese'f a skinful, did ye?" Tuttle called back to him.

"Allus do. Them boys be pow'ful fond o' muh fiddlin', leastaways enough fer makin' 'em part with their sperrits, so's to keep me goin'."

"Reckon so," Tuttle replied, "pervidin' they be awready drunk enough so's they cain't tell how bad yer screechin' be."

"Wagh!" Anse snorted. "If'n ye din't have them'ere tin ears tacked onter that'ere hard Kaintucky haid o' your'n, ye'd know jist how good muh fiddlin' be!"

Such banter made time pass pleasantly on the trail. Neither one took the other seriously. They had been at it for nigh ten years, since they first met on Andy Henry's keelboat on the Missouri.

Dawn had barely broken when we departed the RMF camp and set out upon the northward trail to our cache on the Seeds-kee-dee. Our stock had prospered on abundant springtime grass and their measly loads that consisted only of camp gear and personal plunder burdened them but little. We mostly followed buffalo trails, which are almost always the most direct and passable, often wide enough to allow travelers to ride side by side, passing the long days in idle palaver.

This latest move washed away the last melancholy dregs that had burdened my spirit. I can't say with any certainty what it was during that easy-going journey that let me prosper from the healing powers of the mountains and the prairies. Tuttle's rough-edged philosophy played a part in it. At last I took to heart his advice that the life we lead in the Rockies is precarious. Death is our constant companion, never far off, and a body must grab onto whatever pleasure that comes along.

The fresh mountain air laved away the scales that had clouded my eyes since Rainbow's death and let me count the blessings that still remained to me. In her lifetime, she distilled joy from every minute. I chided myself for ignoring that valuable lessons that I learned from her.

Once again I thrilled to the feel of a good horse betwixt my legs. I drew strength and spirit from Kumskaka's powerful heart and surging muscles. Long-ignored sights and sounds and fragrances enchanted me once more — birdsong and chittering squirrels, the laughter and sharp chatter of our women, even the shrill complaints of fretful kids bouncing on travois, the goodnatured cursing of my fellows, warming sunshine chasing early-morning chill from my back, breeze soughing in tall pines, softly clattering aspen groves, the heady aroma of firs in sunshine, crisp, sweet-smelling mountain air, silvery streams laughing their way down hillsides, booming cataracts tumbling into deep, shadowy pools where trout lurked and flashed in mysterious blue depths, snowy mountain peaks, eternal sentinels looming high above, the musky odor of critters' sweat as they labored on steep trails, even the pungent tang of manure when they lifted their tails and scattered new life onto the trampled earth. The door to my inner being, so long pent up and barred, swung open and warming sunshine flowed into my soul.

I knew pleasure once again in the company of my companions, loyal and reliable, every one. Rough and tough, sometimes casually murderous and mostly uncivilized, they had been curiously considerate whilst I mended, granting me privacy in my grief, giving me time to heal until I was able to reclaim my place amongst our brotherhood.

Powatawa never intruded upon my journey through the pain of Rainbow's death. I had shunned him along with the others. Now I often sought him out, riding at his side, speaking rarely, but renewing my spirit merely from his presence.

Tuttle and Micah welcomed me back without ceremony. Micah resumed our favorite palaver about books and ideas and Tuttle took to joshing me once again.

* * *

Keeping bellies full was no chore. Buffalo drifting northwards on their spring migration kept the herds handy. Cows were stringy, heavy with calves or still nursing newborns, so we harvested fat young bulls, mostly picking them off from cover so as not to alarm the rest.

One day, howsomever, on a flat, open stretch of prairie, Tuttle, Micah, my father, and I surrendered to an impulse to run a sizeable bunch purely for the fun of it. With hardly a word spoken, the four of us spurred in pursuit of the herd, filling the air with whoops and hollers. The buffalo broke into a ground-eating, lumbering gallop, great shaggy heads swinging, stiff tails pointed skywards, grunting and bellowing, squealing and slobbering, as they sought to outrun us. Only one other thing heats up a man's blood and makes him lose all good sense and sound judgment as much as running buffalo a-horseback.

We lost track of one another in swirling dust kicked up by the fleeing herd. I was riding my generally easy-going, goodnatured bay horse Punch. That day he remembered his true calling. I blessed the Blackfoot bravo who first recognized Punch's rare qualities and trained him in his *métier,* as I closed upon a bunch of cows and young bulls, the seed bull chousing up laggards, urging his harem and offspring onward. Punch fairly flew across the prairie, hoofs barely touching the ground, flattened in a surging gallop that had my moccasins nigh combing the grass. He skittered in an arc around the big bull's swinging horns and plunged in amongst the cows and young bulls, then slowed to match their pace. I chose my prey, a rolling fat yearling bull. I barely flicked the rein and Punch nudged his shoulder against the young bull's flank, causing him to swing out and away from the others, still pounding onwards.

Punch eased smoothly forwards, his head just behind the buffalo's, keeping clear of the horns, providing me with a clean pistol shot behind the pumping front leg. I fired and the critter took half a dozen faltering strides, forelegs crumpling, then slid chin-first onto the grass, glazed eyes staring, blood gushing from mouth and nostrils. When the young bull slowed, Punch swung wide to evade the oncoming seed bull and pulled away from the herd rushing pell-mell to safety.

My blood was singing. I reloaded and scanned the prairie for my companions and for possible enemies waiting to take our scalps, as well as some easy meat into the bargain. Punch was breathing heavily but still excited, ready to do it again. There was no need. We required meat only for the present and I could see by then that the others had each downed a critter and were waiting for the herd to pass.

I rode forward with Powatawa and Micah to help Tuttle butcher his kill, a roly-poly youngster that promised tender vittles. We had hardly finished gorging on fresh liver sprinkled with gall and taking the prime cuts, when the caravan caught up with us. The women shooed us away and finished the skinning chore.

The sun was sinking by then, so we retired to a nearby aspen grove and made camp. Sweet, tender, juicy hump and backstrap, boudins sizzling in skillets and smoking on coals, and flavorful tongue boiling in kettles provided royal fare and we did it justice. It is not unusual for a mountaineer to put away as much as eight or ten pounds of buffalo meat at a sitting and then do it all over again a few hours afterwards. We proved the rule again that evening.

The general feeling of well-being prompted Anse Tolliver to bring out his fiddle. This time he played alone, drawing out sentimental tunes from his faraway Tennessee mountains. Those plaintive wordless ballads cast a comforting spell over our company, stilling palaver, provoking reveries. Even the women ceased their nattering and fell into respectful silence. Anse was still at it when I crawled into my robes and surrendered to slumber. Except for Dolly haranguing Tuttle and being alone in my robes, it was a perfect evening.

* * *

Such pleasant interludes became a fond memory when we plodded through a waterless, seemingly endless barren plain devoid of much else besides prickly pear and other cactus, as we pursued a direct route to the cache. Buffalo avoid such country but, happily, so do Blackfoots. At last we put it behind us and arrived on the bank of the Seeds-kee-dee, where grass is plentiful and cottonwoods thrive. Our stock was painfully gant by then but we tarried not, impatiently pushing on to learn if our hidey-hole had escaped springtime floods and the keen eyes of Indians.

Fortunately the cache was dry and still packed with prime plews. Added to what RMF was carrying for us, we were rich, leastaways as a mountaineer reckons wealth.

We lingered there several days to restore our critters on the abundant graze thereabouts. They needed all the good condition we could provide. Lugging that much fur to rendezvous would tax them sorely.

Whilst we waited, we had little to do except hunt and fish and listen to Dolly berate Tuttle for past infidelities, real and fancied, and those she reckoned he would commit at Pierre's Hole. It was nothing new. We had all been punished by her jeremiads for the past year. Even the other women had grown impatient with her rants. Tuttle is Tuttle. Take him or leave him. He is not likely to change his ways.

"If'n she war my woman," Anse declared loudly, more than once, "I'd be lodge-polin' 'er mawnin', noon an' night, 'til she shets the hell up! She ain't jist punishin' Tuttle! It's all of us what's suff'rin'!" Nobody disagreed. Tuttle shrugged and grinned sheepishly, but he never acted on Tolliver's advice.

>

We followed the Seeds-kee-dee nigh to its sources before cutting off west for Pierre's Hole. Near Horse Crick we encountered still another prodigy. Powatawa and I were taking our turn heading up our little caravan when Brass Turtle, Little Mountain, and Ned Godey burst out of the timber and onto the trail, the three of them laughing their heads off. They had been riding in advance, keeping an eye out for hostiles. "Ho, thar, fellers!" Godey hailed us. "Y'ain't never goin' to b'lieve what we jist seed!"

"Hell! We cain't b'lieve it, neither," Turtle interjected, "even if we awready seen it!"

"P'raps ye'd best tie yerse'f in yer saddle," Ned advised, laughing, "lest ye plumb fall off when ye lay eyes on what's waitin' 'round the bend. I damn near did!"

By that time most of our people had ridden forward. We clustered about the scouts, peppering them with questions. Turtle raised his hand for quiet. "You'll see fer yerownse'f's," he announced, "but 'til ye do, suffice it to say thar's a proper tradin' fort a-buildin' jist about a mile up thi'shere trail!"

"Buildin' hyar?" Anse demanded. "Ye gotta be funnin'!"

Disbelieving murmurs rippled amongst us. Paddy McBride was first to voice what everybody was thinking. "Why, they'll surely be after freezin' their arse an' dyin' o' cold, come winter. Surely they will!"

"Ef'n they don't starve fust!" Tuttle averred. "Ever'body knows they ain't no meat critters hangin' hyarabouts in winter!"

"Ner graze fer livestock, neither," Godey added, "leastaways any the critters kin git at, consid'rin' how much snow piles up hyarabouts come wintertime!"

What caused all the commotion was the idea of a permanent trading fort located in a place that is desirable only for a summertime rendezvous. In summer, it affords fresh-running water, tall trees and deadfall firewood aplenty, miles of lush, level pasture up and down the river, and a plenitude of every kind of game in every direction, but, once snow flies, it is one of the coldest, snowiest locations you are apt to find anywhere in the Rocky Mountains, completely devoid of meat critters. Only an ignoramus or a lunatic would think of settling there.

Likely a healthy dose of both. Which was what we decided half an hour later when we dismounted amid a platoon of workmen scurrying hither and thither, felling trees and hauling them to a couple-three saw-pits, digging ditches and foundations, and erecting buildings and palisade walls. Standing in the midst of that frantic anthill were two men, the both of them shouting orders to their laborers. One was tall and broad-shouldered, the other much shorter and egg-bald — which we noticed when he removed his hat to mop his sweating brow.

The tall, dark-bearded man approached us, smiling, and introduced himself. "I be Joe Walker, Joseph Rutherford Walker, lately o' Missourah, an' that'ere be Captain Bone-vee, late o' the Yew-nited States Army. As ye can see, we're settin' up fer tradin' hereabouts. An' y'all?"

We supplied our names and little else. Only Anse Tolliver displayed a willingness to say more. "Walker, ye say," Anse queried eagerly, "an' Rutherford? Ain't I hearin' more'n some'at o' Tinnissee in yer talk? Ye got somebody name o' Sarey Tolliver somewhars 'mongst yer kin, do ye? I be Anse Tolliver, like I said"

The big man laughed out loud. "'Deed I do. Leastaways that's what I recomember from Mama's Good Book. So yew be one o' them'ere Tollivers. Let's yew'n me chaw on it."

The two of them strolled off to engage in what appeared to be a goodnatured chat frequently punctuated with bursts of laughter. The little captain, observing that Walker had departed, abandoned his supervisory ranting and joined us. "Good day, gentlemen," he began, an unmistakeable French accent larding his careful English speech, "I am Captain Eulalie Bonneville — " naturally he pronounced his name properly in French, *Bohn-vee,* which was soon corrupted into *Bonnyville* by a few literate mountaineers. "I am at present on official leave from the Army of the United States. I weesh you welcome 'ere. If you weesh to trade your beaver skins, Messieurs Walker and Cerré will be 'appy to accommodate you on the morrow."

It was plain to see that Bonneville was new to our part of the world. He appeared to be more impressed, unfavorably, by our dirty, blood-stained, trail-worn clothing than by the prospect of doing business with us. We mumbled thanks for his hospitality and allowed that, yes, we would hang on for a spell, but we said neither yes or no about making trade with him, which we had no intention of doing. Up close, with his hat on, we saw that Bonneville was much younger than we had taken him for. He was not very tall but sturdy. His imperious eye and brisk treatment of us suggested that he was no great friend of the common man.

We moved upstream about a quarter-mile and set our camp on the river's edge. On the way, Finn McCool commented wryly, "One thing ye must admit, that popinjay captain possesses one important advantage the rest of us lack. Our Red Brethren'll niver be after castin' a covetous eye upon his hairless pate!"

Cookfires were blazing and the aroma of roasting meat hung over the camp by time an unusually congenial Anse Tolliver caught up with us. "Thar ye be!" Tuttle called out in greeting. "We war thinkin' ye jined up with Cap'n Egg-bald, figgerin' on settlin' daown hyar in Fort Harebrain er whatcha mought be callin' it!"

"No sich a gawddamn thang, as ye know full well," Anse snapped back at him, "but I been larnin' all manner o' thangs from Cap'n Walker. Turns out he be shirttail kin to me back in Tinnissee, nigh Jump Mountain, whar muh daddy come from." Anse was plainly impressed by his Tennessee kinsman. "Ol' Joe mought be new to thi'shere patch o' country, but he shore-as-hell ain't no greenhorn. When he warn't sheriffin' an' marshalin' daown thar in Missourah, he war guidin' traders to Santy Fee an' trappin' thar'abaouts afore he come back to Sain' Looie. Cap'n Joe Walker be the righteous article. Ye kin wager on it!"

"What else did ye larn," Brass Turtle asked. "How come that'ere sojer cap'n plumped hisse'f down whar he did? In mebbe the worst place he's like to find in the whole gawddamn mountains?"

"Cain't be sure. Even Joe ain't sartin-sure. Sez he tol' 'im 'baout how the winters'd be an' all, but thar warn't no steerin' 'im off o' thi'shere partic'lar place. Din't make no nevermind what Joe an' Mike Cerré an' some other freemen an' Dellerwars he's got along with 'im had to say. He war set on settlin' ri'chere an' no buts abaout it, 'spite o'they all be callin' it Fort Nonsense when he cain't hear 'em."

As I have mentioned elsewhere in this narrative, mountaineers are a suspicious lot. Unlettered though most of our fraternity are, they are nonetheless intelligent. Stupid men die off in the first winter, if not before. Anything unusual and out of place attracts our attention and curiosity. Fort Nonsense was onesuch. All sorts of conjecture sputtered throughout suppertime and into darkness.

"Reckon ol' Bonnyville's pickin' up whar Jed Smith left off," Brass Turtle concluded. "Mark me, ye kin wager the guv'mint's ahind it all!!"

"'Pears so," Godey agreed. "Thar cain't be no other good reason fer plantin' hisse'f ri'chere, freezin' an' starvin' like he'll surely be, if it warn't fer keepin' an eye on Aitch-bee-cee an' the rest o' the Brits."

"'Tis true," Finn concurred. "The border is uncertain an' nat'rally the Sassenachs wish to claim this land for their own." He reflected for a spell, then added, "And who better than a military man to be watchin' out for the nation's interest?"

"Howsomever it be, one thing be sartin-sure," Turtle surmised, "competition's gittin' more cut-throat ever' time ye look. Fust it war Amurrican Fur, then ol' Pierre Chouteau an' Joe Robidoux jumpin' in, operatin' on their own hook, 'sides what Chouteau's got goin' with Amurrican Fur, an' now this baldy Frog sojer-boy."

"Don't reckon thi'shere Frenchy be doin' it on his own hook, neither," Anse put in. "Joe Walker's purty sure ol' Jake Astor's puttin' up the stake fer thi'shere whole shebang. Astor's been mad as hell an' frettin' ever since them'ere Nor'westers run him off twenny years ago. 'Pears ever'whar ye be lookin', ol' Jake's got a finger in the pie!"

"Reckon Fitz an' Jim an' the others best be grabbin' off ever' plew they kin afore they git crowded out," Ned opined. "Don't be fergittin' ol' Billy Sublette's still holdin' a passel o' paper on 'em!"

Tuttle had held his peace during most of the palaver. Now he observed shrewdly, "All o' thet mought be so, but whilst they be fightin' it aout, I reckon all of 'em'll be biddin' up the price o' fur an' them as has ther plews'll settin' purty — meanin' us!" He snorted and spat and let out a hearty guffaw before he declared, "But ye cain't be eatin' ner drinkin' plews, 'less'n ye sell 'em! I, fer one, be purely froze fer ronnyvoo! Let's be haulin' arse outa hyar, fust thang t'morry, an' be gittin' on to Pier's Hole!"

Nobody had a better idea. We resolved to get back on the trail first thing in the morning.

* * *

Our early-morning departure was, howsomever, somewhat delayed. Although we had resolved not to trade with Bonneville, an opportunity to acquire gunpowder, galena, percussion caps, and even a few luxuries such as coffee, tea, and honey was too much to resist, for who knew when, or even if, Tom Fitzpatrick and Bill Sublette would show up in Pierre's Hole?

Joe Walker and Mike Cerré were fair, even generous, in grading the few plews we bartered and what they charged for their goods. It was plain to see that both men were experienced in the fur trade, even though they were new to our particular part of the Rockies. They even treated us to a generous round of rum for good measure. We departed Fort Nonsense with good feelings about Walker and Cerré. Captain Bonneville was a horse of a rather different color.

Chapter XVI
Pierre's Hole

We pretty much ran between the raindrops on our westward journey. The three Blackfoot war parties we spied on the way were too few in number to attack a caravan of our size. Our score of guns would surely take too great a toll of their numbers. They let us pass without incident. As we neared our destination we encountered few Indians of any sort. Traveling through Davey Jackson's Hole, only cold firepits and pale lodge-rings on the grass showed where they had camped before moving on, likely to trade at rendezvous in nearby Pierre's Hole. Worn-out moccasins and suchlike discarded trash showed they were Snakes and Crows.

That particular journey was a sentimental one for me and likely for my companions, as well. It was spring of 1832, precisely ten years since we had embarked on Ashley and Henry's first expedition up the Missouri to the Yellowstone, then on to the Rocky Mountains. Except for Powatawa, Micah, Cesár, and Finn McCool, all of the whites and Indians still in our bunch had been part of that initial adventure. Not all of our original companions had survived that decade of hardship, peril, and privation, but the rest of us had been welded into a hardy brotherhood of mountaineers willing, even eager, to take on whatever challenges our mountain wilderness might offer, a band more close-knit than any blood-kin clan you are likely to encounter. I am proud as Lucifer to be a part of it and I daresay every man amongst us feels the same.

Such sentimental thoughts whisked away as we entered upon the final downward slope through the pass in the Tetons that opens upon the broad green basin called Pierre's Hole. The trail was rutted with recent wagon tracks, proclaiming Bill Sublette's passage, not as many, howsomever, as the previous year, nor as deep, likely only light dearborns, not heavy wagons.

When we first spied tents and tall lodges dotting the prairie, every man, and the women, too, sat a little straighter in his saddle and preened in anticipation of our grand entry into rendezvous. Even our saddle horses pricked their ears and livened their gait, responding to the excitement coursing through the legs of their riders.

Earlier that morning, everybody donned his finest clothing, clean calico shirts and leather garments, much of it resplendent with elaborate embroidery of multicolored quills and trade beads. The white bachelors scraped off whiskers and stubble and a few courageous souls even braved the chill waters of the crick to lave away months of sweat and dried blood and accumulated grime. Smelly dogfaces are not popular amongst Indian women. Married men, amongst whom I still counted myself, had long since been bullied into relative cleanliness.

The women were especially colorful, clad as many were in rich silks and satins and velvets, faces painted and hair carefully plaited, shining and redolent of bear grease, soft antelope leggin's bespangled with shiny silver coins and glittering trinkets, moccasins and belts and pokes and knife sheaths agleam with quillwork and beaded embroidery, saddles resting on apishamores bedizened with multi-hued quillwork, pommels and cantles jingling with hawk bells, headstalls festooned with fluttering ribbons, feathers, and plumes, encrusted with quills and beadwork.

Horses sported ribbons in manes and tails and painted designs on shoulders and flanks, hand-prints and symbols that possessed a special meaning for their owners. When we set out on that final leg of our journey to rendezvous, except for the presence of women and kids, our company appeared not much different from a proper Indian war party.

My daughter Iris insisted on riding with me, perched upon the pommel, jabbering a macaroni of tongues in her excitement. She, too, was decked out in her finest raiment, her magical eyes sparkling, swiveling and bobbing about, taking in everything around us. When we reached the foot of the pass and entered level ground, Cat rode up beside me and retrieved a protesting Iris from me, settling her upon the pommel of the handsome Spaniard saddle that Ned had provided for her.

Unencumbered now, I rode forward, trailing my packstring, and joined my fellows. They were already increasing their gait, eager to reach the rendezvous. As we drummed across the prairie at an easy lope, I glanced back and beheld our women not far behind, their hair and all manner of ornaments streaming, mouths open in smiles and laughter, trailing packhorses, travois jolting and bouncing over the uneven ground, some with little kids hanging on for dear life and laughing their heads off. Cat was foremost amongst them, clutching Iris to her breast as she skillfully guided her mount over the rough terrain, trailing half a dozen packhorses, one of them dragging a travois. Her lips were parted in a half-smile over pearly teeth, sparkling black eyes almost lost behind high cheekbones streaked with vermilion stripes, her slim, lithe form responding to every shift and surge of her high-colored paloosie horse. I felt a tightening of my loins and instantly rebuked myself for such an unworthy impulse. Cat is Ned's woman and I will always respect their mutual love and devotion.

I felt a momentary pang when I thought of Rainbow and how she would have gloried that moment, but I reflected that Rainbow's generous nature would never begrudge another's pleasure. Except for Blackfoots. And now, Bannocks, too.

We swept in amongst the Indian camps, scattering kids and dogs and women snatching little ones from our path, all of us whooping and yelling, dodging around old folks hobbling to safety. We slowed at the Snake encampment, where Tuttle's Dolly and Brass Turtle's Tallymesko separated from our merry mob. They reined up to visit with their people and show off their children, who were quickly grabbed from their mothers' arms and passed around amongst admiring female kinfolk. The same thing occurred when we passed the Absóraqa bands of Stone Bird's Sally and Pretty Horse's Bashful Nettie, who was no longer shy. Living amongst our rowdy, democratic crew had long ago erased her timidity.

Iron Bow, straight and tall and strong as a weathered oak, stood before a swarm of Flatheads, raising his arm in greeting, when we thundered into his Salish camp. Cat and Molly drew rein and abandoned our furious charge. They were instantly engulfed in a throng of laughing women who yanked Iris and Paddy's two kids away from them and paraded the children about like treasured trophies. Fast Horse grasped a handful of mane, swung himself onto his buffalo runner, and joined our mad rush into the trappers' sprawling campground. When he caught up with me, he leaned out and nearly dragged me from my saddle with a welcoming hug.

We were late arrivals at the biggest rendezvous I had ever seen. Hundreds of trappers were already there, free men and Company *engagés* from several outfits. So were the traders. Only Bonneville's people were absent. They never did show up. Sublette's carriages and Rocky Mountain Fur's white trade tents were clustered together. We made a beeline for that camp. Our noisy arrival brought the RMF partners pouring out of a big trade tent — Bridger, Milt Sublette, Frapp, and Gervais. Bill Sublette brought up the rear. Only Tom Fitzpatrick was absent.

Milt Sublette called out, "Got all o' yer peltries hyar, safe an' sound an' waitin' on ye!" Which naturally made us feel good.

"Whar's Fitz?" Tuttle demanded. Ain't seen thet'ere Irisher fer more'n a year! Whar's he at?"

The welcoming smiles faded from the partners' faces. Bill Sublette stepped forward. "Don't rightly know," he said solemnly. "We been hopin' mebbe ye seen 'im along the way."

"Nope," Godey said. "Ain't seen nothin' of 'im. Warn't he with you, Bill?"

"He war," Sublette replied, "but he rode on ahead when we got to the Siskadee, so's to spread word amongst the Injuns about thi'shere ronnyvoo an' to let y'all know we war comin' on behind. Took two good Kaintucky hosses with 'im, fer trav'lin fast. Ain't seen ner heard nothin' of 'im since."

Lingering behind the others was a familiar face, Bobby Campbell, unseen since the 'twenty-eight rendezvous. His travels to the East and Scotland and wherever else had done him no harm. His ruddy complexion, robust frame, and cheerful grin bespoke good health and well-being. Most of us remembered the frail, puny young lad from Philadelphia who had come to the mountains in the early 'twenties to remedy his failing health and how he had bloomed on fat cow and pure mountain air. Ned Godey once summed it up neatly. "These hyar parts'll cure ye or kill ye, one, an' Bobby pulled the long straw."

Concern for Tom Fitzpatrick's whereabouts and well-being naturally cast a pall over our high spirits, which Jim Bridger sought to dispel with feigned cheerfulness. "Don'tcha be frettin' over Fitz! If anybody kin be dodgin' Blackfoots an' grizzle b'ars, ye kin wager yer arse ol' Tom'll do it, fust-rate." When that rosy prediction failed to brighten our mood, he called out, "Why'n'tcha step down an' git yer fust drink o' thi'shere ronnyvoo? Our treat! Ye likely worked up a consid'able dry gittin' hyar!" Which invitation greatly improved our dampened feelings and which, naturally, we did.

* * *

By time we left the traders and went in search of a suitable campsite, the women had already picked one on the bank of the Popo-azhieh and put up their lodges. Packs of furs and sundry plunder littered the ground. Cat, likely with Molly's help, had thoughtfully erected the lodge I shared with Micah and my father. There was little left for me to do but unload my packstring, stow my belongings in and around the lodge, and turn my critters out with the huge horse herd that had accumulated in the lush meadows nearby. Naturally I kept one good saddle horse, this time Kumskaka, tethered in camp, as we all did. Dureau and L'Archévêque kept them all well-fed with armloads of prairie hay.

When I returned from the meadow I discovered Tuttle Thompson stomping about, muttering curses, looking forlorn. His lodge, his packs and plunder, and his Dolly woman and daughter Suzy were nowhere to be seen. "Where d'ye reckon she is, Tuttle?" I asked innocently, although I had already guessed where she was. Her Shoshone cousin Tallymesko had already erected Brass Turtle's lodge and stowed their belongings.

"Don't rightly know fer sure, but I got a pow'ful inklin' thet'ere gawddamn woman has gone an' lef' me!" he gruffed. "Splittin' ther sleeprobes an' goin' back to 'er kinfolk, shore as hell!"

"P'raps we'd best be askin' Turtle's Tally woman what she knows," I suggested. "They're both Snakes an' Tally stopped off with her in the Snake camp when we rode in."

Tuttle followed me to Turtle's lodge, where Tallymesko informed us that Dolly refused to put up with Tuttle's philandering ways. She intended to remain with her people. Tally volunteered her own opinion that Dolly's jealous behavior was most unusual and extreme. After all, Tuttle never beat his woman, as Indian men and most white-eyes commonly do, and there was little harm in Tuttle's wandering ways.

"An' whut abaout muh chile, muh li'l gal, muh darlin' Suzy gal?" Tuttle muttered, signing along with his English words, as we always do, out of habit, even with other white-eyes. Anyone who has been in the mountains for very long does it.

Tally replied that the child would remain with Dolly. Which was simple commonsense. How could Tuttle expect to care for a year-old child on his own? Tuttle refused to accept it, leastaways right then.

Half a dozen of us accompanied Tuttle to the Shoshone camp to retrieve his livestock, plews, and personals. Tallymesko, Cat, and Molly came along, too. They tried unsuccessfully to persuade Dolly to reconsider, but she remained adamant. The Snakes were more confounded than we were that one of their women could be so pernickety about her white-eyes husband's harmless extramarital doin's. Several of them signed, behind her back, that she must be crazy. As it turned out, Dolly's family reluctantly let her remain with them and a wifeless Tuttle returned to camp.

On the way back, Brass Turtle sought to cheer him up. "Hell, Tuttle," he offered, "it ain't like ye've gone an' lost a good buffler-runnin' hoss ner a pack o' plews er sumpin' wuthwhile like that! Knowin' you, ye'll be beddin' another afore nex' daylight!" Tuttle just grunted, but I, too, reckoned that my good friend would not mourn overmuch, except for his daughter. He wouldn't tarry long without a feminine companion.

* * *

"Thet ol' Nor'wester Eerie-quah Pier Whatchamacallit shore knew whar to go fer shadin' up, come summertime, din't he naow?" Tuttle opined as he hunkered down at the cookfire and downed a steaming cup of coffee. He was remarkably cheerful for a man who, the night before, had emptied a couple kettles of trader's popskull before wandering off, most likely to celebrate his regained bachelorhood.

"Whar ye been?" Ned Godey asked with a wink.

"Busy," Tuttle replied. Nobody inquired further. We reckoned we knew.

"Ye're right," Paddy said, returning to Tuttle's earlier comment. "'Tis a darlin' place, it is, surely, so beeyootiful I'm wond'rin' why the Good Lord didn't set it down someplace in Ireland, along wid all the other paradises He was always after giftin' the Auld Sod wid."

"If'n ye think so much o' yer Old Country, why in hell didja come draggin' yer Irish arse over hyar, then," Anse asked sourly.

Paddy leveled a cool, blue-eyed gaze at his old friend and everlasting tormentor. "'Cause I got sick an' tired o' livin' on taties, that's why. Lovely an' ferever green as it is, ye can't be eatin' shamrocks an' ye won't be findin' a single buffler in all o' that charmin' isle. Meat's fer the Brits an' us Micks're ferever spadin' spuds jist fer keepin' body an' soul together! Much as I'm after pinin' fer it, sometoimes, leavin' the Sod was the smartest thing I ever done."

The warmth of Paddy's reply brought a halt to Anse's teasing. "Yer right," he said to nobody in particular. "Thi'shere purty place'll do fer me, fer good an' all. It's shorely got ever'thin' a man could be askin' fer." Which was a remarkable pronouncement for our constant complainer.

There was no need, that morning, to rouse ourselves and go hunting. Little Mountain and Acorn had risen early and ridden out to harvest a couple of fat young bulls from the scattered herd that still grazed along the fringes of the lush valley that was old Pierre Tevanitagon's favorite summering place. The aroma of roasting meat on the cookfires had our mouths watering. Further palaver was forestalled when L'Archévêque called out, *"C'est prête! Viens! Viens! Voici le moment! Avant je jete la viande aux chiens!* Nobody challenged Jean-Luc's threat to throw the meat to the dogs. We wasted no time in helping ourselves to slabs of smoking-hot hump and meaty ribs, leaving precious little for canine hangers-on.

Thus fortified, we headed for Rocky Mountain Fur's trade tents, returning a couple hours later with the pack-animals' canvas panniers bulging with our initial purchases, essentials such as gunpowder, caps, galena, traps, and suchlike, goods we can't live without. A second trip to RMF's bustling emporium proved to be somewhat more expensive, leastaways for the married men. That time, the women went along. After the previous year's lack of a proper rendezvous, they were starved for the luxuries they, as trappers' women, had come to take for granted.

Tuttle derived a certain sour satisfaction from the timing of Dolly's impulsive desertion. "Leastaways," he growled, "she din't think fur enough ahaid to wait long enough to steal me blind, loadin' up on foofurraw, afore she run off on me! Reckon right naow she be grindin' her choppers down ter nubbins, settin' over thar 'mongst ther Snakes, frettin' on haow she jumped the gun afore tradin' time! Good fer 'er!"

I had been dreading rendezvous and how it would stir up memories of Rainbow and her delight in dealing with the traders, recalling her innocent greed for their flashy gimcrackery, how her eyes had sparkled with each new trinket and swatch of trade cloth. At first it was so, but as I watched our women bartering and haggling, chattering and tittering and bursting into laughter when they thought they had put one over on the clerks, which was hardly ever so, their innocent enthusiasm seeped into my chilly spirit and warmed me. I vied with Ned to gift Cat with whatever caught her fancy. I owed her more than I could ever repay for the loving care she showered on my daughter. Molly, too, got whatever she wished, for she was ever willing to mother Iris along with her own two little ones.

After a spell I stepped back and observed Indian women of half a dozen different tribes, for the present unmindful of traditional hatreds, crowding up to the trestle tables, happily swapping cased mink and otter pelts and winter-white weasel skins, moccasins, butter-soft brain-tan buffalo robes and elk and deer hides, and gorgeous quilled and beaded belt-pokes, bags, and apishamores in return for Saint Louis mercantile trash not worth a penny on the dollar for the native treasures taken in trade.

When the women acquired a surfeit of traders' treasures, leastaways for a spell, we men handed over our saddle mounts and set out on a stroll through the rendezvous, by far the biggest we had ever seen. Rocky Mountain Fur wasn't the big he-dog trader that Ess-Jay&Ess had been for so many years. They faced stiff competition from half a dozen outfits — amongst them, American Fur, Hudson's Bay, Pierre Chouteau's side venture with Joe Robidoux, and a new outfit called Bean & Sinclair. There was still another, a rank newcomer to the mountains, a hard-nose Yankee name of Nathaniel Wyeth, whom Bill Sublette had unaccountably allowed to tag along with his outfit. They were all doing a brisk business with hundreds of trappers and even more Indians eager to lay hands on whitemen's merchandise theretofore not even dreamed of in the native imagination. Besides useful goods such as trade guns, gunpowder, galena, knives, and the like, they were just as avid to acquire utterly useless frivolities. It was commonplace to see sturdy, painted warriors strutting about twirling frilly parasols and sporting beribboned sunbonnets perched upon their feathered topknots.

Whilst we filled kettles with trader's booze, lest we die of thirst along the way, Brass Turtle spied Milton Sublette seated at the door of a Shoshone-style lodge in the midst of the RMF encampment. "Lookee thar!" Turtle called out gleefully. "I do b'lieve ol' Milton Thunderbolt's gone an' got hisse'f a woman of his own, 'stid o' pickin' a differ'nt prairie flower ever' night!" It appeared to be so. Milt was engaged in earnest conversation with perhaps the most beautiful woman, Indian or otherwise, I had ever laid eyes on.

Joe Meek was standing nigh and he was quick to confirm Turtle's surmise. "That's per-cisely what ol' Milt's gone an' done. Why'n'tcha mosey on over an' gitcherse'f a closer look at 'er? I guar-own-tee it's wuth doin'."

We needed no urging. Half a dozen of us trooped over to Milton's lodge to say hello. Milt greeted us with a broad smile. "Mawnin', fellers! Come to meet muh bride, didja? Wal, hyar she be, purtiest li'l gal anybody ever seen hyarabouts er anywhar's else! An' jist as fust-rate on the inside, too!"

She was indeed comely, roses blooming under a flawless tawny complexion, exquisitely formed under immaculate quilled doeskins, standing now at Milton's side, eyes modestly downcast in the midst of our all-male company. A smile hinted at her lips, howsomever. "She be called Mountain Lamb," Milton was saying, "onliest daughter o' that'ere ol' scoundrelly Snake, Bad Goatcha, what let Meek an' me git out'n his camp still keepin' our ha'r, though I sure-as-hell don't reckon we'll ever be knowin' why he done so. An' Mountain Lamb hyar war the one what made it happen, bringin' up our hosses like she done, so's we could git the hell outa thar!" He winked and added, "I toldja I'd be goin' back to git 'er."

When Milt and Joe Meek told us of their unlikely adventure with the infamous Shoshone chief Mauvais Gauche and his beautiful daughter, we had dismissed it as another of Milton's fanciful tall tales, but here stood living proof of their veracity, rare as that particular commodity mostly is with those two.

When we had feasted our eyes sufficiently, we took our leave, promising to return soon. Considering Mountain Lamb's beauty, that would be no difficult chore.

Once out of earshot, Ned Godey said, "Didja notice ol' Milt never stood up, not even once. Reckon that'ere bad laig o' his'n's still troublin' 'im."

"Hell!" Tuttle snorted. "If'n I had a purty thang like thet'n nigh, I'd not be gittin' up, neither — ner even gittin' out'n ther sleeprobes!"

The distant sound of music turned our steps towards a sprawling aspen grove. On the way, during one of our frequent halts to remedy possible snakebite, McCool inquired, "Has any one o' ye seen Moses Harris? I daresay he'll be knowin' how the land lies concernin' the many tradin' concerns we're seein' here."

Brass Turtle jerked his chin in the direction of the aspen grove. "Reckon ye'll most likely find 'im thar'abouts. Black's partial to settin' up amongst the quakies, when he kin."

Turtle's remark jogged my memory. Harris had once told me, "I git me some extry en-joys outer settin' camp 'mongst them'ere quakies, on account o' them pearly-white tree-trunks allus put me in mind o' purty wimmen's laigs, all smooth an' white like they be, liftin' straight up in the air, like they be waitin' jist fer me, invitin' me in betwixt 'em."

Another man might prefer to camp amid quaking aspens because of the plenitude of deadfall limbs that those trees drop constantly and because aspen wood produces less smoke than pine or fir, helping to escape hostile eyes, but Moses Harris's thoughts are rarely distant from his crotch.

Sure enough, we discovered Black's solitary camp amongst the quakies, but Finn's queries had to wait. Harris was perched on a downed tree trunk, spinning a yarn for a rapt audience of trappers and greenhorn hostlers, all of them hanging onto his every word. The story he told went something like this:

"Wal, arter ronnyvoo a coupl'a years back, by time we got on daown to Sain' Looie, I war feelin' more'n some'at horny, as ye mought be s'posin', so soon's I got done with muh chores fer Billy, I natcherly hotfooted on daown to Veed Poach to Matilda's whorehouse. All the way up an' back from these hyar parts, all I kep' thinkin' 'bout war one o' Matilda's li'l ladies, a purty thang name o' Betsy! She ain't only purty, she be fust-rate at her trade! An' that ain't all! The best thang be, she purely loves doin' it! Which, if ye know anythin' a-tall 'baout sich matters, is more'n half o' what it's all abaout an' twice the en-joys fer yew an' likely fer herownse'f!

"I war in sich a hurry to git on daown thar to Matilda's, I din't even take the time to git m'se'f a bathe at the barber's, ner nothin' else! Jist traipsed on daown like I war, clothes all greasy-dirty an' drippin' hoss sweat an' a passel o' muh own an' totin' half o' the prairie on muh hide.

"Problem war, howsomever, when I got thar, li'l Betsy warn't thar! Matilda tells me she's gone back to Kaintuck fer lookin' arter her ol' ailin' Ma er somethin'! Wal, as ye kin imagine, I war plumb destroyed, carryin', like I war, a britchclout full o' greetin's from the mountains an' naow nobody to be givin' 'em to! Leastaways nobody I been thinkin' 'baout fer nigh half a year!

"Wal, whilst I war commiseratin' m'se'f 'bout li'l Betsy, good ol' Matilda sez, wal, mebbe thangs ain't so bad as I be thinkin' an' she hollers fer one of her new gals. This'n war a dark-eyed li'l Frenchy, name o' Minette, jist come up out o' N'awlins, purty as a pitcher an' frien'ly as hell. Wal, t'warn't no time fer bein' picky an', like the feller sez, any port'll do ye in a storm. Afore ye could blink yer eye, me'n her war traipsin' up the steps to her li'l chamber."

The ordinarily noisy trappers surrounding Harris were silent, hushing anybody who spoke above a whisper, their attention riveted upon every word Black let fall.

"Wal, as ye mought be s'posin', 't'warn't no time a-tall 'til muh clothes war off an' in a heap an' she war washin' up muh nether parts, like any proper tart'll do, don'tcha know. 'Bout then, she cocks up an eyebrow an' smiles all over her purty li'l face an' she sez to me, 'Oh, M'sieu, I seenk I know 'ow all ze squaws at *rendezvous* mus' be callin' you. I seenk zey mus' be callin' you Stovepipe!'

"Well, hell! I reckon ye kin feature how good that got me to feelin'! Why, I could feel muh chest jist a-swellin' up with pride an' I sez to her, 'Ye really think muh pal's that big? I allus thought he's awful purty!'

"'Baout then, she laughs plumb out loud an' winks her eye an' sez, 'But no, M'sieu, he ees not zat *beeg,* but he ees, *certainement,* zat *dirty!'*"

The roar of laughter that erupted from the trappers likely stampeded buffalo a mile away. Moses Harris, the consummate comical tale-teller of the entire Rocky Mountain fur trade, threw back his head and joined the general laughter, obviously pleased with another good story well-told.

We chose not to interrupt Black just then, for, pausing only to take several swigs from the kettles his admirers pressed upon him, he launched into another whopper. As we continued on our way, Ned Godey observed, "D'jever notice how 'most ev'ry comical hist'ry Black tells, 'speshly when he's in it, afore it's over, turns tail an' bites hisownse'f on the arse?"

I had noticed, but Ned's remark made the lesson stick. Bragging is all right in its place, but Harris's way is much more entertaining.

The siren song of fiddles drew us as surely as Odysseus's enchanted crew to a distant part of the grove, where we discovered the fiddlers, Anse Tolliver and Cap'n Billy, Yves Dureau and his little concertina, and the ever-cheerful erstwhile harpooner Harry Yeats, strumming the cittern in his lap, his fine Irish baritone raised in song. The surrounding mob bristled with hand drums, Indian flutes, Jews-harps, and all manner of musical contraptions. In the midst of a score of wildly dancing trappers cavorting in the clearing was red-faced Henry Fraeb, merrily banging on his German infernal machine as he dodged flailing arms and high-kicking moccasins.

Indians greatly outnumbered whites amongst the ring of spectators, most of them standing quietly, arms folded, faces impassive, wrapped in their dignity, likely baffled by the unrestrained merriment of the Americans. Only younger bravos and a few maidens betrayed infection by that wild cacophony, their moccasins shuffling furtively, bodies swaying in response to the alien music.

When he spied us, Anse dropped his fiddle from under his chin and called out in his cracked, high-pitched Tennessee whine, "Thar ye be! An' abaout time, too! A feller mought be dyin' o' the thirsties up hyar, fer all y'all give a good gawddamn! Why'n'tcha pass them'ere kittles up thisaway afore we plumb die o' the dries!"

Naturally we knew better than to turn our kettles loose amongst that ever-thirsty gang, but we did step forward to treat each musician to a healthy gulp or two. Whilst Harry the Harpooner was doing his best to drain my kettle, I observed that he had prospered, both physically and materially, during his three years in the mountains. He glowed with good health and his clothes and trappings were of the finest. He no longer sported a seaman's stubby tarred pigtail. Now he wore his hair long in plaits wrapped in otter fur. "It appears the mountains suit ye, Harry," I ventured.

He grinned almost boyishly. "None better, I warrant ye, Temple," he declared warmly. "I do believe I've discovered hereabouts what it was I was ferever seekin' on land an' sea. What more could a sane man be askin' fer than passin' all o' his days in this darlin' place? A full belly, most o' the toime — an' the best o' meat it is! — an' not a bloody spud fer a thousand miles around! We're blessed wid willin' Injun women what've never studied the occupation o' naggin'! An' niver a bloody priest preachin' at ye, ferever tellin' ye what a sinful blaggard ye be an' how ye'll be after burnin' in 'tarnal hell ferever fer doin' what a proper man does nat'rally!" He tipped up my kettle for another swig, then declared, "An' here, ragged-arse Harry Yeats is after ridin' as high an' mighty as any bloody Sassenach landlord ye'll iver be findin' in all of Ireland — an' doin' it on better horses, too!"

Harry's paean to mountain life was interrupted by Tolliver drawing his bow sharply across his fiddlestrings. "I must be goin' now," he apologized. "Ye know how tetchy the auld blatherskite can be." He returned my kettle with the words, "An' a plenitude o' thankees, Temple darlin', fer the use o' yer poteen."

Whilst Harry was extolling the virtues and blessings of mountain life, I noticed a ragged, unsmiling young man I took to be an American sitting by himself, not far off, at the edge of the crowd. Even amongst that throng of unwashed trappers clad in greasy buckskins, he appeared poor indeed, toes stucking out of broken, ill-made moccasins, his shabby, poorly-tanned leather clothing ripped and stained with dirt and blood and hanging loosely on his scarecrow frame, a truly forlorn character.

On an impulse, I thought to offer him a drink and a friendly word. As I drew nigh, two things belied his starveling appearance — his eyes, quick and bright and intelligent in his thin, unsmiling face, and his battered flintlock rifle, clean and glistening with whale oil, resting against his shoulder. "Howdy," I began uncertainly, setting the kettle down beside him, "ye look like ye mightn't be sayin' no to a drink." I regretted for a moment my forwardness, but the quick smile that lit up his features dispelled my embarrassment.

"Thankee most kindly," he replied in familiar accents. "Much obliged. But won't ye be sittin' down an' joinin' me? T'won't do for me to be drinkin' alone." He thrust out a hand that was remarkably clean. "I be Zenas Leonard, late o' Pennsylvanie. I be new to these partic'lar parts."

I hunkered down, shook his hand, and introduced myself, mumbling something about my having been thereabouts for a spell. We passed the kettle back and forth, mostly palavering about young Leonard's adventures in the fur trade during the past year. He was not one of Sublette's hostlers, recruited in Saint Louis for the journey to rendezvous. Rather, he had been engaged by an outfit called Gantt&Blackwell, now defunct, trapping beaver during the previous year on the prairies east of the mountains.

He told me of that miserable first year, how he and his companions learned trapping skills and did rather well at it, only to lose most of their catch to Indians who discovered the plews hanging in a grove of trees where they had been hung for safekeeping, how all of their horses had starved to death when deep winter snows covered the graze and sweet cottonwood couldn't be found, and how they had spent most of the winter trying unsuccessfully to get to Santa Fe to buy more horses, turned back, time and again, by deep snow in the passes. It was a wonder that he and the other greenhorns hadn't suffered the same fate as their horses. Leonard's present miserable condition argued that they had come close to it.

As he spoke, I recalled our own first winter in 'twenty-two, trapping on the Musselshell. Cold and difficult as it was, good fellowsip, reliable leaders, and lessons learned from more experienced men brought us through it. As I have often done, I thanked my stars for my good fortune in falling in with the men of my bunch. Zenas and his fellow neophytes had not been so blessed. They had been a rabble lost in the wilderness, ill-prepared, and saddled with indifferent leaders who knew little more than their followers did.

Callow as he was and new to the trapping trade, Zenas Leonard was a young man of strong opinions. He hardly knew either Blackwell or Gantt, but he expertly described the partisan of his little band of greenhorn trappers, one Stephens, as a greedy, inept, cowardly, unprincipled, dishonest scoundrel. In the end, Stephens had claimed as his own the measly few plews that his men had harvested in the spring hunt and sold them to Tom Fitzpatrick for his own profit.

Mention of Fitzpatrick's name captured my attention. When my companions beckoned to me, signaling that they wished to move off, I waved them on, promising to catch up later.

I learned that Leonard's outfit first encountered Fitz at the mouth of the Laramie in spring of 'thirty-one, when Tom was heading back to Saint Louis and Gantt and Blackwell were on their way to beaver country. Zenas spoke bitterly about Fitzpatrick's flat refusal to provide helpful advice to the newcomers. "What a hard, selfish, grasping man he is!" he sputtered. "Treatin' us like intruders! Said he'd tell us nothin', that we'uns'd best turn tail and go back to the settlements — an' much more! There's beaver enough for everybody, yet he begrudged our very presence! Imagine! Treating us so after we'uns treated him so kindly in our camp, too!"

I was stung by his attack on my old friend, but I held my tongue until his violent denunciation ran its course. When he paused for breath, I jumped in. "P'raps you'll be seein' Tom Fitzpatrick in a different light after ye pass more time hereabouts, Mister Leonard," I said, trying to rein in my temper. "Ours is a hard trade! Weak men don't survive! You're right that Fitz *is* hard. He's *learned* to be hard, goin' without himself so's his men could make it through, fightin' off Blackfoots an' the Aitch-bee-cee an' cold winters an' dry summers an' money-gougin' traders an' now a bunch o' Johnny-come-latelies come hotfootin' it up here fixin' to cash in on what it's taken us ten hard years to get the hang of! Fitz an' Gabe an' Milt an' the others are just now realizin' their dream of ownin' their own outfit, Rocky Mountain Fur, an' they don't take kindly to a passel o' money-hungry upstarts comin' in an' grabbin' off what we've been workin' so hard to get! Ye can look this whole world over an' ye won't find a braver man, nor smarter, nor one who's more generous or better with his men than Tom Fitzpatrick!"

I fell silent, surprised at the length of my response and somewhat sorry for its vehemence. To make amends, I said, "Why'n't we get outa here an' get on back to camp for vittles? 'Pears ye could do with a bait o' buffler hump." Whatever resentment my tirade might have provoked in Zenas Leonard evaporated at my invitation. He accepted with alacrity, rising and gathering up his few belongings. I realized then that being unfamiliar with the open-handed customs of rendezvous, he had been unwilling to ask for charity and had likely gone hungry since his arrival.

On the way, he told me of his second meeting with Fitz, when his bedraggled crew met up with Sublette's supply train. Scoundrelly Stephens had high-handedly assumed ownership of the few plews his men had garnered that spring, only a couple packs, sold them to Fitzpatrick, and pocketed the cash. His people were penniless after a whole year's hard work, peril, and privation. Fitz offered them employment with Rocky Mountain Fur. Leonard was one of the few who accepted.

Shortly after that, Fitz left Sublette's supply train, riding on ahead to alert friendly Indians as to the where and when of rendezvous, agreeing to meet the train farther up the trail. He was mounted on a fleet well-bred Kentucky horse and was leading another of the same, either one likely able to outrun any Indian warhorse.

Fitz failed to show up at the meeting-place, although Sublette tarried there several days, recruiting his livestock on the good graze thereabouts. That was the last anyone had seen of Tom Fitzpatrick, except for a report from one of Sublette's Delaware scouts, who recognized one of Fitz's horses running in a race in a Blackfoot camp.

It was discouraging news. Even with that report, howsomever, it was hard to believe that our tough, savvy, resourceful Irishman had gone under.

Whatever hardships Zenas Leonard had undergone during his difficult year with Gantt&Blackwell, his appetite remained undamaged. He put away twice as much meat as any man in camp. When word got around about what he had gone through, he was showered with clothes and moccasins, blankets and sleeprobes, most of it used but still serviceable. He is a proud young man and at first he was reluctant to accept our gifts, but Tuttle told him gruffly, "Don'tcha be turnin' daown our horse-pitality! Jest be sure ye pass it along to some other'n's when ye kin!" Which I am reasonably sure that he will do.

There was no thought of inviting Zenas to join our bunch. Such invitations are few and far bweteen. Moreover, he was bound to serve at least a year as an *engagé* with Rocky Mountain Fur until he worked off the cost of the outfit with which they would equip him.

When Simon Pence, a fellow-Pennsylvanian, happened by our camp, I introduced them to each other and Zenas decided to go along with Simon to the RMF camp. We wished him well and I reckon it won't take him long to get the hang of mountain life. He appears to possess smarts and grit enough to make a decent mountaineer, if only he will put aside his rigid settlement notions of right and wrong. From what I could tell, what he lacks most is a sense of humor, a most essential commodity for a mountaineer.

If you can't laugh at peril and privation, you will likely bust out crying and, soon or late, you'll go crazy. For a young man brand-new to the country and the trapping trade, Zenas Leonard's peevish, unbending judgments of people and the way we do things hereabouts are more suitable to a bluenose parson or a hanging-judge.

* * *

In spite of being pelted with much more summertime rain than usual, the rendezvous in Pierre's Hole was much the same as others I have described at length elsewhere in these pages, except that it was larger and more boisterous and bawdy than ever before, swollen by the influx of new traders and the greenhorns they brought with them.

The Rocky Mountain Fur partners were not happy. They were forced to compete in what they paid for fur, as well as what they charged for trade goods. Adding to their gloom, and ours, was increasing concern for Tom Fitzpatrick. He still hadn't shown up. Besides the deep and abiding respect and affection we all felt for the doughty Irishman, Fitz was RMF's only businessman. All of them are proper mountaineers, first-rate trappers and leaders of men, but Bridger can't read or write, happy-go-lucky Milt Sublette lacks his shrewd elder brother's business acumen and cut-throat tactics, and Frapp and Jean Gervais are much more content with their traps and rifles than with inkpots and ledgers.

The most curious of the new traders was a cranky New England Yankee by name of Nathaniel Wyeth. He was determined to lead his pitiful little expedition all the way to Oregon and the Western Sea, where he intended to trap beaver and preserve salmon-fish in barrels of brine, then to ship it all around the Horn to New England. Barely a score of callow Yankee greenhorns made up his party. Most of them were discontented with Wyeth's inflexible rule. They were openly rebellious by time they arrived in Pierre's Hole. Several had already deserted. The gripes and jeers of Wyeth's unruly bunch were nearly as much fun as a string of Black Harris's outrageous tall tales.

"Ye kin allus tell a Yankee," Ned Godey observed dryly, "but ye cain't never tell 'im much!" And so it was, apparently, with Nathaniel Wyeth. Instead of heeding the experienced counsel of Bill Sublette, who had allowed Wyeth's sorry little band to tag along with his supply train, stubborn Nat Wyeth insisted on doing everything his own way. Sublette advised him to build bullboats to ferry his goods across the Platte, but Wyeth built a raft instead. When the raft's tow-rope broke, hardheaded Nat lost a passel of his goods in the muddy waters of the Platte running high in springtime flood. Before that, on their journey to Saint Louis, his men told us gleefully, Wyeth tried to cross the country in one of his inventions which his disrespectful crew dubbed Nat-wye-thiums, wind-powered waterproof wagons, each one equipped with a mast and sails, which were supposed to eliminate the use of horses, mules, or oxen to haul them. Problem was, the outlandish contraptions were top-heavy and mostly unsteerable and they were often either becalmed or stalled in their tracks by a headwind. Wyeth was finally forced to sell them at half their cost.

All of which might suggest that Nathaniel Wyeth was a starry-eyed lunatic. He was anything but. One glance into his steely blue eyes and a quarter-hour of his palaver revealed a man of considerable intelligence and iron will. From what his people told us, Nat had made a tidy pile with his inventions for the ice business in his native Massachusetts. Problem was, Wyeth was a long way from home and ice is an all-too-common commodity in the Rockies.

* * *

Most nights, I had the lodge to myself. Micah and my father were seldom there after dark. More than once I had observed Powatawa strolling purposefully in the direction of the Nez Percé encampment, likely not questing for their well-bred Paloosie horses. My father is always sparing of advice, but Micah frequently invited me to accompany him to the Flatheads. "Don't ye reckon you've been grievin' long enough, Temple?" he asked more than once. "It ain't nat'ral, nor healthy, either, for ye to be keepin' to yourself the way ye do. A man needs a woman an' your woman'd be tellin' ye so, if she could."

I could think of no suitable reply. I simply nodded and Micah continued to make his nightly visits to the Flathead camp alone.

Another night, when Tuttle and I hunkered in a clump of willows on horse guard, I asked him, "How is it, Tuttle, that you got over losin' your Dolly woman so fast, without hardly breakin' stride, as far as I can tell?"

He didn't reply immediately, but at length he said, "'T'war easier'n ye mought be thinkin'. Fer one thang, I war damn glad to be shet o' her everlastin' scoldin' an' bein' s'picious o' muh ev'ry move. Din't matter if'n I done somethin' er no. 'Tain't muh nature to be lodgepolin' 'er, like some war tellin' me I oughta, ner throwin' 'er out, neither, but when she ups an' splits ther robes on 'er own, like she done, I reckon it war fer the best."

He fell silent for a spell. I could think of naught to say in reply. When he spoke again, his voice was hoarse. "Toughest gristle I be chawin' war losin' muh li'l gal agin, like I done oncet'afore back in Kaintuck to ther cholerer." He paused, then declared, somewhat more brightly, "Leastaways they ain't dead an' ther Snakes'll be lookin' arter ther both of 'em better'n I kin, anyways. 'Sides, a feller grows a deal o' callous 'baout sech thangs, 'speshly when it happens more'n once." After a spell of silence, his tone was thoughtful. "Livin' hyar in ther mountains, ye cain't never tell what mought be comin' today, let alone t'morry. Best ye don't hang on ter nothin' too tight."

Tuttle's philosophy is hard and rough as shagbark hickory, but it suits a mountaineer. I reckon Indians live by such a code. I wondered if I could ever adopt it as my own.

* * *

Inevitably, in the midst of that bacchanalia, I strayed onto the primrose path of temptation. One cloudless, warm evening my kettle became disgracefully empty. I repaired to the RMF trade tents to fill it. "Out tomcattin', are ye, Temple?" Doc Newell inquired pleasantly as he sloshed trader's booze to the brim, then scribbled the charge into the ledger book.

"Not likely," I replied.

Grover Weed was standing nearby. "Git it whilst ye kin," the man we call Buzzard solemnly advised. "Long, cold winter's comin' on purty quick. Ye'll be wishin' ye had." He belched and winked owlishly before he added, "Don'tcha never befergittin', ever' poke ye miss out on is a poke ye'll shorely never git." He harrumphed and grinned and folded his burly arms, pleased with his impeccable logic.

"That's fer sartin sure," Doc agreed with a sly smile.

Even through Buzzard's slurred speech, I recognized what was incontestably an unassailable truth. I rewarded Grover for his sage counsel with a healthy slurp or two before I set out on a solitary stroll through the mostly goodnatured bedlam we call rendezvous, stopping now and then to share a sip and a jest with old *compañeros,* stepping clear of rambunctious drunken wrestlers rolling in the dirt, and enjoying the sight and sound of gamblers, red and white, playing the hand game, chanting ancient Indian pleas to Dame Fortune to bless their quick-fingered subterfuges. I spied a grinning Tuttle Thompson amid a circle of eager sheep, dealing Old Sledge from his greasy deck of cards, but I chose not to disturb my friend's shearing of his unwary flock.

Lively fiddling drifted on the warm night air, counterpointed by the hollow boom of dance drums and high-pitched warbling in the

Indian camps. My steps were drawn towards the tall lodges glowing golden in the gloom. I was somewhat tipsy by then but not precisely drunk, still sober enough to step over drunks sleeping it off where they had fallen and to keep a prudent distance from willow groves along the river bank. Muffled groans and girlish giggles, stifled yips, grunts, and passionate whimpers signaled commercial coupling betwixt members of the trapping fraternity and the complaisant copperskinned sisterhood. Not all of my brethren and their temporary lights-o'-love were so discreet, howsomever. Here and there I needed to step off the path, lest I interrupt their amorous congress.

As I drew nigh the village I spied a cluster of women in a clearing, laughing and chattering in what I took to be the Kootenai tongue. They hushed when they caught sight of me. One woman broke away from the group and scampered towards me through the tall grass. When she neared I saw in the pale light of the half-moon that she was young and rather pretty in a round-faced, girlish way. When she drew nigh, walking unsteadily, it was plain that she was no stranger to ardent spirits.

She planted herself in my path and with an impudent grin, tapped on my kettle, as if to exact a toll for the use of her personal turnpike, which I readily granted. After a sip or two, in which I joined her, she held up her hands and brazenly suggested in finger-talk that she might be amenable to more intimate association if I were so inclined. I was not surprised. Such forthright propositions are commonplace at rendezvous, mostly stimulated by unaccustomed spirits and childlike eagerness to acquire white-eyes baubles.

It had been a long spell since I had known a woman and I was more than somewhat addled by the booze. Her feminine fragrance, her firm thigh pressed against my own, and her roaming hand erased whatever reluctance I tried to hang onto. I fingered into my belt-poke and dangled a string of shiny trade beads before her eyes. She snatched them from my hand and, bubbling with laughter, led me off to a willow copse on the riverbank.

Once within the sheltering boughs, she swept her soft doeskin dress over her head, revealing herself completely naked save for moccasins, and pulled me to the ground beside her, fumbling the while beneath my britchclout. Suddenly it was all too businesslike. I lay beside her, inhaling her musky feminine smell, running my hands over her apple-hard breasts and solid rump, tweaking her nipples and stroking her sleek thighs, even kissing her open mouth, but the expected response on my part failed to arrive, much as I wished for it. Eager to please or at least to hold up her end of the bargain, she doubled her efforts, but I was unable to hold up my own. At last I brushed her hands away, lifted her head from my lap, and simply held her close for a spell, wondering the while if I would ever again glory in the flesh and fragrance of a woman as I had with Rainbow and those I had known and loved before her. The emptiness that haunted me for so many dreary months wasn't gone. It had merely retreated to my nether parts.

When at last I rose to my feet, I fingered into my poke and gifted her with an English flint and firesteel, then retrieved my kettle, pistol, belt, and horn, and stumbled off to camp.

On the way, amid the trappers' digs, I came across a bunch of thoroughly drunken white free trappers, old hands who had lately joined up with American Fur. They were gathered around a cookfire, a few playing at cards, most of them frolicking in rough horseplay. Goodnatured curses and loud laughter rang on the night air and kettles passed freely amongst them. My path ran a couple rods distant from their camp, for which I was grateful. Such overly-lubricated gatherings often take an unpleasant turn for no good reason. Suddenly one of the trappers playfully splashed a kettleful of booze onto a tall, lanky, redheaded man. He howled and leaped to his feet, dancing crazily about, long arms flapping, the spirits smarting his hide, prompting roars of laughter amongst his companions. Then one of the drunkards snatched up a flaming brand from the cookfire and touched it to the redheaded man. Flames exploded when the alcohol caught fire. The poor wretch turned into a torch, head to foot. He rolled on the ground in a frenzy, beating at the flames with his hands, whilst his besotted companions laughed in unrestrained glee, until one of them regained his senses and tried to smother the blaze with an apishamore. Another man sobered enough to help. He grabbed up a packsaddle to beat out the flames. At last the poor unfortunate lay unmoving in their midst, a lifeless, smoldering hulk.

I continued on my way. Disappointing as my evening had turned out, I was still better off than some.

* * *

The days of rendezvous passed slowly by, whilst Rocky Mountain Fur cursed the competition and garnered a wealth of peltry, but never enough, to hear them tell it. Late afternoon rainfall often kept me inside my lodge, but that was a pleasant time. When I wasn't reading or scribbling in my journal or swapping books and palaver about them with Etienne LeBref, Iris spent many of those hours with me, learning her letters and honing her English pronunciation, often with Cat at her side doing likewise. When I returned to my empty lodge at night and rolled into my robes, my daughter often crept through the doorflap, sneaked to my side, and snuggled beside me to sleep until daylight. I missed Rainbow deeply and painfully, but my daughter's sweet breath warming my cheek at night and her cheerful presence in daytime helped to keep my demons at bay.

I often rode out to hunt with our Iroquois and Delawares, sometimes with my father and Micah. We rode ever farther out each day, for a rendezvous camp as large as that one requires a plenitude of meat. Nobody went hungry, howsomever, for the rich graze on the far-stretching prairie west of the Tetons keeps it black with vast herds of buffalo and gangs of rolling-fat wapiti. Tender meat hung over the coals of our cookfires day and night. Our camp was festooned with strips of jerkmeat drying in the crisp mountain air on rows of willow racks.

Often I packed a load of choice buffalo cuts onto my Sugarfoot mule and carried it to Iron Bow's camp as a gesture of filial respect. He didn't really need the meat. Flatheads are never behindhand in the hunt. They have spent their life dodging jealous Blackfoots intent on keeping the prairies to themselves. Because their numbers are much smaller than the Píkuni, Káinah, and Síksikah Blackfoot tribes, the Salish, Kootenai, Pend d'Oreille, and Nez Percé long ago learned how to find buffalo quickly, kill and butcher them in a hurry, and retreat to the mountains with their wintertime provender before the Blackfoots tumble to their presence on the plains. Once returned to their mountain strongholds, they have little to fear from Blackfoot bullies.

Iron Bow has always been effusive in his thanks for the meat I bring, but he has made it plain that he would be much more grateful if I would gift him with my handsome Sugarfoot mule. Much as I love and respect my father-in-law, I have been reluctant to do that. Iron Bow and Fast Horse both have horses aplenty, but a magnificent saddle mule like Sugarfoot or Micah's Lightfoot is not to be found in the mountains or hardly anywhere else.

* * *

The sun was high in a cloudless late-summer sky by time Little Mountain and I returned from a successful morning hunt, packhorses fairly groaning under loads of fat cow. About a mile out of camp we spied our own two Iroquois, Acorn and Stone Bird, riding in from northeast'ards, one packhorse piled high with meat, the other burdened with a much smaller load. When they caught sight of us, they commenced waving wildly but they made no move to join us. More curious than alarmed, Little Mountain and I spurred our mounts into a slow lope, closing the distance as rapidly as our heavily-loaded pack animals could manage.

When we reined up beside them, it was plain to see why they were excited. Draped over a packsaddle, head bobbing on the mane, pipestem arms and legs dangling on either side, was what was left of

Tom Fitzpatrick. Fact is, at first, it was hard to be sure just who it was. His long brown hair was white now, matted with mud and tangled with twigs, his brow and upper face burned brown and mud-caked, customarily clean-shaven cheeks sunken to the skull, bristling with scraggly grey beard, his eyes glassy, unseeing. From what we could see under his tattered clothing, Fitz's once-powerful frame was little more than a skeleton. I feared that by time we got him to camp, we would be delivering a corpse.

Little Mountain tossed the lead-ropes of his packhorses to me and galloped off to camp to spread the news, leaving the three of us to transport Fitz the remaining distance as gently as we were able.

All four RMF partners, half gleeful, half fearful, astride bareback horses, met us at the edge of camp, Bill Sublette and Bobby Campbell just behind them, and nigh half the rendezvous in tow. Old Foot and Finn McCool were waiting at the RMF trade tents when we lifted him gently to the ground. His eyes opened then and, through cracked, parched lips, he muttered in a scratchy growl, "'Tis a foine sight, I'm thinkin', to rest me eyes on the lot o'ye. Don't ye be be goin' off, now." His eyes fluttered shut and Thomas Fitzpatrick knew no more.

Finn and Foot were joined by Nat Wyeth's brother Jacob, a medical doctor who served as company surgeon in Nathaniel's quarrelsome battalion. Our two healers quickly shooed him off, howsomever, when the Yankee medico tried to brush them aside and insisted on bleeding Fitz in order to relieve him of "evil humours" Tom might have accumulated during his ordeal. Foot offered to perform a similar service for the good doctor himself, starting with his scalp, but the priggish sawbones departed in a huff before Foot was able to accommodate him.

Whatever heroic ministrations Foot and Finn performed to revive Fitzpatrick, they were eminently successful. When I saw him next, half the day later, the Irishman was propped against a willow backrest, much cleaner now and swaddled in a blanket, and Milton's woman, the Mountain Lamb, was spooning rich broth into him. When he spied Tuttle and me, his blue eyes twinkled and he greeted us with,

"Ye can be goin' back to hell now, ye bloody divils, fer I've surely died an' gone to me Heavenly Reward, as the presence o' thi'shere bee-yoo-ti-ful angel must surely testify." His chuckle dissolved into a fit of coughing and he said no more. It was enough. The rawhide-tough Irisher was on the mend.

*　*　*

From what we were able to piece together, Fitzpatrick's month-long travail amounted to a string of ill-luck and misfortunes hardly equaled since Odysseus's tortuous voyage home from the Trojan War.

Tom's journey commenced well enough. He parted from Sublette's supply train mounted on a fleet, high-bred Kentucky horse and leading another of the same, his mission to apprise friendly Indian bands of the when and where of rendezvous and to announce Sublette's arrival to RMF. Nobody worried. Tom Fitzpatrick is one of the most seasoned, smart, savvy, tough mountaineers in the Rockies. Many, myself included, would call him the best of the lot. Fitz knows the country and its perils and he is as well-prepared to deal with them as any man alive.

The first few days went well enough, but then the sky clouded over, thick as pease porridge, for several days. He was unable to see either the sun by day or stars at night. He lost his bearings and wandered aimlessly, winding up in rough, hilly, forested country, where his misfortunes commenced to accumulate. One early morning, whilst he was munching his meager breakfast, a grizzly came to call, which naturally affrighted his horses and doubtless Fitz, as well. He managed to kill the bear, but his spare saddler, loaded with most of his possibles, ran off and Tom was unable to find him.

About that time he discovered that he had wandered into the midst of a passel of Grovant Indians, so he holed up in a little canyon for half a day, hoping they would move on. They didn't. When he poked his nose out to see if all was clear, a bunch of young Big-belly bucks spied him and gave chase. Ordinarily, in flat country, Tom's high-bred Kentucky horse could have easily outrun their common ponies, but amongst the hills he had no advantage. Boxed in, Fitz tried to lead his horse up a rocky hillside, but the saddler soon played out and Tom was forced to abandon that fine critter, grab his rifle and a blanket, and hotfoot it up the hill with a passel of bloodthirsty Grovants, also afoot by that time, close on his heels.

He had a fair lead on his pursuers, but Fitz realized that trying to outrun them was a losing game. His only good luck during that whole shebang happened then. He spied a measly hidey-hole in the hillside, likely an abandoned catamount den. Quick as scat, he dived in and covered up the front of it with whatever he could lay hands on — rocks, sticks, weeds, and such trash.

I almost sniggered when I heard that part. I had a similar scrape nigh Sweet Lake several years earlier, when Bill Williams and I were forced to hole up in much the same circumstances, chased by a passel of Blackfoots. Scary as it must have been for Fitz, leastaways he didn't have to put up with smelly, cantankerous old Bill Williams lying cheek by jowl with him in a rocky coffin whilst scalp-hungry Indians prowled about day and night.

Except for Old Bill's testy, odoriferous presence, howsomever, Fitz was in pretty much the same fix. There was naught to do but lie there, cold, hungry, shivering with chill and fright, until darkness discouraged further searching by the Atsína scamps. What made it even worse, Fitz had to listen to their triumphant whoops when they captured his horse and led him off to their camp.

When darkness fell, he tried to make a run for it, but he soon found himself smack in the midst of the Grovant camp. He scuttled back to his hidey-hole and passed the rest of the night and next day there, his belly gnawing at his backbone, flinching when his pursuers came nigh. Once, daring to peek outside, he spied Grovants running races with his Kentucky horse — adding insult to injury, as they say. When night fell, he tried it again. That time he succeeded in skirting their camp and got into the woods, but he was hardly better off. All next day he dodged and hid along a crickbank, rarely more than a few rods distant from his enemies, until nighttime let him put some distance betwixt the Big-bellies and himself.

He came to a crick running high in spring flood, but Fitz reckoned he had to cross over in order to escape. Swimming with his rifle and possibles was impossible, so he cobbled together a puny raft, loaded it with his measly belongings, and shoved off for the far bank. The powerful current caught him, howsomever, sweeping him downstream until the raft hit a rock and was smashed to flinders. The water gobbled up everything but poor Tom himself. Rifle, pistols, powder horn, blanket, and capote were gone. Only the knife on his belt remained.

What followed was a month-long nightmare. He lived mostly on roots and rosebuds while he doggedly dragged his tattered moccasins towards rendezvous. Wolves took to tracking him. One time, they treed him, then worried at the trunk and roots for half a day, until they tired of the game and trotted off. The last thing he recalled clearly was finding a dead buffalo with a little meat still on its bones. After that, all he knew was a painful grey nightmare of fear and cold and starvation, until Stone Bird and Acorn found him, which he couldn't remember, either.

Chapter XVII
Grovants

The Pierre's Hole rendezvous commenced to break up in late August. Steadily shrinking supplies of alcohol had reduced trader's booze to an almost tasteless brew not worth its still exhorbitant price. Free trappers grew restless, eager to get to the fall hunt. Indian camps were dwindling. Nez Percés, Kootenais, and Flatheads had by then traded off their extra horses, buffalo robes, plews, and dried meat in exchange for arms and ammunition and other whitemen's goods. The same with the Snakes and Crows. Iron Bow's band still hung on, indulging their headman's affection for his granddaughter. Rocky Mountain Fur had wrung every possible plew out of white-eyes and Indians alike and Bill Sublette was itching to get back to Saint Louis. It was time for moving on.

Milt Sublette was first to gather his brigade and head southwest to harvest whatever plews Aitch-bee-cee's Pete Ogden had missed. We decided not to go with him, choosing instead to tag along with Bridger's crew, heading northwest'ards to the fringes of Blackfoot country. Pickings were likely much better there.

As the custom is, Milt departed at mid-day, intending to travel only half a dozen miles or so before halting for the night, so that necessaries that had been overlooked and left behind could be retrieved from camp, as well as giving drunks time to get sober and laggards a final chance to catch up.

Next morning, having naught better to do, several of us rode out to wish farewell to Milt and his *compañeros*. I rode Kumskaka. He was frisky as a colt that morning, thanks to weeks of little work and lush graze. We traveled at an easy lope, my thoughts straying over the many years since Powatawa had first gifted me with that magnificent animal in Ohio. I was only sixteen and Kumskaka barely a three-year-old. I smiled when I recalled Cesár's practical dictum, long held by Spaniard *vaqueros,* cattle-tenders of his native Mexico, who insisted, "The first seven years belong to the horse. The next seven years belong to you. And the next seven years should belong to your enemy!" Kumskaka gave the lie to that gloomy prediction. He was well into his third seven-year span and going just as strong as ever — better, in fact, than ever he had been.

I rode forward and crowded betwixt Micah and Powatawa, patting Kumskaka's neck as I did so. "What do you think now, Father, of this fine animal you gave me so long ago, when I was but a farm-boy, hardly able to ride a horse?"

Powatawa smiled with evident satisfaction. "I could do no less," he replied. "I knew you for my son. A lesser horse would shame us both." He let his gaze stray over Kumskaka's muscular length before he added slyly, "If I guessed he would turn out so well, I would not have cut his stones. He would have made a worthy sire for my mares. You could have had another."

I shot him a questioning look and realized that he was teasing. Powatawa shared my pride and pleasure in my first and favorite horse.

Ours was not the only group riding to Milt's camp. Several groups of horsemen were heading across the prairie for final farewelling or perhaps to collect unpaid gambling debts, which was Tuttle's main reason for coming along.

When we arrived, Milt's camp was astir with unusual commotion. Early-morning hunters had spied a huge procession of Indians approaching from the eastern hills — not a war party, but an entire village, a couple hundred warriors, their women's ponies dragging travois piled with baggage, children, and old folks. "Blackfoots!" was the first pronouncement, soon replaced with "Grovants!" when we got a better look. "An' they begun flyin' a British flag out in front, quick as they spied us!" someone yelled. "Why'd they be doin' a thang like that'n?" another voice questioned. "Why d'ye s'pose them sumbitches ever do anythang like they do?" somebody else chipped in to nobody in particular.

"Ye'd best be puttin' the women an' kids back in the timber an' get yer arse busy buildin' a fort!" a scratchy, cracked but still-familiar voice rang out. It was Tom Fitzpatrick, leastaways about half of him. "Let ye be lendin' a hand, me bhoys!" he yelled. "'Tis past toime we get to defendin'' oursel's! Getcher back in it, me buckos!" White-haired and scrawny as he was, Fitz darted about Milt's camp, shouting commands, cutting through confusion, putting men to useful chores, restoring order to a flock of hysterical chickens. Fitz had made a remarkable recovery in a few short weeks, although he still resembled a galvanized scarecrow herding a gaggle of giddy geese.

There was nothing funny about the situation we were in. Milt's brigade comprised only sixty or so trappers in all, counting some fifteen led by an Arkansawyer called Sinclair and perhaps a dozen of Nat Wyeth's nigh-useless greenhorns. Those of us come to bid farewell numbered hardly half that many.

"We be needin' lotta more guns!" Little Mountain shouted. "I be gittin' 'em!" He reined his horse about, preparing to return to camp. Brass Turtle checked him and rattled off a passel of Delaware talk, then waved him on his way.

"I told him don't be fergittin' to bring plenty o' powder an' galena 'long when he comes back. 'Pears we'll be needin' it," Turtle explained. "An' here's hopin' thar's a passel o' trappers back thar itchin' fer a fight. We sure-as-hell're gonna be gittin' one!"

I should explain that Grovants, Gros Ventres, are not actually Blackfeet, although most trappers commonly lump them in with the several Blackfoot tribes. The few mountaineers who bother to make a difference amongst them commonly call them Prairie Blackfoots. They are a separate tribe, cousins of the Arapaho, properly called the Atsína, with their own language, customs, clothing, and suchlike. They get along with the Blackfeet only because of fragile treaties, which are often broken. The Atsína got their nickname, Big-belly — *Gros ventre* in French — from neighboring Indians who resent the Atsína custom of descending on their neighbors and, taking advantage of traditional hospitality, eating them out of house and home, then bidding a flippant farewell until next time.   Make no mistake, howsomever, they are fierce warriors, as formidable and cunning in warfare as any Blackfoot.

Most of us farewellers tethered our mounts and pitched in, preparing for a fight, herding women and kids, Milton's Mountain Lamb amongst them, into the woods, together with their baggage, and throwing up a breastwork of downed timber. All the while I marveled at Fitzpatrick's energy and feverish activity after his recent ordeal. Milton Sublette's game leg kept him from getting about much, but his loyal pal Joe Meek more than made up for Milt's enforced idleness. He seemed to be everywhere, relaying Tom's commands, lending his great strength to heaving logs into place, and cuffing loafers into greater exertion. I saw with satisfaction that the newcomer Zenas Leonard was no less helpful, sticking close to Doc Newell and jumping in to assist at every chore.

Once the rude fort was more or less completed, Nat Wyeth wisely sent his quarrelsome Yankee tyros and his horses into the woods with the women and kids, out of harm's way and out from underfoot. He himself remained with us, maintaining a watch on the advancing Grovants with a shiny brass spyglass. They were heading straight for us, but their progress was slow. As they drew closer we saw that many of them were afoot. The straggling column appeared to be endless, a colorful snake writhing across the prairie, outriders dressing its ranks and urging it ever forward.

At last the leaders drew nigh, first amongst them a chief with a bright red blanket gathered around his waist. He was flanked by several of his headmen and a bare-chested bravo clutching the staff of a Union Jack fluttering out behind him in the stiff morning breeze.

"By Gawd! That'ere be ol' Bah-ee-hoh! Damn if it ain't!" someone called out. "I know that sumbitchin' Grovant from a ways back! That'n be a bad'un, fer gawddamn sure!"

Bah-ee-hoh, if that is who he was, drew rein no more than sixty yards distant from our front rank, his well-armed cohort clustered about him. He carried no gun, only a long pipe decorated with scalp hair and eagle feathers dangling from the stem. Horsemen and marchers accumulated behind their chieftains, feathered lances bobbing above their heads and a plenitude of shiny Mackinaw muskets glinting in the sunshine.

"Lookee thar!" a hoarse voice shouted. "Getcherse'f a gawddamn eyeful o' them'ere guns, won'tcha! Them'ere Mackinaws come straight outa ol' Redcoat McKenzie's tradin' fort on the Missourah, sure as hell!"

Which was likely. Word was rampant that Kenneth McKenzie was doing a brisk business at American Fur's Fort Union by trading guns with Blackfoots and Grovants and anybody else who possessed peltry and robes.

More and more mounted warriors crowded into the clearing, those afoot drifting to the far fringe along a tree-grown swamp. It was plain to see by the men's colorful clothing and painted faces that they were gussied up for war. The Atsína ranks continued to swell. Our people, whites and mostly Flathead Indians, braced for what would be an overwhelming attack, if it came. I mounted Kumskaka and made sure my rifle and pistol were capped and ready. My horse fidgeted and rattled his bit, responding to the excitement coursing through my legs. Careful not to move too quickly, I walked Kumskaka slowly to the front of our line, off to one side, where my friends were gathered.

I was better able to see the red-blanketed chief from that position. He was neither old nor young, hawkishly handsome, lean and tough, his face an impenetrable mask. After a spell, he straightened and nudged his horse forward, still unarmed, only his long pipe resting in the crook of his arm. He checked his mount some thirty yards from our line and waited, obviously wishing to parley.

"'Pears he craves some jawbonin'," someone called out. I glanced about, seeking Tom Fitzpatrick, who would be our likely spokesman, since Milt Sublette was still too stove up to get about handily, but Fitz was nowhere to be seen.

Nobody else volunteered to go out to parley until our resident coxcomb, the French-Iroquois hothead Antoine Godin sang out, *"Le*

Gros-ventre canaille weeshes for talk? I weel talk wiz 'eem!" Godin's menacing tone boded no peaceful converse, but nobody else offered to go.

"Trouble's brewin'," Brass Turtle muttered. "Grovants kilt Godin's ol' Frenchy dad over on Godin Crick, years back. Antoine ain't never gonna be fergivin' ner fergittin' it."

Godin, mounted now, resplendent in his quilled and beaded finery, crowned with a jaunty red French voyageur *tuque*, accompanied by a Flathead trapper, crowded past us and halted at the edge of the clearing. He turned to the Flathead and asked, "Your piece, eet ees charged?" The Flathead grinned and nodded yes. "Zen cock eet now an' come wiz me." The two men ambled towards the middle of the clearing, the Salish a traditional enemy of all Atsínas, Godin a hotspur with a family grudge to settle. There could be no peaceable outcome with such envoys.

What the Atsína chief Bah-ee-hoh had in mind when he offered to parley is anybody's guess. What our French-Iroquois firebrand Antoine Godin intended wasn't hard to fathom.

Bah-ee-hoh stiffened when he saw an armed Flathead approaching, but he betrayed no emotion. He sat tall on his pony, his scarlet blanket decorated with a broad band of quillwork draped loosely around his middle, the long pipe cradled on his left arm."

"Git ready," Tuttle whispered hoarsely. "All hell's abaout to bust loose. Them two idjets mean nothin' peaceful."

Godin rode up on the chief's right side, the Flathead on his left. Bah-ee-hoh held out his right hand to Godin, who stared hard into the chief's eyes, grabbed the outstretched hand, held on tight, and yelled, "Fire!" The Flathead brought up his musket, hesitated a moment, perhaps enjoying the chief's surprise, then fired. Bah-ee-hoh pitched backwards off his pony, sprawling headfirst to the ground. The Flathead whirled his horse and galloped to our lines through a hail of galena from the Grovants. Through swirling white smoke, we saw Godin lean from his saddle and snatch at Bah-ee-hoh's red blanket. He dragged it free and sped back to our side, his trophy held high, streaming out behind, whooping and laughing his fool head off. Neither he nor the Flathead executioner received so much as a scratch.

Standing where we were, we were prime targets. I gathered my reins to flee, when Kumskaka suddenly, unaccountably, reared and whirled to face the enemy, front feet pawing skyward. I felt the first ball thud into his broad brisket, another into his throat. His powerful frame shuddered but still he balanced unsteadily on his hind legs, forelegs striking at air, still shielding me, until a third ball smashed into his eye and he fell like a rock.

I barely succeeded in leaping free, then dived back to his quivering bulk, yanked my pistol from its saddle holster, then sheltered behind his carcass, aiming and firing and reloading, weeping and cursing, a monumental anger building in me, choking me. I had lost another irreplaceable belovèd. This time, howsomever, there was no black void, no running berserk amongst his killers, only cold fury aimed against a faceless enemy who had once again stolen a slice of my soul.

* * *

How long I lay there, cursing and firing until my rifle and pistol barrels became too hot to hold, I have no idea. A tug at my foot and Tuttle's strained voice hauled me back to sanity. "Quit it naow, Temple! Ye'd best light a shuck an' git yer arse the hell outa hyar afore ye gitcherse'f kilt!" He lay stretched flat behind me, yanking on my ankle, wincing whenever a ball or an arrow whizzed overhead. "'Tain't wuth it, nohaow, Temple. Let it go fer naow, fer chris'sake, 'fore we both git ourse'fs kilt! Ye kin do better someplace else."

Ever so slowly, my temper cooled enough to let me admit the simple, pragmatic truth in what my old friend was saying. Slowly, reluctantly, I inched backwards on my belly, dragging my rifle by its barrel, hardly daring to raise my head enough to glimpse Kumskaka's sleek, dead body feathered with arrows clustered as thick as quills on a porcupine, Tuttle continuing to encourage my retreat in an urgent, rusty voice, until we reached safety behind the stout logs of the barricade.

We slumped against the logs, breathing heavily. It was amazing that I had escaped unscathed from the fusillade of arrows and musket balls pounding into Kumskaka's carcass. "Ye hurt?" Tuttle demanded when he caught his breath. I assured him that I wasn't, not even a scratch. "Reckon Gawd pertects loonies like yerse'f, but don't be pushin' it!" he advised sourly. "The Big Feller's gonna be busy as hell thi'shere gawddamn day!"

It was likely so. The battle raged on, the Grovants showing no inclination to retreat, still sending clouds of arrows and a hailstorm of musket fire into our ragged defenses. When I rose to my knees and joined the other trappers firing between the piled-up logs, I immediately shared the general fear that we wouldn't be able to turn back an enemy charge if the Atsínas got themselves organized enough to make one.

Women, kids, horses, and travois had vanished from the clearing, likely into the dense thicket that bordered the swamp on the far side of what had become the principal battlefield. Here and there, at a distance, I could hear the sharp crack of rifles and the dull boom of muskets, where scattered bunches of our people were fighting separate skirmishes with the Big-bellies.

Then, above the rattle of musketry and crackling curses, a hoarse voice rang out. "Thank Gawd! Lookee thar, won'tcha! The whole gawddamn ronnyvoo's a-comin' on!" He spoke no lie.

Little Mountain must have punished his horse more than somewhat in covering the six or so miles to camp. An advancing brown cloud was sweeping over the northern prairie, a horde of trappers and Indians of several friendly tribes galloping to join the fight. When they pulled up out of musket range, I spied Finn McCool and Old foot close by Little Mountain. Glad as I was to see those two and the others, I felt a pang of disappointment when I caught sight of Ned Godey not far behind them. I had hoped Godey would remain in camp. If not for Ned and Cat, who else would protect and provide for my daughter if I were killed?

A sudden lull in the gunfire turned my attention to the Grovants. All but a few were scurrying for the brushline at the edge of the swamp, many of them dragging their fallen comrades. Those who remained hunkered down behind dead horses and in shallow hollows soon gave it up and disappeared amongst the willows. Our riflemen were not idle, howsomever, and a couple more Big-bellies headed out along the Wolf Trail to the Sand Hills. Puffs of white smoke commenced to spout along the brushline as the Grovants dug into new positions.

Newcomers eager to do battle quickly replaced us in the fort. I took advantage of the relief they offered and scampered out of those close quarters, keeping low until I was out of musket range, then trotted off to greet my companions. On the way I spied Bill Sublette and Robert Campbell supervising the unloading of half a dozen packmules, distributing jerked meat, horns of gunpowder, and galena pigs, to which I helped myself. My own horn and shot poke were getting light and my belly was growling.

Standing nigh Sublette and Campbell, I overheard them making verbal wills to each other, or what I took to be such. When Bill noticed me there, he called me over and said I should be their witness. When they finished, I said, "Billy, I'd be obliged for the use of a pencil and a scrap. I need to be doin' the same, but I'd best get it in writin'."

Sublette shot me a hard look, but he dug into his pouch and handed me a stub and a wrinkled old trade bill. I thanked him, dropped to one knee, and scribbled on the clean side:

To M. Pierre Chouteau, Cadet

In the event of my death, I, Temple Buck, hereby bequeath all my worldly goods and valuables entrusted to your care to my daughter Iris and to Edward Godey, called Ned, and his natural wife Kathleen,

Cat, a Flathead Indian woman, said monies to be used for the welfare and education of Iris, which I entreat you to oversee.

Sgd: Temple Buck, Trapper

29th July 1832

The chore took but a minute or two. I returned the pencil stub to an impatient Bill Sublette and hustled off to find Godey. When he read my will, Ned was flabbergasted. He stuffed the paper into his poke and said, blushing, "Thankee, Temple. I'm honored, but let's see to it neither one of us gits hisse'f kilt. Tuttle tol' me ye war awready courtin' it this mawnin'."

More than a hundred trappers had ridden in with Sublette and Campbell, besides that many Flatheads and Kootenais, Iron Bow's band amongst them, and perhaps a couple hundred Nez Percés. Now, our side easily outnumbered the Atsína fighting men, but defeating them would not be a simple chore, holed up like they were on that brushy, quaggy riverbank.

I found McCool and Old Foot in a sheltered hollow, patching up a couple men who had suffered wounds in the morning. My father and Micah were with them, huddled over a little fire, melting galena and running a stock of rifle and pistol balls. I joined them to do likewise.

Powatawa looked grave but he said naught about my Kumskaka horse until I spoke of his death. "He gave his life for yours," he said then.

"Yes, I know," I replied, "but how could he know to do that?"

Powatawa was silent for a spell. When he spoke, his voice was solemn, his gaze level and serious. "Many years ago, I entrusted you to him — not him to you. I told him he must care for you. Always he has done so. Today, Atsína meant to kill you. Kumskaka would not allow it. He took the balls. Not you. You live, my son. I'm thinking Kumskaka runs content now in the Grey Land."

I am not equipped to discuss the Grey Land, Heaven or Hell or anything to do with such matters. So I didn't. I merely nodded and held my peace. Just the same, it's comforting to think of that noble horse running free forever in such a place.

By time I ran a sufficiency of balls I heard Bill Sublette's big, raspy voice rallying his men. I reckoned I owed Bill a favor. I ran to join him.

Billy Sublette, for all his rapacious ways, is no coward. He didn't order his people into battle. He led us, cautiously, to be sure, but he was out in front when we plunged into the thicket along the riverbed. Which wasn't the smartest thing I ever did.

Bending low and dodging one way and another, Sublette weaved his way through heavy brush, Bobby Campbell and the Arkansawyer trapper-boss Sinclair right behind him, Joe Meek and I close on their heels. Perhaps a score of free trappers, many of them Sinclair's, were scattered out on either side. We soon came in sight of a hastily thrown-together fort composed of driftwood, rocks, dead horses, and saplings draped with lodge covers, apishamores, sleeprobes, painted shields, bright-colored blankets, and suchlike concealments. These afforded no protection but they kept us from getting a look at our enemies.

There was no chance of surprising them. As we crawled forward on hands and knees, thick brush and tall weeds betrayed our movements. Meek jabbed an elbow into my arm and jerked his head sidewise, calling my attention to Sinclair, who had got out in front. He was crouched, parting the branches of a willow with his rifle barrel, likely preparing to shoot. Smoke bloomed through a blanket, followed by the hollow report of a musket. Sinclair jerked, doubled over, and fell forwards, shot low in the belly.

Campbell lay nearest to Sinclair, who twisted about and strangled out, "Take me to my brother," before he fainted. Bobby wriggled forwards, caught hold of Sinclair's leg, and pulled him back far enough for Joe and me to relieve him of his burden.

"Reckon he be a goner," Joe grunted as we half-carried, half-dragged the big man to the rear, "plugged in the guts like he be." I reckoned Joe was right. Several Arkansawyers offered to care for their wounded leader, so we entrusted him to them, telling them to find the brother, and scuttled back to Campbell and Sublette.

We discovered Bill lying on his belly, scanning the shabby Grovant bulwarks, seeking a target. I heard his satisfied grunt when he shifted his rifle to his shoulder, took aim, and fired. A blanket fluttered and a smothered yelp testified that his shot was true. "Got that'ere sumbitch square in the eye!" Bill announced triumphantly. "Keep an eye on that hole, Bobby, an' you'll get another." He crept behind a cottonwood and stood up to reload. He was fumbling a cap onto the nipple when suddenly he lurched backwards and grunted. A man standing behind Sublette howled with pain at the same time and clutched at his bloody head, possibly shot with the same ball. Bill fought to stand erect, a red stain spreading on the shoulder of his buckskin shirt.

A flurry of shots from our side squelched further activity from that particular quarter, leastaways for a spell. Sublette was tottering but still on his feet, swinging his arm to see if it was broken, before he sagged and collapsed.

"Damn if I ain't gittin' fed up with nursemaidin' cripples!" Joe complained as we lugged Bill Sublette to relative safety. "I come hyar fer fightin' an' all me'n yew 'pear to be doin' is haulin' bleeders!"

"You'll get a bellyful o' fightin' before this day's over, Joe Meek," I assured him. "'Pears there's plenty to go around."

Which was true. By time we left Sublette with Milton and Nat Wyeth's medico brother and trotted back to the Grovant hideout, the battle was on in earnest. Campbell had assumed command and a horde of mountaineers and Flatheads had advanced and were pouring a cloudburst of lead into the barricades. Shifting clusters of white smoke puffs along the makeshift fort showed that the Grovants were shooting in volleys, then scurrying elsewhere to evade our return fire. Well-aimed shots and arrows sent skyward and falling on our fighters, who were mostly lying prone, were exacting a murderous toll on our side.   But diminishing musketry, anguished yelps, and quavering deathsongs from inside the barricade told a story of thinning ranks of defenders and powder and lead running low.

So many trappers, hostlers, traders' clerks, and Flatheads had come to do battle that it became difficult to squeeze in amongst them to do my share. I looked about for my bunch, but I could see none of them. When the shooting lulled for a spell, I crawfished to the rear and trotted off to the far side of the swamp, where, as I drew nigh, a lively din of gunfire and Indian whoops promised adequate entertainment.

I discovered my father, Micah, and Tuttle lying behind a flimsy shield of driftwood and rocks, taking potshots at likely targets, puffs of gunsmoke spurting from the curtained barricade, riddled now, some of it ripped clean away. Lying behind Tuttle was a tidy packet of beaver and otter fur and a pistol. Tuttle had succeeded in settling accounts with Milton's men who tried to renege on their gambling debts. "Whar ye been?" Tuttle demanded, lifting a quizzical eyebrow. "Ye been missin' all the fun."

I assured him that I hadn't missed a smidgeon of fun and told about Sublette, Sinclair, and how the battle was proceeding in that quarter. "Who's runnin' things over here?" I asked.

"Hard to say," Micah offered. "Fitz is, for the most part, when that Yankee know-it-all isn't yelling his fool head off, tellin' 'em to be doin' somethin' else."

Sure enough, just then I caught sight of Nat Wyeth darting about amongst a crowd of Nez Percés, who stood with their arms folded. He was waving his arms and pointing to the Grovant breastworks, likely exhorting them to charge, which the Nez Percés were having none of.

"Ye see thet?" Tuttle cackled. "Them'ere Napercys ain't abaout to git theirse'fs kilt jest fer pleasin' ol' Yankee-britches! They been fightin' Blackfoots long afore ol' Nat begun peddlin' ice!"

Powatawa was saying nothing. He was squinting along the barrel of his Hawken, waiting patiently, then squeezed off his shot. He ducked down behind the log until the gunsmoke cleared, then peered at the barricade, a faint smile lighting his powder-smudged face. "I think mebbe so I count coup this time," he announced. "Mebbe no." Reloading as he spoke, he said, showing he had been listening all the while, "Shahaptin are no damnfools. Injuns don't need white-eyes tellin' 'em how to fight." He glanced towards the Nez Percés and Wyeth. "Not that paleface, anyways."

There was no room for another shooter behind the puny little fort, so I wished them well and hotfooted towards a throng of mostly Flatheads, Kootenais, and Nez Percés. I sidled nigh a skinny, haggard Tom Fitzpatrick, who appeared to be at his wits' end. He was trying to convince the Indians and anybody else who would listen to set fire to the Grovant fortress and burn them out, once and for all, before more of our blood was spilled. Fitz's half-breed interpreters were threading through the crowd, spreading his plea in a couple-three tongues and sign-talk, then bringing back the replies of the various chiefs. Once again, the Indians were having none of it.

Antoine Godin, not so dapper now, his pretty buckskins soiled with dirt and gunsmoke, his Frenchy bonnet gone, summed up their response. "Zey say no burnin'. Zey say *les Gros-ventres* are *riche*, zey say Atsína come from veesit zeir Arapaho brozzers. Zey 'ave breeng *beaucoup cadeaux*, many geeft, from zeir keenfolk, many blanket an' robe, *hache de guerre*, gun, knife, *calumets de paix et de guerre*, pipe, an' all good seeng from zeir keen. Eef we burn zem, all mus' be lost. Zey say no, no burnin'! We mus' nevair burn!" Listening to Antoine's impassioned translation of the Indian chiefs' expressed desire for booty, I wondered about which side he was on.

Fitz threw up his hands in disgust and stalked off, cursing with all his Irish eloquence, waving off a platoon of Indian women who had been set to gathering dry grass and brush for the conflagration. "Bloody, greedy bastards!" he lamented to nobody in particular. "For the sake of a pitiful handful o' bloody rubbish, the bloody red bastards'll be after killin' off a hundred good men! Let 'em all go to bloody hell!" He trudged off towards a meadow where mounted trappers were bunching up half a hundred Grovant horses they had rounded up on the far side of the river, where the Atsína had sent them for safekeeping when the shooting first commenced.

Tom's gloom instantly transformed to glee when one of the horsemen called out, "Hey, Fitz! We been thinkin' mebbe we gotcher Kaintuck hoss back fer ye!" The trapper reined his horse about and crowded a tall, high-headed, clean-limbed, sunburnt black gelding into the open. "This'n be your'n, Fitz?"

Fitzpatrick fairly jumped with joy. "'Tis himself! His very own darlin' self, begawd! Me very own trav'lin' horse! An' ye found 'im where?" The rest was lost to my ears as Fitz went squawking and skipping across the meadow to take possession of his high-bred charger.

Bethinking myself that I had best make myself useful, I turned back to the Grovants' makeshift fortress. Mostly creeping, sometimes crawling on my belly, I made my way to a big driftwood stump and stretched out behind it, seeking a target, a puff of gunsmoke or movement behind a tattered blanket. The pandemonium that had reigned earlier had subsided to sporadic shots from inside the fort, just enough to discourage any foolish ideas of rushing the Grovant defenders. Plainly, their ammunition was running out. Their shouted taunts and dares had mostly dwindled off, as well.

Then, shooting from inside quit altogether. Their cocky gibes and brags ceased completely. Silence reigned. Curious, our people held their fire and quit jabbering. One lone, strong voice speaking in the Atsína tongue came from within the Grovant fort. I couldn't understand a word of it, but, here and there, scattered amongst our ranks, some Flatheads, Kootenais, and Nez Percés commenced looking serious, then alarmed, then gabbling to their neighbors the import of what the Grovant orator was speechifying about. He continued for maybe five minutes, his voice growing louder, his tone more stern, belligerent, threatening as he warmed to his subject, whatever it was. Then, with a final bark, the voice ceased.

A general murmur rippled amongst the Indians ranged around the fort, growing louder as the words of the Grovant were interpreted by those who understood the Atsína tongue. The message spread amongst a growing number of Indians, then to whites when Indian friends passed along what had been said. Chatter increased to a roar. Men deserted their positions, crawling backwards until they were out of musket range, then racing for their horses. Soon I saw a mob headed for camp, accompanied by most of the women and kids from Milton's brigade.

I still had no idea of what the Big-belly chief had said, but I stayed put, lest the Big-bellies come busting out of their fort and take advantage of our confusion. They were eerily silent, howsomever. They had quit shooting and sending arrows aloft, leastaways for right then. Our side also held our fire.

Brass Turtle rescued me from my ignorance. He espied me stretched out behind my sheltering stump and wriggled his way to my side. "What the hell happened?" I demanded. "Everybody gone loony?"

"Pert'near," he replied with a hard laugh. "Best I kin tell, arter gittin' it through mebbe five or six Injuns that don't talk Grovant proper-like, that'ere Grovant chief starts off tellin' how his bunch would'a whupped us, 'ceptin' fer ever'body comin' out from ronnyvoo an' then their powder runnin' out. But he says they don't mind a-tall. They ain't afeared o' gittin' burnt out an' kilt. He says fer us to go ahead an' do it. They be ready fer dyin'. But then he says, if we be lookin' fer some real fightin', we oughta jist stick around hyarabouts, 'cause they awready sent word fer a big bunch o' Grovants to come a-runnin' to git 'em out o' the fix we put 'em in. Says thar's four hunnerd lodges o' Grovants a-comin' thisaway an' they'll sure-as-hell be rubbin' us out!" Turtle paused and grinned at me. "So what d'ye think?"

"Four hundred lodges," I said, trying to chew some sense out of what he was saying. "That's maybe a thousand fightin' men."

"Yep, sumpin' like that," he replied with a bigger grin. "If'n thar's any Grovants comin' a-tall. I reckon they ain't! Shee-it! That'ere ol' Big-belly chief war blowin' smoke up our arse! An' them damnfool ninnies're b'lievin' ever' gawddamn lyin' thang he war tellin' 'em! Look at 'em!" Turtle twisted about and jerked his chin towards the meadow. Scores of trappers and Indians were forking their critters and racing off towards the rendezvous, convinced that their horses, wives and children and their precious plunder were in dire peril, especially their horses and plunder.

I pondered Turtle's words. Then I said, "I'm wagerin' you're right."

"Yer damn right I'm right!" He allowed himself a short, hard laugh before he said, "That'ere Grovant liar kin give ol' Harris a run fer his money when it comes to spinnin' a yarn!" He peeked around the side of the stump, making sure that our unwilling guests remained inside their fort. Dusk was gathering fast. When I glanced over the field I saw few Indians and no mountaineers. Turtle noticed my concerned look. "Yep," he said, "we'd best be haulin' arse outa hyar afore them'ere Grovants git to takin' our ha'r."

Which we did.

* * *

Turtle and I hiked a goodly distance away from the riverbank, detouring to retrieve Turtle's horse tethered in the woods, then heading for a campfire glimmering through the trees. A number of trappers and Flatheads had gathered beside a little stream, amongst them Old Foot and Finn McCool, Cesár, and Simon Pence. Micah, Tuttle, and my father arrived a-horseback about the same time that we did. Iron Bow and a passel of his band were also there. When he espied me, my father-in-law allowed cracked a smile and said in Salish and hand-talk, "It is good you come here." He ran his eyes over me, top to bottom, then, "You lose blood?" He grinned with satisfaction when I assured him that I wasn't leaking anywheres.

I looked about for his son, but before I could ask about him, Fast Horse and another Flathead rode in. My brother-in-law dropped my saddle and bridle beside me, signing and saying in Salish, once his hands were free, "You need these things. No need now to go to your horse." I thanked him for returning my saddle, but I know not enough of his tongue or even the proper signs to thank him enough for sparing me the sight of Kumskaka just then.

Naturally the trappers did their bombastic best to outdo one another, describing their courageous exploits and hairbreadth escapes during the day, and I reckon the Flatheads were doing much the same. It's a common pastime in the mountains and nobody takes such bragging seriously, not even the braggart himself.

There was a sufficiency of guns and sharp eyes in our gathering to discourage any Grovants from attacking us or trying to steal the horses. I filled up on jerkmeat and stood a brief stint at horse-guard with Micah before I curled up on my apishamore and fell into a deep, dreamless sleep, which was a blessing after such a day.

* * *

Not long after daybreak the prairie once again swarmed with horsemen, red and white, riding pell-mell out from rendezvous, not as many as the day before, but more than enough to finish the chore they thought they had to do. Campbell and Fitzpatrick led them, Tom mounted proudly on his handsome charger, followed closely by Milt Sublette and his ever-present shadow Joe Meek. Iron Bow lent me one of his extra horses and we joined the main force, bent now on avenging themselves on the Grovants for their trickery. They had waited in vain, all night long, in the main camp, for the threatened attack, which never came.

We left our mounts under heavy guard in a meadow and crept cautiously forward to the Grovant fort. The front rank, thirsting for blood, commenced shooting and yelling, daring the Grovants to do battle. Nothing stirred. No gunshots. No shrill challenges. Only silence.

Most of the lodge covers, shields, sleeprobes, and suchlike concealing drapery were gone. Only tattered, bullet-riddled blankets fluttered in the crisp morning breeze. Naught else moved.

Joe Meek and a couple others raced to the battlements and peeked inside, then swung about and threw up their hands in disgust. The fort was empty. The Grovants had departed in the darkness.

A howl sent up by redmen and whites alike ripped the sky. They rushed like madmen to the hideout, the Indians especially eager to see if the enemy had left behind anything valuable. They hadn't. Nothing useful remained. No scarlet blankets or pretty shells or aught that anybody might want was there, only a dozen dead warriors and a couple dozen dead horses stripped of their saddles, besides a passel of useless trash, littered the swampy ground. The only valuable commodity left in the fort was likely the couple hundredweight of galena that we ourselves had fired into it.

The Indians and some whites ripped off the scalps of the dead Grovants and several parties set off in pursuit of the fleeing enemy. All they found were a few broken-down horses and the bodies of warriors and women who had died of their wounds. Not surprisingly, they claimed those scalps, as well.

I followed afoot through a forest patch, curious to learn what I could about the Grovant exodus. A low, sing-song moaning caught my ear. I stepped off the path, parting branches as I went, and came upon a tiny clearing. There I beheld a young Atsína woman. She was beautiful, I thought, in spite of her mud-smudged, tear-streaked face. One leg was flung out, all twisted antigodlin. She cradled the head of a dead young warrior on her lap. Startled at my approach, she raised her head and her eyes met mine, defiant yet imploring to be left in peace in her grief. Then she jerked her gaze to my right. A Nez Percé warrior was racing towards her, tomahawk raised, intent on finishing her off.

A vision of Rainbow flashed before my eyes, Rainbow the moment before a Bannock snuffed out her life. I lunged forwards, seeking to block the Nez Percé. Terrified, she misunderstood. She plucked a short-barreled pistol from the dead man's belt and swung it up. Flame blossomed from the muzzle. A punch in my chest flung me backwards and slammed me to the ground. Through drifting smoke and a red haze I saw her brains splatter when the tomahawk slashed through her skull. The crimson veil mingled with her blood, dissolving the gory scene into welcome blackness.

Chapter XVIII
King of the Missouri

First thing I made out in the dim light was Finn's strained, anxious face bending close to my mine. When my vision cleared more, I saw Old Foot's face beside McCool's. There was no telling what he was thinking or feeling, but then, nobody ever can.

"He's after comin' 'round," Finn announced in a hoarse voice. Foot merely grunted. A chorus of approving murmurs and stifled cheers came from somewhere beyond my vision. My chest burned with unholy fire. Cat's voice, from behind my head, commanded, "You go now. He mus' eat." First, the familiar surroundings of my lodge swam into view, then Tuttle, Ned, my father, Micah, and Paddy huddled near the doorway. They made no move to obey. I struggled to sit up, but Cat's strong hands held me down. "You no move," she said in a stern voice. "You bad hurt." I did as I was told.

"I'm wishin' ye might'a held off wakin' up for a spell," McCool said, "'til I finished stitchin' on ye." He sighed. "But no matter. 'Tis what's got to be done." I clenched my teeth as I felt my hide being pierced, then drawn up. It seemed to take forever, but likely not for long. I remembered nothing of his earlier attentions to my wound. Then Foot reached in and laved my chest with soothing balm. He muttered something in Delaware that sounded approving and settled back on his heels. "There now," Finn pronounced, "that'll be holdin' ye fer a spell."

Cat scuttled on her knees to the fire and brought back a kettle. She propped up my head and commenced spooning thick broth into my mouth. "You mus' eat," she said, her tone softer now. "Udderwise you die." Once again I did as I was told.

* * *

Next thing I knew, sunshine was spilling through the smokeflaps and the open doorway. I felt an urgent need to perform my chore. I slithered about, trying to rise, when I felt Cat's firm hand on my shoulder and heard her voice. "You sleep good. Long time. Take!" She shoved a hollow gourd into my hand and retreated out the door, calling back, "I come bye'n-bye."

I was much relieved by time she returned bearing a steaming kettle. My chest ached beneath bandages torn from a calico shirt, but the burning was mostly gone. Cat retrieved the gourd and carried it outside. When she came back, clucking her displeasure, she was not alone. The aforementioned half-dozen friends and my father came crawling in after her. Cat propped me against a willow backrest and commenced feeding me. Between spoonfuls, I managed to ask, "What happened?"

Naturally, everybody except Powatawa tried to tell me at once. Tuttle prevailed. "Wal, arter Foot an' ther Irisher hyar got ther most o' ther bleedin stopped, we reckoned it war time ter be gittin' ye back to camp."

I swallowed a mouthful and interrupted him. "But how did ye find me? Out in the woods like I was?"

"Oh, thet! Wal, fust thang we knew abaout it war thi'shere Napercy comes a-runnin' up ter ther fort, swingin' a bloody scalp an' yellin'! Natcherly nobody savvies no Napercy lingo, but he tells in sign thar's a white-eyes in ther woods bleedin' bad an' we better git a move on! We din't know it war yew, natcherly, but we hotfooted out thar, anyways, an' it war!" The others nodded agreement.

"Wal, like I war tellin', arter they got ye patched up some'at," he nodded at Foot and Finn, "we slung ye in a lodgeskin 'twixt two hosses an' walked 'em on back to camp, fast as we could."

McCool held up his hand, saying, "I'd best be tellin' the rest of it. So ye'll know an' be actin' accordingly."

IIis serious tone caused me to wave away the offered spoon. "Know what?" It sounded ominous to me.

Finn cleared his throat, looking gloomy, hesitating before he plunged into the bad news. "Well now, whilst ye were dreamin' off in Niver-niver Land, Misther Foot here an' meself performed consid'rable surgery on yergoodself, attemptin' to remove the ball from your breast." He looked even more glum. "But I'm sorry to tell ye, Temple darlin', we failed. 'Tis too deep and it's hidin' somewheres deep down. We can't get at it!" He swallowed hard and hurried on. "Furthermore, 'tis likely near your heart an' the ribs're in the way. The short of it is, we lack the knowledge an' the tools an' the skill to mend ye proper-like!"

I refused to come to terms with what sounded like a death sentence. "But couldn't I just go on an' live with it? Let it heal up an' let it stay there? I've heard of others carryin' galena balls inside them for years."

Finn would have looked even more mournful if that were possible. "Ye could, perhaps, exceptin' fer lead poisonin' an' where it lies. Lyin' so close to yer heart an' yer vital organs as it is, that galena ball is sure to be infectin' ev'rythin' nigh until it kills ye."

Still unwilling to surrender, I demanded, "Then what's to be done?"

McCool turned then to my assembled comrades. They looked as grim as the medico did. Their nods told him to go on. "Well now, we've chewed it over an' the only thing we know to do is gettin ye to Sain' Looie as soon as ye can get there. P'raps there's a surgeon there who can fix ye, Temple, afore the bloody lead poisonin' rots yer innards an' kills ye."

I wanted more than anything to stay forever in the mountains, but remaining there in a shallow grave was not what I had in mind. I was faced with Hobson's choice. Stay and certainly die or take a chance on maybe living through it by going to Saint Louis.

I sighed and told them, "All right. If I must, I"ll go. Even Saint Looie ain't as bad as dyin'!"

* * *

Fortunately for me, Bill Sublette is considerably more tender of his own comfort and well-being than ever he is of others. Nursing him back to health from the gunshot wound in his shoulder required much more time than Bill would have allowed anybody else. Which accounts for the delay in his departure for Saint Louis that permitted my wound to heal sufficiently for me to join his eastbound caravan.

Not everyone was content to wait for Sublette. Stephens, the Gantt & Blackwell partisan who had fleeced Zenas Leonard and the other fledgeling trappers, had come along to rendezvous with RMF. Thinking it over, he became dissatisfied with the dishonest deal he had made with Fitz for the peltries he had stolen from his own men. True, Fitz is a hard bargainer, but Stephens had agreed to the terms. Now Stephens thought he could renege on the deal he had made with Fitzpatrick. He was set on getting back to the Laramie and lifting Fitzpatrick's cache, then racing on to Saint Louis and selling the furs, thereby doubling his ill-gotten gains.

Whilst Sublette tarried in camp, Stephens persuaded half a dozen greenhorns eager to return to the settlements to join him in an early departure. One was a young fellow called More, one of Nat Wyeth's rebellious recruits. Somebody said two of the others were Daniel Boone's grandsons, but if so, the old boy's wilderness smarts had washed out of the family bloodstream.

They didn't get far. Just over the hill, in Davey Jackson's Hole, they ran into a score of Grovant warriors, likely still smarting from the drubbing we gave them. When the Indians jumped them, More's horse spooked and threw him. Boone's grandsons turned back to help him and one of them, Foy, was killed, along with More. Stephens got his comeuppance for his lifelong chicanery. A few days after the survivors straggled back to Pierre's Hole, he died of his wounds, all of them in his back.

Anse Tolliver's oft-repeated dictum, "Thar's safety in numbers," had again proved valid. Even aside from the time needed to heal my wound, waiting for Sublette's big caravan was sound policy.

* * *

Rocky Mountain Fur was fed up with American Fur dogging their tracks, the newcomers cashing in on RMF's hard-won knowledge accumulated during ten tough years in the mountains. Bridger and Fitz even offered to split the territory with them, so each could do their trapping separately, but Vanderburgh and Drips scoffed and said they liked the present arrangement better.

RMF's debt to Bill Sublette was looming larger. The partners were desperate, squeezed betwixt the competition and their unforgiving creditor. Fitz and Bridger came up with a solution. They would head far north into Blackfoot country for the fall harvest. If they couldn't shake loose the tagalong American Fur people, Blackfoots would likely do the job for them.

* * *

At last Bill Sublette declared that he was fit enough for the long journey to the settlements. The hole in my chest had healed over and, except for a nagging ache, I, too, was ready for the trail. Old Foot volunteered to accompany me to Saint Louis, in case my condition worsened along the way. When the caravan came to the Bighorn crossing, we planned to split off and follow that river to its mouth, where it spills into the Yellowstone. There we would build a bullboat and Foot and I would float down the Yellowstone to Fort Union and the Missouri, where we would buy passage on a keelboat or mackinaw headed downstream to Saint Louis.

When I questioned the need for half-a-dozen of our people coming along as far as the Big Horn, Tuttle promptly squelched my objections. "Cain't nohaow be trustin' Billy Sublette, cold-hearted, mean, an' hungry as he be, not to leave ye dyin' on ther prairie — like he done ol' Hiram Scott in 'twenny-eight — if'n ye cain't keep up. Nope! Cain't 'low it nohaow! We'll come along 'til we turn ye loose on ther Big Horn, so's ye kin float on daown to ther Yellerstone ter Amurrican Fur an' thet'ere McKenzie feller.　Tight as ye be with Chouteau, McKenzie'll hafta he'p ye, like it or not."

Godey assured me that from the Big Horn to the Missouri the Yellowstone is devoid of waterfalls and serious rapids.　His old boss Manuel Lisa had lugged his keelboats up that far in 'ought-seven and built a trading post there.　"From thar," he said, "all ye got to worry abaout is grizzle b'ars fishin' an' Crows an' mebbe Stonies lookin' fer easy pickin's whilst ye go floatin' by.　They oughta still be out on the prairie, west o' thar, huntin' buffler, but ye never know."

I recalled the Stonies, Rocks — properly Assiniboines — who pirated Andrew Henry's horses from us back in 'twenty-two.　Thieving Crows not above killing are a common nuisance.

After the escort saw us safely on our way down the Yellowstone, they would ride west to catch up with Fitz and Bridger and the rest of our bunch.　They reckoned half a dozen good marksmen mounted on their best horses would be equal to the chore of traveling through hostile Indian country.　I wasn't so sure, but there was no talking them out of it.

* * *

Foot and I would be traveling light, so the day before Sublette's departure I conducted a giveaway in the Indian fashion.　I got rid myself of everything I wasn't taking with me. If I survived, Saint Louis could provide plunder galore to replace it.　Most of what I owned I gave to Cat, to keep what she wanted and give away the rest.　I also presented her with Rainbow's gentle piebald mare, which she had already been using, anyway, and which she immediately gifted to my daughter, who would soon be ready to ride on her own.　My tall bay buffalo-runner Punch went to Tuttle.　He had been covetous of that fine horse from the first day I claimed him from the Blackfoots on the Flathead.　Powatawa said he was content with the critters he already had.

When Iron Bow came to wish me a fervent godspeed, it gave me great pleasure to gift him with Sugarfoot, my well-bred saddle mule that had filled the old gentleman's eyes since he first spied him. Micah immediately offered me the use of his Lightfoot mule for the journey to the Big Horn. "You'll likely be needin' an easy-walker, Temple," he said, "an' ye know he's one o' the best." I thanked him and offered him first pick of my remaining cavayard. The rest went to whoever in our bunch could use them.

My books went to Micah, whom I was sure would care for them and happily share with anyone who wished to borrow one. I promised to bring more from the settlements.

Bidding farewell to my father and entrusting my daughter Iris to the care of Cat and Ned was the most difficult part of embarking on a journey from which I might never return. Iris had shared my robes every night since I mended enough to sleep without an attendant. She refused to be parted from me during daylight hours, chattering away in her faltering English, her chubby little hands seconding her speech, big-eyed and striving to appear cheerful when she and I spoke of my impending absence, keeping a respectful silence when I visited with others, but insisting, nevertheless, on being present. Knowing that Cat and Ned and Powatawa — and Micah, too — would look after her was a comfort, but it was nonetheless painful to part from her.

Powatawa and I often smoked together, mostly in silence, but his mere presence lent me courage during those difficult days. I have often felt fear in the face of danger, but I have never been overcome by it when my actions might save my skin. It was the waiting and not knowing that was disturbing.

* * *

A ragged volley of sour blasts from Gabe Bridger's battered old bugle summoned what was left of the rendezvous to bid farewell to Sublette's packtrain. I was already mounted on my reliable Ready horse, Micah's Lightfoot mule in tow, the packsaddle loaded with my few belongings, which included my precious journals tightly wrapped in oilskin.

A buckskin parcel rode on top of the light load. At the last minute Cat had called me aside and pushed into my hands a beautiful quilled deerskin longshirt, soft antelope leggin's, and elaborately quilled and beaded moccasins. Blushing and looking down, she said, "You mus' walk proud wiv white-eyes." Her hand-signs made it clear that she wanted me to look respectable when I got to Saint Louis. It was a touching gesture and I wanted to hug her for it, but naturally I refrained from doing such a thing to Ned's woman.

Ned and Paddy, as well as Pretty Horse and Stone Bird, had wanted to come along, but the burden of wives and children made that course unwise. It should have kept Brass Turtle with his wife and child, as well, but, as he explained it, "If it warn't fer Cat an' Molly, I reckon I'd'a had to be hangin' back, too, but them two say they'll be lookin' arter Tally an' muh li'l gal better'n I could, anyways, so I mought as well ride along with ye."

The bodyguards — Powatawa, Tuttle, Brass Turtle, Micah, Little Mountain, and Cesár — were passing Anse's kettle amongst them, then on to Paddy and Ned. Anse grabbed it back and brought it to me. "Hyar ye go, Temple! Gitcherse'f a dram fer the trail! I be wishin' ye the best. An' see to it ye gitcherse'f back hyar fer nex' ronnyvoo, do'ee hyar?" Such tender sentiments are rare with Anse Tolliver. I was touched.

Finn McCool caught my shoulder as I prepared to mount. "I'm wishin' I were goin' wi' ye, Temple, but Foot'll be after doin' ye as much good as I could an' he'll doubtless be much better help on the way. Try to get yoursel' to Saint Looie fast as ye can. That galena ball nestin' nigh your heart's doin' ye no good a-tall, a-tall. May the Lord go wi' ye!"

All the sweat-lodge prayers and farewells had been said, all the well-wishing and regrets expressed, all the promises to return next year had been made. It was time to go.

The packtrain was ready. Black Harris would guide it. Bill Sublette emerged from a tent, mounted a stump, and stepped onto his waiting horse, his left arm still in a sling but otherwise looking fit enough. He gave no farewell speech. "All right!" he yelled. "Let's git to it!" Far up front, Harris repeated the command and the packtrain shambled forwards, heavy packs swaying, hostlers waving goodbyes and cursing happily, settlement pleasures likely in mind, critters neighing and braying, harness bells jingling, all the cacophony of a caravan on the move. The two creaking dearborns loaded with furs lurched into line and it was time for us to fall in behind.

Cat had placed Iris in my arms for a final embrace. I hugged my little girl, kissed her chubby cheeks, brushed away the gathering tears, and told her to be a good girl for Mama Cat. She clung to my neck until Cat pulled her down. She looked up at me with desperate eyes, full lips trembling but refusing to cry, one hand waving a feeble farewell, until I lost sight of her when we passed the first bend in the trail.

* * *

The journey through the pass and across Davey Jackson's Hole to the Big Horn was uneventful. That big packtrain bristling with guns was too large a quarry for the scattered bands of Grovants that lurked along our route. A few nighttime attempts to steal or stampede the critters were quickly squelched. The thrashing they had received at Pierre's Hole had left the Atsína with a thirst for vengeance but also with increased respect for white-eyes grit in a fight.

We pitched in with the daily chore of providing meat for nigh a hundred hungry bellies, picking off scattered bunches of kicked-out young bulls wandering mountain trails and meadows. Moses Harris often shared our cookfire, for we kept the choicest portions for ourselves, observing the precept that the workman is worthy of his hire. As always, Black paid his due, filling the nighttime hours with his comical yarns.

We parted with the packtrain at the Big Horn. Sublette continued to South Pass and we struck out northwards, sticking as close as we could to the Big Horn, threading our way around the eastern side of the mountains, aiming for the Yellowstone. The morning we parted, Harris shook my hand and promised, "When ye git to Sain' Looie and gitcherse'f patched up, Temple, c'mon down ter Matilda's so's I kin interduce ye 'round. She's got herse'f a whole new stable o' fillies naow. Better'n ye ever seen thar. We'll gitcha laid good an' proper. My treat." I promised to meet him there, but the charms of Mathilde's *filles de joie* ranked amongst the least of my concerns.

* * *

Traveling the long stretch from where we parted from Sublette to the mouth of the Big Horn was more cautious, less carefree, than the earlier part of the journey. Eight well-armed men would easily discourage roaming bands of horsethieves, who usually conduct business in handfuls of half-a-dozen or so, but running into a whole village could spell sudden death. We kept to woodland trails when we could and scouts spied out open country in advance. We cooked supper in daylight in aspen groves and doused the cookfire before scattering out in the trees around meadows that provided graze for the critters, there to grab a few hours' sleep before saddling up and pushing onward. Such precautions served us well. We accomplished the journey without incident.

"I reckon we run plumb betwixt ther raindrops thi'shere time!" Tuttle crowed gleefully as we neared our destination.

"An' whilst you're at it, ye'd best be wishin' we don't git no wetter joinin' up with Bridger's outfit!" Brass Turtle commented dryly. "Thar's sure to be a passel o' Crows an' ever'body else makin' meat out thar on the prairie, afore we git to the Forks."

We built a bullboat when we got to the Big IIorn, just upstream of where it joins the Yellowstone. First, we harvested a big buffalo bull and skinned him, slicing down the belly to keep the hide in one piece.

We bent and tied stout green willows more or less in an oval and added more to form a bowl, all of it lashed solidly together with sinew and strips of hide. That provided the sturdy frame, over which we stretched and secured the green buffalo hide before suspending it over an aspenwood fire to dry it enough to snug up the hide and lashings. A latticework flooring of willow withes to relieve strain on the bottom completed the chore. The old saw which advises that many hands make light work held true. We completed the task in little more than a day, whilst Cesár and Foot whittled out paddles to aid in steering our clumsy craft downriver.

A fat cow and plenty of jesting enlivened our spirits that final evening, fending off doubts about the downriver trip and what could prove to be a perilous journey westwards for the bodyguards. "'Tain't wuth frettin, nohaow, 'baout neither one," Tuttle declared. "All ye kin ever do is jest do yer best an' let ther cards fall like they come off ther pack. Cogitatin' won't change nuthin'."

"You're right," Micah agreed. "It likely makes it worse. Worryin' makes ye get in your own way."

Powatawa nodded but remained silent. How much Little Mountain, Foot, and Cesár Pérez understood of that palaver, I'm not equipped to say. They, too, held their peace and so did I.

* * *

Horses were saddled and loaded, ready for the trail, when Foot and I stepped into the bullboat bobbing in the shallows, made sure that our plunder was securely lashed in place, and pushed off from the shore into the swift-running current of the Big Horn. A line tied to a tree vibrated and twanged whilst we made sure there were no leaks. I signaled to Tuttle, who cast it loose, and we went whirling downriver, paddling furiously to stay offshore, our *compañeros'* well-wishing fading in our ears. I snatched a final glimpse of those beloved men before they were lost from sight around a bend, wondering if I would ever see them again. The force of the Big Horn's powerful current meeting the Yellowstone sent our light craft skidding towards the far shore, until the Yellowstone caught us up and propelled us out of reach of its mighty tributary. Our watery hike to Fort Union had truly begun.

* * *

Old Foot has proved to be a remarkable compendium of lore and skills since I first met him ten years ago on our keelboat journey up the Missouri in 'twenty-two. Now he revealed himself to be a first-rate waterman, as well as a healer of citters and men, herbalist, fighter, trapper, hunter, cook, unerring pathfinder, and a good-natured, tireless playmate of our children, although he is customarily curt and impatient with the rest of us. He speaks little, which I always assumed was because of unfamiliarity with our tongue, his rare spoken comments usually confined to brief, wry-humored observations on our shortcomings. His accompanying sign-talk, which we all use, unconsciously, without even intending to, even amongst whites, leaves little doubt, howsomever, as to what Foot means to say.

He is short of stature, lean but sturdily-built, strong and agile. His age is a mystery. From the first, we called him Old Foot, but he hasn't changed a mite in ten years. His leathery features frame bright, inquisitive eyes, his fleeting grins reveal strong white teeth, and two tiny streaks of grey in his dark hair haven't increased in a decade. He is ageless.

Save for swimming, I harbor an abiding aversion to more water than I can drink, which accounts for my total ignorance of how to prevent our little nearly-round tub from whirling its way uncontrolled down the Yellowstone. I was getting giddy from its gyrating, until Foot showed me how to dig my paddle deep in the water like a rudder, creating enough drag to keep us from spinning in circles. After that our swift passage downriver became a pleasure instead of the whirligig ride it was at first.

Sometime during the first day, Foot said, "No more you call me Foot. Name be Zeetlah. You call me Zeetlah."

"All right," I replied. "Whatever you wish." I thought for a moment before I asked, "What does Zeetlah mean in Lenni-lenapay?"

He grinned. "Mean 'Foot,' two time." He held up two fingers. So it meant "Feet," but if it made him feel good, Zeetlah it would be from then on. Brass Turtle had told me long ago that Foot — now and forevermore Zeetlah — in his youth had been one of the great runners in what was left of the Delaware nation. I wondered why it had taken him ten years to correct me, so I put that queston to him. "Allus eva'body 'round. Don't matter," he explained. "Now, just you'n me, so you be callin' me Zeetlah, like Dellerware say." That seemed fair enough to me.

Zeetlah was adept at avoiding hazards such as snags, sawyers, and boulders in the streambed, as well as, one time, getting clear of a big grizzly standing up to his haunches in the river, swiping at fish, directly in our path. Zeetlah barked out an order to dig my paddle deep, which I did, then paddled furiously on his side, causing us to skitter sidewise just out of Old Ephraim's reach and leave him pawing air and bellowing imprecations as we swept past to safety.

At day's end he would gauge the river's flow to guide us to a smooth landing in a place where we could haul our water-soaked tub ashore, overturn it, conceal it with branches, and let it dry overnight. We were reluctant to fire our guns, lest we attract attention, so we made do mostly with jerkmeat and fish we caught on grubs dug out of rotten logs.

Abundant rains upstream kept the Yellowstone flowing rapidly, hastening our progress to the Missouri. Twice we were espied by Indians a-horseback on the broad sweep of prairie that bordered much of the river, but by time they were able to gallop to the shoreline we had gained the cover of forest growing down to the bank, which made pursuit impossible.

Thus, in five days' time, the rude battlements of Fort Union hove into view, and Zeetlah actually smiled at a job well done.

* * *

The bottom of our clumsy little ark had scarcely scraped the pebbled beach when a trio of halfbreed servants came hustling down the footpath. They greeted us in French, but their smiling *bienvenues* changed to disappointed looks when they peered into the bullboat. *"Mais, M'sieu, vous n'avez pas des plews?"* their leader questioned. No, I informed him, not this time. No peltries. I have other, more important, business to conduct here, so, if it pleases you, conduct me to Mister McKenzie so that I might get on with it.

They appeared doubtful that anything could be more important than beaver plews, but, cheerfully enough, they emptied the bullboat of our plunder, hauled our tub a distance from the water's edge and flipped it upside down to dry, then shouldered our packs and led us up the hill. Inside the gate of the fort, they piled our plunder in a heap, and one of them trotted off, presumably to announce our arrival to the man in charge. When the messenger returned I rewarded each of them with a few small coins, which happified them to a surprising degree. Evidently Fort Union wages are not lavish. Somebody barked a command from within one of the surrounding buildings and our three helpers jumped to obey, calling out their *mercis* as they disappeared indoors.

Zeetlah and I cooled our heels for a considerable spell, passing the time smoking and taking stock of what we could see of Fort Union from where we waited. The establishment was an impressive affair, far more elaborate than the rude trading fort we had built for Andrew Henry in 'twenty-two. A score of doorways let out on a large courtyard and most of the rooms appeared to possess a second storey, all of them butted against a tall stockade of sturdy pickets, around which ran a walkway nigh the top, likely intended for defense in the event of attack. The clang of hammer and anvil echoed from a blacksmith shop and the air was redolent with cooking smells from somewhere within that sprawling warren. On the hike up to the fort I had observed still more log wokshops and dwellings scattered outside the walls and a number of Indian lodges standing amongst them. What appeared to be a small army of employees and visitors flowed through the courtyard, white-eyes clerks dressed in sober broadcloth and colorful Métis servants scurrying in pursuit of their duties, leather-clad woodsmen lounging in doorways or strolling aimlessly, Indian men and women of half-a-dozen tribes come to trade and get drunk, all of them dodging a regiment of ragamuffin children and barking dogs darting hither-thither amongst them.

At long last the Great Man Himself appeared, truly a spectacle well worth waiting for. Kenneth McKenzie stood slightly taller than most men, but his manner implied that his stature exceeded that of all but a few select mortals upon the earth. Clean-shaven, well-fed, ruddy-faced, he was clad in a bright-blue frock-coat and trousers of the same stuff, a lavishly-embroidered waistcoat, a frilly white shirt, and a lacy stock sprouting at his throat. A gold-knobbed walking-stick completed his ensemble. All he lacked was a coronet perched upon his well-barbered head to assert his claim to be King of the Missouri. Incongruously, howsomever, he was shod in elaborately-quilled moccasins, possibly to accommodate a case of the gout, a common malady amongst wealthy gentlemen addicted to Madeira wine and rich vittles.

He halted some ten paces from us, obliging us to come to him. Which we did. I wasted neither time nor breath with niceties. "I be Temple Buck, free trapper, late o' Pier's Hole, an' this be Zeetlah, my *compañero*, the same. We're headin' for Sain' Looie on personal business of my own. I'd be much obliged if ye'll put us up here — nothin' much required, just vittles and a roof — 'til we can buy passage on a keelboat goin' downriver."

It was plain to see that McKenzie did not recollect our earlier meeting and introduction in Pierre Chouteau's offices in Saint Louis, four years before, and I declined to remind him of it. His stern expression caused me to blurt, "No charity's bein' asked. I've got cash money enough for whatever ye charge!" I rattled the poke on my belt.

The dull clink of gold pieces, not silver coins, captured his interest. "I'll pay ye now, if ye like."

"No need," he replied. "Ye can settle up when ye leave." His icy gaze swept over the two of us and I realized then what a sorry figure I cut after weeks a-horseback and another scudding down the Yellowstone in a bullboat, unwashed and unshaven, my leathers mud-caked and blood-stained. Zeetlah looked somewhat better, but not much. "We'll put you up, but the Injun can sleep in the barn."

I bristled, struggling to keep a civil tongue. "No ye don't! He goes where I go. We'll be lodgin' together."

It was apparent that Kenneth McKenzie was not accustomed to being contradicted, but he harrumphed and replied, "Very well. Hamilton will show ye to your quarters." He jerked his chin in the direction of a tall, somewhat-past-middle-aged man who had followed him into the courtyard, then spun on his heel and left us.

Mister Hamilton was tall and spare and possessed of a most remarkable nose, large and red and pitted in testimony of a lifetime of dedicated dramming. His limping gait as he led us to our quarters suggested that he might share his master's gouty affliction. His manner was dour and officious, but he offered no affront. When he pushed open the door of a windowless little box of a room, he spoke for the first time. "There's but one bed," he announced, "but it must do ye." His accent was unmistakeably British and well-bred. I later learned that he was an exiled English nobleman condemned to spend his life amid the rude company of Americans like myself and savage Indians, whom he abhorred. When he turned to go, he informed me crisply, "Supper's at five. Sharp!" then limped off.

The single bed was no problem. We deposited our belongings upon it and spread our sleeprobes on the plank floor. It was still early in the afternoon, so Zeetlah and I betook ourselves to the Yellowstone and bathed off our coat of grime, after which I scraped away my measly beard and dressed in my second-best raiment. Except for shaving, Zeetlah did likewise.

Naturally neither Zeetlah nor I had any idea when it was five o'clock, sharp or otherwise, but a procession of clerks streaming towards a particular doorway informed us that suppertime had arrived. We joined them and entered a long, narrow, candle-lit room furnished with a single long table fitted with benches on either side, where the clerks jostled one another as they took their places. The table was adorned with a splendid white tablecloth and all manner of bottles and cruets. Two servants, one a Negro, bustled about, preparing to serve up vittles. Kenneth McKenzie was already seated at the head of the table, Hamilton at his side. When the old gentleman spied me, he waved his hand towards an empty bench at the far end — well below the salt, as the saying is — and called out, "That'll be your place, Mister Buck." Just then he spied Zeetlah at my side. He half-rose from his seat, his face coloring, and bellowed, "No red savages allowed in this refect'ry, by God! Begone!"

I felt my temper rising fit to choke me. I fought to control it. Then, ignoring Hamilton, I addressed McKenzie directly in a loud voice, "Your bad manners, sir, will not go unreported!" Evidently my unusual retort sparked McKenzie's curiosity. He stared intently at me down the long table, his face a thundercloud, but he said naught. Blood thumped in my ears. I could not remain silent. "Perhaps you choose not to recall, Mister McKenzie, that we have met before!" An intent look appeared on his face. "Yes," I went on hotly, "in the offices of M'sieu Pierre Chouteau, four years past, when that esteemed gentleman, whose good manners far exceed your own, introduced you and me as *equals!* Which I certainly am, if not moreso!" I struggled to restrain the curses surging in my throat, fortunately successfully. "I shall certainly inform le Cadet of the ill-treatment that I and my companion have received at your hand!"

McKenzie had half-risen from his seat, his eyes bugging. Without waiting for a reply, if indeed one was forthcoming, I stalked from the dining hall, Zeetlah at my side, my ears throbbing with anger and the excited murmurs of the assembled clerks.

We had scarcely regained our quarters and were stuffing our plunder into our packs, preparing to quit the fort, when the Métis servant who had first assisted us appeared with a steaming kettle of fine fat buffalo meat and, amazingly, a napkin that contained four fluffy white-flour biscuits. We asked no questions and he offered no explanation. Hungry as we were by that time, we devoured the meat and savored every crumb of the biscuits, a luxury only dreamed-of in the mountains.

Shortly afterwards, Mister Hamilton presented himself in the doorway and announced stiffly, "Mister McKenzie sends his compliments. He desires that I conduct you to suitable quarters, which I am prepared to do at this time." Surprised and curious in spite of myself, I nodded. Hamilton had brought with him a couple of servants, whom he commanded in heavily-accented bad French to transport our belongings to our new digs. He led the way to a much larger bedchamber that afforded a barred window screened with buffalo hide scraped to vellum thinnness and two narrow wooden beds. His duty completed, Hamilton bowed ever-so-slightly and said, "I trust that you will be comfortable here." I mumbled an indistinct thankee and he departed without further commerce.

A flask of Madeira and half a carrot of fresh tobacco beside one of the beds completed McKenzie's distant apology for the time being. Zeetlah and I drained the flask and filled our pipes before going outdoors to sit in the gathering darkness, smoking, not talking, satisfied that mountaineer honor had been successfully defended.

* * *

Days dragged all-too-slowly by whilst we waited impatiently for a keelboat or mackinaw to carry us downriver to Saint Louis. We took our meals in our room, avoiding further conflicts. Zeetlah was frequently absent from our quarters in the early evening, visiting the Indian encampments on precisely what business I am not equipped to say for sure, but his satisfied look and manner each time he returned bolstered my suspicions regarding his purpose in going there.

Daytimes, whilst Zeetlah was off in the woods gathering herbs and whatnot, I passed time by wandering about McKenzie's sprawling wilderness manor. He presides over a veritable beehive of industry — several smithies, a cooperage, a carpenter's shop, a tannery, and warehouses where plews, pelts, hides, and buffalo robes are graded and pressed into bales for shipment to the settlements. Cultivated fields of corn and garden truck stretch out along the broad finger of land betwixt the Missouri and the Yellowstone to the bordering mainland forest. Hogs snort in styes and chickens, ducks, and geese squawk, quack, and honk in pens, and a sizeable herd of milch cows and oxen and another of horses and mules graze in lush pastures, besides the stables and paddocks in which well-groomed saddlers are kept. I longed to borrow a good horse and join the hunters who keep the establishment supplied with buffalo meat, wapiti, deer, and other game, but pride forbade asking that favor.

Most remarkable of all is Kenneth McKenzie's distillery. Government watchdogs at Army posts along the Missouri forbid the transport of ardent spirits into Indian country, so McKenzie stills his own from corn he purchases from upriver Mandans, Hidatsas, and Gros Ventres, who supply him daily with boatloads of Indian maize they float downstream in dugouts and bullboats. From what I could tell, their payment mostly consists of rotgut booze, the nearly universal coin of the Indian trade.

Indians of every stripe — Mandans, Assiniboines, Big-bellies, and every kind of Blackfoot — find their way to Fort Union to trade and get drunk. Only Crows resist the pernicious, crazy-making brew. And Kenneth McKenzie's warehouses bulge ever more full of beaver plews, fine furs, and buffalo robes, as well as a treasury of Indian art and handcrafts — exquisite quillwork, beaded embroidery, painted robes, traditional weapons, and ceremonial clothing, which drink-crazed warriors and their women gladly swap for just one more swig of popskull.

* * *

Upon my departure from Pierre's Hole, my bookish trapper friend Etienne LeBref gifted me with a well-thumbed English translation of *The Satyricon* of Petronius Arbiter, an old Roman writer who delighted in scribbling florid descriptions of the opulent luxuries, gilded excesses, and licentious orgies enjoyed by the privileged few in the courts of Roman emperors. I particularly enjoyed reading that book at Fort Union, the realm of the King of the Missouri, who, if he had ever read it, must have turned green with envy and striven to emulate the sumptuous style of the Caesars, leastaways as best as the primitive wilderness would allow.

Whenever I tired of strolling amongst the workshops and paddocks of the fort, chatting with mechanics and grooms, I often retired to a shady corner where I divided my time betwixt reading dear old Petronius and scribbling in my journal. One day when I was occupied with capturing my memories on the pale lines of my ledger, I became aware of the approach of Mister Hamilton. I chose not to acknowledge his presence. He, howsomever, appeared to care little about my wish for privacy. He halted beside me, leaned down to peer at the book which lay open at my side, fumbled in his waistcoat pocket for his spectacles and fitted them onto his bulbous nose for a closer look, before he said, "Hmmmmm, oh my! Petronius. Good gracious! I see that you are a man of parts, Mister Buck. Quite unexpected, I daresay, in one of your profession."

I felt my dander rising at his condescension, but I replied coolly, "I reckon it takes all kinds, Mister Hamilton. Circumstances alter cases. I'm not trapping just now and I prefer not to be idle." It wasn't much of a reply, but it sufficed.

"Hmmmmm," he murmured again. "Curious indeed. You are to be complimented, Mister Buck." With that he straightened, pocketed his spectacles, and, without another word, proceeded on his way. I have never, before or since, felt so much like a zoological specimen on public display.

Thereafter, howsomever, Mister Hamilton was much more affable in his greetings when we chanced to meet, the Madeira and fresh tobacco appeared more frequently in our quarters, and, thenceforth, the quality and variety of our vittles was much improved.

He must have spoken of his observations to the Great Man, as well, for after that occasion McKenzie actually deigned to nod and even blessed me with a brief smile whenever we encountered each other in and around the fort.

* * *

Once the wound in my breast healed over my health appeared to be as good as ever it had been, except for an occasional twinge and the knowledge that I carried in my bosom the leaden memento I had received at the hand of the ill-fated Grovant damsel. Finn McCool's dire warning about the danger of galena poisoning my innards was rarely far from my thoughts, but I was powerless to hasten my progress to Saint Louis and the possibility of a cure. Days slipped past and still nary a southbound keelboat or a sizeable mackinaw appeared on the Missouri. All of which likely accounted for my short temper and the grudge I nursed against Kenneth McKenzie and Fort Union in general.

Truth to tell, he deserves much credit for the enormous chore he accomplished in just a few years. I didn't alter my disapproval of his imperious manner or his popinjay costumes and conduct, but there should be no doubt that McKenzie is very good at what he does for a living. I reckon both his efficiency and his high-handed treatment of others likely stem from his early service with the British Nor'westers. And I must admit that ever since the confrontation in the dining hall, for whatever reason, Zeetlah and I were well-treated in McKenzie's little kingdom.

Two unlikely vassals rendering liege to His Self-inflated Highness chanced to cross my path on one of my early-morning rambles. As I neared one of the rude log outbuildings that litter McKenzie's sprawling domain, two big, leather-clad men ducked through the doorway, turned about, and commenced hauling out several long, heavy wooden crates. When I drew nigh, I recognized them as Hugh Glass and Jim Beckwith. They appeared no less surprised than I at our meeting. Glass merely growled something to Beckwith, turned away, and shambled off. Jim, howsomever, lingered and greeted me with a sickly smile, as if I had caught him doing something naughty. Which, as it turned out, I was about to do.

"Mornin', Jim," I called out cheerfully. "Long time no-see-um!"

"Mawnin', Temple," he replied, sidling towards the doorway, as if to block my view. "Ye be a long ways off from your stompin' ground."

"Indeed so," I agreed. "Just stoppin' by on the way to Sain' Looie." The closer I got to him, the more embarrassed he appeared to be. "Still trappin'?" I asked pleasantly.

"Some," he allowed. Then, without my asking, "Mos'ly workin' fer McKenzie. Tradin'."

"Not surprisin'," I replied. "Ye've always been good at it." By that time I was able to make out the lettering painted on the crates, which, I saw, contained muskets manufactured in New Jersey.

I made no comment, but Beckwith likely read the look on my face. "Hell, Buck, somebody's gonna be doin' it!" he declared defensively. "Mought as well be us!"

"Ye reckon?" I replied levelly. There was no profit in my expressing judgment. Glass and Beckwith — and McKenzie, too — would do as they pleased, no matter what anybody might think or say. I turned to go. "Take care, Jim. I'll remember ye to the *compañeros* when I get back."

"Ye do that, Buck," he said in a small voice. I reckon there was still a shred of good left in Jim Beckwith that greed and resentment hadn't smothered.

* * *

Next morning I was strolling on the Missouri bank, peering upstream for the longed-for sight of a keelboat, when I was startled by the strident blast of a boat horn and piercing toots of a steam-whistle. I swung about and beheld a steamboat rounding the bend below the Yellowstone, its enormous paddlewheel churning the muddy water, flinging glittering spray skywards into the sunshine, tall smokestack belching clouds of black smoke and sparks, the high prow thrusting through the yellow river as it surged towards the Fort Union wharf. I had seen a few steamboats before, but only smaller ones near Saint Louis, and never one that was so welcome a sight for my hungry eyes.

As I trotted towards the wharf I was caught up in a mad rush of nigh-hysterical clerks and servants of the fort stampeding to greet the first steamboat to travel this high on the Missouri. As the boat maneuvered nigh the wharf and a hundred eager hands reached to grab mooring lines flung out from the deck, I saw that it had been christened the *Yellowstone*. That day it lived up to its baptismal promise.

The mob of clerks and fort servants went wild with jubilation, as if this were the Second Coming of the Messiah, which in a way it was. Equally impressed by the floating Armageddon, but in a much different way, were the copperskinned heathens gathered at a safe distance amongst the skin lodges scattered outside the fort. Most of their women ran headlong to the forest, shrieking and wailing, dragging their children away from the fire-breathing monster. Horses bolted and yanked up their pickets. The men remained, lest they be considered cowards by their fellows, but strained looks, hands darting to cover their mouths, and shuffling moccasins betrayed their fear of the smoke-belching smokestack and the hissing boiler as it slowly shut down.

The crowd parted behind me as Kenneth McKenzie, Mister Hamilton limping at his elbow, strode forward to welcome the passengers. As he drew nigh, McKenzie flashed a smile and beckoned me to join him. Which I did. "I believe, Mister Buck," he shouted above the hubbub, "that you will be happy to greet one passenger in particular." Whatever else he might have said was lost in the cheering as a plank ramp crashed upon the wharf and boatmen rushed to secure the craft against the Missouri's powerful current.

First to step upon the wharf was Pierre Chouteau, tall, elegant, imperial, a triumphant smile on his lean features, for me a sight even more delightful than his waterborne chariot. Close behind him was a youngish man clutching a portmanteau and what appeared to be a painter's easel.

McKenzie stepped forward, hand extended, mouthing a welcome mostly lost in the hubbub. Whilst they exchanged pleasantries, Chouteau's glance fell upon me and his face took on an even more pleased expression. He clasped me by the shoulders and exclaimed, "M'sieu Bock! Temple, *mon vieux! Quelle surprise!* You! 'Ere! On zis *grande occasion! C'est incroyable!*" Before I was able to reply, he caught McKenzie's arm and my own in his and marched us to the fort, babbling the while his experiences whilst ascending the Missouri and firing questions at us both to which he gave us no opportunity to reply.

We parted in the courtyard, where he insisted that I join McKenzie and himself for supper that evening. Which, naturally, I assured him that I would be happy to do.

* * *

The refectory that evening was reserved for only a few — Chouteau, McKenzie, the gentleman with the easel, the inevitable Mister Hamilton, Captain LaBarge, master of the *Yellowstone,* a couple-three senior clerks, and myself. The others were sartorially splendiferous in well-tailored broadcloth, ruffled shirts, and embroidered waistcoats. I wore what I owned.

The banquet that Kenneth McKenzie laid on in Chouteau's honor surpassed anything that I might have imagined. A seemingly endless profusion of vittles were brought to the table by broadly smiling waiters who doubtless would be first to gobble up the abundant leftovers — roasted buffalo hump, ribs, and backstrap, fresh boiled tongue and marrow, smoked pork cutlets and *médaillons* of tender beef, catfish from the Missouri and trout from the Yellowstone, Polish hams and all manner of pickled and preserved European comestibles, potatoes and an array of garden truck prepared to perfection, sweet fresh butter and a plenitude of piquant sauces, fluffy light biscuits, layer cakes and fresh fruit and meat pies and creamy desserts, and I can't recollect what-all, washed down with red and white French and German wines appropriate, I was told, to the various courses.

That Lucullan supper, worthy of Trimalchio at his most expansive, occupied more than three hours, consumed lazily, richly flavored with conversation both elevated and practical, all of it good-humored. Accustomed as I am to the feast-or-famine life of a mountaineer, where it is not uncommon for a man to consume ten pounds of meat or more at a sitting, I had no trouble holding my own amongst those hearty appetites.

Reluctant at first to join in the palaver, I was continually drawn into it by le Cadet, who kept plying me with queries about life in the mountains, trading practices, Indians, weather, and other matters that only I amongst that particular company could answer. In time the wine and good-fellowship loosened my tongue sufficiently to allow my participation in more general converse, as well. In the course of that supper, I softened my judgment of Kenneth McKenzie, who, temporarily relieved of his daily burden of exercising authority over the vast holdings of Fort Union and its army of servants, proved to be a most genial host and table companion.

The gentleman beside me introduced himself as Mister George Catlin, a painter of portraits and natural scenes. We struck up a chat of our own when he admired my clothing. Wishing to present the best appearance possible at supper, I had laid out my two best outfits, one made by Rainbow, the other that with which Cat had gifted me on the day of my departure. I hated to admit it, but Cat's was the most beautifully quilled and most neatly sewn and decorated.

Catlin asked a multitude of questions regarding Indians and their way of life and explained that he had begged to accompany le Cadet on his voyage in order to capture in his sketchbooks and canvases images of uncivilized aborigines before whitemen's ways corrupted them and erased their native beauty. That appeared to me to be a worthy effort, so I did my sorry best to provide whatever information I possessed.

After supper, several of us retired to McKenzie's comfortable quarters for coffee, cigars, fine French cognac — vastly superior to the raw brandy from Fort Union's still — and more pleasant palaver, until Pierre Chouteau declared that it was time for bed. As I took my leave I promised Catlin that, next day, I would conduct him amongst the Indians gathered outside the fort.

When I returned to my chamber I discovered a tipsy Zeetlah seated on the floor, happily devouring the contents of a large hamper and swigging from a wicker-covered bottle. He regarded me owlishly and announced with a lopsided grin, "Ol' Buffler-nose bring vittle. Plenty ha-ha-ha, plenty drunk, I'm t'inkin'. Huh?" If Mr. Hamilton were indeed drunk, which was likely after our bibulous evening, Zeetlah had plainly caught up. He fell asleep amid the generous leavings of our fabulous feast. As I slid into contented slumber I surmised that Hamilton was likely doing his best to make amends for the initial shoddy treatment we had received and was trying to protect his boss.

* * *

Next morning I drew the old gentleman aside and prayed that he would assure Kenneth McKenzie that I harbored no grudge, that bygones were bygones, and that I would say nothing harmful to them when I spoke with Pierre Chouteau.

I discovered Mister Catlin perched on the bankside, sketching the Missouri and the farther shore, the steamboat in one corner of his drawing. When he completed his picture, we strolled amongst the separate encampments of the various Indians who had come to trade at the fort. Except for the Crows and the Mandans, all of the Indians gathered there had been my enemies for the past ten years — Gros

Ventres, Assiniboines, and the three tribes of Blackfoots, Píkuni, Síksikah, and Káinah. Hidátsas can blow hot or cold.

As you might expect, I was more than a mite nervous as we trod amongst them. Naturally I was armed, rifle slung and my pistol ready in my sash, but nobody challenged us. The uneasy truce that exists amongst tribes come to trade evidently applied to us as well. Except for the teetotaling Absóraqas, they were a surly lot. It was still early morning and most of them, men and women alike, were still suffering the effects of McKenzie's popskull, a goodly number still sleeping it off, sprawled and snoring where they had fallen the night before.

I did my best to point out to Catlin tribal differences in clothing and the arrangement of the men's hair. I explained, howsomever, that it is common practice to strip a fallen enemy and appropriate his garments, especially those of the usually well-dressed Crows. It was a bewildering chore. I likely did as much to confuse Mister Catlin as I was able to enlighten him.

Afterwards, I sat for Catlin whilst he sketched my portrait, but I never saw the picture.

* * *

In spite of all the goodnatured bonhomie I had shared with Chouteau in the company of others, I still had not enjoyed a private moment with him. I needed to ask his help in getting me to Saint Louis as rapidly as possible. I seized an opportunity to address him when I espied him standing alone at the wharf observing the unloading of stores for the fort and taking note of the tremendous quantity of plews, fine furs, buffalo robes, casks of pickled buffalo tongues, and a cornucopia of other wilderness products being trundled to the dock by a seemingly endless procession of servants.

When le Cadet caught sight of me, he beckoned me to his side and commenced to speak to me, in French, as he had begun to do in Saint Louis, four years before. "So, Temple, I have until now lacked an opportunity to inquire precisely why you find yourself here on the

Missouri at a time of year when one would expect you to be in the mountains, harvesting the skins of castors, together with your companions. Is it that you have decided to abandon the trade of the trapper and return to life in a village?"

I assured him, in English, that such a thought had never entered my head and that I intended to remain in the mountains, pursuing my chosen trade, as long as I had breath in my body. Then, aware that his time was precious and fearing interruption, I plunged into a hasty description of my wound and how I had acquired it, McCool's gloomy prediction concerning the poisonous pistol ball, and my desire to obtain passage for Zeetlah and myself aboard his boat when he returned to Saint Louis.

"But of course you weel come wiz me! You are *mon ami!* You weel be my gues' *d'honneur* on ze *Roche jaune* — an' your *Indien, aussi!* I had not *l'opportunité* to tell you zat before now. *Cela va sans dire* you weel come wiz me to *Saint Louis!* I 'ave knowledge of an excellent *chirurgien* newly come to *Saint Louis, un Chinois, bien sûr,* bot he ees known to be ze ver' bes' *médecin* een *Missouri!*" I knew nothing of medical folk of any sort, in Missouri or elsewhere, so Chouteau's Chinese surgeon would do as well as any. Le Cadet's judgment had never wronged me in the past. I would trust him in this matter, as well.

Just then Kenneth McKenzie bustled up, a sheaf of papers in his hand. I thanked Chouteau and hastily excused myself. I had achieved my purpose. There would be ample time for palaver on the journey downriver. The pleasant smile that McKenzie sent my way as I walked off assured me that Mister Hamilton had conveyed my message to him.

* * *

A second lavish supper, even more bountiful than the first one, for McKenzie's cooks had had more time to prepare it, celebrated our departure. Chouteau was anxious to return to his affairs in Saint

Louis and Captain LaBarge was even more eager than le Cadet to get under weigh, lest the Missouri's flow lessen and endanger his precious steamboat. Unusually frequent summertime rains had permitted the voyage upstream so late in the season, but there was no guarantee that such conditions would last.

The *Yellowstone's* storerooms were crammed to bursting with bales, barrels, and chests filled with wilderness products destined for settlement markets. Evidently accounts had been squared and future plans approved. All that remained was a final farewelling.

Earlier that day, McKenzie had drawn me aside and suggested that if I were so inclined there might be a profitable place for me in the mountain operations of American Fur's Upper Missouri Outfit. My response was vague and noncommittal. I wished to maintain our shaky truce but I had no intention of forsaking my bunch or being disloyal to the partners of Rocky Mountain Fur.

* * *

Golden-orange shafts had barely pierced the darkness over the eastern prairie when we trooped across the dock to board the *Yellowstone*. I was groggy from overindulgence in wine, ardent spirits, and rich vittles at the banquet the night before. Zeetlah was nigh petrified, thanks to Mister Hamilton's generous bribes of sweet wine and brandy, but his gait was steady, his features as unreadable as ever. Pierre Chouteau appeared to be chipper and unaffected by the lavish food and drink laid on in his honor. He chattered alternately in French and English, mostly in a macaronic *mélange* of both, issuing final instructions and extending good wishes to the mob of clerks and servants gathered there, even as he stepped aboard the *Yellowstone*. McKenzie and Hamilton positively glowed with relief at having passed muster regarding their conduct of the fort. Captain LaBarge was nowhere to be seen, likely deep in the steamboat's bowels, seeing to the mechanics of his hissing, steaming ark already belching clouds of black smoke skywards, scattering flaming bits of debris over the colorful crowd assembled on the wharf. A stiff easterly breeze carried some of it as far as the Indian camps, where stolid warriors and some of their women stared, arms folded, and waited for our departure, no doubt happy to see the fiery Behemoth departing their neighborhood.

Zeetlah's eyes opened wide when he stepped upon the shifting deck, the only evidence of the doughty Delaware's uncertainty, but he quickly regained his wooden-faced composure. Both he and I jumped, howsomever, when the steam-whistle shrieked and a boat-horn blasted farewell. The deck shuddered as the giant paddlewheel commenced churning muddy water. Mooring lines were cast loose and crewmen pushed the *Yellowstone* free of the dock and into the Missouri current.

The cheering, waving crowd diminished in size, then disappeared as we swept around the first bend, losing sight of the Yellowstone and entering upon our long downriver journey to Saint Louis.

* * *

Most of the time, Zeetlah and I were about as useful as a third stirrup on a saddle. There was naught for me to do aboard the steamboat during most days, other than staying out from underfoot and sitting in the bow, reading or watching the shoreline slide past as the *Yellowstone* plowed through the Missouri's murky waters at a speed that amazed me. "We be makin' 'bout a hunnert miles a day," Mister Stubbs, Captain LaBarge's mate, informed us proudly. I was duly impressed, especially when I recalled fighting for every upstream mile aboard Andy Henry's keelboat ten years before.

Zeetlah soon made himself popular by patching up the crew's scrapes and scratches, sewing up bad gashes and applying soothing balms to burns and minor wounds. Even Injun-haters granted him grudging acceptance.

During the frequent stops to replenish the wood supply for firing the boilers, Zeetlah and I made ourselves useful by harvesting a buffalo cow or two, providing fresh meat for the crew's mess and augmenting Chouteau's plentiful stock of preserved comestibles. We traveled each day from first light to dusk, when it was necessary to anchor, lest the boat run into snags or sawyers or sandbars, dragon's teeth with which the Missouri abounds. When buffalo were scarce, Zeetlah and I threw out lines for catfish at night. One time something huge grabbed the bait and made a terrific run, the stout English silk line scorching our palms, slicing our fingers, threatening to break free, taxing our combined strength. "T'ink mebbe we cotch buffler! Huh?" Zeetlah panted. I thought maybe he was right. Mister Stubbs, wearing gloves, and then one of the crewmen, pitched in to lend their brawn. At last the critter slowed, then stopped and allowed us to haul it slowly and carefully to the boat.

It was a fish, after all, sort of. When we drew it alongside and Stubbs shone the light of a bulls-eye lantern onto it, Zeetlah fell back in horror, clapping his hand to his mouth, screeching fearfully in Delaware. I felt like doing much the same. What lay near the surface, huge fins and tail moving feebly, was a gigantic fish nigh ten feet long, equipped with long snout like a canoe paddle.

I reached out, knife in hand, to cut the line. Stubbs yelled, "Don't ye dare! That'ere be a paddlefish an' thar be mighty good eatin' off'n 'im, 'speshly if he's got aigs! Them's the best part!" I put up my knife, but that was all I was willing to do. Stubbs and the crewman snagged the struggling monster with boathooks and heaved it, flopping and twisting, onto the deck and Stubbs cut its throat. "They don't got much fight in 'em, 'ceptin' at first," the mate informed me with a grin. "Like I say, this'n'll make mighty good eatin'." He was right on all counts. The tender flesh was delicious and the roe was even moreso. There was plenty to go around, but Zeetlah wanted no part of it.

* * *

I reckon I needn't have mentioned that last part about the fish, but catching a fish that big happens maybe once in a fellow's lifetime.

Chouteau and I had plenty of time for palaver during the voyage. He took particular delight in telling me how his wise investments had enriched me during the years that he had husbanded my money, from the very first windfall when I fell heir to the sizeable capital of Mike Fink and his henchman and my fortuitous salvage of a boatload of furs and robes. Like most of my bunch, I had directed to Chouteau whatever profits I made from trapping after the cost of next year's supplies and rendezvous binges were deducted. It has accumulated and grown to a tidy fortune, thanks to le Cadet's careful investments, but I care little for it. All I wish for is a return to my life in the mountains and the fellowship of my friends.

Just the same, I wrote my will again with Chouteau's assistance, consigning whatever wealth I possess to Ned Godey and Cat as guardians of my daughter Iris. Chouteau assured me that he would guarantee Iris good treatment and a proper Catholic education if she should ever make the difficult journey to Saint Louis. I have little regard for the religious part of such schooling, but the nuns and brothers offer the best instruction that I know of. Besides, I am confident that my strong-minded daughter will sort out her immortality for herself.

Unaccustomed leisure afforded me much time to think whilst I perched in the bow, under the *Yellowstone's* pilothouse, watching the prow cleave through the chocolate water, speeding us to Saint Louis, where I would learn my fate, whether I would resume my carefree mountain life or suffer an early death. I concluded that I don't fear death, although I would regret missing out on all the good times that living provides, and I'll take my chances in the hereafter, if there is one. But that was nothing new.

The most valuable thing I gained from my woolgathering was final acceptance of Rainbow's death, admitting that life is fragile and must be lived to the fullest whilst you have it, that there is a time for grieving and a time to return to all the life that remains. Tuttle and Micah and Cat and Ned, and Brass Turtle, too, all told me that Rainbow would wish me to pick up and go on, but my ears had been stoppered up with grief. I couldn't, wouldn't, hear their counsel. Now I could.

Rainbow will always be a part of me, living on in our daughter, but I will do as she would wish, if she were able to say to me, "Time now, Tempo. You got plenty work waitin'."

* * *

From the first, Zeetlah and I shared the master's table with Chouteau, Captain LaBarge, and Mister Stubbs. For sleeping, we were assigned a snug little cubbyhole previously occupied by Mister Catlin. We chose, howsomever, to sleep on deck. That airless little compartment was stifling, unsuited to our habit. Later on, our decision proved to be a wise one.

A steamboat requires a continual supply of firewood for the boiler and to lessen delay, American Fur has established a number of stations along the Missouri, each one staffed by a couple-three woodcutters, where logs are ready and waiting whenever a steamboat arrives. Downstream travel requires less fuel than upriver, so our first stop for more wood was Fort Tecumseh, nigh the mouth of the Little Missouri. My father would enjoy knowing that American Fur named a major trading post after the great Shawnee leader.

One time we were stalled for half a day, blocked by a solid procession of buffalo swimming across the river, great shaggy heads bobbing in the current, cows pushing their calves through the muddy water. They paid no nevermind to the ear-piercing steamwhistle and the bellowing boat horn. There was naught else to do but wait for a break in their woolly ranks.

A couple days later Captain LaBarge guided the *Yellowstone* to a little dock located in Aríkara country. The day was warm but the silence there sent a chill through us. There should have been whooping and hallooing by the woodcutters. Here there was only stillness. The stack of logs ready for the boat was scattered, some of it burned, still smoldering. When the boatmen tied up our craft we stepped out upon the dock, every man armed, rifles, muskets, and fowlers ready, but nothing stirred.

We soon discovered what we feared. The woodcutters' shack was a smoking ruin. Three mutilated bodies, stripped and scalped, lay in the clearing. Nothing of value remained in the rude dwelling.   From my first year on the Missouri, and especially the second, I have held Aríkaras in low esteem. That day, my opinion of Rees plummeted even further, if that were possible.

Zeetlah and I stood guard whilst some of the boatment buried the bodies. Others replenished our wood supply. Then as quickly as possible we cast off and continued our downward journey.

"No good sit one place," Zeetlah observed, once we were under weigh. "Too easy bad'uns come getcha." I nodded agreement. Settlement ways don't work in the wilderness.

Much the same thing occurred in Teton Sioux country. That time, two scalped bodies lay in the woodlot. Again our hearts were small whilst we buried them.

That night Captain LaBarge anchored in mid-river at a wide place, out of bowshot and musket range. He allowed no lights on deck. The crew went to their hammocks and bunks, but Stubbs and the captain kept watch with Zeetlah and me. "We'd'a kept on goin', if we could," Mister Stubbs said to no one in particular, "but what's floatin' an' stuck in the river's worse'n Injuns." Which was true.

Captain LaBarge passed out fowlers, loaded and primed, for extra armament. The four of us scattered throughout the boat, fore and aft and on either side, huddling in darkness, alert to every sound. Whenever a floating log bumped against the hull or a branch scraped alongside, my hackles rose, eyes straining into the darkness, rifle raised, seeking a target, then settling down to wait some more.

When they came, they attacked on both sides, swarming over the rail, wet hides glistening in the light of a half-moon, armed only with knives and tomahawks. Guns and bows would have been rendered useless in the water. Zeetlah's rifle cracked the stillness just before my first Lahcotah heaved himself over the rail and tumbled to the deck.

He never got up. I dropped my rifle and yanked my pistol free, in time to spy an attacker climb up the paddlewheel and cock his arm, preparing to throw his hatchet. He never did. Shots cracked and boomed from every quarter amid the whoops and screams of the invaders. Half a dozen cursing crewmen came hurtling onto the deck, armed with all manner of pistols, knives, axes, and boathooks. Lahcotahs still able to do so dived overboard and swam for shore. Many never made it. They were easy targets until they swam into darkness.

When I turned from dumping the body of my first kill overboard, I spied Pierre Chouteau standing in the doorway of his cabin, clad in his nightshirt and beaver topper, a still-smoking pistol in either hand, a triumphant grin on his lean features. "We keel zem all, *hein?* Temple!" he crowed. "I seenk so zey weel not soon try zere treeks ver' soon again! *N'est-ce pas?*" I burst out laughing, whether from amusement or leftover excitement, I am not altogether sure.

Nobody could sleep after that. Lanterns blazed all over the vessel. Soon the aroma of boiling coffee filled the air. Everybody had a story to tell, even the Johnny-come-latelies. Nobody minded, howsomever, for that shared experience welded the crew of the *Yellowstone* together as never before. LaBarge and Stubbs had chosen their sailors well. Combat fused them into a proper crew as nothing else could do.

* * *

We got under weigh at first light. The rasp of holystones scrubbing bloodstains from the deck kept me from sleeping, but no matter. There would be plenty of time for slumber in Saint Louis. Naturally I hoped that didn't mean forever.

The remaining downriver voyage was uneventful. The *Yellowstone* made a hundred miles a day, sometimes more, LaBarge and Stubbs steering skillfully past snags, sawyers, and sandbars, wood stations fortunately untroubled, even in Pawnee country. The river broadened but remained high enough to hasten our progress and keep us from running aground. First, cabins in clearings, then little hamlets came into view along the shoreline. Here and there we spied a lone hunter or a cluster of villagers and their ragged kids come out to stare and wave at the noisy, whistle-tooting, smoke-belching apparition chugging past, doubtless providing weeks of wondering palaver in their desolate lives.

Settlements became bigger and more numerous, with larger crowds cheering us on our way down the mighty river. At last Independence appeared and Captain LaBarge steered for the wharf, steamwhistle shrieking, the boat horn blasting the *Yellowstone's* brag that it had steamed all the way to Fort Union and made it back again.

A crowd of welcoming townsfolk thronged the wharf and the road behind it. Horses reared and bolted at the sight and sound of billowing smoke, the paddlewheel still churning slowly, and steam hissing from the cooling boiler. Teamsters fighting to control their terrified dray teams added fervent curses to the cheers of drab townsmen, shabby workmen, elegant, top-hatted gentlemen and their colorful ladies in shimmering silks, plainly-dressed women, coatless clerks with bombazine sleeves, Negro servants in livery and blanket-draped Indians, kids of every size and description, and here and there a leather-clad woodsman, all of them surging perilously close to the water's edge, eager to get an eyeful of the waterborne prodigy that had completed a journey nobody thought possible. A hastily-assembled brass band, its members sporting only bits and pieces of their gaudy uniforms, struck up a gay tune mostly drowned in the hubbub. Nobody minded or likely even noticed, so great was the elation of those who came to greet the Conquerors of the Wild Missouri.

A beaming Captain LaBarge and Mister Stubbs stood atop the pilothouse, directing the hands at their tasks, all of them wallowing in the adulation of the mob. As soon as the gangway thudded upon the dock, Pierre Chouteau, dressed to the nines and carrying a portmanteau, strode ashore and disappeared amongst a group of gentlemen come to greet him. Zeetlah and I leaned on the rail, saying little, marveling at the sight and sounds and myriad colors of the settlement town and its people. Gazing over the crowd, it came to me that I had not seen a white woman in more than four years. Zeetlah noticed them, too. "Lotta woman hyar, huh?" he said. I nodded. He frowned and added, "Too goddamn white." I shrugged. He continued to stare at the people, the women in particular, before he pronounced, "Purty, though, huh?"

Chouteau stayed in town that night, but the rest of us, including the grumbling crew, remained aboard. LaBarge was anxious to set a record in getting from Saint Louis to Fort Union and back. If he allowed his sailors to visit the grog shops and brothels of Independence, he wouldn't see them for days. Instead he treated them to good Kentucky whiskey and promised them a bounty when we reached Saint Louis. Which reduced the grumbling considerably but not completely.

Rosy fingers were barely poking through the sky's dark counterpane by time we were steaming once again down the Missouri. Whilst they hustled about their chores, the crewmen gabbled about their anticipated sprees when we docked in Saint Louis. Shoreside towns were numerous now, their wharves often crowded with well-wishers cheering and waving until we passed out of sight. Some places even saluted the *Yellowstone* with a cannon salvo.

Our hearts were big — and in our mouths, as well — when the Missouri's powerful current catapulted the *Yellowstone* into the Mississippi, twisting the steamboat this way and that like a matchbox until LaBarge and Stubbs together at the helm were able to regain control of the rudder and steer our course to Saint Louis.

Word of our arrival had spread through the town, likely carried by horsemen galloping on an overland route. Our reception was magnified tenfold over that of Independence by an even more colorful and enthusiastic crowd of welcomers. The wharf in front of *Berthold et Chouteau's* mercantile threatened to collapse under the weight of the giddy throng. Members of a couple-three brass bands had enjoyed time enough to get themselves gussied up in flashy uniforms and were doing their manful best to outblast one another on their shiny cornets and trombones and drums, each red-faced bunch performing a different tune, much of it lost in the cacophony of the steam whistle and bellowing boat horn. Captain LaBarge refused to be outdone by mere landlubbers. The captain and his mate were literally blowing their own horn. They were worthy of their brag. They had accomplished the perilous journey from Fort Union to Saint Louis in just seventeen days!

Every social class had come to greet us. Frowzy housemaids jostled stylish ladies and many a gentleman's well-brushed beaver topper was toppled by blue-smocked tradesmen, threadbare stevedores, Negro slaves, and nigh-hysterical youngsters darting betwixt their legs, hooting and hollering their glee at witnessing the *Yellowstone's* triumphant return from the wilderness.

Open carriages of the gentry choked the road that ran behind and above the mercantile, crammed with fine ladies shaded by brightly-hued parasols, well-tailored gentlemen teetering on the high wheels, and liveried coachmen standing on their boxes, all straining for a better look as our helmsman swung the *Yellowstone* expertly against the dock.

From my perch in the prow I caught sight of broad-shouldered Israel, resplendent in bright-green coachman's livery. Below him in her open postchaise, Lucette, beautiful as ever, smiled a welcome to her *ancien ami,* her long-time friend and ally, le Cadet, even if she couldn't see him yet. Another carriage shoving past blocked my view, but that fleeting glimpse of Lucette, my first and best friend in Saint Louis, made my heart big.

Chapter XIX
Reprieve

Le Cadet, impeccable in tailcoat and topper, his linen starched and gleaming in soft autumn sunshine, grasped my elbow and marched me down the gangway and through the crowd, which parted respectfully at his approach, Chouteau nodding and smiling, gracefully acknowledging their compliments and good wishes, Zeetlah tagging close behind, gawking at the buildings and the pretty women. I did my share of gawking, as well. Where, four years before, there had been open fields surrounding Chouteau's establishment, now those fields were jammed with workshops, warehouses, and all manner of commercial emporiums lining the waterfront. And, I confess, the comely women thronging our way did not escape my notice.

Chouteau guided us to a large carriage, where he briefly introduced me to his wife and numerous sons and daughters, then assured them in rapid French that he would join them later. After which he led us up the slope at a brisk pace to Lucette's postchaise.

I am well-acquainted with Lucette's mercurial temperament, but I was unprepared for her emotional outburst when she first espied me at Chouteau's side. She ignored her dear friend and benefactor and, I am reasonably sure, steady customer of her *maison*. She shrieked, laughed aloud, burst into tears, then rose to pull me into her arms, babbling the while, *"Est-ce qu'il est vraiment toi? Temple!* Ees it you? *Viens de la desert, les montagnes sauvage? J'ai pensée que tu es mort!* You mus' be dead! *Oh, cheri, je t'ai manquée!* I 'ave miss you so!" All the while nigh suffocating me in her embrace.

I struggled to assure her that I wasn't dead, even though, right at that moment, I wasn't altogether sure that I wouldn't soon be so.

When she calmed down to something like only mild hysteria, Lucette insisted that I come directly to her *maison* to stay with her. Chouteau interrupted then and informed her in mind-numbing rapid French that it was not possible that I should do so, that I had suffered a grievous wound, that I required the immediate care and attention of a surgeon, and that we must proceed immediately to the premises of such a person. Which naturally set Lucette off in another fit, this time one of tearful concern, hugging me to her delicious bosom, kissing my cheeks and mouth, and sputtering macaronic endearments and concern for my well-being. Meanwhile le Cadet gave instructions to Israel to proceed to a certain address. The three of us joined Lucette in the large postchaise.

Zeetlah was fascinated by this very pretty woman who appeared to be enamored of his trapper friend, whom he likely had never considered to be much of a catch for any female, let alone one this good-looking. He continued to stare at her whilst we jolted over cobblestoned streets and soon onto dirt byways. After a brief glance at Zeetlah's weathered face and workaday buckskins, Lucette ignored him completely and lavished all of her attention upon her long-lost swain, who happened, happily, to be myself.

Israel halted his team before a modest house surrounded by a well-tended garden, on the outskirts of the town. Chouteau immediately dismounted and hastened to the entrance, where he impatiently rang the ship's bell hanging there. A tall, slim, pleasant-appearing Chinese gentleman, attired in ordinary settlement clothing, opened the door. His expression was at first cordial, then intent, as le Cadet rattled off information in his quaint Frenchified English. What he was telling the gentleman was an exaggerated version of what I had told him earlier. I learned that I hovered at Death's door and might expire at any moment, that it was a miracle that I had survived the journey from the faraway mountains, and that immediate surgery was required. Fact is, just then, much thanks to Lucette's warm welcome, I was feeling as chipper as ever I had been.

When I joined them on the threshold, Lucette and Zeetlah at my side, the gentleman invited us inside his plainly-furnished but immaculate home. If he was disturbed by the weapons that Zeetlah and I carried, he never showed it. As it was by then late in the day, he suggested that I stay with him overnight, so that he might examine my condition in the morning and determine what was to be done. Chouteau nodded his approval and Lucette reluctantly agreed to depart, promising to return next day. Naturally Zeetlah remained with me.

When they were gone, our host introduced himself as Doctor Yuan in the most perfectly-spoken, unaccented English that I have ever heard. Over a wholesome supper, whilst I struggled to reclaim the table-manners my mother taught me, I described the circumstances by which I had acquired my wound, whilst I silently marveled at Zeetlah, who eschewed tableknife and fork but acquitted himself admirably with his skinning knife and a spoon. Two Chinese servants flitted noiselessly, almost invisibly, whilst Doctor Yuan plied me with questions about the mountains, the plants and animals there, Indians, the fur trade, and the Americans who conduct it. I could tell that he was quietly amused that I found it difficult to reply without also using hand-signs, but he was too polite to comment on it.

During supper, a drayman arrived from the dock with our plunder, which awaited in our quarters when the doctor bade us goodnight at sundown. The sparely-appointed room, which contained two narrow beds and little else, let out on a garden. Neither Zeetlah nor I wished to sleep indoors or on a bed. We spread our robes beside a little pond fed by a measly stream trickling through the garden, grateful to sleep at last on solid earth instead of a wooden deck rolling and shuddering in the Missouri current.

As I slipped into slumber, I was untroubled by what might lie ahead. The morrow would bring what it would. We had completed the long journey. That was enough for now.

* * *

Doctor Yuan interrupted our morning bathe in his fish pond, calling us indoors to break our fast, leastaways Zeetlah's. He restricted me to a single cup of sweet tea. Afterwards, he led us to a mostly bare room with whitewashed walls, where he seated me upon a table and proceeded to examine the healed-over wound in my breast.

His first comment was, "I trust that your wound was sutured — sewn — by one of your large white bears in the mountains."

My temper sparked. I blurted out that crude as the stitchery on my hide might be, the ministrations of Finn and Zeetlah had saved my life. Doctor Yuan wasn't flustered by the heat of my response. He merely nodded and queried me regarding the precise circumstances of receiving my wound, what kind of weapon, where I was standing, in what position I stood, how distant I was from my assailant, and suchlike details. When he was satisfied with my replies, he nodded, looked thoughtful, then laved my chest with alcohol. It stung my nostrils and prickled my hide. I saw that he rinsed his hands in it before he proceeded to dip his instruments into it — little knives, pincers, and similar tools of the surgeon's trade.

"You will need to lie down now, Mister Buck. I will apply these restraints, so that you may remain as still as possible when I attempt to remove the pistol ball." I noticed for the first time broad leather straps attached to the sides of the table on which I sat. "I fear this will cause you much pain," he went on, "but I must remove the bullet. If not, it will quite possibly make your flesh rotten and it will kill you. I am surprised that you are not already suffering infection."

Zeetlah was close by my side, opposite the surgeon, taking in every word, his expression strained, intent. He spoke up then. "No need make Tompo hurt. I feed heem dream-vittle. He sleep." He turned to me and grinned reassuringly. "Like Hoss-face, huh?"

I recalled Tuttle's bout with the toothache and how he had slept through getting four teeth yanked. I was prepared to suffer whatever it might take in order to keep on living, but I could see no harm in avoiding what promised to be a great deal of pain. "Let him do it," I advised the surgeon. "I've seen him do it. There's no harm in it and it might make your chore easier."

Doctor Yuan sighed, obviously unconvinced, but he said, "If you wish." He nodded at Zeetlah, who scuttled out of the room and returned a few minutes later with his parfleche bag of medicaments and a cup of water. Whilst he mixed a potion of powders and pastes from the hollow bones and horns stored in his bag, the tall surgeon hovered over him, observing his every move, sniffing and sometimes touching his tongue to each item when Zeetlah laid it aside. When the Delaware healer was satisfied with his mixture, he dumped it into the cup of warm water, stirred it, and handed it me. "You drink now. Purty quick you go g'bye." I did as I was told.

I gulped down the vile concoction. My ears commenced ringing and buzzing, my eyesight blurred. The last things I recall were Zeetlah's grin and Doctor Yuan snugging up the leather straps over my arms and legs. After that, nothing.

* * *

When I returned to the world I spied the doctor and Zeetlah hunched over the parfleche, pawing through its contents, Zeetlah removing the wooden stoppers and Yuan sniffing and delicately tasting with the tip of his tongue, both of them jabbering, likely without much comprehension on either side. When I hailed them, they looked up, startled, and came to my side.

The first thing Yuan said to me was, "I thank you, Mister Buck, for bringing this remarkable physician to my house." I made an effort to sit up, but they kept me from doing so. The surgeon allowed himself a broad smile and announced, "I am happy to say that I believe you will live without further trouble from this wound." He picked up a little cup from a nearby table and rattled a small pebble against its bloody sides. "This is the culprit, Mister Buck, the author of your misfortune."

I stared at the little round stone and croaked, for my throat was parched, "But where's the pistol ball. Did ye get it?"

Yuan smiled even more broadly. "There was none. You are fortunate that your enemy possessed little gunpowder and no galena. This small stone penetrated your body with little force and hid itself behind a rib, where your colleagues were unable to find it. Fortunately I was able to do so. Your health will soon be as good as ever it was."

Perhaps my life isn't precisely charmed, but I'll settle for whatever brought me through that particular scrape.

* * *

Over Lucette's noisy protests, Doctor Yuan insisted on keeping me with him for the next few days, until my wound healed sufficiently. I suspect that much of his reluctance to part with me was prompted by a desire to keep Zeetlah at hand. The two of them spent hours every day crawling amongst the plants and shrubs in his garden, gesturing and chattering in a tongue I reckon they invented betwixt the two of them. Sometimes they disappeared for half a day, roaming the fields and nearby woods in search of medicinal roots and herbs.

Zeetlah was obviously the guest most preferred by the good doctor. I marveled at the little Delaware's ability to fit into whatever situation in which he finds himself. If I had known the Delaware word for "cat," I would have called him that. He possesses an amazing ability to land on his feet.

I occupied the daylight hours rereading the few books I possessed and catching up on my journal. Anticipating the idle months ahead, I reckoned that I might as well write this book. In the doctor's absence, his shadowy servants lurked outside my door, ready to respond to my slightest need or wish, as well as, I'm sure, to report my frequent breaches of his orders that I remain abed.

Lucette visited each day, flouncing about in her colorful dresses, ordering the servants about, and showering me with her attentions and mostly-unneeded gifts. Chouteau, once assured that my recovery was certain, wished me well, invited me to see him when I could do so, and did not return.

* * *

When at last the good doctor consented to turn me loose, he sent word to Lucette. Within the hour, Israel and the postchaise were at the door. When I offered to pay Doctor Yuan for his services, he shrugged and smilingly assured me that Pierre Chouteau had already compensated him most generously.

Whilst Israel guided his team expertly through crowded streets, I mused on the peculiar relationship I had enjoyed with Lucette during the previous ten years. The shady ambiguity betwixt the meanings of the word *aimer* in the French tongue has always been convenient for the two of us. *Aimer* can mean "to love" or "to like" and that gentle blurring of what I feel for her — and, I believe, she for me — is eminently fitting. Lucette was first my savior and protector, always my steadfast friend, and, whenever opportunity affords, my passionate lover. My feeling for her lies somewheres between the loyalty and affection I feel for my comrades and the true love that Rainbow stirred in me for the first and only time in my life.

Now I wondered how my longtime, even if only sometime, lover would deal with the half-man I had become since Rainbow's death. Ever since Lucette first introduced me to the unashamed delights of lovemaking, I had always been eager, albeit selective, to enjoy fleshly pleasures. Now I was bereft of desire for robe games, hollow where I should have been full and rampant, numb where I had been vibrant. Somewheres in the ragbag of my mind lurked a nagging concern that sharing the bed of another would be disloyal to Rainbow, even though I knew full well that she would have chided me for such unnatural prudery. That conundrum had unmanned me for nigh a year and a half.

* * *

Lucette greeted us at the door with a warm embrace and kisses for me and a perplexed look at Zeetlah, but she faltered not a step. She issued commands to her people to take our plunder to our quarters, mine to her suite, Zeetlah's to a separate bedchamber. We had arrived in the forenoon. The public rooms were mostly deserted, which was just as well. Lucette's refined patrons would surely have looked askance at a pair of wild Indians being treated as honored guests. Our rough clothing, rifles and pistols, sashes and belts bristling with warlike hardware, were remarkably out of place in those genteel surroundings.

When he was shown into his chamber, Zeetlah looked uncertain at first, but he quickly regained his stoic demeanor. He padded about the large room, examining the furniture and appointments, poking and prodding and sniffing, running his hands over the fine fabrics, for all the world like a curious bear cub. He paused to stare at the big bed before he carried his sleeprobes out onto the broad terrace that adjoined his room. Before I departed with Lucette, I assured him that I would be residing nearby. He merely grunted and signed that he was hungry and enquired when dinner would be forthcoming.

During the four years since I had last been her pampered guest, I had almost forgotten Lucette's love of luxury. Now I was purely astonished at the abundance of brilliant carpets from the Far East, delicate European furniture, sofas and padded chairs and ottomans upholstered in soft leathers and rich fabrics, colorful wall hangings and paintings mostly of nudes which bore a resemblance to Lucette herself, glowing whale oil lamps of intricate Eastern design, and a huge canopied bed covered with a silken counterpane. She watched with satisfaction whilst I marveled at that wanton display of oriental opulence before she said coyly, "I seenk eet would be *à propos* of your return to *ma chambre* eef we make *l'amour* on each of zese *chaises* while you are 'ere, *n'est-ce pas, Temple?*"

I quailed inwardly, but I forced a smile and mumbled something appropriate. It didn't feel like the right time to blurt out what I was, or wasn't, feeling.

Fortunately our dinner arrived just then, so I was spared further squirming, leastaways for the time being. We dined out-of-doors, on a broad, shaded verandah that overlooked a courtyard mostly devoted to a colorful flower garden and a large pool with a bubbling water fountain in its center. The meal that arrived in several generous courses was much more substantial and flavorful than the simple, healthful fare provided by our recent host Doctor Yuan and we both did justice to it. As I had done many times before, I wondered how her hearty appetite allowed Lucette to remain as trim and lithe as a schoolgirl, untouched by the years, as beautiful and vivacious and lively as she was the first night she took me to her bed a decade before.

The thought of her bed prompted me to put aside my reticence. She would learn about my condition soon enough, anyway. I needed to make a clean breast of it. I told her everything. In a torrent of words from my innermost being I told her about Rainbow, her beauty and understanding, and the first real, all-encompasssing love I had ever known. I spoke, too, of the love Rainbow returned to me, our life together, our daughter Iris, and, most wrenching of all, the manner of Rainbow's death.

As my words came tumbling out, what I saw across the cluttered table was a Lucette I had never known, never suspected in the gay, pleasure-loving butterfly or even in the intelligent, hard-headed businesswoman she needs to be at other times. She uttered not a word, but she absorbed every syllable I spoke, her expression grave, dark eyes alive with interest, sympathy, and understanding, sensitive lips pursed in concentration, her body tense, strained, as if she were herself present at the brawl with the Bannocks.

Once begun, I could hold back nothing. Most difficult of all was confessing that I was no longer the vigorous, eager young man she had known. Hollow and numb best described me now. My appetite for life had withered. All the delicious flavors had turned to ashes.

Hardest of all to admit to my longtime lover, I was now but half a man.

I fell silent. I had nothing more to say. Lucette spoke now, not with her customary sparkling wit and elfin good humor, but with gravity and understanding and deep sympathy. She spoke in the French tongue, for this was serious business, and she, like Chouteau, had long known that I understand their native language well enough. I cannot render here all that she said to me that afternoon. Daylight drifted into dusk and darkness whilst I sat transfixed by her own tale of a life that began in slavery to a prominent Creole family in New Orleans, of ill-use and broken promises, of unrequited love, then the loss of a true love who died in a duel, of gaining her freedom only to find herself in circumstances more desperate than her servitude had been, and her arduous climb from poverty and degradation to her present state.

"I tell you this sad history, Temple," she said earnestly, "simply to show that only weaklings allow life to trample them. You are strong. You are wise. If you were not, you would have died or become insane in the wilderness in which you have lived and prospered, these past ten years. You have suffered much in the loss of your Rainbow, but the woman of whom you have told me, who loved her life as much as you always have done, that admirable woman would tell you that you have mourned enough. She would beseech you to honor her memory by living on as the strong, wise, brave man she loved, not as a tearful, pathetic wretch who throws himself upon her grave and gives up his life for no good purpose."

Those last words were harsh. Coming from anyone else, I likely would have bristled, but what she said next caused me to ponder them carefully. "When I first took you to my heart," she said earnestly, "— and to my bed," she added with an earthy chuckle, "I saw in you the man you would become. You have proved me right. There are many strong men, many brave men, but to be strong and brave with understanding of others is rare. You possess these qualities. You proved it at our first meeting, before I knew your name, when you —

young, a starveling without weapons, without experience — challenged Fink and his bullies in my defense. Use those qualities now, Temple. Defend your own life. If you do not, this grief will kill the man you are."

Her tone softened then. She returned to her customary easy-going manner, still thoughtful but much less intense. "Many men come to my house," she confided, "with concerns not much different from your own. I tell my ladies — the wise ones — to be gentle, to listen, never to hurry, always to listen. Satisfied lust cures many imaginary ills, but a patient ear is the best medicine for a tortured soul. My ear is patient, Temple." She laughed and added, "Even if the rest of me is not always so."

Still grinning, she pulled me from my chair and led me to the bed, threw back the coverlet, and pushed me down. "There you will stay," she said gently, still in French. "Prepare yourself for sleep. I make no demands on you. You are my cherished friend and I will always be yours." She whirled and left the room, skirts and petticoats rustling, to attend to the affairs of her establishment.

I did as I was told. Naked save for the bandage that protected my recent surgery, I slipped between soft, sweet-smelling sheets and closed my eyes, conflicting notions buzzing like angry bees. Except for Lucette's own history, I had heard it all before from my friends, even from Cat, not so well-said but essentially the same. Lucette let me see clearly the pitiful wretch I had become. Rainbow, most of all, would not approve. I held on to that thought until all the others dissolved and I disappeared into dreamless sleep.

* * *

It was I who awakened her. I opened my eyes in near-darkness. The large room was lighted only by a single lamp glowing in a far-off corner and pale moonlight spilling through the open garden door. I could hear her gentle, regular breathing. I inhaled her fragrance, the delicate scent that stirred memories of youth and discovery. We lay discreetly apart in the huge bed, she careful not to intrude, I fearful to offer what perhaps I could not provide. The temptation was irresistible. I touched her shoulder, then her firm, supple breast, my fingers straying to her nipple. She stirred. Then she giggled and rolled into my arms and kissed my throat. Her moist lips brushed my ear and she murmured impishly, "You called, M'sieu?" and giggled again.

I kissed her then, a long, deep, lingering kiss that erased doubt and regret and guilt for a betrayal that had existed only in my imagination. Her tongue was not idle. Soon, neither was mine. I traced the line of her throat to her breasts, lingering on her nipples. They swelled and hardened under my nibbling lips. I retreated from those delicious knolls and descended to the smooth plain of her taut belly, rediscovering the cherished landscape where I had first learned the delights of generous lovemaking, where she was crisp as fresh parsley and moist with fragrant dew.

Never a malingerer, Lucette was busy elsewhere, until I cried out in alarm, too late, then ceased to struggle and reveled in the pleasurings of her eager lips and tongue, the while returning the favor. Ere long she succeeded in restoring what we both desired and straddled me for a long and pleasurable ride, at first an ambling stroll, then a brisk trot increasing to a rolling lope that tired neither mount nor rider, climaxing in a frantic, pounding, headlong gallop that left both the rider and her all-too-willing critter gasping and drenched in sweat.

We lay quiet for a spell, embracing, nuzzling, legs entwined, speaking softly, Lucette belatedly concerned that our exertions might have damaged my wound, which, I assured her, wasn't so, that Doctor Yuan's expert probing and stitchery had done little damage to my hide, and that her recent ministrations had done wonders for my well-being. Which was so. Shortly afterwards we improved my health still more.

Sunshine streaming into the room awakened us, still twined in each other's arms. Lucette scampered off to her ablutions and I lay musing over the remarkable transformation in my spirit that had occurred overnight. I had made the long journey from the mountains to save my life from what I believed was a mortal injury of the flesh. Now I realized that, if not for Lucette, the wound to my spirit would have proved equally fatal. I silently thanked both physicians.

Being of my peculiar cast of mind, I wondered then if my return to proper manhood was due solely to Lucette's wise counsel or if I had been horny all the while but unwilling to settle for less than superior quality. It's a conundrum.

* * *

Lucette, for all her wanton behavior in the bedchamber, is a serious and ever-busy chatelaine of her *maison,* forever occupied with myriad chores involved in the conduct of her large establishment. She is often absent from the quarters I share with her. I soon chafed at my inactivity. Books and newspapers failed to provide sufficient distraction. I missed the mountains, my work there, my daughter and my companions and my critters. Saint Louis is no good place for a mountaineer. I retrieved my journal from my packs and, for a spell, I amused myself with my cryptic scribbles, reliving the happenings of the previous four years, what I had seen and heard about and done myself. Soon such daydreaming proved inadequate. The several long months ahead, until I could return to the mountains with the springtime packtrain, loomed as a dreary desert. I had already written two books which described my first four years in the fur trade. Now I resolved to write another, even if nobody other than an editor and the printer ever reads it. As you see, if you have made the journey through its pages, this is that book.

Doctor Yuan made frequent visits to my quarters, I daresay as much to confer with Zeetlah as to examine me, as well as whatever other business he might have had in Lucette's establishment. When he pronounced me fit and healthy, I betook myself to a stationer and stocked up on a ream of foolscap, a quart of ink, and dozens of pens and pencils, much to the wonderment of the counter-jumper, who was plainly flustered by a long-haired, leathery mountaineer clad in britchclout and leggin's purchasing such quantities of his wares. So equipped, I set myself, once again, the task of recreating the life I lead amongst the people I know in the mountains, for whoever might possess an interest in such matters.

My chore proved much easier than it was the first time I traded my traps and weapons for pen and paper. The jottings in my journal provided seed that readily blossomed into the verbal pictures that make up this work. It wasn't long, howsomever, until I realized that if my labor would have a result I needed an editor to transform my heap of foolscap into a book.

Choosing onesuch was not an easy decision. Saint Louis supports many newspapers, gazettes, and suchlike publications which employ men well-qualified to perform the tasks I needed. Still, I recollected the difficulties I encountered when I insisted that my former editor in Ohio, Mister Euphemius Hobbes, refrain from altering my manuscript according to his own refined taste and rigid morals and to confine himself only to matters of spelling and grammar and later to oversee the printing of my history. My remaining time did not permit training another editor, so, although I shuddered at the prospect of once again skirmishing with the hardheaded, mulish Mister Hobbes, I sent for him to come from Chillicothe, Ohio to Saint Louis. Naturally I included with my request a generous bankdraught to cover his expenses, for the impecunious Mister Hobbes rarely possesses money enough to pay his rent. With him, it's largely a matter of thirst.

On the other hand, I know him to be an honorable gentleman, downright finical in pecuniary matters. I was confident that he wouldn't cheat me. A further incentive was provided by Pierre Chouteau, who was delighted to learn that I had already written two books, although neither he nor I had seen them. He promised to obtain a position for Mister Hobbes on one of the local journals. Naturally I instructed Hobbes to bring with him whatever copies of *Backbone of the World* and *Free Men* that he possessed.

At first Lucette was pleased that I have my writing to occupy my time whilst she is engaged with the affairs of her *maison*, but ere long she begrudged the many hours I spend every day hunched over her escritoire scribbling my recollections and opinions. Lucette is literate and accomplished at arithmetic, but I reckon the world of letters will be forever remote from her interest. She is nonetheless proud as Lucifer to show off my books to all and sundry since Hobbes arrived with copies of them. Dear as she is to me, and I to her, howsomever, I doubt that she will ever read one of them.

* * *

The hours I spend scratching and scribbling are not the only source of exasperation my presence here has occasioned for Lucette. Zeetlah is her particular anathema. One morning, not long after he and I took up residence in the *maison*, Lucette stormed into the little room in which I work, screaming, "'E mus' go! *Ton Peau-rouge! Ton Indien!* Your *sauvage! Ton viellard!* Your ol' man! Your Zeetlah! Eet ees <u>*intolérable!*</u> *insupportable!* zat 'e should remain 'ere longair!"

I should mention that Lucette and Chouteau, although they know that I understand their tongue, usually prefer to practice their quaint English on me. Nowadays Saint Louis is flooded with Americans from the East and South and English is fast becoming the language of business hereabouts.

I was startled by her outburst. When she ran out of breath, I enquired after the source of her displeasure. She gulped for air and renewed her attack, her vexation mounting with each word. "Your Zeetlah, 'e ees destroyin' *ma maison! Mes femmes de chambre, mes domestique,* my maids, zey 'ave become crazy for 'eem! Already one of zem 'ave become *enceinte,* wiz child, by 'eem! Soon I weel 'ave no maids for to clean ze *chambres ou* any ozzer work!" *Il est très agé, très sale, très mauvais,* but zey find 'eem *aimable!* 'Ow you say eet? Lovable!"

I was stunned. I could certainly agree with Lucette that Foot is old and frequently unkempt and very likely evil, but *lovable?* I am sure that my dear friend and faithful guardian possesses many undiscovered qualities, but I am hard put to include "lovable" amongst them. Then again, I am unable to view him with the same eyes and standards that Lucette's chambermaids might employ.

Before I could frame a reply, Lucette launched into another rant. "Il est un séducteur, ta canaille! 'E seduce mes domestique ever' mornin' when 'e fait sa toilette, when 'e make 'is bat' dans le jardin, dans la fontaine, entierement nu, sans culotte, zey see 'eem! Zey say 'is membre, sa virilité, c'est formidable! Il est irrésistible for zem!"

I tried, unsuccessfully, not to laugh. Evidently my friend's daily nude bathe in the garden fountain has attracted an enthusiastic following of spectators amongst the chambermaids, many of whom find his considerable manhood irresistible. When I was able to quit sniggering, I sought to deflect her ire. I asked, "And you, you never looked?"

Lucette actually blushed. "Only one time," she confessed. "An' yes, 'e ees *formidable.*" Then, recovering her composure, she demanded, "What weel you do wiz 'eem?"

I was in a quandary. It had been difficult enough to convince Zeetlah to use the chamber pot in his room instead of a discreet corner of the garden. Asking him to forego his morning bathe would be too much. My only solution was to remove the both of us to a lodging-house in town, which Lucette absolutely refused to consider. Muttering that she would attend to the matter herself, she swept from the room.

That afternoon I observed a platoon of workmen in the garden, erecting a screen around the fountain. Later, she softened and admitted the comicality of the situation. She even jested about it. "Eet ees enough bad zat ze maids are *enchantée* wiz 'eem, but I cannot permit my ladies to give for free what I sell to my *clientèle.*"

I did what I could to improve the situation. I visited Charlie Bowden, the English horse-coper, and purchased a horse for my horny

Delaware friend. Nowadays Zeetlah passes much of his time with Doctor Yuan, combing fields and forests in quest of the medicinal roots and herbs they prize.

Whilst I roamed Bowden's paddocks I asked him to be on the lookout for a first-rate saddler for myself. As I described the horse I had in mind, it came to me that I was picturing the high-bred charger that Tom Fitzpatrick had lost and then regained from the Grovants. Because I was in no hurry, Charlie assured me that I would return to the Rockies mounted on such an animal.

* * *

The arrival of Euphemius Hobbes on a steamboat occurred sooner than I had hoped for. He had wasted no time in complying with my request. His considerable baggage included few personal belongings. It consisted mostly of several crates containing my books. Few of them had sold. Apparently Ohioans possess little curiosity concerning the fur trade. Perhaps Saint Louis residents will be more interested, awash as they are in Rocky Mountain and Santa Fe commerce.

Hobbes has changed hardly at all. He is still the skinny, knobbly, threadbare, out-at-elbows, down-at-heel, frequently-unshaven, bibulous pedant I first encountered in Chillicothe five years ago. Nevertheless, a quick riffle through the pages of the books he brought with him convinced me that my original choice had been a good one. He has been faithful to his task. The text was unchanged from the final manuscripts I approved and the well-printed books are bound in sturdy buckram and some in elegant morocco. For all his sartorial and tonsorial shortcomings and his frequent lapses from sobriety, Mister Hobbes is a reliable editor.

Besides my own books, Hobbes brought with him two volumes that I treasure more than all of my own, entitled *An American Dictionary of the English Language,* produced solely by Mister Noah Webster, a Yankee schoolteacher, who defines and pronounces seventy thousand English words the way Americans ought to use them. It was neither easy nor cheap getting that treasure away from Hobbes, but he can get another copy, if he doesn't drink up what I paid him for it. If he does, it will take him several sodden evenings to do so.

Hobbes is installed in a nearby lodging-house, for it would be unwise to expose that priggish gentleman to the distractions offered by Lucette's comely *filles de joie,* who often flit about the corridors in various states of *déshabillé.* When he is not engaged in his editorial duties at the *Missouri Republican,* he wades through my ever-increasing manuscript, doubtless blushing and clucking over some of its passages, but steadily rendering them into printable form.

Hobbes is still the same irascible, recalcitrant prude that I battled in Ohio, but nowadays he surrenders somewhat more readily on matters of content and expression. Perhaps at last he accepts that when I describe outrageous mountaineer antics and quote my mostly-unlettered trapper companions, trying as best I can to capture the sound and flavor of their idiom, I am simply soothing the heartache I feel from being so distant from them and our beloved mountains and prairies. Mostly I have refrained herein from quoting the actual language used by Rainbow and Cat, lest I demean them. Our mutual lingo consists of an olio of their Salish tongue and my own, always fleshed out with sign, leastaways in daylight.

* * *

When I grant myself respite from writer's cramp I visit Black Harris, walking to Madame Mathilde's brothel in Vide Poche or, astride a borrowed horse from Lucette's excellent stable, riding to William Clark's large estate. I saw Black first at Mathilde's, where he spends most of his free time and money when he is in Saint Louis, indulging his lust and slaking his thirst and holding court amid a coterie of eager townsmen and trappers willing to buy him drinks in return for his colorful tales. I often wish that he would commit his outrageous yarns to paper, but he'll never do it.

"Thar ye be!" he yelled when I set foot in Mathilde's spacious public room. "Temple Buck! An' lookin' fit as a fiddle strang, begawd!" He shooed away his admirers and yanked out a chair for me. "Ye plumb gave us a heap o' cornsarn over ye! They git that'ere galena pill out'n ye?"

I assured him that my health was as good as ever, described the steamboat trip down the Missouri, and briefly related the circumstances of the surgery, which provoked a roar of laughter from Black and all who overheard it. Then I switched to what was uppermost in my mind. 'When'll ye be leavin' for the mountains, Black? Who's headin' it up an' do ye reckon Foot an' I can come along with ye?"

He replied without hesitation. "We'll be pullin' out soon as prairie mud dries up some'at. Far's I know, Bobby Campbell'll be booshwayin', an' ye kin betcher arse ye'll allus be welcome on my train. Ye ain't never been a'hindhand fer huntin' — ner fightin', neither — an' Bobby knows it, same as me." Which information happified me considerably.

As always, Harris offered to treat me to one of Mathilde's best girls, which, as always, I politely declined and settled for whiskey, explaining the while that I was enjoying as much in the way of robe games as I could desire. "Ye still beddin' that'ere high-yaller Madam Lucette, are ye?" He rolled his eyes and whistled softly. "That'n shorely be somethin' scrumptious! How'd'ja manage it, Temple?"

"Just lucky, I reckon." Then, the whiskey taking hold, I said, "Hell, Black, ye know damn well, if ye ain't payin' for it, it's the women that do the decidin', much as we like to think it's us." Harris grunted and conceded that it's likely so. Which it certainly is.

On the way back to Lucette's I breathed a sigh of relief that Zeetlah and I will soon be shaking Missouri mud off our moccasins. I have been increasingly concerned about my Delaware friend. Zeetlah is getting to be entirely too citified. He is frequently tipsy, much more articulate and rather more presentable in his dress, and slyly affable in the presence of women, for whom he possesses a voracious appetite.

Not long ago he asked me, in a mixture of English and sign, "Tempo, you ever had a white woman?"

Startled, I mumbled out a reply. "Yes. One time."

"How was she? You like?"

"Not much," I replied guardedly, recollecting the loss of my virginity to my aunt-by-marriage. Fact is, it was pretty good but embarrassing to recall.

"Me, too," he agreed. "Injun mos' good. Black purty good, no bad. White woman —" He made a sign indicating so-so.

I wondered how my friend had become such a *connoisseur* of the opposite sex in such a brief spell, but I declined to pursue the matter, lest I encourage him in his lewdness.

* * *

It is April now and Harris is busy preparing the packtrain for the long, hard trip to rendezvous, buying sound animals, recruiting hostlers, storing up supplies and trade goods, seeing to the repair of saddles, harness, and such, and otherwise attending to the countless details essential to a successful journey. I found him at Charlie Bowden's stockyard, dickering for mules. "'T'won't be long naow," he assured me. "Bobby's gittin' itchy to be gittin' on the trail. We awready got nigh all the plunder heaped up out t' the Ginral's barns an' pert'near enough men to see us to ronnyvoo. Ye'd best be gittin' yer plunder an' critters together, Temple, if'n ye wish to come along from hyar. If'n ye don't, ye kin jine us in Lexin'ton, whar we'll be jumpin' off fer the mountains."

"What about Bill Sublette?" I asked. "Is he stayin' down here this year?"

"Oh, hell no!" Black replied. "He be goin', too, but he ain't goin' a-hossback. He be takin' a coupl'a keelboats up the Missourah. Him an' Bobby aim to build theirse'fs a passel o' tradin' forts up aroun' the Yellerstone — stickin' a stob inter ol' Redcoat McKenzie's eye, don'tcha know!" Harris cackled, contemplating Kenneth McKenzie's consternation when he finds himself competing for Indian trade he now considers to be all his own. "Yep! Ol' Billy's been hirin' ever' smith an' joiner he kin pry out'n Sain' Looie, 'long with tools an' sichlike he'll be needin' up thar. 'Tain't easy, neither, findin' men, cornsid'rin' haow they be buildin' up Sain' Looie naowadays."

* * *

During a recent visit with Pierre Chouteau, my friend and benefactor did his best to convince me that I should give up being a free trapper and accept employment with the American Fur Company, leading a trapping brigade and encouraging Indian trade. I was not surprised. Le Cadet has hinted at such an offer before, not only for me, but for Micah, as well. My principal difficulty lay in politely declining his request and the very generous terms he offered without hurting his feelings or, worse, provoking his resentment.

I needn't have worried. I explained that my loyalty lies with the men with whom I have worked and fought and bled ever since our greenhorn days on the Yellowstone and Musselshell in 'twenty-two and 'twenty-three. The five Rocky Mountain Fur partners, hardworking trappers themselves, have always treated us fairly. I refrained from mentioning Johnny-come-latelies eager to cash in now on our early efforts, lest I offend le Cadet's pride in his commercial endeavors. I finished by telling him that if Rocky Mountain Fur should fail, I will be happy to join him, providing that my work is in the mountains.

Chouteau surprised me by his response. *"D'accord!* I commend you, *Temple,* for your *loyauté* to your *ancien compagnons.* I would not expect less of you. *Mais oui! Certainement!* Stay wiz zem, but, as you say, if zey should fail, zen come to me. You are welcome 'ere always."

It was at that meeting that le Cadet hauled out his account books and revealed that I am wealthier than I had imagined, thanks to his prudent investments and careful husbandry of my earnings and fortuitous windfalls during the past decade. The money means little to me, except that it assures that I need never become a grayback farmer scratching out a living in the settlements, if the fur trade should ever peter out.

It was only on the way back to Lucette's that I commenced to wonder about le Cadet's easy-going acceptance when I turned down his offer of employment. Pierre Chouteau is accustomed to getting his own way. He brooks little opposition to his plans. What, then, does he know that I don't? I admit that I'm a babe in the woods when it comes to commerce. What I do know is that Rocky Mountain Fur is deeply in debt to Bill Sublette. Even though Chouteau and Sublette are not friendly, there are few business matters in Saint Louis to which le Cadet is not privy. It is one more conundrum that I am not equipped to puzzle out.

* * *

I reckon that I have by now recounted here every jot and tittle of interest concerning my history during the past five years and much that is of little or no interest at all to anyone but myself. Today I will hand over to Euphemius Hobbes these final pages, along with my inkpot, pens, and unscribbled foolscap. It is time to rise from this escritoire and busy myself equipping Zeetlah and myself for our journey back to where we belong.

Just this morning I received a message from Charlie Bowden, telling me that he has at last found the superior saddle horse I desired of him.

Within a fortnight Robert Campbell's packtrain to rendezvous will be on the westward trail. I mean to be part of it. There is much to be done, buying sound saddle and pack animals and ransacking the bins and shelves of Berthold et Chouteau's mercantile for heaps of essential plunder and gifts for my loved ones in the mountains, visiting Jacob Hawken's gunshop and the old Spaniard saddler's murky lair, and getting it all together to carry to the mountains.

It won't be easy to pry Zeetlah away from his doxies, but I reckon he misses the Rockies as much as I do. He won't remain unpleasured for long, once we get there.

Most difficult of all will be bidding farewell to Lucette. She will always occupy an important place in my heart, but long before now she and I agreed that my remaining here would mean the death of the man that I am. She loves me too much to destroy me. She will survive my departure — likely with tears and tantrums for a spell, for that is her way — but she will soon resume her customary life. Petite and fragile as she might appear, Lucette is made of strong and supple stuff. And I daresay she won't be lonely for long, for that, too, is her way. I am blessed to know her as my friend.

Now, as I pen these final paragraphs, I realize that I haven't put a title to this work. I will call it *Shinin' Times!,* not because all that it describes was what we might have wished. Much of it deals with violence and death, hardship and peril, loss and heartache, but those things are merely part of the rich and rewarding life of those of us who live close to Nature's bosom. I have learned to accept such things, even the death of my beloved Rainbow.

I have told of rich harvests of beaver plews, feasts and lovemaking, unbreakable friendships and rowdy camaraderie, boys discovering their manhood, true love and dedication and the awesome gift of fatherhood, and I have tried to give you glimpses of majesty in snowy mountains, bottomless blue valleys, and shimmering prairies rolling endlessly to faraway horizons. It is there that I return. Wish us well.

FINIS

About The Author

Edward Louis Henry (a.k.a. Poredevil) has been a working cow-hand, rodeo contestant and Wild West performer, WWII infantry sergeant (Pacific), newspaper reporter, U.S. Foreign Service officer, and executive speechwriter, plus thirty years in advertising. A lifelong horseman and outdoorsman, Henry is active in mountain man rendezvous. Western history is his abiding passion. Henry, a member of Western Writers of America, is the author of *Poredevil's Beaver Tales* and the Temple Buck Quartet: *Backbone of the World, Free Men, Shinin' Times!,* and *Glory Days Gone Under*.

Other Books by Edward Louis Henry

THE TEMPLE BUCK QUARTET
A Rocky Mountain Odyssey
1822-1837

Volume I: Backbone of the World, 1822-1824 is a coming-of-age story of the first two years of the Rocky Mountain fur trade, 1822-24. It is told in his own words by Temple Buck, an Ohio-born lad whose rollicking tale begins with growing up in the Ohio wilderness, how he is kidnapped aboard evil Mike Fink's keelboat, is rescued by a beautiful St. Louis madam, and finally enlists in Ashley and Henry's first expedition up the Missouri River to the beaver-rich Rockies and a wealth of adventure and undreamed-of new experiences. This painstakingly researched tale blends historical and fictional characters in a colorful tapestry of actual events spiced with bloody battles, Indian customs and characters, homespun humor, and earthy romance. If you've ever wished for absolute freedom and hair-raising adventure in the early Old West, come along with Temple and his trapper companions and breathe the free, pure air of the Rocky Mountains!

Volume II: Free Men, 1824-1826 chronicles the exploits of Temple Buck and his rowdy trapper companions in the American Rocky Mountain fur trade from 1824-1826. In this, the second volume of the Temple Buck Quartet, they push ever farther west in their quest for beaver pelts, exploring new country and encountering fresh adventures, some of them welcome, others not at all. This well-researched tale, told in Temple's own words, blends historical and fictional characters against a colorful backdrop of actual events,pungently flavored with gory battles with hostile Indians, homespun humor, and earthy romance, culminating in Temple's disappointing return to his Ohio birthplace.

Volume III: Shinin' Times!, 1828 – 1833   Temple Buck returns to the Rockies, rejoining his trapping bunch and picking up the free, unfettered life of the American free trapper where he left off in 1826. He and the other members of his trapping bunch explore uncharted new country and gain new and different experience in a changing and expanding fur trade. Their personal lives change, as well, as they take on new responsibilities while continuing to enjoy the happy-go-lucky life of the Rocky Mountain free trapper, its rich flavor much improved now by their wider knowledge, deeper experience, and greater appreciation of everything that living in the American wilderness can provide for men who possess the the savvy and smarts and courage to surviveon Nature's bosom.

Volume IV: Glory Days Gone Under, 1834-1837, is the fourth and final volume of the Temple Buck Quartet. All things, good and bad, come to an end. Fashions change and human greed injures even all-bountiful Nature. Faraway factors in Europe and the American East destroyed the market for beaver pelts, which occurred just when beaver were growing scarce in the mountains. Without a market, pelts were worthless. The mountaineer's income was wiped out. White settlers, following trails blazed by the early trappers, were moving west, bringing with them families, farming, civilized customs, laws, and missionaries, all of which the trappers despised, corrupting the Indians and crowding them off their ancestral lands, all in the name of a Manifest Destiny that mountaineers, tough, resourceful, and courageous as they were, were powerless to resist.

Poredevil's Beaver Tales   You can almost hear the voice of a tough, experienced early 19th century mountain man in this collection of 24 humorous mountain man tall stories and poems narrated in a loose sort of verse. All of the stories contain glimpses of the difficult and dangerous life of that rowdy breed of men who challenged America's uncharted wilderness and who survived and triumphed because of their courage, fortitude and unquenchable laughter in the face of hardship and peril.

For more information on these and other great books, visit www.christophermatthewspub.c